GOD'S R

A Small Town's Awakening

Tony Tona

DEDICATION

To God, whose guidance and grace transformed my life, my family, and my career.

To my wife, Jeannie, of 38 years, whose unwavering support has carried me through every venture.

To my sons, Ryan and Jesse, for their encouragement, which gave me the confidence to publish and leave a lasting legacy.

To my parents, Fred and Marie, for their steadfast support and pride.

To true friends—Mike, Sam, and Danny—and to Pastor Tom, a mentor of my early years.

And to Pastor Charlie, who led me to the saving knowledge of Christ, changing the course of my life forever.

2 Chronicles 7:14

"…if my people, who are called by my name, will humble themselves and pray and seek my face and turn from their wicked ways, then I will hear from heaven, and I will forgive their sin and will heal their land." (NIV)

Cover illustration and design: Cassandra Sutfin

ISBN: 979-8-218-41326-2

ONE

John Ivan sat alone at a quaint, weathered table, the flickering candlelight casting dancing shadows across his furrowed brow. As a seasoned detective, he had faced countless puzzles in his storied career, but the one before him now stirred emotions he hadn't felt in years. Stapleton, with its rustic charm and winding streets, had become his new home for the past three months. The town's central avenue, adorned with graceful trees and vintage streetlights, was a scene of pure nostalgia. The old brick buildings housed both the cherished First Wiltshire Bank and charming mom-and-pop shops, breathing life and character into the tight-knit community. Yet, even in this idyllic setting, the somber realities of the outside world crept in.

After 14 years of unraveling mundane cases of spousal infidelity, John had yearned for something more profound, a change of pace that would reignite his passion for the job. He had hoped that his move to Stapleton would provide the adventure he so desperately craved. At 40, John's unwavering determination and sharp private eye skills had made him a formidable figure in the world of law enforcement. Although he was highly educated and had a commanding presence, a year of solitude had passed since his divorce, leaving him uninterested in pursuing any serious relationships. In his rare moments of leisure, he embraced the thrill of casual dating as a source of solace.

But today, his unwavering focus was riveted on the intricate puzzle sprawled out before him. He was resolute, driven by an indomitable will to crack the case and serve justice to the elusive perpetrator. Each chess piece he touched was a thread, and as he methodically wove them together, a plan of action began to emerge. This was John's defining moment, an opportunity to prove both to himself and to the town that he was more than capable of tackling the most enigmatic cases. The revival of his career hung in the balance, and he was determined, with every fiber of his being, to emerge victorious.

It had all begun approximately three months ago in the picturesque town of Stapleton. On any given day, the town's rhythm consisted of diligent citizens toiling away, mothers keeping watchful eyes on their children at the sun-dappled park, and elderly residents huddled together, playing chess, exchanging pleasantries, and sharing the latest news on who had taken ill. However, on that fateful morning, one man had awakened to a different, ominous premonition—Pastor Bruce Hutchinson.

Bruce, the devoted minister of a small-town church, possessed an intimate familiarity with every member of his congregation. The church itself was a picturesque example of traditional architecture, with sturdy brick walls, pristine white trim, and a steeple adorned in brilliant white, all framed by meticulously maintained green lawns that cascaded across the rolling landscape. In his mid-thirties, Bruce remained unwed, his heart aflame with a fervent devotion to the Lord. His enthusiasm for matters of faith radiated from him, as clear as daylight. Graduating at the top of his seminary class had been a defining moment, second only to the day he had wholeheartedly surrendered his life to Christ.

Two years prior, Bruce had encountered the woman of his dreams, Jennifer. From the very first moment, she had stolen his heart, and their courtship had been filled with moments of deep connection and profound love. Yet, beneath the surface, they both sensed that God had grander designs for her life. Jennifer had been called to serve as a missionary abroad, a heart-wrenching decision that they had grappled with but ultimately deemed God's divine plan. As she embarked on her mission, Bruce felt his heart shatter into countless fragments. He had held onto the hope of an enduring future together, but with the Lord's guidance, they had managed to move forward. Over the years, Bruce remained in close contact with Jennifer, fervently following her mission experiences, even as the prospect of their reunion seemed to dim. Nevertheless, he never abandoned the hope that one day they might be reunited.

On this particular morning, Bruce's heart weighed heavy as he meditated on a familiar passage: "If my people, who are called by my name, will humble themselves and pray and seek my face and turn from their wicked ways, then will I hear from heaven and will forgive their sin and will heal their land." This scripture had always held a special place in his heart, one he had preached on numerous times. However, today, it was the phrase "will heal their land" that captivated him.

Bruce's garden, a serene refuge just beyond his back patio, was an exquisite showcase of vibrant rose bushes. It was here that he often sought solace and communed with the still, small voice of the Lord. As he leaned in to inhale the fragrance of a rose, his mind wandered back to the morning's scripture, pondering its deeper meaning: what did it truly mean to heal the land?

Amid the rows of roses, one bush stood in stark contrast. Ravaged by aphids and devoid of blossoms or buds, it appeared a mere shadow of its former self. Bruce marveled at its tenacity, considering the pest-ridden foliage and lifeless state. It brought to mind Stapleton, a town barely clinging to life, as he observed the beleaguered rosebush. Visions of the local liquor store, adult magazine outlets, and the sinister Gothic cult that had infiltrated the schools with its dark influence, marked by tattoos and piercings, flashed before his eyes. And most distressingly, the numerous abortion clinics offering empty promises of a brighter future.

Bruce shook his head in dismay, recollecting the countless times he had picketed outside those abortion clinics and confronted the Association for Fetal Research, deeply embedded in every facet of the abortion industry. They convened their pivotal conferences in Stapleton, forging the tools and strategies for the year ahead. A surge of righteous anger welled up inside him, his emotions running wild. Yet, in that moment, an inexplicable peace settled over his soul as he gazed at the flourishing rosebush beside the ailing one, as if God Himself whispered, "...and I will heal their land."

The ringing of the phone inside his house jolted Bruce from his reverie. With no cordless phone at hand, he instinctively opened the kitchen window, his customary method for answering calls. Although he possessed an old-school answering machine, he hurried to pick up the phone before it could intercept the call.

"Hello?" Bruce greeted, his voice tinged with curiosity and anticipation.

"Bruce? This is Maggie," came the voice on the other end.

"Hi, Maggie," Bruce replied, feeling both surprised and pleased by the call. Maggie, a single woman in her forties who attended his church, had faced numerous challenges in life. Sue, another church member, had befriended her and requested the congregation's prayers for Maggie. Her life had taken a difficult turn, and the burden was growing heavier. "How are you?"

"Good... well, not really. Do you have a minute?"

"Of course, what's going on?"

A brief pause followed as Maggie hesitated. "I... I'm not sure where to start."

"Would you prefer to talk in person?"

"Yeah, that would be better. Sue suggested I talk to you. She's been a great help, but she gave me your number to call. I really need to talk to a pastor about this."

"Alright, how about this afternoon?"

"That would be great." Maggie provided her address, and they exchanged parting words.

Bruce then made his way to his study, knelt down, and prayed fervently, "Father, You know how long we've been praying for Maggie. Please use me, for I have nothing to offer except Your guidance." With that, he left to meet with Maggie, a heavy sense of responsibility weighing on his heart.

Later that fateful afternoon, Bruce found himself standing on Maggie Fortunato's inviting front porch. Maggie, a petite Italian woman with a crown of dark, curly hair, greeted him, her appearance belying the turmoil within. Her attire was impeccable, but her eyes betrayed the fear and unease that had evidently plagued her for an extended period.

"I just want to thank you for coming on such short notice," Maggie said with gratitude etched across her face.

Bruce nodded, his heart heavy with the responsibility of helping a troubled soul. "This is a beautiful house you have. How long have you lived here?"

"I've been here for about five years. It was my first house. I've been having some disturbing dreams over the past month," she confessed, her eagerness to share evident in her voice.

"Tell me about them," Bruce encouraged, envisioning nightmarish scenarios involving monsters or harrowing cliffs.

"They started about a month ago," she began, a timeline that coincided with Sue's request for the church to pray for her. "In each dream, I die a different death. But…it's not the dying that's the worst part; it's what happens after."

Bruce maintained a compassionate expression as he listened

intently. "I see."

Maggie hesitated briefly before continuing, her voice fraught with anxiety. "It's hell."

A shiver ran down Bruce's spine. "It must have been awful."

"No, I mean it was really hell," Maggie clarified, her face paling. She spoke as if recounting a chilling encounter with the supernatural. "I was immediately seized by gruesome, dark, malevolent entities against my will, and they carried me away while I screamed and fought to break free. Their laughter... it was hideous, and they only tightened their grip, cutting off the circulation in my hands. I would scream, but they wouldn't listen."

Bruce's eyes filled with sympathy as he tried to fathom the horror she described. "Oh, how terrible."

"It was, and it gets even worse," Maggie continued, her voice becoming more somber. "The place where they took me... the smell was... have you ever come across a dead rat in the attic or a decaying animal?"

Bruce nodded gravely. "Yeah."

"Well, it was ten times worse!" Maggie exclaimed, clutching her stomach as if the noxious odor lingered even now. "You could smell it in your dream?"

"I know, that's what makes it worse. It was so real, just like you and me talking."

Bruce encouraged her to share more. "What else?"

Her voice grew increasingly intense as she recounted her nightmare. "It got even worse. They threw me into a confined space, and the stench was overpowering. I can't even describe it, but it made me feel nauseous." Maggie paused, gathering her strength before continuing, her voice trembling. "It was sweltering, and my mouth was bone dry, like when you're really scared. And then, the worst part happened."

Bruce listened with undivided attention, his expression mirroring her distress as she described the nightmarish moment when writhing worms infested her. Maggie's voice quivered, her movements became more frantic, as if she was reliving the grotesque scene. "That sounds absolutely terrible," Bruce said, his voice filled with empathy. "How long did you say this has been going on?"

"For a month," Maggie replied, her voice heavy with exhaustion. "It started after I talked to Sue about dying. She asked me a strange question about what would happen to me after death.

I wish she had never asked me that question. I can't get it out of my mind."

"Well, maybe it's time to do something about it," Bruce suggested, his eyes radiating compassion.

Maggie peered into Bruce's eyes and found nothing but unconditional acceptance and understanding. "Yeah, maybe it is time," she conceded.

And then, in that quiet moment on her porch, Bruce did what he had done countless times before - he won a soul for Christ. He eloquently explained the necessity of a personal relationship with a personal Savior and conveyed God's boundless love, demonstrated through His Son's sacrifice on the cross. Maggie had many questions, grappling with the notion that simply being good might not be enough.

"It's a gift," Bruce assured her, "a gift that can't be earned or deserved. It is by grace you are saved, through faith, and that not of yourself... no matter what you do, you cannot earn heaven."

As Bruce spoke, Maggie's heart began to soften. Tears flowed freely, and her heart lay ripe for the taking. "I need to do this," she said, her voice choked with emotion. With those heartfelt words, she surrendered her heart to Jesus, and the burden she had carried for so long began to lift.

John Ivan, known for his relentless determination, sat at a cluttered table, surrounded by an overwhelming sea of pictures, reports, notebooks, and tapes. Frustration gnawed at him as he contemplated the mountain of evidence that seemed insurmountable. "Get a grip, John," he chided himself, gripping the edge of the table tightly. "Let's start from the beginning."

Three months had passed since the Association for Fetal Research had enlisted John's services to investigate the escalating problems plaguing their headquarters in Stapleton. In the past, the association had endured the ire of local religious extremists and the resultant negative media coverage, but recent months had seen the situation spiral out of control. They suspected Stapleton was at the epicenter of these troubles, hence the substantial fee they'd offered John to crack the case. He had eagerly embraced the challenge, armed with cutting-edge technology in the field of investigations.

One of the first tools at John's disposal was a device capable of reading ultraviolet waves, enabling him to glimpse people's activities and locations within buildings. This device had revealed that the religious faction seemed to gather concurrently with the Association's events. A creeping suspicion suggested that they possessed some technology for remote surveillance. Among the names, Bruce Hutchinson stood out as the likely mastermind behind this religious faction. John uncovered Bruce's extensive history of picketing abortion clinics in Stapleton, as well as his frequent visits to the local library, where he accessed news articles about the protests, particularly those concerning an abortion clinic operated by the Association.

Despite this mounting evidence, connecting Bruce to the ongoing chaos at the Association had proven a daunting task.

Upon arriving in Stapleton, John had made a beeline for Bruce's church, determined to interview Ms. Maggie Fortunato, a recent addition to the religious group. He sought a fresh perspective from someone less loyal to the pastor. John possessed a knack for extracting information, often without his subjects even realizing it, and he aimed to start with newer members like Maggie.

After a random phone call, they arranged to meet at a local coffee shop, where John adopted the persona of a private company representative conducting a survey. Maggie agreed to the interview, and after some casual conversation, they delved into the topic of the church.

John probed about the day Bruce had visited Maggie, offering his assistance with her psychological struggles. The revelation that a pastor could provide such help, given John's atheism, surprised him. Maggie shared how Bruce had illuminated the significance of knowing her eternal destiny and reconciling with the Lord, a revelation that had brought her a profound sense of peace.

Next, John inquired about the church's activities, particularly whether they engaged in picketing. Maggie disclosed that they had done so in the past but not recently. Bruce had previously organized protests during abortion association gatherings, but this year, they'd refrained. When John asked about any written correspondence, phone calls, or communication within the group over the year, Maggie confirmed there had been none.

Feeling as if he had hit an impasse, John concluded the interview by transitioning into a survey with more general inquiries. He meticulously recorded his notes on his laptop and subsequently emailed a summary of his findings for the week to his client.

Unfortunately, the results appeared to offer more of the same. John ran a hand through his hair, puzzled, and decided it was high time to shift his approach and adopt a more aggressive strategy.

Two weeks had elapsed since Bruce had led Maggie to embrace the Lord, and as Sunday morning dawned, the church pulsed with a heightened sense of God's presence. Despite the church's unremarkable wooden pews, dated orange carpeting, and a centrally placed platform pulpit, it exuded a warm, welcoming atmosphere. For those who crossed its threshold, it felt like home. Testimonies abounded, shared by individuals who had spent years in search of spiritual fulfillment before finding their way to this congregation and surrendering their lives to Christ.

Bruce himself felt an extraordinary stirring of the Spirit within him, unlike any he had ever experienced. He could sense that the roughly 200-strong congregation was attuned not just to him but to God Himself. Pausing for a moment, he spoke with a fiery passion, his words carrying the weight of divine authority. "You can do nothing in your own strength. This is a battle against the roots of carnality, the sinful nature, and the desires that run contrary to the Spirit." His gaze swept across each person in the pews, radiating warmth and love. "Only the Holy Spirit, in His mighty power, can accomplish this profound transformation. All that's needed is your willingness. Once willing, never say, 'I won't do this' or 'I will pray more.' NO! Say, echoing Romans 8:13, '...if by the Spirit you put to death the misdeeds of the body, you will live...'"

The tangible presence of the Holy Spirit enveloped the congregation. Faces bore expressions akin to those of students who had just solved a challenging math problem they had wrestled with throughout a sleepless night. Questions found answers, and expressions of relief graced the countenances of those who had struggled for years to "get right with the Lord." Finally, it all made sense.

Bruce, sensing the Spirit's leading, was compelled to halt his preaching. He stepped back from the pulpit and simply stood there. Oddly, not a single expression among the congregation changed. They welcomed this serene pause, eager to soak in the divine atmosphere.

Then, an unscripted moment unfolded as one of the choir

members rose and approached the pulpit. She gently picked up the microphone and began to sing. The song she sang was unfamiliar, for she had composed it in real-time, inspired by the pastor's message. It wove together verses from Scripture, like "Draw near to God, and He will draw near to you" and "If my people will humble themselves," and once more, the recurring theme emerged, "...and I will heal their land..." The praise band seamlessly accompanied her, as if they had rehearsed this moment for years. It was a profound and deeply worshipful experience, one where the tangible presence of the Lord permeated every heart, and everyone knew that He was well pleased.

Bruce's heart swelled with joy and excitement until he heard those familiar words again, "...and I will heal their land..." within the song's verse. In an instant, his heart flooded with memories, emotions, and the words God had spoken to him earlier in the week. God often employed what Bruce referred to as 'confirmations' to ensure that he recognized His voice. Bruce's mind raced, grappling with the profound question: what did it truly mean to heal their land? Then, his thoughts turned to those exquisite roses he had encountered earlier.

The Association for Fetal Research found itself ensnared in a legal quagmire, besieged by a multitude of lawsuits. Doctors, nurses, and patients who had undergone abortions at clinics owned and operated by the association across the nation had initiated these legal battles. Their allegations painted a harrowing picture of mistreatment, false information dissemination, and procedures that left them unable to conceive. Some of these individuals had teetered on the precipice of death, while others had tragically succumbed. The association's involvement in the abortion industry extended to every facet, from doctor training through textbooks and manuals to the provision of certified educational programs, the sale of medical equipment and specialized tools, and the promotion of a controversial method for disposing of fetuses, designed to sidestep the graphic images typically wielded by the anti-abortion opposition.

John had meticulously sifted through a staggering volume of emails—over 400 in total—and diligently pursued leads in an additional 150 freshly generated ones. He recognized that this phase was of paramount importance and was resolute in his determination to stay focused and undeterred. Yet, amidst this relentless pursuit of evidence, the memory of his interview with Maggie Fortunato nagged at him, invading his thoughts. It wasn't merely her physical attractiveness that lingered; there was an intangible quality about her, an inner radiance that seemed to exude from her very being. And that sparkle in her eye, perhaps it was just a play of fluorescent light, but it had captured his attention. This reaction caught John off guard, for he typically viewed women through the lens of potential romantic interests. However, there was something distinctly different about Maggie that eluded his comprehension, a mysterious allure that left him intrigued and, for the moment, slightly distracted from his relentless pursuit of the truth.

The morning sun bathed Bruce's study in a warm, inviting glow as it streamed through the window. This room held a sacred aura, a space where Bruce met with the Lord each day before diving into the hustle and bustle of his busy routine. It felt like hallowed ground, and every visit, regardless of the hour or reason, drew him into fervent prayer.

Kneeling before the Lord, Bruce's heart swelled with gratitude for the extraordinary work God had wrought within their church the previous Sunday. "Thank You for taking the center stage," he whispered in prayer, his voice filled with reverence. "That's what it's all about, and I'm humbly thankful for Your presence. And thank You for Maggie's remarkable salvation. Her transformation has been nothing short of miraculous."

A contemplative pause hung in the air as Bruce recalled the unexpected revelation that the choir's most moving voice belonged to Maggie, a new Christian of just two weeks. "God's ways are truly mysterious," he mused. "There's no doubt about that."

Continuing his prayer, Bruce sought divine guidance on how to fulfill God's promise to "heal your land." His Bible in hand, he opened it to a page where the words leaped off the page: "If my people...and will heal their land."

Bruce's eyes scanned the sacred text further, "If my people, who are called by my name, will humble themselves and pray and seek my face and turn from their wicked ways, then will I hear from heaven and will forgive their sin and will heal their land." These words resonated with profound meaning, and Bruce knew he had found his answer.

He began to dissect the verse, contemplating each phrase deeply. "My people," he pondered, "the Lord's chosen, His beloved children." The concept of humility struck him, and he saw fasting as a powerful symbol of humility, intertwined with prayer. Recalling another cherished verse, "If we ask anything according to God's will, He hears us," Bruce recognized that healing the land was undoubtedly God's will, given its frequent mention in the Bible.

As his thoughts delved further into the verse, the melody of the song Maggie had sung during the service echoed in his heart. It felt like the prayer he had been uttering daily since surrendering his heart to the Lord, a fervent longing to seek His face. He reflected on the recent service, the manifest visitation of the Holy Spirit, and the collective decision to walk in the Spirit henceforth.

Deep in contemplation, Bruce heard a gentle whisper in his heart, "Apply, don't just preach." He realized that he needn't deliver a sermon but must instead embody the principles he had just meditated upon. As he had seen the light and resolved to walk in the Spirit, he now understood the importance of persistently seeking God's face, humbling himself, and turning from any wicked ways. Only then could he wholeheartedly trust in God's promise to listen, forgive, and bring healing.

His reverie was interrupted by the ringing of the phone, grounding him in the present moment.

John's mind drifted back to those first two weeks in Stapleton, where the relentless pursuit of truth had consumed his every moment. The countless interviews with the enigmatic religious group, the exhaustive email searches, and the meticulous follow-ups on the minutest of details had left an indelible mark. However, it was when he began recollecting the events of the third week that an overwhelming sense of anguish washed over him.

The evening sky was a breathtaking canvas, streaked with hues of red, orange, and delicate shades of purple as John embarked on his drive home—or more accurately, to his high-tech sanctuary nestled within the heart of the town. Every conceivable machine and gadget adorned his office, an arsenal of technology that would have elicited envy even from a seasoned electronics store manager.

Without warning, the world came crashing in as another car violently collided with his own, jolting him from his reverie. A surge of adrenaline coursed through him as he gripped the steering wheel, realizing that this was no mere accident. His assailant was unrelenting. John's eyes darted nervously to the approaching vehicle, which drew closer and closer until the menacing grille swallowed up his car's rear bumper.

"Bam! Bam, slam!" The relentless strikes against his bumper sent his vehicle careening across the road. Panic gripped him as he struggled to regain control, and sparks erupted as his car collided with a speed limit sign. "Who was this guy, and what does he want with me?" John's racing thoughts echoed his escalating fear. Glancing down at his speedometer, he was met with a grim revelation: he was doing a reckless 60 in a 45-mile-per-hour zone.

Desperation clawed at him as he yearned to put distance between himself and his relentless pursuer. It was pure instinct now. The shattering of the back window by a gunshot underscored the urgency of the situation. John floored the gas pedal, grateful for his lifelong affinity for swift cars. This vehicle was no exception, catapulting forward as if fired from a gun. The turbocharger roared to life, propelling him from 60 to a staggering 90 in mere seconds. A quick glance in the rearview mirror revealed the unforgiving streets, designed for far lower speeds, protesting his reckless flight. He darted into the oncoming lane, then swerved back, the other car hot on his trail. As they raced over hills, both cars went airborne for heart-pounding moments before crashing back onto the road.

On one such landing, the car's undercarriage struck the ground with a deafening explosion. John couldn't fathom if his relentless pursuer had planted a bomb in his car or if it was some other sinister mechanism at play. The other vehicle wasted no time in closing the gap, pulling alongside John's car. A resounding thud marked the impact, followed by the staccato bursts of a semi-automatic. Pain seared through John's side, and control slipped from his grasp as he careened into a tree. That was the last fragment of consciousness he could cling to.

Bruce reached for the ringing phone, its sudden interruption slicing through the tranquil atmosphere of his study. "Hello?"

"Pastor Bruce? It's Sue." Sue Billings, a faithful member of Bruce's congregation, greeted him with warmth and enthusiasm. She was a woman in her mid-thirties, her blonde hair radiating under the light, and her beauty was surpassed only by her radiant faith. Sue was a true prayer warrior, gifted with evangelism, and she had a heart for leading people to Christ.

Bruce often found it intriguing that Sue was married to Jerry, a man of stark contrast. Jerry worked in a rugged mining field outside of Stapleton, and he was known for his burly demeanor. But despite their differences, Jerry treated Sue with kindness, even if he hadn't yet found the path to faith himself. Easter Sundays were the only occasions when he made it to church, and Sue's devoutness seemed to make him feel somewhat guilty.

"Sue, how are you doing?" Bruce asked.

"I'm doing great!" Sue's voice exuded excitement. "I was so thrilled when Maggie called me to share the good news! I haven't been able to catch up with you, and when I did, it always seemed to slip my mind."

"Yes, what an opportunity to share the Lord. God had it all planned out, and I was glad that you were a part of that plan."

"I was just glad, period," Sue replied earnestly. "It didn't matter to me who was part of the plan as long as it happened. And, wow, how she has grown in the Lord! What a beautiful song she sang Sunday."

"Wasn't it?"

"Well, I knew that her major in college was music, and that she taught music, but boy, did God get her involved quickly."

"Yes, He did. I always like it when He does that."

"And at the service, God was definitely working. I have talked to a number of people since Sunday, people that have just been playing Christian; and, oh, how they have been transformed! They are on fire for God and His work. Don't be surprised if you start getting calls."

"Boy, that's encouraging. Sometimes I wonder if it's just me. So what's going on with you?"

"Well, the Lord has been putting on my heart something that I wanted to share with you. I have been walking through my neighborhood during the evenings, originally to get a little exercise, you know."

Bruce chuckled. He thought of the need for exercise in his own life and then recalled the lack of it.

"Anyway, as I walked by each home, I began praying for the neighbors by name, and then when I got to the homes that I did not know their name, the urge to pray just became stronger."

"Aha."

"It is as if the Lord is giving me exactly what to pray. They were short prayers, right to the point, you could say. I would pray for their salvation, for their hearts to become sensitive to the Lord's calling, for their children, and for blessings upon them."

"That is neat. What a great time of prayer."

"Well, that is what I originally thought, but it has become more, much more!"

"Oh? What do you mean?"

"I mean that the answers are being seen. I mean really seen. For instance, I prayed for the Baileys down the street, and the other day, they approached me as I was walking. We got into a conversation about our church. They had just recently, since I began praying, to be exact, begun to think of how important it was to have their children brought up in church because of all the TV coverage of school violence throughout the nation."

"Really? That is exciting!"

"Yea, and similar stories can be told about the Johnsons, the Millers, the Wraths, the Stantons, and many others. It's like a spiritual awakening," Sue exclaimed.

Bruce's thoughts immediately went back to his quiet time: "Apply, don't preach." He was filled with excitement at the power of prayer and the transformative work of God in people's lives.

Sue continued to share her enthusiasm, discussing a couple of upcoming church meetings and a few more people in need of prayer before they quickly wrapped up their conversation.

"See you in church!" Sue said.

"Okay, Sue. Thanks for calling," Bruce replied.

"Bye," Sue said before hanging up the phone.

Bruce was accustomed to fasting once a week, either for a meal or for the entire day. As he began his usual Thursday fast, he reflected on Sue's newfound ministry of praying for her neighbors while walking in her neighborhood. He remembered a lesson from the Lord that he had learned before: that one should look for where God was working and then join in, rather than starting a ministry and asking God to work in it. Bruce prayed a simple prayer, asking God to confirm if he too should do the same as Sue.

Later that day, Bruce headed to Albright Nursing Home, located just on the outskirts of town. As he approached, he was struck by the beauty of the trip, with green oak trees lining the streets and hills adding to the enjoyment of the ride. Upon arrival, Bruce was greeted by a picturesque view of the home with off-yellow siding, white window shutters, a wrap-around patio with white trim, and colorful flowers that seemed to receive daily attention.

Bruce enjoyed visiting Marian, a strong witness for Christ who had been in his church's senior adult ministry for years. As her health failed, she moved into Albright's.

He strolled down the corridors and noticed a cozy ambiance. Bruce gently knocked at the open door and said, "Good morning, Marian. How are you feeling today?"

"Pastor Bruce. I'm doing well. Please come in. I was excited and looking forward to our visit."

"How are you coping with your health?"

"Wonderful, you know, I still have some aches and pains, but the Lord helps me get through each day. He has such great plans every day that I'm always eager to see what He will do next."

"Is this why you're excited?"

"Yes, but let me explain. About a week ago, I started walking up and down the halls of the nursing home, and it took me quite some time. I never knew there were so many rooms here, honey."

"I can only imagine," said Bruce, who could relate to her experience from his past visits.

Marian's voice trembled with a sense of wonder as she described her recent experiences. "As I walked down the hall," she began, her eyes alight with fervor, "the Lord directed me to pray for each person in every room. I can pray for them by name because of the nameplates on the door. As I began to pray, it was as if the Lord Himself was leading me. I knew exactly what to pray and how to pray for each person, like the words just came to my heart."

Bruce leaned forward, captivated by her words. His heart raced, knowing that this was the confirmation he had been seeking. "That's amazing," he murmured, his anticipation mounting.

Marian's eyes sparkled with spiritual energy as she continued, "Yes! Sweetie, it was as if God was praying through me."

Bruce couldn't contain his curiosity. "Have you noticed any positive outcomes from your prayers?"

crackled with frustration.

"Well--"

"While I'm waiting, the Association for Fetal Research is going to pot! Our earnings are down, our lawyers are busier than a one-armed paper hanger, and our divisions are failing."

"Sir, I've been diligently investigating, but this takes time."

"Time is a luxury that we don't have, son. We're paying you big bucks, and your expense account has no limit. I expect results, and I expect them now!"

Click.

With an abrupt click, the call ended, leaving John in a state of unease. He had only spoken with Dennis Spence a couple of times before, but it was abundantly clear that the man was in dire straits. The Association for Fetal Research, once a towering titan in the corporate world, was now teetering on the edge of precipitous decline.

John was intimately acquainted with the troubles that had besieged the company. The Publication Division, responsible for distributing textbooks on abortion to medical professionals, had seen sales plummet by a staggering 79%. Simultaneously, the medical equipment division, which had once pioneered cutting-edge tools for every facet of the abortion procedure, now faced an 87% decline in sales.

Even the latest and most advanced fetal disposal equipment, boasting exorbitant price tags, languished unsold.

The company's woes were further compounded by a mounting avalanche of lawsuits. In years past, profits had effortlessly absorbed such setbacks, but now the litigation deluge had swelled to such proportions that the company had to employ additional legal teams simply to keep pace.

Despite the mounting turmoil, John remained in the employ of the Association. He was acutely aware that the generous salary he drew furnished him with the financial freedom to pursue his true passion – private investigation – an indulgence he was unwilling to relinquish.

However, the tides of his allegiance had begun to shift following a recent conversation with his sister, Elizabeth. Possessing an innate allure, her blond hair and captivating blue eyes seemed as though they were plucked from the cover of a glossy magazine. The siblings had shared an unbreakable bond forged over the years, their connection deepening with time.

Elizabeth's life had taken an unexpected turn when she found herself pregnant out of wedlock. In a desperate bid to navigate her predicament, she opted for an abortion, believing it would alleviate her situation. Instead, it had only exacerbated her troubles. In hushed tones, she had confided in John about her post-abortion depression, the life-threatening complications that had ensnared her, and her mounting anxieties regarding her ability to conceive again.

What shook John to his core was the revelation of the ethically questionable practices she had encountered at the abortion clinic. Disturbingly, the clinic was owned and operated by none other than the Association for Fetal Research.

As John cast his gaze back upon the tumultuous sequence of events that had led him to this moment, he realized that there were secrets yet to be unveiled, and it was becoming increasingly evident that Sue Billings had been an unseen force in his life since the day of the accident.

Unbeknownst to John, his circumstances were shifting inexorably, all converging toward a singular, divine purpose – leading him to a saving knowledge of Jesus Christ.

Sue had just returned home from the tumultuous scene of the accident, her heart still racing with adrenaline. Remarkably, she couldn't help but feel an unusual sense of calm despite the chaos that had unfurled before her eyes. Even in the face of the car's explosive inferno, she had remained composed, a testament to her unwavering faith and the divine prompting she believed had guided her actions. As she prepared dinner that evening, her excitement and gratitude bubbled over, and she couldn't wait to share her extraordinary experience with her husband, Jerry.

"Jerry, you won't believe what happened to me today," Sue began, her voice filled with eagerness. Jerry, typically a man of few words and rare expressions of gratitude, momentarily set aside his dinner, sensing that this interruption to their customary routine held extraordinary significance.

"Let me say grace first, and then I'll tell you," Sue said, bowing her head. "Dear Lord, I want to thank you for saving John Ivan's life today." Jerry's head snapped up, his eyes fixed on Sue as she closed her eyes and continued her prayer. "Please keep Jerry and

Bruce sensed the Lord's presence like a gentle, reassuring hand on his heart.

As he meditated on the Scriptures, a profound sense of affirmation washed over him. The Lord had impressed upon his heart and confirmed through the sacred text His pleasure with Bruce's unwavering obedience. At first, Bruce couldn't help but feel a pang of unworthiness, acutely aware of the sins that occasionally ensnared him. Yet, in that sacred moment, the Lord's grace enveloped him like a warm embrace, assuaging his doubts.

The Lord gently reminded Bruce of his humility, of the repentant spirit that resided within him. Bruce acknowledged his shortcomings and sought forgiveness for any transgressions. He knew he wasn't a perfect individual, but the Lord, in His boundless love, sought only one thing: commitment. Bruce's whole being radiated with devotion to please his Creator, and that was enough.

With a heart full of gratitude and newfound vigor, Bruce closed his Bible, laced up his tennis shoes, and headed for the door. His commitment to walk the neighborhood and offer prayers had become a cherished ritual. Today, as he embarked on his journey, he felt that same warm sensation permeating his being—a tangible sign of divine approval.

Bruce knew that this simple act of walking and praying brought joy to God's heart. It was as if the words he should utter for each home he passed were gently whispered into his soul, just as Sue and Marian had shared. Every step was guided by the divine, and every prayer was a heartfelt plea for salvation, healing, and deliverance. Bruce prayed for each resident by name, though he was unfamiliar with their individual circumstances. Each prayer was succinct, yet laden with profound meaning, tailored to their unique needs.

His walk was not only spiritually fulfilling but also counted as exercise, a thought that brought a smile to Bruce's face. He hoped that this newfound routine might help him shed some of the extra pounds he had gradually put on in recent years, though that wasn't his primary motivation.

As he returned home, a blinking light on the old-school answering machine caught his attention. Bruce rubbed his eyes in disbelief, wondering if the machine was malfunctioning. To his astonishment, he discovered thirty identical messages, each one a heartfelt request for a time of prayer on Tuesday nights.

"Pastor Bruce, this is Mary. I feel the Lord impressing on my heart to have a time of prayer. Tuesday nights would be a good time. Talk to you in church." Beep.

"Pastor Bruce, this is William. Could we have a time of prayer, maybe on a Tuesday night? This is really important. Let me know." Beep.

Bruce stood there, overwhelmed by the outpouring of spiritual hunger from his congregation. It was a clear sign that God's presence was moving among them, igniting a fervor for prayer and communion.

The answering machine's messages continued to play, each one a plea for prayer, and it left Bruce in a state of awe. He listened to the earnest voice on the other end of the line, introduced as George Hines. It was a name he didn't recognize, and yet the message carried a profound weight.

"Pastor Bruce, this is George Hines." The name hung in the air, unfamiliar but significant. "I don't know a George Hines," Bruce thought as he listened intently. "You don't know me. One of your church members had begun praying for me as they walked through our neighborhood." George's voice was filled with a mix of humility and hope, a stranger reaching out for something beyond himself. "Anyway, I hope this is not too forward, but I was wondering if you could start a prayer time. Tuesday nights are good. I will see you Sunday, and I am looking forward to meeting you." Beep.

Most of the messages mirrored George's request, coming from members of his church, friends of church members, and individuals whose lives had been touched by the transformative power of prayer during those neighborhood walks. The names Sue, Maggie, and Marian appeared on the list, too, their voices radiating with excitement and expectation. Marian, though unable to attend, had plans for a simultaneous prayer time at the nursing home, perfectly synchronized with Tuesday's gathering.

Bruce was overcome with wonder and gratitude as he considered the flood of inquiries and requests. "Lord, this is unbelievable!" he prayed, his heart swelling with emotion. "What are you doing, and why have you chosen me to start it?" The answers remained elusive, but a profound sense of peace settled over him, reassuring him that he was not alone in this divine endeavor.

The following evening, Bruce stood before the infested rose bush, a living testament to his faith and determination. The ladybugs, released with purpose, were now his partners in this horticultural battle. As he carefully inspected the bush, he couldn't help but ponder the parallel between the ladybugs and the spiritual army God was raising.

Kneeling down beside the thriving rose bush, Bruce witnessed the ladybugs diligently at work, devouring the destructive pests that had plagued the plant. It was a visceral reminder of God's faithfulness, His ability to send the right agents at the right time to wage war against the forces of darkness.

In that moment, he couldn't help but think of the armor of God, the divine weapons that were bestowed upon believers. "Put on the whole armor of God," he recalled, "so that we may stand against the devil's schemes. And pray in the Spirit, using prayer as our number one weapon."

With newfound determination, Bruce rose to his feet, the sight of the ladybugs imprinted on his mind as a symbol of divine intervention. He climbed into his car and made his way to the church, ready to prepare for the impending prayer gathering. With every mile that passed, he whispered a prayer, "Lord, show me how to lead this army in prayer," a humble plea to be an instrument in the hands of the Almighty.

John's mind was a whirlwind of confusion and determination after his tense conversation with Dennis Spence. The investigation had been a tumultuous journey, filled with unexpected twists and turns. As he meticulously sifted through the vast sea of data before him, a pattern began to emerge, albeit a cryptic one that tested the limits of his deductive skills.

Amid the labyrinth of information, John's thoughts wandered back to his days in the hospital, a vivid memory that played in his mind as if it were yesterday. The hospitalization had been a grueling chapter in his life, filled with discomfort and uncertainty. He vividly remembered the haze that had enveloped him upon waking from surgery, a sensation reminiscent of his reckless college days when overindulgence had its consequences the morning after.

The doctor's entrance had disrupted his reminiscing, and John was jarred back to the present. The physician's words had been delivered with clinical detachment. "If you didn't have airbags in your car, you would be dead today," the doctor had said before delving into complex medical terminology. John, though, halted him, demanding an explanation in plain language.

"You had severe internal bleeding from your broken ribs due to the accident. We've managed to stabilize it. Additionally, you sustained a bullet wound in your right arm, but it's not a critical injury and should heal relatively quickly."

Impatient, John inquired about his release date, eager to leave the confines of the hospital. The doctor's response carried a sobering warning. "Probably seven to ten days, depending on how well you respond to the medication. Rush your recovery, and you'll end up with an extended stay. The choice is yours."

A peculiar expression crossed John's face, prompting a knowing smile from the doctor. He recognized the telltale signs of a man who had been in quite the chase.

With the doctor's departure, John's eyes darted around the room, searching for his belongings. The presence of his laptop, seemingly unharmed, surprised him. Questions swirled in his mind. "How did it get here?" he pondered. "Did Sue manage to retrieve it from the wreckage? She had her hands full getting me out of that car. Perhaps it was just a stroke of good luck." Little did John know that it was not mere luck at play.

After a brief nap, John felt well enough to make some critical phone calls. His first call was to a friend on the police force back in his hometown, providing the license plate number of his assailant, a lead that Sue had handed to him. He trusted his friend's ability to trace it efficiently, utilizing the broader police network, all while keeping his presence in Stapleton under the radar.

John couldn't shake the feeling that his attacker wouldn't relent easily, that unfinished business hung in the air, waiting for resolution. Scanning through his phone contacts in a small black book, he came up empty-handed. Frustration gnawed at him, but hope dawned as he retrieved his trusty laptop.

With a quick flicker of its screen to life, he navigated to his extensive database, an archive of essential phone numbers and addresses. There, he found the number he had been searching for, a crucial piece in this perilous puzzle.

It was the contact for a company specializing in the relocation of individuals under the veil of the witness protection program. In

territory. He had never harbored anger towards God; instead, he had chosen to ignore the divine presence, pretending that He wasn't there. The idea of someone praying for him stirred emotions he hadn't explored in years. After a brief moment of reflection, John decided to open up, his voice carrying the weight of sincerity.

"My Mom used to say, 'You can never have enough prayers said for you.' She wasn't religious. Just something she said from time to time," John shared, his words a tribute to his mother's wisdom and the sentiment behind Sue's offer.

Sue's eyes lit up with appreciation, her heart warmed by John's openness. It was a simple gesture, but it meant the world to her, especially considering the circumstances. She couldn't help but feel a sense of gratitude for the opportunity to make a connection with someone who had been through such a harrowing experience.

As their conversation came to a close, Sue left the hospital room, carrying with her the knowledge that she had made a meaningful difference in someone's life through her faith and compassion. John, on the other hand, was still troubled by the enigmatic appearance of his laptop. However, that troubling feeling gradually ebbed away, replaced by a sense of comfort and hope as he contemplated Sue's prayers on his behalf. The power of faith and human connection had left its mark on both of them, and it was a reminder that even in the most unexpected places, miracles could unfold.

John's hospital room was bathed in sterile white light, a stark contrast to the shadowy secrets he was uncovering on his laptop. The soft hum of medical equipment provided an eerie backdrop to the grim discoveries he was making.

His phone rang, jolting him from his digital investigation. With a weak voice, he answered, "Hello?"

"John, it's Joe," came the voice on the other end of the line. Joe was more than just a voice on the phone; he was John's lifeline to the police station, a trusted ally who had aided John in countless investigations.

"Joe, how are you?" John inquired, though every word he spoke seemed to cost him precious energy.

"Good. Listen, I couldn't get a real check on the license you gave me," Joe explained. "The driver got the car from a shady rental lot, and he knew what he was doing. I hope you know what you're doing too. Don't get yourself killed in some small town."

"I'll be careful. Thanks for trying," John replied before ending the call. His inquiries into the license plate number had yielded no results, but he couldn't afford to be discouraged. There was too much at stake.

The room felt claustrophobic as John's thoughts raced. He had a gut feeling that the emails he had received earlier in the week were somehow linked to the danger he found himself in. In an age where technology blurred the lines between safety and vulnerability, he knew that anything was possible.

Summoning every ounce of his strength, John retrieved his laptop and opened the three emails that had piqued his interest. Each word on the screen carried a weight of intrigue and menace.

The first email, signed with the enigmatic screen name "Snag," hinted at a nefarious plan and a potential betrayal. It mentioned sidestepping the Association, a phrase that raised alarm bells in John's mind.

The second email, from someone identified as "Night," spoke of goals and a hidden agenda, urging the recipient to gather vital information.

The third email was the most cryptic and ominous of all. Signed as "Co-warrior," it bestowed a sense of grave responsibility upon the recipient. It demanded secrecy and flawless execution of an undisclosed plan, with the Association remaining blissfully unaware of their existence.

John's heart raced as he read these emails, feeling the noose of danger tighten around him. It seemed that each sender had transformed into a potential suspect, their words dripping with sinister intent.

With trembling fingers, John began his digital hunt for clues, determined to unravel the web of deception and unmask those who sought his demise. The room may have been quiet, but the storm of intrigue and danger was raging within him.

THREE

Restless and anxious, Bruce spent a Saturday night tossing and turning in his bed. The weight of a looming challenge pressed heavily upon him. It was an unprecedented predicament for a seasoned minister like him – he had no sermon for the upcoming Sunday service. This wasn't a result of procrastination; he had fervently prayed for divine guidance throughout the week, yet his efforts had yielded nothing - not a single thought, not a solitary scripture verse, just an unsettling void.

The silence of the night hung heavy around him as he considered his predicament. Bruce knew that he couldn't simply stand before his congregation empty-handed. He had always relied on the Lord's inspiration to deliver his sermons, and this spiritual drought left him feeling bewildered and inadequate.

Finally, unable to endure the restlessness any longer, Bruce arose from his bed and made his way to his study. There, amidst an eclectic collection of clocks, an old cuckoo clock – a family heirloom – hung on the wall. The once cheerful "cuckoo" had been silenced, a testament to his current state of mind.

Bruce was a clock enthusiast with a fascination for timepieces of all kinds – grandfather clocks, anniversary clocks, table clocks, wall clocks, and even a dining room table that doubled as a clock. As he stared at the clock on the wall, he marveled at its intricacies, finding solace in the rhythmic ticking of its hands. Time seemed to move steadily, a stark contrast to the stagnant ideas that eluded him.

Kneeling down in the dimly lit room, Bruce began to pray. His words were humble, an acknowledgment of his inadequacy juxtaposed with unwavering faith. "Lord," he whispered, "I thank you for all that you have done this week. Thank you for allowing me to be such a vital part of whatever you are beginning in the hearts of your saints."

His voice quivered slightly as he continued, "Quite honestly, I feel inadequate and a little ashamed that nothing has come to mind for the sermon tomorrow. But Lord, I know that your ways are higher than my ways, and your thoughts are higher than my thoughts. I place into your hands what you want to say tomorrow. In Jesus' name, amen."

During his prayer, Bruce could feel the heavy burden of anxiety gradually being lifted. It was a sensation he had experienced countless times before, a reminder of God's promise to "guard your heart and your mind in Christ Jesus." His faith in that promise brought comfort, like a soothing balm to his troubled soul.

Returning to his bed, Bruce felt a newfound sense of peace. The anxiety that had kept him awake had now dissipated. He nestled into his covers, his heart lighter, and his mind at rest. Suddenly, like a gentle whisper in the night, inspiration struck.

"Testimonies!" he realized. The idea was as clear as day, a timely revelation. "We haven't done testimonies in quite a while, and what a perfect time to do this with all that is going on! Lord, you are wonderful! Thank you for the answer."

With that, Bruce drifted into a peaceful slumber, his faith reaffirmed and his heart ready to deliver a sermon inspired by the lives and experiences of his congregation.

On that Sunday morning, the atmosphere in the church was discernibly different from the week before. It wasn't just a matter of perception; the pews were genuinely filled with more congregants than usual. Bruce's excitement buzzed beneath his composed exterior. He couldn't contain his anticipation for what the day held, a day filled with God's divine workings in his life and in the lives of at least 30 of his cherished congregants.

Bruce began the service with a heartfelt prayer, his words imbued with reverence and longing. His voice resonated with an earnest plea, "Lord, we thank you for such a glorious day that we can worship You and hear what You have to say to us. Come in all Your power. Come, Holy Spirit. You are welcomed."

The melodies that filled the sanctuary that morning bore a different quality than what Bruce had grown accustomed to. The choir, an ever-devoted source of spiritual resonance, seemed to transcend their usual praise and worship. Their voices carried not only a message of devotion but also an invitation, a beckoning to the divine. It was an unfamiliar yet strangely welcome shift. The hymn, with its revised lyrics of praise and adoration set to a familiar tune, resonated deeply within the hearts of the congregation.

In that transformative moment, something extraordinary occurred, defying rational explanation. A sensation, akin to a gentle gust of wind, seemed to sweep through the sacred space. It was as if the very breath of God was brushing past them, an ethereal presence that left no visible trace – no fluttering robes or swaying scarves. This inexplicable event was unprecedented in the history of this humble church, and the congregation collectively held its breath in awe.

Bruce, overwhelmed with joy, raised his eyes toward the heavens. It felt as though the Lord had chosen this modest sanctuary in the unassuming town of Stapleton, a place known to only a select few, to grace with His divine presence.

As the choir's celestial melodies reached their crescendo and concluded, Bruce stepped forward to the microphone. His eyes, filled with a profound sense of gratitude and humility, gazed upon his congregation. "Lord, welcome," he declared, and the congregation responded with a resounding "Amen."

With deliberate and measured steps, Bruce descended from the pulpit and walked to the front of the church. A hushed and reverent anticipation filled the air as he extended an open invitation to the congregation. "Today," he began, "I want to give all of you an opportunity to share what God has been doing in your lives."

As if moved by an invisible force, one by one, individuals of all ages, genders, races, and socioeconomic backgrounds began to step forward. Their faces reflected a mix of humility, hope, and an unwavering belief in the divine presence that had touched their lives. Today, they were eager to share their stories, knowing that they were about to embark on a sacred journey of testimony and revelation.

Mary stepped forward, her voice carrying both vulnerability and determination as she embarked on the journey of sharing her story. Her forties had unfolded a life marked by the rollercoaster of joys and sorrows, and her marital history bore the scars of a bitter divorce. An air of sincerity surrounded her as she stood before the congregation, her gaze shifting between faces that held both compassion and curiosity.

Bruce, ever the gentle shepherd of his flock, politely interjected, his voice filled with warmth and patience. "Excuse me, Mary," he said with a kind smile, "could you please introduce yourself for the sake of newcomers?"

Mary nodded graciously, her gaze softening as she looked directly at the newcomers. "Of course, my name is Mary," she began anew, her voice clear and resolute.

She continued, recounting her recent interaction with Bruce, a moment of outreach that had sparked a transformation within her. Her story was one of struggle and self-discovery, a journey through which she had navigated the tumultuous waters of faith. Her faith had often felt lukewarm, and she had sometimes veered towards decisions rooted in desire rather than righteousness. Her penchant for shopping, even in the face of mounting credit card debt, was a testament to her vulnerability. Despite her pleasant demeanor, it was evident that her commitment to God's teachings had, at times, wavered.

But her narrative pivoted as she delved into her recent spiritual awakening. Mary described the pivotal sermon on the Holy Spirit delivered by Bruce, a moment that had reshaped her understanding of faith. It was a revelation that had shifted her focus from self-reliance to divine dependency. Her eyes sparkled with newfound fervor as she spoke of the freedom she had found in surrendering to the Holy Spirit's guidance.

The transformation didn't stop there. With unwavering conviction, Mary spoke of a call to prayer that had transformed her daily life. It had begun as a gentle tug on her heart during her morning walks, urging her to pray not only for those she knew but also for strangers. The urgency of the divine directive had led her to pray for hours, the physical act of walking a metaphor for her spiritual journey.

As her prayers unfolded, they took on a life of their own, manifesting as answered petitions in the lives of her neighbors. Mary's words held the power to bring forth living proof of God's grace. She shared the story of the Ross family, whose troubled marriage had been mended through her intercession. As the family stood before the congregation, smiles radiating their newfound happiness, the congregation couldn't help but be moved by the living testament to God's transformative power.

Mary's voice resonated with humility and awe as she shared similar stories of answered prayers. Her testimony was a testament to the profound change that divine reliance had brought to her life. Her final words, spoken with unwavering conviction, stirred hearts within the church.

"I know that God has called all of us to do more wonderful works than His Son. He said so himself in His word," Mary declared, her eyes shining with a newfound sense of purpose. "God has truly been working in my life, and I had a hunch after talking with some of my friends that He was doing the same with others in our church."

As Mary's testimony concluded, a sense of awe hung in the air. Her story was a powerful reminder of the transformative potential of faith and reliance on the Holy Spirit, leaving the congregation with a deep sense of hope and inspiration.

George Hines, a distinguished older gentleman in his late 50s, stood up, his hair graying gracefully, lending him an air of wisdom and experience.

"My name is George Hines," he began, his voice quivering with a mixture of vulnerability and excitement. Bruce felt a shiver down his spine as he recognized George's name from one of the thirty messages on his answering machine. "I would like you all to know that I am new to this church. As a matter of fact, this is my first time here. You may be wondering why I am so bold to come up in front of people that I have never met and bare my soul. It is because of the miracle that God has so graciously granted me."

George paused, and the room held its collective breath, hanging onto his every word. His deep breath resonated through the silence, building a sense of anticipation. "I was only four years old when my parents divorced. I went to live with my mom while Dad would visit once a month. I had heard of a God that did wonderful things, so I asked Him to bring my Mom and Dad back together. God never answered that prayer, so I figured that God was not real. He must not exist, otherwise He would have answered such a noble and pure request."

Tears welled up in George's eyes as he delved into his past, his voice quivering with the raw emotions of a wounded child. "The years passed by, and I made it on my own. I was proud of that fact, however there was something missing in my life, and I would not admit that to a soul. I tried to rationalize with myself. I told myself that I had a successful job, a six-figure income, the nicest house that money could buy, a beautiful wife, and children that any dad would be proud of. So what was it: adventure? No. I had been down that road in my earlier days. All I knew was that there was something missing."

The room seemed to hold its breath, wrapped in George's narrative. His words painted a vivid picture of a man who had it all but felt an insurmountable void within. The audience could almost feel the weight of his unspoken burden.

"During the course of my life, I experienced a tragedy as I am sure many of you can identify with through similar situations. I lost the use of my left leg because of a freak accident."

A collective empathy washed over the congregation as they listened to George's tale of tragedy. His voice quivered with sorrow, and many in the room could relate to the pain of unexpected loss.

"But recently, while sitting on my porch, I noticed a young woman walking through the neighborhood. Her name was Sue Billings, not Mary. She caught my eye and greeted me with a warm smile and a hearty 'Good morning.' For some reason, I got up and walked down to the sidewalk to start a conversation with her. Soon she asked me about my spiritual beliefs, and I told her that I had none. To my surprise, she said that she had been praying for my knee. I was astonished and asked her how she knew about my knee. She explained that she felt compelled to pray for me while walking through the neighborhood and believed that it was Jesus's will for me to be healed."

George's voice filled with wonder as he recounted this unexpected encounter, his words tinged with amazement and gratitude. The audience hung onto his every word, captivated by the unfolding miracle.

"I laughed and said that I would give all I have to God if He were to heal me right there and then. Sue then asked for permission to pray for me while laying her hands on my knee. Without knowing why, I gave her permission, and she prayed for me."

The room seemed to hold its breath as George described the pivotal moment when faith and healing collided. The audience could almost feel the warmth of Sue's touch and the electric charge in the air as she prayed.

"As she prayed, I felt a warm sensation, almost like an electrical current I experienced as a child. The prayer was short, and when she finished, I just sat there, stunned. Without even trying, I knew my knee was healed. After what seemed like minutes of silence, I reached down and undid my leg brace. I stood up, bent down, stretched my leg, and jumped up and down. I was completely and wholly healed, not just partially."

The room erupted with gasps of astonishment and applause, mirroring the joy and wonder that George felt in that life-altering moment. His description transported everyone present into the scene, experiencing the miraculous transformation alongside him.

"With tears in my eyes, I immediately asked her, 'What must I do to surrender everything to God?' She simply replied, 'Place your trust in Jesus for your ticket to heaven and for life's road map. Ask Him to forgive you for wanting to make it on your own. Ask Him to be your Savior.' So that's what I did right there on the spot. And something amazing happened. The feeling of a void vanished! It was gone! All I remember is standing there with a deep sense of well-being, something I had never experienced before. I'd like to thank Jesus and Sue Billings for this life-changing experience."

George's voice quivered with gratitude, his words carrying the weight of a profound transformation. The room was awash with emotion as those gathered shared in his newfound sense of purpose and fulfillment.

"I am overwhelmed with gratitude for the time I have already spent with all of you this morning. I feel God's presence here, just like I did when He reached down and healed my knee. With Sue's encouragement, I was bold enough to call a pastor I had never met before, and ask for a time that we could come together and pray. Tuesday seems to be the perfect day for that."

George's testimony left an indelible mark on the congregation, filling the room with an all-encompassing sense of awe and inspiration. His journey from doubt to faith, from despair to healing, had touched the hearts of everyone present, leaving them with a profound sense of hope and wonder.

With those words, George Hines sat down, his heart brimming with deep emotion, his eyes glistening with tears of gratitude. Sharing his profound journey with the congregation had been a transformative experience, one that had not only healed his body but had also mended his soul. He felt a profound connection to the people in the room, a shared understanding that transcended words.

As the others took their turn to speak, their voices were filled with the raw, authentic emotions of their own stories. The room became a sanctuary of vulnerability and shared pain, a place where the weight of their burdens was lifted, and hope began to take root. It became evident that everyone had a similar story to tell, and there were about thirty tales of faith, struggle, and redemption echoing through the hallowed walls.

When the last person finished sharing, it was a moment of collective catharsis. The room seemed to hold its breath, hanging onto the lingering echoes of those heartfelt narratives. Bruce, the pastor, stood at the pulpit, his face radiating warmth and compassion as he prepared to conclude this extraordinary gathering.

Bruce's voice filled the room, resonating with a quiet authority that commanded attention and reverence. He announced that the church would open its doors on Tuesday night, beginning at around 5:00 p.m., inviting anyone who wished to come and seek solace in prayer. The announcement sent ripples of anticipation through the congregation, and a swell of emotion swept over the assembled worshippers.

A wave of applause, fervent and heartfelt, surged through the building like a tidal wave of gratitude and praise. People stood, their hands clapping rhythmically, their voices raised in joyful exultation. It was a moment of communal celebration, an outpouring of shared faith and belief.

Bruce, too, joined in the applause, his heart swelling with gratitude and awe. He knew, deep within his soul, that something truly remarkable was happening in their midst. God's presence was undeniable, a Godly force that bound them together in a moment of divine connection. As the applause continued and the congregation praised the Lord with all their hearts, a mysterious breeze, seemingly summoned by a higher power, began to waft through the church. At first, it was a gentle caress, brushing against the faces of those gathered. But as their praises grew louder and more fervent, the breeze intensified, becoming a powerful and refreshing gust of wind.

Bruce glanced around, realizing that the church's aging air-conditioning system was no match for this divine breeze. It was a reminder that in their collective worship, they had tapped into something greater, something beyond the realm of the ordinary. This breeze, a gift from the heavens, filled the room with a sense of renewal and rejuvenation, washing away weariness and filling their spirits with a profound sense of peace.

In that moment, as they basked in the gentle embrace of the celestial breeze, Bruce knew that this small town church had experienced a divine encounter, a moment of profound connection with the divine. Their faith had been reaffirmed, their hearts rekindled, and their souls stirred by the inexplicable wonders of the spiritual world. It was a moment they would carry with them, a testament to the power of faith, community, and the boundless grace of God.

John's cramped office felt like a world away from the emotional turmoil he was experiencing. He'd taken a much-needed break from poring over the evidence he'd painstakingly gathered over the past three months, his heart heavy with concern for his sister, Elizabeth. Their last conversation had left him deeply unsettled, and he couldn't shake the nagging worry about her well-being.

Taking a deep breath, John dialed Elizabeth's number, the anticipation weighing on him as he waited for her to pick up. When she finally did, her voice carried a hint of reluctance, and he could sense the unspoken turmoil in her response. "I'm really worried about you," John said, his words laden with genuine concern. "Are you doing okay?"

"It's fine, John. I don't want to bother you," she replied, her voice trembling with uncertainty.

John's heart ached at her response, and he knew he couldn't let it go. He needed to dig deeper, to uncover the pain that lay beneath her facade. "How are you sleeping? Are you still having nightmares?" he asked gently, his voice tender with empathy. Elizabeth had confided in him about the horrifying nightmares that plagued her, and they both knew they couldn't be ignored.

Elizabeth hesitated, her voice quivering as she opened up about her torment. "Yes, they're still happening. You know, it wouldn't be so bad if they were different, but they're always the same, like someone is punishing me for the decision I made to abort my baby." Her words were punctuated by heartbreaking sobs, her pain spilling over into the phone call. "Why did I make that decision? Why? I hate myself for it. I could have done better. I could have raised him or given him up for adoption to a loving family."

Listening to Elizabeth's anguish was excruciating for John. He wished he could reach through the phone and comfort her in person. "Shhh, Lizee, it's okay. You made the best decision you could at the time," he whispered soothingly, his heart aching in tandem with hers.

"Really, Johnny? Do you really believe that?" Elizabeth's voice wavered with vulnerability, seeking validation and absolution.

"Yes, I do. Now calm down. Don't be so hard on yourself. You did what you thought was best," John reassured her, his voice unwavering in its support.

"But the dreams! I can't take any more of these dreams!" Elizabeth's anguish echoed through the line, and her tears flowed freely.

"They'll go away. Just be patient," John replied, his words a lifeline of hope in the midst of her despair. After some time on the phone, she seemed to be feeling better. After saying goodbye, John couldn't shake off her words. "Those dreams... those dreams!" he thought. "If it was the right decision, why is there so much emotional trauma? Am I missing something?"

John's mind wrestled with a deep inner conflict, a gnawing doubt that refused to be silenced. He questioned his unwavering commitment to the company he worked for, one that promoted abortion, profited from it, and pushed its agenda relentlessly. "Maybe Elizabeth is just an exception. Maybe most people who have an abortion are relieved and happy to start anew," he reasoned, desperately searching for reassurance. But despite his attempts at self-conviction, the nagging feeling in his gut persisted, a relentless reminder that something wasn't quite right.

John shifted uncomfortably in his chair, his thoughts pulling him away from the sterile confines of his office. His shoulder, once injured and now fully healed, throbbed with discomfort, serving as a constant reminder of the traumatic accident he'd endured. As his mind wandered, he couldn't help but reflect on those harrowing days in the hospital, where pain and uncertainty had been his constant companions.

Reflecting on his time in the hospital, his mind wandered back to the sterile, clinical environment. The memories were a vivid tapestry of discomfort, exhaustion, and constant interruptions. He realized that what he needed most was rest, a precious commodity that had been in short supply. Nurses would march into his room at all hours of the night, their footsteps echoing through the quiet corridors as they checked his vitals or administered medications. The incessant disruptions left him yearning for the peace and quiet of his own home.

Despite the less-than-ideal circumstances, John knew that he couldn't afford to be unproductive. He was a man on a mission, determined to unravel the mysteries that had brought him to this point. With a sense of grim determination, he rolled his bedside table closer, laptop perched atop it, and got to work. His fingers danced across the keyboard, and he signed onto the internet, his virtual portal to a world of information.

He navigated to a physician referral page, a vast database of medical practitioners across the United States, neatly organized by regions, states, counties, and cities. John's eyes focused intently on the screen as he typed in the last name "Myers." The search yielded twenty results, one of which piqued his interest—there was a Dr. Myers listed in Stapleton. A glimmer of hope ignited within him. "Bingo!" John thought with a surge of excitement. "Now, if I can just get out of here and do some legwork."

His gaze shifted to the address and phone number, and with a few swift keystrokes, he highlighted, copied, and pasted the information into his database. The power of technology was at his fingertips, as he accessed all his vital information with the ease of a well-practiced investigator.

Hours seemed to slip away as John meticulously traced the origin of an elusive email, hunting for the elusive sender. He had been relentless in his pursuit of the truth, and finally, his diligence paid off. The name of the sender emerged—Dr. Kenneth Penkowski, residing in California. John quickly downloaded the address and phone number and initiated a browser search. To his surprise, Dr. Penkowski had his own webpage, a virtual portal to a world of medical possibilities.

John's curiosity was piqued as he delved into the doctor's offerings. Dr. Penkowski's webpage showcased a unique emphasis on biotechnology, with a focus on preserving youthfulness. The range of procedures on display ranged from the simple to the radical, including plastic surgery, liposuction, face lifts, breast reduction, enhancement, and an enigmatic term—rib restructuring. John couldn't help but ponder the latter, his mind wandering to a famous movie star who had undergone similar surgery for a more shapely physique.

As he made notes about Dr. Penkowski's webpage, John was pulled back to reality by a sudden knock at the hospital room door. Startled, he wondered who else might know of his presence there.

"Come in," he replied, his voice tinged with both curiosity and caution.

To his surprise and delight, Maggie entered the room, an ethereal presence in her elegant attire and a hint of perfume that lingered in the air. Her visit brought a sense of warmth and familiarity to the sterile surroundings.

"Hi, John. I hope it's okay to visit you." she said with a disarming smile.

John's heart skipped a beat as he welcomed her into his room. He couldn't deny the thrill of having her by his side, and he couldn't help but wonder what secrets lay behind her enigmatic smile.

It was a Tuesday, and the atmosphere in the church was charged with a sense of urgency and anticipation. Emotions ran high as members began to grasp the profound importance of the impending prayer gathering, especially considering the relentless challenges that had plagued their day. It felt as though, whenever God was poised to unveil something truly miraculous, the relentless adversary, the Enemy, would rear its head to obstruct the divine plan. And in the midst of it all, Bruce stood as a vivid example of this struggle.

The day dawned with a sense of unease at Bruce's home as the air-conditioning unit decided to abandon its cooling duties. The oppressive heat seemed to mirror Bruce's frustration as he reached for the telephone, only to be met with the deafening silence of a dead dial tone. Borrowing a neighbor's cell phone, he embarked on the arduous journey of making the necessary calls, all the while the sweltering heat threatened to overwhelm him.

Upon his arrival at the church, Bruce was greeted by disheartening news. A scheduled missionary group meeting, an event of profound importance, had inexplicably vanished from the church calendar. And if that weren't enough, the electricity had decided to abandon them as well, casting the church into darkness. The late afternoon loomed ahead, and Bruce could only dread the thought of enduring it without the solace of air-conditioning and the comforting glow of lights.

Meanwhile, Sue's day unfolded with its own share of challenges. Her car had chosen this very day to break down, leaving her stranded and disheartened. Desperation led her to call her husband, Jerry, hoping for a glimmer of hope in this sea of adversity. However, Jerry's response was far from enthusiastic.

"You might have to skip the church meeting tonight, Sue," Jerry's voice crackled through the phone line.

Desperation seeped into Sue's voice as she replied, "Jerry, this is crucial! I made a promise to pick up three individuals who are not regular churchgoers. Please, be a sweetheart and come to my aid."

Jerry, torn between his commitments and his love for Sue, finally relented. "I'll see what I can do. I have a friend at work, James, who's quite handy with cars as a hobby. He might be able to help."

Sue's hope rekindled. "Is this the same James who underwent a remarkable transformation?"

Jerry's voice softened. "Yes, the very same. I'll explain the situation to him, and I'm sure he'll be willing to assist you. I'm sorry, Sue, but I have to work late tonight. You know I'd be there if I could."

In that moment, Jerry's love for his wife shone brightly. He went the extra mile by contacting James, even though it was his day off—a gesture that few would have made for a co-worker.

And then, providence intervened. James not only agreed to help but went a step further, arriving at Sue's home to repair the car right in the driveway. Gratitude welled up in Sue as she asked, "How can I repay you?"

With a warm smile, James replied, "How about you give me directions to your church? Your husband told me all about tonight's event. I'd love to attend that prayer meeting."

Sue readily obliged, her heart soaring with gratitude. "You've got it."

As James drove away, Sue bowed her head in prayer, overwhelmed with gratitude. "Thank you, Lord," she whispered. "Thank you for providing the help to fix the car and for allowing me to bring these newcomers to the prayer meeting tonight. Your goodness knows no bounds!"

It seemed as if trouble was hitting everyone in town. One by one, each person from the original group of 30 that called Bruce and stood Sunday morning were experiencing car problems, electrical problems, phone problems, and other obstacles that seemed to detain them.

But one by one, each person prayed, and their prayers were answered.

Bruce also prayed, "Father, how could I have made such a terrible mistake? What am I going to do about the missionaries?" Then a thought came to mind. Why not call them, invite them to the prayer meeting, and reschedule their meeting later in the week? So that is what he did.

He also managed to get everything at home straightened out. The only remaining obstacle was the lack of power at the church. It was 4:55 pm, and there was still no power.

John's face lit up with a radiant smile as he allowed himself to wander down memory lane, retracing the steps of Maggie's visit to the hospital. It had been six weeks and a half since that unforgettable day, but the memory of her graceful entrance through the hospital room door still sent warmth surging through his heart. There was something inexplicably enchanting about her presence that he couldn't quite put into words, but regardless of the reason, he cherished every second of her visit. John's life had been a whirlwind of work and responsibilities, leaving him with no time for dating or the pursuit of happiness.

"I was talking to Sue Billings," Maggie began, her voice gentle and soothing, "and she mentioned that you were here in the hospital. She's a dear friend of mine."

John nodded, a mixture of excitement and apprehension bubbling within him. He wanted to make the best impression, to show her the genuine gratitude he felt for her visit.

"Anyway," Maggie continued, her eyes filled with empathy, "she shared the whole story with me. How are you feeling?"

A sigh of relief escaped John's lips as he realized they were having a normal conversation. "I'm actually feeling better," he replied, grateful for the chance to connect with her.

"That's good to hear. How much longer do they expect you to be here?"

John grinned, and Maggie's smile mirrored his own. "They've hinted that if I play nice and don't stir up any trouble, they might let me go by the end of the week."

Maggie's sincerity touched John's heart. He felt a deep appreciation for her genuine concern, even if he couldn't fully share her faith. "I'd be honored if you prayed for me," he replied, careful not to offend her with his own beliefs.

With a gentle touch, Maggie placed her hand on his, her voice filled with compassion as she began to pray. John closed his eyes, allowing her words to wash over him, not really focusing on their content. His profession as a private investigator made him naturally curious about people's intentions, but he chose to set that aside in this moment, overwhelmed by gratitude.

"Lord, thank You with all my heart for sparing John's life. I pray You would open his eyes and touch his heart, leading him to make a significant decision that draws him closer to You. Stir his spirit, Lord, and guide him on a path that will transform his soul. In Jesus' name, Amen."

"Thank you," John whispered, simplicity and sincerity in his words.

As Maggie withdrew her hand, John felt a pang of longing, as if a breathtaking sunset had just faded, leaving a yearning for more. Maggie mentioned her upcoming meeting at her church and her anticipation for it.

"Thank you for coming," John said, trying to hide the hope in his voice. "Will I have the pleasure of seeing you again?" He cringed inwardly, fearing his words sounded clichéd.

Maggie's response filled the room with an air of promise. "I would love that. How about I visit again before you leave the hospital?"

Excitement surged within John, a sensation he rarely allowed himself to indulge in. It was a departure from his usually stoic demeanor, a refreshing change he welcomed with open arms. "That sounds wonderful! I'll be looking forward to it," he replied, relieved that he hadn't embarrassed himself.

FOUR

Bruce's gaze drifted toward his watch, revealing that it was just five minutes to five, and the oppressive grip of a power outage still held the church in its grasp. Despite the brilliant sunshine streaming through the windows, the interior of the church felt stifling and airless, devoid of the relief that the air conditioning once provided. The stained glass windows, which spanned from one end of the church to the other, appeared washed out, casting an eerie, dimly lit ambiance that obscured the view inside.

As the congregation trickled in, their faces bore no surprise at the continued absence of electricity. Maggie and Sue stood engaged in conversations with others, their voices resonating with stories of the day's trials and distractions, challenges that nearly deterred them from gathering together.

Taking his place before the assembly of 30-40 souls, Bruce began, his voice carrying a blend of resilience and faith, "How many of you encountered obstacles, setbacks, and distractions today that nearly kept you from joining us tonight?" Three-quarters of the hands in the room rose in unison. "I, too, faced similar trials at home and here in the church, and you're living through one of them right now, feeling the absence of air conditioning and light." Heads nodded in understanding and agreement. "I reached out to the electric company, but it seems God has ordained our presence here tonight despite these challenges. We entrust it all into His hands."

With those words, everyone descended to their knees—some at the altar, others in their seats, and a few with their hands raised in surrender. Prayer began silently, but soon a voice broke the stillness, and others followed suit. The room was filled with simple, heartfelt petitions.

Sue Billings, with earnestness in her voice, prayed, "Father, we thank you for guiding us into the neighborhoods of our community to pray for the lost, to bring hope to the discouraged, and to fortify the faithful. Keep using us to make a difference for Christ."

Then, George Hines, though inexperienced, prayed with the candor of a child. "We pray for God's presence to be here with us, to illuminate our path. And let's not forget to pray for Pastor Bruce; he's carrying quite a burden. Amen."

Bruce couldn't help but smile at the simplicity and innocence of George's prayer. "God will indeed honor that," he thought.

Maggie Fortunato initiated her prayer, "Father, we thank you for rescuing us from the abyss of sin and for sending your son, Jesus Christ, to redeem us through his sacrifice on the cross and his resurrection..." Suddenly, her voice gently trailed off, replaced by a soft and melodious song of praise. Her singing was like the serenade of an angel, and as her voice soared, everyone joined in the spontaneous chorus—a simple refrain that resonated with the hearts of all present.

In that moment, the stifling heat dissipated, and an inexplicable coolness enveloped the room, reminiscent of the gentle breeze they had experienced on Sunday morning. As the singing continued, the presence of God became undeniable, and excitement coursed through every heart.

When prayers resumed, a common theme emerged: the plea for forgiveness of sins. As each person confessed their transgressions, it felt as if a floodgate was slowly swinging open, and a torrent of repentance was about to rush in. Suddenly, a brilliant burst of light pierced through the stained glass windows, a radiance that couldn't be attributed to the setting sun. Its pure, white brilliance resembled the searchlights used in the darkest of nights. The light intermingled from window to window near the ceiling before descending toward the praying congregants. Despite its intensity, it didn't hurt their eyes.

As the light touched each person, tears flowed uncontrollably, including from Bruce himself. Amidst the sobs, voices could be heard, uttering confessions such as, "Lord, forgive me for my sins" and "I am so sorry, Lord, for my disobedience." Sins of omission, lust, and selfish ambition—all forms of wrongdoings were laid bare throughout the sacred space.

In the midst of this divine encounter, Bruce's thoughts drifted to an Old Testament passage that described a prophet's awe-inspiring experience in the presence of the Almighty God. "The doorposts and thresholds shook, and the temple was filled with smoke." The prophet Isaiah, humbled by the encounter, had exclaimed, "Woe to me! I am ruined! For I am a man of unclean lips, and I live among a people of unclean lips, and my eyes have seen the King, the Lord Almighty." In this moment, Bruce recognized that God was purifying His people, preparing them for His service.

John's heart raced as he suddenly realized that he had been so engulfed in the euphoria of Maggie's visit that the thought of missing her return hadn't crossed his mind. Anxiety gnawed at him as he contemplated the fragile connection they had forged, but then, like a lifeline, he remembered he had interviewed her and had her contact information tucked away on his laptop. Still, a sense of scattered thoughts and distraction persisted, clouding his focus.

Seeking to regain his composure, John turned his attention back to his work, thankful for the ability to continue his investigations even from the confines of a hospital room. His yearning to move into his new apartment and access his more advanced equipment intensified. His virtual journey led him back to Dr. Kenneth Penkowski's webpage, and this time, he stumbled upon an uncharted path, previously unnoticed. Clicking on it, he found a video of Dr. Penkowski, providing him with the much-needed positive identification and voice recognition. He swiftly downloaded the video, eager to delve into his next lead.

In the afternoon, an unfamiliar male nurse entered John's room and, to his surprise, locked the door behind him. John's sense of unease grew, as the nurse's expression exuded danger rather than care.

"Mr. Ivan," the man began, showing no intention of allowing John to speak. "You've made a grievous error by poking your nose where it doesn't belong."

"I didn't—" John attempted to defend himself but was rudely interrupted by the unknown nurse.

"You should've never been so impudent as to invade people's privacy! Don't you realize that's against the law?" The man's voice grew increasingly agitated.

"Tell me who, and I can—" John tried to interject but was once again cut off.

"You won't do anything!" The man abruptly produced a silenced gun, its ominous presence chilling the air.

"Wait a moment!" John pleaded, attempting to reason with the man.

"Shut up! I don't take orders from anyone but myself."

"Who sent you?" John persisted, desperate for answers.

"Enough!" The man started to pull the trigger, the sound distinct and unmistakable. Panic surged through John's veins; there wasn't enough time to react. Just as the man aimed the gun directly at John, a knock echoed on the hospital door, causing the assailant to glance away.

"Stapleton police."

Swiftly, the man concealed his weapon and opened the door, grinning at the police officers before casting one final malevolent glance at John. John chose not to reveal anything to the police, deciding it was prudent to maintain a low profile.

As the police officers entered, John's heart pounded, and he felt caught off guard. The conversation with them was a blur, and it dawned on him that it was time to vanish and embark on a new life, under a new identity.

Once the police had departed, John sprang into action, hurriedly removing the tubes and detaching the sensors. The machines began beeping and chirping, and within moments, nurses were rushing into the room.

"Mr. Ivan, what are you doing? You're not discharged!" they exclaimed in a panic.

"I must leave. Now," John asserted firmly, grabbing his laptop and hastily donning the rest of his clothing.

"We can't let you go!" one nurse protested, blocking the doorway.

"I'm sorry," John replied, pushing past her. The commotion he left in his wake paled in comparison to the peril he sensed.

With a quick scan of the hallway for any sign of his would-be assailant, John pressed the elevator button. As the doors slid open, he stepped in and hit the button for the ground floor, his heart pounding in his chest.

In the wake of that Tuesday night event, Stapleton came alive with a fervor that couldn't be contained. Phones rang incessantly, neighbors exchanged hushed conversations over fences, and water cooler talk at work was dominated by discussions of the night's mysterious happenings. While a few skeptics mocked the church attendees, the majority found themselves irresistibly drawn to the unfolding events.

The neighborhood prayer walks gained momentum, yielding results that surpassed anything seen before. People joined hands with trusted friends, pouring their hearts out for those in their community who were yet to embrace Christ. They prayed with fervent dedication for the expansion of God's Kingdom and for Pastor Bruce. These prayers were unadulterated, sincere, often accompanied by tears, and they bore undeniable fruit. It was as if each person had a direct line to the Almighty.

Couples who prayed together found themselves gathering with

other couples in their neighborhood, forging bonds as they lifted their prayers and cries together. Soon, groups throughout Stapleton synchronized their prayers, focusing on specific neighborhoods, streets, businesses, and houses. The tangible answers to their petitions came in the form of people surrendering their lives to Christ, ushering in noticeable transformations, even for those who had initially scoffed. Liquor and adult magazine sales dwindled, and the local jails saw fewer inmates with each passing day.

Yet, amid the Tuesday night gatherings that continued to burgeon with each passing week, an unmistakable power emanated from these meetings. Little did they know that the Enemy was surreptitiously moving pawns into place, setting the stage for a spiritual battle that would soon erupt.

One crucial lesson that had momentarily eluded Bruce was the reality that when God moved in mighty ways, the adversary, Satan, would strive to counter and undermine those divine works. Bruce had been so captivated by the manifestations of God's grace in the church and community that he had neglected to brace himself for the spiritual warfare that lay ahead.

Bruce read aloud from his Bible, "For our struggle is not against flesh and blood, but against the rulers and the authorities, and the powers of this dark world and against the spiritual forces of evil in heavenly places." Every morning, he sought solace with God, allowing the Lord to guide him.

One day, as he ventured into his garden, a sudden wave of panic and fear washed over him. He whispered a prayer, pleading, "Lord, either lift this dreadful feeling or reveal its source." However, as he surveyed his once-tranquil garden, his heart plummeted. Instead of the expected beauty and serenity, his eyes met a scene of devastation—his garden lay scorched, as though a malevolent torch had ravaged the entire area. Bruce's gaze shifted towards his home, only to discover that it, too, had fallen victim to vandalism.

Shutters hung askew, symbols of malevolence etched onto walls, patios, and sidewalks. An array of sinister icons had been employed. Overwhelmed by a tumult of emotions—anger, fear, anxiety, and disbelief—Bruce cried out to God, "Lord, what is this?!" Silence greeted his desperate plea, leaving him with the disheartening realization that he was unprepared for the spiritual warfare that had now begun.

As he grappled with the shocking discovery, Bruce tried to

recall the sequence of events. He remembered returning home late the previous night, well past 1:00 AM, in the pitch-black darkness of his unlit street, hoping not to disturb his slumbering neighbors. Fatigue had weighed on him, obscuring his vision, and he had caught a glimpse of something peculiar in the shadows. Fatigued and with red, weary eyes, he had simply retired to bed.

Rushing to the front of his house to assess the damage, Bruce's heart sank further. The mailbox, once a picturesque fixture mounted on a brick structure adorned with vibrant annuals, now bore the marks of a torch's cruel touch. Burn scars and the same symbols that marred his walls littered his once-pristine yard. As he slowly circled his home, he found himself in the back garden, where his cherished collection of roses had once thrived. Despite the radiant sun above, an oppressive cloud seemed to cast darkness over him. Overwhelmed by a flood of emotions, he sank down against the garden wall, buried his head in his hands, and wept. "Lord, why has this happened?" he implored, but no answer came.

Without hesitation, Bruce snatched his keys and fled his home, racing towards the church. His heart pounded with apprehension as he anticipated the horrors that might await him there. Yet, as he drew closer, his racing heart began to steady, and he breathed a sigh of relief. There was no evidence of damage or vandalism at the church. Nevertheless, Bruce wasn't one to leave things to chance, and he meticulously surveyed the entire property, ensuring its safety.

Upon entering his office, he felt compelled to reach out to George Hines, a newer member of the church who, alongside other volunteers, devoted his time and effort to maintaining the church property and aiding those in need. Bruce picked up the phone, his mind racing as he made calls to individuals within the church, informing them of the potential threat looming over the church and its property.

"Hello?" came George's voice on the other end.

"Hey George, it's Bruce," Bruce's voice quivered with worry.

"Bruce, what's wrong? You sound really upset," George responded, genuine concern coursing through his words.

"My home has been vandalized, and I'm worried that the church might be the next target," Bruce explained, his voice laden with unease.

"Your home too?" George exclaimed, his surprise evident.

"What do you mean 'my home too'?" Bruce asked, his heart sinking with apprehension, fearing the worst.

John managed to slip away from the hospital unharmed, fortunate that the assailant had been spooked by the police and made a hasty escape. He opted for the obscure backstreets on his journey, despite the added time and the agony it inflicted on his injured shoulder. Encrypted emails had guided him to his new residence, and he couldn't afford any risks, especially with a cab driver who might be connected to his attacker.

At last, he reached his destination: a picturesque house nestled in a tranquil neighborhood, where meticulously groomed lawns and elegant street lamps painted a serene backdrop. As he approached the front door, John couldn't help but let his imagination wander. What would it be like to have a normal life? To return to a home where a loving wife and children eagerly awaited his arrival?

With a sense of longing in his heart, he located the key tucked away in the porch light. As the door creaked open, a stark reality washed over him. The solitude was piercing, the absence of warm greetings and loving faces left a void that gnawed at him. Desperately, he tried to convince himself that he was content with this solitary existence, reminding himself that he had lived this way for many years. "Come on, John, pull yourself together," he silently admonished himself, fighting back the waves of loneliness that threatened to engulf him.

The moving company John had enlisted proved to be exceptional. Every piece of his life, including the vital equipment he cherished, had been meticulously arranged just as he remembered it. He wandered over to the dining room table, and there, he discovered a plain manila envelope awaiting his attention. Gingerly, he emptied its contents into his trembling hands, revealing a new driver's license bearing the name James Saven. "Saven, almost like Ivan, but they're professionals," he mused, a hint of admiration for the meticulous effort involved in his identity change. Alongside the license lay a passport, complete with his photograph and a new identity to match. It was clear that John had some transformations ahead, involving hair color and style, colored contacts, and a burgeoning goatee that would align with the computer-generated image.

Rummaging further through the materials, his fingers brushed against the keys to his new car. The promise of a fresh start beckoned as he made his way to the garage. Yet, as he stepped inside, a magnificent automobile greeted him—one of the most impressive vehicles ever crafted. Its top speed was poised to push its driver nearly into the realm of mach 1. John had always harbored a deep affection for fast cars, and this one stood as a testament to the utmost extravagance. However, the pain in his arm, a stark reminder of his previous car ride, began to gnaw at him. "That was no Sunday drive," he thought, wincing at the memory.

Overwhelmed by a surge of emotions and fatigue, John retreated from the garage and returned to the interior of his new home. His exploration eventually led him to the bedroom, where he discovered a neatly made bed. He surrendered to the weariness that weighed upon him, collapsing onto the crisp sheets. As sleep swiftly claimed him, his thoughts danced between the anticipation of his new life and the discomfort that still clung to him.

"Unbelievable!" Bruce exclaimed, his voice a mix of horror and disbelief, his eyes wide with shock.

"You knew that eventually the enemy would show his ugly face," George replied, his tone steady and resolute.

As they conversed, Bruce couldn't help but reflect, "George sure has come a long way since the first night I met him." He said out loud, "Of course, but I guess I just didn't think about it much. I was so caught up in the excitement of what God was doing..."

"And that's not a bad thing," George responded, his voice carrying an undertone of acceptance.

Bruce continued, "I just forgot about the other side of it. How many homes did you say were vandalized?"

"Fifteen. All of them bear the same markings as you described."

Bruce shook his head in disbelief. "This is unimaginable! What are we going to do?"

George's response was solemn and unequivocal. "Pray."

Bruce couldn't help but let a hint of sarcasm creep into his voice as he said, "Why didn't I think of that?"

George met his sarcasm with unwavering seriousness. "You would have eventually, but the enemy caught you off guard."

"Yeah, I guess you're right," Bruce conceded, his initial resistance softening.

"Hang in there. I'll call the rest of the folks in the church. We'll start working on your home."

Bruce began to object, but George interrupted firmly, "We'll start with yours first, and there will be no more conversation about it."

"But..." Bruce tried to argue, but George silenced him.

"But nothing. I'll call you later."

"Thanks, George."

"Remember, if the enemy can get the general, the army is weakened. Keep the faith, brother." With those parting words, they bid each other farewell, their voices laden with determination and solidarity.

Bruce drove wearily back home from the church, his energy spent after a long and taxing day. Thoughts swirled in his mind, reflecting on how it often seemed that God's presence was most profound in his life when he was at his most exhausted and drained. His mind drifted to a gas station store he frequently visited, where once, the racks were filled with explicit magazines. Now, those racks stood empty, a testament to answered prayers, and a deep sense of gratitude welled up within him. He noticed C & C Liquors, its neon sign flickering and its walls bearing a dingy yellow hue. It had maintained the same appearance since his childhood, and now it sat locked up and offered for sale. Bruce pondered the significance of these changes, marveling at the undeniable influence of God in his life and community.

As he pulled into his driveway, his eyes widened with amazement at the sight before him. Workers were diligently restoring his vandalized home. They painted the walls with care, tended to the eaves and window sills, and repaired broken shutters and other damaged items. Some were laying fresh sod and planting new shrubs, while others carried rose bushes to the backyard.

Bruce's heart swelled with emotion, a flood of gratitude threatening to overwhelm him. He sat in his car, tears streaming down his face, and whispered, "You are so good to me, God."

A gentle tap on the driver's side window brought Bruce back to the present moment. He rolled down the window, his emotions still raw.

"Bruce, isn't this incredible!" George's voice rang out, his face covered in paint but illuminated by a radiant smile.

Bruce struggled to find the right words, his voice soft and humble as he replied from within the car, "I don't know what to say."

George's smile only widened. "You don't need to say anything. We're having a blast. Besides, it's the least we can do for someone who has shown us how to connect with God in such a profound way," George said earnestly. "People at my job are still talking about those Tuesday night meetings, and it seems like every Tuesday, another coworker joins us. Bruce, if this keeps up, we'll have the whole town down there with us."

At George's words, Bruce looked up, his eyes glistening with tears, and a genuine smile graced his face.

Just a couple of weeks had passed since John's recovery, and now he found himself on the brink of an investigation he had been yearning to conduct. His pursuit of Dr. Myers had been triggered by an internet lead, and despite the lingering soreness that still coursed through his body, the surge of adrenaline more than compensated for the pain. Behind the wheel of his new car, John felt an exhilarating rush, with the tachometer teetering on the edge of the red zone and an engine that seemed eager to unleash its full potential. Exercising a modicum of restraint, John maintained a reasonable speed. The last thing he wanted was to draw the attention of the police, especially with his freshly minted ID, altered appearance, and new identity.

As John approached Dr. Myers' office, his heart quickened its pace. He couldn't help but wonder, "Could this be the man who had orchestrated the attempt on my life by hiring those thugs?"

"Mr. Saven," the nurse called out from the waiting room, and John set aside his magazine, embarking on the short journey towards her. The steps felt like they were leading him not to a specialist but to a figure of dread, Dr. Death himself. Nevertheless, he felt a quiet satisfaction in how seamlessly he responded to "Mr. Saven," a name that bore a semblance to his previous identity.

Once inside the exam room, John settled into the chair, waiting anxiously for the doctor. A man entered, presumably Dr. Myers, and inquired, "What brings you here today, Mr. Saven?" The doctor appeared entirely ordinary—distinguished with graying hair, devoid of facial hair, and clad in the quintessential white medical coat. John had rehearsed his response repeatedly, caught in the liminal space between two possible answers.

"I had an accident as a child," John began, his voice steady and convincing. "In our neighborhood, dogs were allowed to roam freely, and every now and then, a feral dog would mix in with the others. One day, while playing stickball with the neighborhood kids, a wild dog charged at us." John's words flowed smoothly, and the doctor's posture conveyed a sense of acceptance. "It lunged for my right ear and tore it at the bottom. My family didn't have much money, so we made do."

Dr. Myers scrutinized the ear, his gaze thoughtful. "You hardly notice it, really. But I could perform a reconstruction so seamless that no one would ever discern the difference."

Suddenly, a nurse burst into the room with an urgency that filled the air like electricity. "Doctor, we have an emergency in Room 2," she exclaimed, her voice laced with panic.

"Excuse me," John interjected, seizing the opportune distraction. It was a stroke of luck even better than he could have imagined. He had meticulously observed the office layout when he was led to the examination room, noting that the records area was conveniently accessible and tucked away from the doctor's office.

Without wasting a moment, John swiftly made his way towards the records section. The commotion had successfully diverted everyone's attention, leaving the area unattended. Fingers nimbly flipped through files, and John's eyes scanned the yellow copies in the phone message book. "Aha!" he thought with triumph. "Dr. Kenneth Pencowski - 1-2-3,4." Yet, John's count was soon forgotten as he noted two alternating numbers, distinct from the one he had found on the internet. Hastily, he jotted down a phone number, all while avoiding prying eyes.

As John skimmed through the office computer, a document from Dr. Pencowski's office beckoned him. With quick precision, he printed it out and clutched it tightly, hoping not to be discovered.

Then, a chilling voice, colder than ice and as sharp as a dagger, pierced the air. "Can I help you?" The menacing stare that accompanied it seemed capable of delivering a death sentence.

Bruce settled in for the night after an emotionally draining day. The morning had brought devastation to his home, a deluge of anger, fear, and a profound sense of loss. Yet, by the day's end, his heart was brimming with a different kind of emotion – love, gratitude, and a sense of overwhelming blessing. It was as if God had orchestrated a symphony of compassion through His people.

The outpouring of support had been nothing short of miraculous. Friends and fellow believers had rallied to paint his home, repair the damage, replace the ruined lawn, and even gift him a brand-new rose garden. Amongst the blooms, both familiar and novel, Bruce felt a sense of restoration. He couldn't help but reflect on the biblical tale of Job, who had lost so much but received even greater blessings in return. "This is Your way, Lord," Bruce thought, "to take and then bestow more than what we originally possessed."

Walking amongst the freshly planted roses, Bruce's heart swelled with profound thankfulness. He felt cherished by God through the kindness of His people, and his eyes betrayed the depth of his emotions. In a hushed whisper, he uttered, "Lord, You are so good."

Bruce paused to offer up a heartfelt prayer, his voice gentle yet fervent, "I pray that those responsible for this devastation may come to know You as their Lord and Savior. In Jesus' name..."

"I'm looking for the bathroom. I guess I got turned around," John confessed, his voice carrying a tone of complete honesty and sincerity.

The nurse, understanding and professional, kindly directed him to the restroom. Alone inside the small space, John couldn't help but feel a rush of adrenaline coursing through him. His eyes fixed on the printed document left unattended on a countertop. It was a stock report, resembling something straight out of the business section of a newspaper.

His gaze honed in on the details, noting the precise markings of one of the stocks with a date from the previous year. The others, however, were recently dated, indicating a flurry of recent activity. What caught his eye was the dramatic spike in the stock's value, appearing suspiciously higher than any normal stock's trajectory.

With stealth and haste, John slipped the report into his pocket, his mind racing with questions and possibilities. He then made his way back to the exam room, resuming his wait with an air of anticipation hanging in the air.

Dr. Myers returned, apologizing for the earlier interruption, unaware of the clandestine information John now held close.

Bruce settled down in front of his TV, eager to catch the last part of the news. The announcer's voice resonated in the room as he switched on the television.

"Amazingly enough," the announcer emphasized, his tone carrying a hint of astonishment, "Mrs. Downing checked with the Westshire Bank and they said this was no error. Someone has deposited over $1,000 in her account, on purpose. And this is not the only account that experienced this." The news report painted a picture of baffled bank officials and surprised account holders. Jay Ramford, Vice President and Chief Loan Officer of Westshire, weighed in, revealing that they had 120 other customers questioning varying amounts that were deposited by someone other than the account holder.

"In other news today," the announcer continued, "15 homes in Stapleton have been vandalized. One of them belongs to Pastor Bruce Hutchison who pastors a small church in town. It seems this church has had amazing crowds for the past four weeks." The revelation of the vandalism sent a chill through Bruce.

The announcer went on to explain that the vandals had been caught, linking them to a major satanic cult with its headquarters located in a large city outside of town. Bruce found himself gripping the remote tightly, absorbing the implications of the disturbing news. With a resolute click, he turned off the TV.

"Wow," Bruce muttered aloud, the weight of recent events and revelations settling in. He decided to retire for the night, but as he lay in bed, thoughts swirled in his mind. He wondered what God had in store for him on this new day.

The morning sun bathed his bedroom in a gentle glow, and the aroma of freshly brewed coffee wafted through the air. The joyful chorus of birds singing outside filled the room, and Bruce felt a sense of renewal in the air. It was indeed a new day, ripe with possibilities.

Just then, the phone rang, its shrill ringtone breaking the morning calm.

"Hello?" Bruce answered the phone, his voice carrying a sense of curiosity.

"Bruce, it's Sue Billings," came the cheerful voice on the other end.

"Hey Sue, how are you?" Bruce responded, a hint of warmth in his tone.

"Great!" Sue exclaimed with piercing excitement. "By the way, thanks for all the help around the house yesterday." Bruce felt a lump form in his throat, touched by her gratitude.

"Oh, you're welcome; it was a blessing to be a blessing," Bruce replied sincerely. "Did you see the newscast last night?"

"Part of it," Sue admitted.

"The part about the extra money put in folks' accounts?"

"Yeah, I saw that," Sue confirmed.

"Well," Sue's voice took on a tone of anticipation, "the person responsible is Jackson Binsley."

"Isn't he the owner of the mining field that Jerry works for?" Bruce inquired.

"Yeah!" Sue answered excitedly. "Can you believe it?"

"Tell me, why did he do it?"

Sue began to share, her voice carrying the intrigue of an incredible story. "Jackson had been charging more than the average for services and products. Then he came to Tuesday night's meeting, after one of his employees invited him."

"Isn't he the man that helped you with your car?" Bruce asked, remembering their previous encounter.

"That's him," Sue affirmed. "He has completely changed. His demeanor went from an angry scowl all the time to a smile. When you look at his eyes, you can almost see a twinkle, they are so bright! Anyway, he felt convicted for the overcharge."

"How much was it?" Bruce inquired.

"It did not seem like much, but he went back in his records and calculated just how much it was, and he has paid it all back in full."

"Why did he do it so secretly?" Bruce wondered.

"He did not want the publicity."

"Wow, Sue, that is just amazing!" Bruce exclaimed, his voice filled with awe.

"God is doing great and mighty things," Sue affirmed. "I talked with a girlfriend in town that works for a retail store. She said that shoplifting has completely stopped, and there has been no inventory shrinkage for four weeks!"

As the conversation unfolded, Bruce couldn't help but be filled with wonder at the transformative power of faith and the incredible ways in which God was working in their community.

"That's just when we started Tuesday night prayer time. God is amazing!" Bruce exclaimed with heartfelt enthusiasm, his voice reflecting his deep faith and gratitude.

"You know what else? Jackson, Jerry's boss, and Jim, his coworker, have convinced Jerry to come this Tuesday night," Sue added, a note of joy in her tone.

"Oh, Sue, that is just wonderful," Bruce responded, his words laced with genuine happiness. "I will be praying for Jerry." Their conversation carried the warmth of camaraderie and shared faith as they exchanged their goodbyes.

John diligently inquired about Dr. Myers' expertise, the procedure details, and the cost, his voice a mix of curiosity and determination. He probed into the network of physicians Dr. Myers collaborated with, hoping for any information that might lead him to Dr. Penkowski. However, every avenue he explored seemed to lead to a dead end.

Once back home, John punched the numbers he'd obtained from Dr. Myers into a receiver specially designed to intercept phone conversations. He endured a prolonged waiting game, his anticipation mounting. Then, finally, a connection was established.

As he listened in on the conversation, John's heart raced with a mix of anxiety and revelation. He overheard cryptic discussions about someone getting perilously close to the truth, and the ominous mention of the need for an elimination. His mind clicked into place as he realized the true enemy behind the Association for Fetal Research was not Bruce Hutchinson, but rather, Dr. Penkowski.

The revelation was like a bolt of lightning, and John knew he could no longer delay the crucial call that had been weighing on his mind since leaving the hospital. He understood that making this call might jeopardize his precarious position, but it was a risk he could not afford to ignore any longer.

Bruce's heart weighed heavy as he sat down with pen and paper to compose a letter to Jennifer. A myriad of emotions swirled within him. Was this letter yet another burden placed upon him by God's design? Had he faithfully placed his trust in the divine plan all along, only to now find himself emotionally shaken? Or perhaps, in the depths of his heart, he longed for a connection with the one person who knew him best, a sanctuary of understanding amidst the tumultuous waves of life.

"Dear Jennifer," Bruce began his letter, the words flowing from his soul onto the page. "Oh, how I miss you." With each stroke of the pen, he began to recount the incredible happenings within the church, the remarkable transformations unfolding within the community, and the intricate tapestry of his own life. His words conveyed a profound sense of longing and vulnerability. "With all that's going on, I feel like I've been walking on water like Peter. I mean, when Peter took that step, he knew for him alone it was impossible, and when he began to walk on water, he knew it was purely God's doing and none of his. But as he began to look at the waves and hear the wind, he sank. I feel like these past four weeks have been all God, but the waves are splashing in my face, and the wind is causing me to lose my balance. I'm only human. I can't help but lose my focus, and I too am sinking into the watery depths."

As he penned these words, a swell of emotions surged within Bruce, the weight of fear welling up, and tears flowed unchecked. "Oh God, don't let me sink! Keep my eyes on You, oh Lord...on You!" Bruce couldn't help but cry out to his Creator.

"Please pray for me, Jennifer!" Bruce continued to write, his words pleading for support. "I've never needed your prayers more than now! With God working greater than I've ever experienced in my life, I feel so privileged, yet so inadequate. However, I've never experienced evil so greatly either."

Then, as if sent by divine guidance, a scripture surged into Bruce's mind: "Call unto me, and I will do great and mighty things you do not know." With conviction, Bruce shared this sacred verse with Jennifer within the confines of his letter. "Jennifer, why me? Why has God come to my church so dramatically? Why has he picked Stapleton to 'do great and mighty works'? I'm looking forward to seeing you soon. I love you with all my heart!" As he concluded his heartfelt message, Bruce sealed the envelope and sent it on its journey.

"Hello?" A voice answered from the other end of the telephone, and it was a voice that carried a sense of familiarity and warmth.

"Maggie, it's John Ivan," John's words flowed with a mix of caution and reassurance, as he sought to maintain the security of his phone and the secrecy of his newfound identity.

"John..." Maggie's voice, filled with an undeniable excitement, broke through the line. The connection, though distant, seemed to bridge the gap between them.

"How are you? I went back to the hospital, and you were gone. They said you had left in a hurry," Maggie inquired, her concern for him evident in her words.

"It's a long story. I am currently undercover," John responded, his tone carrying a hint of intrigue, the kind that accompanies secrets and hidden missions.

"Won't this compromise your cover?" The question weighed heavily on John's mind, lingering like an unspoken fear that had been haunting him since the moment he left the hospital.

"No, my phone is secure, and no one would know I'm calling you to tap into your phone." John's assurance held a thread of confidence, although the implications of her words lingered, casting shadows on the conversation.

"Tap into my phone? John, what's going on?" Concern laced Maggie's voice, her thoughts racing to the possible dangers that might encircle her, as if her name could be the next on a hospital list she had unwittingly been a part of.

"I can't really get into that right now," John replied, his words weighed down by the weight of secrets he could not yet share.

"Well, I'm glad you called anyway," Maggie's tone shifted, carrying warmth and relief at hearing from him.

"So am I." As those words escaped his lips, John felt an unexpected flutter in his chest, a sensation reminiscent of the hospital room and the connection they had formed there.

"I'll try to meet up with you within a week, if you'd like," John offered tentatively.

"That would be great!" Maggie's excitement bubbled through her voice, the prospect of reuniting with John filling her with eager anticipation.

"I just need to work out the details. I'll talk to you soon," John concluded, his thoughts already racing ahead to the logistics of their impending meeting.

"Thanks for calling. I'm praying for you." The conversation ended with a heartfelt sentiment, and the click of the phone seemed to resonate with a shared connection that neither could fully explain.

"I'm praying for you," John mused as he hung up, his thoughts drifting into uncharted territory. It was a phrase he hadn't expected, given his atheist perspective. Yet, instead of turning him away, it only intrigued him further. "What could a woman like that see in a man like me?" he wondered, his emotions swirling as he contemplated the enigma that was Maggie.

FIVE

As Bruce approached his new mailbox, a warm and overwhelming sense of God's love washed over him. His heart swelled with gratitude, much like it had the day before when he returned home to discover church members laboring tirelessly to restore his once-dilapidated home.

"Good morning, Bruce," a cheerful voice chimed in. Bruce looked up to see George Hines.

"Good morning, George! What brings you out so early?" Bruce's voice brimmed with excitement, his heart still awash with gratitude for George's support during the previous day's flurry of activity.

As they strolled back toward the house, Bruce couldn't help but notice the peculiar box George was carrying. It looked like something out of a science fiction movie. Walking along the freshly refinished sidewalk, Bruce felt a surge of joy having George as his companion for this special moment.

"Everything looks absolutely incredible! I can't begin to express my thanks."

"It was truly a blessing for us, beyond anything you can imagine," George replied with a beaming smile. "We've already started working on three more homes today. The word has spread among those who worked on your home yesterday. By the end of the week, all the homes should be completed."

"That's wonderful," Bruce said, his satisfaction evident.

"I'm eager to hear your thoughts on the new email link I sent you," George added.

Bruce and George entered the freshly renovated home and powered up the computer. George couldn't wait to unveil the new email link he had shared earlier. Bruce opened his email and was astonished to find 200 messages from everyone who had attended the Tuesday night prayer meeting.

"We've been receiving these kinds of emails consistently, and it's simply incredible. It's as if God is answering all our prayers with a resounding 'yes,' not just from Tuesday night but also from the neighborhood's small prayer groups and even through email," George explained with awe.

"Can you believe it? Our prayer request for the closure of the abortion clinics in Stapleton has been answered! God is truly amazing," George exclaimed, showing Bruce an email from Sue.

Bruce approached the computer, feeling a twinge of guilt for not yet offering George a cup of coffee.

"That's amazing; Sue is such a dedicated prayer warrior," Bruce remarked, deeply impressed by Sue's seemingly direct connection with God, even before the Tuesday night prayer meetings.

"I know, right? We're witnessing almost every prayer request being granted. How is this possible?" George asked, still marveling at the power of prayer.

"God has revealed the answer to your question," Bruce said, pausing for a moment. George leaned in, his curiosity piqued. "What is it?"

Bruce walked over to his Bible, opened it, and began to read, "If my people who are called by my name will humble themselves and pray and seek my face and turn from their wicked ways, then will I hear from heaven and will forgive their sin and will heal their land." Bruce explained, "God is simply keeping the promise He made thousands of years ago. You see, George, the people have truly humbled themselves through their tears, confessions, and repentance during our first prayer meeting. God's Spirit has moved among His people, prompting them to pray in alignment with His will."

Bruce flipped through the Bible to another passage and continued reading, "This is the confidence that we have... that if we ask anything according to His will, He hears us. And if we know that He hears us, whatever we ask, we know that we have what we have asked of Him."

"But Bruce, haven't we prayed according to His will in the past?" George inquired.

"Yes, but often we weren't in the right position to receive because we hadn't truly humbled ourselves," Bruce replied thoughtfully. "There were brief moments of genuine humility, and it's during those times that we witnessed the most answers to our prayers."

George was captivated and exclaimed, "Wow!"

Bruce continued, "And there's more to the equation."

"What do you mean?" George asked.

"George, we are in the midst of a divine revival," Bruce said, his voice tinged with awe. He paused, contemplating the magnitude of his words. "It's been centuries since our country experienced a spiritual awakening like this. And to think that God chose Stapleton and our church to be a part of it is simply beyond my comprehension."

George suggested, "Perhaps it's because of your leadership and guidance, Bruce."

Bruce smiled humbly and replied, "I appreciate your kind words, George, but it was God who gave me the scripture I shared with you. He also moved the hearts of the people to call me and start the Tuesday night prayer. This is all His doing."

George nodded in agreement and said, "I remember the first time I attended the prayer meeting. I felt something profound deep within my soul, something I had never experienced before."

Bruce responded, "That was God working within you, George. He initiated this revival, and I'm eager to see what He will do next."

John approached Dr. Stearing's home, the former head of one of the three abortion clinics in Stapleton that had recently ceased operations. An air of curiosity swirled within him, a burning desire to unearth the truth and unravel the enigma surrounding the clinics' closures.

The house stood as a magnificent Victorian-style residence, adorned with an elegant wrap-around porch and bathed entirely in white, complemented by a pristine white picket fence. The yard, a verdant masterpiece, exuded meticulous care, its lush green grass providing a canvas for a vibrant tapestry of flowers and shrubs. Each bloom seemed to sing with a spectrum of colors, painting a serene backdrop against which John's quest played out.

Approaching the front door, he couldn't help but be filled with anticipation—an old sensation, yet one that never failed to quicken his pulse when embarking on a mystery.

John pressed the doorbell, and its traditional chime reverberated through the air. The door swung open, revealing an older gentleman with distinguished gray hair standing in the doorway.

"Can I help you?" inquired the man, his eyes sizing John up with suspicion, uncertain if he was yet another door-to-door salesman.

"Hi, I'm Lucas Manning from the Medical Today newsletter," John introduced himself with a practiced charm. "You must be Dr. Stearing."

"Yes?" The older man's skepticism lingered, but his guard began to lower.

"I was hoping to talk with you about your experience as a physician in the abortion industry."

At the mention of his past, the man's demeanor shifted, a cloud of reluctance enveloping him. "That is not a topic I enjoy talking about. Besides, I've never heard of the Medical Today newsletter."

"We just started publication in this area, but we began in the north about six months ago," John reassured him, his tone earnest. "I'm excited to start at the ground floor."

"Well, young man, I suppose I can give you a couple of minutes, but I warn you, there's no uplifting story to be found here."

Dr. Stearing welcomed John into his home, leading him to a study adorned with shelves filled with books. Among the volumes, John's gaze fell upon a small plaque bearing the words, "To help and restore."

"I noticed that plaque up there, 'To help and restore.' Where did you get that?" John inquired.

The man's shoulders slumped as he sighed deeply. "It was a gift from my first wife. She supported me through medical school, working tirelessly to help pay our bills while I pursued my education full-time."

"She sounds like an incredible woman," John remarked, sympathy in his voice.

"She was," Dr. Stearing conceded. "But I let her down. I became consumed by the pursuit of wealth, losing sight of the dream we once shared—to help and restore. I changed the motto to 'It is your choice.'"

"Is that when you entered the abortion industry?" John probed gently.

"Yes," Dr. Stearing admitted with a heavy heart. "The Association for Fetal Research presented an offer I couldn't refuse."

"What kind of offer?" John leaned in, eager for details.

"They provided all the instruments, the latest techniques, and a convenient and profitable means of fetal disposal if I agreed to perform abortions."

"What do you mean by profitable?" John's curiosity grew.

"They paid me for each filled XM2 I supplied."

"XM2?"

"The XM2 was a machine for storing fetuses during the day. I paid for the machine upfront, and the Association, in return, compensated me monthly for the fetuses I provided and stored at freezing temperatures."

"I see."

"The fees I earned from the company exceeded the machine's cost within the first year. After that, it was all profit."

"What did they do with the fetuses?"

"I assume it was for research," Dr. Stearing replied, his voice tinged with remorse. "But, to be honest, I didn't ask questions, and I didn't care at the time." His tone grew somber. "I wish I could go back and change it all."

"Tell me how your experience in the industry has affected you," John inquired, hoping to steer the conversation toward a more positive direction.

"I can't say the industry has had a positive impact on me," Dr. Stearing confessed. His voice carried a weight of regret. "It has taught me that no matter how long you try to justify wrongdoing, silence your conscience, or evade responsibility, the consequences of your choices will always catch up to you."

"And what are those consequences, Dr. Stearing?" John inquired, his voice laden with empathy.

"For me," Dr. Stearing began, his gaze distant as if peering into the abyss of his own past, "it has resulted in lost dreams, painful memories, regret, and endless nightmares that are worse than any horror movie. Son, that is what the abortion industry has given me. I'm sorry if that's not the upbeat response you were hoping for."

John couldn't shake the emotional weight of the moment. His thoughts shifted to his beloved sister, Elizabeth, who had endured similar torment following her own experience with an abortion clinic.

"You know, Lucas... if that's your name," Dr. Stearing continued, his voice trembling with emotion, "pediatricians have pictures of the babies they've helped bring into the world. One of my recurring nightmares is seeing a poster board in the lobby of my practice with beautiful baby faces, but the rest of their bodies mangled because of the procedures I performed."

With a sudden intensity, Dr. Stearing rose from his seat and demanded, "You must leave!" before retreating into another room.

John understood that Dr. Stearing wouldn't return. He had received the answers he sought, some of which had shaken him to the core. His thoughts couldn't escape the turmoil in his heart. He felt as though he were complicit in the pain his sister had endured. Loyalty to the Association for Fetal Research dissolved, replaced by simmering anger. He faced a pivotal decision. Should he resign from his job? Should he confront his boss about the impact of their work on his sister? Or should he embark on a potentially perilous path of action? As he drove home, he pondered his options, the weight of responsibility heavy on his shoulders, while diligently typing in the final notes for the day.

Bruce stood before the congregation on a Sunday morning, his heart brimming with emotions as he surveyed the gathering before him. The transformation was nothing short of astonishing. It was almost surreal to think that this was the same humble 200-person church he had known; it had now burgeoned to 300 souls. While many familiar faces remained, some had departed. Bruce couldn't help but wonder if the influx of newcomers had made the church feel unfamiliar or if it was the shift in format with the new Tuesday night prayer. In any congregation, there was that unwelcome reality: 20% did the lion's share of the work, shouldered the financial burdens, and were truly dedicated to Christ. It was a truth he reluctantly accepted, grounded in the parable of sowing, where only a fraction of those who heard God's word would bear fruit.

Yet, something profound had shifted. Those who had merely attended Sunday services, never immersing themselves in the church's life, had vanished. In their place stood new faces, individuals Bruce had never imagined would step foot in a church, let alone become fervent participants. A baker, whose shop had been the town's talk for years, the former owner of the local liquor store now beaming in the front row, and even the president of Westshire bank, once preoccupied with wealth, now found themselves deeply involved in Tuesday night prayer meetings. Surveying the 300 souls gathered, Bruce discerned that each person was attuned to God's heartbeat, playing an integral role in Christ's cause.

As the music subsided, Bruce's heart raced, knowing it was his moment to address this remarkable congregation that God had guided to his small church in Stapleton.

"Dear friends," Bruce began, his voice trembling with a mixture of gratitude and awe. "I stand here today in utter amazement. I've experienced personal revivals as a Christian, witnessed the dedication of sold-out believers, read about revivals of the past, and delved into the examples of God's presence in the New and Old Testaments. But never in my wildest dreams did I envision that the Creator of the universe would reveal Himself in such a profound manner to our humble church and the town of Stapleton. Lives have been transformed, businesses have altered their ways, and families have undergone remarkable changes. God has orchestrated something that leaves us all in sheer wonder."

Bruce leaned forward, quoting, "'If my people,' he recited, 'who are called by my name, will humble themselves, pray, seek my face, and turn from their wicked ways, then I will hear from heaven, forgive their sin, and heal their land.' This scripture encapsulates what is transpiring in our church. We see liquor stores closing, new ones struggling to secure permits from City Hall."

His address continued, "Families once torn asunder are now

reuniting, finding healing in their relationships. Individuals once ensnared by drugs and alcohol now stand liberated from their addictions. Those who once grappled with hopelessness and despair now bask in renewed purpose and joy. We have witnessed more baptisms than in the entirety of the past year. All of this is a testament to the incredible work God is doing within our community."

Taking a deep breath, Bruce couldn't help but notice a smile on the face of one City Hall official. He pressed on, "As we remain humble before God, continue to pray, seek His presence, and turn from our wicked ways, we trust that God will keep hearing from heaven, forgiving our sins, and healing our land."

Bruce then shared that three abortion clinics in town had shut their doors for good, their intent not to reopen, and he observed a young doctor from one of the clinics with a grin and a sparkle in his eyes.

"Years of petitions to close those clinics, to halt the annual meetings of the abortion industry's leaders here in Stapleton, fell on deaf ears," Bruce asserted confidently. He paused briefly before concluding, "The transformation in this town is undeniable. Adult magazines have vanished from gas station shelves, restitution is being made for past wrongs, and billboards advertising church services, scriptures, and family support lines have replaced liquor and cigarette ads. The group that restored the 15 vandalized homes also mended fences and other neglected parts of our town."

Tears welled in Bruce's eyes as he realized the enormity of the changes and the miraculous revival that had gripped Stapleton.

Bruce stood there, his chest rising and falling with the effort to catch his breath. An oppressive knot tightened in his throat, threatening to silence him. His eyes slid shut briefly as he fought to regain his composure. With a deep, steadying inhalation, he mustered the strength to continue.

"As I drove through that area just last week," he began, his voice trembling with emotion, "my heart sank at the desolation before me—the once-pristine landscape now marred by hate insignias and sinister symbols. It was a desecration of beauty and love."

Bruce's voice quivered as he continued, "But then, in that very moment, something truly miraculous unfolded before my eyes. Those symbols, those scars of darkness, they started to fade, as though an invisible hand was gently erasing them. Tears welled up, blurring my vision, and my heart ached with the profound significance of this moment."

He paused to regain his composure, his voice barely a whisper, "It was like a sign from above, a whisper of hope, a promise of redemption. The words of that verse, 'and I will heal their land,' they echoed in my mind and pierced my soul. The power of that moment overwhelmed me." Bruce's voice trembled as he fought back tears.

He took a deep breath to steady himself and, with a voice laden with emotion, he continued, "Why, dear friends, has God chosen to grace this church, and me, with all our shortcomings? We are no better than anyone else. We did not seek Him out, but He, in His infinite wisdom, looked down upon us and touched the hearts of our people. They humbled themselves, they prayed, they confessed, they repented, and they sought Him. And, oh, how He heard their cries, forgave their sins, and is now in the process of healing. He is the Lord, the Almighty God of the Universe, and yet, He chose us. It is our sacred duty to go forth in His holy name."

Bruce wiped away the tears that had streamed down his face during his impassioned speech, his heart heavy with the weight of this profound moment of divine grace and calling.

"Hello?"

The phone crackled with anticipation, the brief silence carrying a hint of uncertainty.

"Maggie, this is John."

John's voice quivered with a mix of nervousness and longing, as if his very existence hung in the balance.

"John! I wasn't expecting your call so soon. How are you?"

Maggie's words flowed like a soothing balm, her voice tinged with curiosity and genuine concern. It was as if a lifeline had been thrown to a drowning man.

"Good. I know you may not want to meet me, but if you do, I have a place in mind."

John's heart raced, emotions swirling within him like a tempest. He longed for her to understand the gravity of the situation. His voice trembled with hope and apprehension.

"John, I don't fear for my life or yours. I've thought about it, and meeting you would be great. Just tell me when and where."

Maggie's words pierced through the uncertainty, a beacon of bravery amidst the darkness. She was resolute, her willingness to stand by his side undeniable.

"I'm pleased." John's relief was vivid, his elation tinged with the fear of what lay ahead. He hinted at a meeting in the forest, hoping she'd decipher the unspoken message. The words he chose were carefully veiled, concealing the true nature of their rendezvous. The fear of surveillance weighed heavily on his conscience.

"Okay…" Maggie responded hesitantly. "I'll do that if it comes to me."

Her voice held a quiver of doubt, a cautious dance between trust and skepticism. She was willing to play this dangerous game for John.

"Maggie, your safety is my utmost concern." John's guilt gnawed at him, a reminder of the peril he had drawn her into.

"I understand. Thanks for calling. I'll be seeing you soon." Maggie's determination shone through her words, a pledge to decipher the enigma that surrounded them.

"Thanks Maggie. I look forward to seeing you too." John's hope flickered like a fragile candle in a storm. He yearned for her presence, the warmth of her brown eyes, and the solace she brought. The life of a detective had lost its luster, and he clung to the belief that this meeting would dispel some of the darkness that had clouded his world.

"Sue, we have to figure out where John is meeting me! I've been working on this all week, and I still have no clue. And I'm supposed to meet him within the hour!" Maggie said, sounding desperate.

"Hey Maggie, don't worry. We'll figure this out. You seem so edgy for a date," Sue said with a teasing tone, trying to lighten the mood.

"Oh, Sue, it's not a date! We're just getting together as friends. Nothing more."

"Okay, Maggie, whatever you say. Now let's think about this. He said to meet you in the forest."

"Yeah. But I've been thinking, there's a cafe in town called The Redwood."

"Oh, that's too obvious. Is there a restaurant with some type of outdoor seating?"

"No, outdoor seating. Hmm...he said to meet in the forest, in the foul place."

"The foul place? What a lovely spot for your first date."

"It's not a date." Maggie said with a silly grin. "I wonder if the forest means the outdoors. When I was a kid, I used to love to go to the park and feed the ducks."

"Wait a minute! What's the name of the park in town? Forest Ridge Park."

"That's it, Sue!"

"Yeah, I remember looking over the lake and feeding the ducks. It was so beautiful standing on the white wooden walkway over the water."

"That's it! Sue, I've got to go!"

"Wait a minute, what about the foul place? We didn't figure that part out."

"Gotta go! Don't want to be late!" And with that, Maggie was heading for the door.

"Enjoy your date!"

"It's not a date!" Her voice trailing off as she ran to her car. She jumped in and sped off.

Approaching the park, Maggie found herself entranced by the familiar, meticulously manicured entrance. It was like stepping into a portal to her childhood. Vibrant annual flowers adorned the landscape, standing in contrast to the stately trees that flanked the path, their leaves forming a verdant canopy over the road. Freshly mown grass carpeted the ground, and the red brick walls gleamed as if they had just been subjected to a thorough pressure cleaning. The elegant, bold letters spelling out 'Forest Ridge Park' adorned the walls, a testament to the park's timeless beauty. Memories from her youth surged through Maggie's mind, a mosaic of moments both joyful and bittersweet. It was a rare sensation, feeling so youthful once again, a sentiment she had longed for but thought was lost. Her newfound faith had brought her peace and purpose, and now, God had orchestrated this unexpected meeting. But was it a blessing or a curse? She couldn't deny the rightness of it, even though the looming danger added an edge of uncertainty. Strangely, the prospect of peril did not deter Maggie in the least. She was determined to see this through; it felt undeniably right and good.

As she strolled towards the lake along the serene walkway, Maggie parked her car and took in the tranquil surroundings. The cool breeze whispered through the leaves, not only soothing her body but also calming her soul. Stepping onto the freshly painted, brilliant white path, she savored every detail. The walkway gradually transitioned into a charming bridge that spanned over the serene lake, offering a picturesque view of the water. Just as she reached the apex of the bridge, almost on cue, a parade of ducks swam gracefully towards her.

"Beautiful, isn't it?" A voice approached her, but the man before her bore little resemblance to the John she remembered.

"Yes, it certainly is," Maggie responded politely, but her voice held an air of detachment.

"Maggie, it's me, John."

Maggie scrutinized the man closely and then uttered in disbelief, "It sounds like you, but it sure does not look like you."

"I had to go undercover and change my identity," he explained, his gaze scanning the surroundings. "I dyed my hair, altered my hairstyle, grew a goatee, and got colored contacts."

Maggie blinked in realization. "It is you! I didn't even recognize you."

"That's the idea. How long have you been waiting?"

"I just arrived. Your cryptic clue nearly stumped me. What was that all about?"

"I apologize. I had to speak in code, not just for my own sake but for your safety as well. It's been a while since we last talked, and I couldn't be certain if our phones had been compromised."

"My phone tapped? Why would anyone tap my phone, John? What's going on?"

John reassured her with sincerity in his eyes, saying, "It's okay, Maggie. I don't believe it's tapped. I was merely being cautious."

"John, I understand you're undercover and working for some secretive client, but could you at least give me some context, so I can make sense of all this? To be honest, I don't even know why I'm here."

"Well, I'm grateful that you are," John said, flashing a warm smile at Maggie.

"I can tell you that the client I started with was not at all who I thought they were," John began, his voice tinged with a mixture of intrigue and disillusionment. Maggie leaned in, her eyes locking onto his, captivated by his words. "At first, it was glamorous, with fancy cars and an unlimited budget to purchase any piece of high-tech equipment that money could buy."

Maggie nodded in understanding, her brows furrowing as she sensed the tale had taken a darker turn.

"But then, things began to unravel," John continued, his voice carrying the weight of a man burdened by moral conflict. "I started to see a side of my client - their personality and business practices - that didn't align with my values."

"I see," Maggie replied, her empathy evident in her gentle tone.

"Well, things have changed. It's even affected my personal life and people that I'm close to," John confessed, his thoughts drifting to the pain his sister Elizabeth had endured after having an abortion. He hesitated, questioning his decision to share so much. "I have been...why am I telling you all of this? You don't want to be bored by all this."

"But I do care, and this is very interesting," Maggie assured him, her sincerity reassuring John.

Feeling a newfound sense of comfort, John continued, "I've had a change of heart and can no longer work for my client in the same way I have been."

Maggie offered a practical suggestion. "Well, then you can lose the disguise."

"It's not that easy. I'm going to continue working for them," John replied, a trace of sadness lingering in his voice.

Maggie questioned, "Why would you do that?"

"Because, while I am working for them, I can find out more so that I can put a stop to all they have been doing, the business which I have now come to hate. Maggie, I am so sorry for all of this. I wanted us to just enjoy some time together."

A poignant silence hung in the air, and then Maggie noticed something in John's hands. "What do you have in your hands?"

John glanced at the bread in his hand. "What, this? Oh, I brought some bread. I thought we could feed the ducks."

"At the foul place," Maggie smiled. "You have a waiting audience." From the vantage point of the bridge, it seemed that every duck on the lake had gathered around John and Maggie, their eyes fixed on them with patience. John handed some pieces of bread to Maggie, and together, they tossed them into the water for the eager ducks.

"You know, John, I have lived a very tough life," Maggie

confessed, her voice tinged with vulnerability. "Though I am not proud of it, it is still a part of who I am." John looked at her with surprise, his disbelief evident. "No, it's true. I was caught up in the fast lane, finding pleasures in things that began to tear apart my life. I made a decision recently that changed all that. Decisions are powerful. They are life-changing. I think that the decision you are choosing will also greatly affect your life for the positive."

In that moment, John recalled the brief prayer Maggie had uttered while he was in the hospital: "make a positive decision." Perhaps, he pondered, God had begun to answer that part of her prayer. After all, he had been discharged from the hospital sooner than expected.

"Maybe you're right, Maggie," John admitted. He longed to share more but held back, concerned for her safety. "You know, I would go into detail if I felt you would not be harmed in any way. But I am glad we talked."

Their conversation shifted to lighter topics. John inquired about Maggie's place of birth and upbringing, while Maggie asked him about his experiences in his field. Despite the gravity of his current situation, John found the day to be enjoyable, a momentary escape from the stress of the Association's threats and his conflicted feelings about his work. Maggie, too, relished the opportunity to feel young and adventurous. In the end, both felt that the time spent together was a remarkable experience, a brief respite from the shadows that loomed over their lives.

Bruce had just completed a taxing day at the church, and the exhaustion weighed heavily on his shoulders. The sermon he had delivered on Sunday felt like a relic from a different era, out of touch with the present. As he pulled up to his house, a sense of gratitude welled up within him for the kind church members who had rallied together to repair the damage inflicted upon his home. Walking over to the white mailbox adorned with gleaming gold trim and vibrant, blooming annuals, he couldn't help but appreciate the beauty in this small corner of his world.

Amid the stack of mundane junk mail, Bruce's fingers brushed against a familiar envelope, and his heart skipped a beat. A letter from Jennifer. For Bruce, these handwritten missives held more value than a million-dollar check.

With trembling hands, Bruce tore open the envelope and began to read Jennifer's words as he made his way towards his house. "Dear Bruce," it began, each word a lifeline of connection in the vast sea of his thoughts. "I received your letter the other day, and I can't wrap my head around everything that's happening. While our perspectives may differ, I have faith that God has chosen the right person for the task. Your humility, Bruce, is the very trait that God seeks in a vessel, and you possess it in abundance. I still vividly recall our first date together."

Bruce stood there, enveloped in a world of memories, transported back to that special night. Nervousness had coursed through him like an electric current, but as he relived those moments, he couldn't help but smile to himself. Jennifer's words in the letter brought those cherished memories flooding back to life.

"You opened the door for me and pulled out the chair before I could sit down at the table in the restaurant," Jennifer's words danced off the page and into Bruce's heart. Her description of that evening, filled with life, excitement, and dreams of doing great things for God, made his heart swell with warmth. Her words painted a vivid picture of that night when they had first met. "But you conveyed yourself with such humility, Bruce, that's when I knew you were the one for me."

Tears welled up in Bruce's eyes as he felt the bittersweet sting of their separation. Jennifer's declaration of love, growing stronger with each passing day, tugged at his heartstrings. Her belief in his humility and its impact on their community filled him with a profound sense of purpose and responsibility. He knew that their parting had been necessary, but it didn't make it any easier.

Bruce carefully folded the letter and tucked it into his pocket, the weight of Jennifer's words lingering with him as he made his way inside the house.

However, Bruce's excitement found an outlet when he discovered Jennifer's new email address, a testament to her resourcefulness even in the remotest mission field. With unwavering determination, he settled down to compose a message, eager to share the latest developments concerning the Revival.

Bruce detailed the countless answered prayers, some daily miracles, and the emergence of prayer groups that now dotted the community's landscape. These groups met consistently, transcending boundaries, and permeating every facet of life in Stapleton, from homes to businesses, schools, and government offices.

Bruce went on to describe the remarkable transformations occurring since the Revival's inception. He shared the closure of all abortion clinics in town and the awe-inspiring vanishing of hateful and Satanic symbols. The email was a testament to the undeniable transformation gripping the community, a direct result of God's powerful presence, and Bruce felt deeply humbled and grateful to be a part of it.

As Bruce continued to type, he marveled at the growth of his church and the astounding changes in individuals who had once seemed unlikely candidates for transformation. He couldn't help but express his astonishment at the disappearance of long-standing enmities, complainers, and those who had never previously supported the church in any way. His email to Jennifer radiated joy and gratitude for the miraculous ways in which God was reshaping their world through the Revival.

Reading over the heartfelt message, Bruce felt as though he were skimming through the pages of a dream-turned-reality. His heart brimmed with anticipation and joy for what lay ahead. He concluded his message by expressing the depth of his appreciation for their connection and how thrilled he was to send his first email to her, the digital tether bridging the miles that separated them.

Bruce settled into his armchair after a quiet dinner, the room dimly lit as he turned on the news, hoping for a moment of relaxation. The evening's tranquility was abruptly shattered when the news anchor, in the middle of a sentence, interrupted with a startling report.

"...Mrs. Madelyn Jones," the anchor's voice carried a tone of curiosity, drawing Bruce's full attention, "of Stapleton High was upset today after the students recited the Lord's Prayer before the football game. Our correspondent Ruth Bell has more."

The screen shifted, and Ruth Bell, on-location, appeared, ready to delve into the story. "Mrs. Jones, why are you so angry about a simple prayer that most people learned as children?" Ruth inquired, her tone laced with inquisitiveness.

"I can't believe our school allowed this!" Mrs. Jones' voice resonated with fury as she vehemently expressed her disdain. Her gestures were animated, and her anger was discernible. The camera captured her exasperation and indignation, painting a vivid picture of her frustration. Bruce watched with disbelief as her tirade continued, targeting those with conservative beliefs and condemning religion as a crutch for the weak.

But as Bruce observed, something extraordinary happened. Mrs. Jones suddenly clutched her chest, her face contorted in agony. "My God, the pain, the pain!" she exclaimed before collapsing to the ground. The news reporter, taken aback, hastily announced technical difficulties and shifted to a commercial break.

Bruce couldn't shake the haunting image of Mrs. Jones writhing in pain, her outburst seemingly provoking an unforeseen consequence of divine retribution.

Overwhelmed by a sense of urgency, Bruce began to pray fervently, his words carrying a plea for mercy and understanding. "Lord, please forgive Mrs. Madelyn Jones for her words and actions. Help her find peace and comfort in your presence." In the midst of his prayer, a scripture verse sprung to mind, etching a profound truth on his heart: "Truly I tell you, people can be forgiven all their sins and every slander they utter, but whoever blasphemes against the Holy Spirit will never be forgiven; they are guilty of an eternal sin."

The weight of realization settled upon Bruce like a heavy cloak. He understood the gravity of Mrs. Jones' actions, her blasphemy against the Holy Spirit. There was no turning back, no possibility of redemption. She had unwittingly sealed her fate, an irreversible consequence.

Feeling the immense burden of the situation, Bruce was about to switch off the TV when the news anchor returned with somber news - Mrs. Jones had passed away from a massive heart attack.

With a muted click, Bruce turned off the TV, the room now filled with a somber silence. As he prepared to retire for the night, he contemplated the fragility of life and the profound importance of being mindful of the weight of one's words and actions, especially in matters that touched upon the divine.

The following morning, Bruce awoke with a sense of purpose

that had become an integral part of his daily routine. As the sun's gentle rays filtered through the curtains, he found solace in prayer. These moments were precious to him, transcending the mundane and infusing his life with meaning and anticipation. With each uttered word, he felt a profound connection to something greater than himself, something that had breathed new life into his existence.

After his prayer, Bruce decided to take a leisurely stroll through his meticulously tended rose garden. The blossoms, vibrant in color and delicate in fragrance, mirrored the beauty he felt within. As he ventured out to explore the neighborhood, his heart swelled with a pleasant surprise. Many of his neighbors had embraced the prayer meetings, even those who had never set foot inside a church before. The transformation was evident, with some of the remaining few choosing to put up "for sale" signs in front of their homes, relinquishing their hold on what had once been their safe haven.

During his walk, Bruce paused to exchange heartfelt conversations with friends. His excitement was intense as he shared the remarkable ways in which God was weaving His presence into their lives, like golden threads illuminating the tapestry of their community.

Upon his return home, Bruce reached for the morning newspaper, and his eyes gravitated toward the headline news that promised a revelation. With anticipation building, he tore off the plastic covering and delved into the article, starting from the middle.

"Mrs. Madelyn Jones had disrupted the prayer offered during the Stapleton High School football game this past weekend," the article began. The story unraveled, recounting Mrs. Jones' history of vocal objections to activities with a spiritual focus and her passing from a sudden heart attack at the age of 42. The principal, Joe Benton, had taken a stand in favor of religious activities on school grounds, and the article emphasized that even the most significant events, like the "See You at the Pole" gathering, would flourish without the disruption they had once faced.

The newspaper revealed the remarkable transformation occurring in the school community. High school students were embracing their faith, bringing their Bibles to school, praying during lunch periods, and shedding the trappings of a less virtuous path. A rally had even resulted in the disposal of knives, drug paraphernalia, occult literature, and questionable video games in a symbolic bonfire. The principal, Joe Benton, spoke of the remarkable changes, emphasizing a shift towards abstinence over birth control, resulting in decreased teen pregnancies and a safer, more positive learning environment. Bruce couldn't help but feel a surge of gratitude and hope as he read the tangible impact of God's presence in their lives.

As Bruce gently closed the newspaper and laid it on the dining room table, he pondered the future. Would God's intervention continue to unfold, or would it gradually taper off? The question lingered in his heart, but somehow, he couldn't shake the feeling that what they had witnessed was merely the tip of the iceberg, and the path ahead held even greater wonders.

The sun had just begun its ascent on the horizon, casting a golden hue over the tranquil neighborhood as Bruce concluded his customary morning walk. With each step, he had felt a sense of divine guidance seeping into his soul, outlining his purpose for the day ahead. As he slid into his car's driver's seat, the breathtaking sunrise painted a vivid reminder of fresh starts, reminiscent of the time he embarked on his seminary training or when he first set foot in his church. It also echoed the sense of renewal following the storms that had once raged through his life.

Despite the thrill of this new adventure that awaited him, a flicker of uncertainty danced in his eyes. Questions swirled like a gentle breeze: Would he succeed in this endeavor? Could he accomplish all that he needed to? Would he be embraced or met with rejection? Amidst this whirlwind of uncertainty, the only certainty Bruce clung to was encapsulated in a memorized scripture verse: "For we walk by faith, not by sight."

With this unwavering faith as his compass, Bruce knew exactly how to proceed.

John's heart brimmed with an overwhelming joy, a radiant light that had long been absent from his life, flooding in after his meeting with Maggie. It was a sensation he hadn't truly experienced in years. All the other trappings of his existence now seemed like transient pleasures, fading as swiftly as they appeared. As he navigated the familiar roads homeward from the park, his eyes darted periodically to the rear-view mirrors, ensuring he wasn't being followed. Alongside his vigilance, his thoughts turned to the intricate tapestry of his life.

Approaching his home, he pressed the button, and the garage door glided open with a mechanical hum. He eased his sporty car into the garage, but instead of the customary sense of pride that accompanied this ritual, there was an unsettling emptiness that had infiltrated his being. With a heavy sigh, he sought refuge in the bathroom, craving the solace of a shower to clear his cluttered mind.

The water cascaded over him, a soothing respite, washing away the accumulated layers of tension and doubt. Stepping out of the shower, he stood before the fogged mirror, swiping a hand to reveal his reflection. The gaze that met him in the glass was searching, questioning. Who was this man? What were his aspirations in life? Why had the pinnacle of his career left him feeling unsatisfied, questioning the very essence of his desires? The goals he had once set had materialized, yet the satisfaction, celebration, and pride he had envisioned remained elusive.

With a closer examination, he realized that the man he beheld in the mirror was no longer the John Ivan he used to be. It wasn't the superficial changes - the new hairstyle, altered hair color, and discreet facial hair, or the colored contact lenses that still clung to his eyes. It was a transformation that transcended appearances, a metamorphosis he couldn't quite define.

His thoughts meandered through the corridors of his sister Elizabeth's dreams and a recent interview with a retired, remorseful doctor. An unsettling revelation dawned on him - was this the life he truly desired, one fraught with hollowness and remorse? Was he making a meaningful impact on the world, and how would he be remembered when his time inevitably drew to a close? These questions stirred something long buried beneath the veneer of accomplishments, wealth, and pride. A weighty realization descended upon him, causing him to hang his head low, confronted by the stark truth of his self-centered existence. His pursuit of wealth and success had exacted a toll on his character, a toll he could no longer ignore.

Reaching for the towel on the bathroom counter, John's fingers brushed against a renewed sense of purpose. It was time for him to make a difference, to recalibrate his life's trajectory. Uncertainty clouded his thoughts, the path forward unclear, but determination coursed through his veins.

Amid his contemplations, the shrill ring of the phone sliced through the air, shattering his introspection.

"Hello?"

"John, Dennis Spence here."

"Hello, Dennis," John responded with an air of calm, his thoughts racing as he contemplated the unknown journey ahead.

"I have been reviewing your reports and updates," Dennis's voice crackled over the phone, his tone carrying a weight of contemplation, "and it seems that you are onto something significant. I believe it has great potential." The words hung in the air, charged with a sense of urgency and possibility.

"Hence," Dennis continued, his voice steady but tinged with anticipation, "I am assigning another man to assist you." The revelation was met with a sharp intake of breath on John's end.

"He is the head of our manufacturing facility, George Hines," Dennis revealed, his words carrying a sense of gravity as he disclosed this pivotal information, "and he works for me in town." The implications of this assignment, the collaboration it hinted at, swirled through John's thoughts, leaving him with a mixture of apprehension and curiosity.

Bruce found himself driving along roads that were an unfamiliar yet breathtaking spectacle. The landscape was adorned with the first brushstrokes of autumn, as leaves burst into brilliant reds, radiant yellows, and the faintest hints of purple, casting an enchanting spell over the trees. This was Bruce's cherished season, a time of transformation and renewal. With the windows of his car rolled down, he drank in the invigorating, crisp air, filling his lungs with the essence of the changing world around him.

It had been quite some time since Bruce had ventured into this part of town, an enclave of rich diversity. As he continued along the meandering road, he couldn't help but offer a quick prayer of gratitude, his heart welling with appreciation for the blessings in his life. His gaze was drawn to a cross, looming tall on the horizon, standing sentinel over an approaching hill. The sight never failed to stir deep emotions within Bruce, a poignant reminder of the profound sacrifice made by his Father, granting him not only a divine relationship but also a purpose to fulfill.

Drawing nearer to a modest church, Bruce felt a flutter of anticipation building within him. The church's elegant steeple held aloft the very cross he had spotted earlier. The surroundings were meticulously tended, the church nestled within a vibrant, close-knit neighborhood. His attention was caught by a tall and distinguished figure, an African American man in his late thirties, toiling on the well-kept grounds. As Bruce pulled up, their eyes met, and a radiant smile adorned the man's face. He raised his hand in a friendly wave and began to approach Bruce's car.

"Bruce, it's great to see you!" Wayne exclaimed, his voice alive with genuine excitement as they drew closer.

Bruce extended his hand to greet Wayne, his own face lighting up. "It's been a while, how have you been?"

"Well, I am doing just great! You know you are doing good when you wake up with a heart as light as a feather and no worries in the world," Wayne replied, his grin warm and infectious.

"Glad to see you in such good spirits."

"So what brings you to this neck of the woods?" Wayne inquired, gesturing toward a bench shaded by a sprawling tree. They began to make their way toward it.

"Well... the Lord, you could say."

Wayne's smile waned, and a solemn expression descended upon his features, a shift from the previous lightheartedness.

"Dennis, I'd like to conduct a background check on Mr. Hines before I introduce myself," John ventured cautiously, the weight of his words carried by a measured tone.

"A background check? Do you think he's involved in illegal activities?" Dennis thundered, frustration visceral in his voice, a storm of impatience brewing within him.

"As you're aware," John began, keeping his composure, "I'm currently undercover, and my life isn't as perilous as it once was. This affords me greater freedom to gather information."

"I know you're undercover, and I can read!" Dennis retorted sharply, irritation gnawing at him. "Now, spare me the details. I want results, and I want them now!"

"Yes, sir," John replied, unfazed by Dennis's outburst, his calm demeanor a testament to years of experience.

"Contact Mr. Hines before the end of the week and keep me updated on your progress," Dennis demanded tersely before abruptly terminating the call, leaving an air of tension lingering in its wake.

"Bruce, what's happening in your church? You're all over the news, and many of my congregation have been talking about this Tuesday night prayer group," Wayne asked, excitement tinging his voice, as though he'd been waiting for the right moment to inquire.

Bruce couldn't help but smile, as he had hoped someone would ask. "It all started with a scripture the Lord laid on my heart one morning," Bruce began, his voice carrying the weight of divine inspiration. "It's from 2 Chronicles 7:14, 'If my people, who are called by my name, will humble themselves and pray and seek my face and turn from their wicked ways, then will I hear from heaven and will forgive their sin and will heal their land.'"

Wayne's eyes widened with keen interest as he leaned in, eager to hear the rest of the story. Bruce recounted every remarkable detail, from the initial calls for the Tuesday night meeting to the transformative prayer walks in the neighborhoods and the miraculous answers to their petitions. As he spoke, Wayne's expression shifted from curiosity to awe, as though he were witnessing a divine miracle unfolding before him.

"Brother Bruce! Do you realize what this means?" Wayne exclaimed, his voice filled with passion and conviction. "This is the work of God's hand. This is what I've hoped and prayed for since my early childhood—a genuine revival!"

Bruce's heart swelled with gratitude for Wayne's presence, sensing that God had sent him as a confirmation of the revival unfolding in his church. "I'm glad you came by, Bruce. I've been wondering what's been going on in your church, and hearing about it now...wow! But what brings you to see me? How can I help you?" Wayne asked humbly.

Wayne's expression shifted to one of solemnity, his demeanor indicating that there was more to this meeting than a casual catch-up. "It's not me, Wayne. It's God. He's brought me here to talk to you."

Bruce nodded, his gaze steady as he looked at Wayne, accepting the gravity of the moment. "Go on."

"God wants His revival to spread like wildfire," Bruce explained, his voice laced with deep conviction. "He's already made dramatic changes in our city—closing down abortion clinics, shutting liquor stores, and more. He's doing a great work, and He doesn't want to be limited by human methods. His ways are higher than ours."

Bruce continued, "I would love to take credit for what's happening in my church, but I know this is much bigger than me. Therefore, I won't allow my ego or pride to hinder His will. He's looking for additional space on Tuesday nights."

At this, Wayne's face underwent a transformation, his initial disbelief giving way to a profound realization. "Bruce, you can't be serious," Wayne said, his voice tinged with incredulity. "I can barely manage the humble tasks the Lord has entrusted to me in this modest church. I'm among the least of pastors in Stapleton. Look at the larger churches in town or those on the other side of town. Surely God would choose them over us. Yes, my congregation is good-hearted, but their leader, their janitor, their groundskeeper?"

Bruce couldn't help but chuckle softly, as Wayne's reaction reminded him of Moses at the burning bush, offering excuses and doubt in the face of divine calling. With warmth in his voice, he replied, "Why not you, Wayne?"

Wayne stared at him, still processing the idea that had begun to take root in his heart.

"You're a humble man, Pastor Wayne, and that's exactly the kind of person God seeks to use," Bruce continued. "Have you noticed that since this revival began, some of the most well-known and influential churches and their leaders in town have closed their doors?"

Wayne's eyes brightened as he listened intently, eager to hear more answers to questions he'd been hesitant to ask anyone.

"God is refining His church, not only externally but also internally," Bruce explained. "Some of the long-standing troublesome members in my church have either left or become passionate about serving God. Moreover, He's diligently working to change and transform people, using them more profoundly for His work than He has in a hundred years, since the last revival."

After a brief moment of silence, Wayne responded, "Some of the members in our church have raised concerns about the very things your church is doing, particularly the Tuesday night meeting.

I had dismissed it as just another program, one of many that have come and gone over the years. But something kept telling me this was different. As each day passed and I saw more evidence of God's hand in this, I wasn't entirely surprised by your visit or what I believe your next request will be."

With that, Bruce asked Wayne to start the Tuesday night prayer meeting, encourage his congregation to participate in prayer walks throughout their neighborhoods, and open his church to new people and new works of God.

"You have my word. I'll do as you've asked," Wayne replied, a sense of purpose igniting within him. "I only ask that I be able to contact you regularly because if even half of what's happened to you and your church occurs here, I'll need someone who understands to talk to."

"You've got it, Wayne," Bruce said, sealing their holy agreement —a partnership in the work of God that hadn't been experienced for centuries.

George Hines. John couldn't help but feel a wave of concern wash over him. He was undercover, and involving someone in his mission without their knowledge or consent was a risky move. However, the clock was ticking. Dennis had given him until the end of the week to gather information for the report, and he needed to get started.

Without wasting a moment, John sprang from his seat and rushed over to his laptop. His fingers flew across the keyboard as he initiated a search for George Hines on the internet. He unearthed details about Hines—his age, upbringing, and even his social security number. Hines had spent roughly a decade in the abortion industry after working odd jobs before that. Somehow, he had ascended to the position of general manager at AFT Manufacturing, a prestigious role by all accounts.

Grabbing his coat, John dashed out of his door. The engine of his car roared to life as he maneuvered out of the garage. Time was not his ally; he had to condense a month's worth of investigation into a single week.

As he approached the imposing factory just outside of town, John couldn't help but admire the pristine exterior. The recently painted parking lot gleamed with bright stripes marking parking spaces. The building bore a simple sign that read "AFT Manufacturing," and there was a conspicuous spot reserved for George Hines.

Parking his car, John observed a couple of cameras in the vicinity. He swiftly covered his face and staged a fake coughing fit, concealing his identity with a handkerchief. Approaching the entrance, he noted a security keypad. With a small device meant for overriding such keypads, he quickly input the universal code, granting him access.

Inside, John scanned his surroundings and headed for the staircase. He paused at the door, attuned to any approaching sounds, and slowly pushed it open.

"Perfect," he thought. The vantage point on the second floor offered a panoramic view of the manufacturing plant below. Executive offices occupied the second level, complete with windows, cameras, and TV monitors overlooking the production floor. Staying in the shadows of a dimly lit corridor, John blended into the surroundings.

Nameplates adorned each office, guiding his reconnaissance. George Hines' office, the most luxurious and spacious, was identified by a distinctive plaque on the wall. John noticed the stark contrast between the opulent executive quarters and the bare, industrial setting outside. This incongruity provided an opportunity for some impromptu investigation.

From his briefcase, John retrieved a portable eavesdropping device and aimed it towards Mr. Hines' office. Carefully tuning in, he discerned a voice matching the lip movements of the man he'd researched on the Association for Fetal Research website. Though the voice was somewhat indistinct, it was unmistakably Hines.

Static crackled before John captured a snippet of the conversation. "...production is down, quality is down, sales are down. Is there any good news you can give me?" The voice on the other end sounded frustrated. "We will make quota by the end of this quarter despite the consistent downturn we have seen for the last three months! It's not impossible; we have done it before. Let's do it again." With that, the conversation abruptly concluded. It was a reflection of what Dennis had been saying all along, but John knew he needed more information to form a conclusive report.

John spent the majority of the day operating unnoticed. As closing time neared, he slipped out of the building and surreptitiously trailed Mr. Hines to his car without detection. Hours later, George departed, leaving John behind to scour for any clues that could aid his decision before the week's end.

SIX

George arrived at the church a little earlier than usual, his steps echoing with an eagerness that only a few knew about. As he approached Bruce, his face lit up with an infectious smile that radiated warmth and anticipation. "Bruce, how did the meeting go with your pastor friend across town?" he asked, the enthusiasm bubbling in his voice.

"You mean Wayne?" Bruce replied, his eyes twinkling with intrigue.

"Yes, how did that go?"

"Well, it seemed to go really well. He was open to the working of God but intimidated by the calling of God. He originally thought that all that has been taking place in our church was just another program coming down the line. But after seeing all that God is doing, he confessed it was nothing short of a revival of God," Bruce explained, his tone shifting from cautious optimism to genuine awe.

"Great! I wanted to let you know that the email system is still going strong! We have had a tremendous amount of communication from the folks. It seems to fill in the gaps when everyone is away from the Tuesday night prayer meeting and the daily studies in workplaces and homes," George chimed in, his excitement mirroring the energy of a bustling city.

"I can't believe all the responses we are getting and all the answers to the prayer requests. Speaking of work, I know you work for some large organization in town. What is it called again?" Bruce asked, his curiosity genuine and inviting.

At that question, George's demeanor shifted. He became a bit fidgety, and a shadow of discomfort crossed his face. He had never truly revealed to anyone at the church that he was a key player in the very organization that Bruce and his church had picketed years before. He had always managed to dance around the issue.

"It's AFT Manufacturing," George replied curtly, hoping to change the subject quickly, his voice tinged with apprehension.

"You must be pretty high up in the organization," Bruce remarked, his eyes narrowing with curiosity.

"I run the plant. It's kind of a daily humdrum thing. I wanted to be an air pilot, but my leg held me back from that," George replied, his discomfort now evident as he disclosed a part of his past he'd long kept hidden.

"That doesn't seem to be a problem any longer," Bruce said with a knowing smile. George's brace had been gone since the beginning of the revival, and the transformation was nothing short of miraculous.

George excused himself, feeling increasingly torn by the dual lives he was leading. In one, he had been a victim, but now, in the embrace of the church, he had found joy and fulfillment he'd never experienced before. The weight of his secret was becoming burdensome, gnawing at his conscience like a relentless shadow.

Feeling conflicted, George sought refuge in a small, empty room. He closed the door quietly and leaned against the wall, muttering, "Lord, what am I doing?" But the heavens remained silent, leaving him to grapple with his inner turmoil.

As the Tuesday night prayer began, Bruce's voice resonated with deep emotion, and his words carried the weight of divine purpose. "Ladies, gentlemen, teenagers, boys, and girls," he began, "I want to share with you that I visited a church on the other side of the community where Pastor Wayne Miles resides. He was very pleased to see me and very interested in hearing about the events that have been taking place in our church and in the community at large. He is willing to collaborate with us and is grateful for any support we can give to them."

Bruce's voice quivered with a mix of humility and hope, and as he began to pray, the room was infused with an unspoken warmth. Outside, the chill of fall was creeping in, but within the church, packed wall to wall with people, there was a tangible sense of unity and fervor. Newcomers knelt in tears, confessing their sins, while others prayed with a fervor that could move mountains. Each request, each plea, was offered with unwavering trust and faith, creating an atmosphere of profound spiritual connection. It felt as though the very air within the church was infused with the divine.

Suddenly, three African American individuals rose almost in unison, their voices carrying a blend of joy and wonder. Kenny, the first of the trio, spoke with an infectious enthusiasm, "I'm Kenny Jones, but my friends call me Kenny. This is my first time here, along with Carl Regan and Jeffrey Stacy. We're all from Pastor Wayne's church, and we've been longing to be part of what God is doing in your church."

Kenny's voice crackled with excitement as he continued, "I've seen firsthand the impact that God has had on my children in school. When they stand and recite the Lord's prayer, it's a beautiful thing. And they haven't stopped it. Someone tried to put an end to it, but I saw God strike her dead live right on TV! I'm telling you the God's honest truth."

The room was electric with emotion as Kenny shared his testimony, his words painting a vivid picture of God's power. He took a deep breath before continuing, "And there's more. I've driven by graffiti every day on fences, back walls of buildings, and it's always been a source of hate and anger. But one day, when I was walking and praying for my neighbors, I saw the hate symbols disappear right in front of my eyes. Gone! Vanished! As though someone was erasing a chalkboard."

Kenny's revelation left the room in stunned silence, then erupted in applause as his words resonated with every heart present. Maggie, their gifted songwriter, struck up a new, soul-stirring melody, and the congregation joined in, creating an atmosphere saturated with the spirit of God.

John had left before George arrived home. When John returned, he cautiously ventured further inside, his eyes widened in astonishment when he discovered a treasure chest tucked away in a corner, an unexpected enigma in his otherwise ordinary abode.

As John tiptoed through the house, trying to unravel this mystery, his foot accidentally landed on the tail of their sleepy cat. The feline let out a startled yowl, and both the cat and John jumped in surprise. Their hearts raced in tandem, the element of surprise flooding their senses.

After the initial shock subsided, John's curiosity got the better of him. He decided to explore further, leading him to a secure desk drawer in the den. The anticipation in the air was charged as he attempted to unlock it, his hands trembling with a mix of fear and excitement.

Inside the drawer, John's eyes fell upon a trove of documents, bearing a letterhead from a company he didn't recognize—

"Advanced Medical." The company's logo featured the traditional medical symbol of a snake coiled around a rod. With each page he uncovered, a sense of disbelief settled over him, leaving him reeling with a mixture of confusion and trepidation.

The papers revealed a meticulously crafted plan to utterly obliterate an organization known as the Association for Fetal Research, a name all too familiar to John. The plan was presented with cold, calculated precision, and as he continued reading, John's heart sank with revelations. Here, within the pages, were answers to the enigmatic losses, the surge in lawsuits, and the closure of countless Association clinics.

John's eyes raced through the documents, absorbing the shocking details of how various divisions had suffered losses, the reasons behind the increasing lawsuits, and the calculated strategy behind the clinic closures. The realization struck him like a bolt of lightning; someone had been orchestrating the destruction of the Association for Fetal Research for a considerable period of time. The information was far too valuable to skim; John knew he needed to capture it for posterity, and so he began taking pics.

John's heart raced with a unique blend of excitement and trepidation. It was as if he'd stumbled upon a hidden treasure trove, a secret that held the potential to change the course of events. The adrenaline coursing through his veins was electrifying, and he couldn't help but savor the thrill of unearthing such a profound revelation. It was these moments that made his job seem worthwhile, although he knew the euphoria would be short-lived, leaving him yearning for the next intellectual fix.

Returning to the table, John's eyes remained glued to the papers as he delved deeper into the unfolding plot. The documents contained a detailed blueprint outlining the destruction of the AFT Manufacturing plant. The revelation struck him like a thunderclap, leaving him in disbelief.

To his astonishment, George Hines was revealed as the mastermind behind this nefarious scheme. John's heart sank as he read how George had surreptitiously manipulated the manufacturing process, coaxing his employees into intentionally altering their work, creating inferior products. It was a deceitful act, masked by a facade of high employee morale through frequent task rotation. The deception was veiled by excuses like raw material shortages and a lack of superior materials, making it difficult for anyone to detect foul play.

But George's duplicity didn't end there. He had been manipulating the company's financial records, creating a surplus on paper that didn't exist in reality. The funds were covertly channeled into a 401K program, matching employees' contributions up to 15 percent.

As John processed this sinister revelation, a torrent of questions flooded his mind. "Why would George do all this? What was his motive?" He pondered, wrestling with a sea of emotions. "Is he a do-gooder? No. But why? Why would... wait a minute."

In a sudden burst of insight, John seized his computer, feverishly searching for "Advanced Medical" on the internet. His heart raced as he waited for the results, and his eyes fell upon the printed copy he had taken from Dr. Myer's office, the letters "AM" in the stock numbers. Finally, the computer screen came to a halt, displaying the website of "Advanced Medical: equipment and supplies for all your medical needs." John couldn't help but read the words aloud, a revelation dawning upon him like the first light of day.

Wayne had made an announcement in church on a sunny Sunday morning, igniting a spark of hope for the upcoming Tuesday night prayer meeting. Doubt loomed over him like a dark cloud, uncertain if anyone would grace the church's doorstep tonight. However, as he meticulously completed his chores, emptying the garbage cans and vacuuming the sanctuary, a sight caught his eye that would forever etch itself into his memory.

A group of figures emerged on the horizon, steadily making their way towards the church. At first glance, they appeared as an enigmatic assembly, casting ominous shadows on Wayne's anxious heart. But as they drew nearer, faces began to reveal their true identities – individuals from his very own congregation. Relief washed over him, and his heart swelled with a mixture of gratitude and disbelief.

The approaching assembly swelled into a congregation, and then an assembly of congregations, like tributaries converging into a river. People emerged from the nooks and crannies of the neighborhood, forming an ever-growing procession. It was nothing short of astounding. Wayne's eyes beheld a kaleidoscope of humanity, a vibrant mosaic where African Americans, Hispanics, and Asians intertwined, transcending the boundaries of race and ethnicity.

Wayne's heart raced as excitement surged through his veins, and tears welled up in his eyes, like a river breaking through its banks. The realization of what was unfolding before him was overwhelming. All he felt in that moment was a profound sense of unworthiness, humbled by the unity and devotion of his congregation.

Greeting everyone as they entered the church had become Wayne's customary practice, but tonight was different. The air was charged with a vibrant energy, an electrifying anticipation that tingled in every corner of the room. The expressions on the faces that passed him were a symphony of happiness and determination.

As the flock filed into the church, a rare hush descended upon them, a profound stillness that was anything but ordinary. Wayne, feeling the gravity of the moment, raised his voice, "Ladies and Gentlemen, how overjoyed I am to see each and every one of you here! This is truly a divine manifestation!" Wayne's voice trembled with excitement, and his words were met with resounding amens from all around the room. This was the congregation's way of expressing their fervor for the Lord.

"We have gathered here to do the work of the Almighty. So, let us begin." Wayne commenced the evening with a prayer of heartfelt gratitude for the blessings the Lord had bestowed upon them. Amens reverberated throughout the church, an echo of their collective thanksgiving. There was a moment of stillness, and then, as if on cue, others took the torch of gratitude. Their voices filled the sanctuary with a symphony of appreciation.

Suddenly, an invisible force seized them, an overwhelming surge of emotion that defied explanation. It was as if a tidal wave of divine grace had engulfed them all at once. Tears flowed freely, and each person, amidst the sobbing, began to confess their individual sins. The room seemed to brighten, and an otherworldly light illuminated the space.

In the midst of this spiritual tempest, three individuals, so deeply moved, fell to the ground, yet in the whirlwind of emotions, they went unnoticed. Time passed, confessions filled the air, and the sweet presence of God enveloped the tiny church. People leaped for joy, their voices ringing out with shouts of "Praise the Lord!" that grew louder with each passing moment. An ecstatic fervor had seized the entire congregation, and for the first time, the church witnessed an unparalleled, uncontainable jubilation that was not confined to a select few but embraced each and every soul in that sacred space.

As the fervor of the congregation began to subside, a sudden realization gripped them. Three individuals lay lifeless, motionless, in the midst of the spiritual outpouring. A somber hush settled over the church as Wayne was urgently beckoned over to the scene. Simultaneously, a physician among the attendees stepped forward, his face etched with concern and apprehension. He examined the fallen trio and, after a moment of silence, delivered his grim verdict – they were dead. Wayne's features contorted with shock, his world shifting once again.

"What in the world happened?" Wayne's voice trembled as he questioned the physician.

"I won't have answers until an autopsy is conducted. My initial suspicion is heart failure," the physician replied with a solemn gaze.

"But two of them are still in their twenties!" Wayne's disbelief hung heavily in the air.

The physician offered no comforting words, simply pulling out his cell phone to dial for an ambulance. Wayne's emotions churned like a tempest. From the pinnacle of spiritual ecstasy, he now found himself plummeting into the depths of sorrow and perplexity.

One member who had been present throughout the tumultuous evening, approached Wayne. He bore a look of deep concern and began to speak slowly, as if treading on fragile ground. "Pastor Wayne, I'm not sure how to tell you this, but these three individuals are the same people who were accused of vandalizing Pastor Bruce's house and tormenting his members, yet they were never convicted," the member said, his gaze shifting between the still figures. "They were also suspected of writing the disturbing letters found in our church."

Wayne's countenance darkened at the revelation, his eyes flickering with a mix of emotions. "You mean the letters discovered in the pews a couple of months ago, the ones that spoke of prayers to Satan causing chaos in the church, depleting our budget, and leaving souls unclaimed for two long months?"

The member nodded gravely. "Yes, Pastor, those are the letters. Many of us had our suspicions about these individuals when they were accused, but their alibi was flimsy, and they managed to evade conviction. It seems like they didn't escape justice this time."

Wayne surveyed the congregants, noting the shared sense of realization and apprehension. These individuals had eluded consequences for their actions countless times before, believing they could disrupt the work of God with impunity. Little did they know that this fateful night marked the end of their malevolent endeavors. It was a sobering reminder that, ultimately, God's justice prevails, even in the face of adversity and evasive wrongdoers.

John's fingers danced across the keyboard as he frantically navigated the internet, his heart pounding in his chest like a drum. With each click, he delved deeper into a web of secrets and uncertainties. His eyes fixated on the stock section, where the letters "AM" and their stock price over the last six months materialized on the screen. There it was, the damning evidence: the stock had soared three months ago, aligning perfectly with the time The Association began facing its troubles, leading to a catastrophic plummet in their own stocks.

Overwhelmed and disoriented, he rested his head wearily on the counter. A storm of conflicting emotions raged within him, and the weight of his revelation bore down on him like an anchor. "What am I going to do now?" he whispered to the quiet room, his voice tinged with desperation. The person Dennis had tasked him to collaborate with was a key player in the company's downfall.

John contemplated his options, feeling the walls closing in around him. The situation was dire, and he couldn't see a clear path forward. The thought of approaching George and Dennis to lay bare the situation loomed, but the fear for his safety was paralyzing. In his mind's eye, he pictured George drawing a weapon, and the mere thought sent shivers down his spine.

On the other hand, the option to turn George in and terminate the entire investigation was a heavy burden on his conscience. He wondered if it would make any difference at all. Maggie's words echoed in his mind like a haunting refrain: "Be done with the disguise, the chase, the threat of death." He knew he had to make a decision, but he was mired in a sense of futility.

With a heavy heart, he rose from his seat and approached the TV, a symbol of solace he had rarely enjoyed due to his hectic life.

He sank into the chair, eyes fixed on the screen, which now displayed a breaking news report.

"...this evening's surprise death of three young men," the announcer said, abruptly catching his attention. "What makes this even more of a strange situation is the fact that two of these men were in their mid-twenties, and for all three to have a heart attack at the precise same moment in the same place is quite remarkable."

The anchor's words sent a shiver down John's spine as he absorbed the gravity of the unfolding events. The news story continued, connecting the dots between the school incident, the vandalism of homes, and the tragic deaths of the young men in the church. They had been accused of vandalism, yet escaped justice due to a technicality.

As the news segment concluded, John shut off the TV, weighed down by the realization that he was distanced from the events unfolding in Stapleton. Regret gnawed at him as he acknowledged the haughtiness and self-absorption that had kept him aloof from the town and its people. It was time for a change, a chance to make a difference in a place he had underestimated. If Maggie had chosen to live in this town, it couldn't be as dreadful as he had initially assumed. Memories of the park and its tranquil beauty flooded back, reminding him of what he had overlooked.

Determined, John reached for the phone, his fingers trembling with anticipation, and dialed Maggie's number. It was time to bridge the gap, to connect with the town he had been estranged from, and perhaps, find the answers he sought in the presence of a woman who meant so much to him.

The TV crews bustled about, dismantling their equipment and loading it into waiting vans. The reporters, who had delivered their on-scene coverage, were concluding their segments. An ambulance's doors closed with a soft thud before it slowly pulled away, siren silenced. Wayne remained rooted in place, a solitary figure amidst the aftermath, his lips silently moving in prayer, seeking answers from the divine. Why, he wondered, had this tragedy unfolded on the very first night? Yet, as he beseeched the heavens for clarity, a deafening silence met his cries.

The people who had been part of the prayer night gravitated toward Wayne, encircling him with faces aglow, eyes shimmering with profound emotion. Their smiles and radiant expressions conveyed a shared understanding that God's personal and potent intervention had transpired in their lives that fateful night. Wayne stood in awe of the fervor and intensity of their comments, which surpassed anything he had ever encountered. He couldn't deny that God's presence had manifested itself powerfully, and the divine had confronted those who had strayed to serve the enemy. The consequences of their choice were early and untimely death.

The following day, Bruce's concerned voice resonated through the phone, inquiring, "How are you holding up, Wayne?"

"I'm doing well, Bruce," Wayne replied with a sigh of relief. "I'm grateful you called. What a night it was!" He recounted the remarkable events that had transpired.

"In the midst of all that light, confession, singing, and shouting," Wayne continued, "three men...just dropped dead! I'm sure you saw it on the news."

"Yes, indeed, they ran a comprehensive story about our church and all the events in the community," Bruce responded. "I assume you have an idea of why these men met their sudden, simultaneous demise, don't you?"

"They were on the wrong side, weren't they?" Wayne replied with a chuckle, a fleeting moment of levity amidst the tension.

"Because it was live last night, you probably didn't catch the news, did you?" Bruce inquired.

"No, I missed it," Wayne admitted.

"They linked the vandalism of my home and the other fourteen homes, and how they got off the hook due to a technicality," Bruce explained.

"I heard about it from one of my members. It's just that I've never had anyone pass away in my church before, and it's unsettling," Wayne admitted, his voice trembling with concern.

"Well, you've never experienced God's presence in your church the way you did last night, have you?" Bruce responded.

A prolonged silence followed, and then Wayne sighed deeply. "No, I suppose not. But, Bruce, what does this all mean? What have I signed up for, my brother? More deaths in my church, more media frenzy, more ambulances?" Desperation laced his words.

"Wayne, this is bigger than us! It's a God-sized endeavor. Our finite minds can't fathom God's intentions or His plans. The Enemy despises you and me, and he'll do whatever he can to thwart us and all that God is trying to achieve through this revival. You need to keep doing exactly what God intends, and let Him bear the burdens."

"It's just that, growing up, dreaming of being part of a God-sent revival, I never pictured anything as dramatic as losing three men in my church."

"Brother, you haven't seen anything yet. Remember the woman at the public school's football game who made a fuss about the Lord's Prayer being recited?"

"Yes, I saw that on TV. Then the next thing I know, she's gone."

"She passed away the very next day, just as the papers reported."

"It's just that when these things happen, they seem to occur to other people, not in my little world."

"When God enters your life, your church, He shakes everything. Instead of an earthquake, He disrupts the circumstances."

"Bruce, you're right! Brother, I'm grateful you called today. I'm ready to move forward and do precisely what God intends. Exactly!"

"That's usually how revival ignites within a person's life."

"Who would've thought it would begin in a community, let alone in our small town of Stapleton?"

"God's ways are truly remarkable." With that, they exchanged heartfelt farewells, knowing they were embarking on a journey neither could fully comprehend, yet their faith remained unwavering.

"Hello?" A melodious and welcoming voice greeted John.

"Hey, Maggie, it's John. How are you?" John's voice carried an unequivocal tone of concern, reflecting his inner turmoil.

"I'm good, John. Glad you called. Is everything okay?" Maggie's intuition sensed the underlying worry in his words.

"I really need to talk to you. Could you meet me at the same place in about an hour?" John's urgency was unmistakable.

"Sure, see you then." Maggie agreed, her concern deepening as she hung up the phone.

An hour later, John arrived at their designated meeting spot, his restless steps echoing on the bridge. When Maggie joined him, it was clear that something weighed heavily on his mind, casting a shadow over his demeanor.

"John, how are you? You look good," Maggie greeted him warmly, her eyes reflecting her genuine care.

"Maggie, I'm so glad you came. I need to tell you something, but I'm not sure you'll want to hear it," John's voice held an earnest and serious tone.

Maggie's curiosity grew, mingled with a sense of honor that John had chosen to confide in her. "You have my complete confidence," she assured him.

"I want you to know that what I'm about to tell you could be dangerous. It could even cost you your life. But I have no one else to talk to, and I believe you're a moral person. You're religious, right?" John hesitated before broaching the sensitive subject.

Maggie nodded, her curiosity piqued. "Yes, I am. What's going on?"

John took a deep breath before continuing, his words laden with emotion. "Do you remember how we talked about how my work has negatively impacted my personal life?"

"Yes," Maggie replied, her curiosity now tinged with apprehension as she wondered where this conversation was headed.

"My sister, Elizabeth - I call her Lizzy - has had an abortion. And the client I work for owns the clinic where she had it done," John confessed, the weight of the revelation hanging heavily in the air.

Maggie's heart sank as she put the pieces together. "Your client wouldn't happen to be The Association for Fetal Research, would it?" Her voice barely rose above a whisper.

"Yes, but wait, before you think the worst of me, let me tell you the rest of the story," John implored, his words heavy with regret.

Maggie moved to the side of the railing on the bridge, leaning back, taking a deep breath. Her mind whirred, and she began to realize the gravity of the situation. This was the same organization that Pastor Bruce had picketed years ago.

"Wait a minute," Maggie said, her tone contemplative. "Isn't picketing what you asked me about the first time we met? You said you were doing some type of survey."

"I apologize, Maggie. In my line of work, I can't simply approach anyone and reveal that I'm an investigator asking about someone they care deeply for. They may withhold information and hinder my investigation. I need to uncover every detail to get to the truth," John explained, hoping she would understand his predicament.

Maggie's tense expression relaxed as she comprehended the

necessity of John's methods. "I understand now. Please continue," she urged.

John was unaccustomed to being so open and vulnerable, but he had no other option. "Lizzy has been plagued by terrible nightmares since the day of her abortion up until now," he shared, his voice laced with concern for his sister.

At the mention of the word "nightmares," memories of Maggie's own traumatic experiences flooded back, causing her to turn pale and lean back against the railing once more, her past trauma briefly resurfacing.

"Are you alright, Maggie?" John asked with concern, walking over to her and offering a comforting hand on her shoulder. His presence seemed to help clear her mind.

"This is how I came to make a decision that changed my life. Nightmares," Maggie said, her voice trembling with a hint of vulnerability.

"Maggie, tell me about it," John gently urged.

"No, tell me more, this is more important. Something is really bothering you. Tell me."

John continued to divulge his intricate connection to The Association, the doctors, the attempts on his life, and, finally, his hope that Maggie might hold the answers to the complex puzzle that had ensnared him.

"Maggie, Dennis, the head of the Association, has asked me to partner with George Hines," John revealed, his voice tinged with uncertainty and apprehension.

"George Hines? He doesn't have anything to do with the company that I am aware of," Maggie responded, her puzzlement evident.

"He actually does," John confirmed. "He works for Advance Medical."

Maggie was taken aback. "That can't be right. George is an active member of our church. He's helped us with repairing homes and managing our email communications. He's been a great asset to our community."

John contemplated her words, his mind a whirlwind of questions. Had George managed to deceive everyone at church, or had he genuinely turned over a new leaf? Why was he still working for Advance Medical? These were the thoughts that raced through his mind.

"Maggie, have you ever noticed anything suspicious about

George, something that doesn't align with everything else he's done for the church?" John inquired, searching for insights.

Maggie shook her head, her brows furrowed with deep thought. "No, never. He's been nothing but helpful to our church and Pastor Bruce."

"There's more to the story, Maggie," John said, his voice now marked by a sense of urgency. "Maybe we should take a walk and discuss it."

Maggie regarded John curiously. "What could be more shocking than what you've already told me?"

"There's a lot more," John said gravely. "Let's go to the park and talk about it there."

As they walked, John reached for Maggie's hand, and she held it tightly, their intertwined fingers signifying a shared sense of solidarity and determination. He squeezed her hand, and Maggie gazed up at him, a hint of a smile gracing her lips, reflecting their mutual commitment to unveiling the truth.

Bruce concluded his heartfelt prayer for Wayne, his brother in Christ, as he sat in the quiet solitude of his study. Little did he know that his visit to Wayne would set in motion a chain of events that would impact their lives in unforeseen ways. The weight of the moment lingered, heavy with the unspoken bond of their shared faith.

However, Bruce had another visit to undertake that day, one that he anticipated would be more challenging. He had made it his mission to systematically visit the various prayer groups that congregated in homes during the day, attended by homemakers, as well as the dedicated participants in work bible studies and prayer gatherings throughout the close-knit community. With each visit, he witnessed the remarkable unity and love that characterized these gatherings, whether they were composed of local business people at Westshire Bank or a group of shoppers within the confines of a bustling grocery store. Despite their diversity, each group harbored a common purpose—to pray for their neighbors to find solace in Christ and to celebrate the divine works that had manifested in their lives. Bruce's visits to these groups had become a regular routine since the revival's inception, yet the rapid proliferation of new groups continued to outpace his efforts to connect with them all.

George, with his diligent work, was instrumental in helping Bruce stay informed about the activities of these scattered groups. His work extended to crafting a dedicated web page that promised to go live within a month, further enhancing their outreach.

With all these responsibilities and the ceaseless growth of the movement, Bruce found himself in need of assistance. He contemplated the idea of enlisting Wayne, who had recently initiated a Tuesday night prayer group, to help in visiting these scattered assemblies. The exponential growth of these outside groups had begun to outstrip Bruce's capacity to keep pace. However, Bruce finally conceded that this challenge was something best entrusted to God's guidance.

It was time for Bruce to embark on a visit to a church that held dramatically different theological views but remained united in their faith in the central truth—Jesus's sacrificial atonement for their sins. Despite the theological variance, Bruce had always approached this individual with respect, allowing him the freedom to pursue his beliefs without any confrontation. Remarkably, they had never exchanged words, even though the church had experienced remarkable growth over the years. The impending visit represented an opportunity to bridge gaps and foster connections in the name of their shared faith.

The church in Stapleton stood as a magnificent testament to history, a place of breathtaking beauty adorned with ornate stained glass windows that filtered the sunlight into a kaleidoscope of colors. A majestic pipe organ graced its sanctuary, filling the sacred space with the rich, resonant tones of hymns that had echoed through the ages. The resonating peals of its Sunday bells carried far and wide, reaching every corner of the community. Beyond its role as a place of worship, it held a special allure as a sought-after venue for weddings, attracting couples who felt its timeless charm even if they did not regularly attend the church. During the festive season, it became the heart of the community's Christmas celebrations, offering a live nativity scene and a cherished Christmas show that left a lasting impression on all who attended.

At the helm of this venerable institution was Reverend Richard Stone, a figure who had dedicated over two decades of his life to serving the Stapleton community. His leadership had earned him the deep respect of local officials and business owners alike, establishing him as a pillar of the community. As Bruce prepared for his visit, he couldn't help but feel a sense of intimidation when faced with the towering achievements of Reverend Stone. It was not the content of his message that concerned Bruce, but rather whether Reverend Stone would accept a word from God delivered by a preacher from a small church on the outskirts of Stapleton.

In the midst of these contemplations, a scripture surfaced in Bruce's mind, a passage that recounted the challenges faced by an earlier man of God as he questioned whether his people would accept him and his divine message. The man had been blessed with signs and wonders as validation for his mission. Bruce recognized that God had similarly provided him with signs, the most recent being his conversation with Wayne, who had learned of the Tuesday night prayer group through members of his own church. This would serve as the divine confirmation Bruce sought to share with Reverend Stone. The rest, he understood, was entrusted to the will of God, the ultimate orchestrator of their spiritual journey.

Sue Billings was the driving force behind the neighborhood prayer groups, acting as their dedicated point of contact and the linchpin of communication through email. Her heart swelled with inspiration as she witnessed the tangible answers to their fervent prayers, emanating from the small but devoted groups scattered throughout their community.

Among the numerous emails she had sent, one stood out as particularly exhilarating. It heralded the fulfillment of a prayer she had fervently lifted up for years. The subject of her joy was Jerry, her husband, and his transformation under the influence of Jackson, his boss, and a co-worker named Jim, who had encouraged Jerry to attend the Tuesday night prayer group. It hadn't been an easy feat to convince Jerry, but over time, he had evolved into a new man through the experiences he encountered there.

Previously, Jerry had constructed walls around his heart, cynically dismissing religion as a mere crutch and asserting that he could navigate life independently. He held the belief that women were more susceptible to religious conversion than men. Yet, witnessing the remarkable changes in his wife Sue and his co-worker Jim made him reassess his preconceived notions. And when he observed his own boss, Jimmy, also undergoing a profound transformation, he couldn't deny the profound impact of Christianity.

On a particular Tuesday night, during his second visit to the prayer group, something finally clicked for Jerry. He made the life-altering decision to follow Christ, a moment of profound significance that he kept to himself for days. Jerry was determined to ensure the authenticity of his newfound faith, and as the days passed, it became undeniably real. He began to experience an unshakable peace, a stark departure from his chronic worry that had persisted for years. Even when there was nothing to fret about, he had been consumed by worry. His life acquired new purpose, something that his incessant anxiety had prevented him from discovering. The void within him was now brimming with joy and peace, and his restlessness had evaporated. As he awoke the following morning, the world appeared brighter, more vivid, and he was filled with an enthusiasm for living rather than merely surviving.

With each passing day, Jerry found it increasingly challenging to keep his newfound faith a secret. Finally, the day came when he confided in his wife, Sue, about his transformative experience.

It was a bright morning just before work, and Jerry had risen earlier than usual. Sue, a steadfast early riser, spent her mornings interceding in prayer for those she loved and even those she didn't know.

As Jerry walked in and embraced Sue, she noticed the recent change in his demeanor and couldn't resist inquiring. Jerry took a seat beside her and delivered the news with a radiant smile, "I wanted you to be the first to know. On Tuesday night, I decided to place my trust in Jesus for my salvation."

Sue was overwhelmed with emotion, her eyes glistening with tears. In an attempt to lighten the mood, Jerry teased, "Hey, if I knew you were going to cry, I wouldn't have done it."

Sue assured him that her tears were tears of joy, an outward expression of the years of fervent prayer she had dedicated to Jerry. Jerry confessed that he had been obstinate and had taken an extended period to make this momentous decision. Sue acknowledged her moments of doubt, expressing that at times, it had seemed as though her prayers fell on deaf ears, but she had never lost faith.

Jerry conveyed his readiness for change, even if the path ahead was unclear. He had already delved into a book titled "The Way to God's Success," a recommendation from Jim, his co-worker. Sue recognized the author as a renowned preacher and was deeply moved, enfolding Jerry in a warm, tight embrace.

SEVEN

Maggie and John stumbled upon a breathtaking, idyllic spot beneath the sprawling branches of a majestic oak tree that proudly stood sentinel over the tranquil lake. Despite the crisp chill in the air, the absence of the biting wind made it surprisingly bearable, painting the atmosphere with a serene calmness. As their eyes explored the surroundings, they were elated to discover a bench thoughtfully placed by the park's caretakers in this perfect spot, inviting them to share in its splendor.

Their hearts warmed with gratitude as they approached the bench, only to be taken aback when they spotted a small assembly of onlookers. To their immense relief, it wasn't the malevolent individual who had previously attempted to snuff out John's life through reckless driving, gunfire, or nefarious hospital care. Instead, a charming entourage of ducks had stealthily followed them from the bridge, accompanied by two regal swans that embodied the very essence of gracefulness.

As they made their way to the bench, John, ever the gentleman, gestured for Maggie to take a seat first. This small yet significant act of chivalry sparked a warmth in Maggie's heart. In a world increasingly obsessed with new-age political correctness, this simple display of respect made her feel cherished and deeply valued.

Settling down on the inviting bench, Maggie's gaze alternated between the ducks frolicking in the serene waters of the lake and John, who reached into his jacket and produced a bag of bread. With a shared sense of delight, they cast morsels of bread onto the water, watching as the eager ducks and swans swooped in to snatch them up.

However, their tranquil moment was interrupted when John's demeanor shifted, taking on a tone of gravity. "You know that what I'm about to share may put your life in jeopardy," he cautioned, his voice hushed. "But I have no one else to turn to, Maggie. I need answers, answers that I believe only you can provide."

Maggie's smile vanished, replaced by a look of genuine concern. "What's going on, John?"

In a low, hushed tone, John disclosed, "George Hines is entangled with another company that's actively sabotaging the Association. Their stocks have skyrocketed, and I suspect George's manufacturing practices are deliberately producing inferior products for this other company to profit from."

Maggie's head sank into her hands in disbelief. "George Hines? I can't fathom it. He's such a pivotal figure in our church and our prayer group. Bruce, too, works closely with him."

John nodded solemnly. "I know, Maggie. It's hard to believe. But I have concrete evidence."

John's plea weighed heavy on Maggie's heart as she contemplated the implications. "How can I assist you, John? What do you need?"

John revealed his true intentions. "Maggie, what I really want to know is whether George genuinely wants to be involved in this nefarious endeavor, or if he's trapped."

"I hope he doesn't, but I can't say for certain. You'd think that someone who experienced such a profound miracle would change their life," Maggie replied.

John's confusion was evident as he inquired, "Miracle? What are you talking about?"

Maggie sighed and recounted the miraculous tale. "You see, George couldn't walk without a brace. A woman named Sue, whom you met in the hospital, walked through his neighborhood one day, guided by the Lord. She struck up a conversation with George about his knee, even though she was a complete stranger. She shared that she had been praying for him, which astonished him, considering she was an outsider. In a moment of divine connection, he made a sarcastic comment about God healing him, challenging her to pray for his knee. To everyone's astonishment, he agreed."

She continued, "As Sue laid her hands on his knee and prayed, George felt an electric shock course through his leg. In an instant, he discarded his brace, jubilantly leaping and proclaiming that he was healed. Given this miracle, it's challenging to fathom George's involvement in such a mess."

John looked at her, surprised. This was the most he had heard from her about her church, but it wasn't entirely unexpected, given the hints she had dropped earlier. Her involvement in the prayer group and her comments about a significant decision had piqued his curiosity.

"Do you truly believe he was healed?" John asked.

Maggie nodded firmly. "Yes, I do. And what motive would he have to become entangled in our church's troubles? Why invest all the effort he's put into it? Besides, you saw the news the other night—three men lost their lives during Pastor Wayne's first prayer night."

John raised an eyebrow, conveying a mix of skepticism and curiosity. But instead of challenging her, he chose to smile, respecting Maggie's perspective.

"Regardless of what we think, if you're interested in my opinion, I believe George is genuine. I just can't fathom why he remains embroiled in this mess."

"He's trapped," Maggie replied, her voice filled with empathy and understanding.

John realized the painful truth. "He can't get out. If he tries, they might resort to drastic measures, just as they did with me."

As the pieces of the puzzle began to fall into place, both Maggie and John wore expressions of revelation. "It's all starting to make sense, Maggie. I knew you'd have the answers."

Maggie, still processing the weight of the situation, replied, "I didn't say anything."

John chuckled, an affectionate smile on his face. "But you did. I'm going to approach George with a proposition."

Maggie's worry creased her brow. "What if he gets scared and does something irrational, especially knowing that you're working for the opposition?"

John's determination shone through. "I'm hoping to offer him a way out of this mess, Maggie. It's a work in progress, but I think I might be able to help him."

Maggie leaned in, her eyes searching for the details. "How are you planning to do that?"

John's gaze held a hint of optimism and a touch of uncertainty. "That's a great question, Maggie. I'm still working on that."

The phone rang, shattering the stillness of Bruce's day. He

hastily picked up the receiver, his voice infused with curiosity and anticipation as he answered, "Hello?"

On the other end of the line, a warm and familiar voice responded, "Hey Bruce, it's Sue."

A smile curled at the corners of Bruce's lips as he replied, "Well, isn't that something. I was just about to call you. I wanted you to pray for something for me."

Sue's voice radiated a deep sense of caring and devotion. "I have been praying continually for you. This will allow me to pray more specifically."

Curiosity piqued, Bruce inquired, "Why did you call?"

Sue's excitement bubbled over as she delivered her news, her voice quivering with emotion at the end. "Bruce, I wanted you to be the first to know. My husband Jerry has prayed and asked Jesus into his life!"

A surge of elation and joy coursed through Bruce's veins. "Oh Sue, that is awesome! How long have we been praying for him?"

Sue's reply was tinged with a sense of nostalgia. "Well, since we first got married. I thought Jerry was a Christian because he went to church. Of course, he was just doing that for me. After a while, he just stopped attending."

Bruce's voice brimmed with excitement and pride. "That is great! How is the spearheading of the in-home prayer groups going?"

Sue's words flowed with enthusiasm. "Great! It is so exciting to be an intimate part of the outreach that the Tuesday night prayer group has given. And I can't put into words all the answered prayers, miracles, and changed lives it has produced. God is really using it."

With a thoughtful pause, Bruce broached another topic. "Then you won't mind if you help another church?"

There was a brief silence on the phone as Sue absorbed the revelation. "You mean God is working in another church like ours?"

Bruce's response held a sense of reverence. "Well, it is a church that loves Jesus and worships in its own distinct style."

Sue's unwavering faith and devotion shone through in her reply. "Bruce, anywhere God is, well, that is where I want to be. Count me in!"

A sense of unity and purpose resonated in Bruce's voice. "Great, Sue. That is just great. I have another favor to ask."

Sue's willingness to support and assist never wavered as she encouraged him, "Ask away."

With sincerity, Bruce revealed his need. "I need prayer. I will be approaching Reverend Richard Stone, and I would ask that you pray for God's wisdom."

Sue's curiosity was piqued as she inquired, "What are you going to talk to him about?"

Bruce began to explain, his words carrying the weight of a sacred mission. He revealed everything he had discussed with Pastor Gary, and Sue realized the depth of prayer needed for this situation, considering the differences in worship style between Reverend Stone and their church. Their conversation had transcended the mundane, embracing a deeper connection through faith and shared purpose.

As Bruce concluded his heartwarming conversation with Sue, the weight of responsibility didn't let up. His phone rang once more, and this time it was none other than Pastor Wayne himself. Bruce was swiftly realizing why his trusty answering machine was showing signs of wear and tear.

"Bruce, I need you to preach on Sunday. I don't know what to say after what happened on Tuesday night. You've been doing this for a while, and I'm sure it will come easily to you," Pastor Wayne implored.

Bruce, ever the humble servant, felt the gravity of the situation but remained steadfast. "Wayne, it's your church, and you're a man of God. The Lord doesn't want me to travel and preach. He has given me my church, and with it, all the responsibility I can handle. Besides, this is a God thing, and He is taking it beyond the borders of our church. It's a revival, and God is behind it. He will empower you and give you the words to speak, as He has done years prior."

Pastor Wayne's voice quivered with a mixture of awe and apprehension. "But that was different! I didn't have people dying in my church, God visiting in all His glory, and a congregation that has been so responsive. It's unbelievable!"

Bruce's faith remained unwavering as he assured his friend, "It's God."

Pastor Wayne, now clearly shaken, voiced his anxieties. "Whatever! I can't do this! What if I mess up? I might be the next one they carry out on a stretcher!"

Bruce's wisdom and reassurance shone through as he attempted to calm his friend. "Now you're talking about God's Judgment, not discipline. Wayne, calm down. Work on something and give me a call. I'll be happy to be a sounding board. Keep in mind the verse of scripture that says, 'Do not worry about what you will say at that time. The Father will give you the words at the appropriate time.'"

With a heart full of gratitude, Bruce offered, "Meanwhile, I'll be sending Sue Billings over to help get your home Bible studies going."

Pastor Wayne couldn't help but express his curiosity. "How did you know about that? I just got a bunch of calls today, all about that."

Bruce's light-hearted tone broke the tension as he joked, "Just a lucky guess," and they both shared a hearty laugh.

"Bruce, you're the greatest. Thanks for being here for me. It's great to know that I'm not alone," Pastor Wayne acknowledged, his voice filled with deep gratitude.

The call ended, and Bruce's smile was a mile wide. It was a profound blessing to be doing God's work and to be an instrument of the Creator of the universe. A sense of purpose and fulfillment coursed through him. Most of the time, he felt as though he was cheating because God orchestrated the circumstances in his favor, used his words to accomplish great things, and turned his deeds into remarkable feats. But, in reality, he was simply following the lead of his Master, and everything else fell into place. It was a profound sense of contentment to know that he was precisely where God wanted him to be.

John had bared his soul to Maggie in a way he had never done with any of his previous girlfriends. The sense of relief that washed over him was intense. It was a rare and precious thing to have someone who listened without judgment or the inclination to impose their beliefs and offer unsolicited advice. Maggie was a true friend, a confidant, and it felt like a lifeline in the stormy sea of his life.

As he continued pouring out his thoughts and fears to Maggie, John realized that the time had come to break free from the stagnation he'd been mired in. His self-absorption had reached its limit; his actions were causing harm to others, including his baby sister and all the innocent individuals entangled in the web of the Association for Fetal Research and Advance Medical.

Yet, John was acutely aware that he couldn't tackle this formidable challenge alone. Maggie's unwavering support was invaluable, but he needed a partner in this perilous journey. Would George Hines be willing to join forces with him? John grappled with the nagging doubt – was George genuinely committed to the path of morality or merely putting on a façade for the church community? Nonetheless, his first act of kindness would be to try to liberate George, to give him a chance at redemption if he was indeed in too deep.

Maggie, with her deep wisdom, applauded John's decision, recognizing its daunting nature and moral significance. She stood beside him, firm in her belief that it was the right thing to do. John understood that this decision would upend his life, but the prospect of looking at himself in the mirror as a man who had made a difference in the lives of those affected by the callous actions of the two nefarious companies filled him with a renewed sense of purpose.

John's first order of business was to prepare himself for the challenges ahead. He knew that his appearance needed a transformation, just in case George was the one who had ordered a hit on him. By altering his look, he would have the opportunity to protect his newfound identity if George's change of heart turned out to be a ruse. John was determined to be unrecognizable, a silent guardian of his mission for justice.

On the fateful deadline day that Dennis Spence had set, John's phone jolted to life with an insistent ring, yet he deliberately let the call divert to voicemail. It was none other than Dennis, seeking an update on whether John had ventured to meet George as instructed. Dennis, the voice on the other end of the line, voiced his concern, mentioning that George was generally prompt in his communications, and he was anticipating updates from both of them. "My plant managers are in the habit of keeping me informed about anything new or out of the ordinary. I've always believed in maintaining an open-door policy," Dennis added, before ending the call.

John couldn't help but ponder how Dennis, in his interactions, exuded a veneer of pleasantness, yet the situation at hand was far from ordinary.

The gravity of his mission weighed heavily on John's mind as he contemplated the life-altering decisions that loomed before him. It was crucial to change his appearance, particularly if George had indeed placed a contract on his life. With a sense of purpose, he made his way to the local drugstore and stocked up on an assortment of disguises: hair grease, hair dye, an outdated pair of glasses, and a pocket protector brimming with pens.

A detour to a nearby clothing store was his next step, where he unearthed an ensemble that transported him back to the 1970s – plaid slacks and a button-down shirt with patterns that were an eyesore. He paired these fashion relics with an astonishing discovery from a thrift shop: white and black leather golfing shoes and lime green socks. Surprisingly, the store staff proved unusually helpful during his shopping spree, a detail that didn't escape John's notice. He couldn't shake the feeling that they were somehow connected to the news story he had recently seen about Maggie's church and the transformations sweeping through the community.

Back in the sanctity of his home, John wasted no time transforming his appearance. Hair, eyebrows, and goatee, all underwent a dramatic makeover. He added thick, bushy sideburns, slicked his hair back with a pronounced part, and even went so far as to break his glasses, hastily patching them together with scotch tape to achieve a lopsided effect. A dental piece was wedged into his front teeth, giving his smile a comically exaggerated look. He diligently practiced imitating Jerry Lewis's iconic laugh, finding the sound both absurd and strangely liberating.

John felt a strange lightness as he began to dress in his outlandish ensemble – a jarring combination of mismatched shirt and plaid pants, the awful golf shoes, and the pocket protector housing five pens of varying shapes, sizes, and colors.

To complete his transformation, John liberally sprayed Musk cologne on his cheeks, its fragrance evoking vivid memories of his teenage years. He stood before the mirror and rehearsed his walk, accentuating the exaggerated swing of his arms and donning a goofy smile. His voice took on a slightly whiny, almost cartoonish quality, with just the right amount of absurdity.

As the finishing touch, John concealed a bulletproof vest beneath his clothes, a precaution born of his instinct for self-preservation. The gravity of his task bore down on him, and he couldn't help but wonder if Maggie's intuition about George was indeed accurate. Nevertheless, John was resolute in playing it safe as he readied himself to confront the unknown.

Bruce found himself on the way to meet Reverend Richard Stone, a name that alone stirred feelings of intimidation. As he drove through the picturesque town of Stapleton, the scenery seemed to have taken on a brighter and more vibrant hue, despite the chilly weather. Bruce took advantage of the invigorating cold breeze by rolling down his car windows, allowing the crisp air to energize him for the impending encounter.

The church he was bound for stood as an architectural marvel, reminiscent of old English-style churches, with an elegantly designed circular stained glass window adorning its facade. The level of craftsmanship made Bruce's own church's windows appear childishly assembled by comparison. The church grounds were immaculately maintained, with a diligent lawn crew putting the finishing touches as Bruce arrived.

Upon stepping into the foyer, an inexplicable tension gripped him, making the already intimidating atmosphere feel even more unwelcoming. It was possible that his own apprehension contributed to this overwhelming sense of unease. As Bruce proceeded down the hallway leading to Reverend Stone's office, he couldn't help but notice an open door revealing the clergyman's robes. They were long and gracefully adorned, a stark contrast to the plain attire he usually wore. Bruce couldn't help but wonder how his congregation would react if he ever appeared in such attire.

Continuing his journey down the hall, he happened upon another open door leading into the sanctuary. The sight that met his eyes was breathtaking, causing him to come to a sudden halt, his gaze transfixed by the grandeur before him.

A voice interrupted his reverie, and Bruce turned to find a woman standing there. Her voice held a note of admiration, "Amazing, isn't it?"

Startled by her presence, Bruce could only respond, "Yes, it sure is."

She continued to share her awe, "Those pipes on the pipe organ make the whole sanctuary come alive. You can't go anywhere in the building without feeling their full impact..."

Intrigued by the unexpected encounter, Bruce introduced himself, "By the way, I'm Bruce Hutchinson. I am…"

But the woman cut him off, getting straight to the point, "The pastor from the little church that's having all of the miracles."

Bruce acknowledged, "Yes, I guess you could say that."

Lucie's words resonated with a mix of curiosity and concern as she shared, "Oh, yes. Many of our folks have been attending your Tuesday night prayer meetings. Reverend Stone seems to be concerned about this."

Bruce couldn't help but feel a twinge of trepidation. The knowledge that members of Reverend Stone's congregation had been gravitating towards his church weighed heavily on his mind. This revelation only added to the complexity of the conversation he was about to have.

Attempting to maintain an air of innocence, Bruce inquired, "Why is Reverend Stone concerned?" His heart raced, though he was well aware of the answer.

However, Lucie's response was far from subtle. She cut straight to the chase, her words laced with candor, "Why are you taking his congregation from him!" The bluntness of her question hung in the air, a challenge Bruce knew he would need to address head-on.

Burces's response sent a signal that this conversation might be more challenging than he had anticipated, "Well, that's not my intention at all. As a matter of fact, I've come today to discuss what's really going on in our church."

Lucie's tone softened as she decided to assist him, "In that case, let me take you to Reverend Stone."

"Is he here today?" Bruce inquired.

"Yes, and I'm his secretary," Lucie replied.

With a friendly exchange of pleasantries, Bruce and Lucie embarked down the hallway, finally reaching an elegant door. As they entered the office, Bruce found himself captivated by the sheer beauty of the surroundings. Lucie efficiently informed Reverend Stone of Bruce's arrival, and the anticipation grew. The moment of truth was at hand as they walked down yet another hallway to another door, and Lucie opened it, introducing Bruce to Reverend Stone.

"It's truly a pleasure to finally meet you, Pastor Hutchinson," Reverend Richard Stone exclaimed, extending his hand with a warm and genuine smile. The room was bathed in soft, warm light, casting a comforting glow on the moment.

"Likewise," Bruce replied, his voice tinged with a touch of shyness, but his eyes gleamed with curiosity.

Reverend Stone stood tall, radiating an air of authority, his broad shoulders and stature speaking of his physical well-being. A crown of silver-gray hair adorned his head, a testament to his wisdom and experience. Bruce couldn't help but be impressed by the presence of this formidable figure.

"How can I assist you today, Pastor?" Reverend Stone inquired, his voice gentle and inviting, adding a layer of genuine warmth to the conversation.

As they spoke, Bruce felt a whirlwind of emotions. Butterflies danced in his stomach, and he couldn't help but be nervous, facing such a well-respected figure in the community. His heart raced, and he silently sent up a fervent prayer, "Lord, grant me wisdom and success." The room seemed to shimmer with tension and anticipation.

With conviction in his voice, Bruce began, "I am here because I believe God has sent me."

Reverend Stone's expression, once welcoming, transformed into one of disbelief as he quizzically cocked his head. "Oh yes," he responded, his tone now laced with sarcasm and a hint of disgust. "I've heard it from some of my congregation. Or should I say, some of my ex-congregation members."

Bruce was taken aback, his emotions shifting from anticipation to confusion. "Sir?"

"Don't play coy with me, son," the Reverend retorted, his voice now tinged with sternness. "I've been ministering since you were in diapers, son. Whatever you're doing, or whatever God is doing in your church, it's drawing my members away."

Bruce struggled to clarify, his voice wavering slightly, "I've never solicited any members from any other church in Stapleton. I've only opened up Tuesday nights for prayer, and God seems to be doing amazing things as a result."

Reverend Stone was unrelenting, his voice unwavering. "You're not going to take credit for the good things that have happened, are you?"

"No, not at all. It's God-" Bruce began, his voice shaking with frustration.

The Reverend interrupted with determination, "You know there are other churches in the community, some of which have closed their doors. Perhaps it's a result of your actions."

"No, sir!" Bruce's anger began to well up, and he struggled to keep it in check.

With an unwavering tone, the Reverend's words cut through the air, laden with conviction. Each word resonated like a solemn bell tolling in a sacred cathedral, creating a reverberating atmosphere.

"God demands more than mere prayer," he declared, his voice brimming with authority. The room seemed to be steeped in the weight of his words. "He seeks out those who labor with unwavering dedication in His name. Our Christmas pageant stands as a magnificent testament to the divine. It consumes countless hours and an immeasurable amount of time each year. God hungers for diligent souls, not those who idly gather to utter empty phrases. The divine work demands financial sacrifice. Behold this sanctuary, with its grand pipe organ and pristine stained glass windows – the cost is immense. Have you any inkling of the expense required to maintain this hallowed ground, from the meticulous care of our manicured gardens to the venerable elk tree, casting its shade over our prayer garden? It is pruned by skilled hands, moss removed every three months – all in the name of divine elegance."

The room seemed to pulse with the energy of his words, and each detail painted a vivid picture of the dedication and resources poured into maintaining the church's splendor.

Bruce couldn't hold back any longer. "Reverend Stone, that's not what God is looking for. He wants men and women who surrender their will to Him, allowing His Spirit to guide them according to His purpose, not ours!" His voice rose, filled with fervor, but the Reverend remained unyielding.

"These are just words, good pastor. It's not about words; it's about the work of God. It should be done the way He wants it, with grace and style."

"Style? What do you mean?" Bruce asked, his eyebrows knitting together in a mix of curiosity and confusion. The room felt charged with tension, as if it were crackling with an unspoken debate.

Reverend Stone continued, "In the Old Testament, priests were dressed in the finest garments, woven with pure, refined gold. I wear a robe to please the Almighty."

Bruce was left stunned by the Reverend's perspective.

"Our church is adorned with the richest purple, blue, and red colors, all touched with gold," Reverend Stone added. "This church truly embodies the name 'God's house' more than any other church in the community, including yours, Pastor Hutchinson."

Bruce responded, "God doesn't dwell in a building but in His creation once they invite Him in."

Reverend Stone retorted, "Ah, the born-again philosophy. While I believe in Christ's sacrificial atonement for our sins, this isn't about Christ. It's about the members you're taking from my congregation. I'd kindly ask that you cease."

"But Rev..." Bruce began to protest.

"I said, good day," Reverend Stone interrupted firmly.

Leaving the room, Bruce was overwhelmed by a mix of anger, a sense of failure, and deep frustration. He realized that his words hadn't made any difference for God or for any good, leaving him with a heavy heart as he exited the room.

John, with a determination fueled by both nostalgia and a desire for anonymity, found himself on a quest to rent a car. His last vehicle held sentimental value, and he couldn't bear the thought of history repeating itself with the new one. In his search, he stumbled upon a car lot proudly boasting "Cheap Cars, Cheap Rentals." A wry chuckle escaped him as he envisioned his parents' imagined approval of his frugal choice.

Wandering through the lot, his eyes locked onto his dream car—a late model classic that spoke to his soul. Negotiating with the affable and transparent staff, he even persuaded the dealer to equip the car with a discreet license plate from the hidden stock, ensuring his identity remained veiled. John marveled at the unexpected support from the used car lot, a spark of curiosity kindling within him about the community's unique qualities.

As he pulled up to AFT Manufacturing, a surge of excitement and anxiety mingled within him. John recognized the risks, yet he remained resolute in his mission to speak with George Hines. Approaching the receptionist, he detected a subtle worry in her expression, a detail that strangely boosted his confidence.

"Can I help you?" she inquired, her tone expecting a negative response.

"Hi," John greeted, carefully suppressing his gum-chewing habit as he adjusted his stance. "I'm John Smith with Tech 1, here to see George Hines." He spoke with practiced ease, ensuring his cover story sounded natural while silently reinforcing the role he needed to play.

The receptionist shot him a disapproving look, questioning the presence of an unannounced visitor. Leaning in, John flashed a grin, revealing dental imperfections. "I've been sent by the big guy himself, Dennis Spence!" he declared with a twinkle in his eye.

Skeptical, the receptionist made a call to verify John's claim. As confirmation came through, annoyance etched on her face, John grinned and resumed his gum-chewing routine.

Calling George Hines, the receptionist relayed the message with dwindling enthusiasm. The response came, "Send him in."

Approaching the door, John couldn't shake off the fear of walking into a potential danger zone. Memories of the hospital incident haunted him, but he steeled himself with the confidence befitting a seasoned private investigator.

Inside, George Hines, an attractive figure with distinguished gray hair, rose, extended a welcoming hand, and smiled broadly. "Hello, I am George Hines."

John shook his hand, introducing himself with a firm grip. "John Smith of Tech 1."

"Welcome, have a seat," George offered, unfazed by John's less-than-impressive appearance.

"Dennis Spence sent you?" George inquired.

"Yes, he did," John affirmed.

"Great! Is your specialty computers? I could use some help in our computer department." George's nonchalant demeanor suggested he had dealt with unconventional situations before.

"I assume Dennis has sent people to you before," John observed.

"Oh, yes, many times. That's how I've found some of my best talent," George revealed.

As the conversation unfolded, John carefully observed his surroundings, noting fishing pictures, an old sports trophy, and a particular item that intrigued him.

"I noticed that picture on your shelf. What is it if I may ask?"

John inquired, aiming to delve deeper into George's personality.

George's face lit up with a genuine smile. "That is the first day I attended a church. A church that changed my life." Encouraged, George recounted the transformative story of how a prayer meeting had led him to experience a profound connection with God.

In that moment, John was moved by the sincerity of George's tale, contemplating the significance of decisions. A prayer echoed in his mind, Maggie's voice resonating, "Father, we thank you for saving John's life through the awful car wreck that he had." The memory lingered, a testament to the impact of choices.

Taking a deep breath, John decided it was time to unveil his true purpose for being there.

It started as an ordinary day in Mrs. Hurwitz's class at Stapleton High, the monotonous drone of routine settling over the room. However, the tranquility shattered when one boy, usually only present for an easy credit and to flirt with girls, escalated his disruptive behavior to an alarming degree. Mrs. Hurwitz couldn't ignore the signs—his eyes glazed over and tinged with red, a clear descent into a disturbing state.

In the midst of inappropriate comments that hung heavily in the air, Mrs. Hurwitz's patience wore thin, and she swiftly dispatched the troubled student to the principal's office. Yet, defiance gripped him. Rising with an unsettling determination, he brandished a menacing knife, leveling it at Mrs. Hurwitz with a chilling declaration, "I am going to kill you!"

In that harrowing moment, Mrs. Hurwitz, fueled by fear and desperation, whispered a prayer, the gravity of the situation weighing heavily on her. The rest of the class, frozen in shock, watched as the scene unfolded, the air thick with tension.

Amidst the chaos, Mrs. Hurwitz's gaze fell upon something unexpected. The principal had quietly hung the Ten Commandments on the classroom walls, an act that, in the chaos, went unnoticed until now. Gratitude flooded her heart, unsure of how he managed to implement it, but thankful he did.

As the boy's threatening gaze followed Mrs. Hurwitz's, he bellowed, demanding her attention. When he turned to face the wall, he was met with the glowing Ten Commandments. The letters burned with intensity, emitting a beam of light that etched onto the boy's trembling form. The words "Thou shalt not kill" imprinted themselves onto his chest and face, triggering a guttural scream that echoed through the room.

Struggling to maintain his balance, the boy teetered under the relentless assault of the divine light. Each flicker etched the commandment onto the classroom floor, a stark reminder of the gravity of his actions. "Thou shalt not kill" spelled out in searing letters.

Finally, in a surreal turn of events, the boy stumbled, his hand with the knife colliding with a desk. The weapon flew from his grip, landing in the path of the radiant light. The students, their faces frozen in a mix of disbelief and awe, bore witness to the surreal spectacle. The once-menacing knife, gripped by the troubled boy, began to melt away as if succumbing to an otherworldly force. Its sharp edges blurred into an indistinct mass, leaving behind only a greasy residue on the floor—a haunting echo of the weapon's former menace.

Yet, it wasn't just the remnants of the knife that captivated their attention. Alongside the fading grease spot, the floor bore the scars of divine intervention. The letters, seared into the surface, formed the unmistakable commandment: "Thou shalt not kill." The students, grappling with the inexplicable events unfolding before them, couldn't tear their eyes away from the powerful testament left behind—a tangible reminder of the unseen forces at play. The light, as abruptly as it appeared, vanished.

As the aftermath settled, Mrs. Hurwitz sank into her chair, her mind reeling from the surreal events. The class, gripped by a collective silence, processed the extraordinary scene before them. Mrs. Hurwitz, regaining composure, rushed to check the boy's pulse and, reaching into her purse, dialed 911 on her cell phone, breaking the eerie silence that hung over the room.

"Bruce, I'm grateful you could make it today," Joe Benton, the principal of Stapleton's high school, welcomed with sincerity in his voice.

Bruce reciprocated, "Not a problem, Joe. How are you holding up?"

"I'm doing well. The reason I asked you to come in today is

because I have something significant to share with you."

Intrigue filled Bruce. Whatever it was, it had to be important if Joe specifically summoned him to his office.

"I'll show you shortly, but first, let me share the story that leads up to it. By the way, those Tuesday night prayer meetings have been quite powerful. The answered prayers we've witnessed are beyond belief."

"Absolutely, Joe. It's been extraordinary. Out of curiosity, when did you decide to follow Christ?"

"Around six years old. I've always attended church, but the way God has worked in recent times is unlike anything I've seen before."

"God's revelation and power in our lives—it's a revival," Bruce acknowledged.

"Exactly! I've read about revivals in the past, but to be a part of one…that's why I wanted you to come in."

"Oh?"

"Yes."

"Joe, before you continue, I caught Mrs. Jones, who was causing trouble for the school, having a heart attack on TV!"

"Yes, she had been a hindrance for years. But since she's been removed from the picture, I've been able to do many more positive things, like putting up the Ten Commandments on each classroom wall."

"You're serious?"

"Absolutely. I just put them up one day, and surprisingly, no one has complained. The school board has stayed silent. It's usually only a fuss when parents are upset. Politics, you know."

"That's incredible. How have the teachers responded?"

"Let me share the story of one teacher whose life was saved by those commandments on the wall."

Bruce gave Joe a quizzical look, prompting him to recount the events in Mrs. Hurwitz's classroom.

"She's been part of the Tuesday night prayer group."

"Yes, and I believe it was God who intervened."

"In what way, Joe? How did God intervene?"

"Come with me, Bruce. I'll show you."

As they walked, Joe continued the story until they halted in front of a classroom. Opening the door, they entered, and Bruce's eyes fell upon the words "THOU SHALT NOT KILL" perfectly written on the carpet in front of the teacher's desk. The outline of a knife remained visible, covered by the word "kill." Though the letters had faded, their clarity persisted. Bruce touched the letters and recoiled as though burned, looking up at the Ten Commandments on the wall. Walking over, he touched them with both hands, closed his eyes, and recited, "My word is like a fire," declares the Lord, before letting out a deep sigh.

Joe stood there in awe of Bruce, sensing the presence of God and the sanctity of a truly holy man. Emotions surged in the room, a testament to the profound spiritual experiences woven into the fabric of their lives.

"George, could we take a walk? I need a smoke break," John requested, a subtle urgency in his tone, hoping to find a secluded spot for an unguarded conversation. Even though he didn't smoke, he needed an excuse to get George out of the office, wary of potential eavesdropping from shadowy organizations.

"Sure, we have a designated smoking area just outside. No one will be there since it's in-between breaks," George replied, unwittingly stepping into John's well-crafted plan.

They headed towards the door, John informing George's secretary that they would be right back. As they strolled to the designated area, John keenly observed his surroundings, every detail etching into his mind. Initiating a conversation about the manufacturing process, John noticed George's smile slipping away, a subtle transformation not easily discernible to the untrained eye.

"How is this?" George asked, pointing to a serene garden area with tables and chairs.

"Perfect. But I must confess, I don't smoke," John confessed, a hint of mischief in his eyes.

George looked puzzled.

"I wanted to get out of your office before I told you why I'm here," John explained, though his clarification seemed to add to George's confusion. Settling back, John discarded his gum and got straight to the point.

"I am a private investigator hired about six months ago by Dennis Spence to uncover who has been sabotaging the company."

George's face drained of color, and a heavy silence settled between them. John leaned forward, taking a deep breath before delivering the next revelation. "Mr. Spence has assigned me to work with you, and I'm expected to report my progress to him by the end of the day," he declared. "But before we proceed, I need to tell you that I know about Advanced Medical."

George's reaction was visceral; he covered his face with his hands and let out a heavy sigh. "I always knew this would come back to haunt me," he muttered. "But why does Mr. Spence want you to work with me? Doesn't he want to throw me in jail?"

John, now devoid of his usual geeky accent and irritating mannerisms, met George's gaze. "I haven't told him anything," he admitted.

"Why not?" George inquired. "Isn't this why he hired you?"

"George, I know Maggie," John disclosed, capturing George's attention.

Continuing, he said, "Maggie tipped me off that you attend her church and have been a great help there. I believed your transformation was genuine, that your decision to follow Christ had a real impact on your life. I also suspected you were stuck in a difficult position, torn between your values and your job at Advanced Medical. I know firsthand how ruthless they can be—I've had my own encounters with them, losing my car and nearly my life. That's why I've been in hiding and took a chance in approaching you, an employee of the same company that attacked me."

George leaned back in his chair, taking deep breaths, relieved that John wasn't there to turn him in. He asked cautiously, "What is it you want from me?"

"I want to work with you as Dennis asked," John replied.

George, perplexed, questioned, "To find the saboteur? But I am he. I don't understand."

John responded calmly, "I know, George. I know. Let me explain."

EIGHT

Reverend Stone experienced an unexpected reunion when Lawrence Stein, a cherished friend from their seminary school days, paid him a surprise visit. Many years had passed since they last crossed paths.

As Lawrence entered Reverend Stone's office, a burst of energy accompanied him, infusing the room with vivacity. In his late forties, Lawrence carried an air of distinction, his hair lightly touched by gray. The years had matured him, and his lively personality seemed to transcend time.

"Dick! How are you, buddy! It's been so long since I've seen you!" Lawrence exclaimed, rushing over with an outstretched hand.

"Please, call me Reverend Stone while on church premises," Reverend Stone replied.

"What is this? Are we being formal?" Lawrence asked with a playful grin.

"I believe that I have earned this title," Reverend Stone explained.

"Well, I think I have also...Reverend. But you call me Larry. That's what my staff calls me," Lawrence countered, maintaining the friendly banter with a smile.

Reverend Stone observed Lawrence, who had come to visit him, noticing a subtle change in the atmosphere. As Lawrence delved into the purpose of his visit, Reverend Stone wiggled in his chair, grappling with the first-name basis that Lawrence insisted upon. "The church down the way seems to be having a significant impact on the community," he finally shared.

Lawrence, surprised, responded, "Significant? From the looks of the news, it seems like that little church is affecting almost every aspect of life in Stapleton."

A sudden flush colored Reverend Stone's face. "Dick? What seems to be the problem? Don't you approve of the positive changes?" Lawrence inquired.

Reverend Stone, after a moment, began to calm down. "The pastor of that little church came to see me. His name is Bruce. He wanted some type of involvement on my part. I said, 'No way! I don't want anything to do with a church that would actively entice members from one church to another.'"

Lawrence looked at Stone with a puzzled expression. Reverend Stone continued, "The nerve of that man! It's one thing to do it on the sly, but then to brazenly walk into my office, sit on my chair, and ask for more of my members..."

"He asked for your members?" Lawrence interrupted.

Reverend Stone hesitated before clarifying, "Well, not exactly."

"What did he ask for then?" Lawrence pressed.

"Well, nothing. He never had a chance. I finished the visit. I was not in the mood..."

"Not in the mood? You never gave the pastor a chance to tell you what was on his mind," remarked Lawrence.

"No. Whatever it was could only lead to more problems for me," replied Reverend Stone.

"More problems? What are you talking about, Dick?" Lawrence questioned.

Reverend Stone continued, "I already have trouble getting my remaining members to work for God. And this new pastor emphasizes prayer, which is not what God wants from us. He wants us to get up and make a difference, to change things for Him."

"Dick, prayer is where it all starts."

"Oh, not you too? I know that you pray, but the focus should be on work, not prayer. Prayer is for the lazy who don't want to get their hands dirty."

"Dick, do you really believe that? Look around you. It's not some pastor who's changing this town, it's God's work. The pastor is only a vessel. Have you ever considered that he may have come to you to ask for your help in God's work?"

"I don't want anything to do with a man who steals members from my church!"

"Your church?"

"Yes, my church. I've worked for years to establish a church that this community can be proud of. We have elegant programs such as the arts, and our campus is made picture-perfect with a one-hundred-year-old oak tree and a pipe organ that cost thousands of dollars. We're the envy of every other church in this town."

"Dick, please stop. I've heard enough. I didn't come here to talk about your church. I came here to see what God is doing in this town." At that comment, Stone smiled, convinced that Lawrence had finally come to his side.

"Dick, I came today to warn you," Lawrence said with a serious expression.

"Warn me? Warn me of what?" Stone's smile disappeared, and he looked defensive.

"God is here in this town working, and he has chosen that pastor to start his work."

"What are you saying? Are you for this guy?"

Lawrence raised his hand to stop Stone and continued, "If you don't humble yourself before God and listen to what this man has to say…"

"I will do…"

"Stop! If you don't humble yourself before God and listen to what this man has to say, God will have to get your attention, and based on our conversation, it will have to be a real eye-opener."

Lawrence got up and headed for the door, saying, "If you need anything, call me, and I will be happy to help. It was good to see you, Dick."

Reverend Stone remained silent, his head nodding in acknowledgment as Lawrence walked out. The weight of their conversation hung in the air, leaving Reverend Stone to grapple with the profound implications of the encounter.

Pastor Wayne Miles ushered in the Sunday morning service with a prayer that echoed the fervor of the transformative Tuesday night prayer meetings. The congregation had been caught in the contagious wave of prayer—praying at work, during the day, in various homes, and strolling through their neighborhood in the evenings, covering their community in a blanket of fervent petitions. As Wayne took the pulpit for the preaching portion on Sunday mornings, the weight of leading a divinely orchestrated revival rested solely on his shoulders.

"I have always dreamed of being involved in a revival of God," Wayne began, his voice carrying a blend of anticipation and humility. "I remember as a small boy reading about some of the revivals that occurred hundreds of years ago. I remember thinking, 'Oh, Lord, how I desire to be in the middle of all that excitement!' Well, brothers and sisters, we are now enjoying my greatest dream, revival!"

The congregation responded with a resounding "Amen."

"Now that we are in the middle of all the action, it can be a little overwhelming. I mean, what in the world do I have to say?"

"Say it, brother!" someone exclaimed, followed by affirmations like "We're listening. Speak up, brother Wayne."

"It is God who desires to speak. Not me! He has a message. He wants you to know that you can win the war, the war that wages within each of us. 'You can do all things through Christ who strengthens you!'" More "Amens" resonated throughout the sanctuary.

"Imagine a country at war with itself, good against immoral, the immoral winning most of each battle. Then an outside nation with more military power than both sides put together steps in alongside the good and begins to fight the battles for them. Each and every battle is won. The immoral side has been defeated but not removed, so it is always there as a threat. As a result, the outside nation leaves military power to keep the immoral under control, and as a result, the country at war is now experiencing peace time."

Pastor Wayne paused, surveying the remarkably quiet room. This departure from the usual vocal expressions of excitement concerned him. Yet, as he looked into each face, he discerned that the Lord was at work. Encouraged, he continued.

"God has said to us, 'Are you so foolish, my church? After beginning with the Spirit, my Spirit, are you now trying to achieve your goal through human effort?'" Wayne's voice intensified. "Our weapons are divine in nature for the pulling down of strongholds, strongholds that the enemy has placed in our lives. It is now or never, folks. God has come to us in a mighty way. What are we going to do? Continue fighting the good fight alone only to be defeated every time? Or are we going to finish with the Spirit and take the victory!"

The congregation erupted, shouting back, "Take the victory!"

"Will we take the victory?" Wayne asked.

The resounding response echoed through the auditorium, "Take the victory! Take the victory! Take the victory!" As their voices reverberated, a cool breeze swept through the room, refreshing and invigorating the worshippers.

After the service, a final song, unlike any other the church had ever heard, filled the air. It was a song of worship, and the breeze that had begun as a gentle whisper now blew with greater force. Hair moved, dresses swayed, and lights dangled on their extended wires. As the people left, they murmured to each other, "God has truly been among us." They went home changed, transformed by the radiant presence of the divine.

"George," John spoke, his tone weighted with seriousness. "Something has unfolded in my life that has altered my perspective on the Association of Fetal Research."

George's countenance immediately shifted to one of concern. "What happened?" he inquired.

"Now is not the moment to delve into it," John replied, his expression revealing a complex mix of emotions. "All I can say is that I need a change in my life. I want you to help me dismantle the Association of Fetal Research and Advanced Medical."

"Dismantle them?" George exclaimed.

"Yes," John affirmed. "Bring them both to a halt."

"But they're colossal corporations," George protested. "How can two people like us undertake something of this magnitude?"

"George, you don't have a choice," John asserted firmly. "Unless we execute my plan, you will be ensnared in the middle with no way out."

"I could run away," George suggested weakly.

"Where?" John countered. "Where could you escape to without being tracked down by Advanced Medical? Besides, do you truly want to abandon the church, the people, and all that is transpiring in this community?"

George cast his eyes downward and admitted, "No. That is the primary reason I haven't already tried. Besides, you're right. This fear seems to be governing my life." His face then brightened as he lifted his gaze back to John. "What is your plan?"

"I have information on Advanced Medical that could imprison them for years, but I need more to do the job right. That's where you come in. I need your help," John elucidated.

"And the Association of Fetal Research?" George inquired.

"I might let it self-destruct, giving us time with Dennis Spence, now that I have a new partner and all," John responded. "George, I'll be frank with you; this will be exceedingly perilous. You might even be risking your life."

"John, it has to be better than being confined in this prison, engaging in something I abhor, compromising my conscience every day, sleep diminishing with each passing night," George declared resolutely. "I don't care. I am doing wrong, and I can't continue without a just cause."

"Well, I'm glad you said that. Your just cause will be to stay undercover," John softened his tone.

George regarded John, confusion etched on his face. "Continue to manage this facility, apply pressure on the Association, and work with me to infiltrate Advanced Medical to gather more information to dismantle them," John clarified.

"Infiltrate?" George questioned, still uncertain.

"We're leaving first thing in the morning," John declared,

sidestepping George's question.

At this, George's complexion paled once again. John slapped him on the arm and reassured, "Hey, if your God is big enough to heal you, isn't he big enough to take you through this? Besides, I'll be right beside you."

George simply looked at John, at a loss for words.

"What other choice do you have?" John pressed.

Bruce was en route to the hospital to visit a young man struck down at school when a loud noise pierced the air from behind him. The skies, once serene, now churned ominously, darkening with a foreboding intensity. He pondered if it might be one of the last summer storms, even though an odd coolness lingered. Peering into his rear-view mirror, Bruce's heart plummeted. It wasn't a tempest of rain; it was a tornado of devastating proportions, a force that could make even Dorothy of the Wizard of Oz tremble. The monstrous twister roared like an unstoppable locomotive, obliterating everything in its path, leaving only the haunting echoes of a city that once thrived—homes, buildings, stoplights—all erased in an instant. As swiftly as it had touched down, the tornado ascended into the air, vanishing into nothingness.

Bruce's immediate instinct was to turn his car around, compelled to offer assistance to those impacted. Approaching the aftermath, navigating the streets became an arduous task. Swerving around debris, some recognizable and others unidentifiable, the road became a treacherous obstacle course. Lawn chairs, garbage cans, remnants of what once was a playground, broken tree branches, and leaves cluttered the path. Eventually, the accumulation of debris rendered further progress impossible. Bruce pulled over to the side, staring out of his front window in disbelief. Before him stood the remnants of Reverend Richard Stone's once-majestic church, now reduced to nothingness. The sight left him breathless, his mouth agape at the sheer devastation wrought by the unforgiving force of nature.

Sue visited Maggie's house, a familiar routine born out of deep friendship and shared spirituality. They settled on the porch, where

Sue had first embraced Christianity, overlooking a garden that, despite the encroaching winter, retained its captivating beauty.

"How are you doing, Maggie?" Sue inquired, her concern etched in her voice.

"I'm doing great. It's incredible to witness all the things unfolding in the church and the community," Maggie replied, her eyes sparkling with enthusiasm.

However, Sue's tone shifted, adopting a more serious note. "I'm concerned about Pastor Bruce."

Maggie's expression mirrored the concern. "Why?"

"I feel like the attack on his home was just the beginning. I have a heavy burden to pray for him like never before, and it scares me."

Maggie listened intently, her eyes filled with empathy. "Bruce has been a catalyst for the revival that God has sent to our city. If he's somehow neutralized, the church could be hurt, and God's revival could be hindered."

"Sue, God is able to take care of this. You know He can use evil for good," Maggie reassured her, placing a comforting hand on Sue's shoulder.

Despite the reassurance, Sue leaned forward, burying her face in her hands. "Yes, but that still doesn't keep Bruce from great pain."

"Sue, you know better than anyone that this is going to work out for the best. Someone is tugging on your heartstrings for your prayers. You are a prayer warrior! That is what you do. Of course, you would have this burden. It is right. Let's take care of it," Maggie encouraged, offering unwavering support.

The two women bowed their heads, tears streaming down their faces as they fervently pleaded with God on Bruce's behalf. After they finished, they lifted their heads, hugged each other, and smiled through their tears.

"Sue, how is your husband Jerry doing?" Maggie gently shifted the conversation.

"He's doing great! He has become a new man," Sue beamed with a smile.

Maggie, intrigued, asked, "What do you mean?"

"Well, he doesn't spend as much time with the boys as he used to. He likes to take me with him when he goes to do the things he likes, and he has even started to come with me when I shop or go to the arts and crafts store."

"You're kidding? Jerry?" Maggie exclaimed in disbelief.

"I'm telling you, he has really begun to change. Just recently, I caught him actually listening to me when I was talking," Sue shared, laughter bubbling through her words.

"What do you mean, 'caught him'?" Maggie inquired.

Sue continued, "I usually just talk, expecting him not to listen like he used to. In the middle of a conversation the other day, he asked a question, and I just kept on talking. He stopped me and asked it again! That is when I realized, for the first time since the car wreck incident, that he is actually listening to me!"

"Wow, Sue, that is just great!"

"You know, Maggie, I can accept the crazy things that happen in church, in the community, and even in my own neighborhood, but when they hit as close to home as my husband..." Sue trailed off. Tears welled up in her eyes, but a radiant smile broke through.

"Oh, Sue, I am just so happy for you." They sat in silence for a while, savoring the weight of the spoken words.

"Sue, I have to tell you, I saw John again," Maggie shared, her eyes lighting up.

"Another date?" Sue teased.

"Sue!"

"Okay, I won't start. How is he doing?"

"Well, you know he is out of the hospital, and, well, he has confided in me about his assignment."

"Maggie, that sounds dangerous. Don't you remember the car wreck? It wasn't an accident, you know!"

"Yes, but I think it was important. I think that he is getting closer to making a positive decision."

"Oh, really?" Sue's eyes now mirrored Maggie's enthusiasm as they both looked over the garden.

"Yes, and some of the things that he shared with me I am not at liberty to say, but I can say that I can see why you may have been given this burden for Bruce's safety."

At that comment, Sue quickly turned her head and stared at Maggie, a mix of curiosity and concern in her eyes.

As Bruce surveyed the debris, the once-majestic church now reduced to ruins, he noticed movement in the distance. It was difficult to discern amid the scattered obstacles, but as he drew closer, he saw Reverend Stone and the petite woman who had guided him to the reverend's office a few days prior. The two were engaged in conversation, their voices carrying through the wreckage.

"I'm so grateful we had this basement," the woman expressed her relief.

"If it weren't for your quick thinking, we would both be dead! How did you know the commotion was a tornado?" Reverend Stone inquired.

"When I was a child, a tornado hit our farm. I remember my dad grabbing me and my sister and yelling at my mom as we rushed to the cellar. I recognized the sound as soon as I heard it," the woman explained, a tinge of nostalgia and fear in her voice.

"We'd both be dead if we hadn't made it down here in time! It's a good thing the rest of the staff was off today," Reverend Stone added, a mix of gratitude and distress in his tone.

"Reverend Stone, are you okay?" Bruce called out as he approached them through the rubble, concern etching his face.

As Reverend Stone turned to look at Bruce, his face turned red with anger, emotions boiling beneath the surface.

"What do you want? To sift through the rubble for more members for your church?" he snapped, the bitterness in his words hanging in the air.

Bruce, taken aback by Reverend Stone's harsh accusations, couldn't hide the hurt that flashed across his face.

"Don't give me that look! This is all your doing! Did you pray for the wrath of God to come upon me because I wasn't willing to go along with your ideas like Pastor Wayne?" Reverend Stone continued, his anger escalating.

"Reverend Stone, that's nonsense. I'm here to help," Bruce replied earnestly, his voice carrying a mixture of sincerity and hurt.

"Did the Devil intercept that prayer and send this mess my way?" Reverend Stone retorted, bitterness and suspicion lacing his words.

Bruce spoke solemnly, "I'm here to help. What can I do?"

"You can leave and never show your face around here again!" Reverend Stone exclaimed, the harshness of his words echoing through the desolation.

Even the little woman looked at Reverend Stone in disbelief, her expression betraying her shock. Pastor Bruce turned away, tears welling in his eyes, and slowly walked away, his heart heavy with the weight of unjust accusations.

It was early morning and John was waiting underneath a tree in the parking lot of Stapleton High School for George Hines to arrive. He had intentionally chosen this spot to avoid being detected by anyone. George parked on the other side of the lot and had to walk around the school grounds to meet up with John. As George walked, he couldn't help but notice the remarkable transformation the school had undergone since he last saw it. A year ago, the school was in the news for all the wrong reasons. The courtyard was unkempt, and the students seemed to have no respect for their school or teachers.

But now, the courtyard was pristine, with manicured lawns, newly painted benches, flower gardens, and shrubs. Signs proudly declared that the area was maintained by 10th graders Melissa and Terry. The halls were also lined with attractive landscaping, giving the school a private college's look and feel. George couldn't believe his eyes and whispered, "Lord, what's happening here?" Unexpectedly, he heard the words, "I shall heal their land," in the voice of his beloved pastor.

As George approached the designated bench, a figure emerged from the shadows of the trees. It was a stranger, and as he got closer, George noticed something familiar about him, but couldn't quite place it.

"Are you ready?" the stranger asked.

"Ready for what?" George replied, a hint of nervousness in his voice.

"It's me, John!" the stranger said, revealing himself.

George was taken aback by John's appearance, which was vastly different from what he remembered. John's hair color and style had changed, and he now had facial hair and a confident voice that was a far cry from his previous geeky accent.

"I have to stay undercover because there is a contract on my life," John explained.

George's face went pale at the mention of a contract on John's life, but he quickly regained his composure and said, "Not for long! We're going to change that!"

John was surprised by George's determination and felt even more confident in their partnership. They walked toward John's car, and on the way, John asked if George had informed Dennis about their meeting.

"Yeah, he's a pleasant guy," George replied. "He's on board with us, and we'll be working together to solve this problem."

"Perfect!" John exclaimed. "We'll have the freedom we need to work together. Do you think you can pull this off?"

"Sure, I'll just reverse what I've been doing," George replied.

John cautioned George that their mission would be dangerous and that one or both of them could end up dead. However, George was determined to make a difference and was tired of living a lie.

"This is going to change," John assured him. "I have enough information on both organizations to put them out of business. But we'll need to do some heavy-duty snooping at your former employer's."

"That sounds dangerous," George said.

"It is," John agreed. "But it's what we need to do to get off the hook."

John and George hopped into the sporty car and threw George's suitcase in the trunk. John grinned mischievously at George as he fiddled with the key. "Like fast cars?" he asked, as the engine roared to life and the car shuddered with anticipation. When he shifted the car into gear, it jolted forward, causing George to chuckle.

"Actually, I do," George replied with a smile, as they peeled out of the parking lot.

When they arrived at the airport, they quickly boarded a private jet that looked like a corporate Learjet. George asked, "Is this the company's jet?" to which John replied, "No, I don't like using any company-owned items. I only use the money they give me." With a smirk, he settled into his seat.

As the plane ascended, John began to reveal to George all that he had found out so far, speaking in generalities just in case someone was listening in. He explained the plan and why they were headed to California. After they landed, they exited the plane and found themselves in a bustling airport. George felt out of place in the big city environment, whereas John felt right at home.

They rented a car and drove to Dr. Penkowski's empire, a massive forty-story building with the letters "Advanced Medical" emblazoned in bold print.

Bruce regained his composure and hit the road. He was on his way to visit a young man who had threatened the life of his teacher and received a shocking response. As Bruce mulled over the incident, he wondered about the boy's well-being after the intense confrontation.

Upon arriving at the hospital, Bruce noticed a parking spot designated for clergy, but the nearly empty lot made it seem inconsequential. He greeted Lori, the charge nurse, and inquired about the boy's condition.

"Tommy, is it?" Bruce asked.

"Yes, Tommy," Lori replied. "He's been here many times."

Bruce sensed that there was more to the story than met the eye, and Lori's reluctance to divulge details only reinforced his suspicions. He wondered if the boy had been subjected to physical or drug abuse.

As they continued to chat, Bruce mentioned the tornado that had struck Reverend Stone's church. Lori was surprised to hear about it but assured him that there had been no injuries at the hospital. Bruce then asked about visiting Tommy.

"Is it okay to visit him? What room is he in?"

"He's stable and in room 120," Lori responded, giving him the green light to proceed.

"Thanks, Lori," Bruce said before taking a moment to call George Hines. When there was no answer, he tried Sue and informed her of the situation at Reverend Stone's church. She immediately got on the phone, and within an hour, people were at Reverend Stone's church, lending a helping hand.

Meanwhile, Bruce walked down the hospital hallway, silently praying as he did. When he knocked on the door, a faint voice said, "Come in," barely audible. As Bruce walked into the room, his eyes caught sight of the young man, and his first impression was that he had been hit by a semi-truck.

"Tommy, I am Bruce Hutchinson, the pastor of a little church in town," Bruce said.

Tommy looked up, and his eyes were red and glazed over. Immediately, his face turned red, and he shouted, "What do you want with me, man of God?"

Bruce was caught off guard by the sudden and intense response from the boy, causing him to freeze in fear. The boy started spewing vulgar language and making death threats, sending shivers down Bruce's spine. He was at a loss for what to do when two men dressed in white burst into the room, seemingly out of nowhere. They quickly swooped in and grabbed the agitated boy, who was now poised to pounce on Bruce.

With a sense of urgency in their voices, the men in white gazed at Bruce and urged him, "Pastor, act now and act swiftly, for your safety is at stake."

Bruce looked at them and then back at the boy. The boy was shouting threats. "Let me go! Let me go, you warriors! He is mine. He is mine, I tell you!"

"No!" shouted Bruce. "He rightfully belongs to Jesus!"

"No, he doesn't!" the boy shouted in an eerie voice. "He came to me on his own free will, and he belongs to me!"

"No! He has been bought by the blood of Christ. You have taken what does not belong to you!"

"Listen, you man of God, you have taken enough souls in this community. Your days are numbered! We are shutting down your church, and there will be no more people allowed to slip to your side. You are done, finished! We have won!"

Bruce was taken aback by the threat and accusation, but he remembered the truth and stood firm. The two men holding the boy reminded him to stay strong. "Greater is He who is in me than he that is in this town! Now get out of him!" he declared.

The possessed boy screamed, "No! No! He is mine! Mine!"

"No, he rightfully belongs to Jesus! In the name of Jesus, be gone!"

The boy's body convulsed uncontrollably, his limbs thrashing wildly before he suddenly went limp, as if he had been drained of life itself. The two men who had been holding him, released their grip and nodded silently at Bruce, before disappearing into thin air. Bruce rushed after them, but they vanished without a trace, leaving him standing there in confusion and disbelief.

Bruce rushed over to the charge nurse, Lori, and urgently inquired, "Lori, those two men who just came out of the room... What happened to them?"

Confused, Lori replied, "What two men, Bruce? You're the only one who has been in or out of that room."

Bruce was taken aback. "But they were dressed in white, like doctors."

Lori shook her head. "Our doctors wear blue or green scrubs, Bruce. I'm sorry."

Bruce's mind raced as he looked back at Tommy's room, trying to make sense of what had just happened. He felt a sense of unease wash over him as he headed towards the break room, where he spotted a doctor flipping through some charts. The doctor looked up and greeted Bruce, "Pastor Bruce, what brings you here?"

Bruce swallowed hard, his mind still reeling. "I, uh...just checking in."

As he left the break room, Bruce felt a sense of disorientation and disbelief. Who were those men? And how did they disappear so quickly? He hurried back to Lori and asked her to check on Tommy to make sure he was alright.

As they both entered the room, Tommy opened his eyes, and they shone with brightness. "How are you feeling?" Lori asked. "I feel like I've been given a fresh start in life," he replied, grinning broadly. Then he looked at Bruce, and his smile began to fade.

"Pastor, I owe you a massive apology," Tommy said.

"What for, Tommy?" Bruce inquired.

"I was part of the gang that destroyed your house and the houses of your members," Tommy confessed.

"You have already been forgiven, Tommy. Now I need to ask you something," Bruce said.

"Anything, pastor."

"I want you to start coming to our church, reading your Bible, and talking with God every day," Bruce requested.

"If it makes me feel the way I do now, you got it!" Tommy exclaimed, his face beaming with excitement. But then his expression turned sad again.

"What's wrong, Tommy?" Bruce asked.

"I recall saying to you that your church is going to be closed down. Please tell me that's not going to happen. Please!" Tommy pleaded.

"Calm down, Tommy. I don't know what God's plans are for our church. All I know is that He is in control, and it's not my church; it's His. If He wants to shut it down, so be it. We will still be here for you and each other," Bruce responded.

At this remark, Tommy smiled. Bruce went over to Tommy, placed his hand on his shoulder, and spoke about the significance of making a decision for Christ so that his former roommates wouldn't return to dominate his life. And then, they prayed, and the Devil lost another soul to the kingdom of God.

"Shut him down!" The voice on the other side of the phone resonated with a commanding force, a thunderous call to action that reverberated through the air.

"Reverend Stone, I agree," responded the mayor, his tone carrying a weight of responsibility and concern.

"Mayor, you've been a part of my church since you were a kid. Surely, you must feel something about all the havoc this troublemaker has unleashed," Reverend Stone implored, his voice tinged with a mix of urgency and emotion.

The mayor sighed, revealing the burdens he carried. "I'm under political pressure from the Association for Fetal Research. They've threatened to relocate their convention and withdraw promised funds, all because the abortion clinics have closed. They're even considering moving their manufacturing plant out of our city, jeopardizing jobs."

"Jobs. And what about those vacant buildings?" Reverend Stone interjected, his words filled with a sense of dismay.

"The liquor store and...," the mayor hesitated, "yes, they're empty, and our town doesn't look like the charming place it once was. We're beginning to resemble a ghost town, and that's hardly appealing to newcomers."

"You're right, Mayor. What about my church?" Reverend Stone questioned, his voice determined.

"I won't let this small church pastor defeat us. I've already contacted the insurance company, and construction will begin immediately. Can you pull some strings, Mayor, and secure the school auditorium for our congregation until we're done?"

"I'll have to navigate the separation of religion and state policy, but I believe I can arrange something," the mayor assured, his voice conveying a blend of determination and caution.

"Look at this. Even as I speak, the pastor's people are out here, sifting and searching," Reverend Stone exclaimed, his frustration raw.

"You mean helping with the cleanup?" the mayor clarified, attempting to inject reason into the conversation.

"Whatever! It's just a cover-up. How many more of my members will the pastor get from this disaster?" Reverend Stone retorted, his tone sharp with suspicion.

"It's not like the pastor sent the tornado himself, Reverend," the mayor reasoned, the words hanging in the air, prompting a heavy silence.

"I suppose not," Reverend Stone admitted with a sigh, the acknowledgment of reality carrying a touch of resignation. "But he's going to use any opportunity to take my members. I must stop him. We must stop him. Will you do something, Mayor?"

"I'm not thrilled about losing the funds from the Association for Fetal Research. They're committed to city improvements, and without their support, we'll be in a tough spot," the mayor conceded, his voice reflecting the gravity of the situation.

"So, you'll do something?" Reverend Stone pressed, hope creeping into his tone.

"I'll take care of it," the mayor affirmed, his commitment echoed in the resolute assurance of his voice.

John and George meticulously surveyed the looming structure, each step filled with purpose. John took the lead, his eyes scanning for potential access points, security systems, and escape routes.The weight of their mission hung in the air, an intense tension that fueled their determination.

"Are we going in now?" George's voice wavered, betraying a mix of anticipation and unease.

"No, no, just checking the place out," John replied with a calm assurance, his words attempting to soothe the nerves that lingered in the cool night air. "It looks secure, but I see a couple of flaws."

With the precision of a seasoned professional, John extracted a digital camera, a tool that would document every nook and cranny of the building. He moved methodically, capturing the essence of the structure in a series of snapshots. Each click of the camera echoed in the stillness, punctuating the gravity of their mission.

"Hmm. Yeah. Oh, this looks good," John muttered to himself, the hushed words laden with a sense of urgency and determination. "We need to avoid this area. Okay, I think that does it. Let's head back to the hotel!"

As they retreated, John's excitement bubbled to the surface, a manifestation of the adrenaline coursing through his veins. In contrast, George exhaled a breath he didn't realize he'd been holding, relief flooding his features. The prospect of not entering the building just yet was a temporary reprieve, and George clung to it with gratitude.

Back at the hotel, a new chapter unfolded as John delved into his makeup kit. "Now, this won't hurt a bit," he said with a hint of jest in his voice, attempting to lighten the mood.

George looked up at him, vulnerability etched on his face, and John responded with a comforting smile. "Have you ever been to the main office of Advance Medical?" John inquired as he transformed George's appearance.

"No, never. I'm embarrassed to say how I got the job," George confessed, his voice laced with a mixture of regret and shame.

Silence hung in the room, and John, with a gentle touch, added wrinkles to George's face, each line carrying the weight of a life marked by choices and consequences. "It was a desperate time in my life," George began, his tone reflecting the ache of past wounds.

As the makeup transformed George, John listened intently, the atmosphere thick with emotion. "I was surfing the internet, and I came across a site that offered unbelievable hope to people. The hope of youth," George revealed, his voice tinged with the vulnerability of a man who had once grasped at a fleeting chance for change.

John's smile widened at the revelation, recognizing the significance of this newfound information. "Advance Medical's site?" he guessed, a glint of understanding in his eyes.

"Yes, yes. I was intrigued. I contacted them via email," George continued, unraveling the threads of a story that had led him to this pivotal moment.

As John worked, George's appearance aged, each layer of makeup adding depth to his narrative. "They responded immediately to me. To my shock, they offered me an interview for a top position in their local warehouse," George shared, the memories of that crucial juncture resurfacing.

"Where you work now?" John inquired, his voice holding a quiet sympathy.

"Yes, but at the time, I thought, how could they know so much about me?" George confessed, his eyes reflecting the lingering doubts that had plagued him.

As John continued the transformation, George's voice quivered, unraveling the tale of a choice made in the depths of desperation. "I couldn't believe it when they offered me the job. The salary they offered was ten times more than what I was earning before, and I could finally give my family the life they deserved."

The room fell into a heavy silence, John's hands moving with practiced precision. "But when I asked about the catch," George continued, his voice laden with the weight of a pact with an unseen force, "they warned me that if I wanted to know the catch, I could never tell anyone else. I felt like I was selling my soul to the devil, and I didn't know what to do. I was torn between providing for my family and the feeling that something was terribly wrong."

With each passing moment, John became a silent witness to George's inner turmoil, the makeup serving as a visual narrative of a man's journey into the shadows. "I accepted the job, along with the catch. I just kept telling myself, 'Yes, this is not right, but it is my final opportunity to have all that I ever wanted. It didn't just slip by. My boat had arrived. But, oh, what a mistake I made.'"

John listened, the room filled with the echoes of a life unraveling in the pursuit of elusive dreams. "At first, it was great! A new dream home in the best part of town. A new dream car. All the best computer and software that money could buy! I felt like I had just hit the lottery," George's voice trailed off, the bitter taste of disillusionment creeping into his words.

With the makeup complete, John turned George around, capturing the transformed image with a digital click. The pictures downloaded to his laptop, and John proceeded to change George's attire. "You know, John, I thought I would be happy. I really, really did."

As George donned an outfit that mirrored the passage of time, John felt a connection deepen—a shared understanding of the pursuit of happiness and the harsh realities that often accompanied it. "That's the idea, George. I hope you're not too attached to having hair," John chuckled, introducing a hairpiece that completed the illusion of aging.

"Oh great! The one thing I have been dreading all my life - going bald!" George complained, the humor offering a brief respite from the gravity of his confession.

"Hey, it's not real, George. Calm down and tell me the rest of your story," John reassured, the camaraderie between them evolving into a bond forged by shared struggles.

George's voice quivered as he forged ahead, his story unraveling with a poignant sincerity that exposed the intricate web of his decisions. "I witnessed the realization of all my hopes and dreams. At last, I believed I could do the things I'd always longed to do, possess the things I'd always yearned to have."

"George, I understand. Keep going," John encouraged, his compassion underscored by the gentle cadence of his voice.

As George pressed on, the reverberations of his disillusionment echoed in the room. John, in turn, contemplated the intertwining paths that had led them to this juncture.

NINE

As Bruce navigated the journey back from the hospital, an unshakable sense of disquiet clung to him, casting shadows over the gratitude he felt for the day's triumphs. The celestial assistance, the salvation of a soul—these blessings were overshadowed by the looming threat of the church's closure. The weight of uncertainty pressed heavily on Bruce's shoulders, a persistent question mark lingering in the air. Was it merely another ploy from the adversary, a scare tactic designed to test his faith, or a tangible peril demanding attention?

Upon reaching the church's parking lot, Bruce's determined strides led him straight to his study. Closing the door behind him, he sank to his knees, the worn carpet beneath him a humble sanctuary. In the solitude of his prayer, Bruce poured out his concerns to the Almighty. Gratitude for the day's successes paved the way for a fervent plea for spiritual fortification.

"Lord," Bruce's prayer echoed in the quietude, his voice a mix of earnest supplication and resolute determination, "I am uncertain whether this threat against Your church is real or not. One thing I do know is that You can handle this, and I cannot." With each word, he envisioned the spiritual armor encasing him, an ethereal shield against the unseen forces at play.

"I pray that You put on me the helmet of salvation," Bruce intoned, his hands reaching out to the intangible armor surrounding his head. "'These things have I written unto you that believe on the Son of God that you may know that you have eternal life.'" The words hung in the air, charged with the weight of faith and assurance.

"I put on the breastplate of righteousness," Bruce continued, the imagery vivid in his mind's eye. "'Seek first the Kingdom of God and His righteousness, and all these things shall be added unto you.'" The prayer became a ritual, a sacred dance of words and spiritual symbolism.

"I put on the belt of truth," Bruce proclaimed, the resonance of his voice echoing the foundational tenets of his faith. "'Jesus said, I am the Way, the Truth, and the Life. No man comes to the Father except by Me.'" Each piece of the divine armor seamlessly became part of him, a testament to his unwavering commitment.

"Lord, I put on the shoes with the preparation of the Gospel," Bruce continued, the weight of spiritual readiness settling upon him. "'Be ready in season and out of season to share the hope that is within you.'" The rhythm of his prayer quickened, a cadence that mirrored the urgency of the moment.

"Father, in addition to all of this," Bruce's voice soared, resonating with conviction, "I lift up the shield of faith." The ethereal shield materialized in his spiritual grasp, a tangible manifestation of trust. "'Trust the Lord with all your heart, and lean not on your own understanding...We live by faith, not by sight.'"

Finally, the crescendo of his prayer reached its pinnacle as Bruce proclaimed, "I lift up the sword of the Spirit." The invisible sword materialized in his hands, a divine weapon against the uncertainties that sought to assail him. "'The Word of the Lord is living and active. It is sharper than any double-edged sword. It is able to divide soul and spirit, joint and marrow. It judges the thoughts and attitudes of the heart.'"

As Bruce concluded his prayer, a surge of strength coursed through him, a spiritual energy that fortified his resolve. In that sacred moment, surrounded by the armor of faith, he felt a profound connection to the divine, ready to face whatever challenges lay ahead.

In the dim glow of John's makeshift command center, the air was charged with a sense of urgency and unspoken tension. Both men, consumed by the gravity of their mission, huddled over their electronic devices. John, with an air of seasoned expertise, meticulously organized the images he had captured earlier in the day, each pixel holding the secrets of Advance Medical's formidable fortress.

George, on the other hand, focused on his laptop, a beacon of digital preparation. As he navigated the vast expanse of the internet, a webpage took shape under his adept fingertips—a lifeline for his church in case of unforeseen circumstances. The quiet hum of electronic activity formed a backdrop to their silent curiosity about each other's endeavors.

With the pictures organized, John seamlessly transitioned to another program, his nimble fingers dancing across the keyboard. The room bathed in the soft glow of screens as John revealed a sophisticated 3D rendering of Advance Medical's building, a virtual model that allowed them to scrutinize every angle, every potential entry point.

Curiosity burning within him, George couldn't resist probing, "What do you have there, John?"

John's response was measured, a blend of pride and explanation, "This program digitally scans pictures and creates a 3D rendering, allowing us to see each side of the building, including the top and bottom." Simultaneously, he stole a glance at George's laptop screen, a subtle exchange of curiosity.

"Are you going online?" John asked, attempting nonchalance but betraying a keen interest in George's activities.

"Yeah, I'm creating a webpage for my pastor," George confessed, a touch of vulnerability in his admission. "I've been handling all the computer stuff for our church, and if anything happens to me, they can access this page with step-by-step instructions for the email, instant messages, and web information for our church and more."

John, though outwardly composed, silently applauded George's foresight and meticulous planning, recognizing the significance of these digital contingency measures.

"So, you know a little about computers, do you?" John asked, a playful smile accompanying his inquiry.

"Only a little," George replied humbly, concealing the extent of his tech-savvy prowess. Despite his modest words, George was well-versed in the intricacies of the digital realm, an unsung hero for Bruce's church in matters of technology.

"Come take a look at this. You'll like it," John invited, gesturing for George to join him at the computer. George, eager but cautious not to appear too anxious, rose from his chair and ambled over to John's side.

"Look at this, George! Here is the entrance." John manipulated the mouse, and the building unfolded before them. "And here is a side entrance. The front is heavily guarded, probably with video cameras and the like. But this side entrance, this is where I think we'll have some luck."

George leaned in, captivated by the intricate details of the digital model. As John moved the mouse, revealing a small structure, George's anticipation heightened.

"And you see this structure?" John questioned, a conspiratorial excitement in his voice.

"Yeah."

"This will be a great place to wait. Let's see who goes in and out of it." John, with deft precision, manipulated the digital realm, unveiling a strategic waiting spot on the 3D model.

Impressed, George murmured, "Impressive," a hint of envy coloring his tone.

Just as the gravity of their clandestine preparations set in, John's cell phone erupted into a distinctive ring, signaling a call of utmost importance. George observed the change in John's demeanor, a shift from casual curiosity to a focused intensity.

"What is it?" George inquired, his senses on high alert.

"This ring indicates that we have a tap on Dr. Penkowski's phone line. It's constantly changing frequencies and is difficult to catch. This will be good," John revealed, the gravity of the situation reflected in his gaze.

With purpose, John activated his cell phone, placing it on a holder connected to the computer. A voice emanated from the device, and data streamed down the screen, transforming the room into a clandestine hub of intercepted communication.

"You know you messed up twice now! I want this man dead!" The voice on the other end growled, sending a chill down John and George's spines. The revelation unfolded—a sinister plot, a threat that transcended mere words.

"I just received word that the detective is now working with someone else. Whoever it is, I want them both eliminated," the voice commanded, a cold determination underscoring the sinister plan. ""Yes, boss," the other voice replied, a sense of submission suffocating in the air. "That is what you said last time! Either the next call I get is you telling me that you followed my directions or I will not be getting another call! Do you hear! Yes sir."

The line went dead, leaving John and George pale-faced, the weight of the ominous conversation lingering in the room.

"Well, the good news is that he doesn't know it is you," John offered, attempting to quell the rising panic in George.

George, however, looked at John incredulously. "John, it doesn't matter! He wants to kill me just because I'm with you, not because he knows that I've betrayed him!"

"George, calm down. They are just words. Doing is a lot harder than talking about it, I've found out in this business. We will be just fine," John reassured, his words carrying the weight of experience and resilience.

As George met John's gaze, he saw not just reassurance but a determination to face the dangers ahead. "You're right, John. What's next?" George asked, a newfound resolve in his voice.

"Good, let's get to work," John replied, his gaze unwavering. He proceeded to brief George on the plan and the crucial documents that needed retrieval. "Are you ready?" John asked.

"As ready as I'll ever be," George replied, his determination a spark in the face of impending danger. The room transformed into a battlefield of pixels and data, as the two men readied themselves for the challenges that lay ahead.

Bruce was still at the church, having prayed and feeling at peace about what the demon had said through the teenager at the hospital. He was caught off guard, however, when a young man in a crisp shirt and tie greeted him with a polite smile approached his office. The man smiled and politely asked, "Are you Reverend Bruce Hutchinson?"

Bruce was surprised to be addressed as Reverend, but he answered, "Yes, how can I help you?"

"My name is Carl Milan. I am with the county health department. I have four violations that have been recorded, and one from the Fire Marshall. I will have to close down your building."

Bruce tried to assure him, "Mr. Milan, I'm sure that these are minor and I can…"

"Minor? Do you think I would close a building on minor violations? Maybe one, but Reverend, you have four!" Carl interrupted.

"Well…"

"The one from the Fire Marshall is most urgent."

"I have 500 people coming and they will have no place to meet if you close our building!"

"That is one of the problems. This building is only made for 450."

"Because of 50 additional people, you are closing our doors?"

"That and the electrical service are out of date and should have been replaced a year ago when the new codes went into effect."

"Am I not grandfathered in?"

"For a year! I think we have been fair enough about this issue."

"What are the other violations?"

"They are all listed below." The man handed Bruce a very official looking document with a seal from the Mayor's office, the same Mayor that Reverend Stone had previously talked to about getting his favor.

"Mr. Milan, I need time. I have to..."

"This building is officially closed until the following corrections are made, then inspected and approved by our office."

"This will take at least a month to get all of this work done."

"It usually takes 3 to 4 weeks to get an appointment with an inspector, and then another 4 to 6 weeks to receive an approval."

Bruce looked at the man in disbelief.

"To add insult to injury," the man added, "That's on a good month."

"I can't work out of this office?"

"When a building is closed, it is closed. Any violation of this order will result in financial penalties and possible jail time."

Bruce attempted to continue the conversation, but the man seemed uninterested and walked towards the front entrance. Bruce followed him as he watched the man place chains and locks on the doors. Official-looking papers were posted on the doors with the words "CLOSE TO PUBLIC FOR HEALTH VIOLATIONS" written in red letters.

"You should start packing because once I'm finished with the side doors, you'll need to leave the building unless you want to be locked in here," said the man.

Bruce's heart raced with a tumultuous mix of fear and disbelief, the very core of his being shaken by the unthinkable reality unfolding before him. As a law-abiding citizen of the United States, the notion of being forced to abandon his office, a sacred space for his ministry, seemed inconceivable. Thoughts swirled in his mind like a tempest, but amidst the chaos, a fragment of scripture surfaced: "Submit yourself to authorities." Reluctantly, he bowed to the weight of the command, his hands trembling as he hastily packed his study materials into a box. It felt like he was being uprooted from everything he held dear, each item he stowed away a painful reminder of the disruption.

"Are you ready, Reverend?" inquired the man, his tone carrying an indifferent coldness.

"Do you have a business card?" Bruce asked, seeking a semblance of normalcy in the face of the unfolding ordeal.

"Just call the county health department. They have a file on you," replied the man with a chilling nonchalance.

As Bruce exited with the young man, a sense of outrage and injustice coursed through him. The cold demeanor of his companion made him feel like a criminal, unjustly punished. The trouble he had anticipated from his prior visit paled in comparison to the harsh reality unfolding before him. Walking towards the parking lot, a pit formed in Bruce's stomach, the weight of false accusations and unwarranted punishment pressing down on him. Glancing back at the church, the sight of chains on the doors and government signs turned his once-welcoming sanctuary into a hostile and forbidding place.

Once inside his car, Bruce was surprised by an unexpected flood of peace. It wasn't his usual tranquility but a formidable sense of calm, a fortress within him shielding against negative emotions. Instead of dwelling on the recent events, his thoughts turned to George Hines, a beacon of positivity in the midst of chaos. Recollections of their first meeting, George's boldness in sharing his story, and his instrumental role in the ministry flooded Bruce's mind. The memory of the church group George had organized to clean up his vandalized home brought tears to Bruce's eyes.

Overwhelmed with emotion, Bruce drove straight to his study, knelt down, and poured out his heart in prayer for George's safety. A heavy burden weighed on his heart, as if a looming danger threatened his friend. Unable to bear it any longer, Bruce rose, turned on his computer, and through tear-stained eyes, sent out a heartfelt email to his prayer warriors and network, detailing his own troubles and pleading for prayers for George.

Checking his email, Bruce noticed a message from George. Eagerly opening it, he read George's words of gratitude and the creation of a web page dedicated to the Revival. Each word from George's message painted a vivid picture of commitment and dedication. A smile played on Bruce's lips, but it was short-lived as he continued reading and learned of George's personal struggles and the potential threat to his life.

A profound sense of peace enveloped Bruce as he spent what felt like an eternity in deep prayer. Rising to his feet, he sat down at his computer, marveling at the beauty and complexity of George's website. Tears streaming down his face, he composed an email to George, baring his soul and expressing profound gratitude for the strength and resilience his friend displayed in the face of adversity.

John and George moved stealthily behind the wall, shrouded in the darkness that had settled after the sunset. The majority of employees had vacated the building, leaving an eerie stillness in the air. George's heart pounded against his ribs, a percussion of anxiety, while John, with that familiar twinkle in his eye, seemed fueled by an adrenaline rush.

"What was that noise?" John whispered.

"That was my heart about to burst out of my chest," George replied.

"C'mon now, think of all the conflicts you've faced in the past. How did you handle them?"

"With confidence, knowing that I was in control."

"That's it. Use that same mindset, and you'll be okay."

"Okay? Okay! We're about to break into our employer's headquarters! They want to kill us, and I'm supposed to be okay with this?"

John turned to George, a look on his face that conveyed, "Do we have a choice?"

George calmed down, and they resumed their covert mission. John handed George a small pistol, and then, to George's surprise, pulled out what appeared to be a toy gun with a suction cup on the end. Just then, the door swung open wide, and before the person stepped out, John fired the gun. The suction cup hit the bottom of the door. A head popped out, glancing toward George and John, but they quickly ducked behind the wall. The person, satisfied there was nothing amiss, continued walking in the opposite direction. As the door began to shut, the string attached to the suction cup became taut. Abruptly stopping, the closing door served as their cue to action.

"That's our cue!" John exclaimed.

John sprang to his feet, and George followed suit. George felt like he was in a dream, as if this reality was too surreal to be true.

They found themselves in a dimly lit hallway, the back fire exit revealing itself. Keeping a vigilant eye for any intruders, they ascended the stairs, the quiet building amplifying the sound of their footsteps. John gestured for George to keep moving, and together they climbed several flights of stairs. A distant noise below them signaled the opening of a door, and footsteps echoed. John and George pressed themselves against the wall, watching as the footsteps grew softer and softer before they resumed their ascent.

Eventually, they arrived at another closed door. John turned the doorknob, glancing back at George to ensure his compliance. Fear etched on George's face, but it dissipated when he saw John's reassuring smile.

They opened the door cautiously and peered inside. The office was deserted. John swiftly assessed the security cameras, aimed a laser beam from his keychain at the lens, and draped a handkerchief over the camera, retrieved from his back pocket. George hesitated until John signaled for him to proceed, and they continued down the shadowy corridor.

John appeared confident about their destination, but when George inquired, he received a cryptic response: "Not a clue." Despite the uncertainty, George found himself admiring John's self-assurance. As they walked down the hallway, John suddenly halted and motioned toward an office filled with file cabinets. Checking for surveillance cameras, John cautiously entered the room while George stood guard at the doorway. After five minutes of searching, John's excitement grew, raising George's hopes for freedom. Yet, their relief was short-lived as George noticed a looming shadow approaching. He warned John, and they both sought refuge behind a small cubicle.

Soon, a security guard entered the room, switching on the lights and surveying the office. This was no ordinary guard - he resembled a member of a SWAT team, armed with a pistol and a semi-automatic weapon at his sides. George silently prayed for safety, grateful for all that God had done in his life recently, hoping that if this was the end, his departure wouldn't be too agonizing.

The guard extinguished the light, leaving the room in a cloak of darkness. George's breath escaped in a sigh of relief, the tension slowly releasing from his shoulders. But John's cautionary words pierced the newfound calm, reminding them that the danger still loomed. George, however, welcomed the respite from the oppressive presence of the guard, if only for a fleeting moment. Glancing at John, he found solace in his partner's resourcefulness.

"Is that one digital too?" George asked.

"Yes, and it uploads to the cloud after each click," John replied.

George's satisfaction radiated in a whispered "Nice!" The small digital camera held the promise of exposing the wrongdoings that could potentially bring justice to light. John's excitement was pulsing as he asserted, "This is exactly what we need. Everything is here to put these people away for a long time."

Suddenly, the room erupted in harsh brightness, catching John and George off guard. The same guard had returned, and the reality of being caught red-handed struck them like a lightning bolt.

"Get away from the files!" the guard barked.

John and George edged away, their hearts pounding with fear as the guard advanced, his finger on the trigger of the semi-automatic weapon aimed directly at John's face. An oppressive tension hung in the air, suffocating the room. John, his hands trembling, handed over the camera. With a steely grip on the camera, the guard began to close the cabinet doors, momentarily diverting his attention. In that brief window, John seized the opportunity, kicking out with swift precision, sending the guard's weapon clattering across the room.

The surge of adrenaline flooded John's veins, a mixture of triumph and relief washing over him. "Run for your life!" he screamed, his voice tinged with fear.

George's heart raced, his senses heightened as he followed John's lead. His feet moved faster than he thought possible, the adrenaline propelling him forward. As they fled, a chilling uncertainty hung in the air. George couldn't shake the haunting thought of what horrors lay ahead and questioned whether they would ever escape the perilous situation alive.

As Bruce strolled through the rose garden, he heard the phone ring inside the house. He walked over to the open window and picked up the phone.

"Hello?"

"Bruce, it's Maggie. What's happening at the church?"

"The city has shut us down."

"I saw your email. How can they do this?"

"They found a couple of code violations, and there was no grace period."

"Someone must be behind this."

"You mean the enemy?"

"Yes, but there must be someone in town who instigated this. I don't understand how they can do this when the church has done so much good for the community. Look at the schools - they've been problem-free since the teacher was threatened, crime rates have dropped to zero, and the commitment to purity is inspiring."

"Maggie, I know. The city has seen a positive change, but not everyone has embraced it. Some still cling to the old ways of power, prestige, and money. When you're in a high position, you have the power to do anything."

"We need to come up with a solution for our meeting place. Maybe we could use the school's auditorium temporarily."

"That's a great idea! One of the violations was exceeding the occupancy limit, and using the school's auditorium would provide more space for growth. If it works out, we could even keep the Tuesday night time and continue it at the same time as Pastor Wayne's church."

After they hung up, Bruce called the school principal, Joe Benton.

"Hello, may I speak with Joe Benton please?" Bruce asked when the call connected.

"Speaking," Joe replied.

"Joe, it's Bruce Hutchinson. How are you?"

"Bruce, good to hear from you. I'm doing well, thanks. How about you?"

"Well…not so good," Bruce said, his tone conveying his distress.

"Oh really? What's up?" Joe asked.

Bruce proceeded to tell him all that had happened.

"Oh Bruce, that is terrible. If there is anything I can do, please don't hesitate to ask," Joe said sympathetically.

"Well…there is something that would help immensely," Bruce said, feeling grateful for Joe's support.

"Shoot," Joe said, eager to assist.

"What is the availability of your auditorium on Tuesday nights?" Bruce asked, hoping for a positive response.

"Well, let me take a look at my calendar. Ah, the cheerleaders just changed their meeting time from Tuesday nights to Thursday nights. Perfect. You got it," Joe said, sounding pleased to be able to help.

"How long can we use it?" Bruce asked, feeling a glimmer of hope.

"As long as you need. We will take care of you," Joe promised.

"Well, someone in the community will not be happy. But, that someone is fighting against God Himself," Bruce said, knowing that they were in for a tough fight.

"With all that has happened in this community, how could anyone not believe that," Joe said, sounding resolute.

"Even in Jesus' days with all his miracles performed before the people some doubted," Bruce said, his faith unwavering.

"Good point," Joe said, feeling inspired by Bruce's words.

Amidst the relentless chaos and disarray, George found himself caught in a whirlwind of panic, desperately trying to navigate the overwhelming uncertainty. Fear surged through his veins like a turbulent river, his heart pounding at an alarming rate. The weight of the situation threatened to buckle his knees, yet he pressed on, knowing that collapsing wasn't an option.

In the midst of the tumult, a blur of movement caught George's attention—John, sprinting past him with a velocity that defied the chaos surrounding them. Suddenly, the air was shattered by a deafening explosion, leaving George's ears ringing. Miraculously, he felt no physical pain, and a quick glance assured him that John, too, remained unharmed. Time was of the essence, and without hesitation, John darted into an office, swiftly flipping a metal desk over and motioning for George to join him.

Gasping for breath, George managed to ask, "What now?"

"Take out the gun I gave you," John urgently ordered.

George stared at him in disbelief, the gravity of the situation sinking in. "What? Why?"

"Just do it, now!" John barked, his command reverberating off the walls.

George complied, pulling out the gun, while John pointed around the makeshift barricade. The distinct sound of gunfire echoed once more, this time from John's weapon. Three menacing figures, eerily identical to the one they had just evaded, emerged with semi-automatics blazing. Sparks flew as bullets ricocheted off the desk, providing a crucial shield. John unleashed a barrage of bullets, and George, fueled by instinct, began firing in tandem.

Two shadows crumpled to the ground, but the third sought refuge, frantically radioing for reinforcements. seizing the moment, John leaped up, shouting, "Rush him!" George followed suit, joining the charge as two determined men pounced on their adversary. A brief scuffle ensued, and the opponent was subdued. Yet, as John and George attempted to regain their footing, a commanding voice cut through the chaos: "Don't move! Get your hands up!" Slowly, they rose to their feet, encircled by hostile figures. There seemed to be no escape.

"Get up!" the men barked, their voices dripping with aggression and hostility. The air crackled with tension as George and John stood, trapped in an uncertain fate.

As they were roughly jostled and pushed, George felt as if he had stumbled into the heart of his worst nightmare. John, though visibly discontent, bore a steely resolve, while George, his complexion turned pallid, wore an expression of sheer terror. Amidst the chaos and looming danger, an unexpected sensation swept over George, akin to the rhythmic waves caressing the shore in his childhood days at the beach. It was a profound and oddly familiar feeling, resonating deep within the recesses of his soul. Yet, he couldn't shake the dissonance between this peace and the dire circumstances that enveloped him. It was a surreal moment, as if an invisible barrier cocooned him and the unfolding events. Elevated above the turmoil, he observed the chaos like a detached spectator. George pondered whether John shared this strange sensation, but when he cast a glance in his friend's direction, he saw only a man deploying every learned skill from the harsh school of experience.

Breathing a prayer of gratitude, George beseeched God for protection and guidance, yearning for a way out of this perilous situation.

Roughly shoved into the elevator, the armed men left nothing to chance, pressing their guns firmly against John and George's sides. Expelled from the elevator with swift force, they were subjected to continued shoving and berating as they approached a pair of elegant double doors. The doors swung open to reveal a spacious conference room, with a commanding figure standing at the head of a long table, staring pensively into the night sky.

"Bring them to me," the man commanded, and John and George were unceremoniously dragged and deposited into chairs around the table.

As the man turned to face them, John's eyes widened in shock.

"Dr. Penkowski," John exclaimed.

The man's gaze bore into them, and George couldn't shake a growing sense of unease. An ominous energy radiated from Dr. Penkowski, stirring an instinct honed over years in the cutthroat world of business. It troubled George deeply, and he braced himself for whatever lay ahead.

"John Ivan, we meet at last," the man said. In his early sixties, he possessed neatly combed hair, a clean-shaven face, and glasses absent from his visage. His eyes, however, were the captivating focal point—hazy yet seemingly penetrating the depths of one's soul. Tall and slim, he donned what appeared to be a thousand-dollar suit with a black tie.

"Here I have been chasing you all over Stapleton, and you come right to me. How convenient and polite," he continued.

"I aim to please," John said sarcastically, earning a harsh rifle hit from one of the nearby men.

"My aim will not miss. I will dispose of you, but first, I will do away with the evidence that you have collected. Let me see the camera," he demanded.

One of the men searched roughly until they found the camera and brought it to Penkowski.

"Who is the old man you brought with you, John?" Penkowski asked as the camera was being handed to him.

"My father. I had no one to watch him, so I brought him along."

"Ah!" John yelled as one of the men hit him again.

"Nice camera," Penkowski said, throwing it on the ground and smashing it with his foot. "Must have been worth a fortune. Now, tell me why you are here and who this man is with you. I am tired of playing games," he said with anger in his voice and blazing eyes.

For a moment, George thought he saw the man's eyes glow, but he dismissed it as his imagination playing tricks on him. Despite everything that was happening, he still felt a deep sense of peace, allowing him to remain focused and standing.

"I know that Advance Medical is the leading organization in the world for advanced procedures," John said confidently.

Penkowski looked impressed, but then he quickly grew angry, "Enough! Why are you here and who is this man with you? I will not ask again!" John remained silent, but George surprised everyone by speaking up, "I am Joe Stanton..."

John interrupted him, "Joe, that's enough!"

But George was determined, "No, John, I will tell them what they want."

John protested, "You will not! Ah!" and was hit once more.

"I was assigned to help John uncover..." George started to say, but he suddenly stopped mid-sentence.

"Uncover what?" Penkowski demanded to know.

"Do you hear that?" George said.

"I hear the sound of a gun going off, one at a time, and the sound of a limp body hitting the floor," said Penkowski. "Make it so."

As the men approached John and George, the ominous sound grew louder. The men looked up but continued to proceed. They each held a revolver, one aimed at George's head and the other at John's. They were on the verge of pulling the trigger.

As the moment approached for Bruce's church to convene on Tuesday night, an electric buzz of excitement and anticipation hung in the air. The word had spread, and everyone was aware of the new location, joining their hearts in prayer for the resolution of the city's closure of the church. As Bruce embarked on his journey to the school, an indescribable feeling enveloped him—a sense that change was imminent.

No stranger to change, Bruce understood that God often worked through such shifts. Despite any discomfort, he welcomed this feeling, knowing it carried the promise of hope, excitement, and the anticipation of God's transformative work. After the profound events that had unfolded in his church, neighborhood, and the broader city, Bruce couldn't help but wonder what else lay ahead.

Arriving at the school, Bruce was greeted by a breathtaking sight. Car after car filled the parking area, dwarfing the capacity of his modest church. The auditorium, with its threefold capacity, was now being embraced by a community hungry for spiritual connection. The infectious excitement and hope permeated the air, and Bruce was eager to witness the unfolding of God's plan for his church and community.

Bruce's heart raced with exhilaration and gratitude. This was the very essence of his lifelong commitment to ministry—the joy derived from witnessing God's transformative work in the lives of his congregation. While he had experienced this feeling many times before, it remained potent, fresh, and invigorating, making him feel youthful and vibrant each time.

Taking in the sight of the multitude gathered for prayer, Bruce was overcome with emotion. Each person had come for a singular reason—to unite in prayer, moved by the hand of God. Bruce hadn't coerced or manipulated them; it was the pure power of God at work in their hearts.

Wiping tears from his eyes, Bruce parked the car and stepped out into the chilly weather. The surge of God's power filled him with an unexplainable peace and warmth, a welcome embrace both for his relationship with the Lord and against the wintry chill outside.

Bruce's heart swelled with awe and wonder as he surveyed the diverse crowd emerging from their cars. Among them were unfamiliar faces, and yet, some were familiar—individuals he recognized from the various transactions in town. As he approached the building, he noticed even more unexpected attendees, such as his barber, who had never set foot in a church before, the woman bagging his groceries, and the gas station attendant. It seemed as if the entire town had converged tonight for a common purpose—to pray. Among these newcomers, Bruce also spotted the regular attendees of the Tuesday night prayer meetings, their faithful presence grounding the atmosphere.

Navigating through the crowds, Bruce eavesdropped on snippets of conversations. The tales of intertwined lives, prayers, and the magnetic pull that led them to this gathering left him in awe. Stories unfolded of colleagues working together, drawing others into the fold through their shared witness. It was a tapestry of testimonies illustrating God's extraordinary work in the lives of ordinary people.

Walking through the school's corridors, Bruce was taken aback by the sight that met his eyes. Scriptures adorned bulletin boards, announcements of Bible studies adorned the walls, and godly quotes were displayed. The atmosphere mirrored that of a church rather than a public school, brimming with reverence and awe.

Entering the auditorium, Bruce was greeted by Joe Benton, who was visibly breathless. "Bruce! Hey! Can you believe all these people?" Joe exclaimed.

Bruce surveyed the turnout, his amazement evident. "It's unbelievable," he replied, humbled by the spectacle.

"This is God's doing," Joe affirmed.

"I never thought I'd witness a revival like this in my lifetime, let alone in our city and our church," Bruce admitted, a sense of humility washing over him.

"God knew He could count on you," Joe said, smiling.

Bruce regarded Joe seriously before returning the smile. "Praise the Lord for that."

As the audience settled into their seats, Bruce caught the eye of Tommy, the boy he had visited in the hospital, who beamed with a smile and a thumbs-up. Bruce smiled back and began addressing the audience.

"Thank you for coming tonight and gathering here in the school. I was worried about the church closing, but God has worked everything out for good. It's great to see both familiar and new faces. Why don't we start by hearing from some of our newcomers? Can you share with us what brought you here tonight?"

The auditorium buzzed with emotion as people began sharing their stories. Each testimony unveiled the remarkable transformations that had occurred in their lives, a testament to the power of prayer. The room fell silent as these stories wove together, connected by a common thread of faith.

As prayers commenced, the room crackled with a sense of divine presence. The prayers weren't mere words; they were deeply felt, expressed with tears of joy and sadness. Each person seamlessly passed the baton, their prayers flowing effortlessly from one to the next.

The power of the moment etched itself on every face in the auditorium, an intense sense of unity and love defying verbal explanation. It was an experience that touched the hearts and souls of everyone present.

As the prayers tapered off, those attending for the first time were gently taken aside and spoken to with love and tenderness. These newcomers, who had no prior relationship with Christ, were drawn by an irresistible desire to be part of this gathering. Their shared reasons revealed a missing piece in their lives, one they witnessed in the attendees of the Tuesday night meetings. Thus, more souls were added to the kingdom, and the joy in the room became indescribable.

TEN

Just as the tension reached its peak, the room erupted into chaos. The walls behind the armed men seemed to explode with a force that left everyone in sheer horror. George and John looked up to witness a surreal spectacle—an approaching wall of what resembled a tornado, punctuated by flashes of lightning and enveloped in brilliant light. The raw power of the wind was so intense that it sent the two gunmen flying, rendering them unconscious. As George raised his eyes once more, his heart pounded relentlessly. Was it a figment of his terrified imagination? No, it was undeniably real.

George stood frozen, his senses overwhelmed with fear, alongside the equally stunned John. The incredible force of the windstorm affected everyone else in the room, but miraculously spared both of them. Dr. Penkowski remained unaffected as well. John, bewildered, sought to comprehend the unfolding phenomenon, while George fixated on the enigmatic images within the tempest surrounding Penkowski. Metallic glows, resembling figures, emerged on each side of the possessed man, instilling in George an unexplainable dread. Straining to get a closer look, his eyes widened in terror as he discerned the appearance of humanoid figures. Yet, before he could grasp the details, Penkowski seized his attention.

The once-possessed red eyes of Penkowski intensified and began to protrude from his face. In a chilling twist, another grotesque face materialized over Penkowski's, surveying the glowing entities on either side.

"Let's go!" John's urgent shout jolted George out of his stupor. The monstrous figures lunged at Penkowski, launching a relentless attack. John forcefully pulled George away from the horrifying spectacle, though George struggled to tear his eyes away.

"George, come on! Let's go now!" John yelled above the deafening roar of the windstorm. They hurried to the exit, astonishment painted on their faces as they encountered no resistance while fleeing the building. Outside, they gazed up at the darkened top floor, unable to discern anything amidst the lingering shadows. The tumult of the windstorm gradually subsided, leaving only the echoes of its earlier fury. Silently, they raced to their car and sped away, the profound impact of the unearthly encounter lingering in the air.

Both George and John were still grappling with the shock of the harrowing encounter, their breaths coming in ragged gasps as they tried to comprehend the unimaginable. Approaching the hotel, John cast wary glances over his shoulder, a lingering fear of pursuit etched on his face. The empty street offered no solace.

Upon reaching their room, John broke the heavy silence. "I can't believe what just happened," he admitted, turning to George. However, George, as pale as a ghost, remained silent, his eyes haunted by the horrors they had just witnessed.

"George, it's okay. Take a deep breath and relax. You did great! I'm really proud of how you handled that gun," John offered reassurance in a comforting tone. Still, George's silence persisted as he continued to gaze at John. In the room, John headed straight for his laptop, an unexplained appearance in his hospital room still lingering in the back of his mind. Meanwhile, George sat on his bed, shock still raw.

"It's not here," John mentioned, hoping George would seek clarification. Yet, George remained silent. Concern crept into John's voice as he continued, "I thought the pics would have been in the cloud by now." He couldn't shake the worry settling over George's mental state.

"Hey, are you alright? You haven't said a word since we left the building," John asked, genuine concern etched on his face. Finally, George spoke up, "You didn't see them, did you?"

"See what?" John inquired.

"Them," George replied, still visibly shaken.

"Who, 'Them'?"

"They were in the wind," George explained. "There were two creatures... men... red glowing things. They were on each side of Penkowski. They were about to attack him when all of a sudden, Penkowski's eyes turned redder than ever!"

John's brow furrowed, and he listened intently to George's

unsettling account. Confusion and curiosity played across his face as he struggled to comprehend the vivid and surreal details. "I... I saw lightning," John finally uttered, his voice tinged with disbelief. "But that was it. It came out of nowhere. I mean, I can't explain it. It's like a miracle. It saved our lives, that's for sure," he added, his bewilderment evident in his tone.

"His eyes came out of his head... it reminded me of the old 3-D movies I used to watch as a kid. And if that was not enough to put chills down your spine, all of a sudden this unbelievably ugly face appeared over Penkowski's face," George continued.

"John, that face made all the things you see in horror movies look like children's Halloween masks. And then suddenly the two creatures attacked Penkowski!"

"What... what happened next?" John asked, his voice tinged with concern, reaching out to place a comforting hand on George's shoulder. "Take a deep breath, George. It's alright. We made it out of there, remember? Just try to gather yourself. I'm still trying to process everything that happened," John reassured, his own emotions settling as he grappled with the bizarre events.

"I don't know," George replied.

"What do you mean you don't know?" John pressed.

"Well, at that moment, you were pulling me out the door," George explained.

"We had to get out of there," John reminded him.

"You mean you believe me?" George asked in surprise.

"I'm sure your eyes were playing tricks on you, my friend," John said, attempting to console him. "The situation was extremely stressful for anyone."

George studied John, opting not to disclose more of his strange visions, deeming them too outlandish for a Christian and too implausible for a non-Christian.

"We don't have the pics I was hoping for," John said, shifting the subject.

"So we did all that for nothing," George remarked, the color returning to his face.

"Well, we did have some fun, didn't we?" John smiled.

George regarded him skeptically. "Right," he said sarcastically.

"Get some rest, my friend. You'll feel better in the morning," John encouraged, offering a comforting pat on the back.

The phone's persistent ringing echoed in the quiet room, jolting Bruce out of his thoughts. "Hello?" he answered, his voice carrying a hint of weariness.

"Pastor Bruce, it's Sue," came the familiar voice on the other end.

"Sue, how are you?" Bruce inquired, appreciating the connection amid the tumultuous week.

"The better question is, 'How are you?'"

Bruce sighed audibly, a heavy weight on his shoulders. "Well, it has been an emotionally draining week. I just can't believe that every morning I get up, and I am ready to head for the church, and then the cruel reality hits me: it's closed."

He paused, allowing room for Sue to share her thoughts, but when she remained silent, Bruce continued. "I mean, well... it just doesn't make sense! God has been working so mightily, and then boom, we're hit with this mess."

"Boy, I don't know what to say, Bruce," Sue responded empathetically.

"I am very pleased with the Tuesday night prayer meeting. Sue, it's just that every time I close my eyes, I see 'CLOSE TO PUBLIC FOR HEALTH VIOLATIONS'... those words! The church of God closed by the government! Are we in a foreign country... what is..."

"Bruce..." Sue interjected, sensing his rising emotions. Bruce waited for her to speak, grappling with fear, anger, discouragement, and confusion. Deep inside, he clung to the knowledge that God was in control, yet the closure of the church, a sanctuary of comfort, left a void. What about the members feeling the same way? The situation seemed laden with adversity, bearing the unmistakable signs of the Devil's hand.

"Bruce..." Sue said again, sensing the need to anchor him in faith.

"Yeah, I'm here... I just can't believe it. Closed. No more choir practice, no more kids running the hall to get to Sunday school class..."

"Pastor Bruce, it's all under control. God has a plan. He will use evil for His good."

"I know all that, Sue, but I am not feeling that right now."

"We live by faith, not by sight..."

A contemplative silence stretched between them before a

somber voice broke it. "I miss George."

Sue listened with compassion.

"He is gone on some mission, and I did not realize how important he was to the ministry. He would always encourage me. I will never forget the house ordeal. Here I came home to a totally destroyed home, and before the week was out, George had organized and redid my whole home. It is now more beautiful than it was before it was vandalized."

"Pastor, that is how God works... The Devil ruins it, and God takes what has been ruined and reworks it better, more beautiful, more effective, more powerful... all to His glory. Though the pain is real, the pain you are feeling, God expanded the Tuesday night prayer by relocating us to the school building. And, God is not finished yet. He has only begun. Sit back and get ready for the ride of your life because what you have seen so far is only the beginning... the appetizer. No eye has seen, no ear has heard, no mind has conceived what God has prepared for those who love Him."

At that comment, Bruce couldn't help but smile. Even though it was Sue speaking the words, he knew it was God's voice coming through her. Bruce silently expressed his gratitude to God in his heart.

The phone call cut through like a thunderous storm, leaving frustration and anger in its wake. "I can't believe you allowed this! What were you thinking?" he bellowed into the phone, his voice brimming with raw intensity.

Mayor Johnson, composed on the other end of the line, replied calmly, "Reverend Stone, I had no control over this situation."

The reverend's anger intensified, a storm brewing within him. "What is the purpose of closing his church if we provide him with a place? Not just any place, mind you, but a place even larger than his own church!" He took a deep breath, bracing himself for his next outburst.

"Who is responsible for this?" he demanded, but there was only silence on the other end, leaving him seething with frustration.

Growing increasingly exasperated, he pressed further, "What do you want me to do?"

"Get him out of there!" Reverend Stone's voice thundered

through the phone, the desperation evident in his tone.

The Mayor's response was regretful. "I can't do that. The school is governed by a school board, and I have no control over their decisions."

Desperate for a solution, Reverend Stone suggested, "What about some city official who can intervene?"

The Mayor's interruption was firm. "Now you're asking for a miracle, and I am not God. I can't change the way things are run."

Reverend Stone's frustration boiled over, his words falling on deaf ears. "Err... this is so frustrating!" he exclaimed in defeat, a defeated tone underscoring his helplessness.

With a note of apology, the Mayor said, "I'm sorry, Reverend. I have done all that I can do."

The gravity of the situation lingered in the air as the call drew to a close, leaving Reverend Stone grappling with the weight of his powerlessness.

The early morning sun cast a soft glow, painting the room in hues of dawn. It was around 7:00 AM, and the world was just starting to stir. Despite the hour, John and George were already up and about, their faces carrying the weight of the events that transpired the night before. Sleep had eluded George, haunted by the unsettling image of the face emerging from Penkowski's face. The profound sense of dread lingered, making it one of the most disturbing encounters he had faced in his fifty years. Even with the flickers of sleep, his rest was disturbed by the symphony of his roommate's snoring.

With the dawn light streaming through the window, George opened his Bible. The first verse he read seemed to echo in the quiet room, "Not by might, not by power, but by my Spirit," said the Lord of hosts. In the solitude of the early morning, George turned his thoughts to his Father. "Father, I need you desperately! I have never been so frightened in all my life. I feel exposed, as if I might come face-to-face with you at any moment. I pray that you would deliver me from this mess I have created in my life, and in return, I will serve you wholeheartedly for the rest of my days."

Aware of the weight of his words, George knew making promises to God wasn't always the wisest course of action. Yet, in that vulnerable moment, it felt right. The life he had led before encountering God was a long, painful journey, and the prospect of a faraway mission trip seemed a more palatable alternative.

"Buddy, are you ready to get going?" John's voice cut through the quiet, breaking the solemnity of the moment.

George looked at John, a grateful smile breaking across his face. In that moment, John seemed to be the answer to the turmoil in his life.

"You bet!"

"Great! Let's go and have some more fun. But before we leave, it's time for a makeover."

John pulled out his kit, and within half an hour, George was transformed. As they left, the dawn unfolded, painting the world with a promise of new beginnings. They set off on their next adventure, the dawn of a new day symbolizing hope in the midst of uncertainty.

On yet another Tuesday night, the gathering mirrored the one before, but this time it seemed to carry an added layer of divine intensity. The room swelled with even more eager hearts, fervent prayers, and an undeniable presence of the Holy Spirit. The atmosphere crackled with an energy that transcended the physical space. As powerful testimonies echoed through the room, souls found salvation, and the very air seemed to vibrate with a divine resonance.

Bruce, seated among the congregation, leaned back, his eyes surveying the scene before him. A tear welled up in his eye, not of sorrow but of overwhelming gratitude. His heart was a tapestry woven with threads of emotions—joy, awe, and an undercurrent of yearning. In the midst of the ongoing prayers, a gentle, cool breeze brushed through the gathering, carrying with it a sense of divine approval. Smiles graced the faces of those in attendance as if God Himself was bestowing His blessing upon the assembly.

Yet, amid the blissful celebration, a lingering question danced in Bruce's mind like a distant melody. "Lord, will You continue to manifest Your presence, work Your miracles, and draw men, women, and children to Yourself?" The weight of uncertainty pressed upon him until, in that very moment, the Holy Spirit touched his spirit with an assurance that resounded like a firm "YES." A warm wave washed over his soul, dissolving worries about the closure of the church, George's absence, and the potential dangers he might face. A profound sense of peace settled within him, for he knew that God orchestrates all things for the good of those who love Him.

By the time Bruce arrived home, the evening had grown late, and weariness crept into his bones. Yet, he carried with him the lingering excitement from the Tuesday night prayer meeting. In his study, he settled in front of the computer, recalling the computer skills George had imparted. Opening his email inbox, Bruce meticulously read through each message, recognizing the increasing importance of checking them twice a day. Each email held its own weight—a life-changing story, a biblical inquiry, prayers for George's well-being, and pleas for the church's situation.

However, amidst the sea of correspondence, one particular email captured Bruce's attention. Leaning back in his chair, he let out a deep sigh, staring in disbelief at the screen.

John and George executed their departure from town with a stealth that belied their desperation. They ventured to a neighboring city just beyond the reach of the ominous Advance Medical building, leaving the chaos and danger behind. Emotionally drained, George clung to a thread of hope as he placed his trust in John, electing not to pry too deeply into their escape plan.

Their journey led them to a gated community on the outskirts of the city, where John seamlessly produced a card from his pocket and swiped it through the card reader. The imposing gate swung open, revealing a world that left George in awe.

"How did you do that?" George asked, his curiosity piqued, knowing that John wasn't a resident of this exclusive community.

"Do what?" John responded innocently.

"You don't live here, do you?" George pressed, already anticipating the answer.

"No, not at all. Oh, the card," John explained with enthusiasm. "You see, these gates all have a master key system. Each key shares similarities with others in its combination. So, I programmed those similarities into this key, and voila, it works every time!" John's eyes sparkled with a youthful excitement, reminiscent of a boyhood filled with dreams of unlocking mysteries with gadgets.

A warm smile tugged at George's lips. Witnessing John's real-life detective skills, complete with modern-day devices, was a nostalgic and exhilarating experience.

As they delved deeper into the community, opulence revealed itself at every turn. Grand homes nestled far back from the street, shielded by majestic fences adorned with ornate gates and meticulous landscaping, painted a picture of affluence.

"Many movie stars reside in this community," John remarked casually, prompting George to scrutinize their surroundings more intently.

The car meandered through streets lined with magnificent trees, vibrant landscaping, and an array of colorful flowers that captivated George's senses. The sheer beauty of the environment began to alleviate his tension, granting him a fleeting moment of relaxation. Their drive continued until they approached an extensive stretch of fence that seemed to extend endlessly. A monumental entrance came into view, boasting a gate large enough to accommodate a semi-trailer.

Suddenly, realization struck George, and panic surged within him. He pleaded with John, "Please tell me this isn't Penkowski's home."

John merely smiled, but George's heart plummeted into the depths of his stomach. Panic and fear welled up, and he silently thought, "If I don't get shot and killed, I might die from a heart attack!" George knew he had no other choice but to trust John with his freedom.

The subject line of the email caught Bruce's attention, reading, "To the town troublemaker..." Taking a moment to gather his thoughts, he offered a silent prayer, "Lord, help me see through Your eyes." As he clicked to open the email, a mix of emotions washed over him. On the positive side, it wasn't from anyone who attended the Tuesday night prayer meetings; the sender had signed their name. Unfortunately, it was a name that didn't evoke warm feelings within him—it was Reverend Richard Stone.

The contents of the email unfolded before Bruce's eyes:

"Pastor Bruce, why do you persist in seeking new ways to steal the very congregation I've devoted my professional life to building? You've taken people who were once part of my church, a church that earnestly serves God and works diligently to advance His kingdom. You've initiated a non-work-oriented group during the week, causing local businesses to collapse and transforming our once quaint community into a ghost town. This has led to a loss of financial support for our city, directly impacting the livelihoods of our people and their families. It's the children in these families who suffer the most when money becomes scarce. And you, above all, should know that financial issues are a leading cause of marital strife and divorce."

Bruce leaned back, trying to fully comprehend the weight of the words on the screen. What bothered him the most was that a part of him, albeit small, began to entertain the notion that Reverend Stone's accusations held some truth.

The email continued:

"For this reason, I will do everything in my power to counteract your disruptive actions. I will launch a campaign to expose this weekly wasted energy and bring people back to God's work, restoring normalcy to our hometown of Stapleton. I will rebuild the church you've cursed, which once stood prominently in this community as a beacon of hope for the desperate and a source of comfort for the afflicted. God will once again be proud of our community, our church, and the work that will resume. Mark my words."

The email concluded with the signature: "God's workman unashamed, Reverend Richard Stone."

Bruce leaned back once more, letting out a sigh. He understood the principle well—whenever God is at work, the Devil tirelessly opposes Him. Witnessing the Devil's influence in a fellow clergy member was always disheartening. Despite immersing himself in the teachings of God's Word, Bruce found it challenging to dispel lingering memories of his upbringing. Those recollections painted a picture of well-meaning ministers, dressed in robes, delivering eloquent speeches against the backdrop of intricately designed stained glass windows. However, these experiences seemed to lack a genuine connection to the core message of the Gospel of Christ.

Suddenly, a Bible verse sprang to his mind: "For such men are false apostles, deceitful workmen, masquerading as apostles of Christ. And no wonder, for Satan himself masquerades as an angel of light."

"Wow!" Bruce thought, taken aback by the harshness of those words. "But they're words I need to hear."

"George, I know things are getting out of hand—breaking into the main Advance Medical complex, risking our lives back there, and now heading to Penkowski's home..." John's words hung in the air, and George stared at him, desperately hoping for some explanation or reassurance. How had he ended up in this mess? His greed for money, fame, and material possessions had led him down this self-destructive path. In truth, George longed to give it all up, even if it meant being destitute, just to break free from this self-imposed bondage.

"But trust me," John interjected, a determined look in his eyes. "I've been doing this my whole life, and I can guarantee you true freedom. I mean real freedom. No more looking over your shoulder. No more worrying about tapped phones. You'll be able to go wherever you want, whenever you want. Be the person you want to be, have the job you want, without anyone dictating your life. However, George, freedom always comes at a cost. And right now, that cost is doing something unthinkable—breaking into your enemy's home. It's like a slap in his face. But rest assured, we won't get caught. We'll go in, get what we need, and get out. Penkowski won't even know we were there."

George let out a sigh, the weight of their precarious situation sinking in. John was right. Everything he said, from the dangers involved to the bondage they sought to break, it was worth it. The price of freedom had always been high. For America, it was the lives of their forefathers. Then George thought about his newfound freedom in Christ—it had cost him nothing, but it had cost his Father His very own Son, Jesus Christ.

Nodding in agreement, George looked at John, who smiled confidently. They continued driving, with John carefully observing their surroundings as they passed the entrance.

"Where are we going?" George asked, curiosity tugging at him.

"Well, in big homes like this, there's often a back entrance that's not as heavily monitored or known to many," John explained.

After a few minutes, they reached a point where the fence stopped, and they came across a concealed side road. It was well-hidden among dense, beautiful trees and shrubs. They proceeded cautiously along the back alley, surrounded by nature's camouflage. Suddenly, John brought the car to a halt, jolting them against their seat belts.

"What's wrong?" George asked, concerned.

"Wait here for a second," John replied, stepping out of the car. He scanned the area, moving slowly towards the front. To George's surprise, John squatted down and disappeared from view. Curiosity got the better of him, and he leaned forward to see what was happening. John had located spikes protruding from the road and managed to retract them using a nearby switch. John returned to the car, saying, "Spikes. Bad for my tires." George couldn't help but smile, appreciating John's resourcefulness. They resumed their cautious journey.

As they continued, the road curved, revealing a building that appeared more like a storage facility than a home. Despite its unassuming appearance, they parked the car and proceeded on foot. The building was nestled amidst dense vegetation, giving John hope that security would be minimal.

True to his expectations, they found only one outdated security camera hanging from a corner of the building's roof, covered in black mildew. John quickly covered it with a small camera case he had brought along. He motioned for George to join him.

Moving around the front, they encountered a sealed entrance blocked by a hefty steel bar—a clear indication that someone did not want visitors. For John, the challenge only fueled his excitement. They explored the side of the building and discovered a small window near the roof's top.

The nearby fence once again served as a makeshift ladder for climbing. John retrieved a small glass cutter from his pocket, accompanied by a suction cup that he affixed to the window. With one hand, he skillfully cut through the glass while using the other to remove it. George couldn't help but recall seeing similar techniques in spy movies from his childhood. Despite the advancements in technology, this simple and dated approach remained remarkably useful. John used his pocket knife's file to smooth the edge of the glass.

They swiftly made their way through the newly created window opening. The dense trees and shrubs surrounding the building limited the amount of light inside. John cautiously lowered himself to the ground, keeping a low profile. George followed suit. Dim lights illuminated the back of an old table, displaying the marks of years of use. Towering before them were the familiar tall file cabinets, clearly having been there for quite some time. As John began searching through the files, George alternated his attention between the window and the door. The screech of an old file drawer opening startled George, making him jump. Papers rustled as files were removed and replaced—it was a sight that could even make an executive secretary blush.

Suddenly, a branch outside the window cracked, prompting George to signal John. However, John had instinctively halted his movements before George could even raise his hand. George peered outside but saw nothing. Then, it happened again! His eyes widened as he spotted the source—a squirrel foraging for its dinner. Giving the OK signal, George indicated that it was a false alarm.

John resumed his search. After some time, a smile crept onto his face, signaling to George that they were making progress. George felt a growing sense of relief, knowing that the sooner they completed their mission, the better off they would be.

With their task accomplished, they hastily exited through the window, returned to the car, and sped away. Impatiently, George asked, "What did you find?" John, however, remained tight-lipped, wearing a big, teasing grin on his face.

Finally, John glanced over at George and said, "Jackpot!"

It was late in the afternoon, and the winter sun offered little warmth despite its presence. Sue sat at the table, her eyes darting anxiously towards the window. Then, a sight brought relief to her restless heart—Maggie walking towards the house. Sue waved enthusiastically, hoping to catch her attention. Maggie spotted the gesture and waved back, her presence bringing a sense of comfort. The twinkle in Maggie's eye and the lightness in her step were a stark contrast to the old Maggie—desperate, unhappy, and miserable.

"Sue, how are you?" Maggie asked, her voice filled with genuine warmth.

"Great! It's so good to see you!" Sue replied, her face lighting up. "Having dinner together was a brilliant idea. How are you doing?"

"Well, super! Remember the song I composed that first night at the revival?" Maggie's eyes gleamed with excitement, her face on the verge of bursting with joy.

"How can I ever forget? Pastor Bruce was in awe of it," Sue

reminisced.

"I got a recording contract!" Maggie exclaimed, her voice brimming with exhilaration.

"You got a recording contract?" Sue's brow furrowed with curiosity.

"Well... a Christian label approached me to sing that very song with other Christian artists," Maggie explained, her words slightly rushed.

"That's fantastic! How did this happen? Who contacted you? How did they discover your song?" Sue's questions spilled out without pause.

Maggie took a breath, her gaze fixed on Sue. "Well, I was singing the song in the shower..." Sue's puzzled expression made her backtrack. "No, no, I mean, I was thinking about the song as I sang it in the shower, and the Lord impressed upon my heart to record it on my computer. So, I did. While surfing the web, I stumbled upon this Christian label that accepts submissions from new artists. I uploaded my recording, and within a week, they reached out to me."

Sue listened intently, captivated by Maggie's story.

"They told me that in all their years of listening to new music, this song struck their hearts deeply," Maggie continued, tears welling up in her eyes. "They said it moved them to tears." She paused, overcome with emotion.

"What else did they say?" Sue's anticipation was evident.

Maggie wiped away a tear and spoke with a quiver in her voice, "They said, 'This song will change the hearts of men and women all over the world.'"

"Wow!" Sue exclaimed, awestruck by the magnitude of the moment.

"Yeah, can you believe it? I thought it would be a dead end... I only did it for God, and then this happens!" Maggie's words spilled out, a mix of astonishment and gratitude.

Sue smiled warmly. "God works in ways we could never fathom, doesn't He?"

"I guess so, Sue. You would know better than I," Maggie acknowledged. They shared a brief pause, and then Maggie's expression turned somber. "I miss John."

Sue gazed at Maggie, her smile filled with warmth and understanding.

"I keep replaying that day we met in the park. Oh, Sue, it was so romantic!" Maggie's voice carried a mixture of nostalgia and longing. "He showed up with his clever disguise. I remember wondering, 'Who is this guy approaching me?' Then, the ducks swam up to us, and he had bread for us to feed them. I truly miss him. I hope he's alright."

"Have you received any news from him?" Sue inquired gently.

"No, and I'm worried. What if he gets into trouble? What if he ends up in another car accident... What if he doesn't make it this time?" Maggie's voice trembled with concern.

"Those are things you'll have to entrust to God's hands," Sue replied, offering words of reassurance.

Maggie's gaze drifted out the window, lost in her thoughts. Eventually, she turned her attention back to Sue and made a heartfelt request. "Would you pray, Sue? Out loud?"

"Of course, Maggie," Sue responded, her voice filled with compassion. And so, she began to pray, offering their concerns and fears to the One who holds all things in His hands. The atmosphere in the room became infused with a sense of peace as the heartfelt prayer echoed in the quiet space.

"I demand immediate action! I'm fed up with the deception, the lies, and everything else that led to the loss of my congregation!" The voice thundered through the phone, directed at Allace Construction Company. They had been tasked with the daunting job of clearing up the aftermath of the devastating tornado that had completely ravaged Reverend Richard Stone's church. Acting swiftly, the construction company worked tirelessly, and within a single day, the site was cleared of debris.

Simultaneously, a vast tent was raised, reminiscent of the old-fashioned revival tents from yesteryears. The area buzzed with bustling activity. Chairs were meticulously arranged, a stage was erected, complete with microphones, speakers, wires, and dazzling lights. Sound checks reverberated through the air. Carnival rides were transported in, accompanied by candy and game stands. As evening approached, the radiant glow of lights beckoned inquisitive onlookers.

The preaching commenced, drawing people with curious minds who gradually gathered and found their seats.

"As the people of Stapleton, we must put an end to this chaos!

We can no longer afford to witness our stores and businesses closing down. We can't bear the shame of our residents perishing on national television! And we certainly cannot stand idly by as the church, which God intended to be built in our community over the past two decades, crumbles due to the actions of a small-town preacher! This man prays, but where is the fruit of his labor? What has he done for our community? What tangible contributions can he show for the betterment of our city? It is we who will demonstrate our work—the work that God truly honors."

"Friends, Bruce's church has been forcibly closed by the county, citing health risks! Is this how they claim to care for their flock? Endangering them with the possibility of fire and inhabiting an unsafe building? A building that is meant to be dedicated to God? This is an absolute outrage! We are grateful that the city intervened when it did, preventing a potential catastrophe!"

The impassioned speaker's words echoed through the crowd, stirring a collective sense of indignation. Faces contorted with varying degrees of disbelief and anger. The abrupt closure of Bruce's church had become a rallying cry, uniting the community against what they perceived as unjust interference.

"Now, let us come together and enjoy the festivities of the carnival! Spread the word to your friends and neighbors who have strayed from our church to return and experience the joy we once shared as a God-fearing family. And if they refuse to return, then shun them. We have no need for them or the influence of their business."

The announcement hung in the air, a divisive directive that drew a clear line between those within the fold and those deemed outsiders. Murmurs of approval and disquiet rippled through the crowd, sowing seeds of discord within the once-tight-knit community.

The crowd was in a state of unrest. They longed for the liquor store and the provocative magazines they had grown accustomed to. The few positive changes couldn't outweigh the numerous negative transformations that had taken place in their small town. Eventually, the crowd dispersed, indulging in the rides, games, and some winning cash prizes while purchasing an abundance of candy, beer, and other treats.

Before departing, each person was given a handful of pamphlets. These pamphlets were to be placed on the cars, trucks, mailboxes, and business entrances of their friends and neighbors who were absent from the evening gathering but were part of the Tuesday prayer group. Everyone traversed the entire town, strategically distributing these brochures to ensure maximum visibility. The pamphlets straightforwardly delivered a message encouraging people to become part of Reverend Stone's church. Additionally, they carried an implication that those who did not align with Reverend Stone's congregation might be viewed as opposing God and consequently treated as adversaries. These pamphlets also included a cautionary note about the potential consequences, warning of the divine anger that could be unleashed upon them.

The distribution of pamphlets continued into the early hours of the morning, leaving no corner of the city untouched. Some individuals, influenced by the alcohol sold at the carnival, became unruly, leading to their apprehension and overnight stay in Stapleton's seldom-used jail.

It had been a significant event, as the jail had remained unoccupied for an extended period of time. The echoes of discontent lingered in the quiet streets, leaving Stapleton shrouded in an unsettling atmosphere, its sense of community now fractured.

ELEVEN

It was early the next morning when the phone began to ring in Bruce's home. He had gone for an early stroll, pouring out his prayers along the way, most of which centered around George. Bruce deeply missed his presence during this challenging time. It seemed that whenever he formed a close bond with someone in ministry, God would inevitably lead them elsewhere.

The lingering ache in Bruce's heart was the scar left by Jennifer. Not only had they become friends, but he had also fallen in love with her. Bruce had wrestled with the temptation to disobey God, especially when Jennifer was sent overseas while he remained in the States. Sometimes, he felt as if his heart had sinned, entertaining thoughts of "what if" instead of focusing on God's will in the present moment.

Another weight on Bruce's heart was the person responsible for all of this—George. Missing George had proven to be incredibly difficult. There were moments when George made Bruce feel less alone in the midst of this extraordinary journey of revival, a concept he had only read about in historical accounts of bygone centuries in America. He had heard stories of powerful revivals happening overseas as well. Jennifer had often shared her experiences of the small revival in her village where she had been working. Bruce had fervently prayed to be a part of a revival, but never in his wildest dreams did he imagine being part of one at this stage of life, in this small town, and especially not in his own modest church.

And then there was the church—or rather, the lack thereof. How could God be glorified when the doors of the church remained closed, seemingly useless? Oh, how Bruce longed for George's companionship. At least he could confide in him. Despite George being a young Christian, he always had an uplifting word to offer, shedding new light on moments of darkness or challenges.

Bruce continued down the streets of his neighborhood, praying and communing with God in the depths of his heart. What would be his next step? And what about the email he had received from Reverend Stone? What plans did the reverend have up his sleeve?

As Bruce approached his house, the windows were open, and he could hear the recording on the answering machine playing...

"...and this note was right on my windshield this morning when I woke up! Can you believe the audacity? Who do they think they are? Threatening me just because I left a church? I always had a feeling something was amiss with Reverend Stone and his congregation. I only attended because of my husband. Now he's resorting to threats?"

Bruce walked over to his chair, almost missing it despite its familiar presence in the room. He couldn't believe what he was hearing. This was unprecedented. Just in time, he closed his mouth to prevent any embarrassment, holding back the words that almost escaped. He sat there in stunned silence, listening to the rest of the message.

"Pastor Bruce, what am I going to do? My husband and I own a small business, and we're barely making ends meet as it is. This would ruin us. And my husband is excited about Tuesday night, and he's not going to give it up for this!"

The message continued, but it was abruptly cut short as the machine had a time limit for recording each message. Once again, as this whole ordeal began, the answering machine sat there blinking with a string of messages. Bruce hurriedly grabbed a pencil and legal pad, pressing the play button to transcribe the notes. It felt like an eternity as he jotted down the details, constantly interrupted every 15 minutes by live calls.

It was the final straw that broke the camel's back. How could one person be expected to handle so many problems? Bruce fled into his praying room, ignoring the ringing phone and allowing the now silenced answering machine to collect the messages.

"God, what am I supposed to do?" Bruce cried out in desperation. Tears streamed down his cheeks, and the weight of each person's burden fell heavily upon him. The world's troubles rested upon his shoulders, and he knelt there in silence, groaning in his spirit, finding solace in this release.

"Father, I need help! Even Moses had help. Please send assistance!" He paused and then whispered aloud, "Lord, I miss George. Help him, keep him, save him wherever he is. Enable him to fulfill Your purpose, and bring him back home. I need his assistance."

Bruce continued to pray, and although the answers to the numerous questions didn't immediately appear before him, he felt a profound peace enveloping him like a comforting cloud. All he could do was lean back and bask in the presence of God.

"Thank you, Father, in Jesus' name."

"What does 'jackpot' mean?" George inquired, curious to understand the context.

"It means that if we uncover the root of this problem, we can resolve it. Personally, I'm tired of playing games with old Penkowski. It's time to finish him off and bring down the Association for Fetal Research in the process," John replied with a serious tone. His enthusiasm was still present, but he was dead set on accomplishing his mission. It was now or never.

They proceeded up the street, passing through gates that proved ineffective at deterring curious detectives, and continued into the city until they reached a large warehouse. It bore a striking resemblance to the one they had just left, only much larger in scale. Cameras were still present, but they appeared to be better maintained. John parked the car a safe distance away from the warehouse, retrieved a small briefcase from the trunk, and quietly instructed George, "Follow me."

This time, their task wouldn't be as simple. It was broad daylight, and they were clearly entering a place where they didn't belong, according to Advanced Medical's perspective, despite their altered appearances since encountering Penkowski.

Once again, they encountered a rear entrance, covered by a camera. John skillfully bypassed the lock, and they entered the building. Although there was no bustling crowd, it was evident that some individuals were present. They passed what seemed to be a break room, with a blaring TV, dirty plates from lunch, and the lingering aroma of over-brewed coffee that had been brewing since the early morning.

George stuck close to John, both of them adopting stealth mode. George chose not to ask any more questions, hoping it would help calm his nerves, but it proved unsuccessful.

They ventured from one room to another, with John appearing as if he had been there before. He seemed to possess knowledge of the layout, guiding them with confidence.

John suddenly froze, his hand signaling for George to do the same. George reminded himself that this wasn't as dire as having a gun pointed at him, but his heart continued to race nonetheless. Peeking through the doorway of the room they had stopped short of, George cautiously backed up behind a corner, waiting for the coast to clear before making his move. He followed John's lead, albeit with a bit less confidence. John confidently walked into the room they had avoided, instructing George in a hushed tone, "Watch the door."

Opening his briefcase, John retrieved a number of flash drives and methodically inserted them into the computer positioned in front of him. His typing speed rivaled that of an executive secretary, swiftly swapping flash drives with each keystroke.

Once he finished with the computer, John glanced up at George and nodded, then proceeded to another area of the room. From his briefcase, he produced a small digital device, which he placed on a wall-mounted safe. The device emitted a ticking sound and displayed a digit, indicating the need to turn the safe's combination. With each twist, it ticked and revealed a new combination. Eventually, the safe clicked open. John glanced at George, signaling him to keep watch, while he removed copies of government-issued documents from inside. He returned the remaining documents to the safe, closed it, and locked it once more.

Then, seemingly on a whim, John began rummaging through

file drawers, boxes, and crates that were stored in the room.

"Bingo!" John exclaimed with excitement. He swiftly handed his briefcase to George and grabbed a crate, lifting it up. George couldn't believe John intended to take the crate with them. If they were stopped, there would be no concealing John carrying such a bulky item.

George discreetly signaled to John, and they both sought hiding spots, reminiscent of roaches scurrying away when a light is switched on.

In the dimly lit room, shadows played on the walls as two men entered, their hushed conversation carrying an air of secrecy and guilt.

"...my job at night. I only do this to help make ends meet."

"You mean a little drinking money, don't you? What the wife doesn't know won't hurt her?"

"Hey, my wife knows I drink. Just not the amount I drink."

The conversation carried on for about 15-20 minutes, the tension building in the cramped space. The clandestine atmosphere hung thick in the air, making every passing second feel like an eternity.

As the men finally departed, John and George emerged from their hiding places, a silent exhale of relief accompanying their swift movements. George felt a sense of redemption, as if he had paid his dues by remaining concealed for the past 20 minutes. The narrow escape heightened his senses, his heart beating in synchrony with the rapid pace of their exit.

Navigating the corridors felt like a high-stakes game, the exit door gleaming like a beacon of freedom at the end of a tense tunnel. Every room they cautiously checked added to the suspense, their senses on high alert, listening intently for any signs that would prompt them to retreat into the shadows.

Finally, they reached the door and emerged into the radiant embrace of the afternoon sun. The relief was profound as they hurriedly made their way to the car, stashing the crate and briefcase in the trunk. The engine roared to life, and they sped away, leaving the covert operation behind.

"What did you get?" George asked, breaking the silence inside the car.

"Oh, my friend, I got everything. I obtained documentation that will not only shut them down but might also bring down The Association," John replied confidently, his eyes reflecting the triumph of their mission.

George couldn't help but smile, a rare sight since he had met John. There seemed to be nothing to smile about, and yet, the success of their daring venture brought a brief moment of respite.

"That seemed too easy," George expressed, his words tinged with a mix of disbelief and caution.

"Well, even dogs have their days. Relax, I think we're in the clear this time. Penkowski would never have expected us to find this warehouse," John reassured, his eyes glistening with a combination of satisfaction and adrenaline.

"He probably assumed that after our last attempt, we would lay low for a while. I'm almost certain he never even considered the possibility of us visiting his private residences," John continued, relishing the thrill of outsmarting their adversary.

John let out a deep sigh, the tension of the operation releasing like a held breath. "Thank God... We were bold, and it paid off!"

George echoed John's comment, saying, "Thank you, God!" John glanced at George and smiled, the camaraderie between them deepening with each successful mission.

"George, I'm glad you're here," John expressed, his face showing appreciation. "You've been a tremendous help, and now we have the key to free you from the prison created by Advanced Medical..." John paused, "...in more ways than one." He chuckled, the weight of their shared burdens momentarily lifted.

George chuckled along, savoring the rare moment of accomplishment. "What's our next step?" he asked, eager to continue their journey against the powerful forces they were up against.

"Well, now we need to find qualified and trustworthy legal assistance. We have everything we need to take down both companies, but we require someone who can't be swayed, threatened, or silenced."

"Silenced?" George questioned, his brows furrowing with concern.

"Yes, silenced. They need to be sharp, knowledgeable about the law inside and out. We'll need to protect them and the evidence at any cost."

"Shouldn't the government handle the prosecution?" George inquired, navigating the moral and legal complexities of their mission.

"No. We need someone for the people—the patients, the

physicians, the employees, the businesses... This is massive! If we play our cards right, the house of cards these companies have built upon will come crashing down."

"Do you have someone in mind?" George inquired, curiosity coloring his tone.

John paused for a moment, the weight of the decision apparent on his face. "Hmm... I do! I know the perfect person for this mission."

"Who is it?" George asked, anticipation building in the air.

"She is the best lawyer I know, and she has personally been affected by these companies. My sister, Lizee..." John paused, correcting himself, "Elizabeth."

"Are you out of your mind?" George fumed, a mix of concern and disbelief coloring his expression. "Why on earth would you want to involve your own sister in this mess, no matter how skilled she is?"

John inhaled deeply, sensing the weight of George's unease. "I understand your concern, George, and it might seem risky, but let me explain. Elizabeth is not merely a good lawyer; she's exceptional. I trust her implicitly. Given her personal ties to these companies, I believe her motivation to bring them down will be unparalleled. George, we're in this for the long haul. The lawyer we choose needs protection, and the evidence we hold must be safeguarded. It's going to be a challenging journey, and we need someone we can rely on. Besides, you still have to keep up your facade at Advance Medical, ensuring they don't suspect your role in their imminent downfall."

George, though, remained skeptical, his gaze fixed straight ahead. The idea of entangling Elizabeth in the same nightmare he had endured for years weighed heavily on him. The prospect of putting her at risk troubled him to the core. What George failed to grasp was that Elizabeth was already ensnared in her own harrowing ordeal, courtesy of these very companies.

"We have limited funds to donate this year, Reverend Stone," came the voice on the other end of the line.

"I need your donation more than ever! I have a church that is non-existent because of a tornado. My congregation has strayed, and to bring everything back together, I need to rebuild this church even better than before!" Reverend Stone pleaded.

"I understand the situation. I will see what we can do," the other person replied before the call ended abruptly.

With the insurance money approved and the assistance of Allace Construction Company, Reverend Stone was finally able to initiate the construction of his new church. The construction work commenced near the area where the temporary tent had been set up. The construction crew worked tirelessly, making progress at a steady pace. Meanwhile, the tent meetings continued with a small core group of individuals who remained loyal to the church.

However, a malevolent undercurrent infiltrated the group. Lingering remnants of the original church fostered sinister intentions and actively resisted the burgeoning revival in Stapleton. Their threats materialized, precipitating a discernible dip in business activity. Despite the ominous challenges, the facade of normalcy persisted, concealing the internal strife and discord brewing beneath the surface.

As Pastor Bruce drove past Reverend Stone's church, he gazed upon its progress, his heart heavy with a mix of emotions. He couldn't resist the urge to halt and reflect, the weight of his thoughts evident on his furrowed brow. "Why, Lord? With all that You're doing, why allow this?" The wind carried a sense of melancholy as he grappled with the unfolding events. Suddenly, a scripture verse flashed across his mind, "Jesus answered them, 'Have not I chosen you twelve, and one of you is a devil?'" The words resonated, stirring a complex blend of sorrow and determination within him.

Despite the burden of shouldering the majority of the ministry responsibilities in George's absence, the day unfolded with a glimmer of positivity for Pastor Bruce. In the afternoon, he decided to pay a visit to Pastor Wayne Miles' church, guided by a sense of curiosity and hope. Pastor Miles had maintained regular communication, sharing tales of remarkable growth within their congregation.

Upon reaching the church, Bruce spotted Pastor Wayne diligently tending to the garden. The cool weather, though hindering flower growth, failed to dampen Wayne's unwavering commitment to his gardening endeavors. Pulling up beside him,

Bruce witnessed a moment of connection as Pastor Wayne looked up and greeted him with a warm smile.

"Pastor Bruce!" Pastor Wayne exclaimed, his excitement evident as he leaped out of the garden. "How are you?"

Bruce couldn't help but reciprocate the enthusiasm with a heartfelt smile. "Wayne, how are you?" he responded, stepping out of the car. "You're looking great. Enjoying some outdoor gardening?"

"I love the outdoors," Wayne replied, his tone taking on a hint of solemnity. "I'm so sorry about your church. Any progress on reopening since we last spoke?"

Bruce sighed, a mixture of frustration and determination in his voice. "No, they're still dragging their feet. But the school has been going well. We're seeing more and more people attending."

"That's great! Actually, I've been thinking... maybe we could join you on Tuesdays. And if you need a church for Sundays, you know you're always welcome here."

A renewed sense of hope flickered in Bruce's eyes. "I've been overwhelmed since George Hines left. He used to take care of the computer aspects and so much more."

"You know, Bruce, I could help you with that. In fact, I could assist you with many things. I understand there's a lot going on right now, and you must feel like Moses. Well, let me pitch in and help with this revival."

"I'm no Moses, but I am overwhelmed. That sounds great. What's new since we last spoke?"

Wayne's face lit up with enthusiasm, mirroring the spark in Bruce's eyes. "Well, you remember the incident with the men who passed away in our church."

"Yes!" Bruce exclaimed, a mix of curiosity and anticipation in his voice.

"Well, since then, everyone has become more serious about their faith. We've witnessed healings and salvations—it's been remarkable! But honestly, a lot of the things you're doing, like the website and prayer walks in the neighborhoods, we need to implement in our own church. How about we partner together and cover more ground?"

Bruce's heart swelled with gratitude. This was an answered prayer, a ray of hope breaking through the clouds. They promptly sat down and discussed everything that was happening, sharing the various areas of ministry. Then Wayne interjected with an idea, sparking a collaborative vision for the future.

"You know, Bruce, I love working outdoors. How about I swing by your church and breathe new life into the exterior? When God reopens it, it will look not just functional but truly fantastic," Pastor Wayne suggested, his eyes reflecting a genuine passion for the idea.

A warmth spread through Bruce as he considered the proposition. "I love that idea," he responded, humbly accepting Wayne's offer. The thought of their church receiving a revitalized touch brought a glimmer of anticipation to his eyes.

"In fact," Wayne continued, a spark of enthusiasm in his voice, "I'll bring our church members along, and we'll gather there to pray for God's glory to reopen the church. Let's make it a collective effort to usher in a new season."

Bruce's face lit up with gratitude and hope. "Let me know when you want to do this, and I'll gather our congregation as well," he eagerly replied, a sense of unity and purpose threading through his words. The prospect of joining forces for a shared cause filled the air with a renewed spirit of collaboration and camaraderie.

The foundation of Reverend Stone's new church had been laid and the walls were beginning to be erected. The tent had modest crowds, and a banner was placed over the entrance. It read, "ALL ARE WELCOME TO SERVE GOD." It was a white banner with black bold letters. Despite being blown off the front several times, it was now secured more firmly. As it was time for the church service, people started gathering. The crowd grew larger and larger in the tent, but the atmosphere was filled with anger rather than a spirit of worship. Murmurs of discontent spread throughout the space as people complained about the changes the revival had brought to their hometown, workplaces, and personal lives. They grumbled about having to travel out of town to get alcohol, cigarettes, tobacco, and mainstream magazines. Of course, nothing offensive was mentioned within the church, only the mention of mainstream magazines that had become ingrained in society.

Reverend Stone stood up, trying to quiet the crowd. Eventually, the noise subsided, and the silence allowed the sound of the wind whipping through the tent to be heard, whistling ominously. The visible evidence of the wind could be seen as people's hair and clothes blew around.

"I am shocked at the defiance of this community!" Reverend Stone began, his voice filled with emotion.

"We have warned them of God's impending judgment upon this idle and unproductive town. Now, we have no choice but to put our faith into action. We must take matters into our own hands," Reverend Stone paused, letting his words sink in.

"Their church has been closed by God's own hand, but they still fail to understand the message. We will make it crystal clear. This Tuesday night, we will gather together and not only picket but also prevent the defilement of our own town's school!" As he spoke, the crowd began to chime in, voicing their agreement with enthusiastic shouts of "Yes!" and "That's right!"

"We will not put up with this man-made 'revival' that is nothing but a counterfeit! It's an excuse for lazy Christians who refuse to work for God, wasting valuable time instead of bettering our town!" Reverend Stone's voice grew more intense as he launched into a tirade, targeting Bruce, his followers, the Tuesday night prayer meeting, and the changes taking place in the school system and their community.

As the wind roared with intensified fury, lashing at the trembling tent, Reverend Stone's voice reached a crescendo, saturated with anger and rage. "We will not tolerate this man's corruption in the name of God! We must obliterate it, using whatever means necessary. I don't care if it sounds threatening! We will unleash hell if it means obliterating this deceitful impostor!"

The crowd, fueled by the reverend's fury, erupted in a cacophony of shouts and curses. Fists clenched tightly, veins bulging on their foreheads, they vowed vengeance. Reverend Stone's malevolent grin widened, mirroring the darkness that consumed his soul. The wind's assault intensified, battering the feeble structure of the tent, yet the reverend remained undeterred.

"We shall crush him and his followers, leaving nothing but remnants of their pitiful existence!" Reverend Stone's voice boomed, drowning out the tempest's fury. His eyes burned with a twisted fervor as he reveled in the chaos he had summoned.

The crowd erupted, their shouts punctuated by death threats. Fists were raised, and anger filled the air. Reverend Stone's first smile of the night cracked across his face. Meanwhile, the wind grew even fiercer, capturing everyone's attention, including the reverend's. People looked around, contemplating whether they should seek shelter. But before a decision was made, the back of the tent tore open, capturing the gaze of all. A hushed silence fell, accompanied only by the relentless howling wind. Through the tear, a blinding white light flooded into the tent, brighter than anything they had ever seen.

The wind continued its assault, yet miraculously, the tent held together. People's hair whipped around, their bodies swayed, but they couldn't tear their eyes away from the spectacle unfolding at the back. As the radiant light persisted, squinting eyes caught sight of a figure emerging through the torn fabric. Cloaked in the light, the figure wore a pure white robe, and it was apparent that the light emanated from within. Slowly, the figure walked past the crowd, and one by one, each person fell to the ground in sheer terror.

Drawing nearer to the stage, the figure did not ascend but remained on the same level as the people. In one moment, it was grounded with them, and in the next, it stood on the stage, facing them. Reverend Stone, filled with terror, retreated backward, step by step, until the platform's edge prevented any further retreat. Then, he tumbled off the back of the stage, landing on the dirt floor below. Rising from the dust, his once-flowing robe now soiled, he pressed one hand against the floor, the other raised in desperate attempts to discern the nature of this enigmatic figure.

The voice that emanated from the figure reverberated through the air with a raw intensity, piercing the eardrums of all who heard it. It carried the weight of a thousand trumpets blaring in unison, its sound reminiscent of the relentless rush of water cascading down a thunderous waterfall. The sheer volume and power of the voice sent shockwaves through the trembling tent.

As the words reached their ears, those still on their feet instinctively clutched their ears, desperate to shield themselves from the overwhelming force. The anguish etched on their faces was raw, their eyes wide with a mix of awe and torment. Even those attempting to rise from the ground, disoriented and off-balance, succumbed to the compelling urge to cover their ears. Their efforts proved futile, causing them to lose their tenuous balance once more, their bodies crashing back onto the soiled floor of the tent.

The words reverberated in Hebrew, carrying a mystical weight that transcended linguistic barriers:

"'I ẏkâbôd kâbôd gâlâh!"

The figure's voice grew in intensity, repeating the phrase with escalating volume:

"'I ẏkâbôd kâbôd gâlâh!"

"'I ẏkâbôd kâbôd gâlâh!"

"'I ẏkâbôd kâbôd gâlâh!"

"'I ẏkâbôd kâbôd gâlâh!"

Each utterance pierced the air, carrying an enigmatic power that resonated deep within the souls of those present. The melodic rhythm of the ancient language held a mysterious cadence, captivating their attention and invoking a sense of reverence.

The foreign words, laden with meaning and significance, seemed to vibrate with an otherworldly energy. Their meaning eluded most, yet their presence evoked a sense of divine power and profound mystery. It was as if the very fabric of reality quivered under the weight of these sacred words, permeating the atmosphere with a transcendent aura.

Reverend Stone's complexion turned ashen, his face drained of all color. He recognized the Hebrew words and their profound meaning, sending a chilling realization down his spine.

"That's not true!" Reverend Stone bellowed, his voice strained with desperation and defiance. Half on the ground, half sitting up, he vehemently denied the truth that had been unveiled before him.

"No! No! The glory has not departed! This false prophet, this so-called pastor, has stolen it from our midst! He has robbed us of God's presence and glory in our town!" Reverend Stone's voice quivered with a mix of anger and anguish, his accusations reverberating through the silent air.

His gaze fixed upon Pastor Bruce, Reverend Stone's voice dripped with desperation and accusation. "Why have you done this to us, Pastor Bruce? Cursed be you and all your evil followers!"

The sudden silence engulfed the scene as the wind ceased its howling. All eyes shifted between the figure on the stage, radiating a divine presence, and their fallen leader on the soiled floor of the tent, defiantly confronting this celestial being. The crowd, momentarily stunned, quickly regained their anger, fueled by Reverend Stone's impassioned words.

"Yeah! We've done nothing wrong! Judge us and see! We've toiled for years in this community, making a difference through action, not mere words and empty visits!" Voices joined Reverend Stone's outburst, a cacophony of anger and renewed threats filled the space, fists raised defiantly in the air. Reverend Stone's smile, twisted with vindication, spread across his face, silently condoning the fervor and aggression of his followers.

In the midst of this collective rage, the tent bore witness to the clash of opposing forces—an encounter charged with emotion and escalating tensions.

"Ichabod!" The figure's voice thundered, and with a pointed gesture, drew the attention of the crowd to the tent wall behind the stage where Reverend Stone stood. Slowly, methodically, the word "Ichabod" materialized on the surface of the wall, each letter seared into place by a creeping fire. Yet amidst the chaos and uproar, the people scarcely noticed this supernatural occurrence, lost in their own tumultuous yelling.

"As requested, you are judged," the figure pronounced in a low, resonant voice that reverberated through the tent. In an instant, the figure transformed into a roaring blaze, engulfing everything within the tent. The flames devoured all, leaving nothing behind. The fire surged outward, consuming the newly laid foundation of the church, reducing construction materials, machinery, tools, and even the bulldozer and dump truck to ashes. Not a single plant, tree, blade of grass, or weed remained. The church property now lay in ruins, a vast expanse of desolate black ashes.

As the smoke gradually dissipated in the coolness of the night, a white object came into view, resting just off to the side where the tent once stood. It was a portion of the tent, bearing the word "ICHABOD" boldly inscribed upon it. Though scorched around the edges, the rest of the fabric remained untouched, pristine and white.

Amidst the arrival of fire trucks and ambulances from the town, the doors of the vehicles swung open, and the men within stared in disbelief at the smoldering aftermath. Soon, news crews descended upon the scene, representatives from the local TV station and the town paper, their cameras capturing the shocking sight. Once the initial shock subsided, a collective curiosity compelled everyone to gravitate towards the sole object that had withstood the inferno.

Bruce relished his time spent with Wayne, the day's events replaying in his mind as he made his way home. Nightfall had descended by the time he stepped into his house, a sense of tranquility washing over him. However, his peaceful demeanor shattered as he noticed the blinking light on his answering machine.

With a mix of anticipation and unease, he pressed the button and listened intently, his disbelief growing with each message. The urgency in the voices hinted at something grave, prompting Bruce to swiftly turn on the television and switch to the news channel. And there it was, displayed before his eyes, confirming the startling messages he had just heard. The screen portrayed the charred remnants of the land that Reverend Stone's church had once occupied.

"We are yet to determine the cause of the fire," the news reporter relayed, their voice tinged with uncertainty. "All we know is that the tent typically hosted small gatherings of devoted followers, ranging from 60 to 80 individuals. It appears that during tonight's meeting, an electrical fire erupted, engulfing all those present and eventually spreading throughout the area."

Bruce sank into his chair, his body barely making contact with its surface. Briefly realizing the need to rearrange the furniture to avoid these near misses, he then fixated his gaze on the TV screen, his mind grappling with the magnitude of what had occurred. The profound shock left him momentarily speechless, his thoughts racing to comprehend the inexplicable events unfolding before him.

"What remains unknown is the exact identity of those present inside the tent when the fire broke out. Authorities are receiving calls even as we speak, providing information about the individuals who had tragically attended this horrifying event," the reporter's voice trembled with a sense of urgency.

The reporter's tone shifted to one of perplexity as they continued, "What continues to baffle investigators is the disappearance of the newly laid church foundation, the construction fence, materials, and even the construction trucks that were on-site earlier today! All that remains now is this immense heap of ashes." The reporter's voice quivered with disbelief.

Amidst the ashes, there lay a solitary object that had managed to survive the inferno. The camera zoomed in, casting a bright light on it, revealing a fragment of the burnt tent with a word seared into it. Regrettably, the word was not in English or any recognizable language. It spelled out I-C-H-A-B-O-D, echoing with an eerie significance.

Upon witnessing this sight, Bruce's heart sank, his face drained of color, and his body went limp, overwhelmed by a profound sense of dread. "Oh Lord, what have you done?" he whispered in prayer, his voice filled with a mix of anguish and confusion.

Bruce slumped out of the chair and collapsed onto the floor, his gaze fixated on the TV screen. Acting swiftly, he rose to his feet, rushing over to grab his Bible. Frantically flipping through its pages, he located the passage he sought: "And she named the child Ichabod, saying, the glory is departed..." Bruce closed the Bible, his eyes returning to the television. The reporter's voice became a distant murmur as his mind raced. The words "the glory has departed... the glory has departed..." echoed relentlessly in his thoughts. Then, a realization struck him with such force that he fell to the floor once more, dropping to his knees in fervent prayer.

"Father God, you couldn't have..." Bruce couldn't bring himself to utter the words. Deep down, he already knew the answer. "Lord, you have judged those who opposed this revival, Your revival, Your very presence in this community. They went to great lengths to hinder it, and perhaps they were planning something that crossed the boundaries of grace." A scripture verse began to flood Bruce's mind, etching itself into his consciousness: "It is a fearful thing to fall into the hands of the living God." And another verse followed, "If we deliberately keep on sinning after we have received the knowledge of the truth, no sacrifice for sins is left, but only a fearful expectation of judgment and of raging fire that will consume the enemies of God."

"Lord, is this Your doing? Is it Your raging fire that consumes the enemies of God?" Bruce's voice trembled with a mixture of awe and apprehension. From the depths of his soul, beyond the realm of emotions and external influences, a resounding answer echoed within him. It was a resolute "Yes." Bruce remained seated on the floor, his gaze fixed on the TV screen, overwhelmed and bewildered. Time seemed to pass as he contemplated the situation.

Thoughts raced through Bruce's mind, a cascade of sermons and teachings unfolding like scenes from a vivid movie. Each sermon spoke of God's judgment, drawing parallels to His dealings with His people Israel, the inhabitants of Sodom and Gomorrah, and countless others. Bruce recalled the countless remarks he made about the punishment of the wicked, the inevitable fate of evil, and the eternal torment of Hell for those who opposed God and His kingdom. He never imagined witnessing such events in his lifetime, let alone in his own town. The unfolding revival had taken him by surprise.

Uncertain of what lay ahead, Bruce pondered his next course

of action. The idea of visiting the site, witnessing firsthand what had been broadcast on the TV, crossed his mind. Yet, he hesitated. It was late at night, and he questioned whether his emotions could withstand the experience. Nevertheless, he mustered enough resolve to call Pastor Wayne, engaging in a lengthy conversation about the shocking events. Once their conversation concluded, Bruce remained close to the phone, the TV providing a continuous stream of updates on the unfolding situation. He knew more phone calls would follow, keeping him informed and connected to the evolving reality.

TWELVE

The cell phone rang, and George glanced at John, a hint of surprise in his eyes.

"Well, aren't you going to answer it? It's your phone, not mine," John urged.

"This is the phone Advance Medical uses to contact me discreetly. They avoid using the business line to minimize the risk of being discovered," George explained. The ringing persisted as George picked up the call and cautiously said, "Hello?"

George's face turned pale, burdened by the weight of his emotions. It seemed that his emotional resilience was being tested lately, and this phone call only added to the already heavy load. His anxiety was overwhelming as he listened intently to the voice on the other end.

"Mr. Penkowski, what a pleasant surprise," George responded, attempting to maintain composure. John quickly retrieved a small device from his briefcase and discreetly attached it to the back of the cell phone. With a press of a button, he activated an earpiece, enabling him to listen to and record the conversation.

"Yes, sir. Everything is proceeding as planned. We are on track to achieve a disruptive rate of 75% in the existing inventory," George reported, his voice steady and professional.

"No, sir. The Fetal Research department remains oblivious to our actions. As our stock skyrockets, theirs plummets, just as we intended," George continued, a faint hint of color returning to his face. However, his demeanor remained impassive, his poker face perfected. This call marked a significant milestone for George; he had always interacted with vice presidents, assistant vice presidents, and similar figures, never directly with the owner of the company that had held him captive for years. It was a first for him, but given the unprecedented events of the day and his encounter with John, it was just another extraordinary development in his life—an unexpected but fitting addition to the chain of remarkable occurrences.

"You're coming for a visit to our facility? That's great! I'll make sure everything is in order for your arrival," George responded, his voice filled with anticipation. John listened intently, intrigued by the conversation unfolding.

"Will you be in disguise?" George inquired, curious about the owner's plans.

"I see. That should work well. I've been looking forward to finally meeting you," George replied, a hint of excitement in his voice.

"I'll be happy to pick you up at the airport. We'll talk more then. Goodbye," George concluded the call.

"Well, that was quite something," George remarked, still buzzing from the conversation.

"I can't believe he called you! Have you ever spoken to him in person before?" John asked, amazed by the turn of events.

"No, this was the first time," George confirmed.

"He didn't sound agitated. I wonder if he's gotten over the break-in and the destruction of his office," John pondered, a smile playing on his lips.

"Who is Dr. Myer?" George inquired, curious about the individual mentioned during the call.

"Dr. Myer is one of Penkowski's associates in town. He's a plastic surgeon involved in their operations. I managed to secure some of the financial stock awards you were discussing with Penkowski during my last visit with him," John explained.

George looked at John, a mixture of curiosity and amusement on his face. "Official work, of course. I like my face just the way it is... well, when it actually looks like me and not someone else. You know what I mean! Man, I'm confusing myself!"

The two friends burst into laughter, savoring the much-needed break from the intensity of their recent adventures.

"So... he's coming to town," John stated, placing a finger on his lip, lost in thought. He then moved his hands to his forehead, rubbing it as he contemplated the situation.

"You know, George, I don't think he cares so much about the facility as he does about getting to me. I can't believe he's coming in person! We must have really gotten under his skin," John mused, a mischievous grin forming on both their faces.

"Alright, we have a lot of work to do before Penkowski arrives. Since he didn't provide a specific time or date, let's assume we have a week. The more time we have, the better," John suggested.

"What's our first move?" George asked, eager to tackle the upcoming tasks.

"First things first, we need to get you back to your job. You can check in with Denis Spense, oversee the operations, and ensure everything is in order for Penkowski's visit," John replied.

"And what about you?" George inquired.

"I'll let Dennis know how instrumental you've been in assisting me. I'll handle any ongoing investigation questions he has. I'll also contact my sister, Elizabeth, or as we call her, Lizy, and see if she's up for the challenge. I'm willing to bet she'll take it on. It might even help alleviate some of the guilt she's been feeling. I'll get started on this right away," John outlined his plan.

As they continued their discussion, George and John packed up their belongings and checked out of the hotel. Soon, they found themselves aboard a plane, leaving sunny California behind as they embarked on the next phase of their adventure.

Bruce awoke this morning with a sense of impending change. The absence of Reverend Stone's constant presence was a relief, but the circumstances surrounding his departure sent shivers down Bruce's spine. It instilled a deep fear within him, reminding him of the awe-inspiring nature of the God he served. The words of a verse echoed in his mind: "The fear of the Lord is the beginning of wisdom." Bruce had always held a reverential fear of God, or so he believed. However, this recent event elevated his understanding of God's power and presence.

Setting aside these thoughts, Bruce resolved to move forward with his day, starting as he always did—with dedicated time spent in communion with God. After concluding his devotional time, he turned his attention to his computer. As he went through his emails, he noticed the absence of the nagging fear of receiving unwelcome threats. There was no reason to fear anymore. God had intervened, removing his most dreaded adversary from the equation. Bruce leaned back, contemplating this realization. But before he could fully process it, the phone rang, interrupting his thoughts.

"Hello?" Bruce answered the phone.

"Mr. Hutchinson?" the voice on the other end confirmed.

"Yes," Bruce replied, his voice filled with anticipation.

"This is the Department of Health."

"Yes," Bruce responded, his excitement growing.

"We have thoroughly reviewed your case regarding the closure of your church, and we have determined that all requirements have been met. We have dispatched someone today to remove the sign and unlock the front doors."

"That's fantastic news! I only wish this had happened sooner," Bruce exclaimed, his elation evident.

"Your file was held up in a... department. It was discovered this morning when one of our employees failed to show up for work," the voice explained, pausing for a moment as if regaining composure.

"In any case, we apologize for the delay. Have a pleasant day." With that, the call ended with a click.

Bruce's mind spun with confusion. What had just transpired? The memories of the church's closure, the locked doors, the chilling encounter with that man—everything flooded back. But something didn't add up. The voice on the phone was different from the person who served him the closure notice. Carl Milan, that was the man's name. Bruce sprang to his feet and hurried outside to retrieve the morning newspaper, faithfully placed on the front patio step as always.

Ripping open the plastic wrapping, Bruce turned to the front page, bypassing the accompanying photos, and delved into the continuation of last night's tragic incident. As his gaze traveled downward, he came across a list of names. These were the individuals believed to have attended the meeting in the tent. Swiftly scanning through the names, he found the one he sought—Carl Milan.

Carl must have been responsible for obstructing the church's reopening, Bruce surmised. However, his excitement for the church's revival overshadowed any lingering concerns about Carl Milan or the harrowing episode the church had endured. Finishing up reading and responding to his emails, Bruce hopped into his car and sped off to the church.

Upon arrival, a bustling group of people greeted his eyes. They were diligently working on the church, tending to the grounds, and the doors stood wide open. Gone were the locks, and individuals flowed in and out with their arms full of paint cans, brushes, rollers, vacuum cleaners, and various cleaning supplies. Bruce recognized the familiar faces and their leader—Pastor Wayne and his devoted congregation. As Bruce pulled up to the church, Wayne spotted him and sprinted over, radiating joy. Once again, a sense of profound gratitude washed over Bruce, and memories of his transformed home flooded his mind.

"Bruce! Bruce!" Wayne's words were a blur as Bruce tried to decipher them through the closed car window.

Finally, the window lowered, rendering lip-reading unnecessary.

"Bruce! You won't believe what happened!" Wayne's excitement was contagious.

"Hey, Wayne. What brings you here?" Bruce replied, his face breaking into a wide smile, a familiar tear glistening in his eye.

"Brother, I told you we were coming over with our church to help prepare yours for the grand reopening," Wayne exclaimed, his grin matching Bruce's.

"This is incredible! Just look at all these people... Wait, is that my carpet?" Bruce's eyes widened as he noticed the distinctive orange hue stretching out like a beacon from afar.

"Yeah, one of our members owns a carpet store, and they had a massive clearance sale. Hope you don't mind us choosing the color," Wayne explained, his own smile undeterred.

"Mind? Anything is better than that outdated, burnt orange shag carpet. It has served us well over the years," Bruce chuckled, shifting his tone to one of gratitude. "We are truly thankful."

Bruce's grin widened, his heart filled with a renewed sense of joy and anticipation for the church's resurrection.

Bruce stepped out of the car, still engaged in conversation with Wayne.

"When did they open the church?" Bruce asked, curious about the timing.

"We arrived bright and early this morning. We gathered around the church, holding hands and praying. We asked God to open the doors and bestow His blessings upon this church, now that His people have returned. As we started working on the exterior, a car pulled up. The driver asked if Mr. Hutchinson was here. I informed him that you would be arriving shortly. Apparently, he didn't want to wait and assumed we were part of your congregation. So, he opened the lock, took down the sign, and wished us a good day," Wayne explained.

"They called me this morning and told me the same, which is why I rushed over," Bruce replied.

"Well, we've been busy ever since, and we're almost finished," Wayne replied, gesturing towards the bustling crowd of people carrying tools, paint, and fresh flowers.

"Wayne, this is amazing! I'm thrilled! Our church has needed some repairs, and this is exactly what we needed," Bruce exclaimed, gratitude shining through his words.

"I've been working closely with Sue and Maggie. They've helped revitalize my church with neighborhood walks, home Bible studies, emails, and we've also collaborated to assist you in George's absence," Wayne said.

Bruce's smile faded momentarily, but Wayne's reassurance brought it back.

"Hey, I've been praying for George. He'll be fine. He's in God's care," Wayne reassured Bruce.

Bruce's smile returned, and his excitement peaked.

"Come on! Let me show you what we've accomplished!" Wayne said, eager to share in the joy of the church's transformation.

Wayne turned and briskly walked towards the church, enthusiastically explaining all the exterior work that had been done, including landscaping, painting, pressure cleaning, and even the replacement of the floodlight that illuminated the cross on the steeple.

As they entered the church, Bruce noticed the beginning of the installation of the new carpet, which looked beautiful. The walls had a fresh coat of paint, and every piece of wood, including the pulpit, had been newly varnished, giving them a brand new appearance. Bruce also noticed that the heating system was working efficiently, providing warmth on this cold day. The heating and air conditioning units had been replaced as well, leaving nothing untouched.

"Wayne, I'm at a loss for words. Thank you so much," Bruce expressed his gratitude sincerely.

Wayne smiled warmly in response.

Curiosity sparked within Bruce as he pointed towards the stained glass, where activity was taking place.

"What are they doing up there?" Bruce asked, observing the transformation of the stained glass.

"One of our members stumbled upon a new chemical compound that can be purchased online. He's an avid tinkerer and enjoys restoring antiques. Well, he found this website promising to restore stained glass to its original state. He bought the product, tried it in his shop, and it worked wonders. So, he brought it here to the church, and as you can see, it has breathed new life into the stained glass," Wayne explained.

"It's beautiful. I never knew what it looked like when it was new. By the time I arrived, it had lost its luster and colors. This is simply amazing!" Bruce stood in awe before the meticulously restored stained glass, marveling at how it brilliantly glistened with a kaleidoscope of colors, each hue captivated and intensified by the warm embrace of sunlight pouring through.

Feeling overwhelmed by the changes, Bruce walked over to a pew and sat down, taking in all that had been done.

Finally finding the courage, Bruce managed to utter the heartfelt words, "What can I do to help?"

In response, Wayne's face lit up with a warm smile. "You can start by putting your belongings back in your office."

With a nod, Bruce made his way to his car. Opening the trunk, he carefully retrieved a box while Wayne handled the other. As they exchanged smiles, a silent understanding passed between them. Together, they walked into Bruce's office.

The room had undergone a remarkable transformation; every detail, from the freshly laid carpet to the newly painted walls and the gleaming furniture, had been meticulously redone. It surpassed even its previous state. Bruce gently set down the box, sinking into the welcoming embrace of his familiar office chair. It had been a while since he had occupied that sacred space, and the sensation of returning felt more comforting than he could express. Here, in the heart of God's house, Bruce knew he was where he truly belonged.

"Hello?"

"Elizabeth, it's John."

"John, how are you? I've been thinking a lot about you. Is everything okay?"

Her voice held a mix of concern and anticipation, eager to

unravel the mystery behind John's call.

"It's funny you ask."

A sigh slipped through John's words, carrying the weight of untold stories and concealed worries.

"What do you mean?"

"Well, since we last talked, I didn't want to burden you with everything that has been going on, but yes, I've been evading danger."

The word 'danger' lingered in the air, casting a shadow over their conversation.

"John, are you okay? Tell me what's happening. Is there anything I can do to help?"

Elizabeth's voice trembled with genuine worry, an unspoken promise to stand by John's side.

"As a matter of fact, there is something you can do to help me, a friend, and many others who are contemplating..."

John hesitated, delicately avoiding the term that had once brought Elizabeth to tears.

"Lizzy, you can help me. But I must warn you, it's very dangerous. You may even risk your life."

A heavy pause settled between their words, the gravity of the situation sinking in. Then, with unwavering determination, Elizabeth responded.

"John, you know I would do anything for you. You're my brother. I love you, and if I can help you get out of harm's way, I would do it in a heartbeat."

"Let's meet in person. I'm in Stapleton. Could you come here and spend some time?"

"I'm in between cases right now. I'll be there tomorrow. Let's meet at the airport."

"Lizzy, if you change your mind, I'll understand. But you're my only hope."

The vulnerability in John's plea echoed through the phone, forging a bond of trust and reliance between siblings.

George returned to his job swiftly. Despite being away for only a short time, his role as the boss meant he frequently moved in and out of the office. As he settled down at his desk, conflicting emotions washed over him. It felt good to be in a place where bullets weren't flying and life seemed somewhat normal again. However, it also reminded him of the sense of entrapment he had experienced. Going through his files and reports, he discovered that inspections continued to conceal the truth, claiming everything was fine despite the production of subpar products.

The revival had caused a reduction in his staff. While most workers were unaware of the underlying situation, some had figured out the connection to The Association for Fetal Research, the parent company, and wanted no part in it. George walked through his plant, observing the machines, assessing productivity, and avoiding prolonged eye contact with his employees. Maintaining a distant, superficial relationship with his colleagues made it easier to deceive, although it was difficult for him to continue the charade.

George longed to call Bruce and inform him of his return to town, but he couldn't risk exposing his closest and dearest friend to the dangers that had closely followed him in recent days. No, he decided to wait until more of the mystery was unraveled and he could regain the freedom he had once cherished before joining Advance Medical. He understood that things would likely worsen before they improved.

With determination fueling her every step, Elizabeth embarked on the first plane to Stapleton, her heart set on reuniting with her brother. The small airport welcomed her, revealing a unique aircraft feature—a door that opened directly to the ground, its attached stairs guiding passengers towards the terminal. Amid the bustling crowd, John's anxious eyes darted, desperately seeking the familiar face of his sister. Deep in cover, he understood the need to stand out to Elizabeth.

And then, like a captivating vision, there she emerged. Gracefully descending the stairs, Elizabeth exuded a striking beauty, her attire balancing professionalism with a hint of femininity. In a world fraught with challenges, she radiated resilience—a woman unafraid of the risks and dangers that lay ahead in John's mysterious proposition. As she drew nearer, their eyes briefly locked, a fleeting connection before she looked away.

"Lizzy, it's me, John!" he called out, his eyes alight with a mixture of relief and excitement.

Elizabeth did a double take, recognizing the mischievous nature that had often fooled her in their younger days. A wide smile broke across her face as she enveloped him in a long, heartfelt hug.

"John, you're at it again!" she exclaimed, holding onto him tightly, savoring the joy of their reunion.

"I had to, Lizzy. My life is in danger. It's so good to see you!" he replied, the embrace offering a moment of solace and reassurance amid the turmoil.

Reluctantly parting, John guided his sister toward the airport, attending to her belongings before leading her to his home. During the drive, he shared a detailed account of the unfolding events, conveying the gravity of the situation and outlining what he needed from her in terms of legal expertise. The air hung heavy with a mixture of emotions—fear, relief, and the unbreakable bond between siblings.

Arriving at the house, a profound sense of tranquility washed over John. For the first time in a while, he felt a glimmer of contentment as he stepped through the familiar threshold. The solitude that once pervaded these walls would now be replaced by the comforting presence of someone he held dear to his heart. Though his soul yearned for a true companion, his thoughts turned to Maggie, envisioning her as the perfect soul mate to complement his life.

"Are we safe here, John?" Elizabeth asked, her voice tinged with concern.

"Oh, yes. I've taken all the necessary precautions. We have new names and identities," John reassured her, his confidence a shield against the uncertainties that loomed.

As they settled down, John retrieved the stack of papers they had obtained with George's assistance during their trip to California. Elizabeth sifted through the documents, her admiration growing with each passing page.

"You've gathered enough evidence to bring both of these companies down," she remarked, impressed by the extent of their findings.

"That's the plan," John affirmed, determination evident in his voice.

Curiosity danced in Elizabeth's eyes as she questioned, "Why?

What have these companies done?"

John had intentionally shielded Elizabeth from the specific details, wanting to spare her further pain. However, the time had come for her to understand the gravity of their actions. With heartfelt sincerity, he began to disclose the truth.

"I know you've endured immense hardships recently, and I don't wish to add to your suffering. But I cannot bear to let these companies continue inflicting pain on innocent lives."

Elizabeth's gaze grew more intense, awaiting the revelation that would unsettle her.

Meeting her eyes, John took her hand, his voice filled with compassion as he continued, "The Association for Fetal Research is the owner of the abortion clinic you visited."

Elizabeth recoiled, pulling her hand away and turning away from John, overwhelmed by the realization.

Undeterred, John pressed on. Taking a deep breath, he resumed, "Advance Medical has been undermining The Association in their quest for dominance. However, Advance Medical is even more malevolent than The Association. They have my friend trapped, and if he resigns from his position, they will kill him. They have already made numerous attempts on my life."

Elizabeth turned around, her once vibrant blue eyes now reddened and brimming with tears. After a moment of contemplation, she reached out, gripping John's shoulder tightly, and held him in a warm embrace.

"I will help," she declared, determination shining through her tears. "Together, we will ensure that neither of these companies can inflict harm on anyone ever again."

After exchanging updates on family news and regaining composure, they returned their attention to the papers, sorting them into different piles, each document representing a crucial piece of the puzzle they were determined to solve. The air was thick with a sense of purpose, and the room echoed with the weight of their shared mission.

Seated together, Wayne and Bruce delved into a conversation about the unfolding events within their community. Wayne shared the happenings in his church, underlining the interconnected nature of these occurrences.

"We need a collective effort," Wayne stated, his gaze wandering briefly up and down. A sigh escaped him before he continued, "Bruce, we have access to a spacious location at the school, larger than both our churches combined. We need a headquarters where we can gather and oversee all aspects of community activities."

Bruce regarded Wayne thoughtfully, a smile of agreement shaping his face. "You're absolutely right! This will help us organize various events, discern God's work, and find ways to join Him," Bruce responded, his mind already brimming with ideas, echoing Wayne's enthusiasm.

"Why not invite all the community leaders to meet there? We can offer support and assess their needs," Wayne proposed.

And so, they forged plans—plans that felt divinely inspired.

Their first call was to Sue, who enthusiastically received their call and volunteered to reach out to all individuals responsible for neighborhood walks and prayer groups.

Next, they contacted Maggie, who assumed responsibility for connecting with individuals involved in musical activities, including those participating in new performances at the local theater. Maggie also extended her outreach to the international recording agency she collaborated with for her music project.

Their efforts continued with calls to all those who initiated the 30 prayer groups in various workplaces and schools throughout the community.

Finally, Bruce brought up the internet site that George had recently completed. Each area now had its independent page, featuring information on prayer walks, specific groups, instant messaging for fostering connections, and even a section dedicated to music and plays. George had done an exceptional job. Now, Wayne and Bruce faced the task of introducing these new tools to people in each area.

Sue and Bruce had used the internet informally before, but now it would become a valuable asset for all leaders to monitor, communicate, and offer specific prayers for the entire community.

Lastly, Wayne sent an email to everyone in the community, introducing himself to those who may not have known him. He shared his new involvement and emphasized that Bruce's church would be there to support every individual engaged in the revival in any capacity. The email was signed off as a joint message from Bruce and Wayne, symbolizing their united efforts.

In the wake of their strategic plans, a sense of purpose and anticipation filled the air, carrying the promise of transformative unity within their community.

George sensed the approaching moment, the time to face the man who had nearly snuffed out his life—saved only by divine intervention. As he shuffled papers and organized files, a sense of urgency hung in the air. With a watchful eye, he scanned his personal computer, searching for any anomalies. Logging into the company's network, he meticulously inspected for red flags, addressing minor issues along the way. Yet, there was nothing of significant concern.

Next, George accessed the church's internet site, curious if Bruce had initiated its use. Navigating through the pages, he detected signs of activity—a glimmer of hope amid overwhelming darkness. Checking his email, he found a message notifying him of the newly reopened headquarters at Bruce's church. A smile formed on George's face, absorbing the news like a beacon of reassurance.

"Mr. Hines? Mr. Penkowski and Doctor Myers are here to see you," the voice on the intercom announced.

George's breath caught in his throat. "Mr. Hines? Are you there?" the voice persisted.

Breathe, George. Just breathe, he thought, attempting to steady himself.

"Yes... Please, let them in," George managed to reply, his voice betraying the mix of emotions swirling within.

A significant disadvantage without his partner by his side, George felt vulnerable—emotionally and physically. He took a deep breath, summoning the courage to stand up and face the impending challenge.

As the door swung open, Penkowski entered, accompanied by an unfamiliar man. Penkowski wore an expensive suit, while the doctor still sported his white smock, likely coming straight from his office.

"Good morning, gentlemen. How are you?" George forced out, masking inner apprehension.

"Good morning, George. This is Dr. Myers, a local physician and a personal friend of mine," Penkowski introduced.

George extended his hand, shaking hands with Dr. Myers.

"Good morning, Dr. Myers. Welcome to AFT Manufacturing."

Each man exchanged smiles, but these smiles seemed akin to the smirks worn by successful bank robbers who had gotten away with their heist. Not a hint of recognition crossed Penkowski's face from their previous encounter. John's disguise had worked marvelously, and George now appreciated the effort put into his transformation. The room held an air of tension, a silent dance of hidden truths and concealed identities.

They gathered around a small conference table in George's office, the hum of the computer screen providing a backdrop to their unfolding plot. As George navigated through various screens, a sense of satisfaction ripened on their faces. And rightfully so, as each screen unveiled the damning impact of Advance Medical on AFT. Decreased production led to a scarcity of products, and the use of subpar materials resulted in shoddy workmanship despite the facade of superiority.

Charts and diagrams sprawled across the screen, allowing Penkowski to trace the descent outlined by bare charts and shrinking pie charts. Dr. Myers expressed contentment with the evidence presented.

Seated beside them, George silently prayed for continued success. Though everything seemed to be progressing well, a vigilant air lingered. Occasionally, their gazes would shift towards him, prompting George to conjure a forced smile, concealing any signs of worry.

"How do you maintain morale and prevent the workers from discovering our activities here?" Dr. Myers inquired, prompting George to draw a deep breath before responding.

"I ensure constant and frequent rotation of our employees across different production lines," George explained. "This keeps them engaged in new tasks, maintaining a dynamic pace and boosting morale. It also prevents them from seeing the bigger picture. They assume there are always some products that fail inspection, never suspecting that it's every product in one way or another. Additionally, we provide them with a robust 401K program and other benefits to deter them from seeking trouble. Occasionally, someone starts to piece things together, but before they can do so, I dismiss them. It's a rare occurrence, though."

Dr. Myers further probed, "Have you encountered any issues with unemployment compensation for these individuals?" Penkowski smiled, glancing back at George.

"No, we haven't," George replied confidently. "We have a lenient clock-in system for our employees. It's not the most accurate, you know." A wave of nausea washed over George as he forced yet another smile and continued, "The employees who were let go had falsified their clock-in and clock-out times. The papers they signed upon hiring explicitly stated that such behavior would result in immediate dismissal."

As those words left his lips, George felt a weight settle in the pit of his stomach. Perhaps it was because both Penkowski and Dr. Myers exchanged satisfied glances. It was time to extricate himself from this self-created nightmare. This encounter felt like the climax, leaving George to wonder how things could possibly get any worse. Despite his commitment to God, here he was, face-to-face with Penkowski, forced to confront the magnified consequences of his actions.

"Shall we take a tour of the facility?" Penkowski suggested, and George took a deep breath as they embarked on the tour, each step echoing the unsettling journey into the depths of moral compromise.

As Wayne and Bruce meticulously worked on their plans in Bruce's newly remodeled and reopened church, an unexpected weight settled upon them, casting a pall over their surroundings. Instinctively, they paused in their tasks, seeking solace in separate chairs. A chilling awareness gripped them, unmistakable and foreboding—the unmistakable presence of evil.

"I can't shake this unsettling feeling, Bruce. It's incredibly dark and malevolent," Wayne confessed, his eyes casting an expectant glance at his companion, yearning for reassurance.

"Absolutely! I feel it too. It's deeply unsettling. Let's turn to prayer," Bruce responded, his voice laden with concern.

Both pastors lowered themselves to their knees, the emptiness of the church amplifying the intensity of their encounter. As they began to pour out their hearts in prayer, everything initially seemed ordinary. They started with adoration, expressing their reverence for God. They moved on to gratitude, offering heartfelt thanks. Then, with unreserved passion, they engaged in worship, exalting their Savior. But suddenly, an unforeseen disturbance shattered the tranquility of their prayer time.

Wayne abruptly ceased his prayer, freezing in mid-sentence. Bruce, sensing the disruption, raised his head to investigate. However, upon opening his eyes, he realized his vision was impaired, clouded by an inexplicable haze. He closed his eyes once again, rubbing them fervently, desperate to restore clarity. When he reopened them, he beheld a startling sight. His pastor friend remained kneeling motionless, accompanied by an extraordinary presence. This was no ordinary man.

The pastors stared in awe, beholding a figure resembling the Son of Man. He was clothed in a robe that cascaded to his feet, a resplendent golden sash adorning his chest. His head and hair gleamed white as wool, while his piercing eyes blazed like flames of fire. His feet radiated a radiant glow, resembling molten metal, and his voice resonated like the thunderous roar of a mighty waterfall.

Bruce and Wayne remained frozen, their bodies paralyzed in awe. In fact, their faces turned blue as their very breath was robbed from them. They gasped for air, desperately struggling to fill their lungs. Just when they thought they couldn't endure it any longer, the man blew upon them, and a rush of air surged into their chests, reviving them. Relief washed over them as they took in deep, life-giving breaths.

"I am the First and will be the Last. I am the One Alive, though I was dead, and I tell you, I will live forever and ever!" The words reverberated through the air, resonating with power and resounding volume, causing their hearts to tremble.

"I am aware of the insults and character assassination of those who claim to be Christians but are not. They belong to the church of Satan. I have removed them from this community. Now, I tell you, do not be afraid of what you are about to suffer. The devil will fiercely oppose you and your ongoing work for Me. You will face greater persecution in the days to come than you have ever experienced in your lives. Remain faithful to Me, even unto death, and I will bestow upon you the radiant crown of eternal life."

Bruce and Wayne remained immobile, their bodies transfixed in the presence of the glorified form they believed to be their Lord and Savior. The man extended His hand, gently touching both pastors, and then, in an instant, vanished without a trace.

As their muscles slowly regained their functionality, Bruce and Wayne mustered their breath, attempting to articulate their bewildering encounter. The air in the church felt charged with an otherworldly energy, and the echoes of divine words lingered, leaving an indelible mark on their souls.

"I... can't... believe... was that who I think it was?" Bruce stammered, his mind struggling to comprehend the magnitude of the ethereal encounter.

"Yes... I... believe we just heard... saw..." Wayne's voice faltered, overwhelmed by the extraordinary reality of their encounter.

"Christ?"

And then, an indescribable joy enveloped Wayne, spilling over in unrestrained elation. "Jesus! Jesus! We just saw Jesus! Hallelujah!"

Gradually rising to their feet, albeit with aching bodies protesting the extended period of kneeling, Wayne couldn't contain his excitement. He began to leap and bound, exclaiming, "Hallelujah! We saw Jesus! My precious Jesus! My Savior! The one I've longed to see all my life... Jesus... we just saw Jesus!"

Bruce, however, settled into a chair and gazed pensively out the window. He would occasionally steal glances at Wayne, offering a fleeting smile before turning his attention back to the world beyond the glass.

"Hey, Bruce, aren't you excited? Jesus! We saw Jesus!" Wayne asked, puzzled by his companion's subdued demeanor.

"I can't fathom why the Lord God Almighty would grace me with His presence in all His glory. Wayne, who am I? Who am I to receive such an honor?" Bruce questioned, his voice tinged with humility.

Wayne's smile conveyed the profound truth he was about to share. "You are a blood-bought, God-chosen, divinely created individual who has willingly embraced not only the right but the narrow path, meticulously mapped out by the Lord God Almighty. You have made yourself available to God as a commanding officer in His spiritual army, and now the Chief in Command has personally conveyed His orders to you."

"Personally? Why personally?" Bruce stood attentively, awaiting Wayne's response.

"Because, my friend, He is a Personal God."

Bruce's smile flickered momentarily, his expression shifting to contemplation. "What about the evil we sensed and prayed about? I still perceive its presence, although not as strongly as when we began praying."

"I believe Jesus' presence quelled the intensity of that evil presence. However, He did forewarn us that we would face suffering. But what will we suffer from? The troublemakers are no longer among us."

Yet, the lingering question remained: Were the troublemakers truly gone, especially with Penkowski's presence in town? The room held the echoes of the divine encounter, a blend of elation, humility, and an underlying sense of foreboding that lingered in the air.

THIRTEEN

George proceeded with the tour that Penkowski offered, but deep inside, he couldn't shake the blatant audacity of Penkowski's presence in their own manufacturing facility, owned by The Association. The tension in the air was tangible, like a storm brewing on the horizon. What if Dennis Spence suddenly appeared today? The resulting chaos would be explosive. Penkowski didn't even bother hiding his identity or the companion he had brought along. They moved through each area, from assembly lines to the stockroom, accounting department, and even the shipping area. No corner was left unseen.

As Penkowski and George approached the front door of AFT, they exchanged handshakes, preparing to exit. In that critical moment, George's gaze lifted, and he witnessed a sight that petrified him in place. It was like witnessing an inevitable car crash, where you see it coming but are utterly powerless to intervene. Dennis Spence, the head of The Association for Fetal Research, was walking towards the building. This was the moment of reckoning. The charade would soon be over. Surely, they would recognize each other, and George's life-altering mistake would be exposed.

The door swung open, and before Penkowski could glance up, he bumped into Dennis.

"Excuse me," Penkowski muttered, swiftly moving on with Dr. Myers in tow.

Dennis looked at Penkowski, but Penkowski arrogantly brushed him off, engrossed in conversation with Dr. Myers.

"Business is good, as I was saying, and I can see how..." The conversation faded as the door closed behind them, leaving Penkowski and Dr. Myers outside the building.

Dennis continued peering through the window, attempting to

discern the identities of these unfamiliar figures. Then his gaze shifted towards George, and in that moment, George contemplated reverting to his old habits of drinking. The weight of the situation tempted him to seek solace in the familiar embrace of a bottle once again.

Lord, George prayed silently, please forgive my jesting. And with renewed determination, George began his prayers anew, starting from the moment Penkowski walked through the door with his doctor friend. The air in the room was charged with a mixture of fear, anticipation, and the gravity of the choices made and yet to be made.

Penkowski sped through town with an air of urgency, the weight of undisclosed motives resting heavily on his shoulders. Dr. Myers, keenly observant, couldn't ignore the restlessness emanating from Penkowski's demeanor and cautiously inquired, "Are you okay?"

"Oh, just fine," Penkowski replied, attempting to conceal the true intentions that fueled his visit to the town. "I've never been to this town before, and I think I'll spend the day here."

"I could show you around," offered Dr. Myers.

"No, I want to explore the potential for growth...do some research at City Hall...all that stuff," Penkowski deflected, evading any offered assistance. "Alright then. Let me know if there's anything I can do. Call me later, and we can have lunch or dinner. By the way, I'm extremely pleased with our stock. I've already made a fortune from it," Dr. Myers exclaimed.

A sly smile crept across Penkowski's face as he dropped off Dr. Myers at his office. Then, Penkowski set out to explore the city. His gaze intensified with curiosity whenever something caught his attention. He first noticed the closed liquor stores, then drove past boarded-up abortion clinics. While stopping to refuel, he observed the lack of vibrant magazine choices and the presence of Christian merchandise strategically placed throughout the store by the employees.

As he returned to the car, his eyes were drawn to an unusual sight. Amidst the bustling cityscape, there stood a large open area, completely shrouded in darkness. It was as if a mountain of ashes had accumulated, forming a blackened expanse. Penkowski halted the car, his gaze fixed upon the enigmatic scene, his brow raised in bewilderment.

Someone approached the car and gestured towards the site. Penkowski rolled down his window, intrigued by the unfolding story.

"This used to be our biggest church in town," the person began, pointing at the blackened expanse. "First, a tornado destroyed it. Then the Reverend tried to rebuild it. The other night, they were having a service in a newly erected tent, and bam! It all went up in flames. Nothing left. Even the construction equipment burned up! If you ask me, it's strange, weird, like something out of the Twilight Zone or something."

Penkowski nodded, absorbing the information. "Can you tell me if you know a John Ivan who lives in town?"

"No, sir, never heard of the man," the person replied.

"Thank you for your time," Penkowski acknowledged, rolling up his window and waving to the individual.

With a determined stride, Penkowski parked his car on the street near the area. Stepping out, he made his way towards the center of the ashes. Each crunch of the ashes beneath his dress shoes seemed to beckon him closer. His gaze fell upon a fragment of the tent, its white fabric displaying the words "ICHA BOD." He picked it up, studying it momentarily before dropping it without a care. Stepping on the tent piece, a realization dawned upon Penkowski. As he slowly looked up from the ground, a mischievous smile curled on his lips. The sight before him held a deeper meaning than he had initially grasped. The air hung heavy with an unspoken tension, as Penkowski navigated the town, uncovering a narrative that promised both intrigue and potential danger.

"I am pleased to see you, Dennis. What do I owe the pleasure to?" George's voice carried a mixture of relief and cautious anticipation. The weight of the situation hung in the air, and George was acutely aware of the gravity of his words.

Dennis's curiosity burned bright as he inquired, "Who were those people that I bumped into?"

George's mind raced, searching for a believable response. "They are distributors. They were very impressed with AFT and wanted to visit our facility."

A glimmer of satisfaction flickered in Dennis's eyes. "They will be doubling their orders as a result of what they saw today."

Suppressing his guilt, George fervently prayed for forgiveness. Though he was lying to the enemy, his desperation justified his actions. "Impressed they were, to say the least."

The two men embarked on the tour once again, retracing the steps George had just taken with Penkowski and Dr. Myers. But this time, George had to weave a web of deceit, offering a contradictory narrative to protect the plan he had devised with John. The urge to call John and share the events with Penkowski tugged at George, fueling his desire to unburden himself. Now, he had a double story to tell, with Dennis's unexpected visit adding a new layer of complexity.

Dennis's prideful smile faded, replaced by a grave seriousness. "George, let's go back to your office. I have some things I want to talk to you about."

As they made their way back, George's heart raced, uncertain of what awaited him in the private conversation with Dennis. The weight of their secrets bore down on him, amplifying the intensity of the moment.

"I am excited about our Lord, yes, very excited. But, I was hoping for a positive message. Wayne, God has just told us that we are in grave danger, and that our lives may be lost in the upcoming days. Doesn't that shake you up a little?" Bruce's voice quivered with a mix of fear and urgency, his words cutting through the air like a chilling gust of wind.

Wayne's smile faded, replaced by a somber expression. He met Bruce's gaze, searching for words that could bring solace in the face of impending danger. But in that moment, even Wayne found himself at a loss for what to say.

"Well, I am usually the one to get a little shaken by things, but, you know, I am just fine," Bruce responded, his voice carrying a tinge of reassurance.

Confusion etched Wayne's face as he probed for further understanding. "What do you mean?"

Bruce's unwavering faith shone through his words as he sought to quell Wayne's concerns. "Well, I just know that everything we have been through to this point, God has been faithful to take care of us, even when we couldn't figure out how He was going to do it."

Wayne remained skeptical, but Bruce pressed on, determined to strengthen their resolve. "He said to be faithful. He is only asking us to do what He has done."

A glimmer of understanding flickered in Wayne's eyes as the weight of Bruce's words sank in. A smile tugged at the corners of his lips. "What do we do next?"

Bruce's voice resonated with conviction as he declared their course of action. "We keep doing exactly what God has called us to do. We will not do anything different."

In the face of impending danger, their faith anchored them, like a lighthouse guiding ships through treacherous waters. The storm may rage, but their unwavering commitment to their calling remained steadfast.

Penkowski's desperate search for any trace of John Ivan consumed him as he drove through Stapleton. Every street, every building, held the potential to unravel the mystery he was determined to solve.

Finally, he parked his car and entered a barber shop, hoping to gather information from the locals. Taking a seat, he anxiously waited for his turn while scanning a newspaper, his ears tuned to the snippets of town gossip floating around.

"I've seen a lot of things happen throughout the years I've lived here, but I just can't figure out what is happening," an old man remarked, his voice tinged with bewilderment, as the barber worked on his remaining hair.

"You're telling me!" exclaimed the barber, commiserating with the old man. They delved into discussions about recent events—the distribution of threatening brochures, the intimidation tactics employed, the changes in the school system, and even the remarkable decrease in crime rates. Then, the conversation veered toward Tuesday night prayer meetings.

Penkowski froze in his seat, his body stiffening with an intensity that bordered on rage. He remained motionless, hiding his face behind the newspaper, as the men shared stories of God's mighty work in Stapleton. Each word they uttered pierced through

Penkowski's facade, striking at the core of his being. His face flushed crimson, drenched in a sheen of perspiration. The redness in his glazed eyes intensified, reflecting the turmoil within him. Gripping the newspaper tightly, his fingers bore into the pages, leaving imprints of his frustration.

Just as the tension in the room reached its peak, Penkowski's cell phone shattered the momentary silence. The men fell silent, and Penkowski excused himself, stepping outside the shop to take the call. His voice carried little emotion as he conversed with the person on the other end.

"You don't know? How can you not know when that is your only job at this moment in time?" Penkowski's voice crackled with anger, seething with disappointment. "Have I asked you to do something in addition to this task? I have only asked you to do one thing, and you can't even accomplish that. I have sent others to this wretched town to find John and eliminate him, and they have failed. Now, here I am, forced to take over their responsibilities. They, of course, won't be needing their jobs any longer. Today, they are more in need of a coffin."

Penkowski's voice grew colder, his threats laced with a chilling determination. "So, if I find John before you, then, of course, there is no need for your services any longer either." With a click, his cell phone cut off the connection. Yet, as some of the anger that had consumed him in the barber shop dissipated, Penkowski glanced back at the window of the shop while pulling away, and a renewed wave of fury crashed over him.

John clenched his cell phone tightly, his face a mask of terror and disbelief. Elizabeth, sensing his distress, leaned in, her eyes wide with concern.

"John, what's wrong? You look like you've just seen a ghost!" she exclaimed, her voice trembling.

"He's here," John replied, his voice barely above a whisper, laden with fear. "Penkowski. He's in town, and he's looking for me. I have to find George, and fast. But if Penkowski finds him first... Oh God, I hope George is alright."

"Call him, John. We need to reach him," Elizabeth urged, her own anxiety growing tangible.

John swiftly retrieved his cell phone from his pocket, fingers shaking as he speed dialed George's number. The agonizing seconds ticked by, but there was no answer on the other end, only the haunting silence of uncertainty.

Desperation etched across his face, John turned to Elizabeth, his voice quivering with urgency. "What are we going to do, Elizabeth?"

"We can't stay here. We need to go, John," she responded, her voice tinged with a mix of fear and determination.

Without wasting another moment, John made a swift decision. "Grab your belongings. We have to leave, now!" Their hearts pounding, they hastily gathered their things, casting worried glances over their shoulders as they hurriedly departed, their only solace the hope that they could outrun the imminent danger that loomed over them.

"Sit down, George," Dennis commanded, his voice carrying an air of authority as he closed the door to his office behind him.

George couldn't decide which company he found more unsettling - Penkowski's or Dennis's. Neither option was ideal, and right now, he yearned to escape it all, picturing himself lounging on a serene beach in Hawaii.

"How's the partnership with John going?" Dennis inquired, his tone hinting at the gravity of the situation.

"Very well! John and I are completely aligned," George replied, relieved that he no longer had to fabricate his responses. Thank you, God, for sparing me from lying.

"Good. You must understand, George, that what you and John are working on is crucial to the survival of this company. It's a matter of keeping your job or losing it," Dennis stated with a seriousness that hung in the air.

"The company is in dire straits, George. John must have briefed you on the extent of the troubles we face. If things continue as they are, we won't last beyond the start of next year."

George mustered a look of surprise and anguish, concealing his inner turmoil.

"I know, it's hard to believe given how smoothly things appear to be going at AFT. But the truth is, we're on the brink of collapse," Dennis continued, his gaze fixed on George.

"Follow John's instructions to the letter. I understand the

dangers involved, but if you and John can pull this off... well, let's just say you'll both be swimming in wealth," Dennis said, his words ringing hollow in George's ears. That was never his intention. It was precisely the pursuit of riches that had entangled him in this mess in the first place.

George switched to a mischievous smile, masking his true feelings. "Working with John is a dream. If anyone can crack this case, it's him."

"Excellent. He's on the verge of a breakthrough, which is why his life is in greater danger than ever before. Just be careful not to get yourself killed. What you're involved in is extremely dangerous," Dennis cautioned, unaware of the depths of peril George had already experienced. Memories of a gun pressed to his head flashed through George's mind, a vivid reminder of God's intervention that had spared his life and allowed him to stand here, conversing with Dennis.

"And remember, money means nothing if you can't enjoy it," Dennis added, his smile displaying a hint of irony as he rose from his seat.

Penkowski continued to navigate through the town, his singular objective becoming increasingly clouded by the overwhelming surge of anger within him. With school being out, he veered into the high school parking lot and decided to explore the halls. As expected, Christian propaganda adorned the walls and flower beds, just as he had heard during his encounter at the barber shop. Intrigued, he made his way towards the auditorium.

As he reached for the door and began to step inside, an inexplicable force halted him in his tracks. Despite his surprise, his curiosity overshadowed any concern, and he took in the sight before him. The auditorium was adorned with pictures, scriptures, posters, and even the Ten Commandments. The anger that had swelled within him at the barber shop resurfaced, but this time it surged with an uncontrollable fury. Faint murmurs reached his ears, and as he turned his gaze, he spotted a small group gathered in the far corner, kneeling and praying aloud.

"Err!" Penkowski let out a ghastly yell, causing the group to cease their prayers and glance in his direction. He attempted to move forward, but once again, a paralyzing sensation gripped his legs. Frustrated, he made a final desperate attempt to break free but met with failure. In a fit of rage, he cursed and blasphemed, uttering the Lord's name in vain. Instantly, an unseen force propelled him out of the auditorium, sending him crashing onto his back. As he lifted his head, he witnessed the auditorium door slam shut with a resounding force.

Penkowski rose from the ground, consumed by disgust, and hurriedly sprinted back to his car. With tires screeching, he peeled out of the parking lot, leaving behind yet another set of dark skid marks on the pavement—testimony to the departure of an adult rather than a teenager, fueled by frustration and defeated pride.

John and Elizabeth sped toward the airport, their destination set.

"Elizabeth, let's go back to your city. I doubt Penkowski would ever think of looking for me there."

Elizabeth nodded in agreement as they raced through the streets. John managed to grab his laptop but left behind all the fancy belongings at his house.

Suddenly, John's cell phone rang, interrupting the tension-filled atmosphere.

"Hello?" John answered.

"John, it's Dennis Spence."

"Dennis, hello," John replied.

"I want to meet up with you, but I need to catch a flight. So, I'd like you to meet me at the airport."

"Not a problem, I'll be there," John agreed, receiving the time details before hanging up.

"The airport?" Elizabeth questioned.

"Yeah, how convenient is that? His flight leaves just before ours. It's a perfect setup. Looks like someone is looking out for us," John remarked.

Elizabeth glanced at John, taken aback. Her brother had never made comments alluding to any higher power. He had always been focused on his own interests.

"You know, John, this must be some friend to get you involved in such a deep mess," Elizabeth remarked.

"He's a good guy who's found himself in a bad place," John tried to downplay the question.

"You've never cared about ethical issues before. Since when did you start playing the part of Sister Theresa?" Elizabeth inquired, suspicion lacing her words.

"Lizzy, things change. I've changed. I'm tired of looking in the mirror and seeing a face that's only out for itself," John admitted, pausing briefly to gather his thoughts before continuing.

"Your ordeal really affected me," John said, his gaze shifting away from Elizabeth and down to the floor.

"I want to make a difference, not chase after money anymore. I have all the wealth and material possessions I ever dreamed of, yet I'm more miserable than ever before in my life! When I look at you, I see how my relentless pursuit of money has blinded me to the true realities of life. People are suffering, and it's the very clients I was trying to help who are causing their pain. And all for what? To have a bank account overflowing with money? To own faster cars, bigger houses, and fancier clothes? No! That shallow existence doesn't cut it for me anymore. I'm tired of being superficial, of watching people get hurt while I remain on the sidelines. I want to make a genuine difference in my life, in your life, in George's life. God knows, I'm trying. And speaking of God, I've witnessed some extraordinary things in this town that can only be attributed to a higher power... Yes, God. I know, it sounds crazy coming from me, but listen to this," John began, recounting all the remarkable events taking place in their town. It was no longer just a town; it had become his town. He continued to share with Elizabeth about George's miracle, Sue's incredible strength in saving him from a burning car, and finally, about Maggie.

"Brother, you're in love! That's what all this 'God' talk is about. You're in love," Elizabeth exclaimed.

John blushed, feeling both vulnerable and elated. "Maggie is an amazing person, but it's more than just that. Haven't you heard what I've been telling you about this town?"

Elizabeth gave John a skeptical look, reminiscent of the one he had given George when he spoke about Penkowski's face transformation during the windstorm. Suddenly, realization dawned on him, and he shifted his gaze forward, falling silent.

"John, you've been under a lot of stress. I'm sure there's a logical explanation for everything you've told me," Elizabeth remarked, her voice filled with uncertainty.

John knew exactly what Elizabeth was thinking, for he had experienced the same doubts during the windstorm incident with

George. Deciding to handle it as George had done, he mustered a smile and replied, "You might be right, Lizzy. But you did ask," their eyes met, and the smile was returned, their unspoken bond speaking volumes.

As John and Elizabeth arrived at the airport, John began to explain the plan to his sister, keeping her involvement hidden from Dennis.

"Okay, Lizzy, do you know where to meet me?" John asked, a tinge of concern in his voice.

"Yes, John. It'll be alright. I trust you," Elizabeth reassured him.

Those words weighed heavily on John's shoulders, instantly erasing his cocky attitude. He was left solely focused on completing the task at hand.

Navigating through the airport, John noticed its small size, but it provided enough space for Elizabeth to remain out of sight. He settled at a small table intended for paying customers of a food vendor.

"John," Dennis approached, and John stood up to shake his hand.

"Dennis, hello," John greeted him. To his surprise, Dennis quickly shook his hand.

"We're in a worse state than when I first hired you, but I see progress," Dennis remarked as he motioned for John to walk with him. "John, we need to act swiftly! To be honest, we have a couple of months, at best, before we're forced to file for bankruptcy... We have to uncover the truth behind all of this, and we have to do it fast!"

"Yes, sir," John replied.

"Keep relying on George; he's exceptional. I just came from AFT, and he's really turning things around there."

With that confirmation, John knew that George was making significant headway. A smile formed on his face.

"Dennis, we should have this resolved in less than two months."

"Good. Good. Make sure you do," Dennis responded, then turned and walked away.

Penkowski drove, glancing up at the speed limit sign, realizing that his anger wasn't worth risking a speeding ticket. He decided to ease off the accelerator, slightly reducing his speed. Navigating through the town, he eventually reached 62nd Street. His eyes scanned each house as he drove, meticulously studying them. Retrieving a picture from his pocket, he compared it to the houses, searching for a match. Finally, he found it. Swiftly, he pulled his car into the driveway.

Approaching the front door, Penkowski shot the doorknob with his gun and forcefully kicked the door open. It swung open with a resounding slam as he arrogantly entered, holding his gun at his side instead of in a ready position. He stormed through the house, wreaking havoc on everything in his path, from electronics to appliances. Desperately, he searched every nook and cranny, hoping to find the stolen paperwork that John had taken from his very home.

From his pocket, Penkowski produced a lighter and ignited anything flammable before walking out of the house. As he drove away, he glanced at the rear-view mirror, witnessing flames erupting from the open front door he had left behind.

Continuing to drive through the city, Penkowski meticulously scanned each block, searching for any clue that could lead him to John. Spotting a church ahead, he slammed on the brakes. Fortunately, no one was behind him, allowing him to swiftly reverse and redirect his car toward the church. With each passing moment, his anger intensified, and his blood pressure surged. Sweat trickled down his forehead, his eyes grew even redder than usual, and the imprints of his hands remained on the steering wheel as he released his grip.

"Hello, can I help you?" Bruce asked as Penkowski entered his office, his demeanor tense. Bruce's attention was focused on deciphering some papers, but he acknowledged the presence of the approaching footsteps. Wayne had already left, leaving Bruce alone in the office.

As Bruce looked up, he was taken aback. In that moment, he understood why Wayne and he had been sensing a malevolent presence. This man exuded pure evil.

"Are you Pastor Bruce?" Penkowski asked, his words dripping with malice.

Uncertain if this was the right answer, Bruce replied cautiously, "Yes."

"So... you're the one responsible for the closure of all the abortion clinics," Penkowski stated, each word laced with accusation.

Bruce remained silent, seizing the opportunity to intensify his desperate, silent prayer. The weight of the situation sank deeper into his being, overwhelming him with emotions.

"And... all this Christian propaganda around the city," Penkowski continued, slowly inching closer to Bruce with each step. "I drive around this town, and everywhere I go, I see the signs of church dominance."

Bruce's surprise transformed into worry, etching lines of concern on his face.

"I enter a gas station, hoping to find some reading material for my flight home, only to be bombarded with religious garbage. I thought it was a mere coincidence. Then, I visit the Barber Shop, and once again, it's nothing but talk about religious indoctrination."

Bruce's expression shifted back to surprise, his mind racing to comprehend the intensity of Penkowski's resentment.

Penkowski advanced, drawing nearer to Bruce, who remained seated, unable to utter a word. Speaking seemed futile, given the circumstances.

"Don't give me that look of surprise! You're no different from my parents. I was forced to attend church, even when I was gravely ill. Forced to endure Sunday school where the other kids despised me... And speaking of Sunday school..." Penkowski's voice grew louder, his perspiration more profuse, and his eyes now glowed with an eerie red hue.

Bruce maintained his silence, knowing that any attempt to speak would prove futile at this point.

"I HATE church... God... religion!" Penkowski's voice boomed with uncontrollable rage. "I despise this town and its feeble, pathetic inhabitants who rely on religion as a crutch. GROW UP! It's not time for Sunday school lessons... class is over... get a life!"

Penkowski loomed over Bruce, who remained motionless, his body frozen in place.

"Your church will suffer the same fate as the one in town—burned to the ground! That's what we should do to all churches... reduce them to ashes! Then, perhaps, we'll experience true freedom to live as we please, without judgment constantly pointing our way... Freedom! REAL freedom!"

Bruce took a deep breath, summoning his resolve, and slowly

rose to his feet. In that moment, Penkowski stood so close that he failed to anticipate what would transpire next. All he felt was searing pain, and then everything faded to black.

As John walked away, his phone began to ring, breaking the silence around him.

"Hello?" he answered.

"John, it's George."

"You okay?" John asked, concerned.

"Yeah, a little shaken. You wouldn't believe what happened over here."

"Let me guess. First, Penkowski shows up with his doctor friend."

"Yep."

"Then, right as he's leaving, Dennis shows up."

"They actually bump into each other on their way out!" George exclaimed, his voice reverting to its teenage days.

"You've got to be kidding me!" John said, trying to match George's excitement to lighten the mood.

"No, I'm dead serious. My heart was pounding a mile a minute!"

"That must have been quite a spectacle."

"You can bet on it."

John found Elizabeth and motioned for her to join him. They walked together while John continued his conversation with George.

"Listen, buddy, you handled Dennis well. I just finished talking to him at the airport."

"The airport? Where are you going?"

"I've got Elizabeth with me, and she's agreed to help us out."

"John, I really wish you hadn't involved your sister in all of this. It's dangerous. It's not a game!" George's concern resonated in his voice.

"I know the risks, George, but I believe I made the right decision. Lizzy... she's willing to help, and she understands the dangers involved."

"Of course she would agree. She loves you."

John stopped walking and looked at his grown-up baby sister. She stopped too and smiled back at him.

"George, I made the right choice," John affirmed, and they

resumed their walk.

"How did it go with Penkowski?"

"He and his doctor friend were thoroughly impressed with the operation, or lack thereof, the accounting books, and how unaware the employees were of Penkowski's true intentions."

"Good. Hopefully, we can drive him out of here. I have a hunch he knows where I've been living."

"Man, John, I can't stand all this lying. It's like a cancer eating away at me. I'm lying to Dennis, Penkowski, even the people working for me."

"Hang in there, George. This will all be over before you know it, and you won't have to lie ever again."

On the other side of the phone, George let out a sigh.

"Thanks, John. I don't know what I would do without you."

Those words caught John off guard. For the first time in his life, he felt like he had made a difference in someone else's life, beyond just his own. As he looked at Elizabeth, he saw yet another opportunity to help someone. Then, he thought about all the women who would benefit from the closure of both The Association for Fetal Research and Advance Medical. He also considered the people at AFT being deceived and working under false pretenses, along with the countless others who would be positively affected.

"John, you still there?" George's voice brought him back to the present.

"Yes, sorry. I was just thinking about everything we have to do."

"Take it one step at a time. Get yourself on that plane and call me as soon as you're out of harm's way. Let me know what I can do to help."

"Just keep doing what you're doing. You're doing an incredible job."

"Thanks, John. I'll talk to you later. Say hi to your sister for me."

"I will. Take care, George."

Bruce's eyelids fluttered open, his vision hazy and disoriented, struggling to make sense of his surroundings. A wave of uncertainty washed over him as he cautiously attempted to move his battered body. Agonizing pain surged through every fiber, confirming his worst fears. It felt as though a monstrous semi-truck had callously crushed his face, while his limbs and ribs throbbed relentlessly, each pulse a reminder of the brutality he had endured. Summoning every ounce of strength, he mustered the will to rise from the floor, his first instinct urging him to reach out to Pastor Wayne for help.

The phone rang persistently, but there was no comforting voice on the other end, no answering machine to offer solace. Bruce, overwhelmed by the intensity of his agony, remained frozen in the position he had assumed to make the call, allowing the shrill ring to reverberate unanswered through the desolate room. The sound seemed to mock his suffering.

"Click... Hel... l... o?" a voice quivered, resembling Bruce's own as it trembled with uncertainty.

"Wa... yne... now!" Bruce managed to speak, each syllable accompanied by a searing pain shooting through his side.

"Man, are you okay?" Wayne's concerned voice crackled through the line.

"What happened?"

Wayne implored Bruce to recount the events leading up to his devastating blackout, his tone filled with a potent blend of curiosity, compassion, and his own underlying pain.

"Go on."

"He blasphemed the Lord's name. It infuriated me... until I noticed his eyes."

A pregnant pause enveloped the conversation, a shared understanding passing between the two men.

"They glowed red," Bruce interjected, his voice strained.

"This man exuded pure evil! No wonder we felt the weight of darkness earlier. Then, he kept advancing toward me, and I was gripped by paralyzing fear."

"And then?"

"As he drew nearer, he continued to berate me, his words cutting deep, calling me weak and labeling our entire community as feeble. He taunted me with the memory of our burned-down church, threatening that mine would be next."

"Yeah."

"He was right in front of me, and I mustered every ounce of strength to defend myself, but the next thing I knew, the phone was ringing. Despite the excruciating pain, I fought against it, desperately trying to answer."

"You know what's really strange?"

"What?"

"Not a single thing in my office is damaged."

"Let me go check the rest of the church. I'll be right back."

"Okay."

Bruce gingerly rose to his feet, each movement sending shockwaves of pain through his battered body. He cautiously surveyed his immediate surroundings, stepped outside, and to his relief, everything appeared as it should be. The church stood unscathed, as if untouched by the terrifying encounter that had unfolded within its walls.

"Wayne?"

"Yes?"

"Everything is in order here."

"It's as if this guy was in a rush or something."

"Yeah... I wonder where he went."

As the pastors concluded their conversation, Bruce reached out to the police, his voices filled with a mixture of urgency and a desire to report the harrowing, otherworldly encounter that had shaken his faith and scarred their souls.

Penkowski sprinted down the street, a cacophony of flashing red and blue lights and blaring sirens following in his wake. Chaos ensued as he careened through the parking lot, colliding with a car, leaving a trail of destruction in his path. Glancing over his shoulder, a wicked grin danced across Penkowski's face. The police car pursuing him lost control, flipping violently amidst the chaos of the lot.

Reaching the front of the airport, Penkowski abandoned the damaged vehicle and bolted toward the security checkpoint. His heart raced as he scanned his surroundings, desperately seeking any sign of suspicion. Suddenly, a security officer's frantic voice pierced through the airwaves, causing Penkowski's blood to run cold. The officer's gaze darted around until it landed on Penkowski, who, defying all human limits, leaped impossibly high over a counter intended to redirect traffic towards the security checks.

The security officer gave chase, but Penkowski swiftly disappeared into a dense crowd of people. As the officer scanned the mass of bodies, his target eluded him. Frustrated, he rushed toward the crowd, his attention fixed on the search for Penkowski.

Once again, the officer reached for his radio, relaying urgent messages.

Meanwhile, John and Elizabeth stood in line, waiting to board their airplane. Despite the throngs of people around them, John couldn't shake his unease, continuously scanning the area for any sign of Penkowski.

"John, calm down. It's going to be okay," Elizabeth reassured him, her voice filled with a mixture of concern and determination.

John glanced at Elizabeth, attempting a smile. However, before he could fully register the situation, a man materialized behind him, seizing his arm and pressing a cold, menacing gun against his back. In a twisted turn of events, the assailant also had a grip on Elizabeth's arm.

"Move!" the man barked, shoving them out of line and forcefully propelling them towards a door leading to the airfield. John strained to catch a glimpse of his archenemy but was met with a tighter grip on his arm and a surge of pain that echoed through his body.

This was precisely what John had wanted to avoid. Now his sister was entangled in the dangerous web he had been desperately trying to untangle.

Navigating their way across the airfield, they spotted a corporate jet with its door ajar. A figure stood on the stairs, frantically beckoning them to hurry. Glancing behind them, they saw police cars hurtling towards them, lights flashing and sirens blaring.

"Hurry up! Run!" the figure shouted, urgency permeating his every word. John and Elizabeth complied, sprinting towards the waiting plane.

The police cars drew nearer as they ascended the stairs, their pulsating lights and screeching tires attempting to cut off any escape route. Just as they thought they were out of reach, the door slammed shut, thrusting John and Elizabeth into plush seats. As they regained their composure, they glanced up at the figure who had brought them on board, his back turned, barking orders.

The plane swiftly gained momentum, its engines roaring to life. Outside the pilot's window, the sight of police cars in hot pursuit filled their view. The cars swerved and screeched, desperately trying to outmaneuver the aircraft.

Yet, the pilot was no novice. With remarkable precision, he deftly maneuvered the plane, countering every move the police cars made. Finally, with a calculated positioning, the pilot outsmarted the pursuers, leaving them trailing behind on the runway.

John and Elizabeth's hearts sank as they caught sight of the relentless police cars through the plane's window, doggedly giving chase. Looking ahead, their dread intensified as they spotted the imposing figure of a large, burly man brandishing an automatic weapon, stationed to ensure their compliance. Casting a desperate glance behind them, they could see the pursuing cars inching closer, the threat growing more intense with each passing second.

Suddenly, a bone-jarring impact shook the plane as one of the police cars grazed the landing gear, jolting the aircraft to the left. Yet, the resilient plane swiftly regained its steady course down the runway, its determination unwavering. Just as the police car prepared to strike again, the engines roared to life, unleashing an immense surge of power that propelled John and Elizabeth forcefully back into their seats. Gasping for breath, John's eyes met the unwavering gaze of the man before them, his grip on the gun unyielding.

As the relentless police cars fell farther and farther behind, their futile pursuit fading into the distance, the plane approached the end of the airstrip. With a final, defiant stand, the police cars came to a halt, their mission thwarted. And in a breathtaking moment, the plane defied gravity, soaring into the sky, leaving behind the chaos and danger that had threatened to consume them.

FOURTEEN

"Pastor Bruce," the police officer's voice carried a genuine tone of regret, "I am deeply sorry we couldn't reach you sooner. It appears that whoever targeted you also ignited a devastating fire in one of our affluent neighborhoods. The flames quickly spread, engulfing numerous homes, and our firefighters are currently battling to bring it under control."

Bruce lifted his gaze to meet the officer's eyes, assuring him that he was fully attentive, even though his focus was divided between the conversation and the excruciating pain coursing through his body, reminding him of his frailty.

"One of the neighbors witnessed him leaving a house, and as he drove away, the house erupted in flames." Bruce shook his head, overwhelmed by the senselessness of the situation.

"To compound matters, Pastor, we did catch up with him after the attacks. He was heading for the airport, but despite our best efforts, he managed to elude us."

"Can't you track him using radar or some other means?" Bruce asked, his frustration seeping into his voice.

"Well, it's a private jet, and there are ways to fly under the radar, making it difficult for us to maintain a constant track. Moreover, he likely used a false identity when registering the plane."

Bruce turned away, his expression filled with disappointment. In that moment, he didn't feel very spiritual. The anger he had experienced when his house was vandalized resurfaced, but this time, it wasn't just his property that was violated—it was his own body, and the perpetrator had managed to evade capture.

Bruce completed the police report, following the officer's advice. However, before getting into the car to head to the hospital, he stepped into the restroom and looked into the mirror. The reflection staring back at him was a far cry from the man he had seen that morning. This person was a disheveled mess, with a swollen eye, a gash leaving a trail of blood down his face. Unbuttoning his shirt, he revealed black and blue bruises lining his side, providing an explanation for the throbbing pain he had endured.

His head drooped, and he collapsed onto the floor, overcome by a wave of emotions. He sat there, tears streaming down his face, as the weight of the ordeal and the emotional overload consumed him.

Once he composed himself, Bruce slowly rose from the floor and made his way to the hospital, determined to seek the medical attention he so desperately needed.

George frantically attempted to reach John, but his calls wouldn't connect. Unbeknownst to him, Penkowski's henchmen had rendered his phone useless. Anxiety gnawed at George's mind as he pondered the potential dangers that John and his sister might be facing.

"Come on, snap out of it, George!" he admonished himself, realizing the need to regain his composure. He turned to prayer, seeking solace and guidance, but in the depths of his heart, he couldn't shake the growing sense of unease surrounding John and his sister.

A profound sense of loneliness enveloped George, leaving him feeling utterly isolated. With John evidently in peril and George's hesitance to reach out to Bruce for assistance, he grappled with a deep sense of vulnerability. Despite his relentless efforts, George's attempts to contact John proved futile, leaving him frustrated and filled with apprehension.

"Where do you think they are taking us?" Elizabeth asked John as she leaned over to him and whispered into his ear.

"I think we are going back to California. That is where Penkowski's headquarters is." John whispered back.

"What are we going to do John, I'm scared."

"Hang in there. Let me tell you why I asked you to do this."

They looked up to the gun man and he was allowing the conversation so John continued. John began from the beginning. Then, he told her of how he began to change his attitude and how she was the catalyst that started the change. He told her of George, of his newly involvement in his church and how he is trapped in this mess. Finally, John finished with an emotionally charged story.

"One of my interviews was with a man named Dr. Stearing. He was an older man that was retired. As we sat down Lizzy, I noticed on the shelf a small plaque that read, "To help and restore.""

"I noticed that plaque up there, "To help and restore." Were did you get that?" I asked.

At that, the man hung his head low. Then after a big sigh he said, "It was from my first wife.' He paused for a moment and then he went on. "When I was first married, my wife helped me get through medical school. It was grueling but she stuck by me, even worked to help pay for some of the bills while I attended medical school full time."

"He told me of how he ruined his marriage. He said, 'I was concerned about the almighty dollar, Instead of keeping my eyes on the dream we both began with, to help and restore. I changed the motto to 'It is your choice'." His search for money led him to The Association for Fetal Research. They offered him a deal he could not refuse he said."

John and Elizabeth continued to look up at the gun man to make certain he was not getting agitated.

"He talked about how being a part of the Association was profitable. He said they paid him to use a machine…what was the name of that machine?" John looked at Elizabeth and she just shrugged her shoulders.

"Man! What was the name of that machine? Wait! It was the XM2. They used for the collection and disposal of fetuses."

John gazed out of the window, lost in thought, before whispering, "I wonder who he sold the fetuses to."

And then it struck him. "Advance Medical!" John's voice dropped to a hushed tone.

The gunman glanced up, sensing the gravity of John's words. John continued, his voice barely audible, "The Association must have sold the fetuses to Advance Medical. But that's illegal. I suspect they disguised it as a disposal fee to circumvent the law."

Curiosity piqued, Elizabeth leaned in closer, her voice filled with concern. "John, what happened during the rest of your conversation with that doctor? He sounded so miserable."

A heavy sigh escaped John as he recounted, "He said, 'I wish I could turn back time,' with his head hanging low."

Eager for a glimmer of positivity, Elizabeth asked, "Tell me, did anything positive come out of his involvement in the industry?" hoping for a glimmer of hope.

John's expression turned somber as he recalled the doctor's response. "Do you know what he told me, Lizzy? He said, 'It has shown me that no matter how much you try to justify wrong as right, no matter how hard you ignore your conscience, no matter what kind of seeds you sow, you will always reap what you sow.'"

John's voice trembled with emotion as he continued, "He went on to say, 'For me, it has resulted in shattered dreams, haunting memories, unbearable regrets, and nights plagued with nightmares that make horror movies look like Saturday afternoon cartoons, son. That's what the abortion industry has given me.'"

Silence enveloped them as the weight of those words sank in. Elizabeth's face softened, understanding the profound impact of the decisions her brother had been facing, decisions that were far from his usual character.

Bruce had returned from the hospital, his injuries tended to and deemed cosmetic, nothing serious. As he tried to process the events that had unfolded, the ringing phone interrupted his thoughts.

"Hello?" Bruce answered eagerly, recognizing the voice on the other end.

"Hello, Bruce, it's George," came the somber reply.

"George! Oh, it's good to hear your voice! Are you okay?" Bruce's excitement was electric, momentarily overshadowing his pain and trauma.

"Bruce, I'm okay, but you may not want to get involved with me," George said, his voice heavy with concern.

Confusion and worry crept into Bruce's tone. "What are you talking about? I'll do whatever I can to help you, my friend. You've done so much for me."

George's voice trembled as he spoke, "This is very dangerous. Your life could be at stake."

Silence enveloped the line, and in that moment, all the pain inflicted by a stranger surged back, overwhelming Bruce. He thought of the personal visit he had received from his Lord and Savior, recalling His words, "Do not be afraid of what you are about to suffer. I have come to tell you that the devil will try to stop you and your work for Me. You will face greater persecution in the coming days than ever before in your life. Remain faithful, even unto death, and I will bestow upon you the radiant crown of life." Those words solidified Bruce's decision, "...even unto death."

Resolute, Bruce spoke firmly into the phone, "I will do it."

George felt a mix of relief and concern for his beloved pastor. What would it mean to involve him in this mess?

"Bruce, I had no one else to turn to... I didn't want to drag you into my troubles, but..."

"No need to say more, my friend. I have the green light from my Commander, and I'm ready to assist you, whatever it takes."

George's heart swelled with gratitude. He proceeded to provide Bruce with a time and place to meet, and they bid each other goodbye, hanging up the phone.

"Come on, get up!" the gunman barked, pointing towards the front of the plane. Bruce and Elizabeth, filled with trepidation, rose from their seats and obediently walked in the indicated direction. As they passed through a door, they entered a small area with a table. Seated at the end of the table was Penkowski.

"Glad you could join us," he sneered.

"Did we really have a choice?" John responded, devoid of any sarcasm. His bravado from the encounter at Penkowski's office building had dissipated. Having his sister by his side amplified his concern for their lives, particularly hers.

"Not quite as cocky as before, my friend. Is it because of the connection between you and the young lady accompanying you?" Penkowski taunted.

John remained silent, his face a mask of stoicism. It was perhaps the first time he found himself at a loss for words.

"Ah... there is a connection. Even better," Penkowski remarked, relishing the revelation. "We'll take both of you. We should have done this from the beginning. Keeping you alive seems to be more challenging than expected."

"Tell me, Dr. Penkowski, what have you done with all the fetuses you acquired—or rather, offered to dispose of—for a fee from The Association?"

A heavy pause filled the air, and then Penkowski rose from his seat.

"Okay, John. We've been through a lot together. You're no longer a threat to me. Fine... yes, you're referring to the XM2. Yes, I paid The Association for the disposal of the fetuses, and they couldn't care less about the methods we employed."

John asked with utmost seriousness, "And what exactly did you do with them?"

"The fountain of youth, my friend," Penkowski declared with perverse delight. "I am creating the fountain of youth!"

"Experimentation on human flesh," John uttered, his voice heavy with disgust. Elizabeth shared his revulsion, her expression mirroring his.

"No! You people always focus on the negative side!" Penkowski retorted, his tone defensive.

"Paying for dead babies is not negative?" John countered, and Elizabeth nodded in agreement.

"Paying for the key to youth, that's what I've done! And now, I am so close to finding the answer..."

"Until I came in and disrupted all your plans," John interjected.

"Tried... to mess up my plans. But now I have you and your lawyer. You can't do a thing," Penkowski gloated.

"What happens when you put The Association out of business? Where will you get your supply of dead babies from then?" John questioned.

"We will take over The Association and turn everything around," Penkowski proclaimed.

"You mean you'll stop sabotaging the company?" John pressed.

"We'll resolve all the problems and make a fortune," Penkowski confirmed.

"So, it's all about the money? It's always about the money," John commented, leaving Elizabeth astonished to hear such words from her own brother.

"Of course! What else is there?" Penkowski responded callously. "Look at you. You have more money now than when you first started working for The Association. Your husband's days of spying are over, and you know you'll never go back. The ethics of abortion didn't stand in the way of your personal pursuit of money and success."

John's gaze dropped to the floor, consumed by a sense of self-disgust. The comment struck a painful chord within him. It was all true, and it hurt. His sister could see the guilt etched on John's face, witnessing the profound change in her brother.

"I thought so," Penkowski continued, his tone growing increasingly excited. "Listen, I'm in this to bring youth to the aging. I've spent years masking the symptoms of age with facelifts, lotions, and all the rest. But it's been an illusion! I haven't reversed time. I've been selling my patients lies, and I'm tired of it."

John gazed up at Dr. Penkowski, his eyes filled with disbelief and incredulity. As Penkowski paced back and forth, his words spilled out with a mix of desperation and anger.

"I want to bring my patients a new hope, a chance to start over," Penkowski proclaimed, his voice tinged with fervor. "I despise the midlife crisis, men leaving their wives for women half their age. Now they can be younger, alongside their wives. They can be more youthful not just in appearance but also in health and physicality! This life, this so-called God, what kind of cruel joke is it?" Penkowski's anger seethed through his words.

He continued his tirade, his frustration mounting. "You work tirelessly throughout your youthful years—learning, growing, practicing—for the promise of adulthood. And what happens when you finally get there? Everything begins to fail you! The aches and pains set in, your eyes require glasses, your back protests against hard work... It's an endless list! What kind of loving God plans our lives this way?"

Although Penkowski's question was rhetorical, he awaited a response. When none came, his anger escalated further.

"I've had enough of religion and churches that promise a happier life, answers to our questions... Are we supposed to be content with the doom this hateful God has bestowed upon us? Spare me the excuses!" Penkowski's voice dripped with disdain for faith.

John and Elizabeth watched in silence, their eyes fixed on a man clearly tormented by his own thoughts and beliefs.

"John, you've spent time in that town, Stapleton, haven't you? How do you endure all that religious propaganda?" Penkowski asked, seeking confirmation of his own biases.

John found himself trapped in a disorienting time warp, where it felt as if everything around him had come to a sudden halt. His mind raced back to his initial arrival in Stapleton, and in a rapid succession, the events that carried the unmistakable mark of God played out before his eyes. The mysterious appearance of the laptop stood out prominently, as did the weighty decisions he had recently made, seemingly influenced by a heartfelt prayer from a woman he would never forget.

"John! Please don't tell me you're falling for all that religious nonsense too!" Penkowski's voice pierced through John's thoughts, snapping him back to the present. John looked up at Penkowski and managed a smile.

"Fine then! Let's see if your God can save you from this mess. We'll see who gets the last laugh," Penkowski declared, his words laden with contempt.

John was taken aback. Accusations of him believing in a god were rare, let alone the Almighty Himself. Nonetheless, he composed himself and met Penkowski's challenge head-on.

At that moment, Penkowski's anger reached a crescendo. His voice rose to a deafening volume, sweat pouring down his face, fists clenched, and his eyes shifting from bloodshot red to an eerie glowing red. John noticed the transformation and exchanged a concerned glance with Elizabeth as Penkowski stormed away.

The armed man escorted John and Elizabeth back to their seats, and once they were settled, John couldn't help but ask Elizabeth about Penkowski's eyes.

"They were bloodshot. He looked like a deranged man,"

Elizabeth replied, her voice filled with fear.

"But...you didn't see them...glow...red?" The words slipped out of John's mouth before he could stop himself.

As soon as he uttered those words, he regretted it. He could sense the unease in Elizabeth's response.

"John, are you alright? I know you've been under tremendous pressure. Sure, I'm scared too, but...are you seeing things?"

Elizabeth's words struck a chord within him. They reminded him of his previous encounter with Penkowski, where his friend-turned-partner had also witnessed a similar phenomenon on Penkowski's face. John realized that his sister's reaction mirrored his own at the time, causing him to sink back into his seat, enveloped in silence. Elizabeth welcomed the respite from conversation, allowing her to catch her breath and regain some semblance of calmness.

George met up with Bruce in the High School Auditorium, and together they made their way to George's car. As they drove off, the day appeared bright, but there was an underlying chill in the air, hinting at the impending snowfall. The sun cast its radiant glow, seemingly painting a picture of a flawless day. They exchanged words about Bruce's new appearance while driving, but deep down, both knew that something was amiss. Finally, they arrived at Forest Ridge Park, stepping out of the car and strolling through the serene surroundings until they reached a park bench overlooking the tranquil lake.

"I find solace in sitting here from time to time. It helps me clear my mind and realign my focus on God and His work in my life," Bruce shared, settling down on the bench with a slight wince of pain.

"Are you alright?" George asked with concern etched on his face.

"Yeah, I'll be fine. That guy really did a number on me," Bruce replied, masking his discomfort.

"And the police have no idea who it was?" George questioned, frustration evident in his voice.

"No. They said he managed to escape," Bruce responded, a touch of disappointment in his tone.

George cast a disdainful gaze over the peaceful lake, then

turned back to Bruce.

"Bruce, what I'm about to disclose may jeopardize our friendship," George hesitated, his voice tinged with apprehension.

Bruce looked at him intently and asked, "Did this happen BC?"

"BC?" George queried, puzzled.

"Yeah, BC. Before Christ. Before you became a Christian," Bruce clarified.

George took a deep breath, grappling with the weight of his confession. "Yes, but still, it's not something to be proud of."

"Did you harm or kill Christians?" Bruce inquired, his voice filled with genuine curiosity.

"No! No, nothing like that," George quickly assured.

"Well, even if you did, I would forgive you," Bruce responded calmly, surprising George with his unwavering compassion.

"How could you? That's...terrible!" George exclaimed, taken aback by Bruce's extraordinary capacity for forgiveness.

"That's what the Apostle Paul did BC. Not only did our church forgive him, but we owe him for writing half of the New Testament. God forgave him too," Bruce explained, his words filled with grace and understanding.

George couldn't help but smile, overwhelmed by Bruce's remarkable perspective in the face of challenging circumstances. He realized what a blessing it was to have such an extraordinary person in his life.

George started from the beginning, recounting his introduction to Advance Medical. He went on to describe his involvement with John and how he believed that God had sent John into his life as a direct answer to his prayers.

"God is still actively working on that prayer, even as we speak," George said, his voice filled with anticipation.

"What do you mean?" Bruce questioned, his curiosity piqued.

"Well, John and his sister were supposed to be on a plane heading to Elizabeth's home. They were working on exposing Advance Medical's deceit and shutting down The Association. But when I checked with the airline, they informed me that they never boarded the plane," George explained, his tone laced with concern.

"Where are they, then?" Bruce asked, his voice tinged with worry.

"That's the million-dollar question. "I'm afraid they might be with Penkowski," George admitted, his apprehension evident.

"The owner of Advance...Medical," Bruce struggled to recall

the name.

"Exactly," George confirmed, pleased that Bruce was following the conversation.

"Pastor Bruce, can you find it in your heart to forgive me for all the wrong I have done and for my current involvement?" George asked, a glimmer of hope in his eyes.

"You mean the wrongs you're desperately trying to escape while preserving your own life?" Bruce questioned.

George smiled, relieved to hear Bruce's response. "Yes."

"Absolutely, my friend! Your wrongs are no worse than mine or anyone else's. We are all sinners saved by grace... grace that transforms us into saints," Bruce declared, placing his hand on George's shoulder, offering reassurance. George reciprocated the gesture, sighing deeply with a sense of relief.

"This Penkowski... Hmm, what does he look like?" Bruce inquired, a flicker of recognition in his expression.

George vividly described Dr. Penkowski, emphasizing his eerie presence.

"I'm telling you, this guy was downright spooky. I swear I saw his eyes glow, but I chalked it up to my mind playing tricks on me considering the chaotic situation," George recounted, his voice filled with a mix of awe and fear.

"The same thing happened to me as he kept getting closer and closer to me!" Bruce interjected, his voice reflecting the intensity of the encounter.

"Yes, but it gets even more bizarre," Bruce looked at George, conveying his understanding that glowing eyes were far from ordinary.

"As I glanced up with a gun pressed against my temple, I could hardly believe my own eyes. I mean, everyone else felt the impact of the windstorm that tore through the wall, but somehow it had no effect on both those creatures that materialized out of thin air! And it didn't affect Dr. Penkowski either. John stood there in shock, trying to make sense of it all, while I kept staring at those apparitions in the midst of the swirling storm. They appeared like glowing metal. As I focused, I could see they had the semblance of men, but before I could discern their exact features, Penkowski seized my attention. His once possessed eyes turned even more intense, jutting out from his face. And as they did, another grotesque face emerged, overlaying Penkowski's own, peering back and forth at each of the glowing entities flanking him. What I witnessed took me aback, freezing me in place. Those two creatures lunged at Penkowski, engaging him in a ferocious battle," George narrated, his voice filled with astonishment and disbelief.

"George, this is unbelievable!" Bruce exclaimed, struggling to comprehend the magnitude of what George had witnessed.

"You're telling me! I told John, not even considering how it would sound to someone who isn't a Christian, and he simply dismissed it as my imagination running wild," George replied.

"I bet the man who attacked me was Penkowski. He matched your description exactly," Bruce remarked, his expression filled with recognition.

George examined Bruce from head to toe, his anger simmering just beneath the surface.

"George, what can I do to help?" Bruce asked, his voice filled with compassion.

George composed himself and replied, "We need to find John so we can bring Penkowski to justice."

"What about the Research Association?" Bruce inquired, striving to recall the details.

"Ah, we can tackle two problems at once. Advance Medical has practically driven them out of business," George suggested.

"Good. Let's get right on it," Bruce responded, his determination evident.

"Um... Bruce, would you mind?" George's voice quivered with raw emotion.

"What is it?" Bruce asked, his tone compassionate.

"Could you pray out loud, right now? I've really missed your prayers, and I know we need them desperately," George requested, his vulnerability exposed.

"You bet," Bruce affirmed, and together they turned to the Lord in prayer.

As Bruce and George made their way back to the church, they unexpectedly found themselves driving through a neighborhood that had been diverted to an alternative route. Their eyes widened in disbelief as they witnessed homes engulfed in flames evidently a result of fires lit of the other day. Bruce urged John to halt the car, and without a moment's hesitation, he leaped out and sprinted towards the scene, driven by an instinct to assist in any way he could. Firefighters scrambled between fire engines and fire hydrants, scaling ladders to combat the raging inferno. The smoke hung heavy in the air, choking their lungs. George followed closely behind Bruce, his heart pounding in his chest.

"Do you hear that?" Bruce shouted over the commotion.

"Hear what?" George replied, struggling to make himself heard above the deafening noise.

"That cry. I hear it. It's a baby," Bruce exclaimed urgently.

"How can you hear that amidst all this chaos? I can barely hear you!" George questioned, his confusion evident.

Undeterred, Bruce raced from one blazing house to another, with George closely trailing behind. George gazed at Bruce, then glanced towards each burning structure, his face etched with bewilderment as he desperately strained to discern the sound his pastor friend was attuned to.

"Here! It's coming from here!" Bruce announced, pointing towards a house consumed by flames.

Flames flickered menacingly through the windows, while the firefighters were occupied elsewhere. Bruce sprinted to the front door and forcefully kicked it in, leaving George momentarily startled. However, George swiftly remembered that a life was at stake, and saving lives was Bruce's life's calling. Spotting a woman lying unconscious on the living room floor, Bruce motioned to George, who hurried to her side. As George looked up, he witnessed Bruce advancing towards a hallway ablaze with fire. Amidst the clamor, Bruce discerned the cries of a helpless infant echoing from the end of the corridor. Time was of the essence, and the only way to reach the child in time was to traverse through the wall of flames. Bruce halted momentarily, contemplating his own life, then drew strength from the story of Shadrach, Meshach, and Abednego. As he fervently prayed, he glanced upward and beheld a sight reminiscent of his encounter with Pastor Wayne back at the church—a figure at the end of the hallway with flowing white hair, fiery eyes, and a robe as radiant as lightning. The figure's feet gleamed like burnished metal, one hand extended towards Bruce, while the other pointed to the bedroom door. This was the moment. Bruce knew that stepping into the flames meant almost certain death. George had just lifted the unconscious woman into his arms when he witnessed Bruce about to embark on his sacrificial mission.

"No, Bruce, no!" George cried out, his voice filled with desperation and choked with smoke. But before George could take a step towards him, Bruce fearlessly strode into the wall of fire. Overwhelmed by the heat and fumes, George had no choice but to flee the house before succumbing to unconsciousness.

As Bruce took his first step into the engulfing flames, his unwavering gaze remained fixed on Christ. He refused to let his attention waver, determined not to repeat the mistake Peter made when he walked on water. The roar of the fire filled his ears, and though he could feel the intense heat, he resolved to keep his focus solely on Christ amidst the chaos surrounding him. Adrenaline coursed through his veins, his heart pounding with urgency. Despite the scorching temperatures, he felt no pain. With each stride forward, the figure of Christ grew clearer, and Bruce noticed that Christ was blowing towards him, creating a cool breeze that shielded him from the fire's destructive power.

Bruce couldn't help but smile. As he obediently carried out Christ's command, a way was miraculously provided for the impossible task before him. Energized by this realization, he quickened his pace. As he reached the end of the hallway, Christ vanished from sight, but Bruce wasted no time. He forcefully broke down the door, revealing a nursery adorned with love and care. The sound of a baby's cry pierced the air, and Bruce located the infant in the crib. Gently and swiftly, he scooped the baby into his arms, wrapping him snugly in a blanket, before making his exit through the window. Racing around to the front of the house, he spotted George, visibly distressed, tending to the woman who was regaining consciousness. She repeatedly murmured, "My baby... my baby..."

"It's okay, it's okay. Your baby will be just fine," George reassured her, uncertain of why he spoke those words, but understanding that it was what a mother needed to hear in such a moment.

As George continued to comfort the woman, a baby was placed in her arms from behind. George looked up, overcome with joy.

"You made it! You made it! How did you do that? I saw you walk into the fire with my own eyes! No one could have survived that! No one!" George exclaimed, his voice filled with astonishment.

Bruce smiled and pointed upwards, causing George to regain composure, rise to his feet, and embrace his beloved pastor and friend. The baby, sensing the love and relief in the air, began to calm down as the mother wept, cradling her child and expressing gratitude to the men who had rescued them.

As they looked up, they noticed news trucks lining the street, and people rushed towards them, armed with microphones and TV cameras. The media personnel listened intently to the mother, glanced at the baby, and then turned their attention to Bruce and George, eager to conduct interviews.

Bruce seized this opportunity to give all the credit to God for the extraordinary events unfolding in Stapleton. The news reporters were delighted to have such a captivating story, and because the broadcast was live, nothing could be edited or omitted.

"We are reporting live from Stapleton, where an extraordinary act of heroism unfolded as a local pastor rescued a baby from the engulfing flames," the news anchor announced on the national network, their voice trembling with a mixture of admiration and awe. The story spread like wildfire, capturing the attention of viewers across the nation.

Meanwhile, in his secluded area in the jet, Penkowski was engrossed in his nefarious schemes, his attention fixated on his computer screen. Suddenly, a flicker of movement caught his eye, and he swiveled around in his chair to face the TV monitor mounted in the corner of the room. The news report seized his attention, causing his heart to skip a beat.

As the anchor described the selfless actions of Pastor Bruce Hutchinson and his loyal companion George Hines, Penkowski's fury ignited, surpassing any rage he had exhibited earlier in the day. Rising from his chair, his trembling hands reached for it, gripping it tightly before hurling it toward the TV in an explosive display of anger. The chair collided with the screen, causing a shower of sparks and shards of glass to scatter through the air, engulfed in a fiery display.

In an instant, the room was flooded with the presence of armed henchmen, their guns drawn and ready. They observed Penkowski's seething anger and glanced at the smoldering ruins of the television set, now reduced to a charred relic. The tension in the room was crushing, hanging heavy like a storm cloud ready to unleash its fury.

"Get out!" Penkowski's voice reverberated with a venomous intensity, his fury demanding obedience. The gunmen swiftly retreated, leaving Penkowski alone with his simmering rage.

With a sense of urgency fueled by his seething emotions,

Penkowski snatched the phone and dialed a number, his voice trembling with a mix of anger and desperation. "Get me George Hines now!" he barked into the receiver, his words laced with an intensity that betrayed the fear and determination driving him in that moment.

"I...I don't know what that was, but it was terrifying," John stammered, his voice trembling with a mix of fear and uncertainty.

Elizabeth, her eyes wide with apprehension, sought reassurance from her brother. "Do you really think the plane is safe? After that explosion and the ominous silence from the gunman, can we really believe we're okay?"

John gazed into Elizabeth's eyes, sensing the weight of her trust in his judgment. With a deep breath, he summoned every ounce of courage he had left. "I believe...I believe the jet is still intact. We're still flying smoothly, and the gunman hasn't made any aggressive moves since he spoke into his walkie-talkie. I think...I think we might be alright, Elizabeth."

Elizabeth's tense expression softened slightly, a glimmer of hope peeking through her anxiety. She nodded, finding solace in her brother's assessment, even amidst the chaos and uncertainty surrounding them. In that moment, their unyielding bond became their lifeline, providing a semblance of strength in the face of the unknown.

"He's not in his office? That's painfully obvious! Instead, he's gallivanting around the city with some religious fanatic! I want him on the phone immediately!" Click. He got on the phone once again.

Bruce's eyes met George's, and in that moment, a sense of urgency permeated the air. "Your phone is ringing," Bruce informed, his voice tinged with concern. George's gaze flickered up, his expression riddled with worry.

"What is it?" Bruce inquired, his voice laced with anticipation.

George's fingers clutched his cell phone, his heart pounding in his chest. "It's Penkowski, the head of Advance Medical," George responded, his voice laden with trepidation. Bruce's memory was still hazy about the details George had shared, but one thing was clear—they both knew exactly who Penkowski was, the man responsible for Bruce's ordeal.

George took a deep breath and answered the call, the weight of impending confrontation hanging in the air. "Hello?" he said, his voice quivering slightly.

"George?" Penkowski' voice boomed through the phone, dripping with anger. The words hit George like a verbal assault, triggering a wave of anxiety within him.

"Yes?" George managed to respond, his voice strained.

"I look up at the news, and I see YOU running around town with some religious freak when you're supposed to be managing AFT's facility?" Penkowski' voice crackled with fury, each word like a lash of a whip.

George tried to offer an explanation, but Penkowski' rage cut him off. "I am furious, and I am about to make your life miserable!" Penkowski bellowed, his words punctuated with venom. "You are on my blacklist, my friend, and I use the word 'friend' loosely! Not only..."

Feeling overwhelmed, George decided to take a different approach, attempting to deflect the mounting wrath. "Dr. Penkowski, I can't hear you. You're breaking up. It must be a bad cell zone," George interjected, desperation tainting his voice.

"Don't give me that line, I—" Penkowski' voice crackled before fading away. The call ended abruptly, leaving George with a mix of relief and unease.

"I need to get back to the office, Bruce. I'm sorry," George said, his voice appearing more composed than he truly felt.

"What was it? What did he want?" Bruce probed, his voice tinged with worry.

"Apparently, Penkowski saw us on the news, and now he's furious. I need to make a few changes at the office to cover my tracks before we take off," George explained, his tone carrying a sense of urgency. His cell phone rang once more, and George glanced down, swiftly silencing it.

"Penkowski?" Bruce inquired, his voice laced with concern.

"Yeah, I'll let it go a couple more times, and then I'll have to answer it. I don't want him to think I'm pulling a fast one with the bad cell excuse," George responded, his words infused with a mixture of determination and caution.

George and Bruce hurriedly hopped into the car, their hearts pounding in sync. Bruce was dropped off at the school, and as George sped off towards his office, his cell phone chimed once more, a final futile attempt from Penkowski to reach him. Eventually, the calls ceased, leaving behind an unsettling silence that seemed to mirror the turbulent emotions swirling within George.

"Did you or did you not work with George Hines in Stapleton?" Penkowski interrogated John, the atmosphere in the room growing increasingly tense. The weight of the situation bore down on John, realizing his vulnerability as his sister remained in the other room, her safety beyond his control. His primary concern was to provide quick answers and return to her side.

"No, I don't know any George," John responded, his words devoid of sarcasm. Yet, beneath his composed exterior, he couldn't shake the feeling of vulnerability. The intensity of the situation made him yearn for swift resolution, to protect his sister from harm.

"Do you know about our manufacturing plant in Stapleton?" Penkowski pressed further, his tone laden with suspicion.

"No, I was only hired to gather documentation on the demise of The Association. It didn't require delving into the details of your company's operations," John explained, attempting to clarify his limited involvement.

"You must be hiding something, John. You're being too cooperative. I'm not accustomed to this absence of sarcasm," Penkowski remarked, a hint of skepticism lacing his words. John glanced up at him, his gaze revealing a mixture of defiance and frustration.

"I have downloaded and wiped everything off your laptop," Penkowski declared, a bombshell that left John visibly shocked. The revelation hit him like a punch to the gut.

"Did you really think we would simply return your laptop with all its contents intact? Please! I want to know if you're withholding anything beyond what was on the laptop. We have gathered a significant amount of information, to say the least," Penkowski asserted triumphantly, turning his monitor to face John, who now felt a growing sense of indignation.

"Ah! Finally, I've got you! Good, good. It's about time. Now, you'll be taken somewhere where you won't cause me any more trouble!" Penkowski taunted, relishing in his perceived victory.

"Where are you taking us?" John inquired, his voice tinged with apprehension.

"I'm taking you somewhere remote. I have a friend who will be doing me this little favor," Penkowski replied, his tone oozing with a mix of malevolence and satisfaction.

The plane began to bank to the right, signaling their approach to the airstrip. "Ah, we're approaching the airstrip. Guard!" Penkowski called out, summoning one of the gunmen to secure John back into his seat, cementing his lack of freedom.

FIFTEEN

George was engrossed in his work in the office when his secretary entered, interrupting his focus. The urgency in her voice caught his attention.

"George... Dr. Penkowski is on the phone. This is his third call within the hour. He said it's urgent," she informed him.

"Thanks. I'll take it in here."

Taking a deep breath, George prepared himself and picked up the phone. "Hello?"

"George! I see you do work in the factory once in a while!" Dr. Penkowski's voice boomed through the receiver, filled with annoyance.

"I was on lunch," George offered, attempting to justify his absence.

"I don't care! I despise that town and its obsession with Christianity! You need to cease all involvement in any religious nonsense, or mark my words, George, I will personally descend upon you and subject you to relentless torment!" Penkowski threatened vehemently, leaving George taken aback. He bit his tongue, refraining from saying what he truly wanted to express. Instead, with the help of God, he mustered a composed response.

"That sounds like a threat," George calmly stated.

Penkowski cursed in frustration. "You're darn right it's a threat, and I will follow through with it without hesitation if necessary!" With that, he abruptly hung up the phone.

"What a beautiful day this has turned out to be," George mused with a touch of sarcasm. "Not only did I receive a scolding, but I also endured a threat." Despite the unsettling encounter, George found solace in the fact that Penkowski had not yet connected him to John. "That's good," he thought, relieved to have avoided further complications.

Bruce assembled all the necessary materials and met with the leaders of each ministry group. He informed them of his temporary absence from the circle and revealing the necessity of addressing some precarious issues. Though the ministry heads inquired, Bruce steadfastly protected the confidential information entrusted to him by George. Throughout the process, he couldn't help but reflect on the divine encounter with his Savior and the profound words spoken to him and Wayne. Recognizing the increased danger that Wayne would now face, Bruce included him in their prayer sessions. As a member of the group, Wayne was prepared to confront the challenges ahead. With his preparations complete, Bruce set off, understanding the urgency of rescuing George from a potentially life-threatening situation.

Meanwhile, George concluded his tasks at work and hit the road. He picked up Bruce once again at the high school, and they embarked on their journey together in the car.

"I thought we could head to the airport and do some reconnaissance," George suggested.

"Have you tried reaching John on his cell phone?" Bruce inquired.

"Yeah, it just keeps ringing until his voicemail kicks in. I've also attempted to text and email him," George replied, his worry evident. He paused, focusing on the road ahead, and continued, "I'm really concerned."

Bruce struggled to find the right words. This whole situation was new to him, and he was still piecing everything together. He asked a series of questions in an attempt to fill in the gaps and understand the complete story. Gradually, it started to make sense. In fact, it made enough sense for Bruce to recognize how God was calling him to be part of it all.

"You know, George, one of the most exhilarating moments during the Revival was the closure of the abortion clinics," Bruce shared, his voice filled with passion. George listened attentively as Bruce continued.

"We used to protest those clinics every year, but it felt like we were making no difference. Even when the Association held their meetings in town, we protested those too. At the time, we couldn't see the impact we were making. Yes, we occasionally saw an abortion being prevented, but nothing as significant as the closure of all the clinics in town. It's truly remarkable."

"And to think, while you were fighting for the lives of unborn babies, I..." George's voice trailed off, leaving his unfinished thought hanging in the air.

Bruce interjected abruptly, cutting George off. "Lost and clueless? That's not the case anymore," Bruce asserted, a smile lighting up his face. "You've already made a significant impact on our church and the God-ordained Revival of Stapleton. Just look at the houses you restored after they were vandalized, the lives you've touched there, and the website that serves as the backbone for our leaders involved in every aspect of the revival." Bruce glanced over to gauge George's reaction, pleased to see that his words were resonating.

"You know, Bruce, you're absolutely right. God has a greater purpose for you beyond just helping me, although I'm immensely grateful for your support. He has placed you here for a specific reason. I wonder what that might be," George mused, a sense of curiosity and anticipation building within him.

George and Bruce delved into the details surrounding John's disappearance. Eventually, Bruce posed a question, "Is John a believer?"

George hesitated momentarily before responding. "I don't think so, but he's witnessed a lot of God's work in Stapleton, including our own experiences together."

"Well, let's pray for him now," Bruce suggested, offering a novel idea. George had been praying for John, but this particular prayer was different.

As they concluded their prayer, George felt a newfound peace regarding John's situation. However, he suddenly remembered that his sister was also involved, causing his anxiety to resurface.

"John is with his sister," George shared with a hint of concern in his voice.

"Why did he involve his sister in all of this?" Bruce questioned.

"He believed that her personal encounter with the Association's abortion clinic would not only bring her on board but also empower her to overcome the horrors inflicted upon her by these organizations."

"Hmm, that's interesting. What's her name?" Bruce inquired.

"Lizzy... no, Elizabeth," George corrected himself. Bruce proceeded to pray for Elizabeth as well.

Once again, George's worries began to dissipate, replaced by a newfound confidence and a sense of divine guidance.

"Thank you, Bruce. That's exactly what I needed. Now, let me share with you our plan of action," George said, his voice filled with gratitude and determination as he outlined their next steps.

As the plane touched down, John and Elizabeth braced themselves for the anticipated rough handling until they reached their undisclosed destination. True to their expectations, they were swiftly escorted from the plane to a waiting limo and then to an unfamiliar building on the outskirts of town. Throughout the journey, an eerie silence enveloped them, with no words exchanged. Penkowski had left them at the airport, leaving them to navigate their way alone from that point forward.

John discreetly scanned his surroundings, his eyes darting to absorb the details of the streets, landmarks, and any distinctive features. Occasionally, the armed guard would glance in his direction, but John managed to avert his gaze, focusing it instead on the floor in front of him, ensuring he didn't arouse suspicion. Elizabeth recognized her brother's intent observation and refrained from interrupting him. She shared his desire to escape this predicament, though she still questioned whether she had made the right choice. However, every time she looked at John, her love for her brother triumphed, even surpassing her reservations about his newfound religious fervor.

As they arrived at a warehouse-like building, they were promptly ushered inside. The atmosphere resembled that of a hospital—everything pristine white and sterile, with a distinct clean scent permeating the air. The security guard at the information desk motioned them forward, and the hallways they traversed mirrored those of a hospital.

John couldn't help but smile, unnoticed by the gunmen but detected by his sister. Elizabeth looked at him, and he responded with a reassuring wink. Though she tried, she couldn't summon a smile herself, weighed down by the gravity of their situation.

They were escorted to another section of the building, where a group of desks in cubicles awaited. People dressed in white lab coats occupied the workspace. Two imposing figures approached and led them to a door that opened into a room. Once again, the dominant color was white. The room contained a bed, a chair, and a small restroom. Before John and Elizabeth could react, the door closed with a resounding echo that reverberated throughout the halls and within the confines of the room. It felt cold, and for a moment, both siblings surveyed their surroundings.

Then, John's investigative nature kicked in. He approached the door, examining its security features—a conventional handle, a deadbolt, and wires attached to the top and bottom. His eyes scanned the corners, spotting sensors, but he discerned no cameras in sight. The restroom, although compact, appeared clean, devoid of any windows. John crouched and checked beneath the bed, feeling its stability with his hands. As he rose slowly, his gaze fixated on the window—a small opening that would have been large enough to escape through if not for the iron bars that thwarted any such attempt. Lost in contemplation, a hand suddenly rested on John's shoulder. He turned, and Elizabeth fell into his embrace, her tears flowing freely.

"Shhh... it's okay. Trust me. Once we escape from this place, we'll dismantle these criminals and make the world a better place. I promise," John whispered, seeking to instill confidence in his sister. He channeled all his emotional concerns into a determined energy, fueling his resolve to find a way out. Even as he held and reassured Elizabeth, his eyes wandered up to the ceiling. He noticed an air vent, large enough for someone to crawl through, along with a fire sprinkler and a ceiling light fixture. Taking Elizabeth's hand, he led her over to the bed where they both sat down.

As Elizabeth regained composure, she asked John, "Why did you smile when we first arrived here?"

"Well, remember on the plane how we heard about Advance Medical buying fetuses and claiming to dispose of them for research?" John recalled. "I have a feeling this is where they conduct their so-called research."

"Really?" Elizabeth questioned, her curiosity piqued.

"Yeah, but it makes me wonder why Penkowski placed us here. He mentioned putting us with a friend," John pondered aloud.

Elizabeth looked at John, offering no immediate answer, prompting him to fill the silence. "Maybe he doesn't have any friends," he quipped, eliciting a chuckle from both of them. The lighter moment helped alleviate some of the guilt John felt for involving his sister in their perilous circumstances.

George and Bruce arrived at the airport, where they were startled to see the overturned police car involved in the chase with Penkowski. Both of them stared wide-eyed at the scene before continuing through the airport. They noticed groups of people gathering around police officers, evidently being questioned about the abduction of two individuals from the airport to a jet. As George and Bruce approached, they caught fragments of conversations.

Among those interviewed, one person seemed to have the most relevant information for George and Bruce. Once the police were done with them, George and Bruce approached to intercept them.

"Hi, I am..." George began, but was promptly interrupted.

"Pastor Bruce! Hello. Oh, what happened to your face?" the woman exclaimed.

"Well, I'd like to say that the other guy looks worse, but I'm not sure that's true," Bruce joked, though the woman appeared concerned.

"I'll be okay. We believe the person who did this is the same person you discussed with the police," Bruce explained.

"But why would they target you? Why abduct those people?" The woman inquired.

"I don't know, but we think the abducted individuals might be our friends," Bruce replied. She glanced around and added, "Can you believe all of this? It feels like we're in the big city or something."

"Yes, it's quite chaotic, Beth. How is your class doing after all the excitement?" Bruce asked.

"Are you referring to the miraculous intervention by God with His word, the Ten Commandments?" Beth replied.

"Yes! Tommy was the young boy. I led him to Christ in the hospital, with more of God's intervention," Bruce shared happily.

Beth smiled and tried to extract more details from Bruce. "I'd love to hear the whole story, and I will. But right now, we might have information about the abducted individuals, and you might be able to help us find them."

"Well, what can I do to assist?" Beth asked.

"First, let us ask you some questions. Oh, where are my manners? Mrs. Hurwitz, this is George Hines," Bruce introduced.

"Please, call me Beth. I prefer being addressed by my last name by my students," Beth replied.

"Beth, it's nice to meet you. Due to time constraints, I'll pester Bruce to share your miracle story with me later," George said, expressing his eagerness to learn more about her experience.

"George, yes, I remember during Sunday service when you shared your joy about the brace coming off and how you were jumping up and down," Beth reminisced. Her words caused George to pause and reflect. In the midst of his sin, God had come to him and met his physical need, making him feel incredibly special.

"Well, let me begin by telling you that this man looked truly evil. I mean, his eyes were red, bloodshot, glazed... it almost seemed like they..." Beth hesitated, unsure of how her next comment would be received.

"Glowed?" Bruce interjected.

"Yes! That's it. They glowed. So eerie! Anyway, he must have had a gun pressed against the man's back..."

"What did the man look like?" George inquired.

"He was in his early sixties, had most of his hair, and it was very neatly groomed," Beth described.

"Did he have any facial hair?"

"No, none at all. He was slim and tall, dressed in what appeared to be a very expensive suit."

George exchanged a knowing look with Bruce and smiled.

Beth continued her account, saying, "But I'm telling you, those eyes seemed to peer right into your soul."

"Did he say anything to the people?" Bruce asked.

"Just 'Move.' And they did. They went right out that door over there," Beth pointed in the direction.

"Could you see them from the window?" George inquired further.

"Oh, you bet! I rushed over to the window and witnessed everything!" Beth replied, her excitement growing. She needed no invitation to continue; her words rushed out like a racehorse.

"I saw them running towards a small jet, you know, one of those owned by corporate executives?"

"Yes, go on," Bruce encouraged.

"Well, I could see a man waving them on and pointing behind them. And suddenly, all our police cars came speeding in as fast as they could..."

"Did you notice any writing on the jet?" George questioned.

"Oh, let's see... um... it was something like 'A period M.' A peculiar name for a jet."

"Bingo! Beth, you've been a tremendous help," George expressed his gratitude.

"But wait, I haven't told you the best part!" Beth exclaimed with excitement in her voice. Bruce and George couldn't bring themselves to interrupt her, so they let her share the thrilling details of the cars chasing the jet. She was pleased with their interest. After thanking her, they moved on from their conversation.

"John, what are we going to do?" Elizabeth asked anxiously.

"Well, the good news is that we're still alive, and it seems like Penkowski has no intention of killing me," John replied.

"John! Being optimistic doesn't help us right now. We need a plan, not empty reassurances," Elizabeth snapped.

"Hold on, sis. I'm thinking," John said, trying to gather his thoughts.

"Even if you manage to get us out of here, they've wiped your laptop clean, and they've taken away all the paperwork we had to incriminate them. We're left with nothing, John," Elizabeth exclaimed in frustration.

"We have everything, sis! Look!" John pointed to his heel.

"What? Shoes? Do you have shoes? What does that have to do with anything?" Elizabeth questioned, perplexed.

"You're not looking closely enough. Look," John urged, a twinkle in his eye. Elizabeth realized he was up to something. John had a way of making you figure things out on your own, just like in their childhood days. Familiar with his tricks, she slowly bent down to the floor and examined John's shoe. He raised his foot onto its toe, revealing a fake heel. Inside, there was a cleverly designed display of circuitry covered in clear plastic. A small USB connector awaited use, ready to download all the saved files from the hardware. Elizabeth looked up, and her brother was beaming.

"This little device contains every file that was on my computer. The other heel holds all the necessary programs. Just plug it into any computer, and I'll have access to everything that was on my laptop," John explained triumphantly.

Elizabeth stood up and tossed the fake heel into the air, which John caught skillfully.

"That solves one problem, but what about the documentation we lost?" Elizabeth asked, still concerned.

"I've got that covered. In the meantime, I've scanned all the information you need to bring these crooks down for good and saved it on my computer... uh... heel... well, you know what I mean," John reassured her.

Elizabeth smiled. "Now, all we need is a computer so I can start working. Any idea where we can find one?"

John pointed towards the door. "It's on the other side of this door."

"And how exactly do you plan on getting to the other side of the door?" Elizabeth inquired skeptically.

"I enjoy a good challenge," John replied confidently.

"Please! This isn't a game, John. Let's just focus on getting out of here," Elizabeth urged.

"Not so fast. As long as we're in here, they won't be actively searching for us," John explained.

"Now I think you've lost it! Of course, they won't be looking for us while we're locked up," Elizabeth retorted.

"That gives us a chance to get some work done," John added.

"I give up. I can't always follow your reasoning," Elizabeth admitted.

"Trust me. I know what I'm doing," John assured her.

"You always made me nervous as a child when you said that to me," Elizabeth confessed.

"Did I ever let you down? Wait, before you answer that, remember, I love you, sis," John said, seeking reassurance.

"No, you've pulled me through a lot of tough times. I owe you a lot. That's why I agreed to help you. I felt it was my turn to pay you back," Elizabeth replied, her voice filled with gratitude.

John looked relieved. He wasn't entirely sure if he had ever let his sister down, so it was comforting to know that in her eyes, he hadn't.

"So, now what?" Bruce asked, standing on the runway with George.

"Well... I'm not really the detective here. John is. So, we've got things a bit backwards," George admitted.

"What do you mean?" Bruce inquired.

"I mean, we're searching for the detective when it would be better if the detective needed to find us. You know what I mean?" George explained, and they shared a laugh at the irony.

"Okay, let's think about this. The tire marks are heading west. Of course, the plane can change direction in the air. Hmm... west," Bruce pondered.

"Maybe California?" Bruce suggested cautiously, trying not to sound patronizing.

"Yeah, what was I thinking? Of course, that's where Penkowski is. But where in California?" George mused.

They walked back into the airport and returned to their car. George took out his laptop and took a shot in the dark. He entered "Advance Medical" into a search engine and found their official website. There, they saw a picture of Penkowski.

"That's the man! He's the one who caused all the trouble!" Bruce exclaimed.

"Yeah, and he fits the description given by Beth Hurwitz," George confirmed.

"That's right!"

Bruce noticed an icon with the word "abortion" on it and pointed it out to George. "George, click on that icon for a moment."

As George clicked, pages upon pages of abortion clinic locations throughout the nation appeared.

"Are you telling me that if we shut down Advance Medical, all these clinics will close their doors?" Bruce asked in disbelief.

"Yes, and The Association for Fetal Research has its own extensive list of abortion clinics, even longer than this one," George replied.

"I think I now understand God's purpose for me in all of this. This is the opportunity I've dreamed of every year as I picketed those clinics and attended meetings. Wow, what a difference we could make!" Bruce exclaimed with determination.

"We will make a difference, no doubt about it. We have all the necessary documentation," George assured him.

George searched for the site map, clicked on all the divisions, and a list of 15 divisions appeared. Bruce watched in amazement as George effortlessly navigated the technology. George stared at the list.

"Well, I don't think he's going to take him to his main office," George concluded.

George copied and pasted the list into a word processor, deliberately removing the main office.

"These four are out, too much traffic," George analyzed.

Bruce chimed in, "These are designated headquarters for clinics and reconstruction surgery centers... Look at the pictures of the buildings. They're also too small."

"Yeah, I think you're right. Well, that leaves us with just four buildings," George determined.

"Great! But how will we figure out which one they're in?" Bruce wondered.

"We'll have to pay each one a visit," George suggested.

Bruce grew concerned. "That sounds dangerous. I'm still in a lot of pain from our last encounter with this Penkowski character."

"I'm sorry, Bruce. There is no other way. If you don't want to come, I understand..." George hesitated.

"No! If it means rescuing your friend and getting his sister a lawyer, if it means closing down these places, then count me in!" Bruce interrupted passionately. "I'll be honest with you, George. Year after year, I stood in those picket lines, praying and wishing I could do more to save those women from the regret of killing their own babies. I must confess, some of my thoughts were not very Christian. But now, I have an opportunity to do more than picketing. Even though there's great danger involved, we can make an impact not just on one clinic, not just in our city or our state, but in the whole nation! Did you see that list? It's a dream come true! I've always wanted to do something as significant as this. I'm ready! Let's go take down these companies for the Lord!"

George was impressed, to say the least. He had no idea his pastor had so much fire within him. He didn't know about Bruce's involvement in picketing before joining the church, nor did he realize how strongly against abortion his pastor was. This newfound knowledge changed George's perspective on involving Bruce in this situation. He was now grateful that he had given

Pastor Bruce the opportunity of a lifetime to dismantle the two largest abortion companies in the world.

"Be careful, that metal is sharp!" Elizabeth cautioned as her brother removed the vent cover for the air-conditioning.

"Okay, Mom!" John replied playfully.

His sister smiled shyly, knowing that her brother had been doing this kind of work for a long time. It was just part of their family dynamic, looking out for one another.

John peered up through the opening and turned until he could see the light, which came from the direction of the door and the area with desks and cubicles.

"Perfect!" he whispered.

"John, get down! I hear the door!" Elizabeth warned.

Quickly, John descended, ensuring he made little to no noise as he replaced the vent cover.

Then, the door swung open. A slender man dressed entirely in white entered. He exuded an attractive presence and wheeled in a table covered with a white linen tablecloth. John glanced toward the door but dared not take any chances that might jeopardize their situation. As nice as the man seemed, his sister was with him, and John had to consider both of their safety.

"Thanks," John muttered, surprising Elizabeth.

"You're welcome. Godspeed," the man replied before exiting the room and locking the door behind him.

John and Elizabeth exchanged bewildered looks.

"Godspeed? What on earth does that mean?" John pondered aloud.

"Why would he say that when he's holding us prisoner?" Elizabeth added, her confusion evident.

Shaking off their perplexity, they turned their attention to the table. It boasted silver platters with elegant covers, far fancier than their circumstances warranted. As they lifted each cover, they discovered high-quality food fit for a five-star restaurant. Their curiosity got the best of them, and they couldn't resist sampling the delicacies. It was the most delicious food they had ever tasted. Without exchanging words, they both loaded their plates and savored every bite. The extravagant treatment left them baffled, yet the meal lifted their spirits despite being locked away. As they finished, Elizabeth settled into a chair while John perched on the edge of the bed. They found themselves feeling content, grateful for the food that had brought some comfort amidst their confinement.

As John sat there, he noticed something black at the bottom of the tablecloth. Intrigued, he stood up and lifted the tablecloth to investigate.

"I don't believe it," he exclaimed.

"What is it?" Elizabeth asked, growing curious as John remained silent, staring intently.

John continued to say nothing, prompting his sister to join him and see for herself.

"That's your laptop case," she observed, picking it up.

John looked at his sister in disbelief as she unzipped the case, revealing his laptop. He was rendered speechless.

"How did this end up under the table?" Elizabeth wondered aloud.

John had a hunch, but expressing it would sound far-fetched. Before Elizabeth could press for an answer, the door locks began to turn. In a hurry, both John and his sister concealed the laptop under the bed. When they looked up, the table had vanished, and the door started to open, revealing one of the men who had initially escorted them into the room. His gaze darted from them to his feet, where two covered dishes sat on the floor. He nudged them with his feet towards the center of the room and placed a metal pitcher of water beside the door before slamming it shut.

John and Elizabeth exchanged puzzled glances and simultaneously asked, "Where did the table go?" They burst into laughter briefly, but their faces quickly turned serious.

"John, we put the laptop under the bed, and before the door even opened, the table with all the food vanished, just disappeared!" Elizabeth exclaimed.

John retrieved the laptop from under the bed, holding it up for both of them to see.

"Here's the laptop," John confirmed. "But where is the table?"

They moved from the edge of the bed to its center, leaning their backs against the wall. They kept pondering the whereabouts of the table, but neither of them had an answer. They stared at the spot where the table had once stood, hoping for some clarity, but it proved fruitless.

George and Bruce boarded the first plane to California. It felt a bit strange for Bruce, as he wasn't accustomed to traveling. Being a small-town pastor for many years, he never gave much thought to how Jennifer, his true love and a missionary, managed life on the go. As he settled in his seat on the plane, the overwhelming excitement of finally making a difference in the cause he had passionately pursued over the years overshadowed his nervousness about flying to an unfamiliar state.

"How should we go about looking for your friends?" Bruce inquired.

"That's a good question. I'm not entirely sure how to answer it, but we'll figure it out together as amateur detectives. I do have one request, though," George replied.

"What is it?" Bruce asked, intrigued.

"Just promise not to disclose all the mistakes we make along the way to John. We wouldn't want to disappoint him. After all, he's the one who taught me everything I know about this," George said playfully.

Their laughter broke the tension, lightening the mood. Bruce continued to update George on the latest happenings back home.

"I'm glad you're in good spirits. I don't want to dampen the mood, but we must acknowledge the danger involved in this mission, just as I mentioned earlier at the park," George said, pausing for emphasis. "It could cost you your life."

"Yes, I believe you," Bruce replied thoughtfully. "I feel like God has already proven Himself through the burning house experience." George recalled the account Bruce shared about seeing Jesus through the flames and the miraculous outcome that saved a baby's life.

As the plane touched down, the men embarked on their California journey. They rented a car, with Bruce taking the wheel.

"Turn here, and keep an eye out for 54th Street. We need to head west," George guided Bruce, navigating their way through the unfamiliar streets.

George used his GPS to pinpoint each destination they planned to visit. They drove up and down streets until they finally arrived at the first location. It was situated in a more upscale part of town and appeared to be open to the public, which raised doubts in the minds of both George and Bruce. However, their confidence in their detective skills was not yet fully established, so they decided to enter with boldness.

"Hi, my name is Mr. Stine, and I would like to take a tour of your facility," George stated confidently, with Bruce standing beside him, hoping George had more expertise than he had initially let on.

The receptionist looked up with a smile and responded, "Mr. Stine, we typically require appointments for facility tours. Would you like to schedule one?"

"Dr. Penkowski specifically directed me to come here," George swiftly replied, pulling out his ID card and flashing it before her. The receptionist caught a glimpse of the picture, and it seemed to satisfy her.

She made a phone call, and without delay, a young woman arrived to escort them throughout the building. The tour left no area unexplored. Once they had seen everything, they expressed their gratitude to the woman and headed towards the exit.

"Well, that was certainly an interesting way of gaining entry," Bruce remarked.

"I didn't really expect him to be here, but I thought it would be an opportunity to gather some clues," George explained.

"And...?" Bruce inquired, eager for further information.

"I believe it's worth visiting the other buildings. In the break room, I noticed some pictures with addresses on them, and those locations are where we should go next. They appear to be more industrial, which could serve as better hiding places," George elaborated, outlining his reasoning.

"What have you come up with so far?" John asked his sister as she worked on the laptop. He had just finished recovering all the information that Penkowski had erased from his own laptop.

"Well, take a look at this," Elizabeth said, pointing at the screen. "In addition to the obvious illegal activities we've encountered, such as kidnapping and assault, it seems that Penkowski has also violated national laws."

On the laptop screen, there were legal terms and documents displayed. Some of it made sense to Elizabeth, but it was clear that John, not being a lawyer, struggled to fully comprehend it.

Elizabeth began taking notes, but suddenly she paused and looked at John.

"You can save this on your flash drive, right?" she asked.

"Yes, sis, no problem," John replied.

With that assurance, Elizabeth resumed her typing, determined to document their findings.

SIXTEEN

After Penkowski's visit, things began to settle down in Stapleton, but the city was still abuzz with excitement. The local papers featured headlines about the recent fires, the heroic acts of saving a baby's life and rescuing a mother from a burning house, as well as the airport escapade that involved a police car flipping in the parking lot. The news caught the attention of everyone in town, and Stapleton continued to have the most eventful news in its history. Today was not going to turn the town back into the sleepy, quiet place it once was.

It was time for the Association for Fetal Research to hold their annual meeting in Stapleton. It was unusual for such a large company to choose this location, but they had maintained this tradition since the company's inception, and it remained unchanged till now. However, on this trip, the Association had decided that this meeting would be their final one.

"Mayor, I wanted you to be the first to know," Dennis Spence said to the mayor in his office shortly after arriving once again in Stapleton.

"What is it, Mr. Spence?" the mayor inquired.

"We have been sold to a California-based company called Advance Medical," Denise stated.

"Oh, I'm sorry to hear this. Will you still be part of the company?" the mayor asked with concern.

"No, they have only acquired the name and assets. Everything and everyone else will have to leave," Dennis said with a hint of disappointment.

"You mean... we won't be able to rely on your financial support anymore?" the mayor sounded disappointed.

"That's exactly what it means for you. For me and the employees of our company, we'll be out of a job," Dennis explained, expressing his disappointment.

"What about your local manufacturer, AFT?" the mayor inquired.

"Advance Medical will replace them with their own people," Denise stated.

"Wow," the mayor was taken aback.

"This shouldn't have come as a surprise to you. The closure of the abortion clinics in this town was the first sign of trouble," Dennis stated.

"Well, I didn't realize the severity of the problem," the mayor admitted.

"Nevertheless, my colleagues and I have come for one last meeting. We need to discuss the dismantling of the company, and we thought it would be appropriate to do it here, where we first started meeting when the company was founded," Dennis continued.

"I remember when I suggested having our meetings here in my hometown. It felt fitting and brought back so many memories. As our company grew, that little church down the road used to picket every meeting we held here for years," Denise recollected.

"That little church has been causing quite a stir lately," the mayor remarked.

"I have no doubt about that. That pastor was relentless. If it wasn't our annual meetings, he was protesting the abortion clinics we had here. He never gave up. But I wasn't willing to give up either. I grew up here, and I started our meetings here. I wasn't going to let some small-town pastor change that," Dennis stated passionately.

"When does your annual meeting start?" the mayor asked.

"We start today. It will give us time to say goodbye. I just wanted all of us to gather here one last time," Dennis explained.

"I'm sure it will be a memorable experience," the mayor commented, although deep down, he felt remorse for lying.

Wayne gathered all the leaders in Bruce's church, his heart heavy with a mix of responsibility and longing for Bruce's presence. It felt awkward for Wayne to take charge, as if Bruce should be the one leading this meeting. However, he understood that it was his duty, especially since Bruce was out of town. Wayne took a deep breath and tried to settle everyone down, knowing that he needed to step up in Bruce's absence.

He addressed the gathered leaders, his voice filled with both concern and hope. Wayne shared that he hadn't heard from Pastor Bruce and urged them to continue praying for him. He explained that Bruce had specifically asked them not to expect any communication for a while. The room filled with questions and uncertainty, but Wayne did his best to reassure them, even though he couldn't disclose the details of Bruce's whereabouts or activities.

"Today, the Association for Fetal Research is holding their annual meeting in our town," Wayne announced, a flicker of determination in his eyes. "I believe we should gather volunteers to picket the meeting, just as Bruce has done in the past."

"I'm on it!" Sue exclaimed with unwavering enthusiasm. "I'll email everyone and rally them in prayer on my end."

Maggie chimed in, her voice filled with determination, "I'll prepare some of the music I've been working on and get the choir ready."

Wayne's face brightened with a sense of unity and purpose. "Perfect! Let's show them a presence they've never encountered in the life of their company. Who knows, with all that God is doing in our community, this may be the last time they come here for their meetings. Together, let's make a powerful statement and stand firm in our faith." Emotions of determination, hope, and anticipation echoed through Wayne's words as he envisioned the impact their united front could have.

Dennis approached the usual hotel where his meetings were held. As he neared the entrance, he glanced up and noticed the picketers, marching back and forth with their signs. These picketers had always been there, a minor annoyance that he had grown accustomed to over the years. Once inside the hotel, they posed no threat. Two sleek stretch limos pulled up in front, and Dennis, along with 20 men, stepped out of the cars, all impeccably dressed in suits. They walked toward the curb, deliberately avoiding eye contact with the homemade signs held by the picketers. Dennis's focus was fixed solely on the hotel's entrance, knowing that once he crossed that threshold, this external disturbance would be left behind.

As the men followed Dennis, they entered through the doors and proceeded down the hall until they reached a small banquet room. They made sure to lock the doors behind them, just in case the picketers decided to intrude. The room was tastefully decorated with white tablecloths, artificial plants, and tables arranged in a boardroom style, facing each other.

Once everyone had settled in their seats and engaged in some light conversation, Dennis took charge and began to speak. All eyes in the room were fixed on their leader and boss, their gazes filled with years of loyalty and respect.

"The Association for Fetal Research has been sold to an up-and-coming company called Advance Medical, based in California," Dennis announced, his tone filled with a mix of resignation and determination. "It was our only choice, short of going out of business."

He continued, reminiscing about the early days when he had started the company from scratch, pouring his sweat and dedication into its growth. Over the years, he had realized the need for assistance in achieving his grand goal of becoming the number one provider in sales and services in the abortion industry.

"Men, we have made a difference. We have outperformed every other national medical abortion company in America, conquered numerous markets within the abortion industry, and established a name that reverberated throughout the nation. We have savored the sweet taste of success, unmatched by any of our competitors."

"But, for some reason, the tide has turned. Despite our relentless efforts to find resolutions to our problems, all our attempts have proven futile. Even my suspicions of external sabotage were debunked by a private detective service."

"So here we are, gathered for our final meeting, and I wanted us to convene where it all began—my hometown of Stapleton. I want to spend this time..."

Suddenly, the locked door swung open slowly and silently, interrupting Dennis mid-sentence. He stared wide-eyed, astonished by this unforeseen development.

"I thought we had locked that door?" Dennis exclaimed, his frustration tinged with surprise.

"We did," replied one of the men in the room. "I personally checked it myself."

An elderly man stepped into the room, carrying a large cork-board turned away from view. Dennis's frustration shifted to disbelief as he recognized the face.

"Dr. Stearing? Is that really you, Dr. Stearing?" Dennis blurted out.

"Yes, your former employee," Dr. Stearing responded with a solemn voice, his presence shrouded in an air of mystery.

"What are you doing here, and how did you manage to get through that locked door?" Dennis demanded, his voice trembling with a mix of confusion and concern.

Dr. Stearing paused for a moment, his gaze shifting towards the door Dennis had mentioned. Then, he returned his attention to Dennis and replied, "I thought it was fitting to express my gratitude for everything you have done for me over the years by presenting this collage of pictures to you."

Dennis's eyes widened with anticipation, ready to question Dr. Stearing's unexpected presence. But before he could utter a word, the man stepped closer to the group of men, gradually turning the cork-board around.

Dennis let out a gasp, and an overwhelming wave of emotions washed over every individual in the room. Some turned away, unable to bear the sight, while others stared in stunned silence, as though witnessing a beheading right before their eyes.

"You granted me a lifetime of memories, and these pictures capture them all. I decided to compile them in a visual format and share them with you and those who aided you in achieving your goals and dreams," Dr. Stearing explained, his voice filled with a mixture of gratitude and distress.

These men had become desensitized to the sight of abortion images over the years, but they had always been presented in a clinical context. These pictures, however, were grotesque beyond imagination. Not a single word was uttered, only the sound of their collective breaths held, as they fixated on the images displayed on the cork-board. Each picture depicted a beautiful baby's face, full of life and joy, juxtaposed with mangled and bloodied bodies. The infants were cradled in their mothers' arms, who were in a state of hysterical anguish. Different faces, different babies, different mothers, each one filled with despair. Blood was splattered everywhere, staining the baby, the mother, and even dripping from their blankets onto the floor.

"I thought it was only fair to share the moments of joy that you have bestowed upon me throughout the years with each and every one of you. These memories are etched in my mind, accompanied by recurring nightmares that have haunted me even in my retirement," Dr. Stearing confessed, his voice tinged with the weight of traumatic experiences.

The men remained frozen, unable to move or speak. Something had rendered them immobile, their voices silenced. As Dr. Stearing stood at the front of the room, he too fell into a hushed silence. His gaze traveled across the faces of the men, each one reflecting the horror he himself had endured for years. In the background, faint singing could be heard, its lyrics distinct and piercing. The words carried a profound message, touching the depths of their souls like only music could. It spoke of life, of children, and the precious opportunity to exist. It continued to lament the lives denied a chance to live, leaving an indelible mark on their hearts.

As the music swelled, the locked doors swung open once again, and one by one, the individuals with their signs entered the room. But these were not the same homemade signs that had been seen outside the hotel. Each sign displayed images, almost like video tapes playing on miniature television screens. As the people moved closer, some of the signs turned sideways, revealing that they were the earlier versions made of simple cardboard. Yet, the mere sight of those images on a cardboard sign was enough to captivate everyone present.

The images on each sign flickered and changed as they were moved. One sign depicted a partial birth abortion, unfolding from conception to development and culminating in the gruesome procedure. The images laid bare the agonizing truth of innocent children struggling to enter this world, only to be mercilessly snuffed out before fully emerging from their mothers' wombs.

Each sign portrayed the killing of innocent children, one heart-wrenching story at a time. The images grew increasingly intense with every cycle, playing out the horrifying scenes repeatedly. Dr. Stearing, too, could see the signs and their video projections looping incessantly. He began to scream, his words laden with desperation and remorse, "No, no more dreams! My dreams have become reality! Oh God, please forgive me! Jesus, please forgive me!"

Dr. Stearing collapsed to the floor, dropping the cork board he had been clutching. It landed against an empty chair, standing upright. As he gazed up at his cork board, he succumbed to hysteria. Each picture on the board also came to life, animating before his eyes. He screamed and scrambled away on all fours, overcome with terror.

The images on the signs accelerated, playing faster and faster, their repetition relentless. The men in the room continued to stare, becoming increasingly emotional. Some broke down in tears, while others buried their heads in their hands. Dennis, their esteemed leader, fixated his gaze on the signs, then on Dr. Stearing's cork -board, and finally on Dr. Stearing himself, his own emotions threatening to consume him.

The singing, growing louder by the second, reached a crescendo, and then abruptly ceased, along with everything else. The signs' images froze, capturing the most haunting and disturbing frame from the clips. Silence enveloped the room, broken only by a voice that reverberated like an earthquake, shaking the very foundation of the building. The windows shattered, sending shards of glass cascading onto the men from the association and Dr. Stearing.

The voice declared with unwavering authority, "THOU SHALL NOT KILL."

In that moment, every man seated around the table reached his breaking point, including their once indomitable leader, Dennis Spence. Slowly removing their hands from their heads, they implored the people at the front of the room to save them from this force that spoke with such commanding power, shaking the room and shattering the windows.

"What must we do to cleanse our hands of this blood?" Dennis cried out, his plea echoing in the hearts of all who gazed at him, waiting for an answer. The people at the front composed themselves, still reeling from the intense experience. As they gingerly set their signs down, the images vanished, replaced by the familiar homemade signs. Simultaneously, Dr. Stearing looked up at his cork board, and the images reverted to the ones he had carefully arranged for his demonstration. He rose, the first to step forward, with the rest of the men following suit, moved by an overwhelming sense of transformation and redemption.

"Hello?" George answered his phone, his voice filled with curiosity and apprehension.

"I wanted to inform you that we have just acquired The Association for Fetal Research."

"You're kidding?" George's voice betrayed his shock and disbelief.

"No, they were on the brink of bankruptcy, and we saw the chance to acquire all of their assets and customer base," Penkowski explained, a hint of satisfaction in his voice.

"What about the employees?" George inquired, concern evident in his tone.

"They will all be terminated. I want everyone working for us to be loyal, without any lingering resentment. Besides, this will allow us to eliminate anyone who may have been aware of our activities," Penkowski responded, his words carrying a chilling sense of ruthlessness.

"Will you still require my services?" George's voice held a glimmer of hope, tinged with trepidation.

"My friend, you will always be required to work for us. You possess too much information. Moreover, where else could you find the treatment and privileges I offer?" Penkowski's tone was both reassuring and menacing.

George swallowed hard, feeling trapped, before reluctantly conceding, "You are absolutely right."

Penkowski seemed pleased by George's compliance. "Before we end this call, I want you to look into a piece of land for purchase in that wretched city."

"For what purpose?" George asked, his curiosity piqued.

"I intend to expand our manufacturing operations. Now that we have acquired The Association, we want that business to thrive. This new facility will work in conjunction with AFT but produce different products. And, George, due to your outstanding performance, I want you to oversee both facilities."

George's mind raced, realizing that this was indeed a promotion. "Thank you, Dr. Penkowski. I genuinely appreciate the confidence you have in me."

"There will be a significant increase in your salary. I believe you will be pleasantly surprised," Penkowski added, his voice hinting at the lure of financial reward.

After Penkowski provided George with the property details, he ended the call. Bruce, who had been holding his breath during the conversation, finally exhaled and bombarded George with questions.

"That was Penkowski, I presume. What did he say? Did he know we were out here? Did he realize you were on your cell phone? And why did you thank him?"

George began cautiously, choosing his words carefully. "Well... He just acquired The Association."

"You're joking, right?"

"No. And he just promoted me to oversee the existing AFT plant and the new one he plans to build in Stapleton."

"Stapleton? Where?"

"Bruce, you won't believe it," George paused, his voice heavy with disbelief. He then continued, addressing Bruce's growing anticipation, "He wants to purchase the land where the church burned down."

"Reverend Stone's church?" Bruce asked, utterly astonished.

"Yes." George confirmed.

Bruce took a moment to process the information before responding, "What does he intend to do with it?"

"Build another manufacturing plant," George revealed, a sense of urgency creeping into his voice.

"Oh no, we cannot allow that," Bruce declared, a mix of determination and concern in his tone.

George pondered for a moment before a spark of inspiration lit up his eyes. "You know, I could come up with various excuses to hinder the purchase of that property, but... I have an idea."

George shared the idea with Bruce, and a glimmer of hope illuminated Bruce's face. "Now, let's look for John and Elizabeth," he suggested, his voice brimming with excitement and determination.

"Wayne, you should have seen it! It was absolutely incredible!" exclaimed one of the picketers, their voice filled with awe and excitement. The group had returned from the demonstration, and each member was eager to share their experience.

"We were picketing outside when suddenly, this man appeared with a cork board," one person began.

Another chimed in, "I recognized him. He used to be the doctor at the abortion clinic we protested years ago."

Wayne's anticipation grew, and he urged them to continue, saying, "Go on, I'm listening." He could sense the immense impact of the events that unfolded, as everyone was on the verge of bursting with emotion.

"He walked right past us, as if we were invisible. We peeked into the hotel and saw him entering the room where the men were having their meeting."

"Yeah," added another person. "The door was locked, as usual. They always keep it locked."

Wayne interjected, "But how did he get in?"

No one had an answer.

"Then what happened?" Wayne probed further.

"Well, Maggie started to sing, and it was so moving. Next thing we knew, we found ourselves inside the hotel, walking down the hallway, singing. And when we reached the door, it was open. We expected to be kicked out."

Someone else spoke up, "That's right. But instead of kicking us out, they looked at us as if we were apparitions! I mean, they turned pale. They couldn't take their eyes off our signs, like they were staring at monsters or something. It made me question if I had misspelled a word or made a mistake."

"And..." another person interrupted, "the man with the cork board completely lost it!"

Wayne felt a surge of overwhelm as he tried to take in everything he was hearing. It was almost too much to comprehend. Then came the recounting of God's intervention, an event so powerful it seemed to shake the very foundation of the room, causing the windows to shatter.

Feeling the weight of it all, Wayne took a few steps back and sank into a chair. The revelations were astounding. They continued discussing how God had touched each man in that room, inspiring them to make life-altering decisions for Christ. They all joined together in prayer, expressing their gratitude to God for making such a profound difference. Little did they know that God had transformed their handmade signs into moving pictures, a powerful testament to His presence.

"Bruce, we're approaching the building... to be honest... I'm not sure what we should do," George admitted, his voice tinged with nervousness. Sensing George's unease, Bruce silently prayed for guidance.

"I got it!" George exclaimed suddenly. "Let's go around the back, just like John and I did when we snuck into Penkowski's place of business."

Bruce felt a rush of gratitude for the swift answer to prayer. They maneuvered around the back of the building, even though it was broad daylight. George seemed to gain confidence and make decisions more assuredly. Parking the car up the street, they navigated through the backstreets until they reached a locked back door. Bruce glanced at George, silently questioning their next move. In response, George gestured toward a nearby dumpster. Bruce obediently made his way there while George stayed behind.

As Bruce reached the dumpster, he turned around to find George still positioned by the door. Confusion crossed Bruce's face, but George simply smiled. George positioned himself against the right side of the door, waiting patiently. After about 15 minutes, the door swung open, nearly crushing George in the process. Bruce, wide-eyed, peered through a crack from his hiding spot behind the dumpster. The door remained ajar, and George slowly emerged, motioning for Bruce to join him.

Once they were reunited, they swiftly entered the building. George skillfully led the way, finding dark corners and maintenance rooms to pause in between their search for their friends. Despite his evident worry, George impressed Bruce with his determination and ability to keep up.

The building they entered was dingy and neglected, with an air of neglect. George and Bruce meticulously explored the entire premises but found no trace of their friends. Exiting through the back door, they set off towards the next building. As they approached, they were greeted by a stark contrast. The new building appeared modern and well-maintained from the outside. George followed the same procedure as before to gain entry, and it worked seamlessly.

However, this building proved more challenging to navigate, bustling with people and resembling a hospital. Its sterile environment, from the pristine white walls to the scent of disinfectant, filled the air. As the men stealthily moved from one hallway to another, they stumbled upon what seemed to be a nurse's station. Many individuals, both men and women dressed in white, occupied the area.

George and Bruce positioned themselves within hearing range but out of sight.

"How long does Penkowski want them here?" one worker's voice could be overheard.

"Indefinitely," came the response.

"Well, it's not like this place is hidden away... Eventually, someone will come looking for these people, I assume."

"Who are they, anyway?"

"I don't know, but they must pose a significant threat to Penkowski for him to go to such extremes."

As the conversation continued, George and Bruce exchanged knowing glances, their smiles conveying a mix of relief and determination. They had found their friends, which proved to be the easy part. Now came the challenging task of extracting them from this place, ensuring their safety and escape.

"Well, I think I've got the preliminary work done," Elizabeth said, her tone filled with a mix of relief and determination. "I still need to get back to my office."

"That's good because I'm ready to get out of this place. I'm going stir-crazy!" John exclaimed, his frustration palpable. Although the room had provided Elizabeth with valuable time to work on her case, it had been driving John crazy, leaving him unable to accomplish anything.

They carefully packed up the laptop, each movement deliberate, a sense of urgency electric in the air. John meticulously reopened the air vent in the ceiling, his hands steady despite the flutter of apprehension in Elizabeth's eyes. Sensing her reluctance, John gently reminded her of the grim alternatives they faced. Reluctantly, Elizabeth nodded her agreement, steeling herself for what lay ahead. With a reassuring squeeze of her hand, John hoisted her up into the narrow vent entrance, his muscles straining against the weight.

Once Elizabeth was safely inside, John followed, his heart pounding against his ribs as he navigated the cramped space. He silently thanked his dedication to his exercise routine, grateful for the strength and agility it afforded him in this critical moment.

"Where to now?" Elizabeth's voice echoed softly in the confined space.

"Shh! Keep your voice down. It carries," John cautioned in a hushed tone, his words a stark reminder of their precarious situation.

"Sorry," Elizabeth replied, her voice barely above a whisper.

"Continue straight, and then at the end, turn left," John instructed, his voice steady despite the adrenaline coursing through his veins.

John and Elizabeth moved with painstaking caution, their movements slow and deliberate to avoid any sound that might betray their presence to those below.

"Okay, I'm turning," Elizabeth whispered, the tension evident in her voice.

"Good," John responded softly, his reassurance a beacon of hope in the darkness.

"I see a vent up ahead," Elizabeth murmured, her voice barely audible over the sound of their own breaths.

"That's the one we want," John affirmed, his heart pounding with a mixture of anticipation and apprehension as they pressed on into the unknown.

George and Bruce found themselves concealed in a dimly lit corner, desperately trying to avoid detection.

"Now what?" Bruce whispered, his voice filled with apprehension.

"Well, I'm not sure. I don't have a gun or any means to defend ourselves," George replied, his voice tinged with concern. "They have our friends exposed, and my guess is that the door over there is where they're being kept."

Bruce bowed his head once again, seeking divine intervention through prayer. Suddenly, a startling noise echoed from above in the ceiling.

"What on earth?" Bruce exclaimed, startled.

In a swift reaction, the air vent came crashing down, hurtling towards the ground. With remarkable reflexes, George managed to catch it in mid-air.

"I'm sorry, John," Elizabeth whispered, her voice laced with regret, as the vent slipped from her grasp, the metallic clang echoing softly in the narrow space.

"For what?" John's voice held a note of confusion, his brow furrowed in puzzlement.

"I... I dropped the vent," Elizabeth admitted hesitantly, her cheeks flushing with embarrassment.

John shook his head, his expression unwavering. "I didn't hear anything," he reassured her, his tone gentle yet firm.

As Elizabeth cast her gaze downward, she spotted the vent securely cradled in George's hands, his reassuring smile offering solace amidst her turmoil.

A wave of relief washed over Elizabeth, mingling with a newfound sense of gratitude towards George. Turning back to John, her thoughts raced as she sought clarity. "Um... John, what does George, the friend you're trying to help, look like?"

Quickly, John provided a description, realization dawning on him as he understood the significance of Elizabeth's question.

George flashed Elizabeth a thumbs-up, his silent assurance calming her nerves. With his approval granted, Elizabeth began her descent, her movements deliberate and steady.

Meanwhile, Bruce observed the scene with a sense of encouragement, offering his assistance to George as he handed off the vent to facilitate Elizabeth's safe passage.

As Elizabeth successfully reached the ground, John emerged from the A/C duct with a triumphant grin, sharing a moment of camaraderie with Bruce before refocusing on their mission.

Handing his laptop to George, John met his puzzled expression with a knowing smile, silently communicating their next steps. With George's guidance, they navigated the shadows with practiced precision, moving stealthily through the corridors.

Approaching an exit, they encountered unexpected obstacles, forcing them to reconsider their strategy. Despite their setbacks, John remained resolute, his determination unwavering as he sought a secure location for their discussion.

With John leading the way, albeit with dwindling confidence from the group, they sought refuge in a nearby room, sheltered from prying eyes and eavesdropping ears.

Elizabeth, her frustration mounting, broke the tense silence. "This is your plan, brother?" Her words hung in the air, a challenge to John's leadership, surprising the others with her boldness.

"It's okay. This room won't allow our voices to carry," John reassured them, his confidence unwavering in the face of adversity.

Elizabeth's persistence echoed through the room, her determination a testament to their shared resolve. "Well!"

"Hey, I'm open to anyone else's ideas right now. We have no

weapons for defense, guards blocking the only two exits, and surveillance everywhere you look. It feels like we're in Fort Knox!" John exclaimed in frustration.

Then, he turned his attention to George and Bruce, curiosity evident on his face. "How in the world did both of you end up here?"

George glanced at Bruce, and Bruce looked upward, silently acknowledging divine guidance.

"John, allow me to introduce you to my pastor, Bruce Hutchinson," George said.

John looked dumbfounded. He knew Bruce was George's friend, but amidst all the chaos, he hadn't given much thought to who Bruce was or why George had brought him.

"Your pastor?" John expressed his surprise before quickly regaining his composure. "Forgive me, Pastor. I'm John Ivan." He extended his hand. "I am very pleased to meet you. I've heard how great of a friend you've been to George."

Elizabeth interjected, introducing herself, her disappointment apparent for not being introduced alongside John. "My name is Elizabeth. I am John's sister."

George and Bruce were pleased to meet her, noticing her beauty. Bruce's recollection of the story George had shared became blurry when it came to Elizabeth's involvement.

"How did you..." Bruce began to ask, but Elizabeth cut him off, completing his sentence.

"...get involved in all of this?" Elizabeth finished his question, smiling.

Bruce paused, glancing at John, and then asked, "Well, do we have time?"

"My plan right now is to observe if the guards take shifts or if they are relieved at some point during the night," John explained. "If they do, I'd rather deal with the surveillance systems than confront people directly. Besides, we have valuable individuals with us, and we shouldn't take unnecessary risks." Elizabeth smiled at her brother, while George looked at Bruce. After that, Bruce began sharing his story of how he first met George.

SEVENTEEN

Construction commenced on the property where Reverend Stone's church once stood. The charred remains and black ashes were carefully moved aside, revealing the bare dirt underneath. The piles of black ashes seemed never-ending, a testament to the abandoned construction project from the past that had never reached completion. Curious passersby couldn't help but stop and gaze at the peculiar scene, causing near accidents on the road due to their distraction. Each time a mound was shifted, a sinister cloud of dark dust billowed into the air, casting an eerie presence over the town, settling particularly heavily on the façade of City Hall.

The Mayor stepped outside the grand building, his eyes scanning the street before him. His heart quickened its pace as he beheld the mounds of ashes and witnessed the rising dust cloud. Slowly, he turned his gaze towards City Hall, now shrouded in a disconcerting blanket of black dust. The once-proud structure appeared aged and dilapidated, evoking a sense of foreboding that gripped his very spirit.

It began with the unsettling surge of religious fervor sweeping through his city. Then came the dreaded reality of losing funds from The Association for Fetal Research. And now, observing the remnants of his church, along with the Reverend's tragic and enigmatic demise, the Mayor wondered when this onslaught of calamities would finally cease.

With a heavy sigh, the Mayor retreated into his office building. As he entered, his receptionist broke the silence with an air of curiosity, "Well, is it the last days? Is the world going to end?" She was a somewhat disheveled young woman in her mid-20s, her unkempt appearance betraying her eccentricity. This was her first job after college, and she relished her prestigious position in Stapleton.

"Yep, at noon today," the Mayor responded in a teasing tone, rolling his eyes at her as he made his way back to his office. Today, he felt a profound sense of loneliness. Most of his comrades, the ones with whom he had once shared laughter and camaraderie, had met their untimely demise during the catastrophic incident at the tent. He silently expressed gratitude that he hadn't succumbed to the zealous fanaticism that had consumed his friends that chilling and mysterious night.

What had transformed this town so drastically in the span of six months? It was as if an entirely different city had emerged. The people had changed, the school system had changed, and even the concept of church had transformed. Once upon a time, Sundays were reserved for attending church, while the rest of the week carried on with little thought given to religious matters until the following Sunday. Now, Bible study infiltrated workplaces, prayers were uttered on Tuesday nights, and even the Ten Commandments found their way into classrooms. When would it all end? Why had this town become so utterly captivated by religious fervor? These were the questions swirling through the Mayor's mind as he gazed out of his window, tainted by the dark residue of black ash, surveying the town he had once joyously governed over for many years.

"So, you see, George has not only been a tremendous testament to how God can radically transform a life and sometimes employ miracles to bring about change, but George has also been an indispensable pillar of support in our ministry, playing a vital role in all the remarkable works that God has been orchestrating in the town of Stapleton," Bruce passionately concluded, his voice infused with deep conviction and emotion.

Elizabeth and John remained silent, their countenances frozen in a mix of awe and disbelief. In unison, their eyes met, mirroring the shock they felt within. It was as if they had just glimpsed a spectral apparition, a presence from another realm. Overwhelmed by the encounter, they hesitated, unsure of how to express their inexplicable experience.

Sensing that he may have unintentionally crossed a threshold of religious comfort, Bruce cautiously ventured, "Did I inadvertently say something that offended either of you?"

John, his vulnerability laid bare, began, "No," his voice trembling with a mixture of astonishment and trepidation. Elizabeth swiftly interjected, "No, no, not at all. It's just... well, something inexplicable transpired while we were imprisoned."

"Yeah, it was absolutely mind-boggling. I doubt you'd believe us," John confessed, his vulnerability further deepening. He remained silent, awaiting George and Bruce's approval before sharing their otherworldly encounter.

George, his eyes brimming with curiosity and compassion, implored, "Please, enlighten us. I genuinely want to understand what occurred."

Bruce, nodding in agreement, looked to John and Elizabeth, silently conveying his support and eagerness to hear their story.

Taking a deep breath, Elizabeth began, "Well, there was this slender man, dressed entirely in pristine white attire. He exuded an extraordinary allure. He was pushing a table with wheels, adorned with a white linen tablecloth. John expressed gratitude to him, and that's when he uttered the most bewildering statement."

"What did he say?" Bruce pressed on behalf of both George and himself, captivated by the unfolding tale.

"He said, 'You're welcome. Godspeed.' And then, the man calmly walked out the door, which immediately locked behind him," John recounted, his voice filled with a mix of wonder and bewilderment.

"We were left standing there, dumbfounded, exchanging bewildered glances," Elizabeth added, her voice tinged with a mixture of incredulity and intrigue. "What on earth did he mean by 'Godspeed'?"

George and Bruce leaned forward, their anticipation heightened. In recent times, they had grown accustomed to the divine intervening in their lives, often manifesting in miraculous ways. As John and Elizabeth continued sharing their remarkable account, including the episode with the laptop, they skillfully held the attention of the two men. And then, with a stunning revelation, they unleashed the ultimate bombshell.

"After we had hidden the laptop under the bed and looked up, before the door opened, the table with all the food was gone!" Elizabeth paused, her eyes locked on George and Bruce, awaiting their reaction to this extraordinary revelation. John, too, was fixated on his newfound friend and the pastor whom he had already grown fond of.

Bruce, with a warm smile and a glimmer in his eyes, simply responded, "Sounds like a divine intervention." His words carried a sense of assurance and affirmation.

Relieved that they were not dismissed as delusional, both John and Elizabeth yearned for further understanding.

"But where did the table go? I mean, seriously! One moment it was there, and the next, poof! Gone! Vanished! This is like something out of the Twilight Zone, you know what I mean?" Elizabeth exclaimed, her voice laced with a mix of astonishment and disbelief. John nodded in agreement, his head moving in sync with his sister's passionate gestures. Then, a sudden realization struck him.

"Wait a minute... George!" John called out, his eyes fixed on his friend.

George turned his gaze towards John, curious about what he was about to say.

"Didn't you share a similar mind-boggling experience with me when we faced Penkowski in that fierce windstorm?" John inquired, his voice tinged with excitement.

George averted his eyes, momentarily lost in the memory, before responding, "Yeah, back then, you thought I was out of my mind."

"Not anymore, my friend," John proclaimed with a wide grin. "I think it's time for me to get acquainted with God. He has brought my laptop back to me not once, but twice now. The least I can do is acknowledge Him and express my gratitude."

John proceeded to share the remarkable story of how Sue rescued him from his exploding car, unable to retrieve his laptop at the time, only to find it miraculously intact in his hospital room. Elizabeth stood in awe, her mouth agape, struggling to comprehend the inexplicable events unfolding before her.

John beamed at his sister, then turned to Bruce, a newfound determination shining in his eyes. "Pastor Bruce, what must I do to be saved?" Elizabeth's astonishment grew, her jaw dropping in sheer disbelief.

Bruce's initial concern about crossing religious boundaries had long faded, replaced by an overwhelming sense of privilege at the prospect of leading a soul destined for hell to a heavenly eternity, with an unshakeable guarantee.

"All have sinned and fallen short of the glory of God. Do you believe that, John?" Bruce queried, his voice gentle yet unwavering.

"Yes, I do. Although I've never contemplated it in those exact terms, I know that no one on this earth is perfect. No one. Well... except for one person who, in my opinion, fulfilled the standard of perfection," John reflected.

"Who?" Bruce inquired, his eyes fixed on John, eager to hear his response.

After a brief pause, John looked up at George and Bruce, his voice filled with conviction as he declared, "Jesus."

Bruce's face lit up with a radiant smile, as he proceeded to share the life-changing and redemptive message of the gospel, offering John the good news that had the power to transform his life forever.

"Mayor?" a voice crackled through the intercom system, breaking the silence in the mayor's office.

"Yes?" Mayor Thomas responded, his attention captured by the unexpected interruption.

"A Doctor Kenneth Penkowski is on the line for you," the voice on the intercom informed.

Curiosity piqued, Mayor Thomas picked up the phone. "Hello?"

"Mayor Thomas?" the voice on the other end confirmed.

"Yes, speaking," the mayor replied, wondering about the purpose of the call.

"It's Doctor Kenneth Penkowski, president of Advance Medical," the man introduced himself.

Recognition flashed across the mayor's face. "Ah, yes. How can I assist you today, Doctor Penkowski?"

"It's actually what I can do for you," the doctor clarified. "I have recently begun construction on a property within your community and wanted to ensure that you are satisfied with the architectural plans. We aim for the building to seamlessly blend in with the existing structures."

The mayor nodded, appreciating the doctor's thoughtfulness. "Well, Doctor Penkowski, I am grateful for your consideration. Much obliged."

"My pleasure," Penkowski replied warmly. "By the way, I heard about the fire that occurred in your neighborhood. I sincerely hope there were no casualties."

Thankful for the concern, Mayor Thomas responded, "Fortunately, we had a close call with a mother and her baby. They managed to escape unharmed."

A brief moment of silence followed, accompanied by a barely audible sigh on the other end of the line. Unaware of the significance, the mayor continued the conversation, oblivious to the doctor's underlying emotions.

"I'm pleased to hear that. The incident made national news, and it was quite a first for Stapleton. Although, with all the peculiar occurrences happening in town lately, I wouldn't be surprised if it were to attract attention again... soon."

Curiosity sparked in Doctor Penkowski's voice. "Oh? Could you elaborate on these happenings?"

The mayor proceeded to recount the series of inexplicable events that had unfolded since the inception of the prayer meetings. Penkowski masked his anger, forcing himself to engage in the conversation and feign interest, all the while growing increasingly infuriated with each passing moment.

"That must have wreaked havoc on the local economy," Penkowski interjected, his words laced with forceful intensity.

Caught off guard by the sudden shift in tone, Mayor Thomas matched the doctor's energy, his voice growing more assertive. "It most certainly has! We've just lost our largest source of funding for community development, The Association for Fetal Research. Furthermore, the future of their AFT manufacturing plant is uncertain, and that facility employs a significant number of people in our community."

A glimmer of satisfaction danced in Doctor Penkowski's voice as he responded, "Oh, Mayor, I believe I have some excellent news for you!"

"Well, I know I'm far from perfect, and if Jesus wants to take my place, I'm more than willing. I trust Him to secure my ticket to heaven," John declared, his voice filled with a newfound surrender.

Pastor Bruce gently interjected, "Remember, John, 'Lord' means 'boss.' That's why we refer to Him as Lord Jesus. You must be willing to follow His lead."

John pondered for a moment, contemplating the implications. "Will He provide guidance for me?" he asked, seeking assurance.

Bruce nodded. "Yes, He will."

"Like a mission, a purpose, a divine plan?" John inquired further.

Bruce smiled, affirming his question. "Yes, He has a plan for your life, John Ivan."

Reflecting on the emptiness he felt and the lack of purpose in his previous pursuits, John thought back to the times he looked at himself in the mirror, searching for his true identity. He remembered how his accomplishments in status and wealth left him hollow, still yearning for something more. The overwhelming sense of loneliness that greeted him every day in his empty home served as a stark reminder. Having a God-given purpose, one that made a meaningful difference rather than self-centered goals, now made perfect sense to him. It all became clear.

Recalling the miracles he had witnessed in Stapleton and the encounters he had, John's mind raced. Thoughts of Maggie and their initial meeting flooded his consciousness. He remembered the prayer that had lingered in his mind, refusing to fade away. And then it hit him—the decision Maggie had prayed for was more significant than his choice to help his newfound friend George. No, the decision she had prayed for was for him to surrender his life to God. Everything suddenly fell into place. The reason he had been led to this small town, the close call he had in the accident, and the impact of the woman's prayer on his life—it was all part of a divine orchestration. God had been working through every event to bring him to this pivotal moment of decision. This same God, who had even taken care of his laptop and provided a sumptuous meal for him and his sister, demonstrated a personal interest in his life.

Lost in his thoughts, John gazed into the distance, immersed in the revelations flooding his mind. Everyone around him sensed the significance of the moment and remained respectfully silent. Even his sister, Elizabeth, recognized the transformation occurring within John and cherished the positive changes. Though different, her beloved brother had become more lovable, shifting his focus from himself to others.

Finally, breaking the silence, John spoke with determination, "Well, since moving to Stapleton for this job, I've embarked on a profound soul-searching journey. It's time for me to make a change in my life. I no longer want to follow my own path. Despite achieving everything I set out to accomplish, I find myself more miserable now than ever before."

George chimed in, empathizing with John's sentiment. "I can relate to that," he acknowledged.

John glanced at George, a smile gracing his lips as he remembered the similar story George had shared about his own life. If it worked for George, why wouldn't it work for him? The possibilities of a transformed existence filled him with hope and anticipation.

"Pastor Bruce, what do I need to do?" John asked earnestly.

Bruce replied with conviction, "Ask Jesus for forgiveness, cleansing, and commit to following His guidance and plan for your life continually. Rely solely on Him for your ticket to heaven. You can't afford it on your own, so don't even try. And then, get ready for the most incredible journey of your life!"

A warm smile spread across John's face. He found solace and clarity in Bruce's words—they resonated deeply within him. It was time to make the decision that Maggie had fervently prayed for him to make. The joy and fulfillment he experienced from his first selfless act of helping George were just a glimpse of what awaited him with this life-altering decision.

After John had prayed alongside Bruce, Elizabeth suddenly burst into uncontrollable tears. Confusion and concern filled the room.

"Sis, what's wrong? What's the matter?" John asked, his voice full of worry.

Elizabeth couldn't find the words to respond, her tears flowing relentlessly. The men sat in silence, their hearts heavy with compassion. Sensing the need for divine intervention, George and Bruce began to offer prayers of comfort and supplication. John, still attempting to console his sister, longed for her anguish to subside, desperate for understanding and solace.

"Yes! We have successfully acquired The Association, and AFT now belongs to us," Dr. Penkowski announced with enthusiasm.

The Mayor's curiosity piqued as he inquired, "Will you be shutting down the facility?"

Dr. Penkowski shook his head, replying, "Oh, no, not at all. On the contrary, we have plans to expand it, which is why we've initiated construction in town."

Delighted by the news, the Mayor pondered for a moment before posing his next question, "Is there any possibility of redirecting some of The Association's funding to support the development of our town?"

Dr. Penkowski's face lit up with delight. "That would be fantastic! We are always seeking ways to uplift the community, and what better way than utilizing those funds to benefit the very town where our employees reside."

The Mayor's heart swelled with gratitude. "Thank you, Dr. Penkowski! On behalf of myself and the entire town, we extend our deepest appreciation."

Dr. Penkowski proceeded to reveal the generous contribution he intended to provide, leaving the Mayor momentarily speechless.

Overwhelmed, he struggled to find the right words.

"Mayor, are you still there? Perhaps that amount wasn't sufficient," Dr. Penkowski interjected, promptly increasing the donation to an even higher figure.

Finally regaining his composure, the Mayor exclaimed, "Oh, Dr. Penkowski, this is incredibly gracious! With this amount, we can accomplish extraordinary things—dreams we've nurtured for years. I can't thank you enough!"

Dr. Penkowski expressed his gratitude, acknowledging the Mayor's support and willingness to collaborate. He particularly emphasized their new facility's architectural design, assuring the Mayor that it would seamlessly blend into the downtown area and enhance its overall aesthetic. Before concluding the conversation, he requested a picture of the original church building, which had unfortunately been destroyed.

"Yes," the Mayor responded somberly. "It burned down, igniting the beginning of new construction."

Surprised, Dr. Penkowski inquired, "What happened to the original church?"

The Mayor explained, "A tornado struck it. It was an odd occurrence—the tornado spared everything else in the community, but it targeted that historic church. It was a landmark, deeply rooted in our town's history."

Concealing his satisfaction, Dr. Penkowski feigned sympathy. "I am truly sorry to hear that."

Swiftly changing the subject, Dr. Penkowski wrapped up the conversation. The Mayor was assured that the funds would be wired into the city's account later that afternoon. Ecstatic about the prospects ahead, the Mayor's heart overflowed with joy.

Pastor Wayne stood in stunned silence, grappling with the whirlwind of events unfolding before him. First, he learned about the dramatic clash at the hotel involving the picketers and The Association for Fetal Research. Then, Dennis Spence, the Association's head, dropped a bombshell: the company had been sold, and he had found faith in the Lord. With his entire staff in tow, Dennis sought out Pastor Wayne, a meeting that left an indelible mark on both parties.

Over the phone, Sue's curiosity bubbled over. "Pastor Wayne, how did he even find you?" she inquired, referencing an email she had received from the pastor, rallying prayer warriors to intercede for the newly converted men.

"They asked one of the picketers where they were from and who their pastor was," Pastor Wayne explained simply. It was a straightforward connection.

Sue's eagerness was vivid. "And then? What happened next?"

Excitement laced Pastor Wayne's voice as he recounted the encounter. "Dennis came to me, and as we spoke, he broke down in tears. It was a rare display of emotion from a man who had long been numb to both joy and sorrow. He admitted that his emotional detachment, once an asset in his work, had left him hollow in his personal life, unable to experience the warmth of family or the joy of connection. He envied those who spoke of family with love and longing."

"Go on," Sue urged, captivated.

"He confessed that the sale of the company had left him feeling empty, his years of boasting about success ringing hollow," Pastor Wayne continued. "And then, amidst their despair, something miraculous happened. The picketers breached the room and there was something extraordinary about their signs, Sue." Pastor Wayne exclaimed, a sense of awe infusing his words. "They weren't just signs, they were like miniature movies, flickering with scenes that seemed to dance across the cardboard as if woven by the very hand of God Himself." Sue's disbelief was evident. "But how? They were just signs."

"It seems the Lord worked through even the simplest of means," Pastor Wayne explained. "Those signs became instruments of divine revelation, paving the way for Dennis and his colleagues to embrace the good news."

In awe of the divine intervention, Sue and Pastor Wayne paused to reflect, their thoughts eventually turning to Pastor Bruce Hutchinson, the catalyst behind this extraordinary chain of events.

They finally managed to calm Elizabeth down, though she remained quiet, visibly upset. Her distress was evident on her face as she mustered the courage to speak.

"John, you know the problems I've had after my..." Elizabeth paused, glancing around at the men gathered in the room.

"You know you're among friends, Elizabeth," reassured her brother.

"I know," she replied. "It's just that I had no idea that a single decision could wreak such havoc on a person's life."

The men remained silent, their eyes filled with compassion and care.

"You see, one of the reasons I agreed to get involved with my brother in this dangerous job was because..." Elizabeth hesitated.

"We are here, listening without judgment," Pastor Bruce interjected, providing her with a sense of comfort and support.

Encouraged by his words, Elizabeth found the strength to continue. "I had an abortion. It has been the single worst thing I've ever done in my life. I pay for it every day. There isn't a moment that passes without something reminding me of this terrible decision. Every time I come home from work, I inevitably see children playing in the streets, playing with their parents."

Elizabeth began to cry again, and John placed his arm around her while Bruce gently held her hand.

She carried on, her voice trembling with emotion. "The nightmares have subsided somewhat, but occasionally they resurface, and it feels as though I am reliving my abortion all over again. Every pain, regret, and remorse resurfaces, as fresh as the day after I made that choice. The depression has never left. I try to conceal it with my busy work schedule."

"When John approached me and told me that I could put out of business the two biggest contributors to my personal hell on earth, I was willing to risk my life. I thought, just maybe, this would be the answer that could free me from the emotional torment that has consumed my life."

"My daughter, there is only one answer that can truly set you free," Pastor Bruce spoke with conviction. "As your brother has recently discovered, Jesus is the only one who can truly satisfy and deliver you from all this pain."

"Can He truly set me free from this mess I've created?" Elizabeth asked, her sincerity shining through.

"Jesus said, 'If the Son sets you free, you will be free indeed,'" Pastor Bruce responded.

"How can you be so sure?" Elizabeth inquired.

"I am certain because He has done it repeatedly in countless lives throughout the years. He has proven Himself faithful to His word. He is not only the Savior of our souls for eternity but also the Savior of our present lives," Pastor Bruce explained.

Elizabeth had exhausted every other option, and witnessing her older brother's decision, she felt compelled to follow his lead. If this Jesus could remove the pain and remorse that had plagued her daily, she was ready to wholeheartedly follow Him each day of her life.

After Bruce had led Elizabeth to a saving knowledge of Christ, and she embraced Him as her Savior, John's voice cut through the solemn air with unwavering determination. "Let's go, now." His urgency startled the room, drawing all eyes to him as he repeated, "Now!"

John had been vigilant, his gaze fixed on the door, noting the guards outside checking their watches. Though uncertain of the remaining time, he sensed the need to act boldly. With his sister's newfound faith lending her courage, he felt a surge of confidence, lessening their vulnerability. It was evident from Elizabeth's resolute demeanor that she was committed to this perilous mission. Gathering everyone, John led them to the door where the guards stood watch.

Anxious glances darted around the room as they surveyed their surroundings, finding no one in sight. John approached the security camera, swiftly concealing it beneath a pillowcase commandeered from the room. From his laptop case, he produced a mirror and a small bag of white powder, scattering it near the door to create a billowing cloud. As anticipated, the telltale red laser beams materialized. With a knowing smile directed at his companions, John meticulously positioned the mirror to redirect the beams, ensuring their seamless path remained unbroken.

A silent signal passed between John and George, who grasped the doorknob and eased it open. George sidled through cautiously, the widened gap allowing him to pass without triggering the alarm. Extending his hand to Elizabeth, George sought assurance from her brother, who nodded reassuringly, granting permission to proceed. Bruce followed suit, stepping through the doorway with cautious determination.

As John began to retreat, he carefully manipulated the mirror's position, inching it closer until the door could be closed without disruption. With a swift motion, he released the mirror and sealed the door behind them. Rushing to join the others in the safety of their chosen corner, relief washed over them in an undeniable wave.

For a fleeting moment, they remained fixated on the building they had just escaped, collectively holding their breath. Seeing no signs of pursuit, they exhaled in unison, enveloping each other in a shared embrace. Believing the worst was behind them, they couldn't fathom the trials still lurking on the horizon.

The money arrived shortly after Mayor Thomas had spoken with Penkowski. The bank notified him that it had been deposited into a miscellaneous account. Uncertain about which account to transfer it to, the Mayor instructed the bank to leave it where it was for the time being. The bank officer informed him that such a substantial amount could generate enough interest to cover several people's salaries for years. They strongly recommended investing it right away. However, the Mayor respectfully declined their suggestion.

EIGHTEEN

A lone figure stood at the edge of the bustling sidewalk, his eyes fixed on the rising walls of the old church property. Dust danced in the sunlight as construction workers moved with purpose, each hammer blow echoing against the backdrop of the city's clamor. Sensing his contemplation, a stranger approached, drawn by the spectacle unfolding before them.

"It looks like they're building another church," the stranger remarked, his voice carrying a hint of curiosity.

A wistful smile played at the corners of the man's lips as he replied, "Yes, indeed."

The stranger's skepticism hung in the air like a shadow, his doubt heavy as he voiced his thoughts. "They tried that before and failed. I wonder what makes them think they can pull it off this time."

With a quiet resolve, the man turned to face the stranger, his gaze steady and unwavering. "Because I'm building it."

There was a weight to his words, a conviction born of determination and faith, as he stood firm in his belief in the project's success.

After the brief exchange, Penkowski's attention shifted to City Hall, where the grand facade was undergoing a meticulous cleansing. The Mayor emerged, a figure of authority and influence, engaging in animated conversation with the overseer of the cleaning operation. A sense of anticipation stirred within Penkowski as he observed the interaction, a smile tugging at the corners of his lips.

With purposeful strides, he approached the Mayor and the cleaner, his demeanor exuding confidence and assurance.

"Mayor Thomas?" Penkowski's voice cut through the air, a deliberate interruption that drew the Mayor's attention like a sudden gust of wind.

The Mayor turned, his eyes meeting those of a tall, imposing figure clad in an impeccably tailored suit, a black tie adding a touch of formality to his attire.

"I am responsible for this man's services to you, and I will cover the expenses. I thought it only fair that since I caused the mess with all the ashes and fallout, I should clean it up," Penkowski explained, his voice carrying a note of sincerity amidst the lingering tension.

The Mayor extended his hand, a gesture of welcome and acknowledgment. "Dr. Penkowski, I presume?"

"Mayor Thomas," Penkowski replied, accepting the Mayor's hand with a firm shake, a shared smile bridging the gap between them.

As they made their way into the building, the Mayor introduced Penkowski to his receptionist. However, her stunned expression left an awkward silence hanging in the air, a ripple of discomfort that colored the encounter.

Proceeding to the Mayor's office, they settled into their seats, a sense of camaraderie beginning to take root despite the initial unease. The Mayor offered Penkowski a drink, and they indulged in the momentary reprieve, their conversation flowing with ease.

"It's becoming increasingly difficult to find this stuff," the Mayor commented, his expression reflecting a mixture of nostalgia and resignation as he took a sip, the taste evoking memories of simpler times.

"Rare year?" Penkowski inquired, his curiosity piqued by the Mayor's cryptic remark.

"No," the Mayor replied, struggling to articulate the complexities of their situation. "We don't have a liquor store in town, and none of the grocery stores carry liquor anymore."

Penkowski's surprise was vivid, his brows furrowing in disbelief. "What about convenience stores or gas stations? Don't they sell it?"

"No. You have to go out of town to get it. No cigarettes, no racy magazines..." the Mayor explained, a hint of resignation coloring his words.

A surge of irritation tinged Penkowski's voice as he interjected, his frustration bubbling to the surface. "You must be joking! What do you all do for fun in this town?"

"Well, it wasn't always like this. It started about six months ago..." the Mayor began, his voice trailing off as he launched into a narrative that spoke of a small-town pastor and a community transformed by faith.

Penkowski listened, his anger simmering beneath the surface as the Mayor's words stirred memories of encounters long past. With each passing moment, his resolve hardened, a silent vow forming in the depths of his being. He despised everything associated with Christianity, yet beneath his composed facade lurked a darker truth —an embodiment of pure malevolence.

His mind raced, a torrent of thoughts swirling in a tempest of rage and determination. His face flushed crimson, his eyes betraying the storm raging within as he struggled to maintain the facade of civility.

"Doctor, are you alright?" Mayor Thomas's voice was laced with concern as he observed the flush creeping up Penkowski's cheeks. He hesitated, wary of causing offense to the man whose generosity had breathed new life into Stapleton. "You look... well... very flushed. Would you like some water?"

For a moment, silence hung heavy in the air, broken only by the faint hum of activity outside the mayor's office. Penkowski's breath caught in his throat, his mind swirling with a tumult of emotions. "I'm sorry. I detest when people's freedom of choice is taken away," he finally confessed, his voice tinged with a hint of bitterness.

Regaining his composure, Penkowski forced a smile, his resolve hardening as he prepared to unveil his plan. "But I have a remarkable idea."

Mayor Thomas leaned forward, his interest piqued by the promise of innovation, his mind already racing with the possibilities. "Go on," he urged, eager to hear Penkowski's proposal.

"I intend to make my workplace not only the highest-paying jobs in town, but also reward my employees—the town's residents working for me—by restoring the very things that have been taken away from them," Penkowski declared, his words brimming with conviction.

The mayor's brow furrowed in curiosity. "What do you mean?"

A spark of enthusiasm ignited in Penkowski's eyes as he painted a vision of transformation, his words carrying the weight of his determination. "I will create a space where employees can enjoy a drink after work, peruse books and indulge in an assortment of magazines, and purchase any tobacco products they desire. Furthermore, I will provide recreational opportunities on the premises for their enjoyment after hours, of course."

"Recreational opportunities?" Mayor Thomas echoed, his intrigue growing with each revelation.

Penkowski nodded, a sense of purpose infusing his words. "You know, games like bingo, poker, and other card games. Your people will once again find joy in their lives and regain the freedom of choice that was unjustly snatched away from them."

As the conversation unfolded, Penkowski's mind buzzed with anticipation, his objectives aligning with his deeper motives. He needed the mayor's support to lay the groundwork for his plans, but he also harbored ambitions beyond mere business ventures.

"That sounds fantastic! What can I do to assist?" Mayor Thomas's eagerness mirrored Penkowski's own, his commitment to restoring normalcy evident in his words.

"Your support is all I require," Penkowski assured him, his smile genuine as they sealed their agreement with a firm handshake.

With a sense of purpose driving them forward, Penkowski and Mayor Thomas embarked on a journey to reshape Stapleton, their shared vision offering a glimmer of hope amidst the shadows of uncertainty.

"Well, how much more time do you need?" John anxiously inquired, his voice filled with concern, as he spoke to Elizabeth over the phone.

"This is turning out to be much more challenging than I anticipated. This guy is a mastermind, and it will take considerable time to unravel his web of deceit. I need to meticulously construct a case around his cunning maneuvers, and that will require more time and possibly additional information," Elizabeth responded, her voice carrying a hint of frustration.

John listened intently, realizing the gravity of the situation. "I understand," he replied, his voice tinged with determination. "As much as I worry about your safety, we can't afford to take any shortcuts. We need to ensure every detail is thoroughly examined and accounted for. If we lose this case... well, the consequences could be devastating. We must do this right, not only for George's sake but for our own well-being."

John concluded his call on his cell phone, the familiar streets of Stapleton passing by in a blur as he navigated his way home. The journey had been a welcome respite, the quality time spent with his sister on the plane a balm for his weary soul. Their conversations had meandered through myriad topics, but this time, they had delved into matters of faith, exploring the depths of belief and the essence of God and His Son, Jesus.

Lost in thought, John's mind wandered through the labyrinth of memories that had woven themselves into the fabric of Stapleton's once-tranquil existence. Amidst the cacophony of peculiar events, one conversation resonated—the heartfelt exchange with Pastor Bruce. It had transcended mere religious discourse, delving into the very core of John's being. As he reflected, he felt a peace settle over him, an inner tranquility that seemed to emanate from the depths of his soul.

Memories of Maggie's prayer at the hospital stirred within him, her words a whispered invocation that had lingered in the recesses of his mind. Had her true intent been to guide him towards a path illuminated by faith?

A shift had occurred within him—a subtle yet profound transformation. He felt lighter, as though a burden he hadn't realized he'd been carrying had been lifted from his shoulders. Despite no tangible change in his physical being, he sensed a newfound clarity, an appreciation for the beauty that surrounded him.

The prospect of a future filled with love, family, and blessings beckoned to him like a distant beacon, promising a life infused with purpose and meaning.

However, as he approached the spot where his home once stood, his heart plummeted. Instead of the stately house he had left behind mere days ago, all that remained were charred remnants—

the blackened husk of what had once been his sanctuary. Anger surged within him as he immediately assumed Penkowski's hand in this destruction. In a fit of vindictive rage, Penkowski had likely orchestrated the destruction, his failure to locate what he sought driving him to such extreme measures.

Unbeknownst to John, Pastor Bruce and George had recounted tales of a fire that had ravaged houses, including one where a baby had been miraculously saved. Little did John realize that his own residence had been consumed by those flames.

Overwhelmed by despair, John found himself offering a silent prayer, the words escaping his lips like a whispered plea for guidance. "Lord, what do I do now?" In that moment of vulnerability, Bruce's name surfaced in his mind, a beacon of hope amidst the chaos.

Instinctively, John chose to bypass his ruined home discreetly, a sense of foreboding gnawing at his insides. As he did, he noticed a car turning onto his street, a sinking feeling settling in the pit of his stomach. His pulse quickened as the vehicle slowed near his desolate property.

Without hesitation, John retrieved a pair of binoculars, his hands trembling as he peered through the lenses. There, amidst the wreckage, stood Penkowski, his gaze piercing through the distance as if searching for something—or someone.

With a heart heavy with uncertainty, John lowered the binoculars and drove away, the weight of unanswered questions pressing upon him like a suffocating shroud.

Bruce returned home to a chorus of warm greetings from Wayne and the other leaders, their relieved smiles reflecting the shared joy at his safe return. Maggie, Sue, and the others who had stood alongside him during the picketing welcomed him eagerly, their eyes filled with curiosity and concern. As Bruce's gaze swept over the familiar faces, he couldn't hide the traces of Penkowski's recent visit etched into his expression, a silent testament to the turmoil he had endured.

Fabricating a tale to shield them from the harsh realities he had faced, Bruce concocted a story of aiding a friend in need, leaving his audience puzzled yet reassured by his commitment to lending a helping hand. "If this friend needs help again, I will be there for them, just as Jesus has been there for me," he declared, his voice imbued with unwavering resolve.

Amidst the lively conversation that followed, Bruce struggled to keep pace with the flurry of inquiries and anecdotes. The atmosphere shifted as the discussion turned to a national news report detailing the rescue of a baby from a burning house. Bruce's face lit up with a radiant glow as he recounted his own encounter with Jesus, redirecting praise to the Almighty for His divine intervention. A reverent hush settled over the room, each heart humbled by the miraculous workings of God.

Suddenly, the door burst open, a familiar voice cutting through the stillness. "Hello, Pastor Bruce?" It was John Ivan. Bruce's eyes met John's across the room, a silent acknowledgment passing between them as Maggie rushed forward to embrace the newcomer. All eyes followed the unfolding scene, the air thick with anticipation as Bruce approached John, his hand extending in a gesture of welcome.

In that moment, John felt the weight of his emotional burdens lift, the warmth of acceptance washing over him like a gentle embrace. It was as if every worry and doubt he had carried had been swept away in an instant. Here, in this room filled with love and understanding, he found solace and belonging.

"I'm so glad to see you! How are you?" Maggie's voice rang out, her eyes searching John's face with genuine concern.

"I am fine," John began, but the gaze he shared with Maggie and Bruce sparked a deeper realization within him. "I am better than fine," he amended with a smile. "I'm home."

Maggie's eyes sparkled with understanding as she exchanged a glance with Bruce, their smiles mirroring John's newfound sense of belonging. In that moment of revelation, John understood that while a house may burn, the true essence of home lies in the embrace of community and the unwavering presence of God's love.

It was an old-fashioned barber shop, steeped in nostalgia and history, its charm accentuated by the iconic revolving pole adorned in the patriotic colors of white, red, and blue—a beacon of tradition barely visible in the daylight. Through the window, the rhythmic snip of scissors and soft murmur of conversation could be heard, hinting at the timeless rituals taking place within.

As another customer approached the shop, the creaking door swung open, ushering in a breath of fresh air along with the newcomer, dressed in blue jeans and a button-down plaid shirt. Today, he appeared different, a subtle shift in demeanor noticeable to anyone who cared to look. The door closed behind him, its gentle jingle of bells announcing his arrival as he exchanged a nod with the barber.

"Good day," the barber greeted, his voice warm and inviting.

Penkowski nodded in acknowledgment, settling into a worn leather chair as he awaited his turn. His fingers idly traced the edges of a newspaper, but his attention was drawn more to the lively banter between the barber and the previous customer.

When his turn finally came, the barber gestured for Penkowski to take the vacant barber chair, his gaze curious but friendly. "New to town?" he inquired, his tone filled with genuine interest.

"Just visiting. It's a beautiful town," Penkowski replied, his voice carrying a note of polite admiration.

"It sure is. I've been here my whole life. Though things have changed quite a bit recently," the barber remarked, his eyes reflecting a mixture of nostalgia and resignation.

Intrigued, Penkowski leaned forward, feigning casual curiosity as he probed for information. The barber, a repository of local lore, shared insights gleaned from years of close observation, his words painting a vivid picture of the town's evolution.

Seizing the opportunity, Penkowski steered the conversation towards the Tuesday night prayer ritual, his interest piqued by the mayor's cryptic remarks. With each detail shared, his curiosity deepened, his mind racing with possibilities.

Then, with calculated precision, Penkowski broached a specific name, his gaze intent as he awaited the barber's response. The mention of John Ivan sparked a flicker of recognition in the barber's eyes, and he shared a tale of heroism, recounting how a woman named Sue Billings had saved a man named John Ivan from a car accident.

As their conversation was interrupted by the arrival of another customer, Penkowski's impatience grew, his fingers tapping restlessly against the armrest of the chair. Sensing the conclusion of his visit, he settled his bill with a generous tip, expressing his gratitude to the barber.

"You're welcome," the barber replied warmly, but Penkowski

wasn't finished yet. With a practiced smile, he seized the opportunity to inquire about Sue Billings, his mind already racing ahead to his next move.

As he exited the barber shop, the wheels of his mind spun with newfound information, his determination unyielding as he set his sights on his next target.

Things began to settle down after John had arrived. Bruce simply introduced John to the group by his first name as a new believer. He was welcomed by everyone.

"Can I talk with you for a moment?" John asked Bruce, hoping he hadn't put his newfound pastor friend in an uncomfortable situation.

Bruce's face lit up with enthusiasm. "Absolutely!" he replied, leading John to a quiet room away from everyone after excusing himself.

Bruce gestured toward a nearby chair, inviting John to sit beside him. As they settled in, a tangible sense of camaraderie filled the room, amplifying the weight of the conversation that was about to unfold.

"I wanted you to know how much I appreciate what you did for my sister and me," John began, his words laden with gratitude and concern. He underscored the risks involved, acknowledging the bravery and sacrifice Bruce had displayed by standing by their side.

For a fleeting moment, Bruce's smile faltered, a brief glimpse of vulnerability flickering across his features before he regained his composure. "God did not give us a spirit of fear but of power, love, and a sound mind," he reassured, his voice infused with unwavering faith.

John met Bruce's gaze, a flicker of uncertainty dancing in his eyes as he grappled with the weight of Bruce's words. Could God truly offer protection in the face of such peril? The question lingered, stirring a mixture of hope and apprehension within him.

"Is God bigger than Penkowski in my life too?" John's inquiry was earnest, his voice tinged with a newfound sense of urgency.

Bruce chuckled softly, his laughter carrying a reassuring warmth. "Of course he is," he affirmed, his words a beacon of comfort in the midst of uncertainty. "You belong to him now, and he will never abandon you."

As Bruce outlined his vision for the church's involvement in John's fight against Penkowski, a surge of purpose welled up within John. Here, in this moment, he realized he was not alone in his struggle. Together, they would stand as a united front against injustice and oppression.

John's eyes widened with a mixture of surprise and curiosity as Bruce continued to speak. "How so?" he asked, eager to understand the depth of their shared mission.

Bruce's response was resolute. "We are all in this together. Your battle aligns with our core beliefs and values," he explained, his words infused with unwavering conviction.

John pondered Bruce's proposition, a sense of humility shining through his gaze. "But can you truly help me?" he asked, his voice tinged with a hint of uncertainty.

In response, Bruce began sharing a new story—a recent development involving the former heads of the Association for Fetal Research. As Bruce recounted the remarkable transformation that had taken place, John felt a rush of emotions welling up inside him. Unable to contain his tumultuous thoughts, he stood up abruptly, walked over to the window, and gazed outside. With his hand pressed against his face, he rubbed his temples, trying to process the magnitude of what Bruce had just revealed. Meanwhile, Bruce remained seated, his eyes fixed on John with a mixture of empathy and anticipation.

"It's true," John murmured, his voice trembling with a mix of awe and realization. "Every member in that room made a decision for Christ."

Bruce nodded solemnly, affirming John's revelation. "Yes."

The weight of this revelation washed over John like a tidal wave. The knowledge that God had used him and the prayers of the faithful to enact such profound change overwhelmed him. A surge of hope welled up inside him, dispelling the shadows of doubt and fear that had lingered in his heart.

As John grappled with the enormity of what he had just learned, his thoughts turned to the sinister figure of Penkowski—the embodiment of pure malevolence. The memory of those bloodshot eyes, brimming with malice and darkness, sent a shiver down his spine. It prompted him to voice a question that had been gnawing at his mind.

"So, the devil is real, just as real as evil itself?" John asked, his voice quivering with a mixture of fear and curiosity.

Bruce's response was solemn yet resolute. "There is a real devil, and he is the author of evil. It's a harsh truth, but it's one we must acknowledge."

Lost in thought, John pondered the complexities of good and evil, grappling with the newfound understanding that the battle he faced was not merely physical but spiritual in nature.

With a renewed sense of purpose, John returned to the gathering, his heart heavy with the weight of the mission entrusted to him by God. As he shared his story and pleaded for their prayers and support, John felt the warmth of their hands laid upon him, their fervent prayers enveloping him like a protective shield.

With a newfound clarity and determination, John knew that he was not alone in this battle against evil. God was working within him, filling him with courage and resolve. As he bid farewell to the gathering and left with Maggie by his side, John was ready to face whatever challenges lay ahead, fortified by the unwavering support of his newfound faith community.

"Hi, my name is Kenneth," he introduced himself to the thrift store worker with a polite smile, masking the urgency in his voice. "I'm a friend of Maggie. Is she available for a couple of moments?"

"I'm afraid she is not here today," the worker replied apologetically, her tone tinged with regret. "She left earlier, said she had to get to her church. She will be back tomorrow. She is our best volunteer, you know."

"I bet she is," Kenneth said, his disappointment overwhelming beneath his courteous facade. He thanked the worker for her time and hastily exited the thrift store. The encounter had left a sour taste in his mouth, the contrast between his opulent lifestyle and the humble surroundings of the thrift store exacerbating his discomfort. The thought of wearing second-hand clothes repulsed him, a stark departure from Penkowski's usual pride in his appearance. Witnessing the less fortunate forced to wear castoffs only added to his disdain. But amidst his revulsion, his determination remained steadfast—his sole objective now was to find John Ivan, no matter the cost.

With each lead he pursued turning out to be a dead end, frustration festered within Penkowski, a simmering impatience gnawing at his resolve. Determined not to be defeated, he made a calculated decision: he would attend the prayer meeting that night. Surely, he believed, he would find some answers there. Little did he know the magnitude of what he was about to walk into. The air crackled with tension as he prepared to step into the unknown, his mind ablaze with a cocktail of anticipation and apprehension.

The Tuesday night prayer meeting was nothing short of awe-inspiring. The once-humble school auditorium now strained to contain the swelling sea of attendees, a testament to the city's fervent hunger for spiritual connection. Overflowing from Pastor Wayne and Pastor Bruce's modest church buildings, the assembly gathered with an intense energy that crackled in the air.

As each person stepped into the auditorium, they were enveloped in an atmosphere charged with anticipation and hope. Conversations swirled like a whirlwind, carrying tales of divine intervention and miraculous transformations. Stories of lives rescued from the depths of despair mingled with accounts of God's unmistakable hand at work—stories that echoed the recent deliverance of a helpless infant and the resolute stand against the forces of darkness at the Association of Fetal Research's meeting.

Penkowski, still dressed in the same attire he had worn throughout the day, experienced a sudden flashback as he approached the door leading to the auditorium. He recalled the last time he had tried to enter and had been barred from doing so. He cleared his mind, took a deep breath, and cautiously stepped through the door. This time, he made it inside, but a wave of nausea overcame him. He fought to maintain his composure, his face turning pale. Gradually, color returned to his cheeks, but his eyes now appeared bloodshot and glassy. He wandered through the crowd, listening to conversations, but none of them mentioned John Ivan. Despite his growing anger, he held onto his objective and pressed forward.

This time, Penkowski chose to ignore the Christian propaganda displayed on the walls, the very sight of which had infuriated him on his previous visit. He began inquiring about Sue Billings, knowing that many in the room knew her. However, the sheer number of people made it difficult to locate her. Then, someone pointed him in her direction, and he set his sights on Sue, determined to find her.

"I don't feel right," Bruce confessed to Wayne, his voice filled with concern and unease.

"What do you mean?" Wayne inquired, sensing the seriousness in Bruce's tone.

"I feel... evil," Bruce admitted, his words heavy with the weight of his emotions. "It's a darkness that I've never experienced before."

Wayne understood the gravity of the situation. "God's Spirit is present, but so is the presence of evil," he concluded, realizing the spiritual battle that was taking place.

With a deep sense of caution, Bruce made a firm decision. He instructed George and John to retreat to the back room, away from the prying eyes of the congregation. It was a precautionary measure, a way to shield them from any potential harm or interference. Bruce's protective instinct urged him to keep them hidden, ensuring their safety amidst the spiritual turbulence that permeated the atmosphere.

"Sue?" Penkowski called out, his voice dripping with an air of malevolence.

Sue turned to face him, mustering a forced smile despite the unsettling aura surrounding him. "Kenneth, a friend of John Ivan's," he introduced himself with an evil grin.

Sue's heart skipped a beat as she sensed the darkness emanating from him. She maintained a composed expression, concealing her unease. "Well, welcome," she managed to utter, her voice strained.

"Thank you. It's been so many years since I last saw John. I heard you know him? Helped him out of a car accident?" Penkowski inquired, his voice laced with curiosity.

Sue's surprise was evident in her response. "Yes," she replied cautiously.

"The barber mentioned it, said it was the talk of the town.

When I heard John's name, I thought I'd see if I could catch up with him," Penkowski explained with a sly smile.

Curiosity mingled with apprehension, Sue continued the conversation, praying silently for guidance and protection. "How do you know him?"

"We were old high school friends. Bet he looks different today," Penkowski remarked, his eyes narrowing.

Sue attempted to deflect further questions, not wanting to arouse suspicion. "Never went to any high school reunions?"

"Nah, those are just bragging opportunities," Penkowski responded, waiting for Sue to provide more information.

Sue decided it was best to change the subject, relying on her prayers for wisdom. "When I pulled him out of the car, he was pretty bloody," she shared, purposely giving a description that deviated from John's actual appearance, hoping to throw Penkowski off track.

Penkowski seemed satisfied, convinced that John might have disguised himself during their last encounter. Still, a nagging familiarity lingered in his mind, though he couldn't quite place it.

Meanwhile, Bruce rose to the podium, capturing the attention of the congregation. Seizing the opportunity, Sue excused herself, her heart pounding with a mix of anxiety and determination. Penkowski, on the other hand, remained in the back, scanning the crowd in a desperate search for any sign of John's newfound religious devotion.

As he stared at the podium, Penkowski could feel his blood pressure rising, a physical manifestation of his mounting frustration. The figure before him represented the catalyst behind what he perceived as religious enslavement. Struggling to regain his composure, he focused on observing his perceived enemy, all the while battling a growing sense of nausea that threatened to overwhelm him.

"I want to begin by thanking all of you for coming, inviting your friends, neighbors, and co-workers," Bruce's voice resounded with heartfelt gratitude, permeating the air with an electric energy. "I want to give God the glory for our baby that was saved from the burning fire and how God received glory on national TV."

Penkowski squirmed uncomfortably in his chair, each word slicing through his ears like a deafening buzz saw in stereo. A wave of nausea churned in his stomach, intensifying with every passing moment.

The mother of the rescued baby stood up, her voice trembling with emotion as she shared her personal story of past mistakes, a life driven by self-centeredness, and the transformative decision to follow Jesus. With each mention of that name, Penkowski felt an increasing pressure weighing heavily on his chest, making it difficult for him to draw a breath. The afflictions he had inexplicably acquired since stepping foot inside the auditorium only compounded his discomfort.

"I also want to inform each of you about a recent encounter I had with someone I believe to be the same individual responsible for the arson attacks in our community and the endangerment of our police force," Bruce began.

A sinister smile crept across Penkowski's face, hidden amidst the pain he endured. He relished in the thought of the chaos he had caused, convinced that this gathering would provide him with a front-row seat to their collective anguish.

Bruce stepped forward, sharing the harrowing details of his own encounter with Penkowski, recounting the violence and malevolence he had experienced firsthand. The smile on Penkowski's face widened, feeding off the fear he hoped to instill in others.

Then, Wayne joined Bruce at the podium, their voices intertwined, delivering a powerful message. "Love your enemy and only do good toward them. Forgive those who persecute, hurt you, and cause you pain because of me, Jesus," they declared in unison.

The mention of that name, Jesus, reverberated through the auditorium once more, eliciting an intensified pressure on Penkowski's chest. The weight of those words and the concept of forgiveness seemed to suffocate him.

"I forgive you in Jesus' name," Bruce proclaimed, his voice resonating with unwavering resolve echoing the power of forgiveness.

Bruce continued, his voice growing stronger, "The enemy boasted, 'I will pursue, overtake, divide the spoils, and my hand will destroy them.' But you, oh Lord, blew with your breath, and the sea covered them... Oh, the pressure of gallons and gallons of water upon these, God's enemy. 'It is mine to avenge, I will repay,' says the Lord."

As Bruce spoke those words, the weight of divine justice and retribution pressed down upon Penkowski, amplifying his discomfort and igniting a flicker of unease within him.

"Ahhh!" Penkowski let out a guttural, otherworldly scream, his voice a grotesque distortion that sent shivers down the spines of those nearby. The man beside him cowered in fear, clutching his Bible tightly.

Bruce halted his speech, his eyes fixed on the disturbance unfolding before him. Penkowski's rage consumed him, his eyes glowing a menacing red as he directed his anger towards the trembling man. In a sudden outburst, Penkowski lunged at the man, attempting to tear his Bible to shreds.

The entire auditorium was now captivated by the unfolding chaos. All eyes were on Penkowski, their gazes filled with shock and disbelief. In the blink of an eye, the Bible, once under attack, burst open, revealing its contents. A blinding, pure white light radiated from within, pouring forth from God's holy words and flooding the entire auditorium.

As the radiant light washed over Penkowski, his human form dissolved, replaced by a monstrous creature of immense size and grotesque features. His damp, black, scaly skin marred with imperfections stretched across his face, revealing a sunken nose-like cavity. His mouth, lined with razor-sharp, oversized teeth, displayed only a few yellowed remnants amidst the dark stains, and drool dripped menacingly from his maw. Each breath he exhaled expelled a repugnant yellow sulfurous smoke, filling the air with a foul stench. The once-red eyes now burned with an ominous blend of red and yellow, radiating an otherworldly malevolence. His unearthly growls reverberated throughout the auditorium, filling the space with a chilling, otherworldly resonance.

As the spectators recoiled in terror, confused and transfixed by the blinding light enveloping the creature, the luminescence extended beyond Penkowski, illuminating the entire area, reaching even the farthest corners of the auditorium.

But amidst the blinding radiance, three majestic figures emerged. Clad in radiant robes that gleamed like the sun itself, they exuded an ethereal brilliance, their presence electrifying the atmosphere. Each warrior wielded a sword of extraordinary luminescence, emanating colors that defied human comprehension. With every movement, they tore through the fabric of reality, leaving behind fleeting seams of darkness that swiftly vanished.

Positioning themselves strategically, the angelic warriors flanked the creature, their swords poised for action. The divine blades blazed with resplendent hues as one of the warriors thrust his sword into the chest of the monstrous being, while the others stood guard on either side of its head. The air crackled with celestial energy, and the clash of cosmic forces resonated throughout the auditorium, heralding a battle of epic proportions.

Overwhelmed by the cacophony of otherworldly sounds reverberating through the auditorium, John and George burst out of the back room and rushed towards the spectacle unfolding before them. Their eyes widened in disbelief as they took in the scene. There, in the midst of the chaos, they beheld the terrifying creature, the three angelic warriors, and the radiant light emanating from what appeared to be a book lying on the ground. The light, however, seemed to extend only halfway across the auditorium, creating an eerie and unsettling contrast.

John exchanged a bewildered glance with George, their astonishment mirrored in each other's eyes. It was a stark reminder of the truth George had shared about Penkowski's monstrous countenance during their initial encounter. They hurried over to where Bruce stood, their minds unable to comprehend the extraordinary sight unfolding before them. In the depths of their being, they engaged in fervent, desperate prayer, seeking divine intervention in the face of this unimaginable confrontation.

Throughout the auditorium, voices rose in unison, proclaiming the name of Jesus. With each utterance, the angelic warriors, bathed in radiant sunlight, thrust their swords towards the creature's head. The creature's screams grew even more intense, reverberating through the walls of the auditorium. The sheer force of its cries sent vibrations coursing through the chests of every person present, like the resonating bass of a deafening rock concert. The intense tremors momentarily caused everyone to pause, their hearts pounding in their chests. Yet, undeterred, they quickly resumed speaking the name of Jesus, their voices united in unwavering faith and conviction.

As the radiant light reached the back doors, two more majestic figures materialized, adorned in resplendent luminescence. Their presence commanded awe and reverence as they stood guard over the entrances, their towering swords extending from the ground to high above the door frames. With their swords crossed in front of the openings, they formed an impenetrable barrier, ensuring that nothing could pass through.

The sight of these magnificent swords alone was captivating, defying description with their breathtaking colors and ethereal beauty. It was impossible not to be transfixed by their sheer magnificence, as if they held within them the very essence of divine power.

Bruce seized the hands of George and John, their connection strengthening their resolve as he lifted his voice in prayer. The words spilled forth, fervently acknowledging the sovereignty of God and the trust placed in His unwavering control. Though George and John were reluctant to close their eyes during the prayer, they stood alongside Bruce, fully engaged in the moment.

Unable to endure the searing pain inflicted by the spoken words any longer, the creature crouched low and then leaped into the air, executing a somersault that left behind a trail of sulfurous breath. As he landed, his knuckles firmly pressed against the ground for stability, the three angelic warriors maintained their unwavering hold, their swords pressed against his head and chest. The warriors moved with supernatural speed and agility, as if they had never left the creature's side.

On the other side of the auditorium, Maggie and Sue clung to one another tightly, their hearts pounding in their chests. Throughout the ordeal, they had remained locked in silent prayer, their breath catching in their throats. They watched with a mix of fear and awe, their voices silenced, unable to articulate the overwhelming emotions surging within them.

"Lord, in the mighty name of Jesus Christ, our Savior and the Son of the God of Abraham, Isaac, and Jacob, I beseech You to remove this beast and the imminent dangers it poses!" Bruce fervently exclaimed. George chimed in agreement, their voices blending in a chorus of determination. John, overwhelmed by desperation, could only utter a plea for God's help, his words hanging in the air.

In an instant, a powerful gust of wind rushed toward them, forcefully impacting their backs and whipping their clothes, hair, and bodies in the direction of the creature. The wind surged through the auditorium, starting from the front and surging toward the back. Clothes billowed, hair tangled in the tempest, and women clutched their purses tightly, fearing they would be torn from their grasp.

As the wind reached the angelic warriors, they remained steadfast, their forms unyielding to its force. Yet, the creature on the floor fought to maintain balance, struggling against the relentless assault of the swords. Though pushed backward by the wind, he continued to resist, battling against the blades that assailed him.

The wind grew fiercer, its intensity increasing. People clung to their stadium-style seats, straining to catch a glimpse of the tumultuous scene unfolding at the back of the auditorium. The creature, buffeted by the relentless gales, inched ever closer to the guarded doors, his attempts to stabilize himself proving futile.

Bruce, his voice raised in prayer, expressed gratitude to Jesus. Yet, as the howling wind enveloped them, George and John could only see Bruce's lips moving, for the cacophony drowned out his words, preventing them from hearing his prayer, despite standing in close proximity.

The warriors raised their swords in unison, and as the gleaming blades made contact, a resonating sound reverberated throughout the auditorium, surpassing the tumultuous noise of the wind and the creature's cries. With the swords now at their sides, the warriors stood aside, allowing the creature to pass through the doors. Inch by agonizing inch, the creature advanced, emitting unearthly screams and growls that pierced the air, accompanied by the relentless presence of the warriors and their ever-present swords.

As the creature traversed the threshold, the warriors withdrew their swords, sheathing them once more. The guards stationed at the door replaced their swords, their movement producing an audible echo that resonated throughout the auditorium. The three radiant figures dissipated, but the guards remained, unwavering sentinels. Gradually, the wind subsided, and a hushed silence descended upon the place as the congregation began to regain their composure, catching their breath.

Meanwhile, the Bible on the ground continued to emanate a gentle glow, though its light gradually diminished. The guards stood firm at the closed double doors, while a cacophony of multiplied cries from the retreating creature echoed through the still-opened portal. Peering through the doors, onlookers could discern the presence of numerous other grotesque beings in the wake of the receding white light.

Abruptly, the doors slammed shut, severing the connection to the outside world. The radiance from the Bible diminished further, and the guards, like ethereal apparitions, dissolved into the replacement of ordinary, mundane lighting fixtures within the auditorium.

Outside, Penkowski lay sprawled on the ground, his outstretched hand futilely grasping towards the doors that had slammed shut in his face. As he rose to his feet and approached the doors, a searing pressure compressed his chest, his head throbbed with pain, and the heat emanating from the doors scorched his hands, causing him to think twice before attempting to enter again.

Penkowski seethed with fury, his anger intensifying as the pain coursed through his body. Reluctantly releasing his grip on the doors, he glared at them with seething hatred. "This is not over yet! It has only begun!" he proclaimed, his voice dripping with venom. With a final burst of rage, he turned away and stormed off, consumed by his seething anger.

NINETEEN

It was a new day in Stapleton, and the streets gleamed with a renewed vibrancy. The old, worn-out lampposts had been replaced with elegant, modern designs, casting a warm glow on the sidewalks. The once-tattered walkways had been revitalized, showcasing a hint of color that paid homage to the town's historical charm.

Brick storefronts, courtesy of the city's generous funds, had been meticulously pressure-cleaned, restoring them to their original grandeur. The buildings looked as if they had just been constructed, their facades radiating with newfound splendor. A couple of abandoned structures that had succumbed to neglect during the revival had been torn down, making room for lush landscaping and vibrant trees.

Forest Ridge Park boasted new park benches, swings, and playground equipment that beckoned children with their inviting allure. The roads had been freshly paved, and the bridge had undergone a stunning renovation. The entire park was a sight to behold, surpassing its initial glory.

However, the most remarkable addition to the community's beauty was Penkowski's own creation. The building stood proudly in the city square, seamlessly blending with the surrounding architecture while exuding a captivating charm of its own. Though it was expansive, its true size remained hidden from the front, revealing itself only gradually as one ventured inside. The structure boasted a modernized interpretation of a steeple, a testament to Penkowski's dedication to craftsmanship and aesthetics.

Today marked the grand opening of this remarkable facility, and its ornate double doors stood wide open, welcoming the entire town. Curiosity drew in the residents, one by one, as they entered and were greeted by a carefully selected staff, handpicked from Advanced Medical's main office in California. Balloons were offered to the little ones, free sodas served from a tastefully arranged bar, and gift cards distributed for a charming bookstore located within the facility.

Beyond the bustling entrance, a separate door led to a private clinic at the back, ensuring utmost privacy. The facility boasted an elaborate workout room and a recreational area, complemented by the presence of knowledgeable staff members ready to answer any questions about potential job opportunities. Advanced Medical seized the moment to promote their expansion plans, showcasing their commitment to providing exceptional job perks and growth prospects through multimedia presentations and informative literature.

As the people explored the facility, a sense of wonder and excitement filled the air. The new chapter in Stapleton's history had begun, leaving behind a legacy of revitalization and promise for a bright future.

Guided tours were conducted throughout the facility, leaving each visitor in awe of the expansive rooms and impressive size. Separate training rooms and board meeting spaces were available, while the spacious cubicles provided a comfortable working environment. An air-conditioned area had been designated for manufacturing, complete with state-of-the-art equipment. Vibrant colors adorned the walls, complemented by elegant light fixtures and stylish décor. Even the flooring exuded a sense of luxury.

The facility boasted numerous computers, allowing visitors to access online applications and explore estimations of the impressive salaries offered for each position. These wages far surpassed the typical jobs available in Stapleton, capturing the attention of those seeking greater financial opportunities. When inquiring about the products being manufactured, visitors were informed that the focus was on medical equipment.

Off to the side, Penkowski engaged in conversation with George Hines, the head of his other plant, AFT, who now also held a leadership role at this new facility. George had been the recipient of fervent prayers from his fellow believers, who were fully aware of the true purpose behind the facility—to manufacture medical equipment specifically for the abortion industry.

This posed a significant dilemma, as while a significant portion of the community had embraced the revival and its principles, there remained a segment that continued to hold out due to their apathy. Despite the widespread presence of the Ten Commandments in schools, Bible studies, prayers at school gatherings, and the integration of faith into the fabric of the community, some individuals—among them employees of AFT and other community members—were still enticed by the allure of the new facility owned and operated by Advanced Medical. Its attractiveness, perks, and the promise of significantly higher wages tempted those who had yet to fully align themselves with the revival's values.

"We have a nice crowd today, don't you think, George?" Penkowski boasted, his tone dripping with self-satisfaction.

"Yes, indeed. Thanks to your vision and this remarkable facility you've built," George replied, mustering up his best acting skills.

"And you, my friend, are the one overseeing it all, including AFT," Penkowski remarked, ensuring that George knew his value had been recognized through fear and intimidation.

George forced a smile and said, "Thank you, sir. I truly appreciate this incredible opportunity and the advancement in my career." But deep inside, he felt a profound unease, a sickening sensation in the pit of his stomach.

"And I will quadruple your income and enhance your bonus accordingly. You will lack for nothing," Penkowski declared confidently.

"But I will lack my freedom," George thought to himself. He

knew that somehow, in some way, God would intervene and bring about a resolution. However, he began contemplating the possibility of disappearing and running away. Yet, the thought of letting down his friends and the potential to put an end to abortion nationwide, considering Advanced Medical's near-monopoly in the industry, seemed worth the sacrifices. Little did he know just how dire the situation would become. Today was merely a prelude to the storm that lay ahead.

"John Ivan. Does that name ring a bell?" Penkowski suddenly asked, catching George off guard.

"No, I haven't heard of John Ivan. Should I have?" George responded, feigning calmness.

"He possesses damaging information about our company, and we must find him and put a stop to it. The plans I have for this facility and the entire community are far greater than anything he can do, and he will not be allowed to ruin them for me," Penkowski explained with a sense of urgency.

"If you could provide me with his description, I will keep an eye out for him," George replied, hoping to maintain his composure.

Penkowski retrieved digital pictures from his pocket—one taken at the main office, another aboard a plane, and a third computer-generated based on Sue Billings' description.

"May I have these?" George blurted out, realizing it might sound overly eager to obtain them.

"Of course. I have distributed copies to my staff at the main office, and they are on the lookout as well. I would like you to give them to your people at AFT and offer a cash reward for his capture," Penkowski instructed.

George maintained his well-practiced poker face, prompting Penkowski to continue.

"The reward is set at $50,000. Let them know that he possesses trade secrets and intends to sell them to startup companies. This would seriously harm our business and potentially lead to our downfall," Penkowski stated, without a hint of deceit.

George's surprise was evident.

"Do you think that's not enough?" Penkowski questioned, his tone slightly challenging.

"No, it's just that I've never been involved in a reward for someone... alive or otherwise," George replied, attempting to inject a touch of humor.

Penkowski's expression remained stoic. He simply stated, "If I have him, I will gladly pay the money."

George regretted asking that question, realizing the gravity of the situation he had inadvertently stepped into.

Thoughts weighed heavily on Sue as she spoke to Bruce over the phone. The events that had transpired seemed surreal, like something out of a twisted science fiction movie. Yet, they couldn't ignore the truth that lay before them.

"I don't know how all of this happened," Sue confessed, her voice filled with bewilderment.

"What do you mean?" Bruce inquired, trying to make sense of the situation.

"I was talking to that man...or rather, creature," Sue replied, struggling to find the right words. "He asked me questions, and as I spoke, I could feel the power of God flowing through me. It was as if my words were not my own."

Bruce, attempting to lighten the mood, quipped, "Well, isn't that what usually happens?"

Sue's response was laced with frustration, "Yes, but not when you're staring evil in the face! I mean, if I were to describe a true encounter with evil, it was right there, in that man's eyes."

Bruce contemplated the situation and offered a possible explanation, "He must be a part of some cult or extremist group."

Confused, Sue sought clarification, asking, "What do you mean?"

Bruce elaborated, "Think about it. This man didn't just randomly decide to beat up me. He happened to drive by a church and thought, 'Oh, let me stop and attack a pastor?' No, his actions were driven by pure evil. We have no connection to his personal vendetta against John and Elizabeth."

Sue's voice trembled as she contemplated the depths of evil at play, "So, you believe he is...possessed?"

"Yes, I truly do," Bruce affirmed. "What other reason could he have to not only harm clergymen but also show up at a prayer meeting? His presence reeks of something far more sinister."

Sue's tone turned somber as she recalled a chilling thought, "I'm surprised he didn't meet the same fate as those three men who attended Tuesday night's prayer meeting at Pastor Wayne's church...

they were found dead."

The weight of the situation hung in the air as both Sue and Bruce grappled with the implications of what they had witnessed and the evil that seemed to be lurking in their midst.

Bruce pondered for a moment, his voice filled with a mix of intensity and urgency. "I've been reflecting on it, Sue, and I believe God permitted Penkowski's presence within our sanctuary. Despite the resistance from the angelic warriors guarding the revival, it was part of a larger message from God to His people."

Sue's voice trembled as she asked, "What kind of message, Bruce?"

Bruce took a deep breath, his words infused with a profound sense of wonder. "Penkowski was cloaked by a multitude of angels, revealing the spiritual realm that coexists with our own. It was an astonishing sight, one that left us feeling as if we had entered the realm of the supernatural."

Sue nodded, still awestruck by the extraordinary events they had witnessed. "I can't deny it, Bruce. It felt like we were trapped in some kind of surreal dimension."

Bruce continued, his tone gaining intensity. "And when Penkowski was escorted out, do you remember the forceful gust of wind that swept through the open doors?"

Sue's eyes widened as the memories flooded back. "Yes, I do. The blinding light streaming through the entrance and the eerie cacophony of the demonic forces outside..."

Bruce's voice grew resolute. "Exactly. It was as if the enemy had unleashed an army of darkness against us, trying to break through the barriers. But who prevailed? The angelic warriors held their ground, pushing back the forces of evil."

A heavy silence filled the air as Sue grappled with the weight of their reality. "The thought of those malevolent beings lurking around us is unsettling, even now," she admitted, her voice laced with unease.

Bruce's response came with a reassuring certainty. "But remember, Sue, the strength and power of the angelic warriors far surpassed that of the creature. They are the guardians of God's people, ever ready to defend and protect us."

Sue took solace in Bruce's words, finding a glimmer of hope amidst the darkness. "You're right, Bruce. Our faith in God's ultimate power should give us courage."

Bruce nodded, his expression resolute. "Indeed. With the old church gone, Reverend Stone and his followers removed, and the Association for Fetal Research dismantled, the enemy needed a new strategy to counter God's work."

Sue struggled to comprehend the magnitude of the spiritual battle they were facing. "I still can't fully grasp all of this. It feels like a whirlwind of chaos."

Bruce's voice grew fervent. "That's because the enemy is intensifying his efforts. He lost the battle against God's saints before, and now he's escalating the war, seeking new ways to undermine and corrupt."

Silence hung heavy in the room as Sue absorbed the weight of their conversation, contemplating the sinister forces at play.

"So, Penkowski is the new war strategy for the enemy?" Sue's voice quivered with a mix of fear and disbelief.

"Exactly!" Bruce exclaimed, a mixture of concern and determination evident in his tone. "Let me tell you, Sue, after witnessing that new facility rise in the heart of our town, replacing Stone's dead church... it's nothing but trouble with a capital T. George informed me that the medical equipment they're manufacturing is intended for abortion clinics across the nation. The Association may be gone, but this 'Advanced Medical' that George warned me about will provide a significant boost to the abortion industry. It's exactly what we don't want."

Sue's voice trembled as she responded, "We squash one cockroach and find ten more, even bigger than the first."

Bruce nodded solemnly, his frustration overwhelming. "That's exactly it. And I must say, I have an uneasy feeling about all the so-called 'perks' they're offering."

"It's strange to have a bar at work," Sue remarked, her tone filled with unease.

Bruce added, "Not to mention a 'clinic' within the facility."

Suddenly, realization struck Sue. "You don't think they might turn it into an abortion clinic, do you?"

"Well, considering they're leaders in the industry," Bruce replied, continuing the train of thought.

Sue's confusion was evident as she struggled to grasp the full extent of the situation. "But I don't understand..."

Bruce took a deep breath, gathering his thoughts before responding. "He wants to reclaim this town for the enemy. By utilizing that facility, offering higher pay, and enticing perks, it becomes a stronghold for the enemy's influence in Stapleton. We need to remain vigilant and ready for action."

They continued their conversation, discussing their plans for increased prayer support and reaffirming their faith in God's ultimate control over the situation. Though uncertainty lingered, they held onto hope, trusting that God would guide them through the trials ahead.

"Thanks again for meeting me here, Maggie. I hate feeling like I'm putting you in harm's way, but I really wanted to see you," John expressed, his voice filled with gratitude and concern.

Maggie nodded, her face showing a mix of understanding and determination. "We've been over this, remember?"

"Yes," John replied, his voice laced with emotion. He paused, taking a moment to gather his thoughts before continuing. "You are a very special woman, you know that?"

Maggie's heart skipped a beat. Never before had a man spoken those words to her. She looked up at John from the lakeside, a tear of joy glistening in her eye. With a mix of overwhelming emotions, she smiled and embraced him tightly.

"So... tell me more about what you and Bruce discussed... about your decision," Maggie gently inquired, not wanting to push but eager to understand.

John's smile deepened. It felt like just yesterday when Maggie had uttered that prayer over him in the hospital. Since then, everything had changed. It was incredible how one simple prayer could transform a person's life.

They spent hours conversing about their individual journeys, the emptiness they had felt, and the moment their paths intertwined. Maggie blushed as John spoke of her impact on his life. Then, they delved into the struggles they had both faced, the mistakes and challenges that had defined their pasts. They marveled at the profound simplicity of finding answers in Jesus.

As their conversation continued, John opened up about his job, his encounter with George, and the fear that had initially gripped him. He shared his concerns for George's safety, feeling a strong sense of responsibility to protect his newfound friend, even though he couldn't fully explain why. John admitted to the lack of genuine friendships in his adult life, longing for a deeper connection. He contemplated the idea of running away himself, seeking a semblance of freedom. But the thought of losing George weighed heavily on his heart.

"He will find freedom soon," Maggie reassured John, her voice filled with assurance. "Be patient. He is doing what needs to be done, and if he can bring about some good for you and Elizabeth, it's incredibly important."

John looked at Maggie with a mix of concern and gratitude in his eyes. She could see the depth of their friendship and understand how much George meant to him, and he didn't want to lose him.

They continued discussing John's plans to take down Penkowski, his worries about the timeline, and the immense pressure he felt. In a moment of solace, Maggie reminded him, "Remember, John, you have someone on your side who is not only your best friend but also your advocate."

John looked at Maggie, waiting for her to mention Pastor Bruce's name or some other name that would give him guidance and direction. Instead, Maggie smiled and looked surprised as she spoke those powerful words to him, "God."

John's heart skipped a beat as he realized the weight and truth behind her words. He sat there, his mind racing, trying to comprehend the enormity of what she was saying.

"The same God that has orchestrated all the miraculous events in this community, the same God who has shown His power and presence, He is with you even now," Maggie continued, her voice filled with conviction.

A flood of emotions washed over John. He recalled the conversation he had with Bruce, surrendering himself to God's care, but now, in this moment, hearing Maggie affirm the very same truth, it felt both overwhelming and comforting.

"He will work on your behalf. He will give you wisdom," Maggie reassured him.

Time seemed to stand still as they continued their conversation, the hours slipping away unnoticed. In that space, John found solace, knowing that he was not alone in his journey. God was with him, guiding him, and he had a faithful friend in Maggie who understood the depth of his struggle.

The facility that Penkowski had built stood as a stark contrast to the beauty of the community. Its presence began to draw in a different kind of crowd, one that brought chaos and disturbance wherever they went. Rowdy and loud, these new residents were causing trouble throughout the town, tarnishing its peaceful atmosphere.

Inside the facility, the hum of activity echoed through the halls as the newly hired employees received training from the staff brought in from Advance Medical's main office. But as the workday ended, the atmosphere transformed into something entirely different. The expanded bar now offered an extensive selection of alcoholic beverages, enticing the employees to stay and indulge. A stage was set for entertainment, and vending machines promised rewards for those who trusted them with their quarters. The bookstore had also experienced growth, and it now offers a selection of erotic magazines, books, and additional items. Although company policies turned a blind eye to some employees using these facilities during working hours, the uproar in the community was undeniable.

Bruce and Wayne met to discuss the growing problem that had befallen their beloved community. Concern filled their voices as they tried to make sense of the situation.

"I knew something like this would happen," Bruce said with frustration evident in his voice.

"They had the open house, but none of this was revealed. They deceived our people, luring them with money and false promises," he continued, his anger building.

In contrast to Bruce's exasperation, Wayne remained remarkably calm. He offered a simple response, "God is in control."

Bruce looked at him, perplexed. How could Wayne remain so composed in the face of such turmoil?

"God works in mysterious ways," Wayne said, his voice filled with faith. "If this is truly a revival, we must trust that He will bring about good from even the darkest of situations."

Bruce's thoughts began to clear as he contemplated Wayne's words. He realized that he had let his emotions dictate his actions, clouding his judgment. A smile crossed his face as a newfound clarity emerged.

"You're right," Bruce admitted. "God can use even the evil for good. But how?"

Wayne paused, deep in thought. He pondered the unfolding

events, contemplating the greater purpose behind them.

"It may not be our role to figure it out right now," Wayne said with solemnity. "But what we can do is increase our commitment to the revival."

Bruce understood the significance of Wayne's words. "Prayer support," he said, the realization sinking in.

"Yes," Wayne affirmed. "And it's also time to rally the people and take a stand. It's time to picket."

Bruce had assumed that with the downfall of The Association, picketing would become a thing of the past. But as he listened to Wayne's determination, he realized he was mistaken.

Together, they made the necessary arrangements, gathering the support needed to protest outside the facility, united in their mission to preserve the integrity of their community.

"I can't believe I'm still stuck in this mess, and I feel so ashamed," George poured out his frustration to Bruce over the phone.

Bruce offered reassurance, knowing the weight of George's past. "We've already discussed this, George. Remember, everything that happened before you found your faith is in the past. You're right where you need to be now."

"But it feels like I'm working for the devil," George lamented, his voice filled with distress.

Bruce couldn't help but make a grim observation, remembering the unsettling transformation he witnessed. "Well, after seeing your boss transform the other night, it seems like you might be."

This remark only deepened George's despair. He reached a breaking point. "That's it! I'm done. I'm walking out. Let him kill me... I don't care anymore. I'd rather be dead than work for the devil!"

Bruce urgently interjected, trying to calm George down. "Hold on, George. Hold on. You'll be more effective serving the Lord alive than dead. Besides, John needs you inside there, and I need you inside there. I have a plan."

The following morning arrived, cold and devoid of snow. The

bare trees stood as a testament to the impending winter. People gathered around the newly constructed facility, known simply as AFT Manufacturing Building 2. As each person picked up the signs distributed by Pastor Bruce, Pastor Wayne, and the leaders of the revival, they began their peaceful march back and forth in front of the building.

Most of the employees had already arrived for work prior to the picketers' protest. However, during their lunch break, some of the workers ventured outside to confront the picketers, unleashing their frustration.

"Go home, you jealous religious freaks! We've had enough of your interference in this town. You're not going to take away jobs that pay better than any other in this place!"

Another person shouted, "Yeah, mess with me and my job, and you're messing with my ability to provide for my family! Go home! Get out of here!"

The picketers remained silent, continuing their peaceful walk. The shouting grew more intense, and the crowd from AFT began to confront the picketers more aggressively. The police and firefighters swiftly arrived at the scene, attempting to control the situation. Yet, the crowd persisted, determined to intimidate the picketers.

Suddenly, a burst of water shot into the air from a firefighter's hose, connected to a nearby fire hydrant, creating a mesmerizing rainbow in its spray. However, even this display failed to disperse the crowd. The firefighters redirected their efforts toward the AFT workers, effectively separating them from the picketers. Many of the picketers had been injured and were rushed to the hospital. Others began to disperse as the police managed to apprehend the AFT workers responsible for the assault. They were loaded into police cars, and order was gradually restored.

That very day, news of the events in Stapleton reached Penkowski's ears, and he wasted no time in taking action. He boarded his private jet and hurriedly made his way to the AFT facility. Once there, he called for a meeting with all the employees, except for those who had been taken away to jail. George found himself in attendance, filled with apprehension.

Penkowski, dressed in his usual expensive suit, wore an unusually wide smile. It seemed out of place considering the recent turmoil. George couldn't help but feel puzzled by this unexpected display.

However, the smile quickly vanished, and Penkowski began to speak with a stern tone. "I am outraged by what has transpired in this facility today," he declared.

Initially, the employees believed Penkowski was upset with the conduct of the individuals who had been escorted to jail, causing a collective hush to fall over the room.

Penkowski's anger shifted direction. "Who do these religious people think they are, coming to your workplace and attempting to dictate how you should live your lives?" His words became more forceful, making George increasingly tense.

"They have taken control of this town as if it were their own personal sanctuary. Let me tell you, when people start losing their freedom of choice, this is no longer a democracy—it becomes a socialistic society."

As Penkowski's message resonated with the employees, relief transformed into anger, mirroring the feelings of their impassioned leader.

"When you strip away the simple joys from people, what is left? Unhappiness, miserable lives... no reason to live," Penkowski continued, his voice growing more fervent.

The employees became swept up in Penkowski's rhetoric, and he seized the moment. "This needs to stop. I believe it is important to provide you, my employees, with these pleasures. That's why I have built these additional areas—for reading, recreational drinking, a free clinic. And now, I would like to introduce a new space..." He paused, relishing the moment, and then announced, "...a place where you can collect your thoughts, meditate..."

George's head shot up, his eyes fixated on Penkowski. His spirit sank, knowing all too well where they were headed. He had been granted full responsibility for the facility, and he had initially been told this room would serve as a meeting space for employees and staff. Once again, he had been deceived.

As the group followed Penkowski, he led them through the corridors until they reached a set of double doors. With a flourish, he swung the doors open, revealing an impressive sight that left everyone in awe. The room was a testament to extravagance, from the meticulously crafted floors to the ornate ceilings, and from the carefully chosen decor to the soft, inviting lighting. The visual appeal captivated all who entered.

Penkowski walked confidently to the front of the room, a smile returning to his face as he relished each step. Then, facing the crowd, his smile vanished, replaced by a serious expression. "Isn't this beautiful?" he asked, and the room responded with unanimous agreement.

"This is all yours! Enjoy it, make use of it as you see fit. It will be open 24 hours a day," Penkowski proclaimed.

He paused, shifting his tone, and then suggested, "Let's observe a moment of silence to commemorate this new meeting area."

As Penkowski bowed his head, George felt his stomach churn, a wave of nausea washing over him. His face turned pale, his thoughts involuntarily shifting to his first encounter with Penkowski, the horrifying transformation he had witnessed alongside John at the main office of Advance Medical, and the demonic presence Penkowski had displayed during the Tuesday night prayer meeting. And now, here they were, in the very place where George worked. He berated himself for not heeding his pastor's warnings. With his eyes closed, he envisioned an idyllic lakeside retreat nestled deep in the mountains, far away from this monster. "Why did I have to stay here with this monster?" he asked himself repeatedly. After that question, an unsettling feeling of evil washed over him, the very presence his pastor had warned him about when he was ushered into the back room during the prayer meeting. It frightened him.

"Ahh, I already feel better," Penkowski remarked, opening his eyes. George glanced at him and was met with a chilling sight. While everyone else only saw bloodshot eyes, George perceived the all-too-familiar glow of red emanating from Penkowski's eyes, a sinister sign of something far more malevolent lurking within him.

Hospital visiting hours were drawing to a close, but the influx of people desperate to see their injured loved ones showed no signs of abating. Among them was John, a bundle of nerves, knowing that his presence at the hospital could potentially expose him to Penkowski and his associates. In the chaos, he couldn't ascertain whether Maggie or Pastor Bruce were present.

John entered through the front door, his eyes scanning the surroundings for any signs of danger. The hospital was abuzz with activity, and he followed the crowd, room after room, searching for Maggie or Pastor Bruce. Each chamber was packed with visitors, but neither of them was in sight. Finally, he arrived at the last room, and there he found Pastor Bruce, looking even worse than their initial meeting with George. John wove his way through the crowd, and as he drew closer, he locked eyes with Maggie, who displayed a mix of surprise and concern. She hadn't expected to see him there, given the circumstances. John offered her a smile before redirecting his gaze to Bruce. In his heart, he silently questioned, "Lord, why Pastor Bruce? Why not me?" Approaching the bed, Bruce looked up, equally taken aback by John's presence.

"John? What are you doing here?" he asked, his voice laced with concern.

"The real question is, 'What are you doing here?' How did you end up in such a state? You look worse now than when we first met," John stumbled over his words, realizing his phrasing wasn't the best.

"I understand what you mean," Bruce replied with a smile. "You don't need to explain."

John felt a wave of relief wash over him.

"We decided to picket the AFT facility, and everything was going well until lunchtime when the employees came out, and things turned ugly," Bruce explained, his voice trailing off.

"Ugly? That's an understatement," John interjected sarcastically. "A hamburger falling apart after the second bite is 'a bit messy.' You look like you've gone ten rounds with a champion boxer, and he emerged victorious!"

"Well, yes, I suppose I do," Bruce admitted.

"And all the other rooms I passed on my way here, those people don't look any better," John remarked, aghast.

Bruce abandoned his attempt to keep the tone light.

"They injured us severely. The police tried to intervene, but they couldn't stop the onslaught," Bruce revealed.

John's expression shifted to one of shock.

"Thank the Lord the firefighters stepped in; otherwise, I fear we would have had many more people in the hospital than just those in this room," Bruce concluded, the gravity of the situation settling upon them.

John lowered his head, his hands gripping his hair as he let out a heavy sigh. The weight of the situation bore down on him, and he couldn't help but blame himself. "Maybe if I hadn't come to this town, taken on this assignment..." His words trailed off, consumed by self-doubt.

"Nonsense!" Bruce interjected, cutting John off mid-sentence. John looked up, taken aback. He had expected pastors to be more composed, not prone to anger.

"Whether you came here or not, this Penkowski character would have seized control of The Association, purchased that property, and done as he pleased. Don't shoulder blame where it isn't warranted," Bruce reassured him, his voice firm yet compassionate. John sighed once more, finding solace in Bruce's words. He glanced at Maggie, who nodded in agreement. "He's right, you know," she affirmed.

As John looked at Maggie, a flood of memories and emotions surged through his soul, harking back to the time they had first met in this very hospital. There was something about her presence that brought him comfort. With a serious expression on his face, John turned to Bruce. "Pastor, what can I do?"

"You can ensure that this man is put away for life," Bruce declared, his tone filled with righteous determination. "This will allow the people of Stapleton to continue growing and moving forward with their lives. Penkowski is the embodiment of evil. If he had the opportunity, he would have me, Pastor Wayne, and all those who follow Christ eliminated, legally if possible."

At the mention of death, a sharp pain shot through John's shoulder, a haunting reminder of why he found himself in the hospital. His demeanor shifted, and he spoke with unwavering confidence, "I will do it."

"Good. In the meantime, George is working on the inside for us," Bruce divulged, capturing John's attention. "He has vital information and is making a difference beyond mere gathering intel."

A smile spread across John's face. His friend was playing a significant role, not only in obtaining information but also in effecting real change from within.

Suddenly, the door swung open, and George stepped into the room. John and Bruce's faces lit up with excitement, and the others in the room cleared a path to make way for George.

"What are you doing here? Are you crazy? If Penkowski finds out, you'll be fired!" John exclaimed, concern etched on his face.

George raised an eyebrow and replied, "Well, what are you doing here? If he discovers you, he'll stop at nothing to end your life."

John's expression softened, and a chuckle escaped his lips. The tension was momentarily lifted as they embraced, a sense of camaraderie and understanding passing between them.

George placed a hand on Pastor Bruce's shoulder, his gaze filled with concern. "Are you alright?"

"A little sore... again. I really need to avoid physical conflicts," Bruce admitted with a wry smile.

George couldn't help but jest, "Well, if you can walk through fire, a few punches should be a breeze to avoid."

Bruce's smile widened, the memory of his encounter with Jesus flooding his mind. He also recalled the words his Lord had spoken to him. Now seemed like the opportune moment to share what Jesus had conveyed, not just with John and George but with everyone gathered in the room. Bruce began from the beginning, recounting Jesus' words, "I am the First and will be the Last. I am the One Alive, though I was dead, and I tell you I will live forever and ever... I have come here to tell you that the devil will do everything in his power to hinder and oppose you in your ongoing work for Me. You will face greater persecution in the days to come than you have ever experienced before. Stay faithful to Me, even to the point of death, and I will bestow upon you the radiant crown of life."

"I consider it a privilege to lie in this hospital bed for my Lord and Savior," Bruce proclaimed, his voice filled with conviction. "I know that those here with me share the same sentiment. There is no higher calling than to endure suffering for the sake of Christ. Just as the Apostle Paul did for the early Christian church, so shall we for the revival that God Himself has chosen to ignite here in our hometown of Stapleton. No matter the form the devil takes, he will not succeed. All glory be to God." The room echoed with resounding agreement, united in their unwavering faith.

TWENTY

The room was shrouded in darkness, enveloped in an oppressive atmosphere. There were no windows to let in even a glimmer of light, and the air was heavy with a musty stench, akin to the odor of death itself. The flickering glow of candles provided the sole source of illumination, casting eerie shadows on the walls and revealing the red-robed figures standing amidst the dimness. Their faces concealed by hooded cloaks, they held candles that accentuated the macabre scene.

As the dim light danced on the walls, obscured shapes emerged from the shadows. Knives of various shapes and sizes adorned the walls, their blades stained with dried blood, a testament to unspeakable acts committed in this sinister chamber. The chant of the hooded men filled the room, a low and ghastly sound that sent shivers down the spine.

At the forefront, behind an altar marred by old and fresh blood, lay a small animal sacrifice. The voice of one of the hooded figures pierced through the somber atmosphere, uttering words that dripped with an unholy reverence, "For unto us, a child is born... my sweet Satan."

With fervor and devotion, the congregation implored their malevolent deity, beseeching for favors and power beyond their wildest dreams. Their voices rose in unison, echoing through the chamber, "We choose you! We choose you!"

The man leading the ritual removed his hood, revealing his face as the ceremony concluded. Accompanied by his companions from the altar, they discarded their dark attire and transformed into businessmen dressed in suits. Together, they exited the room, navigating the halls, seamlessly blending into their respective roles within the organization.

The heavy door closed behind them, and they found themselves in a room that had once been devastated by a tornado. Now, it stood repaired and renovated, a testament to the influence and resources at their disposal.

Penkowski's frustration and anger simmered beneath his words. "I can't believe he has eluded us. Is there no one who can get hold of him? Is he some sort of escape artist? A modern-day Houdini?"

"You should have eliminated him when you had the chance, sir," one of the men dared to suggest.

Penkowski's voice dripped with contempt. "Enough! I know what I'm doing! Do you not remember the last time we tried to eliminate him in this very room? How successful were we then?"

Silence hung in the air, each participant in the room witnessing the demonic activities that had often served their sinister cause.

Yet, doubts began to creep in, casting shadows of uncertainty over their allegiance.

"Besides," Penkowski continued, seeking to justify his decision, "he will serve me more alive than dead."

"He's hiding in Stapleton," Penkowski declared with conviction.

"How do you know this?" one of the men inquired.

"I can feel it. Every time I set foot in that accursed town, I sense his presence, lurking in the shadows like a cockroach, evading my every move. But mark my words, I will crush him like a bug beneath my foot," Penkowski declared, his voice filled with dark determination.

Seated around a grand oval table, the men gazed out of a towering window that offered a breathtaking view of the sprawling city below. It was a scene of magnificence and power, a stark contrast to the darkness that brewed within the room.

Curiosity got the better of one of the men who had never experienced the town of Stapleton firsthand. He mustered the courage to ask, unaware of the storm he was about to unleash. Another man, sensing the impending chaos, shot him a desperate glance, silently pleading for him to remain silent.

"Why do you dislike that town, sir?" the naive man inquired innocently, his voice filled with genuine curiosity.

Penkowski's face contorted with anger, his complexion turning a fiery shade of red. His eyes, once again bloodshot, betrayed a deep-seated rage that simmered just beneath the surface. Rising from his seat, he unleashed his fury upon the room. His fingers dug into the chair before him, tearing through the leather upholstery, his knuckles white with intensity. The man who had given the cautionary look now sat frozen, praying that this outburst would be the extent of the turmoil.

"I despise that wretched place!" Penkowski bellowed, his voice filled with venomous disdain. "The weak and pitiful excuses for human beings who inhabit it!" He seized the chair, his grip tightening, threatening to crush it in his rage. The cautious man could only hope that the situation wouldn't escalate further.

"Their shallow and pathetic existence!" Penkowski's grasp on the chair tightened even more. The cautious man braced himself for the worst.

"And they have the audacity to impose their pathetic ways upon everyone else!" The chair now seemed to tremble in Penkowski's grasp. The cautious man held his breath, praying for a reprieve.

"And that God they worship! A liar!" Penkowski's gaze shot toward the ceiling as he hoisted the chair upward. "I HATE YOU!" With a mighty swing, the chair crashed through the newly replaced window, shattering it into a cascade of fragmented glass that rained down upon the men in a lethal shower.

Penkowski continued his tirade as if nothing had happened. The wind now whistled through the broken window, tousling his disheveled hair and accentuating his wild appearance.

"I will claim that town for myself! Yes, I will! I will ensnare its inhabitants, stripping them away from their feeble God, and they will be under my control. They will be putty in my hands, leashed and subservient to my every whim. It will all unfold right before their beloved yet pitiful churches. So help me, Satan." Penkowski concluded with a somber tone, and then he exited the room.

The man who had posed the initial question glanced at the one who had given him the warning look, shrugging his shoulders in confusion. The latter man wore a look of disgust, unable to comprehend the madness that had just unfolded. As shards of glass were brushed off their clothing, a sense of unease lingered in the room, a reminder of the unhinged power that Penkowski possessed.

"Mayor, I just don't understand. We have people hospitalized because of this establishment. My dear Pastor friend is lying beaten in the hospital because of this place, and you're simply going to allow them to continue promoting gambling, drinking, and all sorts of vices?" Pastor Wayne's voice was filled with frustration and concern as he confronted the Mayor.

"I hear your concerns, but there's no law in this city that forbids alcohol, and as for gambling, it's just quarters on a glass slider. Didn't you used to try knocking those quarters off when you were a kid?" The Mayor attempted to dismiss the gravity of the situation, brushing off the Pastor's arguments.

Pastor Wayne realized he wasn't making any headway with that approach, so he shifted his strategy. "The small local businesses are struggling. They can't compete with what AFT can offer."

"That's business, my son. Competition is what this great country is built upon. Without competition, we'd still be riding around in horse and buggies," the Mayor replied dismissively, sensing his inability to sway the Pastor's stance.

"Pastor, have you taken a good look at Stapleton lately?" Pastor Wayne walked over to the window, letting out a sigh of frustration. "Have you seen the newly laid sidewalks, driven at night under the glow of freshly installed streetlights? Have you taken a stroll in Forest Ridge Park and witnessed the beautifully renovated bridge, the shiny new playground for our children? Look outside, observe the storefronts and buildings. They have never looked better. And with the construction of the AFT building, that eyesore of a lot is now gone. This facility has contributed to the beauty of our community. The owner has funded all these improvements voluntarily, out of the goodness of his heart. This company has brought well-paying jobs to our town, wages that have never been seen before. And you want me to put a stop to all of this? You must be joking." The Mayor halted at that point, realizing he may have crossed a line of respect. Disrespecting a Pastor was the last thing he intended to do.

"But what about all the people in jail who caused the disturbance?" Pastor Wayne, still gazing out the window, asked, his frustration heavy.

The Mayor approached this sensitive topic with as much diplomacy as he could muster. "Pastor, I understand that you mean well, and peaceful picketing is within your rights, but you're protesting against an employer that has shown great potential for the people of this community... for their families. Many of those who work at AFT have never had such opportunities before. This is their chance."

Pastor Wayne had reached his breaking point and headed towards the door. As he walked away, he uttered, "Mayor Thomas, I'm afraid you've put a price tag on yourself. You've been bought."

The Mayor tried to formulate a response, but Wayne had already left the room, leaving the Mayor to contemplate the weight of his decisions.

"Sis, I don't know what is going on…Pastor Bruce is lying in the hospital. In fact, we have many from our church that are in that hospital." It sounded funny to John when he heard himself say 'our church'. It sounded funny to Elizabeth too.

"Well, here's the deal, he has hidden his research behind the

XM2 machine and this has made it legal for him. His company says that it is used only for disposal in a non-biochemical dangerous manner. He then sells the fetuses but I have no evidence that will stand up in court to prove this." Elizabeth said with a business tone of voice.

"I remember when I talked with Dr. Stearing about that. He was a former doctor of an abortion clinic in town here that was linked to Advanced Medical. He said that he, 'paid an out of pocket fee for the machine and the Association would in turn pay me each month for the fetuses that I supplied to them that were harmonically stored in temperatures below freezing.'"

"Did he say anything else?"

"When I asked him what they did with the fetuses they said, 'I assume research.'" John knew what was coming.

"'Assuming' is no help to us." Elizabeth said.

"Well then what? What is it going to take to put this guy away?"

There was silence on the other side of the phone.

"Tell me more about this facility in town, what is it called?"

"AFT manufacturing. Looks more like a church from the outside and a casino on the inside."

Elizabeth began to give John things to look for; hints of illegal activity that would give them the evidence that they need to put Penkowski away.

"Its lunch time, where are you going?" one of the workers at new AFT said to the other as he left for a different area of the building.

"There is someone speaking in the new quite and mediation room…remember, the room introduced to us the other day. He promised a power to help with day-to-day problems. I sure can use that."

"So can I." said the other and both were off.

When they entered through the double doors, it was dark and candles lit the way all throughout the room.

In the front of the room were the same robed and hooded men that previously were heading the gathering in the main office of Advance Medical's quite and mediation room.

"Please, come in, all are welcome." came the familiar voice. "Come and see the power you can have to overcome so many of lives difficulties."

The room continued to fill with more and more people. Even those that had found themselves in jail the other day were there.

"I want to welcome you but I must say, if you are soft, please leave. Any soft or doubting force here will ruin what I want to accomplish for each of you today."

No one left.

"Good, good," Penkowski exclaimed, his voice filled with a charismatic fervor that stirred the emotions of those gathered in the room. "Now is the time for freedom of choice. Now is the time to make a profound difference in your community, in your town, among the very people you share your lives with. Many have reached a point of despair, where a lack of purpose has driven them to seek solace in religious crutches. It is one thing to rely on these crutches in private, but to influence others to lean on them as well is unacceptable. Each of you has suffered enough from walking on crutches that belong to someone else! You have no need for them anymore! Today, I will remove your crutches and propel you beyond mere survival. It is time to seize your life by the horns and transform it into the extraordinary existence you have always dreamt of. Cease dreaming and start living, for I have come to set you free, and you shall truly be free. I have come to bestow upon you an abundant life. Fear should no longer dictate your existence; instead, you shall embrace power!"

As Penkowski delivered his passionate speech, he held a small bird captive before him. With his hands raised, the bird soared upward, mirroring his movements. As he lowered his hands, the bird descended. Then, he took the delicate creature in his hands, crushing it mercilessly until life slipped away from its fragile frame. Placing the lifeless bird upon the altar adorned with flickering candles, he raised his bloodied hands toward the ceiling, proclaiming, "For unto us a child is born... my sweet god."

As those words left his lips, the bird miraculously revived before the astonished onlookers. A sense of awe filled the room. Anger towards the religious entrapment Penkowski spoke of had clouded their judgment, while the allure of this newfound power had numbed their conscience to the brutal demise of an innocent creature.

"This power can be yours!" Penkowski declared, his voice dripping with temptation. "Each of you can wield it in your daily lives, choices, and struggles. Just as I have demonstrated the power to bring life from death, you too can infuse vitality into your dying lives. Stop withering away, embrace life! Seize control of your existence through the power I offer you today. Will you do it? Will you regain the freedom to make choices? Will you?"

The room resounded with fervent agreement. "We will! We will! We will!" they chanted in unison, caught up in the intoxicating moment.

Then, Penkowski's voice took on a sinister quality. "Take this sacrifice and do as only you can do. Embrace the fame, power, and success that lie beyond your wildest dreams! In this land of freedom, where you are free to choose what and who to worship, we choose you!"

A sense of comfort washed over each individual as they departed the room, enticed by the promises of power that men have waged wars over throughout history. Now, they all bore the same telltale eyes as Penkowski — red and bloodshot. The eyes of those who had been imprisoned were even more intensely crimson, reflecting their seething anger and their newfound purpose fueled by the promised power.

The phone call shook Pastor Bruce to his core. The voice of Mrs. Hurwitz, filled with urgency and distress, echoed through the receiver. He could sense the gravity of the situation before even hearing the details.

As Mrs. Hurwitz continued, her words painted a bleak picture of the state of affairs. The scriptures that once adorned the school's halls had been stripped away, and the prayer groups were now confined to a small designated room, unable to accommodate all the children who sought solace and guidance.

"Who? Who has done this?" Pastor Bruce's voice trembled with disbelief and frustration.

"The principal, Joe Benton," Mrs. Hurwitz replied, her voice laced with disappointment.

Pastor Bruce's heart sank. Joe was a friend, someone he had trusted to uphold the values that the community held dear. "Joe, that can't be," he murmured, struggling to comprehend the situation.

But the news only worsened. Mrs. Hurwitz revealed that even the Ten Commandments, the very foundation of their faith, had been removed from the school. The weight of the loss left Pastor Bruce speechless, his mind spinning with a mix of sorrow and anger.

"He said he was forced to. Is there anything you can do?" Mrs. Hurwitz pleaded, her voice desperate for a glimmer of hope.

Bruce, gathering his thoughts and emotions, mustered a response. "I'm not sure what I can do, but I will talk to Principal Benton," he assured her, his determination shining through.

Once he hung up the phone, Bruce braced himself for the next call. As it came, he couldn't shake the foreboding feeling that accompanied it. Wayne's voice, usually filled with excitement and energy, now carried a weight of concern.

"What is it?" Bruce asked, bracing himself for another blow.

Wayne delivered the news, and it hit Bruce like a punch to the gut. The graffiti that had disappeared, a symbol of hope and renewal, had resurfaced with a vengeance. Hatred and bigotry now marred the city's walls, casting a shadow over their community.

Bruce couldn't contain his anguish. "What is going on? I just spoke to Mrs. Hurwitz, and she told me that everything Christian has been erased from the school, including the Ten Commandments."

Wayne's revelation continued, plunging Bruce deeper into despair. The Mayor, someone entrusted with the well-being of the community, had succumbed to the influence of Penkowski. The promises of prosperity and development had clouded the Mayor's judgment, leaving Bruce feeling disillusioned and betrayed.

Bruce took a moment to steady himself, drawing strength from his faith. "Isn't it clear that God is sovereign, that He holds all things in His hand?" he asked, his voice a mixture of conviction and longing.

Wayne understood the truth in Bruce's words, but it was difficult to reconcile with the reality they faced. "I had hoped that with the revival, things would improve, not worsen," he confessed, his voice heavy with disappointment.

Determined to confront the mounting challenges head-on, Bruce made a resolve. "I'm going to pay a visit to Principal Joe Benton and see if I can make some sense of all this," he declared, his voice resolute, guided by a flicker of hope that still burned within him.

Bruce felt a heavy weight on his chest as he drove through the town. The once vibrant and inviting atmosphere now seemed shrouded in darkness. It was as if a sinister presence lingered in the air, suffocating the sense of goodness and replacing it with an overwhelming evil. The absence of God's presence, which he had taken for granted, now gnawed at his soul.

He tried to pray, desperately seeking solace and the strength to overcome the oppressive feeling. But with each passing moment, the intensity of the darkness grew. The town's pristine appearance, with its sparkling sidewalks and newly lit streets, only served as a stark contrast to the underlying malevolence that now permeated everything. Even the sight of the imposing AFT building sent a chill down Bruce's spine, filling him with a sense of imminent danger that he couldn't shake off.

Bruce parked his car outside the school, noticing the signs of Penkowski's influence everywhere. The school, too, had undergone a transformation, its outward beauty concealing the loss of spiritual nourishment. The walls, once adorned with colorful scriptures and invitations to Bible study, now displayed a dreary off-white paint, devoid of warmth and life. With a heavy heart, he hurried towards the gym, dreading what he might find.

Inside, the emptiness of the gym mirrored the emptiness in Bruce's soul. Every trace of the student-led efforts to spread faith and love had been erased, leaving behind a void that echoed with despair. The realization hit him like a blow to the chest: this might have been the last Tuesday prayer night, the final gathering of souls seeking solace and revival.

Principal Benton approached Bruce, his voice tinged with regret. "Bruce, I see you've learned of what transpired here," he said, his own demeanor reflecting the weight of their predicament.

"Joe, what happened? Where are all the invitations, the Bible verses, the Ten Commandments?" Bruce's voice wavered, a mix of confusion and disbelief.

"Gone, thanks to me, the man of the day who supposedly brought hope, prosperity, and a religion-free public school to this community," Joe replied, his tone heavy with self-disgust.

Bruce struggled to comprehend the depth of betrayal. "How

could this happen?"

"Do you remember when I mentioned that as long as no one filed an official complaint, we could continue as we were? Well, he filed it," Joe explained, his frustration evident. "He doesn't even have a child in the school, but according to Stapleton law, his voice holds weight due to the taxes he pays for his properties."

As Joe guided Bruce back to his office, their conversation delved into the disturbing turn of events. Passing by Mrs. Hurwitz's open classroom door, Bruce's spirits lifted slightly. She noticed him and warmly invited him inside, introducing him to the class. The presence of their trusted pastor provided a glimmer of relief amidst the pain and uncertainty that had enveloped them all since the changes took place.

"Hello Pastor Bruce." A bright, young voice resonated from the class, catching Bruce's attention. He turned and a smile spread across his face. "Well hello Tommy, it's great to see you!"

Tommy beamed with pride, grateful that the pastor had called him by name. His eyes sparkled with joy, a small beacon of light amidst the prevailing darkness that surrounded them.

Bruce's gaze shifted towards the back of the room, where the Ten Commandments had once stood. But now, they were gone. He cast his eyes downward and saw only new carpeting, devoid of any trace of the miraculous encounter with God that had transpired in this very room through the young boy named Tommy.

As they left the classroom and entered Principal Benton's office, Bruce mustered the courage to ask the burning question that lingered in his heart. "Joe, how about Tuesday nights? Has he stopped those too?"

A knowing smile formed on Joe's face. "No, as a matter of fact, he hasn't."

Bruce's spirit lifted at the unexpected news. Hope flickered within him.

"But don't get me wrong, he's certainly tried," Joe continued. "I believe he has a personal vendetta against you."

"I haven't done anything to him! I don't even know the guy," Bruce exclaimed, frustration etched in his voice.

They exchanged a meaningful look, both pondering the motive behind this relentless opposition. Then Joe attempted to inject some humor into the situation. "Maybe our Tuesday night gatherings just rubbed him the wrong way... you think?"

"He assaulted me even before he showed up here!" Bruce's anger flared, his patience worn thin. He had strived to forgive his enemy, but witnessing the man's relentless attempts to obstruct God's work filled him with righteous indignation.

Joe sensed Bruce's distress and halted their walk, offering him a sympathetic look. "I'm sorry, Joe. It's not you. It's... it's just the fact that..." Bruce's voice trailed off as he hesitated, fully aware that what he was about to express could come across as self-centered and selfish.

"Go ahead, Bruce. We're friends," Joe encouraged, genuine concern etched on his face.

With a deep breath, Bruce mustered the strength to articulate his innermost feelings. "All my life, I have dreamed of, hoped for, and prayed diligently to be a part of a true revival of God. You know, it doesn't just happen. It's a divine gift, wrapped in beauty and rarity, like the merchant finding that precious pearl... For centuries, America has yearned for a revival, and here in our little, quiet, out-of-the-way town of Stapleton..." Bruce's voice trembled with emotion, tears welling up in his eyes. "God chose us. The God of the universe chose us to bestow His presence, His love, His power, His awe, His everything. And we have tasted and cherished every single moment of it... I just... I don't want to lose it."

Overwhelmed by his own vulnerability, Bruce broke down, releasing his pent-up emotions in tears. He felt conflicted, believing that his desire to preserve the revival was selfish and unworthy.

But Joe, witnessing the remarkable transformation that had swept through their town under Bruce's leadership, saw a man who had profoundly impacted the lives of nearly everyone in Stapleton. He empathized with Bruce's anguish as it seemed that the extraordinary revival they had experienced was slipping away.

As Bruce continued to sob, a comforting hand landed upon his shoulder. He heard Joe commence a heartfelt prayer, and gradually, he felt the reassurance of God's presence soothing his spirit. In that moment, Bruce knew deep within that everything would be somehow okay.

The two men embraced, finding solace in each other's arms. Joe assured Bruce that Tuesday nights would remain unchanged. The stronghold of God's presence had been secured and would not be relinquished without a fight.

"I need more information," John stated, his voice filled with urgency. He and George were speaking on their cell phones, aware of the need for security due to the sensitive nature of their conversation. John was inside his office at AFT, contemplating the daunting task ahead.

There was a brief pause on the other end of the line, and then George responded, "I understand."

However, John sensed a deep discouragement in George's voice, something he had never quite detected before. It stirred a compassion within him, and he felt compelled to offer words of encouragement. "George, hang in there. I know it's tough."

"John, Penkowski has started what I believe is a... satanic church right here with the employees of AFT," George revealed, his tone grave and serious.

John's mind went blank for a moment, completely taken aback by this revelation. "You have got to be kidding," he exclaimed. A strange sensation coursed through him, reaching beyond his emotions and touching his spirit. He couldn't quite put it into words, but he knew deep within that this was exceedingly bad, perhaps worse than he had imagined.

"Is he crazy? With everything that is going on in this community..." John trailed off, struggling to articulate his thoughts.

"That's why I think he has taken such a liking to this town. I hate to burst your bubble, but I don't think it's all about you and the information you have. I believe he despises what is happening here, and he has made it his personal agenda to stop it," George explained with utmost seriousness.

The weight of the situation settled heavily upon John's shoulders. "Wow. How did you find all this out?" he inquired, his voice tinged with disbelief.

George proceeded to recount a series of events that sounded more like a scene from a poorly made movie than reality. It seemed surreal, and the response of the individuals involved was unfathomable.

"John, all I can tell you is that after it was over, my skin was crawling, my spirit was screaming, and my stomach was turning..." George paused for a moment, gathering his thoughts.

"Go ahead, I'm listening," John encouraged, eager to hear the rest.

"...and... with everyone in agreement, they walked out... John, their eyes were bloodshot red, glassy, just like Penkowski's," George revealed, his voice filled with a mixture of fear and astonishment.

"Oh, George, this is not good. We need to get you out of there," John exclaimed, his concern for his friend growing by the second.

"Exactly. I am working for the devil," George confessed, his words filled with resignation.

"Hmm. But he doesn't know that your allegiance is to God," John pointed out, attempting to offer a glimmer of hope.

"I know, I know what you're going to say... You have a plan, right?" George responded, a slight hint of anticipation in his voice.

"Yeah, how did you know?" John asked, slightly surprised.

"Pastor Bruce said the same thing, and that's why I'm still here. I would have run away a long time ago, but... I don't want to let our pastor down," George explained, a sense of loyalty evident in his words.

The mention of "our pastor" struck a chord within John. He was still adjusting to the fact that he was now a follower of Christ, and these newfound emotions, as well as the presence of a pastor and supportive friends, were overwhelming at times.

"We need to pray about this," John suggested, surprising himself with the statement.

"Well, that was Bruce's plan, but before we do, what is yours?" George inquired, seeking guidance.

"Let's pray that you will be able to find the evidence we need to put Penkowski away forever," John proposed.

"That will definitely align with Bruce's plan. He has me praying that God will cause this facility, and Advance Medical, to reap the full harvest of destruction it has sown in the lives of unborn babies, mothers, and now our own townspeople who have been lured by the hope of a better financial future," George responded, his resolve evident in his voice.

There was a momentary pause before George concluded, "I will see what I can find."

As they ended their call, John could sense that his friend's spirits had been lifted, if only slightly. This realization not only brought him joy in his newfound faith but also reinforced his admiration for George as a person.

"I want that Tuesday night shut down," Penkowski asserted boldly to the Mayor, his visit intended to express gratitude for the progress they had made in enforcing secularism within the school. There was no hesitation in his request.

The Mayor, however, appeared puzzled by Penkowski's vehement opposition. "Why are you so against it?" he questioned, trying to comprehend Penkowski's fervor. "We have already taken extensive measures to eliminate any religious influence. We removed all religious documentation, put an end to the Bible studies, and even took down the Ten Commandments displayed in each classroom. Your complaint was sufficient to achieve all of this."

Penkowski maintained his air of superiority, unwilling to back down. "I don't like the fact that religious fanaticism is emanating from a public school protected by the laws of separation of religion and state," he replied sharply. "I find it unacceptable that religious dogma is being propagated within our school facilities. Let them practice their faith in their churches, not in a public institution governed by the state."

Mayor Thomas, not wanting to engage in a lengthy legal discourse, as he had already been less accommodating than desired to the man who had revitalized the old school building, decided to approach the matter from a different angle. He contemplated an alternative strategy.

"We can effectively force them out," he suggested. Penkowski's curiosity was piqued. "Legally, of course. Allow me to explain. We can create such chaos and disturbance that they will be compelled to leave voluntarily. They will beg us to let them go. And the beauty of it all is that it will be perfectly within the bounds of the law."

"I don't care what you do, Mayor," Penkowski responded dismissively. "But for the sake of our town, for the sake of our children, let's restore the freedoms that Stapleton once enjoyed and allow the people to once again revel in the rich heritage that this town has cultivated for decades."

Those words struck a chord with the Mayor. Although Stapleton had its imperfections, its deep-rooted history and close-knit community were what made it uniquely Stapleton. And in the Mayor's eyes, the recent changes seemed to deviate from the town's cherished normalcy. It was time to reclaim Stapleton's heritage, and Penkowski's words resonated with that sentiment.

"I will see you at the gathering at AFT?" Penkowski aked, shifting gears in the conversation.

"Yes. More in touch with my spiritual self, you say?" The Mayor responded, his interest piqued.

"Yes. There is untapped power waiting to be harnessed," Penkowski confirmed.

"I could use a little extra help, considering the problems I have faced recently," the Mayor admitted, hoping he had not pushed the boundaries too far.

"Thanks to your religious leaders?" Penkowski remarked with a tone that assured the Mayor he had struck a nerve. "Yes, the religious leaders," he continued, acknowledging the effectiveness of his plan with a touch of satisfaction.

The atmosphere within AFT was electric with excitement. The employees were living the high life, reveling in the unprecedented financial gains they had achieved. The allure of the job was enhanced by the incredible perks that seemed too good to be true. It seemed like ages since they had enjoyed any alcohol, given that the nearest city was quite a distance away. But now, within the confines of the building, they could easily sneak away during breaks and partake in the forbidden elixir. The designated area provided a sanctuary where they could escape the pressures of work. However, a troubling pattern was emerging. People began relying on alcohol as a crutch to navigate through the days. Without it, they found themselves unable to function, their dependence growing stronger. Many stayed late after work, engaging in drinking sessions, deceiving their families with false claims of working overtime.

Behind closed doors, concealed from prying eyes, clandestine gambling sessions unfolded after hours. While the front area of the facility offered seemingly innocuous activities like Bingo and online gambling, it served merely as a façade for the real action taking place in the hidden back rooms. Some individuals experienced remarkable success, amassing considerable wealth and deriving immense pleasure from their newfound employer. However, not everyone was fortunate. Many fell into the trap of accumulating substantial debts that would take years to repay. Eventually, the consequences caught up with every player who lingered too long. Yet, the intoxicating allure of the illicit activities made it difficult to walk away.

The magazine and book store, typically bustling during lunch breaks and after hours, concealed secret chambers where patrons could engage in morally questionable activities such as viewing explicit movies. The depths of Penkowski's plan became increasingly evident as he successfully won the favor and loyalty of every employee in the town, extending his ownership over them just as he had controlled George Hines, the long-time general manager.

Bruce found solace in his rose garden, seeking respite from the overwhelming emotions that had consumed him throughout the day. The weight of the setbacks had taken a toll, making it feel as if he were spiraling backward instead of progressing forward. It was a tumultuous ride that left him feeling utterly distraught. One moment, he displayed unwavering faith, quoting scripture to Wayne to bolster their confidence in the Lord amidst the onslaught of bad news. Yet, in the next moment, he couldn't contain his tears, pouring his heart out to his friend and the school's principal, Joe Benton. Seeking a moment of solitude with God, he ventured into the midst of his rose garden in the greenhouse sanctuary, where it all seemed to have begun. In the midst of these vibrant and delicate creations, he had experienced divine communion.

As Bruce walked among the garden, he couldn't resist the allure of the roses' captivating aroma. Their colors were a sight to behold, ranging from radiant yellows to deep reds, from pristine whites to delicate pinks. Some blooms displayed mesmerizing combinations of hues, painting the garden with an enchanting palette of colors. Silently, Bruce offered a prayer, his thoughts directed toward the heavens: "Father, have I done something to hinder Your Spirit, to extinguish the fire that You have ignited?" Deep down, he knew the answer, sensing that perhaps the revival had begun with him, and now he questioned whether he had unintentionally quenched the Spirit's flame. It seemed as if God was trying to capture his attention, as well as that of the townsfolk.

An inexplicable draw led Bruce toward a particular rose bush. He bent down and gazed intently at it, unsure of the reason behind this specific attraction. It appeared familiar, a sight he had encountered countless times while tending to his roses over the years. However, upon closer inspection, he recognized the need for pruning. The shoots growing from the lower portion of the bush were siphoning vital nutrients, hindering the growth pattern and preventing the bush from realizing its full potential. Wild shoots sprouted uncontrollably, while dead roses remained attached to the bush, occupying the space where new, vibrant blooms could emerge. The rose bush's appearance was far from beautiful, failing to evoke the usual sense of delight Bruce experienced in admiring their exquisite beauty. In contrast, a well-tended garden, with every bush meticulously pruned, rewarded its caretaker with full bushes adorned with abundant roses, evoking a profound sense of awe and joy.

As Bruce worked in his garden, a realization struck him like a bolt of lightning. The words of Jesus echoed in his mind, "I am the true vine, and my Father is the gardener. He cuts off every branch in me that bears no fruit, while every branch that does bear fruit, he prunes so that it will be even more fruitful." The truth of these words resonated deeply within Bruce, piercing past his emotions and stirring his spirit.

In the depths of his contemplation, Bruce recognized the significance of those who belonged to Christ and those who did not. The non-believers were like the branches that were cut off, removed from the true vine. And for those who followed Christ, there was a divine process of pruning and refinement, akin to being tested by fire. His thoughts harkened back to his encounter with Christ, where he was forewarned of the impending persecution and the call to remain faithful, even to the point of death. But it wasn't just his life that was at stake; it was his life's work—a mission dedicated to the glory of God.

Driven by this revelation, Bruce reached for the pruning shears and began the deliberate act of pruning the rose bush. As he carefully removed the dead branches and withered rosebuds, a transformation unfolded before his eyes. The bush started to regain its allure, taking shape as he removed the unnecessary lower branches. Yet, despite his efforts, it didn't quite match the splendor of his other fully blossomed bushes, filled with vibrant colors.

Surveying the pruned bush and the scattered cuttings on the ground, Bruce couldn't help but acknowledge the current state of their town. It seemed to mirror the bush—far from its full potential, a mess in need of restoration. However, he held onto hope, recognizing that sometimes things need to look worse before they can become better. Stapleton, too, would experience a similar process of refinement. It would take time, faith, and the glory of God to bring about a more beautiful and complete transformation—a town sold out to the Lord.

With a renewed sense of purpose, Bruce left the garden and sought solace in his Bible. He eagerly searched for the verses that God had brought to his attention, delving deeper into their meaning. Each passage unveiled new insights, and peace flooded his soul. He was ready to press forward, trusting in the Lord's guidance, as he embarked on the journey ahead.

TWENTY ONE

It was Tuesday night, and the parking lot was already packed with cars. Finding a spot was a challenge as more and more people arrived. To their surprise, the football field was teeming with activity—a game was underway. It was unusual to have a football game on a Tuesday night, and the presence of the AFT community added to the intrigue. Parents brought their children, while others watched attentively, regardless of whether they had kids playing. The air buzzed with excitement, amplified by the marching band's energetic performance. With each touchdown and field goal, fireworks lit up the sky, painting it with vivid colors and punctuating the atmosphere with booming explosions. The game had just begun, but the energy was already evident.

As people stepped out of their cars and made their way towards the auditorium, they were struck by the chaos that surrounded them. Their eyes darted from one spectacle to another, unable to fully comprehend the scene unfolding before them. The sound of revving engines, blaring radios, and coins clattering on car hoods reverberated through the air, assaulting their senses. The noise was so deafening that it reverberated in their chests, and their ears throbbed in protest.

Navigating through the hallways towards the auditorium proved to be a challenge in itself. Students and participants from AFT were scattered everywhere, engaged in various games and activities. Shouts and yells filled the air as people tried to communicate over the cacophony. The halls were filled with games designed to raise funds, but they all seemed to revolve around noise. In one corner, a screaming contest ensued, complete with a sound meter to determine the loudest participant. In another area, sirens blared, police lights flashed, and strobe lights created a disorienting atmosphere, as people scrambled to locate a specific object amidst the chaos. Each hallway presented its own flurry of activity and noise, making it nearly impossible to hold a conversation without shouting directly into someone's ear.

Finally, as the attendees entered the auditorium, a sense of relief washed over them. The space was still available for use, but the relentless noise infiltrated every corner. People glanced around, bewildered, as they took in the bare walls and wondered how such a racket had permeated the entire area.

"I don't understand, Joe. What happened?" Bruce raised his voice, struggling to be heard above the relentless noise surrounding them. He was engaged in a conversation with Principal Joe Benton, desperately seeking an explanation for the chaos unfolding before their eyes.

Joe wore a perplexed expression, his face a mixture of frustration and confusion as he attempted to offer an explanation. "I... I knew we had the auditorium booked, but someone should have approached me about these changes."

Bruce's eyebrows furrowed as he tried to grasp the situation. "So, we have the auditorium, but what about all these people and the overwhelming noise?"

Joe's embarrassment grew evident as he hung his head low. "I made a mistake. I assumed the fundraisers and football game would follow the usual Friday night schedule. I didn't think to check the details thoroughly. This is entirely my fault."

Bruce was not interested in assigning blame; he simply wanted to understand how the events had unfolded in such an unexpected manner. The atmosphere at Stapleton's high school games had never been like this before.

As Bruce explained his concerns, Joe began to share the information he had received. "I was informed that some parents would be 'helping out with the activities,' but I had no idea they would bring in such elaborate fireworks, fire sirens, and other noisy elements."

Bruce's mind raced as he considered the implications. "Fireworks and these kinds of expenses... Who has the resources for that?"

The shared understanding between Bruce and Joe was evident in their expressions. They were both thinking of the same person.

Bruce pondered for a moment before asking, "Can we prevent this from happening in the future?"

Joe's embarrassment deepened as he responded, "No, once an event is on the calendar, it's set. The time to stop it was before, and that's where I made a mistake."

Bruce reached out, offering a reassuring smile as he placed his hand on Joe's shoulder. "Joe, don't be too hard on yourself. God is greater than this situation." With that, Bruce turned and walked away, feeling a renewed sense of hope. He was grateful for the conversation he had with God before arriving, and now, things were starting to look brighter.

George and John stealthily made their way into the crowded auditorium, blending in with the bustling crowd. Spotting Bruce amidst the chaos, they shouted to get his attention above the deafening noise. "Bruce, should we go to the back room tonight?" They knew it wasn't the ideal location, but it provided safety whenever Penkowski made an appearance.

"No need! Tonight will be awesome!" Bruce's response left George and John puzzled. Perhaps Bruce's hearing had been affected, preventing him from fully grasping the gravity of the situation. Regardless, John sought out Maggie, finding solace in her presence even amidst the cacophony that surrounded them.

The confusion in the room grew as people stood bewildered by the overwhelming activities taking place. Some considered leaving, but before they could, Bruce stepped forward to address the crowd. "Folks, don't leave. That's exactly what the enemy wants you to do. He wants you to have little faith. But God wants you to have great faith, and He will only meet you where your faith takes you."

Bruce's voice struggled to be heard over the noise, prompting him to turn up the amplification system and repeat his message. "The enemy wants you to leave. He wants you to have little faith. But God wants you to have great faith, and He will only meet you where your faith takes you."

Gradually, the people began to focus their attention on Bruce, straining to hear his words amidst the clamor. "Did we not witness God casting out the devil the last time we gathered here?" A resounding chorus of "yes" reverberated throughout the auditorium.

"If God can silence the devil, can't He silence this noise?" Bruce's question elicited an enthusiastic "yes" from the crowd.

"Then let us ask Him." Bruce led the congregation in prayer. As he began to pray, the noise gradually faded until complete silence enveloped the room. Curious onlookers near the door opened it to see if everyone had left, only to be met with a surreal sight—those inside were motionless, making no sound. Those outside gazed in astonishment while those inside waved, seemingly invisible to the outsiders.

"Thank you, Lord, for meeting us at the level of our faith." Bruce's voice filled with gratitude as he praised the Creator. Finishing his prayer, he said, "Father, we have a problem." The room fell into silence as every person held their breath, eager to hear how this man of God would approach the chaos that had consumed their hometown.

"Father, you are the Almighty, ruler of all, in control of everything. You are the Creator and Sustainer of all existence. Without You, nothing would be or continue to be. Lord, You initiated a spiritual awakening in this town, and I believe that the work You have started, You will bring to completion. As Your word says, 'He who began a good work in you will carry it on to completion.' We trust in this."

The voices of agreement echoed throughout the auditorium as people responded to Pastor Bruce's words.

"We know that You work all things out for the good." The agreement grew louder.

"Father, prune us, shape us, mold us to bear more fruit than we ever imagined. Help us to reach heights far beyond our hopes and dreams, and let Your name be glorified in all corners of the earth!" Bruce's voice resounded with passion and conviction, inspiring everyone present to join in the heartfelt prayer

As the prayers filled the room, a sense of boldness and surrender permeated the atmosphere. Each person poured out their hearts, some in quiet whispers, others with fervent cries. The presence of the Holy Spirit was electric, evoking both familiarity and awe, especially for those who were new to this powerful experience. God remained faithful, faithfully drawing more people into their midst with each passing week.

The rumbling grew in intensity, reverberating not only in the voices but throughout the entire building. The lights hanging from the ceiling swung and swayed erratically. Vibrations traveled through the chairs, causing them to tremble, and those kneeling could feel the powerful tremors emanating from the floor, resonating through their bodies.

Eyes met across the room as each person sensed the weight of God's presence and His indescribable power. Doubts about who truly held control of Stapleton were shattered, replaced by an overwhelming certainty that their God reigned supreme.

The earth trembled, the room quaked, and objects toppled off tables. Yet, miraculously, nothing broke. Bruce couldn't help but smile as he looked at Wayne, George, John, Maggie, Sue, and the other leaders. God was not a God to be ashamed of; He was mighty and worthy of their service. Bruce felt honored to serve the living and all-powerful God.

The rumbling persisted for an extended period before gradually subsiding. As the vibrations ceased, people rose to their feet, embracing one another and lifting their hands towards heaven. Their praises filled the room, each person offering their unique expression of adoration to the Lord.

Anticipating what lay beyond the back doors, everyone made their way to the parking lot. To their surprise, they discovered that the sudden departure of the crowd had left personal belongings scattered and abandoned. As God's people ventured outside, the screeching sounds of cars speeding away filled the air. The football field bore the brunt of the damage, with fallen lights strewn across the area, some landing in an adjacent vacant lot that happened to be occupied that night. The individuals responsible for launching the fireworks now lay beneath the fallen poles.

Bruce and a group of fellow believers hurried over, hoping to render aid. However, it seemed too late to help them now. The scene before them stood as a stark reminder of the clash between the darkness and the light, a testament to the power and sovereignty of the God they served.

Bruce stepped wearily into his home, drained both physically and emotionally from the events of the night. As he closed the front door behind him, he let out a heavy sigh and tossed his keys onto the table. Collapsing onto the couch, he switched on the TV, eager to glean any information that might shed light on the bewildering events that had unfolded before him.

His fingers brushed against the remote, a thin layer of dust serving as a testament to his recent preoccupation. Click. The news anchor's voice filled the room, speaking of a seismic event that had rocked the town. Bruce struggled to comprehend the extent of the devastation, hoping that the news report might provide some clarity.

The camera shifted to a reporter on location at Stapleton High School, capturing the chaotic scene that unfolded before them. Fallen lights cast an eerie glow, while emergency vehicles, their lights flashing in hues of red, blue, and white, surrounded the area. Bruce's heart sank at the sight, realizing that the damage had hit the school the hardest.

The reporter's voice broke through the air, delivering the grim news. Three men were pronounced dead, while a fourth clung to life in critical condition, whisked away by the waiting ambulance. A fleeting glimpse of the injured man caught Bruce's attention, and recognition flickered across his face. It was the same man who had caused him distress with his quiet, yet painful picketing outside of AFT. A strange mix of emotions welled up within Bruce—surprise, contemplation, and an unexpected urge to pray for his enemy.

With a heavy heart, Bruce confessed his own sinful thoughts and lifted up a prayer for the man's well-being. As he concluded his prayer, a sense of cleansing washed over him, providing a momentary respite from the weight of the night. He settled back into his chair, closed his eyes, and allowed weariness to overtake him. Sleep enveloped him, transporting him into a realm of dreams, where the events of the night blended with the mysteries of the subconscious.

As Bruce descended deeper into sleep, his consciousness was enveloped by vivid and immersive dreams. In this realm of slumber, the events of the fateful night replayed with astonishing clarity. Every detail, from the scent of sulfur lingering from the firework display to the pungent exhaust fumes emanating from the cars, permeated Bruce's senses.

In his dream, Bruce found himself back on the platform, speaking the same words he had uttered on that unforgettable night. But to his astonishment, the words materialized as ethereal swords, each one floating into the air. Sword after sword appeared, each drawn towards different individuals throughout the auditorium. As the words of faith resonated within the hearts of the believers, they reached out and seized the swords, wielding them with conviction. The swords sliced through the air, striking the foundation of the auditorium, causing cracks to spiderweb throughout the entire structure. The impact reverberated, unleashing powerful tremors that rattled the very core of the building.

Suddenly, Bruce's spirit detached from his physical form, still speaking from the front of the auditorium. His ethereal self soared through the double doors, gazing back at his earthly body, continuing to speak. As he looked ahead, his spectral presence observed a scene of panic and fear. Each face bore the weight of distress, and people scrambled in a desperate attempt to escape the chaos. Their cries reached the heavens, but their pleas for divine intervention were devoid of genuine longing for God's help.

In an instant, Bruce's spirit traversed the field, witnessing the mayhem unfold beneath the bleachers. He hovered over the frantic crowd, watching as people stumbled down the stairs, scrambling over fallen bodies in their desperate bid for safety.

Next, Bruce's ethereal form stood on the field itself, observing the violent shaking of the earth. Yet, amidst the chaos, he remained still and unaffected, while the boys who had previously played the game now sprinted to preserve their lives.

The perspective shifted once more, elevating Bruce to the top of the stadium lights, granting him an expansive view. He witnessed the descent of the other lights, crashing down and intensifying the panic that gripped the crowd below.

From this vantage point, Bruce's gaze descended upon the men responsible for igniting the fireworks. Trapped amidst the fallen debris, they were confined to a perilous maze of boxes and wreckage. Bruce observed it all, feeling helpless as events unraveled before him.

Then, abruptly, everything began to rewind. The lights ascended, people ran backward, and the sequence of events raced by at a dizzying speed until it melded into a blur before coming to a halt.

Bruce found himself back on the ground, standing amidst the men preparing the fireworks. Unseen and unheard, he strained to comprehend their slurred words, their intentions laced with malice. They spoke of causing harm to him and his devoted followers, their voices echoing with malevolence. Laughter echoed through the air, growing louder and more sinister.

Suddenly, Bruce was back on top of the stadium light, thrown and pulled through a bewildering sequence of transformations, his spirit moving at a speed that defied logic. Chaos reigned, and Bruce was caught in its tumultuous grip.

Crack! The light post teetered, on the brink of collapse, and Bruce found himself perched precariously upon it. Looking down, he saw the very men he had overheard, speaking ill of him and those he cherished. He attempted to shout a warning, but his voice remained silent, lost in the abyss of his spiritual state. Time seemed to slow as the men drew nearer, their arms shielding them from the impending danger. Bruce's heart sank, the weight of impending doom settling heavily in his stomach. Not only was he teetering on the edge of demise, but he also held within his grasp the instrument of their destruction. The ground loomed closer, their bodies came into focus, and just as the inevitable collision neared...Bruce abruptly jolted awake, a scream of anguish escaping his lips. Beads of sweat drenched his body, evidence of the intense turmoil that had plagued his slumber.

He found himself back in the familiarity of his home, the stark reality of his surroundings contrasting sharply with the nightmarish visions that had consumed his dreams. Trembling and disoriented, Bruce sat in his chair, grappling with the remnants of his harrowing encounter, his mind and body throbbing with the weight of the experience.

"I will not allow this setback to crush our ambitions!" Penkowski's voice reverberated through his California office, filled with frustration and determination. His eyes burned with an unwavering resolve. "I am determined to claim this town as my own, but that religious group stands in our way, in the way of our complete domination."

One of his staff members stepped forward cautiously, the weight of their words heavy with a mix of fear and reluctant honesty. "Sir, you hold a firm grip on those who toil for you in this town. Many are indebted to you, trapped in a cycle of insurmountable debt. Others seek solace in intoxication just to survive, while some seek refuge in hedonistic pleasures to escape the harsh realities of life."

Penkowski's jaw tightened as he absorbed the reality of his hold on the townspeople. "I want that town!" he exclaimed, his voice resonating with a desperate determination. Without wasting a moment, he sprang to his feet and commanded, "Let's go!"

As if choreographed, the entire staff rose in unison, their expressions a mix of loyalty and trepidation. They followed Penkowski obediently, their footsteps echoing in the office corridor as they descended towards the basement. It was here that Penkowski intended to summon the aid of his malevolent forces, to harness a power beyond the mortal realm.

The Mayor's office was in complete chaos, the incessant ringing of the phone becoming an overwhelming symphony of frustration. The young receptionist, just twenty years old, struggled to keep up with the constant barrage of calls.

"Hello... Can you please hold for a moment?" she pleaded, her voice tinged with exasperation. "Yes, I understand your concerns about the noise from Tuesday night while your church was trying to pray. Can you please hold on... Oh, your front window was shattered by the earthquake? Give me a moment... And you're questioning the legality of the drinking and gambling at the new AFT facility? Hold, please."

The Mayor's patience wore thin, and he finally snapped, "Put all the lines on hold!" His voice carried a mixture of exhaustion and frustration. "I can't handle this anymore. It's only 10:00 AM, and that phone has been ringing nonstop since we started our day!"

Complaints flooded in about the noise, the immoral activities at AFT, and the puzzling occurrence of the recent earthquake. The Mayor's office was inundated with irate citizens, each demanding his attention.

"Mayor... I've put all the calls on hold," the receptionist's whiny voice crackled over the intercom. "But there are about twenty people waiting to speak with you out here, and... there's a crowd of around a hundred or so outside."

The Mayor felt trapped, his office door shut as if it were a prison cell. He slumped in his chair, rubbing his temples and burying his face in his hands. Slowly, he rose from his seat and made his way to the window, cautiously parting the blinds to avoid drawing attention. What he saw outside was a sight that fueled his anxiety—a seething mass of angry people, their voices raised in protest, fists clenched in defiance. This was the very scenario that Mayor Thomas had always feared.

The weight of the Mayor's personal struggles compounded his distress. His wife's mysterious illness tormented her, causing immense suffering and plunging her into deep depression. His eldest son had found trouble with the law in another state, and his daughter, who had recently undergone an abortion, battled with crippling guilt and contemplated taking her own life. The Mayor's personal and professional lives were unraveling simultaneously, entwining in a web of darkness.

Gazing at the turbulent crowd outside, the Mayor's hopes for a brighter future shattered. The promises of prosperity, improved city infrastructure, and contented citizens now seemed like cruel illusions. Despair settled heavily upon him, casting a shadow over what was once a glimmer of hope. This was undeniably one of the darkest days in the Mayor's life.

"George, I want every employee to attend the gathering daily!" Penkowski's voice boomed through the phone, filled with authority and control. "I have put Linux in charge, and he will be leading each meeting every day."

George's response was laced with a sense of unease, feeling as though he was complicit with the devil himself. The weight of his role in enforcing these orders settled heavily on his conscience, causing his stomach to churn with discomfort.

"Sir, yes sir," George acquiesced, his voice tinged with reluctance. "If they refuse to attend, I will inform them that they will be stripped of all the privileges and amenities that AFT has to offer. And if they still won't comply, I will dock their pay. Full attendance will be enforced."

As George ended the call, a faint glimmer of solace flickered within him. It was the only consolation he could find in the midst of his turmoil, a small assurance that his prayers were beginning to bear fruit. He had noticed a decline in productivity due to the staff's indulgence in drinking during work hours, as well as the company's willingness to turn a blind eye. The products being produced were becoming as inferior as when Penkowski had intentionally sabotaged AFT's output during its previous ownership under The Association.

The issues extended beyond product quality. The new building itself was plagued with major problems. The air conditioning and heating system had broken down multiple times, the phone lines were unreliable, and the plumbing emitted a persistent sewer odor that defied detection. It wasn't just the new facility; even the old one was experiencing similar issues. The mounting bills indicated the cost of these problems, yet no effective solutions were implemented. George, having done everything within his power to rectify the situation, could not shoulder the blame for these persistent failures.

The employees found themselves toiling in a bitter and inhospitable environment. They would arrive at work with cleanliness, only to be enveloped by the stench of sewage by the day's end. Frequent fluctuations in electricity wreaked havoc on their computers, despite the installation of top-of-the-line surge protectors. Repair and replacement costs, loss of productivity, and the spread of computer viruses further exacerbated the issues. The IT department was at their wits' end, grappling with the incessant challenges.

Even the after-hours perks were marred by AFT's ongoing problems. Faulty computer and electrical glitches resulted in lost bets, incorrect book and magazine orders, and the inadvertent shipment of religious materials instead of explicit content. Liquor orders went awry, with truckloads of club soda arriving instead of the intended alcoholic beverages.

Each new predicament demanded George's attention as he scrambled to rectify the situation, careful to avoid arousing Penkowski's suspicion. Little did the owner know that it was God orchestrating the chaos, and George found solace in thanking God for sending turmoil to a company owned by the devil himself.

Sunday morning dawned, and the church was abuzz with anticipation. Despite the need for four consecutive services, each lasting an hour and commencing early at 8:00 AM, the pews were brimming with devoted congregants. Wayne's church mirrored this pattern, attracting a diverse multitude of individuals from various backgrounds and denominations. Bruce and Wayne, like kindred spirits, relished the opportunity to exchange sermon notes, finding joy in the undeniable similarities that often emerged. Their hearts swelled with gratitude, recognizing that God had orchestrated their paths, and as humble servants, they wholeheartedly embraced their role in carrying out His divine will.

With a mixture of reverence and affection, Bruce began the fourth service, his voice resounding throughout the sanctuary. "Lord," he began, his voice quivering with deep emotion, "as we embark on this service today, we want to declare our love for You and extend our heartfelt gratitude for all that You are accomplishing within our community. In humble acknowledgment, we recognize that Your ways surpass our understanding, and though we may strive to unravel the mysteries of Your work, we accept that true comprehension eludes us. So, Lord, we entrust our hearts to You completely, relinquishing our limited human understanding."

Bruce's voice quivered with reverence and awe as he continued, "We are compelled to thank You, Lord, for the awe-inspiring manifestation of Your power during last Tuesday night's prayer meeting. In that sacred moment, You revealed Yourself as the Awesome and Powerful God that we serve. Our spirits were stirred, and our faith deepened as we beheld Your might. We implore You, Lord, to continue working through every facet of the ongoing events at AFT and among the individuals in our town who are intertwined with it. Unfold Your purpose and divine will in their lives, guiding every step along the way."

With hearts intertwined, the congregation joined their pastor in fervent prayer, their voices blending in harmonious unity. Bruce's intercession extended to John and Elizabeth, two faithful souls who bravely stood against the injustice prevailing at Advance Medical under the ownership of Dr. Penkowski. "We lift up John and Elizabeth to You, O Lord," he beseeched, his voice marked by compassion. "Grant them the wisdom they need as they press forward in their pursuit of justice. Be their guiding light amidst the complexities they face. In the precious name of Jesus, we offer this prayer. Amen."

The sanctuary reverberated with a sense of sacred expectation, as the prayers of the faithful rose heavenward, intertwining with the fervent desires of their hearts. The congregation stood united, embracing the profound understanding that God's sovereign hand was at work, weaving together the tapestry of their lives according to His divine purpose.

"Ahh!" Penkowski's anguished cry reverberated through his office, the echoes bouncing off the walls as he found himself alone after hours on this solemn Sunday. A wave of intense discomfort washed over him, causing his hand to instinctively clutch his chest, just as it had during that fateful Tuesday night gathering. The same nauseating sensation surged within him, accompanied by a pounding pain that reverberated through his temples. With a sudden burst of urgency, he leaped to his feet, propelled by an inexplicable force that compelled him towards the gathering room within his California headquarters.

In the dimly lit room, the flickering glow of candles cast eerie shadows on the walls. Penkowski hastened his steps, his heart pounding with trepidation. As he approached the altar, a mixture of fear and desperation welled up within him, finding expression in tearful supplication. "You, the one I worship," he cried out, his voice quivering with a potent cocktail of defiance and anguish. "You are more powerful than this impostor of a God who only attracts the weak as followers! Why do you allow Him to taunt me? I am carrying out your commands!"

As Penkowski lifted his gaze upwards, a haunting sight unfolded before him. Suspended in mid-air above the altar, an apparition materialized—a grotesque manifestation of evil. Its malevolent presence was suffused with a reddish glow, emanating an otherworldly aura that instilled terror within Penkowski's trembling frame. The diabolical figure laughed, a sound that echoed through the room, resonating with a sickening delight reminiscent of a child tormenting a helpless creature. The laughter grew louder, mocking Penkowski's despairing cries for help, exacerbating his feelings of hopelessness. Lost in a whirlwind of desperation, he cast his eyes skyward, seeking solace, unsure of where to turn. But with each plea, the laughter intensified, reverberating through his very being, a relentless reminder of his tormented state. And then, as abruptly as it had appeared, the apparition vanished, leaving behind an eerie silence that hung heavily in the air.

Penkowski remained alone, his torment unabated. The pain, both physical and emotional, clung to him like a persistent shadow, a constant reminder of his entangled existence. In this desolate moment, he realized that nothing had changed, leaving him adrift in the abyss of his own torment.

As Bruce concluded his final sermon, a profound sense of excitement coursed through his being, witnessing the extraordinary works of God. The weight of divine inspiration propelled him forward, igniting a burning passion within his heart. After the service, George swiftly caught up with him, and the two friends eagerly embarked on a lunch outing. Aware of Penkowski's absence from town, a comforting assurance enveloped them, fostering a newfound sense of security and peace.

During their meal, George began updating Bruce on the myriad challenges plaguing their facility, delving into the depths of their troubles. As George recounted the litany of issues, a heavy silence settled between them, pregnant with unspoken emotions. Yet, Bruce, intimately acquainted with the unspoken language of friendship, discerned the source of George's distress even before he voiced his concerns. Empathy welled up within Bruce, a deep understanding of his friend's struggles, forging an unspoken bond between them.

"I feel a profound sense of guilt, burdened by the weight of responsibility for the shattered lives of those under my employ... Penkowski, I yearn to sever ties and resign. I would willingly forsake my livelihood and face the uncertain perils of a different path, rather than remain entangled in the malevolent schemes of the enemy."

Bruce was poised to respond, but George refused to let him interject.

"You witnessed his true nature! He embodies evil itself! We beheld it firsthand, right there in the Tuesday meeting! Am I losing my sanity? Working under his command feels like being trapped in a poorly scripted horror film, cast as the hapless accomplice to a monstrous villain!"

Bruce recognized that words alone would not suffice in this moment, so he leaned closer to George, gently placing his hand on his shoulder. He bowed his head, seeking solace in prayer. "Father, You are the ultimate purifier, a divine wellspring that refreshes and cleanses with Your touch. I beseech You to bestow upon George the touch of Your Holy Spirit, purifying his innermost being and instilling him with unwavering confidence that Your divine will is unfolding in his life at this very moment, in the name of Jesus."

As Bruce concluded his prayer, he raised his gaze and met George's eyes. A radiant smile adorned George's face, accompanied by a solitary tear that shimmered with a mix of emotions. "I felt His presence, Bruce," George whispered, his voice filled with awe. "I experienced His Spirit washing over my own spirit, purifying and rejuvenating me. I feel a profound sense of cleanliness, peace, and assurance that I am walking in alignment with God's purpose for my life." Bruce's smile widened, mirroring the profound joy in his friend's eyes. In that sacred moment, silence enveloped them, allowing the weight of divine transformation to settle before George finally broke the silence, expressing heartfelt gratitude, "Thank you."

John was engrossed in his task, diligently gathering the additional information that Elizabeth had requested. The convenience of finding most of it on the internet brought a sense of relief, creating a safer working environment for John. Safety was now a paramount concern that loomed over him. Though he had never been particularly worried about it in the past, the gravity of the dangerous situations he could potentially face to acquire the crucial evidence to bring Penkowski down compelled his thoughts to drift towards Maggie. The thought of losing her or causing her pain by putting his own life at risk weighed heavily on his heart. However, he found solace in the belief that things had changed, and changed for the better. In those moments of introspection, he turned to prayer, humbling himself before God. Although his prayers felt elementary compared to the profound supplications he had heard from Maggie, Bruce, and others, God would answer him in the simplest, most childlike ways. John cherished his newfound life as a Christian and eagerly looked forward to the future, experiencing a newfound sense of hope for the first time.

Suddenly, the phone broke the tranquility of his thoughts, and it was Elizabeth on the line. As they engaged in conversation, John listened intently, absorbing her words.

"This is great information, John. Thank you. However, I need you to return to Penkowski's main headquarters..." Elizabeth paused, an incredulous tone lacing her voice. "...I can't believe I just said that."

"Lizzy, I'm okay with it," John reassured her. "We have to put an end to this man. His influence is not only affecting this town and its people, but it's destroying lives across the entire nation."

Elizabeth contemplated her own journey since embracing Christ, and the gradual healing of the pain from her abortion stirred within her. The lingering ache fueled her determination to play her part in this fight with unwavering dedication. She knew her baby brother, John, shared a similar resolve.

"I know. I despise all of this and I can't wait for it to be over," Elizabeth confessed, her emotions raw.

"It will be over soon. What exactly are we searching for?" John inquired, seeking clarity.

"Money laundering," Elizabeth replied, her voice void of any emotion.

"Money laundering? Are you kidding me? He already has enough money. Why this?"

"I believe he's using a significant portion of his business empire to conceal illegal activities such as gambling, drug money, and much more. You mentioned earlier that he has gambling in the AFT facility, didn't you?" Elizabeth stated matter-of-factly.

"Yes, but..."

"It's just the tip of the iceberg, bro."

"Will this be enough to put him away?"

"Oh, yes. This, combined with all the other illegal activities we have on him, will be the deciding factor. We'll present everything, and this revelation might seal his fate. With the weight of these charges, he'll be locked behind bars for a very long time."

"How long?" John inquired, a mix of curiosity and concern in his voice.

"Probably 50 to 70 years," Elizabeth responded, her tone reflecting the gravity of the situation.

"That will work. I will fly out today. Thanks, sis, for all you have done and all you will be doing," John acknowledged gratefully, his voice tinged with anticipation.

"You're welcome. I genuinely feel a sense of fulfillment in doing this. It's like I'm finally making a meaningful difference in my life. All the other cases I've worked on... they seemed so hollow. They started off exciting, but in the end, even when I won, I felt unsatisfied. I know it might not make much sense to you," Elizabeth expressed, a mix of vulnerability and conviction in her words.

"Believe me, it makes more sense than you can imagine, more than you can imagine. Hey, how about you join us for the next Tuesday prayer meeting?" John suggested, hopeful.

Elizabeth paused, contemplating the invitation. She recalled all that John had shared with her about the meeting, and though some aspects seemed peculiar, a deep inner pull urged her to participate. Before she could overthink it, she found herself responding, "Yes. I will be there."

John found himself seated on an airplane once again, the familiar hum of the engines filling the cabin. This time, however, he made a conscious decision to embark on this mission alone. He had tempted fate too many times before, endangering those he cared about, and he couldn't risk it again. As the plane taxied on the runway, John took out his phone and dialed Bruce's number, seeking his support in prayer. He needed the assurance that his journey would be safe and successful. The conversation with Bruce brought solace to John's anxious mind, soothing his fears and instilling a sense of peace within him. Deep down, he carried an unwavering belief that he would accomplish his mission. The determination coursing through his veins only strengthened his resolve. He could sense it in his very being — this endeavor would be a triumph.

TWENTY TWO

Midweek had arrived, and the town was abuzz with preparations. Streets were cordoned off, and police officers roamed the streets, their parked cars adorned with flashing red and blue lights. Eighteen-wheeler semi-trucks maneuvered into position, parking behind the buildings that lined the town's center. With a synchronized opening of the truck doors, vibrant parade floats of varying sizes and colors gracefully rolled out. The floats formed a majestic lineup behind the buildings, poised to make a grand entrance from behind the AFT building.

In front of the AFT building, a massive stage took shape, rising to prominence. Adjacent to it, an ornate fountain, freshly constructed, added an air of elegance to the scene. On the rooftop of the AFT building, workers meticulously installed laser lights, confetti drop mechanisms, and booming speakers. Inside the building, powerful lights were strategically positioned, their beams cascading through several front-facing windows. At the back of the building, a truck had parked, carrying a trailer adorned with numerous colossal spotlights.

All was in place, and the festivities were on the verge of commencing. Bruce received numerous calls from members of his congregation and church leaders, all informing him of the unfolding events. Amidst the clamor and excitement, they gathered, eager to witness what Penkowski had planned this time.

"You know what I don't understand?" Sue, one of the church leaders, addressed Bruce, surrounded by their peers and other churchgoers who had assembled at the scene.

"What's that?" Bruce replied, contemplating the myriad of things he himself struggled to comprehend.

"If so many people in our town are part of the revival, why does Penkowski still hold such popularity?" Sue's question resonated with Bruce, and he sensed an answer brewing within him.

"Not everyone in town is involved in the Tuesday night gatherings, although we have seen a significant turnout. I believe God is working in a unique way," Bruce explained, his thoughts guided by his recent conversations with Wayne, Principal Benton, and his heartfelt exchange with God during his walk through the rose garden.

"But what good could possibly come from all of this? It feels like we're regressing instead of progressing," Sue expressed her concerns.

Bruce began sharing his belief in God's plan to bring complete cleansing to the city. "I firmly believe that when everything is said and done, God will receive all the glory. The entire town, every individual, will experience salvation and be set ablaze for God."

"A total revival!" Sue exclaimed with elation.

Bruce's heart swelled with joy, witnessing the deep love and devotion others held for their Savior. With unwavering confidence, he replied, "Yes."

Penkowski's spontaneous nature seemed to be his modus operandi. He never bothered to announce any of the events he organized, making it challenging for Bruce and Wayne to rally any form of protest. They were well aware that this was precisely why he operated in this secretive manner.

As the evening progressed, the edges of the streets became increasingly crowded as people poured in from their workplaces. Employees began streaming out of the AFT building, some stumbling from the day's events and the indulgences offered by the onsite bar, while others wore mischievous smiles on their faces. Similarly, attendees from the other facility arrived in high spirits, ready for a night of revelry.

Winter had settled in, and a light dusting of snow filled the air. With the sun now below the horizon, the spectacle of lights illuminated the scene. Colors of the rainbow burst forth from the pinnacle of the AFT building, casting a vibrant display into the night sky. The lights danced through the streets as the accompanying music commenced.

The introductory music reverberated, reminiscent of the opening chords of a rock concert. It steadily built in intensity, reaching a climactic peak. As the music crescendoed, a figure emerged onto the stage, their silhouette casting an enigmatic presence. Making their way toward the front, where a waiting microphone stood, the final chord resonated, triggering a dazzling showcase of strategically positioned lights. The powerful lights inside the building burst through the windows, laser lights shot from the rooftop, and spotlights from the rear pierced the night sky, accentuating the grandeur of the entire building. Silence fell as the lights now revealed the man at the center of attention.

It was Penkowski, donning his impeccable $1,000 suit, exuding an air of suavity like never before. Bruce glanced at Sue and Wayne, sighing in exasperation, and uttered, "Oh brother."

In the midst of the crowd, George managed to slip away and catch up with his group and his pastor. Rushing over to Bruce, he whispered into his ear, "I had no idea about any of this until the trucks arrived this morning." His frustration evident. Bruce raised his hand, offering a reassuring smile to George, assuring him that he was not to blame. Without hesitation, George promptly called John to relay the news that Penkowski was in town, ensuring John wouldn't need to worry about running into him in California.

"I would like to thank Mayor Tomas..." Penkowski's voice resonated through the streets, carrying its weight for blocks. His arms stretched out in the air, gesturing towards the mesmerizing display of lights.

"It is a new day in Stapleton. A time for celebration... a celebration of life," Penkowski proclaimed, his voice filled with enthusiasm. "This is your life. Are you living in freedom? Are you indulging in life's pleasures? Are you truly free to follow your desires? Your hard work has earned you the right to enjoy all that life has to offer, to savor its mysteries, and to marvel at its beauty. Your town has been transformed under the guidance of Mayor Tomas, and I am privileged to be a part of its financial prosperity."

"As we embark on tonight's festivities, I want each of you to look deep into your hearts. What do you desire most in life?" he paused, allowing the question to sink in.

"Is it not control? There is nothing more disconcerting than losing control. Perhaps you have experienced the loss of control while driving a car at some point in your life. The feeling was horrendous. You were utterly powerless," Penkowski continued, emphasizing each word for maximum impact. Again, he paused, relishing in the anticipation.

"Maybe that's how you feel right now, in this very moment, out of control and teetering on the edge of madness. Well, let me show you something."

Penkowski retrieved a sizable cut-crystal object, resembling a bowling ball, from behind the illuminated water fountain. Placing it atop the fountain, the water ceased its flow. The crystal caught the light, refracting it into an array of dazzling colors.

Standing behind the crystal, Penkowski raised his hands and spoke slowly, yet firmly, "It's time to take control of your life!" As he did, the crystal began to ascend into the air, gradually rising higher and higher. Bruce and the others exchanged glances, then refocused their attention on the stage. The music swelled, accompanying the ascending ball, which now hovered approximately 8 to 10 feet above the ground. At the pinnacle of the music, laser lights aimed directly at the crystal, bathing it in brilliant white light. In an explosive burst, the crystal fragmented into a shower of colors, illuminating the town square in a breathtaking spectacle. The crowd gasped in awe. Bruce leaned over to Wayne, whispering, "Impressive magic show." But with a serious tone, he added, "I hope his words don't deceive these people."

The crowd consisted of a mix of the Tuesday night regulars and other townsfolk who were not acquainted with the truth Bruce referred to.

Penkowski snatched the ball from mid-air as the laser lights shot back into the sky, creating a dazzling display. With the wireless microphone enabling his mobility, he carried the ball into the crowd, leaping off the stage. Randomly selecting a person unaffiliated with the Tuesday night prayer group, he handed them the ball.

His voice echoed throughout the square as he commanded them, "Take control of your life!" The crowd erupted with excitement as the person held the ball high in the air, following Penkowski's gestures. Illuminated by a spotlight, the ball began to rise from their hands, captivating the onlookers. People around them instinctively searched for any strings, but their gaze always returned to Penkowski. With a nod of affirmation, they explored every angle, yet found no strings. As the person signaled, the ball slowly descended.

Penkowski repeated this process, moving through the crowd one person at a time, offering men, women, and children the opportunity to take control of their lives. Each time, his command remained simple, "Take control of your life!" However, he never chose anyone from the Tuesday night prayer group. Despite their attempts to catch his attention as he drew closer, he consistently passed them by.

"I would like to invite each of you to come and experience for yourself what these individuals have just encountered," Penkowski announced as he made his way back to the stage. Holding the crystal object overhead, he released it, and it hovered in the air like a helium balloon tied to a string, capturing everyone's attention.

"Every day at 12:00 noon, in our beautiful facility, we gather to learn how to take control of our lives, to savor life's pleasures. If you are weary of being constrained by outdated traditions that lead to unhappiness, join us! As mature adults and grown-up children, you deserve the exhilaration of a lifetime, unburdened by archaic restrictions."

As his speech concluded, Penkowski threw the object towards the crowd. As it approached, the laser lights illuminated it once again, causing it to burst into a vivid display of color. Then, it erupted with hundreds of rose petals that cascaded down over the crowd. The ball vanished, leaving behind a fragrant aroma that wafted through the air.

"Enjoy your life!" Penkowski declared before stepping off the stage. Behind the facility, magnificent floats began to emerge, adorned with a myriad of colors. They released a flurry of what appeared to be confetti into the air, but upon closer inspection, revealed themselves to be rose petals. Machines positioned atop the facility shot even more rose petals into the sky. The air was filled with music, dancing lights, and the contagious joy of the people reveling in the festivities.

With each float that emerged, a different theme was showcased, representing the illicit activities available to AFT employees and now open to anyone in the town seeking to indulge in worldly pleasures. The floats depicted scenes of gambling, accompanied by the hypnotic allure of rock music with dark lyrics. A bar-themed float enticed people with provocative dancing and behavior. As the parade continued, most of the Tuesday night crowd had departed, leaving behind a throng of individuals reveling in the spectacle.

One of the final floats glorified adult activities, crossing the line of acceptability. Bruce and the other leaders had seen enough. They distanced themselves from women flashing for bead necklaces and made their way through the crowd. After their unsuccessful attempt to protest, they had come to the realization that it was not yet the right time to demonstrate. They understood it was not in accordance with God's timing.

"I can't believe we went from Bible studies in businesses and the Ten Commandments on school walls to floats in a parade showcasing nothing but physical pleasures," Sue seethed with anger. The leaders of the revival displayed expressions of frustration, anger, and confusion. What was once a town welcoming the presence of God now resembled a scene from an adult film.

As they walked back home, each leader shared their feelings about the situation. In the midst of their discussion, Bruce had an epiphany. "You know, I'm reminded of another group of God's people who witnessed His miraculous works. However, they became complacent and built an altar, creating a false god and indulging in wild celebrations in the streets." He paused briefly and continued, "Just as we have witnessed here tonight. This pattern is not new for mankind. It seems to be a recurring trademark of human behavior. God blesses, people grow complacent and sin, God disciplines, people repent and obey, and then the cycle repeats itself."

"But these people aren't solely from the Tuesday night prayer group," Wayne interjected.

"True, but some of them were part of it, and others have benefited from the move of God without truly aligning themselves with the Almighty. I believe now is the time when individuals will be tested to reveal where their true allegiances lie," Bruce stated resolutely. As he glanced back at the scene unfolding in the distance, he concluded, "And I believe we have seen their true allegiances tonight."

John returned from California, his excitement evident as he eagerly sought to deliver the information he had obtained to his sister. As Elizabeth had suspected, the evidence pointed to money laundering—a part of the expansive gambling operation that penetrated both AFT facilities and the company, Advance Medical. With the recent acquisition of the Association, they now held the title of the largest enterprise in the nation.

Exiting the airplane, John scanned the airport in anticipation. He grabbed a cup of coffee, taking a sip as he looked up and spotted his sister standing there. Overwhelmed with joy, he rushed towards her and enveloped her in a warm embrace. As they held each other, John's mind couldn't help but replay the harrowing moments of their previous trip to California—their encounters with Penkowski and the unsettling experience of being confined in a room designed for the mentally unstable. Sometimes, John wondered if that room was fitting for him, as it seemed like everything he once knew had vanished, leaving behind a profound and unsettling change in his life.

As they finished their embrace, John gazed into Elizabeth's eyes, noticing a glimmer he had never seen before—a twinkle of clarity, brightness, and hope. Even as they began to walk, he observed a newfound spring in her step. This reassured him about having her by his side during their last encounter with Penkowski. Perhaps it was the right circumstance for her to meet Bruce and join in the same prayer he had offered. It certainly felt right for John.

As they continued their walk through the airport, Elizabeth grew increasingly concerned, her gaze shifting back and forth. John reassured her, "It's okay. Penkowski just left. He was here last night, hosting some spiritual party in the street. I spoke with George earlier."

"Spiritual? I thought he was nothing more than a thief dressed in a business suit," Elizabeth remarked with skepticism.

John chuckled, "Well, I suppose he's after more than just money... and us, of course. George mentioned that Penkowski wants every person in town to have 'freedom'—to take control of their lives, in his own twisted way."

"What?" Elizabeth stopped in her tracks, lowering her head momentarily. Looking up at John, she confessed, "That way didn't work out well for me."

John placed his hand on her shoulder and comfortingly responded, "Me neither. And it's not going to work for the people of our town either." They resumed walking. "What Penkowski truly desires is control over them. George told me that alcohol is now being served rampantly, and people are becoming dependent on it to cope with their days. Many are burdened with debts they can't repay due to gambling. He has a hold on every one of those people... including George."

"A party in the street," Elizabeth mused.

"Yes. Floats, music, lights—the whole extravaganza. But wait until you hear about this," John said, proceeding to recount the spectacle of the floating object.

"People actually fell for that?" Elizabeth inquired, disbelief evident in her voice.

"Hook, line, and sinker. George mentioned that the gathering room was packed to capacity as a result. People are starving for the truth, and sometimes they settle for counterfeit experiences because they appear more exciting and cater to their base desires."

John and Elizabeth delved into discussions about their plans to take down Penkowski, intertwining it with business matters. The topic of Maggie arose, and John's expression transformed into that of a love-struck young man, reminiscent of his college days.

"You really like her, don't you, bro?" Elizabeth playfully teased.

John, having kept his feelings for Maggie to himself until now, felt slightly strange voicing them aloud. "I do. I really do. She's sweet, beautiful, and full of life. Just being around her makes me feel alive! And her friends—the people from the Tuesday night prayer group—they welcomed me with open arms. They prayed for me during this last trip, and everything worked out miraculously. Doors unlocked at precisely the right time—it wasn't mere coincidence; it happened one after another. I kept thanking God, and His assistance kept growing. This trip should have taken at least a week, yet here I am, already back." John paused, his eyes welling up with tears. With a quivering voice, he added, "I feel so special... I've never felt this way before."

Elizabeth, aware that this was not a moment for teasing, simply smiled, sharing in her brother's happiness.

The gathering in AFT had finally concluded, leaving a raw atmosphere of restlessness and dissatisfaction. George, burdened by mounting frustrations, found himself teetering on the edge of breaking. As the invited guests from the town mingled with employees from both AFT buildings, the weight of his responsibilities threatened to consume him. The thought of attending the gathering was overwhelming, and George simply could not bring himself to do it.

Although he took a small measure of satisfaction in witnessing the turmoil unfolding within the facility, George recognized the need to maintain appearances and portray an image of diligently addressing the issues at hand. Despite his internal struggles, he resolved to continue fighting to set things right, even if it meant enduring further hardships and challenges.

"Oh no! You have got to be kidding? Please, oh Lord, let it not be true!" Mayor Thomas exclaimed in distress, his voice filled with anguish as he spoke with his wife over the phone. The news he had just received was devastating, adding yet another calamity to his already troubled life.

"He said that I have about two months to live," the mayor's wife sobbed, her voice trembling with fear and sadness.

"But he said that this was a normal test that usually showed false results, a 'False Positive' he said, and he was not worried about it... he told us not to worry!" Mayor Thomas retorted, his frustration and anger piercing.

Amidst the sobbing on the other end of the line, the mayor made a firm declaration, "Look, I will be right there, don't move!" He hurriedly dashed out of his office, brushing past his concerned secretary and instructing her to hold his calls.

As he emerged from his office, a chaotic scene awaited him outside. A furious mob of people had gathered, chanting and making noise with drums and garbage can lids. The lids bore inscriptions that condemned the actions of AFT, demanding a cleanup of the alleged garbage being spread. News crews swarmed around the mayor, thrusting microphones in his face as he pushed through the crowd.

"Mayor Thomas, why have you allowed such questionable activity? And why have you even allowed it to be promoted throughout the streets of Stapleton?" an assertive young news woman pressed, her stern expression adding to the intensity of the moment. Mayor Thomas was taken aback by the aggressive questioning but continued to forge ahead, with the press hounding his every step.

"Mayor, is it that you have taken all the money from AFT as a bribe to allow them to engage in what is normally illegal activity, specifically gambling?" another reporter probed. The mayor's face turned pale, the weight of the accusations leaving him momentarily speechless. "No comment," was all he managed to utter as he hurried toward his waiting car.

Before he could close the car door, another persistent reporter seized the opportunity to pose one final question, their voice cutting through the air, "Sir, did you not take an oath in office to serve the City of Stapleton? And does allowing your citizens to become indebted to AFT's gambling services, suffer from substance abuse, and promote a cult that prioritizes having fun at any cost to themselves or others not concern you at all?"

Once again caught off guard, the mayor instinctively replied with the same refrain, "No comment." With the sound of the car door slamming shut, he sought refuge from the intense scrutiny and mounting pressures, leaving behind a whirlwind of unanswered questions and the weight of his responsibilities.

"Do you care?" The haunting question echoed through Mayor Thomas's mind as he maneuvered his car through the crowd that had gathered, blocking the street leading to the doctor's office. His heart pounded in his chest, the weight of the situation bearing down on him. He was leaving behind one immense problem at work only to confront another personal crisis that he still couldn't bring himself to fully believe. It hadn't sunk in yet.

As he drove, his thoughts bombarded him, the problems he faced seeming to have arisen after AFT had entered the life of Stapleton. His personal debt had spiraled out of control, mounting hospital bills for his wife consuming more of his income than he could handle. Desperate to make ends meet, he had made the ill-advised decision to dip into the funds provided by Penkowski for city renovation. The guilt and anxiety that followed kept him up at night, plagued by dreams that reminded him of his failure as a husband and provider for his family.

His children had also experienced their fair share of difficulties, their lives marred by poor choices and problems that had eroded any semblance of parental pride he once held. Even his home had begun to crumble, plagued by electrical, heating, and plumbing issues that required costly repairs. To make matters worse, the termite damage had caused a portion of the kitchen wall to cave in, necessitating extensive repairs that he simply couldn't afford.

But his wife... he loved her deeply. They had spent over 40 years together, and now this devastating news. She would be gone in less than two months. "No!" he thought, desperately clinging to denial, refusing to accept the reality of the situation. He needed to summon every ounce of courage for the difficult conversation that lay ahead with his wife.

He hurriedly parked his car and practically leaped out, not even waiting for the door to close on his jacket. His chest tightened, and he found himself gasping for air. Yet, he remained resolute in his determination to be strong for his wife, his lifelong companion.

Approaching the receptionist, he was swiftly ushered to an examination room where his wife sat, tears streaming down her face. As she caught sight of him, she leaped up, and they embraced tightly, seeking solace in each other's arms. Tears welled up in the mayor's eyes, but he composed himself before releasing his wife and guiding her to a chair. He sat down beside her, their hands intertwined, their connection providing some semblance of comfort in the sterile room that carried the familiar scent of hospitals. It had always given him an eerie feeling, but now that unease was mingled with overwhelming fear, anticipation of the doctor's impending entrance into the room, and the news that would change their lives forever.

"Mayor Thomas," the doctor's voice resonated through the room as he entered and closed the door behind him, shutting out the clamor of the Mayor's cell phone incessantly going off. Despite the urgent business emergency demanding his attention, the Mayor made a conscious choice to prioritize his personal family crisis above all else.

"As you are aware, this test we have performed is routine and typically yields false positive results. However, upon using a more advanced test, it also yielded a higher positive result…" The doctor paused, hoping he wouldn't have to utter the disease's name, but seeing the puzzled expression on the Mayor's face, he pressed on. "...positive for cancer. I'm sorry."

The Mayor summoned all the courage within him, ignoring the tightness in his chest and the knots in his stomach, and asked, "How certain are we? Are there any further tests we can explore?"

"This is the most accurate test available. When it comes to life-threatening diseases, I prefer not to play games," the doctor replied, understanding the Mayor's need for clarity and assurance.

The Mayor placed his hand on his forehead, gently rubbing it in a futile attempt to alleviate the immense headache that had seized him. It offered no relief, so instead, he continued to rub his wife's shoulder, seeking solace in the comforting touch.

"I'm sorry. If there's anything I can do..."

"You can have my wife retake the test," the Mayor interjected, interrupting the doctor's words.

Understanding their desire for further confirmation, the doctor nodded with empathy. "I will be more than happy to accommodate that request," he said, offering a reassuring smile. They delved into a discussion of the limited options available to them, bracing themselves for the grim reality that loomed if indeed his wife was afflicted with cancer.

Once they returned home, the Mayor assured his wife not to worry about her car; he would take care of it. After settling her down, he informed her that he would be back soon, urgently needing to attend to a pressing matter back in town.

He kissed her gently, embracing her tightly, suppressing the tears that threatened to spill over. With a final reassuring squeeze, he whispered, "I love you. I will be back," before heading towards the door.

As soon as he closed the door behind him, the floodgates opened, and tears welled up once more. He managed to reach his car and set off down the road, but the overwhelming surge of emotions grew uncontrollable. Anger, fear, gloom, and profound sadness swirled within him, tormenting his weary soul. His heart raced, his chest remained constricted, and the throbbing in his head transformed into a debilitating migraine. He swiftly pulled into the town square, parking at the rear of the building, and slipped inside through the back door. Pressing the button to summon his secretary, he saw her hurriedly rush into his office, barely opening the door.

"Where have you been? There's a mob out in the street! I..." His secretary's voice trailed off as the Mayor held up his hand, signaling for her to stop.

"I am well aware of the situation, but I had a personal emergency," he explained firmly, crossing the line with his tone. She hesitated, realizing the gravity of his words, and awaited his request.

"I need you to call all the voluntary police and firefighters, please. Also, fetch me the bullhorn. I must go out and try to calm everyone down," he instructed, the weight of his responsibilities evident in his voice.

His secretary's concerned expression betrayed her worry for her boss. "Are you sure you'll be fine?" she asked, her voice laced with genuine concern.

The Mayor reassured her with a solemn nod. "Most of these people actually like me," he quipped, unintentionally injecting a touch of humor.

Stepping out onto the front steps, the Mayor grasped the bullhorn and pressed the siren, capturing the attention of the unruly crowd. Gradually, their commotion subsided, leaving behind a low murmur.

"People of Stapleton, please settle down," the Mayor pleaded, his amplified voice carrying over the crowd. "Good people of Stapleton, please calm down."

The crowd continued to quiet, allowing the Mayor to continue his address. "I understand that our town has undergone significant changes this past year. Some changes were so profound that they made headlines. I recognize that we have witnessed many peculiar occurrences, including the new city renovations, the addition of the magnificent AFT building, and the sponsored parade..."

Interrupted by the mob's angry shouts, the Mayor listened as their voices grew louder. "We don't want them in our town! They are ruining our citizens' lives!" cried one person. Another voice chimed in, "We don't want these religious do-gooders! We want our freedom to choose back!"

As if summoned by the urgency of the situation, the volunteer police and firefighters arrived, joining forces with the full-time crews. Witnessing their arrival, the crowd began to settle down, allowing the Mayor to resume speaking through the bullhorn.

"I understand your concerns. I have been entrusted to govern a town filled with diverse and vibrant individuals, not clones or robots. Each of you has different preferences, views, and beliefs. We don't aim to impose our viewpoints on each other. I have been elected to help us coexist, to embrace our diversities and differences, and to create a harmonious environment where we can all live happily, enjoying our American freedoms."

The crowd remained unconvinced, prompting the Mayor to cut to the chase. "I need each of you to go home now. Reflect on what I've said, and let's strive to get along and celebrate our differences. Let's cease bickering with one another." With a pointed gesture toward the Firemen and Police, he smiled as they slowly moved into the crowd. The sight convinced the remaining individuals, and they began to disperse.

The TV reporters, capturing the Mayor's speech on tape, seized the opportunity to question him further. Yet, he swiftly shut them down, declaring, "I've said all that needs to be said. Good day." With those final words, he walked back into his office, leaving an impressed secretary behind. She smiled, recognizing that her boss had come through for her and the town.

But Mayor Thomas had something else weighing on his mind. He left the office and returned home to be with his wife, determined to put aside his own pain and provide her with undivided attention and care. Throughout the entire journey, he couldn't escape the reporter's haunting words echoing in his mind: "Do you care?"

Bruce's heart sank as he hung up the phone with Wayne, who had filled him in on the mob that had gathered downtown. He had caught a glimpse of the chaotic scene on the news earlier. Thoughts of organizing picketers crossed his mind, but the memory of their previous attempt weighed heavily on him. He couldn't bear the thought of putting his people in harm's way again. Instead, he needed to come up with a different approach, one that would protect his followers while still making a meaningful impact. With a determined resolve, he switched on the TV to gather more information.

The news anchor's voice filled the room, reporting on the day's biggest story. "...no comment was all the Mayor had to say today as he was questioned about the strange happenings there in the town. He was asked, why have you allowed such questionable activity and allowed it to be promoted throughout the streets of Stapleton? He then was asked a more pointed question, 'Is it that you have taken all the money from AFT as a bribe to allow them to engage in what is normally illegal activity, specifically gambling?'"

The screen shifted to show a recording of the Mayor's speech, highlighting his persuasive words that had managed to disperse the mob. The news anchors praised his oratory skills, analyzing his ability to calm the situation.

"With all that is taking place in the city of Stapleton, one may wonder, is this a holy war?" one anchor speculated. The other anchor responded, "Well, that is a good question. It seems that we had a rash of religious activities throughout the community, in businesses, in schools, in churches, and even weekday services had to be held in the high school's auditorium to accommodate everyone. And now, we have the AFT building, recently built and owned by Dr. Kenneth Penkowski from Advance Medical, based out of California. It has seemingly changed the dynamics, fostering a more 'care-free' lifestyle with all the activities that had seemingly vanished from the city."

Bruce couldn't bear to listen to any more of the news commentary. He clicked the TV off and turned his attention to prayer. Seeking guidance and strength, he connected with each leader, outlining his plan. Their unanimous agreement provided a glimmer of hope in the midst of uncertainty.

It was a solemn and determined gathering at the church the following day. The atmosphere was heavy with a sense of urgency and a deep desire for change. Bruce, the leader, stood before the crowd, acknowledging the sacrifice they were making by taking time away from work to be present.

"Folks, thanks for coming. I know some of you are taking time away from work, and I appreciate it. It is time that we take a new line of attack," Bruce began, his voice filled with conviction. The weight of the situation was intense.

He continued, "As each of you are aware, our town has fallen into the hands of a cult. AFT seems to be a front for a most severe cult. We have come to the conclusion that Dr. Penkowski, who is the head of this company, is also the head of this cult. I believe that he is demon-possessed... of course, this is no surprise to any of you as you saw his true colors on Tuesday night. But what you may not realize is the fact that... he wants this town. I have sensed this from the beginning and even more now. We have seen the evidence. Those people that were on the fence have not only been swayed to his side by appealing to their fleshly desires, but now these people that were once decent citizens are not. We have Penkowski to thank for this."

A voice from the crowd interrupted, filled with frustration and doubt, "What can we do? We tried to peacefully picket, and you and others were beaten in the streets and hospitalized!"

Bruce paused, taking a moment to gather his thoughts before responding with unwavering determination, "Ah! This time we will do it God's way. I want each of you to take these maps. I have outlined where to walk throughout the city, and we will have the entire city covered in prayer by late this afternoon. After everyone is finished, let's meet up at the AFT building."

Concern filled the voice of another participant, "We're not going to picket them again, are we?"

"No," Bruce assured, "We are going to walk around the entire building once, and we will pray. And before the employees have time to come out, we will be gone. We are going to do this every day from here on. We will surround the enemy's camp just as the Israelites walked around Jericho, and this facility, this cult will fall. I don't know how or when, but we will be faithful, and we will continue to do this until this cult loses its grip on this community.

And I can assure you, once it falls, God will have complete control of this entire city. Complete control. What we thought was a revival of God will pale in comparison to what God has in store for this city, for us as his people. Let's go!"

With renewed determination, each person filed out of the church, ready to embark on their mission. The resolve in their hearts was unwavering. They understood the significance of their task, even if it seemed unconventional to some. They paired up and dispersed into the city, committed to doing God's work, God's way. The atmosphere was charged with the collective determination to rid their town of the evil that had taken hold. They were willing to do whatever it took, no matter how unconventional or seemingly insignificant, to restore their community to righteousness.

"You know, Sue, I cannot believe all that has taken place lately. I mean, to see God working with such power and might, and then to see the Devil come in and make such a big impact in such a small time... How can that be?" Maggie asked, her voice filled with genuine confusion and concern.

Sue sighed, her face reflecting a mixture of understanding and sadness. "Well, here is the deal. Man is fickle. Just like Pastor Bruce said the other night at the parade, one minute we are worshiping, and the next minute we are turning our back on Him," she explained, her voice tinged with a hint of disappointment.

Maggie's eyebrows furrowed as she tried to grasp the complexities of human nature. "Yeah, but why? Why do we let ourselves be swayed so easily?"

Sue's eyes filled with empathy as she replied, "It's the sin nature. It is still pulling and tugging, and when it sees an opportunity of a lifetime to be fed with money, fun, and pleasure, it will jump at it. That is why we are cautioned over and over in the Bible to put the flesh to death and keep in step with God's Spirit."

Nodding in agreement, Maggie reflected on her own journey of faith. "I remember when I was first saved, Pastor Bruce talked about that. I did that, and it seemed that all the 'stuff' that cluttered my life just... lost its appeal."

Sue smiled, appreciating Maggie's understanding. "Well, that's it. And the problem we have here is that most of these folks had never really made any type of real decision to follow Christ, to have

His Spirit day in and day out, directing..."

"...and empowering them to overcome those things that seemed to trip me up over and over before," Maggie finished Sue's thought, her voice filled with conviction.

"Exactly!" Sue exclaimed, her passion for the message growing. "Well, some were religious, but that is not what it will take. Jesus even said to those who called Him Lord, performed miracles in His name, to depart from Him, for He never knew them."

Maggie nodded, her heart stirred by the truth of their conversation. "It's a relationship with Christ, not just a religion about Christ."

"Well said!" Sue affirmed, her voice full of enthusiasm. "That is exactly what it is, and to be honest with you, Maggie, I am so excited to be a part of this revival. I feel like I am in a war, and I know we will have the victory!"

With renewed determination, they continued walking, talking, and praying. Each step they took was filled with purpose and resolve. They carefully consulted their maps, making sure they were in the right places, ready to fulfill their role in the spiritual battle they were facing. The weight of the task ahead was evident, but their faith and commitment remained unshakable.

"Bruce, George will be just fine," Wayne said, his voice filled with conviction as he tried to encourage Bruce in the midst of their conversation.

Bruce's face reflected his worry and concern. "He won't be able to take it much longer. He won't even appear at the gathering, and it's only a matter of time before Penkowski realizes he is absent. What will happen then?"

Wayne placed a comforting hand on Bruce's shoulder. "God will be his strong tower, Bruce. He will shield him from the monster that Penkowski is."

Taking a deep breath, Bruce's gaze shifted to a nearby home. It stood tall and imposing, with a grand front yard. "We need to go up to this home and ask if there is anything we can pray for them," Bruce said with determination in his voice.

Wayne followed Bruce's gaze and recognized the home. "Bruce, I think this is the Mayor's home."

Bruce shrugged his shoulders, a resolute expression on his face.

They knew they needed to do what they believed was right.

Ding dong—the doorbell rang. They waited patiently, and after a moment, the door creaked open, revealing the red-haired, puffy-eyed figure of Mayor Thomas's wife. Her tear-stained face spoke volumes about her pain and sorrow.

"Ma'am, I am Pastor Bruce Hutchinson, and this is Pastor Wayne Miles," Bruce introduced himself, striving to maintain a gentle and compassionate tone.

The Mayor's wife's voice quivered as she responded, "Well, hello. What brings you here?"

"To be honest, the Spirit of God," Wayne chimed in, a hint of hesitation in his voice. Bruce's approach sometimes crossed into unfamiliar territory, but it had a way of paying off.

"We wanted to ask if you have any pressing issues that we could pray about for you or your family," Bruce explained, his eyes filled with genuine concern.

Virginia, the Mayor's wife, couldn't hold back her tears any longer. Bruce and Wayne exchanged glances, their concern deepening.

"It's okay," Bruce reassured her. "We would be honored to pray for you right now."

Overwhelmed by their offer, Virginia extended her hospitality, inviting them into her home. They settled into the living room, and Virginia offered them refreshments.

Virginia, no longer hiding behind her title, shared her story with intermittent sobs. Bruce and Wayne listened attentively, their hearts breaking for her pain.

"How would you like Wayne and me to pray for you?" Bruce asked gently, offering her the opportunity to express her desires.

Virginia, unafraid to voice her deepest longing, spoke with conviction. "I want to be healed."

"Very well, let's do it right now," Bruce responded, his voice filled with faith. Virginia looked surprised, perhaps expecting a more elaborate religious ritual.

"Stay right there in your chair. We will place our hands on your shoulders as we pray. You don't need to say a thing," Wayne reassured her.

Bruce and Wayne approached Virginia, their hands resting on her shoulders. Bruce began to pray, his words carrying a powerful plea for healing and deliverance. They invoked the name of Jesus, the Great Physician, believing in His power to heal.

As they finished praying, Virginia stood there, stunned. Gratitude filled her voice as she expressed her thanks. "Thank you... Thank you. I can't thank you enough. I have to say... I felt very weird."

Bruce and Wayne exchanged knowing glances, their smiles growing wider as they anticipated what she would say next. "How so?" they asked calmly.

"I felt like... electricity went through my body," Virginia admitted, her eyes widening with awe. Encouraged by their supportive presence, she continued, "It started at the tip of my head, moved through my body, to the tip of my fingers, down to the tip of my toes. Wow! I have never felt like that before in my life!"

Bruce responded with gentle affirmation. "That is God's touch on your life, Virginia." Her smile spoke volumes, and they continued to discuss the experience, sharing their joy and thanksgiving.

Before bidding their goodbyes, Virginia asked for the locations of their churches. "I will try to make it this Sunday! I feel... great! I mean, very great!"

Bruce and Wayne exchanged grateful glances, silently offering prayers of thanksgiving as they said their farewells. Their hearts were filled with hope and renewed faith as they left, knowing they had witnessed a divine encounter.

TWENTY THREE

Mayor Thomas trudged along the dusty road, feeling a heavy weight of loneliness pressing upon him. The scorching heat seemed unbearable, making each breath a struggle. His parched throat yearned for relief, and in the distance, he spotted a pool of water shimmering like a mirage. With renewed hope, he pushed himself forward, desperate to quench his thirst. Hours seemed to pass, but finally, he reached the water's edge.

Eagerly, he reached down and dipped his hand into the cool liquid. However, his anticipation quickly turned to horror as he pulled up a black, writhing mass of worms and maggots. A gut-wrenching scream escaped his lips, echoing through the desolate landscape. He looked up, and to his astonishment, there stood his home in the midst of the desert. Confusion etched across his face, he saw his wife waving to him from the doorway, a warm smile on her face as she held a glass of iced tea.

Driven by a mix of relief and urgency, Mayor Thomas sprinted towards his home, only to find himself moving in slow motion, as if trapped in a never-ending nightmare. His wife slowly slipped inside, and the door slammed shut, leaving him frantically pounding on it, calling out her name. Darkness enveloped him, and he stumbled from room to room, futilely searching for a light switch. Panic gnawed at his insides, his desperate pleas for Virginia met with deafening silence.

Eventually, he found himself drawn to a dimly lit room, emanating an eerie glow from scattered candles. As he cautiously entered, his heart sank. The familiar study had transformed into a macabre scene of horror. Where once there were plaques and pictures, now hung bloody knives, dripping crimson onto the floor below. Mayor Thomas felt a cold, sticky sensation on his shoulder, and as he wiped it away, he realized it was blood.

The dripping intensified, transforming the room into a gory spectacle. The rhythmic drip, drip, drip echoed in his ears, growing louder and more menacing. Suddenly, the ceiling crumbled, and he was thrust outside, staring in shock at the ruins of his former home. Among the debris, he saw the lifeless bodies of those he had governed, trapped in a cycle of debauchery and self-destruction.

Overwhelmed with remorse, Mayor Thomas turned away, catching a glimpse of his wife walking towards a small church in the distance. Desperation surged within him as he tried to catch up, but the more he ran, the farther she seemed to drift away. Eventually, she reached the church and vanished behind its double doors, leaving him alone in his torment. Just before disappearing, she turned and waved, her voice ringing in his ears, "He's healed me!"

Mayor Thomas mustered all his strength to reach the church doors, his desperation compelling him forward. But as he grasped the handles, they transformed into searing flames, consuming him instantly. The pain was unbearable, and he found himself trapped in a hellish existence beyond comprehension.

Gasping for breath, Mayor Thomas awoke drenched in sweat, his body trembling with fear. Virginia, concerned for her husband, quickly turned on the light and checked the clock—it was 3:00 AM. Worriedly, she rushed to fetch a cold glass of water, which he downed as if he had emerged from the depths of the inferno. Finally finding his voice, he spoke, his words heavy with realization.

"Those men who visited you today, what were their names?"

"Pastor Bruce and Pastor Wayne," Virginia replied, her voice filled with concern. In that moment, the memory of Wayne's previous visit, urging him to reconsider Penkowski's activities, resurfaced. And then, the vivid image of the church consumed by fire flashed through his mind. Mayor Thomas understood the significance, realizing that perhaps it was time for him to show a little more respect towards these religious figures who had entered his life.

"I know these men," Mayor Thomas finally uttered, his voice filled with a mix of astonishment and realization.

"You do? How?" Virginia questioned, her curiosity piqued.

He proceeded to recount the events that had unfolded, connecting the dots and piecing together the puzzle. Virginia listened attentively, her own recollection of the encounter aligning with his narrative. The pieces fell into place, and the gravity of the situation sank in.

Mayor Thomas, his tone now filled with humility and respect, mustered the courage to broach the subject that had previously been met with sarcasm.

"You really think you are healed?" he inquired, his voice laced with a hint of hope.

Virginia, her eyes shining with gratitude, could only respond honestly, "All I know is that I felt like electricity surged through my body, and then I felt a sense of well-being I haven't experienced in a long time."

Curiosity consumed Mayor Thomas as he sought to deflect attention from his own dream, dismissing it as insignificant. "Oh, just a stupid bad dream, you know," he muttered, hoping to divert the conversation away from his troubling visions.

Unfazed by his attempt to downplay the dream, Virginia pressed further. "I'm going to church on Sunday morning. Would you like to come?"

Mayor Thomas was taken aback by the suggestion, the image of his haunting dream flashing through his mind. A momentary hesitation lingered before he replied, "I think I will pass."

Deep down, he wrestled with conflicting emotions, torn between the disquieting dream that seemed to hold a warning and the flicker of curiosity sparked by his wife's transformation.

Meanwhile, in the depths of Penkowski's gathering, an atmosphere of darkness and malevolence prevailed. The room was shrouded in an ominous silence, broken only by the flickering candlelight and the faint sound of whispered incantations.

Penkowski stood at the center, his face contorted with a mix of twisted pleasure and sinister intent. His eyes gleamed with a wickedness that sent shivers down the spines of those in attendance. The sacrificial altar before him bore the gruesome evidence of his maleficent rituals, staining the air with a sickening scent.

As the chants intensified, Penkowski's voice echoed through the chamber, filled with malice and venom. He cursed the town of Stapleton and the mayor, whom he had manipulated as his unwitting pawn. Every word dripped with a potent blend of hatred and satisfaction, his intentions clear—to bring chaos and despair to the once peaceful community.

"I just don't know," Sue's voice trembled with frustration as she spoke on the phone early the next morning.

"What do you mean?" Maggie's voice conveyed genuine concern.

Sue took a deep breath before replying, "Here we are, making a difference for God, and then the devil himself bullies his way into our town...it makes me furious!"

Maggie's response cut through the tension, "Well, then I guess the devil has accomplished his objective with you."

Silence hung heavy on the other end of the line, as Sue absorbed Maggie's words.

Slowly, the realization dawned on Sue—she was a prayer warrior, a steadfast intercessor who had witnessed God answering countless prayers. It was no wonder that the enemy of their souls was attempting to distract her, pulling her away from the very area where she could make the most impact—prayer.

"You're right," Sue admitted, a hint of confession in her voice. "What am I thinking? I've been so consumed by anger as everything started falling apart—the loss of the Ten

Commandments in schools, the new AFT building, the commotion during our Tuesday night prayer time, and that chaotic parade...I felt like we were not only taking steps backward, but that our town was worse off than ever before."

Maggie offered her understanding and encouragement, validating Sue's emotions and urging her to continue sharing her thoughts.

"My prayer life has turned into a constant stream of complaints rather than true intercession. This needs to stop. Maggie, I commit to praying fervently for...John. Ever since Pastor Bruce introduced us to him and said he would be the one to bring Penkowski to justice and put him behind bars, John has been on my heart."

Maggie sensed a lingering trace of anger in Sue's words and addressed it cautiously, "Sue, I still detect a hint of anger in your prayer."

Realizing her lingering resentment, Sue quickly adjusted her prayer request, seeking to align her heart with God's purposes. "You're right, let me rephrase that. I will pray that God uses John as an instrument of justice against Penkowski and his company. How does that sound?"

Maggie's chuckle conveyed warmth and understanding, "Much better."

Sue's voice softened, filled with gratitude, "Maggie, I'm so grateful to have you as my friend."

Maggie reciprocated, "Not as grateful as I am to have you in my life, Sue."

They concluded their conversation by praying together over the phone. Sue's voice carried a depth of conviction as she addressed her Heavenly Father, acknowledging His sovereignty and purpose in the midst of the challenges Stapleton faced. She pleaded for God's intervention, asking Him to cleanse the city, to bring justice through John and Elizabeth, and to deliver the people from the bondage of sin perpetuated by AFT. Sue called upon God's power to shake the city, causing evil to repent and urging those who refused to repent to leave.

After the call, Sue continued to pray throughout the day. She diligently attended to the prayer requests on George's internet site, interceding for each person who reached out for help. She lifted up the Bible study leaders in local businesses and those organizing prayer walks in different neighborhoods. Sue fervently asked God to make a tangible difference, to use their prayers and spoken words to touch lives and bring transformation. Engaging in this meaningful work for God brought a sense of fulfillment, replacing worry with a renewed sense of purpose.

"I am pleased with how everything went with the prayer walk," Bruce expressed to Wayne, as they met in Wayne's church to discuss and pray over the ongoing events.

"Yes, I am too! We had a powerful walk, and others shared incredible stories of how God worked through them. We even have a testimony of our own with the Mayor's wife!" Wayne responded excitedly.

"Yes! And we were able to walk around AFT, pray, and not encounter any harm."

"They didn't even glance out the window," Wayne added.

"No, and I believe this is where we will witness the victory for God. Let us pray now," Bruce suggested.

"You're right," Wayne agreed.

Bruce initiated the prayer, his voice carrying the weight of authority, "Father... You are fully aware of the deeds committed by Penkowski. In the name of Jesus, I ask that you expose him, revealing to the public the illegal, immoral, unethical, and sinful acts he has orchestrated both in Stapleton and back in his home in California. Lord, you hold all things in your control, and I pray for John and Elizabeth's investigation. Grant them success and enable them to make a significant difference."

"Yes, Lord," Wayne chimed in, his voice resolute. "You are the Holy One, the Mighty One, the Glorious One. You have graced our community with your presence for a time. Oh, how we long to have that time back, basking in your presence. We were overjoyed witnessing your supernatural works in our hometown—lives transformed, miraculous healings, and ancient wonders unfolding before our very eyes. We were filled with excitement and exhilaration. We trust that you work all things for good, and we pray for John and Elizabeth to bring about change in our town, to expose Dr. Penkowski, his company Advance Medical, and his AFT facilities for what they truly are—a cover-up for the works of your archenemy, the devil himself. May they dismantle the schemes that rob souls and destroy lives, causing them to become ensnared in the sinful desires of the flesh. In the name of Jesus, I stand against the works of the enemy and all those who align with him. May they all fall, bringing glory to God and proclaiming victory to the Most High, my Lord and Savior, Jesus Christ. Holy Spirit, I pray this in Jesus' name."

At that moment, the phone rang, interrupting their prayer.

"Hello?" Wayne answered the call.

"Yes," Wayne responded, his voice filled with encouragement. "That sounds great! You most certainly have our prayers. God will make a way; He has gone before you. Let us know what else we can do from our end."

There was a brief pause, and then Wayne continued, "We just finished praying for both of you. You're welcome. That's God's work. We will keep praying; keep in touch." Wayne hung up the phone.

"That was John. They are ready to build their case. He mentioned that they will be issuing a subpoena for Penkowski to appear in court sometime today. We need to pray again," Bruce said urgently, prompting them to resume their prayer once more.

In California, a man dressed in a sharp suit walked up to the receptionist's desk, his presence commanding attention. He confidently requested to see Dr. Penkowski.

"May I ask who you are?" the receptionist inquired, curiosity evident in her voice.

"Yes, I am an old high school friend, Mike Leon," he replied smoothly.

The receptionist picked up the phone and relayed the message, "Dr. Penkowski, there's a Mike Leon here to see you. He claims to be an old high school friend." After a brief pause on the phone, she spoke again, "I will send him in."

Guided by the receptionist, Mike Leon walked down a long corridor, his steps filled with purpose. Finally, they reached a set of imposing double doors. The receptionist opened them, allowing Mike to enter the room. Dr. Penkowski's face displayed a mix of curiosity and suspicion as he extended his hand to greet his unexpected visitor.

Without hesitation, Mike placed an envelope in Dr. Penkowski's hand, his voice firm and resolute, "Kenneth Penkowski, I hereby serve you with this subpoena. The trial date is specified in the document. The plaintiff is the state of California versus the defendant, Kenneth Penkowski, on charges of money laundering, illegal gambling, and 23 counts of malpractice, including the illegal use and disposal of human fetuses."

Penkowski's eyes darted from the paper to Mike, his features contorted with rage as the fury of hell seemed to course through his veins. With a voice tinged with venom, he snarled, "Who are you, Mike Leon?"

"I was the geek that you tormented during high school gym class," Mike responded, a triumphant smile gracing his face. "I suppose now, I get the last laugh." With that, he turned and walked away, leaving Penkowski seething in his wake.

"So how is all of this going to happen?" John asked his sister, their voices filled with a mix of anticipation and concern, as they sat in a small diner in town. From their window, they could see the quaint yet beautiful town square, providing a serene backdrop to their conversation. John, although knowledgeable about certain aspects of the legal system, knew that he was not an expert in this field.

With steaming cups of coffee in front of them, his sister leaned forward, her eyes reflecting determination. "I contacted the attorney general of California and shared all the evidence you gathered for me. The moment I mentioned Penkowski's name, he became fully engaged. He admitted that they had long suspected much of what I presented, but lacked sufficient evidence to hold up in court. That's when I took the opportunity to sing your praises."

A smile of satisfaction tugged at the corners of John's lips.

"He assured me that they would issue a subpoena today. I expressed my concern about whether they could effectively deliver it into Penkowski's hands, but he assured me he had a plan. I'm waiting for a call from him any moment now."

"I did mention the kidnapping incident, but the attorney general assured me that the evidence we've presented will be enough to put Penkowski away for life without the possibility of parole."

John nodded, a sense of relief washing over him. It was a fitting outcome for the man who had caused so much harm and destruction. The wheels of justice were finally turning in their favor.

Elizabeth's cell phone rang, and she quickly answered with a mixture of excitement and gratitude evident in her voice. "This is Elizabeth. Oh, that is great! Thank you so much for calling. When do you need me to appear? Okay, and what about the investigator? Alright, any other witnesses? Oh, sure, I am sure that Pastor Bruce would be happy to testify in court for assault and battery. That will be icing on the cake! You bet. I will be there with bells on." With a sense of satisfaction, she ended the call, her mind filled with the impending courtroom battle.

"Well, he has been subpoenaed, and he has already contacted his lawyer," Elizabeth shared with her brother, her voice carrying a mix of determination and anticipation.

John's brows furrowed as he asked, "Now what?"

Elizabeth leaned back in her chair, her expression a blend of weariness and resolve. "Well, he will appear in court, and then it all begins."

John's confusion was evident as he sought further clarification. "What do you mean?"

Elizabeth's sarcasm laced her response. "You know, the 'Perry Mason' drama," she quipped, referring to the fictional lawyer renowned for his courtroom triumphs. "So this could drag on."

A tinge of frustration colored John's voice as he inquired, "Well, can't they put him in jail?"

Elizabeth shook her head, emphasizing the reality of the situation. "No, we have to prove that he has done all of this. Once we have proven our case beyond a reasonable doubt, then we will be able to put him away for good."

John's concern was evident as he pressed for reassurance. "How good does the evidence look, legally speaking?"

Elizabeth's conviction radiated through her words. "He does not have a chance."

A semblance of relief washed over John's face, and a glimmer of a smile appeared. He then remembered a Bible verse he had recently heard and recited it aloud. "Do not take revenge, my friends, but leave room for God's wrath, for it is written: 'It is mine to avenge; I will repay,' says the Lord."

Elizabeth looked at her brother, a mixture of surprise and

warmth in her gaze. She never expected to hear Bible verses from John, and it stirred memories of their childhood attending Sunday school together. A nostalgic smile crossed her face as she recalled the day he excitedly shared the verse John 3:16, a cherished memory from their upbringing. Reflecting on the verse he had just quoted, she found solace in its wisdom. The pain inflicted by this man would not be avenged by them alone; the legal system would have its role to play, guided ultimately by God's hand. It brought a sense of peace and reassurance amidst the turmoil they were facing.

Sue found herself in the comforting embrace of her home. Having completed her daily tasks, she knew it was time to focus on prayer. Making her way to her small den, she knelt down, ready to engage in a more profound connection with the divine.

As Sue delved into prayer, a sense of weakness overcame her. Gradually, she found herself lying prostrate on the floor, carried away in the spirit of the moment. In an instant, she stood on the other side of a magnificent river, surrounded by lush green trees and sparkling blue water. Across the riverbank stood a figure dressed in radiant linen, adorned with a belt of the finest gold. His presence was awe-inspiring, his body resembling chrysolite, both glass-like and translucent. His face radiated with brilliance, his eyes resembling flaming torches, and his arms and legs shimmered like burnished bronze. When he spoke, his voice resonated like the sound of a multitude.

Overwhelmed by his words, Sue's strength faltered, and she blacked out momentarily. Soon, a gentle touch on her shoulder revived her, and she regained her trembling composure. The man reassured her, saying, "Susan, pay heed to the words I am about to speak, for they are true." Sue struggled to rise, her whole being trembling with anticipation.

"Do not fear," the man spoke with calm authority. "Your prayers, which you offered on the very first day when God's work in this town was disrupted by the vile enemy, have been heard. It was he who hindered me, but Michael, the chief prince, came to my aid, for I was detained. Now I have come to inform you that victory is within reach. Embrace it with unwavering faith, and you will find satisfaction and bring glory to your Lord—Jehovah God,

His only son Jesus, and the eternal Spirit of God."

With these profound words, Sue opened her eyes and found herself once again in the familiar surroundings of her den. A surge of emotions coursed through her, but above all, a profound sense of peace enveloped her being.

The designated time arrived for everyone to gather and walk around the AFT building as Pastor Bruce had planned. As the group assembled, Pastor Bruce noticed a noticeable change in Sue's demeanor. Her complexion had paled, and her expression appeared to be a mix of excitement and fear. Concerned, Bruce approached her and discreetly pulled her aside.

Sue confided in Bruce, sharing the profound experience she had during her prayer time. The intensity of her encounter left her visibly shaken, yet there was also a glimmer of excitement in her eyes. Bruce couldn't contain his own excitement, feeling overwhelmed by the significance of Sue's encounter.

After their conversation, Bruce rejoined the group, his enthusiasm barely contained. He knew that Sue's story had the potential to impact the entire congregation. With Sue's consent, he made his way back to the group, eager to share the extraordinary experience she had just recounted and inspire the church community with her powerful testimony.

John and Elizabeth had joined the group, bringing along the incredible news about Penkowski's impending legal actions. Sue's smile grew wider, reflecting the elation that everyone felt. The sense of victory and justice filled the air, but they remained focused on their mission and continued with their prayer walk.

Walking around the AFT building, Elizabeth couldn't help but feel a sense of unease. John noticed her discomfort and instinctively drew her closer, providing comfort and support. Although John was still getting used to this new environment and the Tuesday night church gatherings, he understood the importance of standing together as a family and supporting the community's best interests.

As they completed their prayer walk, something seemed off.

Despite the building being after hours, there was still a noticeable amount of activity inside. However, nobody paid them any attention, as if they were deliberately being ignored. It felt peculiar, as if people were intentionally looking the other way, avoiding any interaction or confrontation.

Curiosity stirred within the group, but they remained steadfast in their purpose. They trusted that God's guidance would unveil the mysteries behind the building's activities, and they continued to pray fervently, believing that their collective prayers would bring about transformation and redemption for the town.

Pastor Bruce, Pastor Wayne, George, Sue, and Maggie gathered together for a dinner to celebrate the progress made since the revival began. The atmosphere was filled with excitement as they filled Elizabeth in on all the significant events that had taken place within the church. John, eager to understand and absorb everything, listened attentively alongside his sister, their eyes wide with wonder. The conversation flowed effortlessly, carrying them deep into the night. Elizabeth's heart swelled with joy as she got to know these incredible individuals, strengthening her resolve in her decision to follow Christ.

As the evening unfolded, Elizabeth felt comfortable enough to share her personal journey with the group. Sue and Maggie, empathetic and compassionate, immediately connected with her story, offering their support and understanding. Elizabeth then explained the upcoming legal process and the necessary steps to ensure justice prevailed. Everyone present listened intently, fully absorbed in the details and complexities of the situation. They vowed to stand by Elizabeth and John, promising their unwavering prayers at every stage of the legal proceedings.

Realizing the gravity of the situation, they made a collective decision to keep Elizabeth and John hidden from Penkowski's reach. They understood the increased risk they faced now, knowing that Penkowski would likely intensify his pursuit of them. It was a necessary measure to safeguard their safety and allow the legal process to unfold without interference.

As the evening came to a close, a profound sense of unity and determination enveloped the group. They knew they had each other's unwavering support and God's guidance as they faced the challenges ahead. The journey toward justice and redemption had only just begun, and they were ready to face it together, strengthened by their shared faith and commitment to making a difference.

Penkowski's fury reverberated through the office building in California. The employees could sense his rage as he stormed by, leaving an ominous energy in his wake. Summoning them for an impromptu gathering, he unleashed his anger and disgust with an intensity that sent chills down their spines. Knives flew through the air, narrowly missing those brave enough to face him. His wrath was unlike anything they had ever witnessed, a tempest of fury engulfing his being.

Amidst the flickering candlelight, Penkowski's eyes seemed to transform, glowing with an eerie red hue. Suddenly, he dropped to his knees before the altar, his voice trembling with desperation as he beseeched the spirits for justice. But all he received was an eerie silence, amplifying his frustration and despair. Perplexed by his distress, one of his subordinates leaned in, inquiring about the source of his turmoil. After hearing the explanation, he proposed an alternative solution.

"Dr. Penkowski, why not seek justice from those who have wronged you, the town of Stapleton?"

Those words immediately captured Penkowski's attention, causing his anger to subside and a wicked smile to spread across his face. "You're right, my friend," he declared, standing tall once more and concluding the twisted ceremony. The next course of action was clear. Penkowski wasted no time, summoning his private jet and assembling a team of five ruthless hitmen to accompany him on his journey to Stapleton. As he settled into his seat on the plane, his mind churned with seething anger, making it impossible to focus on anything but revenge.

The jet descended toward the airport, each passing second fueling Penkowski's anticipation. Engaging in conversation with his companions, he issued instructions, ensuring they were prepared for the mission ahead. As they touched down on the runway, adrenaline coursed through their veins. The hitmen grabbed their weapons from the cabinet at the back of the plane, strapping themselves in, ready for action upon landing.

Disembarking from the aircraft, the team scattered in different directions, each venturing into the heart of the town, determined to find the one responsible for their boss's foul mood. They combed through diners, barber shops, engaging in conversations with locals, but nobody seemed to possess any knowledge of their target. They visited both churches, arriving at an empty hour, and even stopped by the five and dime shop, the antique store, schools, and grocery stores. Their search extended into the neighborhoods, engaging with neighbors, seeking any shred of information, yet their efforts yielded no results.

Undeterred, Penkowski's attention turned to the AFT building, an ominous presence in the town. With a mixture of anticipation and vindictiveness, he approached the stronghold that symbolized his power and influence. The stage was set for a confrontation that would test the mettle of everyone involved.

Deep beneath the sacred walls of Pastor Bruce's church, a small group of five individuals huddled together in the dimly lit underground space. Their voices, filled with a mix of determination and trepidation, resonated through the chamber as they discussed their roles, prayed fervently, and contemplated the uncertain duration of their confinement.

"Sue will remain vigilant in town," Pastor Bruce informed the group, his voice laced with a sense of urgency and responsibility.

"Maggie will continue to keep watch at the airport," Pastor Wayne added, acknowledging her pivotal role in alerting them about Penkowski's arrival. Her presence had been a providential gift.

George, with a glimmer of hope in his eyes, shared his contribution. "I have a janitor at AFT who recently embraced the Lord. Despite his desire to quit, I convinced him to stay a little longer and assist us. He works double shifts, allowing him to monitor both facilities. Penkowski typically visits the new building, so Billy, the janitor, can trail him discreetly to the old one once he departs."

John, brimming with optimism, couldn't contain his enthusiasm. "I love it when a plan comes together!" His words echoed with a sense of triumph, knowing that their carefully orchestrated strategy was falling into place.

Elizabeth, her voice tinged with a mixture of hope and weariness, shared her heartfelt sentiment. "I believe this will somehow put an end to the nightmarish existence I've endured. And, let me emphasize, Penkowski is not allowed to leave California."

In the midst of their conversation, a cell phone pierced the air, breaking the solemn atmosphere. George swiftly answered the call, his voice filled with anticipation. "Hello? Billy, it's good to hear from you. Thank you for the update. Remember, once Penkowski leaves, make your way to the old AFT building discreetly. We don't want him to suspect anything. Keep me informed of any developments."

George's words were filled with gratitude and reassurance. "That's all you need to do. Just keep me informed. We're okay. Thank you for your prayers. Talk to you later."

The group exchanged glances, their faces revealing a mix of determination, reliance on one another, and the power of their collective faith. In the midst of uncertainty, their unwavering trust in God and their unified purpose gave them strength to persevere.

Penkowski's rage intensified as he searched desperately for George, but the man was nowhere to be found. Frantically, he dialed George's number repeatedly, but there was no answer. Seeking answers, he approached George's secretary, who could only offer a vague explanation. She assumed George had been shuttling between the facilities, moving his belongings accordingly.

Sinking into George's vacant seat, Penkowski found an empty desk devoid of any remnants. The emptiness before him only fueled his anger and deepened his sense of betrayal. As his emotions spiraled, the situation took an even darker turn. Opening the accounts, Penkowski discovered glaring deficits that shouldn't have existed. Summoning the trembling accountant, whose breath reeked of alcohol, Penkowski interrogated him and unearthed a shocking revelation—the accountant had embezzled hundreds of thousands of dollars.

Without hesitation, Penkowski dialed the authorities and ordered one of his trusted henchmen to detain the accountant in a separate room until the police arrived. As he delved further, he realized the repercussions of the accountant's actions. Other accounts, including utilities and electricity, were severely delinquent. The power was scheduled to be disconnected that very day, and the penalty would result in a three-day delay for reconnection.

Overwhelmed by the mounting chaos, Penkowski decided to survey his once magnificent establishment. He ventured into the leisure areas, starting with the bar. The once vibrant space was now dilapidated, bearing the scars of countless drunken brawls. Moving through the gambling areas and adult section, he encountered vandalized machines and torn, tattered books.

In the work areas, the scene was equally distressing. Employees stumbled between workstations, engaging in heated arguments and physical altercations. Penkowski observed the final products of his enterprise—a shoddy, substandard piece of equipment designed for the elite medical industry.

Descending further into the building, Penkowski reached the gathering room, which had devolved into a pit of darkness. Swastika symbols adorned the walls, floors, and ceilings, accompanied by profanity scrawled across every surface. The stench of decay hung heavy in the air.

Returning to the main work area, Penkowski was confronted by an enraged man who unleashed his pent-up frustration. The man's voice reverberated through the room as he denounced Penkowski, blaming him for the destruction of his life. He recounted how he had been trying to rebuild his life in a small business before Penkowski's enticing offer derailed his progress. The open bar during work hours proved irresistible, leading him back into the clutches of addiction. He had lost his wife, his family, and everything he held dear for a mere extra $12,000 a year. The man's grievances resonated with others nearby, who joined in the chorus of discontent.

The crowd grew more aggressive, fueled by shared grievances. Sensing the impending danger, Penkowski urgently called for his men, but they were scattered throughout town, delaying their arrival. Only the henchman tasked with watching the accountant swiftly responded, but the situation quickly escalated beyond his control. Penkowski and his henchman found themselves overwhelmed and at the mercy of the furious mob.

"Billy, you have got to be kidding!" George again was on the phone with the janitor as he was informing him of what was happening at AFT.

"Well, stay far away from that mess. I don't want anything to happen to you!"

"Yes, we will continue to pray for you." and everyone began to lift Billy up to the Lord as George stayed on the line with Billy.

The police swiftly moved in to break up the chaotic brawl, their authoritative presence creating a momentary sense of relief in the midst of the madness. Penkowski, bloodied and battered, felt a surge of gratitude wash over him, though his anger still simmered beneath the surface.

As Penkowski attempted to inform the officers about the accountant's whereabouts, his hands were forcefully restrained, handcuffs tightly secured around his wrists. Frustration and disbelief coursed through him, intensifying his wrath.

"You fools! The accountant is upstairs, not me!" Penkowski shouted, his rage escalating, his voice tinged with a blend of desperation and fury.

The officers recited the Miranda rights, their words falling upon deaf ears as Penkowski's anger consumed him. In a sudden burst of strength and defiance, he forcefully shrugged off the grip of several police officers attempting to escort him to the waiting squad car. Even his henchmen, eager to assist, found themselves subdued and handcuffed by the authorities.

Undeterred, Penkowski fought back with a ferocity that seemed otherworldly. He hurled several more officers aside, their bodies flung in different directions across the room, adding to the already chaotic scene. A moment of tension filled the air as the room plunged into darkness, the main power abruptly cut off. Dim emergency lights cast a ghostly glow, illuminating the space with eerie beams.

In this unsettling ambiance, Penkowski's anger transformed into an eerie, hellish presence. His bloodshot eyes blazed like fiery coals, reflecting his unleashed fury. The officers, employees, and henchmen who had previously assailed him now recoiled, fear driving them into a corner. Their collective gaze was fixated on Penkowski, whose body became a canvas for an otherworldly display.

Finally, one of the police officers, realizing the need to regain control, swiftly retrieved an electric stun gun. With a resolute aim, he unleashed a powerful surge of electricity, sending hundreds of volts coursing through Penkowski's convulsing body.

A jolt of intense pain shot through Penkowski as the electric current surged through his muscles, causing him to convulse uncontrollably. The room was momentarily filled with a blinding display of electric arcs and flashes, creating a vivid and disorienting spectacle. Penkowski's screams merged with the crackling sounds of electricity, creating an eerie symphony of agony

Amidst the surreal light show, Penkowski's screams seemed to blend with an otherworldly chant, evoking an unknown deity. The room was held captive by this bizarre manifestation, the employees who had once assaulted him now reduced to cowering onlookers, their expressions a mix of fear and awe.

"Pray harder, Billy says, guys!" George urgently relayed the message, his voice filled with a mixture of desperation and determination. The gravity of the situation had intensified, and the need for divine intervention became even more apparent.

As the words resonated through the room, a collective sense of urgency enveloped the gathering. One by one, they knelt down, their hearts burdened with the weight of the battle they were waging. With eyes closed and heads bowed, they entered into a sacred communion with the God of the universe.

Eventually, the electric stun gun accomplished its purpose, forcing Penkowski to collapse to the ground in a heap of defeat. The room fell into a tense silence, broken only by the heavy breaths of the bewildered witnesses. The air hung heavy with a mixture of relief, trepidation, and an unsettling sense of the supernatural that had unfolded before them.

Penkowski lay on the floor, his body battered and broken, his face etched with a twisted expression of pain and defiance. The room slowly returned to a dim illumination, the emergency lights casting long shadows over the aftermath of the encounter.

"Is he still alive?" one of the police officers asked, his voice filled with astonishment and disbelief, as the other cautiously approached Penkowski's motionless body to check for a pulse.

The officer looked up at his companion, his eyes wide with a mixture of shock and confusion. "He is. I can't comprehend how anyone could withstand such an intense surge of electrical voltage coursing through their body for as long as he did. More than 10 seconds of that level of electricity would be fatal for even the strongest of individuals."

With a mixture of caution and urgency, the police officers proceeded to carefully lift Penkowski's limp form and place him inside the police car. In a surprising turn of events, Penkowski's loyal men offered no resistance or protest, seemingly stunned by the dramatic turn of events.

The remaining members of Penkowski's entourage, who had witnessed the commotion from a safe distance, stood in a state of shock and disbelief. As they observed their once formidable and feared leader being carried away in the squad car, a sense of powerlessness washed over them, their confidence shattered in the wake of this unexpected defeat.

"It's over," George said, his voice filled with a mixture of relief and exhaustion, as he ended the call with Billy.

As Elizabeth and the rest of the group finished expressing their gratitude to God for His intervention, a sense of calm settled over the room. The tension that had been weighing on their shoulders seemed to lift, replaced by a feeling of profound gratitude.

Elizabeth, her voice steady and resolute, began to address the group, her words carrying a sense of wisdom earned through trials. "As I mentioned earlier, Penkowski was not permitted to leave California, let alone his own city."

John, feeling a mix of frustration and concern, couldn't help but voice his question. "So why would he do something so reckless?"

Bruce, with a compassionate understanding, replied, "Anger can drive a person to act in ways that defy logic or reason."

John, his face flushing with embarrassment, recalled his own impulsive actions. "Like punching cement walls with your bare fists, right?"

Elizabeth nodded, her gaze filled with empathy. "Exactly. It's the destructive power of unchecked anger."

George, wanting to understand the next steps, asked with anticipation, "What happens now?"

Elizabeth's voice held a sense of certainty. "He will be escorted back to California and placed in jail until the trial next week."

A solemn silence settled in the room as the weight of the situation sank in. After a while, John broke the silence, his words filled with a mix of relief and gratitude. "My friends, we are finally free to leave this hiding place." In that moment, his heart overflowed with joy, not only for the physical freedom he now possessed but also for the deep connection he had found with his newfound companions. True friendship, he realized, was the ultimate source of freedom and happiness.

TWENTY FOUR

Sunday morning church was filled with an electric atmosphere of excitement and joy. Bruce stood before his entire congregation, sharing the incredible news that had unfolded. The room erupted in rejoicing and praise as the people celebrated the victory they had witnessed.

Bruce knelt in prayer, expressing heartfelt gratitude to God for honoring the obedience of His people. He thanked Him for the courage to step out in faith, even when it seemed irrational, as they had walked around the imposing AFT building. He reminded everyone that their work was not finished, as Penkowski still needed to be convicted of every charge brought against him to ensure he remained behind bars.

The church continued to grow with each passing Sunday, defying the darkness that Penkowski had tried to cast over the town. Among the congregation, a distinguished woman stood near the front, radiating joy and anticipation. It would have been even more perfect if her husband, Mayor Thomas, had been by her side.

The church was packed to the brim, and Bruce and Wayne had been conducting multiple services to accommodate the influx of new attendees since the revival had begun. Both pastors were grateful for the school auditorium that still served as the gathering place for Tuesday prayer meetings, despite the tight space that barely accommodated everyone from Bruce's church to Pastor

Wayne's.

Bruce invited Sue to stand alongside him, encouraging her to share the vision God had given her. With a mixture of trembling and boldness, Sue recounted the encounter she had with the heavenly messenger. She described the man's appearance and the overwhelming fear that had gripped her. But as she spoke, the memory of his touch filled her with newfound strength, allowing her to stand before him.

"He said to me, 'Susan, consider the words I am about to speak to you for they are true. Do not be afraid. For I have heard your prayer from the very first day when God's work in this town was disrupted by the vile enemy. It was he who delayed me. But then Michael, the chief prince, came to my aid because I was detained. Now I have come to tell you that victory is at hand. Hold onto your faith, and you will be satisfied, bringing glory to your Lord, Jehovah God, His only son Jesus, and pleasing the eternal Spirit of God.'"

"I was pale white when I got up from the ground back in my den," Sue shared, her voice filled with awe and wonder. The memory of that powerful encounter still sent shivers down her spine. "I had to force myself to breathe because I had no breath. After that, I knew without a shadow of a doubt that everything was going to be okay. I knew God had taken care of it all."

Sue's excitement was contagious as she couldn't contain her joy. "Next thing I know, Pastor Bruce is telling me this great news of Penkowski being taken away by the police! Praise the Lord! God is so good and so faithful," she exclaimed, her words filled with gratitude and praise.

Virginia, filled with newfound hope, couldn't contain her eagerness to share her own story. Ignoring the nagging voice of doubt, she raised her hand and made her way to the front of the church. Pastor Bruce, brimming with excitement, welcomed her warmly, grateful that their visit had made an impact.

"Hello, Madam Mayoress," exclaimed Pastor Bruce, his enthusiasm shining through. "So glad to have you here. Would you like to share?"

Virginia's voice trembled slightly as she began to speak, her heart racing with anticipation. "I wanted to thank you and Reverend Wayne for stopping by the other day and asking if there was anything you could pray for me," she started slowly, her voice filled with both vulnerability and gratitude. The congregation leaned in, captivated by her words.

"I have been feeling very low lately... I have been diagnosed with cancer," she revealed, and a wave of sorrow washed over the congregation. However, Virginia's smile began to light up her face, perplexing those who couldn't understand her reaction in the face of such devastating news.

"Reverend Bruce and Reverend Wayne came to my home," she continued, her voice quivering with emotion. Her eyes met Bruce's, and his smile offered her comfort and encouragement. "They were a Godsend, angels sent at just the right time... Oh, how I needed someone to talk to, someone who could share hope with me in the depths of my despair."

Virginia's emotions overwhelmed her, and Sue approached her, offering support and understanding. The two embraced, and Virginia regained her composure to share the miraculous turn of events.

"I shared with him the most personal thing: my impending death in two months," she revealed, tears streaming down her face. "And they... they prayed for me, for God to heal me, and... well... He did... He did! He healed me! I got my test results back after the pastors prayed for me, and the test showed that... I am completely clear of cancer! It's gone! Oh, thank you, Reverend Bruce! Thank you Reverend Wayne!" She rushed over to Bruce and Wayne, embracing them tightly. "Thank you for your prayers, thank you that God heard you and answered you... thank you."

The room erupted in excitement, applause echoing throughout. It was a moment of pure joy, another opportunity to praise and give thanks to their loving and faithful God.

As the cheers and applause subsided, Virginia, with a grateful heart, expressed her desire for everyone to pray for her husband, the Mayor of Stapleton. She longed for him to share in this happy occasion, to be part of a church community once again. With a touch of nostalgia, she remarked, "I miss going to church. It is good to be back."

Pastor Bruce led the congregation in a unified prayer, each person finding a place to kneel and lift their voices in intercession for Mayor Tomas. The sanctuary reverberated with heartfelt petitions and thanksgiving, a powerful moment of unity and faith.

At the AFT facility, the atmosphere was eerily quiet, with the power still not restored even long after Penkowski's removal. The once bustling workplace now lay dormant, its machinery silent and lifeless. It became increasingly apparent to the remaining workers that the prosperity they had enjoyed was abruptly snuffed out, leaving behind only shattered lives in its wake. A sense of disillusionment hung heavy in the air.

Unable to find similar opportunities within Stapleton, many of the factory workers decided to leave, seeking employment and stability in larger cities. Though deeply rooted in their hometown, they believed that escaping the problems was their best chance for a fresh start.

The AFT building, once a symbol of hope and economic growth, now stood vacant, a haunting reminder of what had been lost. From inside his car, a man gazed out the window, his eyes fixed on the motionless structure. The weight of disappointment settled upon him as he reflected on the shattered dreams and the bright future that once seemed within reach for him and the entire community of Stapleton.

With a heavy heart, the man slowly drove away, his destination set for city hall. Parking in a reserved spot, he stepped out of the car, his demeanor solemn and contemplative. As he entered through the front doors, his head hung low, his thoughts consumed by the burden of the situation.

"Good morning, Mayor Thomas," greeted the receptionist with a warm smile.

"There's nothing good about this morning," the mayor responded, his voice tinged with sorrow, as he closed the door behind him.

In his office, Mayor Thomas sank into his chair, feeling the weight of the world upon his shoulders. His gaze fell upon the local newspaper, carefully placed on his desk by his diligent secretary.

The headline caught his attention: "Mayor Thomas calms crowds amidst conflicting views of AFT manufacturing, now defunct." The mayor's mood didn't improve as he continued reading. The article dismissed the opposition's claim of ousting AFT, attributing its downfall to the nefarious actions of its owner,

Dr. Kenneth Penkowski. The state of California had convicted him on various charges, ranging from money laundering and illegal gambling to multiple counts of malpractice, including the illegal use and disposal of human fetuses.

Penkowski had been escorted from his local manufacturing plant, AFT, with witnesses claiming he endured an extended electrical shock from the police. The authorities were puzzled by his ability to withstand such punishment without losing consciousness or perishing.

The mayor's thoughts drifted, contemplating how something that seemed so promising for the people of Stapleton had turned into a catastrophe. The allure of good income, newfound freedom, and a departure from traditional religious practices advocated by the African American pastor had initially captivated him. He reminisced about Pastor Bruce's persistent picket lines and demonstrations, causing disruption and aggravation in the community, only to end up in the hospital. In Mayor Thomas's mind, it served him right.

A pang of nostalgia washed over him as he reflected on the days when life was simpler, under the guidance of Reverend Stone and his church. But his reminiscence was interrupted by the unsettling revelation from his wife—that she had been healed by the troublemaker, Pastor Bruce Hutchinson. The mayor's thoughts wandered to a recurring dream, where his wife waved goodbye, vanishing into a church, possibly Pastor Hutchinson's church. His eyes widened, and visions of hell flooded his mind, despite his previous efforts to suppress them. Fear gripped him, causing his once confident demeanor to crumble, reducing him to a frightened child cowering in a corner.

"If this man could heal by God's power," the Mayor thought, his mind consumed by a whirlwind of disturbing thoughts. He contemplated the devastating earthquake that had struck Stapleton on the night of their prayer meeting, the tornado that razed the church belonging to the man who had shut down Pastor Bruce's church, and the tragic fire that claimed the lives of Reverend Stone and his congregation during their tent service. The vision of hell loomed before him, refusing to fade from his mind's eye. Beads of sweat formed on his forehead as he desperately tried to shake off the disturbing images.

In a futile attempt to clear his mind, the Mayor shook his head and anxiously wrung his clammy hands. But the thoughts continued to flood his consciousness, one after another, relentlessly. The liquor stores had vanished, the abortion clinics had closed, and the once-disruptive school disturbances were no more. Children transformed school halls into spaces of worship and Bible study, not only in the schools but also in businesses throughout the community. Even the jail sat empty, its vacancy a testament to the transformative power of the revival. Try as he might, the Mayor couldn't escape these thoughts that haunted him.

"No... stop!" he exclaimed aloud, his words falling on deaf ears. Each thought intensified the vividness of his vision, his impending damnation. His eyes squeezed shut, his temples throbbing as he pressed his hands against them with all his might. His face turned crimson from the exertion, yet he persisted. Deep within, he yearned to see the name of the church that condemned him to eternal torment before he stepped foot inside.

Through the grip of paralyzing fear, with eyes clenched tightly, he finally looked up, and there it was—clear as day—the name of the church from his vision: Reverend Stone's church. A horrified scream escaped his lips as he bore witness to this chilling revelation.

The sudden intrusion of his secretary jolted him from his distressing thoughts. She burst into the room, her face etched with concern. Mayor Thomas appeared visibly unwell, his complexion pallid and his face drenched in sweat. He stumbled to his feet, desperately clinging to his desk for support, his chest heaving, but words eluding him. Fear was etched deeply into every line on his face as he gazed at his secretary.

"I'll call an ambulance!" she cried out, rushing to his side and frantically dialing the emergency number.

Mayor Thomas struggled to maintain his balance, leaning against the desk, gasping for breath, his inability to articulate his distress rendering him silent except for occasional grunts. The wail of an ambulance siren pierced the air as the vehicle swiftly arrived. The paramedics promptly attended to the Mayor, attaching wires and IVs. Their urgent actions were a testament to the severity of his condition.

"Is he going to be okay?" the secretary inquired, her voice laced with concern.

"He's having a severe heart attack. It's touch and go," the paramedics responded in a frenzied manner, diligently working to stabilize him.

With great care, they transported him into the back of the ambulance, their urgent mission to rush him to the hospital, where his life would hang in the balance.

The Mayor lay motionless on the operating table in the hospital's Emergency Room, his unconscious form a stark contrast against the bustling medical personnel surrounding him. The heart monitor displayed a chaotic pattern, reflecting the desperate struggle within his body. People in scrubs hurriedly moved about, their voices filled with urgency, until suddenly, a piercing, continuous beep drowned out all other sounds. The monitor's flatline sent a wave of panic through the room.

"Clear!" shouted the doctor, his voice laced with determination, as he applied an electric shock to Mayor Thomas' chest. In response, the Mayor's body jolted off the table, momentarily suspended in the air before forcefully crashing back down. All eyes turned to the monitor, hoping for signs of life, yet the line remained stubbornly flat.

An ethereal light beckoned the Mayor, its brightness gentle and inviting. As he gravitated toward it, he felt an indescribable pull, but he resisted, acutely aware that reaching the light would diminish his chances of returning to the earthly realm and mending the wrongs he had committed. Tremendous perspiration poured from his brow, his fear escalating to unimaginable levels. The closer he ventured toward the light, the more his trepidation intensified. Immersed within its radiance, he beheld a sight that no mortal could gaze upon and survive—the glorious countenance of God Himself.

Overwhelmed by the intensity, the Mayor screamed in agonizing pain, averting his gaze. His heart sank as his life unfolded before him in a rapid succession of images, each one evoking the accompanying emotions he had experienced. The first lie, the initial profane word, the earliest immoral thought—all resurfaced with vivid clarity. He witnessed his first encounter with the teachings of Jesus Christ and his subsequent rejection of salvation. The images whirled faster, evoking a torrent of regret, shame, and a profound sense of unworthiness that steadily intensified until it became unbearable.

"Ah!" he cried out, hoping to alleviate the torment, only to find himself immersed in an even deeper anguish. The images continued to surge, approaching the present day, rekindling memories of his involvement with AFT and the lives ruined by the company. He confronted the realization of his failure to govern with fairness and integrity, as the sting of greed and self-interest pierced his conscience.

Suddenly, the ground beneath him vanished, and the Mayor plummeted through the abyss, hurtling downward at an accelerated pace. The once-glowing light faded into obscurity, replaced by a noxious atmosphere, searing heat, and agonizing screams reverberating through the air. With each passing moment, the intensity of his torment amplified. Every organ within him throbbed with excruciating pain, as if stabbed by a thousand knives. His dry eyes refused to produce tears, his ears distorted by the clamor exceeding any rock concert he had ever attended, and his tongue felt like a parched desert, barely capable of muttering what he believed to be his final comprehensible words:

"What about grace..."

In an instant, Mayor Thomas's eyes fluttered open, his gaze met by the sights of the Emergency Room. The voice of relief reverberated through the room as someone exclaimed, "We have a heartbeat!"

"Pastor Bruce!" The urgency in Virginia's voice caught Bruce's attention as he answered the phone, momentarily surprised by the use of the title "Pastor" instead of "Reverend" as before.

"Yes? Is everything alright?" Concern laced Bruce's words as he sensed the distress in Virginia's tone.

"No! My husband has been rushed to the hospital. He just suffered a severe heart attack. Could you pray... could you please come as well? I'm at a loss of what to do," Virginia pleaded, her voice trembling with anxiety.

"Take a deep breath. Everything is going to be alright. I will pray for him as I make my way to the hospital. I'm leaving right now," Bruce assured her, his voice filled with compassion and determination.

Bruce was on his way to the hospital, his heart heavy with concern and fervent prayers for the Mayor's well-being. As he drove, his gaze caught sight of newly painted swastikas, symbols of hate and bigotry, gradually fading away as he passed by. A sense of relief washed over him, a small victory against the darkness that had plagued their town. His spirits lifted momentarily, even as his prayers intensified for the Mayor's recovery.

Upon arriving at the hospital, Bruce swiftly maneuvered into the reserved parking for clergy, his footsteps quickening as he made his way to the bustling emergency room. The charge nurse recognized him and led him directly to the Mayor's room, where medical staff continued their frantic efforts, though the monitor displayed an almost normal heartbeat. Bruce approached Virginia and offered her a comforting embrace, their shared concern etched on their faces as they stood together beside Mayor Thomas.

"He's been asking for you, Pastor, ever since he regained consciousness," the charge nurse informed Bruce, her voice filled with a mix of hope and gratitude.

Bruce was taken aback by the Mayor's request, leaning closer to him with eyes filled with compassion and understanding. As their hands clasped, Mayor Thomas smiled, expressing gratitude for Bruce's presence.

"It's my pleasure. Shh, you need to rest," Bruce replied softly, his eyes darting to the medical staff to ensure he wasn't disturbing their patient. Their smiles reassured him, many of them familiar faces from the Tuesday night prayer meetings.

Desperation filled the Mayor's raspy voice as he whispered to Bruce, expressing his desire for salvation, an urgent plea to escape the torment he had experienced.

"What do I need to do to be saved, Pastor? I don't want to go to hell again!" Mayor Thomas's words were fraught with fear and an overwhelming sense of urgency.

Bruce exchanged a puzzled glance with Virginia, trying to make sense of the Mayor's words. Virginia tearfully explained that the doctor had declared his heart had stopped, rendering him clinically dead.

"Pastor, please, I want to be saved. I don't ever want to go back to that place!" Mayor Thomas pleaded, his desperation mirroring someone being dragged away against their will.

Bruce nodded solemnly, realizing the gravity of the moment. He knew he had to act swiftly, guiding the Mayor in a heartfelt prayer of repentance and surrender to Jesus Christ. Moved by the intensity of the moment, Virginia, too, placed her faith and trust in the Savior.

Tears mingled with relief as the room filled with an atmosphere of hope and transformation. The weight of their salvation journey had begun, and Bruce knew that this pivotal moment would forever change the trajectory of their lives.

In his cramped cell, Penkowski was visited by a constant stream of lawyers throughout the day. They spoke with confidence about the intricacies of litigation, assuring their client that he would soon be set free. Yet, beneath their confident facade, a sense of uncertainty lingered. Penkowski, in the midst of these legal discussions, anxiously made phone calls to check on the state of his company, Advanced Medical.

The news was grim. The closure of the two AFT manufacturing plants had sent shockwaves throughout Advanced Medical, impacting the entire company. Orders remained unfulfilled, customers were abandoning ship, and financial constraints prevented the payment of bills. The repercussions reached beyond the realm of regular business operations. Abortion clinics struggled without the necessary equipment, facing difficulties in the removal of fetuses. The fees for removal went unpaid, exacerbating the mounting problems. Even worse, Penkowski now faced calls from unsavory individuals associated with his illegal operations, those who had always relied on him for funds. With the sudden financial crisis, these criminal elements were becoming increasingly restless.

Fueled by frustration and anger, Penkowski sat in his cell, indulging in the rituals and ceremonies that had accompanied him for years. He chanted, focusing his rage on the town that he believed was responsible for his downfall: Stapleton. In his prayers, he cursed each prominent figure in that town, his eyes occasionally opening to reveal an eerie glow that disturbed the guards who watched over him.

Allowed to watch TV during designated hours, Penkowski eagerly monitored news channels, both local and national, searching for any information related to his crumbling empire. It didn't take long for him to find what he sought: a sensational story about the rapid decline of the world's leading medical company, led by its imprisoned president and owner, now facing 23 counts of malpractice and other criminal charges.

Penkowski struggled to contain his fury, his grip tightening on the table before him. With an unnatural strength that surpassed the table's capacity, he squeezed, causing it to splinter and break. The guards, ever watchful, grew increasingly intimidated by the man's supernatural power and his unsettling, fiery gaze. The aura of danger surrounding Penkowski became crushing, unsettling those tasked with his confinement.

"I can't believe I'm going back to California. It feels like I was just there," John exclaimed as he boarded the plane alongside George, Elizabeth, and Pastor Bruce. The mixture of anticipation and anxiety filled the air as they settled into their seats, preparing for the journey ahead.

Elizabeth sensed the need to clarify the upcoming proceedings. "This is just the preliminary hearings. The Burden of Proof will lie on the state of California, specifically the Attorney General," she explained, noticing a few puzzled expressions. Determined to ensure everyone understood, she continued, "In legal terms, the Burden of Proof refers to the responsibility of proving a fact or facts in dispute during a lawsuit. It determines which side must establish certain points. They will call us as witnesses and question John extensively on the stand, utilizing the evidence he has compiled."

"There will be a jury," Elizabeth confirmed. "The court will ensure the selection of an impartial jury. The Attorney General has been working on this case for years but lacked the expert evidence necessary. John's background as a detective will make him a valuable expert witness."

As the plane's engines whined, the group found themselves fully onboard, ready for departure. The aircraft taxied down the runway, steadily gaining speed. Bruce gazed out of the window, his eyes fixed on the shrinking view of Stapleton below. It appeared so small from above, a realization that never failed to astonish him whenever he flew. In that moment, he contemplated how this tiny town must appear in the eyes of God. Though small in size, Stapleton held immeasurable worth, having been graced with the presence, glory, and divine works of God. A smile tugged at

Bruce's lips as he silently offered a prayer of gratitude, acknowledging all that God had accomplished in their midst. His thoughts then shifted to the upcoming trial, prompting him to pray fervently, seeking guidance for each step of the process. He understood that by asking the right questions, his prayers could become more aligned with the specific needs of the trial.

Pastor Wayne, Sue and Maggie, alongside other dedicated individuals in the community, tirelessly worked to advance the ministry. The prayer walks had multiplied, and nearly every household on every street eagerly attended the Tuesday night prayer meetings. Business establishments throughout the city hosted prayer groups and Bible studies, from small mom-and-pop stores to gas stations and even industrial manufacturing plants.

Principal Benton at the schools could hardly contain his excitement as the Ten Commandments were reinstated on the classroom walls, lovingly placed there by parents from all walks of life. Bible study groups resurfaced and their numbers doubled. The students were once again filled with joy, and the divisions among different social groups dissolved. Friendships blossomed among the strong and weak, the rich and poor, and the color of one's skin was no longer a barrier.

Fundraisers were held in the schools not only to support various activities but also to contribute to local charities. The Salvation Army received an overwhelming amount of donated items, many of which had never been used before.

Those living in the least expensive homes experienced an unexpected influx of visitors. George had been overseeing home renovations in the community, and in his absence, the community members took it upon themselves to continue making a difference. Houses in desperate need of painting were given fresh coats, new flowers were planted, mailboxes were replaced, brick homes were pressure-cleaned, and lawns were beautifully manicured. The previously dilapidated houses now outshone the rest on the block, much to the delight of the homeowners. Some who had not previously attended the Tuesday night prayer meetings or any church at all were inspired to come, eagerly anticipating the chance to meet others like those who had generously given them this incredible gift.

The widows in the community received personalized visits, along with financial assistance checks aimed at alleviating any outstanding debts they may have been facing. Food was purchased for them, and general maintenance was performed throughout their homes.

The jails were once again empty, as the former employees of AFT had left the city. The Tuesday night prayer meeting had gained such widespread participation that only a few individuals remained unaware or were physically unable to attend.

The influx of prayer requests, praises, and thanksgivings via email became so overwhelming that ten individuals were required to read and respond to each request around the clock. Testimonies poured in, with people sharing stories of being healed from long-standing illnesses. Many spoke of friends and neighbors accepting Jesus into their lives, breaking free from addictions and bondages. They marveled at how their desires for substances like tobacco, alcohol, and drugs had completely vanished after receiving prayer from a neighbor during their walks around the neighborhood. Chains were broken, whether they were related to excessive credit card debt, overeating, or any other form of addiction.

Without a doubt, God's presence was once again tangible in this community, and the people joyfully reaped the benefits, continually glorifying their God on a daily basis.

Virginia and Mayor Thomas were finally back home. The Mayor had undergone two operations during his hospital stay – one on his physical heart and another on his spiritual heart. The transformation within him was evident, and he could sense the difference.

As he lay in bed, a rare sense of peace washed over him. It was a feeling he hadn't experienced in a very long time. He believed deep in his soul that everything was going to be alright. The fact that he had briefly died during his ordeal no longer troubled him. The troubles he once had with AFT, the threat of demonstrations, and the lack of funds to revitalize Stapleton seemed insignificant now. His focus had shifted to the people in his community and how he could positively impact their lives. The weight of the harm caused by AFT stirred a genuine desire within him to make amends and bring about positive change. As he contemplated his upcoming reelection, he wondered if the community could forgive him for the past, knowing that God had already forgiven him. Only time would reveal the answer, but in that moment, he was committed to serving the people's interests and making a difference in their lives. These thoughts brought him even greater peace.

"Honey, how do you feel?" Virginia asked, entering the bedroom.

Mayor Thomas turned his gaze away from the window, his eyes twinkling and a gentle smile playing on his lips. He replied, "I have never felt better."

Elizabeth, John, George, and Bruce, stepped off the plane, their anticipation palpable in the air. They were immediately greeted by a sleek black limousine with tinted windows, exuding an aura of secrecy and importance. The door swung open, revealing a man dressed in a dark suit and sporting dark sunglasses.

He extended his hand towards Elizabeth, his presence exuding confidence. "You must be Elizabeth," he said with a firm voice.

Elizabeth, maintaining her composure, shook his hand and replied, "Yes."

"Attorney General Stan Robinson," he introduced himself, his tone leaving no room for doubt.

Elizabeth greeted him with a polite smile. "Nice to meet you," she said, acknowledging the weight of his position.

As each member of the group was introduced, Attorney General Robinson shook their hands, showing a professional courtesy and genuine interest in their presence. His smile and nod conveyed a sense of welcome and camaraderie.

"I have made arrangements for your stay. First, we will go to the office to discuss the preliminary matters. My team and I will review the evidence you have provided, and based on that, we'll determine the best course of action. Elizabeth, I will be spending more time with you, going over the legal process in detail to ensure we don't overlook anything. I believe in the power of collaboration; two heads are better than one," Attorney General Robinson explained, emphasizing his collaborative approach.

Elizabeth nodded in agreement, appreciating his thoroughness and dedication to their case. With a sense of unity and purpose, they all entered the luxurious limousine, ready to embark on the next phase of their journey. The vehicle smoothly glided through the city streets, carrying them towards the office where they would delve into the intricacies of the legal process.

Mr. Robinson sat across from the men, positioned next to Elizabeth, his eyes focused on her with a mix of curiosity and admiration. He leaned in slightly and asked, "Tell me, Elizabeth, how did you become involved in all this when your law offices are not located in Stapleton or even California, for that matter?"

Elizabeth took a moment to collect her thoughts, her gaze drifting briefly as memories resurfaced. "My brother..." she began, her voice carrying a hint of emotion, "John Ivan. He reached out to me, informing me about this case and how it had put his life and the lives of his friends in jeopardy."

Mr. Robinson's brows furrowed, a mixture of concern and intrigue evident in his expression as he glanced towards the other men. "These gentlemen," he acknowledged, his gaze shifting from John to the rest of the group.

Elizabeth nodded in affirmation, grateful for their presence and unity. "Yes," she confirmed, her voice filled with a mix of admiration and gratitude.

"Penkowski is a very dangerous man," Mr. Robinson affirmed, his tone tinged with gravity. "Even working for him puts your life at risk. But to go against him... I must commend all of you for the incredible courage it took to take that step. We have lost men in the past who were gathering information far less damning than what you have brought forward."

John's confidence radiated as he spoke up, conviction evident in his voice. "He will be put away for life," he asserted.

A smile played on Mr. Robinson's lips, a glimmer of satisfaction shining in his eyes. "Yes, Mr. Ivan, I believe you are absolutely right. We now possess more substantial evidence than we have ever had before, thanks to all of you," he acknowledged, his voice laced with genuine appreciation.

George couldn't help but let out a smile, infectious joy spreading throughout the limousine. In that moment, a sense of triumph and camaraderie permeated the atmosphere, bolstering their resolve for the arduous battle that lay ahead.

The limousine glided towards the imposing government building, its grandeur accentuated by the security detail awaiting their arrival. As the group stepped out of the vehicle, the presence of bodyguards served as a stark reminder of the gravity of the situation.

"We can't take any chances," Mr. Robinson asserted, his voice filled with a sense of caution. The expressions on everyone's faces shifted, transitioning from excitement to trepidation. The glamorous image of a sunny California beach vacation was quickly replaced by the realization of the arduous and high-stakes nature of the trial they were about to face.

Nevertheless, the thought of dismantling an industry giant that had amassed billions through the profits of the abortion industry spurred a sense of determination within them. They understood that their efforts would have a far-reaching impact, transcending the boundaries of a mere picket line. The magnitude of the task at hand overshadowed any desire for leisurely beach days.

Leading up to the trial, the attorneys delved deep into a labyrinth of scenarios, meticulously examining documentation, accounting books, and the intricate laws governing the medical and abortion industries. They uncovered a web of illegal activities, from gambling and money laundering to unscrupulous fees and concealed malpractice suits. Each revelation further fueled their resolve to ensure that Penkowski would be held accountable and his company permanently shut down.

Throughout this process, Elizabeth found herself increasingly drawn to Mr. Robinson's presence. There was a sweet spirit about him, an unwavering dedication to ensuring justice prevailed. As they worked side by side, their connection grew, and Elizabeth couldn't help but wonder about his faith.

"Do you attend church anywhere?" she asked, her boldness tinged with curiosity.

Mr. Robinson looked up, a warm smile playing on his lips. "I do," he replied, his response evoking a reciprocal smile from Elizabeth. Their conversation continued over dinner that evening, and Elizabeth marveled at the way God was orchestrating not only the trial but also the unfolding of her personal life.

TWENTY FIVE

"Please rise for the honorable Judge Leonard Stepson," the bailiff's voice resonated through the room. With a collective rising, everyone stood, their gazes shifting to the angry figure on the other side of the room, clad in handcuffs and flanked by two lawyers. Among the onlookers were four individuals, their nerves tightly wound, their hearts burdened with the memories of life-threatening encounters with the man now on trial. Anticipating this day, they yearned for its conclusion, yet dread clung to them like a suffocating fog. Even in custody, the menacing presence exuded by Penkowski cast an ominous shadow, penetrating the depths of their beings from the distant recesses of the room. As far as they knew, Penkowski did not recognize them as he entered the courtroom.

The atmosphere was suffused with official solemnity, adorned with government emblems and an American flag standing proudly in the corner. Judge Leonard Stepson, adorned in a black robe with his distinguished gray hair, emanated an intimidating aura. The bailiff announced his presence, and the room hushed in response.

Attorney General Stan Robinson, accompanied by two additional lawyers, stood on the opposite side of the courtroom. His professional demeanor exuded unwavering determination, the culmination of a long-awaited moment finally realized. The weight of anticipation hung in the air, as all eyes turned to the judge.

"Mr. Robinson?" Judge Stepson addressed the attorney general.

"Yes, your honor?" Stan Robinson responded, his voice filled with respect.

"Please make the first opening statement," the judge requested.

"Thank you, your honor," Robinson acknowledged, stepping forward to address the jury.

The jury consisted of a diverse group, both men and women, seemingly representing the working class with their blue-collar attire. Having undergone the rigorous screening process, they were believed to possess the impartiality required for a fair decision.

"Ladies and gentlemen of the jury, what you are about to hear will shock some of you," Robinson began, his tone grave. "For others, it will awaken you to the cruel reality of what people will do to amass wealth, prestige, and fame. It is disheartening to shed light on the heinous acts committed in darkness, but to render judgment, one must confront the full extent of the facts, no matter how gruesome, disgusting, or detestable they may be."

He paused, allowing the weight of his words to sink in, his eyes searching the faces of the jury.

"Remember, as you listen, you will encounter medical and business jargon cleverly employed to conceal immoral, unethical, and illegal activities. Do not allow anyone in this court to rationalize what is right and wrong, what is legal and illegal. If you believe in your heart that it is wrong, that it has caused harm to another individual, that it is a crime against humanity, then let your judgment reflect that truth."

He emphasized each word, his conviction seeping into the minds of the jury members.

"You will not lack evidence in this case. In fact, the evidence presented will be irrefutable. However, be prepared to navigate through confusing terms and emotionally charged narratives designed to distract you from the true issue at hand: whether the man seated in the judgment seat today is innocent or guilty. Thank you."

Penkowski's anger continued to smolder, his gaze fixated on Stan Robinson. If looks could kill, the attorney general would have met his demise a hundred times over. Despite his lawyers' efforts to contain him, they realized their main concern was preventing him from erupting in the courtroom. Observing John's smile, George felt a surge of confidence, a glimmer of hope that this trial would finally rid their lives of this menacing figure. Returning the smile, George silently conveyed his shared determination.

"Mr. Taylor?" the judge called out.

"Yes, your honor?" Mr. Taylor, the lawyer representing Penkowski, replied.

"Please make your opening statement."

With a confident air, the lawyer for Penkowski, impeccably dressed in a dark suit and power tie, rose from his seat. His tone was smooth yet charged with a hint of skepticism as he addressed the jury.

"Ladies and gentlemen of the jury, as you can see, the prosecuting attorney is smooth. Very smooth. You will witness no mistakes from him in this case. Every word has been rehearsed, and his objective is simple: to prosecute, regardless of the truth. Let me make it clear that the truth is not the focal point for him in this trial."

"But for the opposing side, prosecution lies at the heart of this trial. The Attorney General has been relentlessly searching for years to find something that would put my client, a respected medical doctor and owner of the leading medical company in America, behind bars. Why? Mostly, I believe it stems from jealousy. Jealousy that my client, a successful doctor, is more accomplished, affluent, and esteemed in his industry than the prosecuting attorney is in his."

"I believe his bias against the abortion industry in general has clouded his ability to fairly judge this case. As a member of an evangelical church, his disdain for this thriving and life-saving industry is apparent."

Bruce and George exchanged glances, their smiles fading slightly as concerns about the potential impact on Mr. Robinson's credibility with the jury arose in their minds.

"It is also evident that my client's business approach, which includes providing leisure activities and additional perks to his employees, though perfectly legal, does not align with the standards of the very church the Attorney General attends. These practices are frowned upon."

"Lastly, you will come across evidence that may seem suspect at first glance. However, as with everything in life, one should not judge a book by its cover. A discerning eye will reveal that there is no wrongdoing. Thank you."

"The court will adjourn. We will reconvene at 8:00 AM sharp tomorrow."

As everyone stood up, Penkowski turned and glared at the audience. Spotting George, he made an aggressive lunge forward, but his lawyers swiftly intervened, gripping his handcuffed hands and whispering fervently into his ear, urging him to comply.

George stood frozen, a wave of fear washing over him. John immediately grasped his arm, pulling him away from the menacing presence of Penkowski. "Come on, buddy," John reassured him. "It's going to be just fine." George looked at John, his face mirroring the vulnerability and unease he had felt during their initial encounter with Penkowski. This time, George had no disguise to shield himself, leaving him exposed and defenseless. Reluctantly, he followed the others out of the courtroom.

"An evangelical church! Did you hear that? I had no idea," Bruce exclaimed, his enthusiasm evident.

"Why didn't he tell us? He knew I am a pastor," Bruce questioned, a hint of disappointment in his voice.

"Calm down, folks," John interjected, attempting to pacify the growing concern. "I'm sure he wants to ensure that the facts and figures remain objective and unbiased. He doesn't want anything to cloud the case."

"I knew," Elizabeth admitted shyly, speaking up among the group.

"You did? Why didn't you tell us?" Bruce inquired, his tone polite yet curious.

"I, too, wanted to avoid any chance of bias. The jury can see right through that kind of stuff, and I don't want anything to jeopardize our opportunity to bring justice against this man who has personally harmed each of us and countless innocent people... including babies," Elizabeth explained, her lawyer instincts shining through.

They stepped out onto the outdoor steps, their gazes drawn to a car surrounded by policemen. Penkowski was being placed in the back of the vehicle, his attention not directed toward them. Relief washed over each of the four individuals, grateful that Penkowski had not noticed their presence.

As they turned around, they were greeted by Attorney General Stan Robinson, a wide smile adorning his face. Anticipating his thoughts on the proceedings, they eagerly awaited his assessment.

"Let's go to my office, and I'll share what my attorneys and I found promising about today," Stan suggested, his voice filled with optimism.

They pushed open the grand doors, stepping once more into the office where they had gathered for countless meetings in preparation for this momentous day. The group settled down in the expansive boardroom, their anticipation undeniable as they awaited Mr. Robinson's remarks.

"I must say that today went... well... different, but well," Mr. Robinson began, taking his seat alongside his team of lawyers. He looked at the expectant faces before him, sensing the question they all had in their minds. Anticipating their thoughts, he addressed their curiosity directly.

"About six years ago, I gave my life to Christ. My colleagues have been Christians since childhood," Mr. Robinson revealed, his voice carrying a mix of emotion and sincerity. "As Elizabeth may have already shared with you, I wanted each of you to answer the questions my lawyers and I had objectively, and you have. So, I feel comfortable sharing this fact about me and my colleagues with all of you. I had every intention of revealing it after this morning's hearing. I didn't anticipate it coming up sooner, or I would have told you beforehand. I am even more excited about... how... God has answered my prayers that I've been lifting up for years." His voice quivered slightly, revealing the depth of his gratitude.

"To have a pastor on my side in this trial, a pastor who initiated what I believe to be the first revival this country has seen in hundreds of years... wow," Mr. Robinson expressed, visibly taken aback by the profound significance of their presence.

Bruce offered a humble smile, acknowledging that the glory belonged to God and not him.

"Elizabeth has shared with me everything you all have been through, in addition to what you've shared for the trial. It's truly incredible. Though the media may not cover the remarkable events unfolding in your community, there are occasional slip-ups, and I find myself sitting there, amazed, wishing I could be a part of it," Mr. Robinson admitted, his smile fading.

"You are now," Bruce declared, catching Mr. Robinson's puzzled expression.

"The purpose of God's hand in this revival is not only to draw people closer to Him and bring His people together but, to the best of my knowledge, to bring an end to this dreadful industry that is destroying lives and denying babies the chance to live," Bruce passionately affirmed.

"I am one of those lives," Elizabeth unexpectedly revealed, sharing her personal connection to the cause. Although unintended, her disclosure deepened the sense of personal investment in their mission.

Mr. Robinson's smile vanished, replaced by a visible anger etching itself onto his face. "I despise the fact that people have been harmed by those whose sole interest is making money. I detest how they try to hide behind legal loopholes and act smug about getting away with... murder. I abhor the shattered lives left in the wake of this industry. I promise each and every one of you whose lives are endangered today because of this monster, Penkowski, he will be put away... for life."

One of the other lawyers interjected, "Mr. Robinson has received numerous death threats and narrowly escaped multiple attempts on his life. So, he is not just speaking to each of you but also to himself."

"Nothing compared to what these people have endured," Mr. Robinson deflected, shifting the focus away from himself. "The priority here is simple: convict Penkowski of the crimes he has committed and, in doing so, restore each one of your lives, allowing you to live freely as American citizens should... as God has promised in His Word."

They delved deeper into their discussions, examining what went well, what caused concern, and revisiting everything they had tirelessly worked on throughout the week.

"Pastor Bruce, would you pray for our success?" Mr. Robinson requested as they concluded their day's work.

"I would be honored to," Bruce responded and begin the prayer. A sense of peace enveloped every soul present, and the victory had already been won even before the battle had truly commenced.

"Yes?" Virginia answered the door to her home. It was the mailman, and he had two large bins of mail.

"I can't place this in your mailbox," he said, a warm smile gracing his lips.

Virginia's face illuminated with delightful surprise as she swung the door open, inviting the mailman, Norman, inside.

"Thanks, Norman," she said gratefully.

"You're welcome, Mrs. Thomas. I will pick up the bins tomorrow."

Virginia carefully carried each mail container one at a time into the mayor's bedroom. As the mayor turned to look at his wife, a surprised expression crossed his face.

"These... are all for you, my love," she said, her heart filled with warmth.

Mayor Thomas brightened up and patted his bed, inviting Virginia to place the tote on it. She sat down next to him as he began opening each letter.

Tears welled up in his eyes as he read through the heartfelt messages. After reading each one, he passed it to his wife, causing her eyes to well up with tears as well.

"Honey, these are from the people I thought were causing all the problems in town. I've complained about them and viewed them as a nuisance, and now... look at this... the kind words... the caring attitude..." His voice trailed off, overcome with emotion. "I don't deserve these. I've been a horrible mayor," he confessed, dropping his hands along with the letters onto the bed.

"That was then," she gently reassured him. "And this is now. How can you change that fact?"

"I can't go back and undo all the rotten stuff I've done," he lamented.

"No, but you can make a difference now and from now on. It's your choice," she encouraged him.

Mayor Thomas pondered for a moment, wrestling with his thoughts. Then he spoke with determination, "You're right! I can't change the past, but I can change the future. And... I will. I want to give these people the type of mayor they deserve."

As the mayor gazed out of the window, he let out a sigh.

"What is it, honey?" Virginia asked, concerned.

"How can I just change? I've been this way for years, and now I'm expected to change?" he questioned, wrestling with self-doubt.

Virginia seized the opportunity and replied, "Church has seemed to change people all over this city. Maybe you should start there." She waited, unsure of his response, hoping for a more favorable reaction this time.

The mayor looked at his wife with a whimsical expression, fully aware of what she was trying to convey. But then, he began to contemplate, thinking about Pastor Bruce and the transformation he had witnessed in the community, in people's lives, and even in his own life during his time in the hospital. The assurance of heaven and the freedom from fear of hell had deeply impacted him. Maybe, just maybe, church held the answer.

"Then I will start there. Will you join me?" he said, looking at his wife with a genuine smile.

"I would be most happy to!" she exclaimed, leaning over to hug her husband with excitement and joy.

The court resumed the following day, filled with anticipation and tension. Penkowski entered, his eyes immediately searching for George. However, the police officers accompanying him redirected his attention elsewhere.

"Please rise for the honorable Judge Leonard Stepson," the bailiff announced. Everyone stood as the judge took his place on the bench.

"Mr. Robinson, you may call your first witness," Judge Stepson instructed.

Mr. Robinson stood up and confidently said, "I would like to call John Ivan to the stand."

John walked to the witness stand, his gaze briefly meeting Penkowski's puzzled expression. This was the first time Penkowski had seen John without a disguise.

"Do you swear to tell the truth, the whole truth, and nothing but the truth, so help you God?" the bailiff asked as John placed his hand on the Bible.

"I do," John replied solemnly.

"You may be seated," the judge permitted.

John took his seat, bracing himself for the questions to come.

Mr. Robinson approached John with a serious expression on his face and began questioning him. "John, state for the record your line of work."

"I am a private investigator," John replied, his voice steady.

"And how long have you been in this line of work?" Mr. Robinson inquired.

"I have been in this line of work for nearly 15 years," John responded.

"And prior to that?" Mr. Robinson pressed further.

The defense attorney objected, interjecting, "Objection, we don't need to hear the man's whole life story."

"Your honor, my intention is simply to establish that this man is an expert witness," Mr. Robinson explained.

"Overruled," the judge ruled, allowing the line of questioning to continue.

"What did you do for the company prior to becoming a private investigator?" Mr. Robinson asked.

"I audited accounts and worked in search and inquiry, responsible for detecting security leaks that could endanger both the company and the military," John explained.

"So, you were essentially an 'investigator'?" Mr. Robinson clarified.

"Yes, that is correct," John affirmed.

"And you performed these investigative duties for ten years?" Mr. Robinson further probed.

"Correct. I worked as an investigator for ten years," John confirmed.

"So, all in all, you have been an investigator for 25 years," Mr. Robinson concluded.

"We get the point!" the defense attorney interrupted angrily. "Can we move on?"

Ignoring the outburst, Mr. Robinson turned back to John. "Tell me, Mr. Ivan, what brought you to Stapleton?"

"A company called 'The Association for Fetal Research' hired me," John replied.

The defense attorney objected once again, expressing his frustration. "Your honor, this is irrelevant!"

"Mr. Robinson, what is your point?" the judge inquired.

"Your honor, I am simply pointing out that John had previously investigated the wrongdoing of Advance Medical, Dr. Penkowski's company, before bringing the evidence to the State of California," Mr. Robinson explained.

"This has nothing to do with the case at hand," the judge ruled firmly. "Please move on, Mr. Robinson."

"Yes, your Honor," Mr. Robinson acquiesced. He then refocused his questions on John. "Mr. Ivan, the evidence presented in court today, did you secure it yourself?"

"Yes, I did," John confirmed.

"I would submit to the court and the jury that the documentation submitted by Mr. John Ivan provides evidence of money laundering, illegal gambling, and 23 counts of malpractice, including the illegal use and disposal of human fetuses," Mr. Robinson declared boldly.

"Mr. Ivan, please explain the documentation that has been submitted," Mr. Robinson prompted.

"There are accounting records that clearly show the source of funds for all illegal gambling activities. Bank records demonstrate the flow of these funds back into Advance Medical, making it appear as legitimate profit and concealing their illicit origin. Additionally, I possess documentation for 23 unresolved cases of malpractice, each indicating negligence on the part of Dr. Penkowski," John explained confidently.

Dr. Penkowski's anger grew intense as he glared at John, but John refused to meet his gaze. He had no desire to give Penkowski the satisfaction.

"No further questions, Your Honor," Mr. Robinson concluded,

taking his seat.

The defense attorney stood and approached John, his disdain evident in his tone. "Mr. Ivan," he began, "is it not true that prior to taking this case for The Association, your usual work involved mundane tasks such as spying on husbands or handling domestic disputes?"

John hesitated for a moment, knowing the line of questioning was designed to undermine his credibility. "Yes," he reluctantly admitted.

"Then why should we consider you an expert when it comes to investigative work?" the defense attorney pressed.

The prosecutor quickly objected, arguing, "Objection! The defense is attempting to discredit the witness's experience in investigative work."

The judge calmly intervened, saying, "Sustained."

Undeterred, the defense attorney continued his line of questioning. "Is it not true that you took this case for the prestige and financial gain it would bring?"

The prosecutor objected again, stating, "Objection, Your Honor! The defense is attempting to make unfounded assumptions."

Once more, the judge sided with the prosecution. "Sustained. Mr. Taylor, I recommend you move on from this line of questioning."

Mr. Taylor, the defense attorney, looked at the judge, attempting to conceal his anger but failing to do so entirely. "Your Honor, I am merely trying to highlight the lack of experience Mr. Ivan has, thereby proving that he is not an expert witness."

The prosecutor objected once again, and this time the judge firmly addressed Mr. Taylor. "An expert witness is determined by their time and experience, and Mr. Ivan has demonstrated both. Move on with your questioning, Mr. Taylor."

Undeterred, Mr. Taylor shifted his approach. "Mr. Ivan, is it not true that your sister, who supplied you with the information for this trial, holds a personal grudge against the abortion industry?"

Before John could respond, both the prosecutor and the judge objected simultaneously. The judge then announced, "I would like to see Mr. Taylor and Mr. Robinson, the prosecution, in my chambers."

The tension in the courtroom was tangible as the judge's decision left everyone speculating about the nature of the meeting and its potential impact on the trial.

It was Tuesday night, and the auditorium that had once seemed spacious now struggled to contain the massive crowd that had gathered. The air crackled with excitement, and restlessness permeated the atmosphere. Joe Benton, a regular attendee of Tuesday nights, was approached by Sue, who seemed unsure of what to do.

Pastor Wayne felt uneasy with the crowded auditorium and approached Joe Benton for guidance on what to do.

"Let's move everyone out to the football field. There should be plenty of room there," Joe suggested, trying to find a solution.

As the sea of people was redirected to the football field, the excitement only intensified. There was an electric sense of anticipation, and a surge of energy ran through the crowd. A stage was swiftly brought out from the sidelines, typically reserved for school events, and a sound system was quickly set up. People filled the bleachers, lined the sidelines, and filled the expanse of the football field. All were on edge, waiting for something momentous to unfold. Pastor Wayne stepped forward to the podium and began to speak.

"Folks, as most of you are aware pastor Bruce, George and others are currently in California. They will be testifying as witnesses in a court case against AFT and its owner for their illegal activities," Pastor Wayne announced, his voice carrying over the hushed crowd.

Silence fell over the gathering. Faces were devoid of smiles, words unspoken.

"We will pray for Dr. Penkowski, the owner of AFT, that God may work in his life during this trying time. I also ask that we continue to pray for our pastor and friends. May God perform His great and mighty work to bring an end to one of the most devastating industries our nation has ever known," Pastor Wayne continued, his words laced with hope and determination.

As Pastor Wayne surveyed the crowd, he spotted Mayor Thomas and his wife, Virginia, standing on the sidelines. With a sense of conviction, he turned towards them and spoke, "Mayor Thomas, it is an honor to have you and your lovely wife with us tonight. Would you please come forward and share a few words?"

Mayor Thomas was taken aback by the invitation. He had hoped to remain inconspicuous, knowing this group was opposed to AFT, and he had been publicly associated with them. But then he thought of the countless letters he had received from these very individuals. A smile formed on his face as he squeezed his wife's hand, and he stepped forward. This was his opportunity to express his gratitude.

The microphone was handed to the Mayor, and he began to speak, his voice filled with a mixture of gratitude and emotion. "Thank you," he said, taking a moment to compose himself.

"I want to take this opportunity to express my deepest gratitude to each and every one of you for the overwhelming support and well-wishes I have received through all the cards and letters," the Mayor continued, his voice quivering with emotion. The crowd erupted into applause, and the Mayor struggled to regain his composure as tears welled up in his eyes.

As the applause subsided, the Mayor spoke again, his voice filled with remorse. "I don't deserve all the love you have shown me. I have been a terrible Mayor, putting my interests and agenda ahead of the well-being of the people of Stapleton. I have let you down, and for that, I am truly sorry."

A profound silence fell upon the football field, the weight of the Mayor's words hanging in the air.

"From this moment on," the Mayor continued, his voice filled with newfound determination, "I will listen to the people, I will serve the people, and I will love the people—each and every one of you—as you have shown your love for me. Together, with the guidance of God, we will make a positive impact and bring about meaningful change not only within our community, but also in the surrounding areas."

Thunderous applause and cheering erupted, filling the stadium with a resounding roar. The Mayor paused for a moment, allowing the wave of support to wash over him, before he spoke again. "My eyes have been opened. I now see what is truly happening in this community, and I can't believe I was so blind," he said, his voice filled with sincerity. More applause followed.

"To each of you, I solemnly promise to uphold the Judeo-Christian principles on which our country and its laws were founded," the Mayor declared, his words met with enthusiastic clapping. "I will champion religious freedoms that are unparalleled in any part of this country."

The applause swelled, and the Mayor, his smile genuine, expressed his gratitude. "Thank you for your forgiveness, your thoughts, and your prayers throughout my medical crisis."

With those final words, the Mayor took his seat, and the crowd erupted into a thunderous applause, cheering and celebrating his newfound commitment. Virginia, the Mayor's wife, placed her hand on his, her eyes filled with pride and love.

"Mr. Taylor, I am dismissing you from this case," the Judge stated firmly as he and Mr. Robinson stood in his chambers.

"You can't do that!" Taylor responded angrily, his frustration evident.

"I just did. I have had nothing but problems from you in the past, and I am not about to let it happen again. Please leave," the Judge commanded, his tone leaving no room for argument.

Taylor glanced at the Judge, knowing better than to say another word. He realized the severity of the situation and the potential consequences for his career. With his head hung low, he silently exited the chambers.

Returning to the courtroom, the Judge called Taylor's assistant to the bench and explained what had transpired. Mr. Millen agreed to follow the Judge's direction to prevent further complications. As he rejoined the proceedings, Penkowski leaned over and whispered in Mr. Millen's ear, his frustration evident.

"You may continue questioning the witness," the Judge directed Mr. Millen, bringing the focus back to the trial.

Standing up slowly, Mr. Millen approached the witness with caution, keenly aware of the consequences he could face if things went awry.

"Mr. Ivan," Mr. Millen began in a calm and respectful tone, "How did you acquire the evidence in question?"

"Through investigative means," John replied.

"Did you take it from my client?" Mr. Millen asked, his tone probing.

"I made copies," John responded.

"With his consent?" Mr. Millen pressed, hoping to undermine

the credibility of the evidence.

"Objection," the prosecution interjected. "Mr. Ivan is a professional investigator who adheres to a code of ethics."

"Sustained," the Judge ruled, supporting the objection and disallowing the question.

Mr. Millen shifted gears, attempting a different approach. "Tell me, Mr. Ivan, why would a multibillion-dollar company like Advance Medical involve itself in petty theft schemes?"

"I don't know. Maybe for some extra cash?" John answered, not offering much satisfaction.

"Is it not true that your colleague felt wronged by the abortion industry and had a personal motive to target the nation's leading abortion company?" Mr. Millen questioned, insinuating ulterior motives.

"Objection," the prosecution objected again, attempting to protect the witness.

"Overruled," the Judge surprised the prosecution with his decision, allowing the defense to proceed.

"Isn't it true?" Mr. Millen repeated, his voice devoid of emotion.

"My colleague assisted me on this case as a favor, as I requested her help," John clarified, defending his colleague's involvement.

"I see," Mr. Millen responded with disbelief, his line of questioning not yielding the desired results.

"How would you describe your relationship with your first significant client, The Association for Fetal Research?" Mr. Millen asked, changing his approach.

"Fine," John replied, his tone guarded.

"Fine?" Mr. Millen repeated, his skepticism evident.

"Yes," John said, trying his best to maintain a poker face. He couldn't help but wonder how this man knew so much about him. It was evident that Penkowski's associates had a keen eye on him, given the incidents he had experienced in Stapleton. The feeling of being constantly watched and monitored sent a shiver down his spine, but he tried not to show it. He avoided looking in Penkowski's direction, knowing that the man's smug grin would only add to his discomfort.

The defense attorney, Mr. Millen, continued his line of questioning, attempting to connect John's personal life to the case. "And haven't you started attending Stapleton's evangelical church?" he asked, insinuating some hidden agenda.

"Objection! The witness's religious beliefs are irrelevant," the prosecution objected, trying to protect John from personal scrutiny.

"Sustained," the Judge ruled, agreeing with the prosecution's objection.

Seemingly content with making his point, Mr. Millen announced, "Your honor, I have no further questions at this time."

"You may be seated," the Judge said to John, who felt a sense of relief as he returned to his seat.

Mr. Robinson called his next witness, Pastor Bruce Hutchinson, to the stand. The tension in the courtroom was intense as the pastor was sworn in.

"Pastor Hutchinson, is it true that a man personally assaulted you in your church?" Mr. Robinson asked, getting to the heart of the matter.

"Yes," Bruce responded firmly.

"Can you point out this man in the courtroom for the court and the jury?" Mr. Robinson asked, seeking to establish a direct connection between Penkowski and the assault.

Bruce pointed towards Penkowski, making it clear that the man on trial was indeed the one who had attacked him.

"Objection, Your Honor, this is irrelevant!" Mr. Millen objected, trying to undermine the significance of the pastor's testimony.

"Sustained," the Judge ruled, disallowing further questioning along that line.

"No further questions, Your Honor," Mr. Robinson said, accepting the Judge's ruling.

The tension in the courtroom was evident as George Hines took the stand. All eyes were on Penkowski, who seemed visibly agitated. His eyes turned red, or at least it appeared so in the eyes of the onlookers, as he swayed back and forth, unable to hide his frustration. The jury grew uneasy, exchanging concerned glances with each other. Murmurs spread throughout the courtroom, causing the judge to intervene, hammering his gavel for order.

"Order! Order in the court!" the judge commanded, trying to restore some semblance of decorum.

Mr. Millen, Penkowski's defense attorney, leaned over and whispered in his client's ear, trying to soothe him, but the attempt seemed to be in vain. Despite the effort to quiet the courtroom, the atmosphere remained charged with tension.

As the prosecution resumed questioning, George recounted his work for Penkowski, explaining his role at AFT Manufacturing and his prior connection to The Association for Fetal Research and Advance Medical. Penkowski's discomfort grew as George revealed that Advance Medical had hired him to undermine The Association, without the latter's knowledge.

The prosecutor delved deeper into the illicit activities, probing the gambling, funds, and accounting books used to launder money. George provided detailed accounts that incriminated Penkowski and his company. The evidence presented seemed damning and left little room for doubt.

During the proceedings, George Hines portrayed himself as a witness committed to truth, determined to reveal the illegal activities he had been involved in. The prosecution skillfully presented a mountain of evidence, exposing the shady dealings of Advance Medical.

As the trial recessed for lunch, the courtroom was abuzz with discussions about the explosive testimony. The weight of the evidence was overwhelming, and many began to anticipate the outcome.

Outside the courtroom, Penkowski was escorted by the police, a visible sign of the gravity of the charges against him. The lawyers requested a private moment with their client, and they were allowed into a secure room. Meanwhile, other imposing figures stood nearby, ensuring Penkowski's confinement.

The atmosphere in the room was tense, as if a storm was brewing. The uncertainty of what might happen next hung heavy in the air. As the lawyers and their client conversed behind closed doors, the anticipation for the trial's continuation grew among the spectators. The fate of Dr. Penkowski and his empire hung in the balance.

It was after a much-needed lunch break, and the tension in the courtroom reached a new level as the trial resumed. The defense team's turn to cross-examine the witness, George Hines, had arrived, and the atmosphere crackled with anticipation.

With an air of confidence and determination, Mr. Millen, the defense attorney, began his questioning, aiming to challenge George's credibility. His voice held a hint of skepticism as he asked, "Mr. Hines, is it not true that while you worked for Advance Medical, you became disenchanted with AFT due to its involvement in manufacturing equipment used for the abortion industry?"

The prosecution immediately objected, trying to protect their witness from potential manipulation. The judge, with a thoughtful expression, allowed the line of questioning to proceed, aware of the high-stakes nature of the trial.

Continuing his line of inquiry, Mr. Millen asked, "Were you not unhappy about working for AFT?"

George, composed but with a touch of hesitation, responded, "I did not have warm feelings, no."

Mr. Millen pressed further, infusing his tone with a sense of moral indignation, "Not only did you not have warm feelings, but it went against all your moral values also, did it not?"

Caught in a moment of vulnerability, George admitted, "Yes."

The defense attorney, Mr. Millen, persisted in his line of questioning, determined to challenge George's credibility. With a hint of accusation in his voice, he asked, "Is it fair to say that you were looking for something to close down this plant and ultimately to close down the entire company?"

The prosecution swiftly objected, accusing Mr. Millen of leading the witness. The judge, with a stern expression, agreed, sustaining the objection, thus preventing the defense from manipulating the witness's responses.

Undeterred, Mr. Millen tried again, pressing George with a sense of urgency, "Well, weren't you, Mr. Hines?"

George took a moment to gather himself, and a hushed silence fell over the courtroom. He closed his eyes briefly, offering a silent prayer for guidance, before firmly responding, "Though admittedly I was not happy working for a company that made its money through the abortion industry, it was only when I saw the law being broken that I felt it was time to come forward."

The weight of George's words hung in the air, resonating with the jury and everyone present. It was evident that his actions were motivated by a sense of moral responsibility, rather than personal vendetta.

In a last-ditch effort to cast doubt on George's testimony, Mr. Millen made an accusatory statement, insinuating that George had planted misinformation to achieve his own ends. The prosecution quickly objected, urging the judge to intervene.

"Your Honor, I object," the prosecutor declared with fervor, "he is accusing a witness who is not on trial, someone who has not broken any laws. This line of questioning is entirely inappropriate!"

The judge promptly agreed, sustaining the objection and putting an end to the defense attorney's accusatory remarks.

The courtroom was tense and somber as the defense attorney conceded defeat, stating, "I have no further questions at this time." The look on Penkowski's lawyer's face revealed the gravity of the situation, indicating that the evidence presented was undeniably against them. Penkowski had anticipated this outcome, feeling a sense of impending doom.

Before the witness could be excused, chaos erupted as the back doors flung open, drawing everyone's attention. Even the police officers who were meant to be guarding Penkowski turned to see what was happening. In a stunning display of supernatural power, Penkowski broke free from his handcuffs, overpowered the officers with superhuman strength, and sent them flying through the air.

George, seated in the witness stand, couldn't believe his eyes. The extraordinary scene unfolding before him resembled something straight out of a superhero movie, but now it was happening right in front of him, leaving him utterly speechless and in disbelief.

Reacting quickly, John sprang from his chair, attempting to apprehend the escaping Penkowski, but his efforts proved futile. Penkowski easily tossed John aside like a mere rag doll, displaying his overwhelming strength and prowess.

With guns pointed at their heads, Penkowski's henchmen took John and George hostage, forcing them to move towards the court house's front doors. As they stepped outside, they were met with a lively parade filled with music and jubilant people celebrating on the streets. The chaotic scene became even more frenetic as Penkowski's captors weaved through the parade, using the festivities as a shield.

Despite the terrifying situation they found themselves in, both John and George felt an unusual sense of calm, almost a divine reassurance that they were not alone. Deep within their beings, they sensed a connection to their home city, Stapleton, where countless people were praying and supporting them in their hour of need.

Penkowski continued to threaten the police with the lives of his hostages, the urgency in his voice barely audible above the uproar of the parade. The police had called for backup, but their arrival was delayed due to the parade obstructing their path.

In the midst of the chaos, John managed to trip one of the henchmen, using the diversion to roll behind some bushes, with George following suit. Concealed for the moment, they hoped to find an opportunity to escape from their captors' grip and bring this dangerous situation to an end. The stakes were high, but their faith and determination were stronger than ever.

The men frantically searched for John and George, their faces etched with determination and fear. Despite the urgency, Penkowski managed to direct them towards a helicopter, which was just beginning to lift off the ground. The deafening noise of the rotor blades filled the air as the helicopter gained altitude, ready to make a daring escape.

In the midst of the chaos, the police officers retrieved their guns and fired at the helicopter in a desperate attempt to stop the fleeing criminals. The bullets, however, merely hit the helicopter's bulletproof glass, rendering them ineffective. In retaliation, the henchmen unleashed a torrent of machine gun fire, causing destruction and tearing up the concrete beneath the police officers' feet.

Unaware of the gunfire outside, Elizabeth, and Bruce rushed out of the courthouse, their hearts pounding with worry for John and George. They sprinted over to the bushes where the two were taking cover, but John tried to warn them to stay back. It was too late; the sound of machine gun fire reached their ears, chilling them to the core. As they looked up, a heart-wrenching sight greeted them – both police officers lay motionless on the ground, victims of the merciless attack.

The panic among the parade attendees reached a fever pitch as they scattered in all directions, seeking safety from the deadly hail of bullets. Elizabeth and Bruce exchanged worried glances, unsure of what to do next in this terrifying situation.

Meanwhile, high above in the helicopter, Penkowski's eyes gleamed with malice. The pilot was preparing to leave, but Penkowski's thirst for vengeance was far from quenched. With a venomous yell, he demanded that those who had found refuge in the bushes, referring to John's group, be killed. His pointed finger singled them out, and they could be seen clearly from the air, vulnerable and exposed.

TWENTY SIX

With a heart brimming with determination and a touch of anxiety, Mayor Thomas stepped into his role as a community savior. The sight of the large, desolate AFT building at the heart of the town square spurred a mix of emotions within him – a symbol of both opportunity and challenge.

The once-thriving AFT building now stood in abandonment, mirroring the neglect that had plagued the community for weeks. It seemed like the right place to start, and the mayor decided to take a leap of faith, reaching for the phone with a sense of resolve.

"Hello, could I speak with the commercial lending department?" Mayor Thomas inquired, his voice carrying a mix of authority and hope.

As the voice on the other end recognized him as Mayor Thomas of the city of Stapleton, a glimmer of anticipation flickered in his eyes. "Yes, I would like to inquire about a loan made to Advance Medical in the city of Stapleton... its public status?"

Inwardly, his heart raced with excitement, but he composed himself not to give it away. His quest for redemption was tied to the information he possessed about businesses and mortgage companies in Stapleton. He had a hunch that Advance Medical's financial troubles were linked to embezzlement, possibly by the deceitful accountant he had heard about.

"Hmm. Let me ask you then, what if the city of Stapleton came up with the full amount? Could the city purchase it?" he inquired with a hint of eagerness, trying to convey how vital this move was for the town's aesthetic and community spirit.

The person on the other end put the mayor on hold, and the wait felt like an eternity. But when they returned with a positive answer, Mayor Thomas couldn't contain his elation. "It can?" he exclaimed, a mix of joy and relief flooding his tone.

"I will have the money wired this afternoon! I'll sign the documents as soon as you email them, and I'll overnight them to you!" The mayor's voice trembled slightly with excitement as he eagerly embraced this unexpected triumph. "This is great! By the way, what is the status on the other building in Stapleton?"

As he hung up the phone, a profound sense of gratitude

washed over Mayor Thomas. His bold decision had paid off, and the prospect of revitalizing the town square filled him with immense satisfaction. He turned his chair around to face the window, gazing at the AFT building. It seemed poetic and ironic that the very funds he had received from Penkowski's shady dealings would now be used to rescue the community.

With a serene smile, Mayor Thomas closed his eyes for a moment, silently thanking God for guiding him on this path. This endeavor was more than just about buying buildings; it was about restoring faith in the community, and he was determined to see it through, come what may.

The bullets descended from the heavens, raining down upon John and his friends, and fear clutched his heart like a vise. His concern wasn't solely for his sister's life; it extended to the lives of his dear friends. In a desperate move, he grasped George's trembling hand, and together they leaped out into the open, zigzagging frantically, each step laden with the weight of their lives.

As they dashed through the chaos, a chilling voice pierced the pandemonium. Penkowski's cold command targeted them specifically, making their escape all the more urgent. The duos heart-pounding plan was underway, redirecting the gunfire away from Pastor Bruce and John's sister, but it replaced one danger with another. The relentless helicopter now pursued them with unyielding determination.

Emerging from their concealed spot, they sought refuge in the safety of a nearby building. From its vantage point, they beheld an almost surreal scene unfolding before their eyes. The helicopter hovered menacingly above the parade crowd, the whirling blades stirring up a tempest of chaos, tossing clothes, hair, and festive streamers into a wild dance. The once-celebratory atmosphere had turned into an eerie spectacle of confusion and fear.

Amidst this madness, John couldn't escape the pang of guilt for endangering innocent bystanders. Yet, they had nowhere to hide, and their instincts drove them to keep running, with the relentless chopper hot on their trail.

Desperation fueled their actions as John spotted two large cymbals discarded by a fleeing band member. He snatched one, tossing it to George with a fervent hope. The sound of gunshots erupted, and in perfect unison, they raised the cymbals as makeshift shields, clinging to them like a lifeline.

The bullets tore through the parade balloons, unleashing a storm of colorful fragments and grey dust upon the terrified crowd. Panic and terror reverberated through the air like an eerie symphony.

The helicopter's relentless assault narrowed the distance between the assailant and the fleeing duo. The bullets found their mark, striking the cymbals with a deafening clang that reverberated through the cacophony. Yet, their makeshift defense held, offering them a fleeting moment of respite.

Summoning every ounce of courage, John plunged under a passing motorized float, seeking cover from the unrelenting barrage. With a painful cry, George followed, taking a bullet to the shoulder that sent searing pain through his body. But the stakes were too high to surrender to the agony. Survival depended on their relentless will to press on, even as George's strength waned, and his determination screamed louder than his wounded body.

As the two women entered the Mayor's office, their anticipation and nerves were electric, their hearts beating with a mix of excitement and hope. They approached the secretary with a sense of purpose, announcing their appointment with Mayor Thomas. The secretary acknowledged them with a warm smile and gave the go-ahead to enter the inner sanctum.

Upon entering, they were greeted by Mayor Thomas, who extended a friendly handshake, instantly putting them at ease. They settled around a round table, and the Mayor began to delve into the plans that lay ahead. As the discussion unfolded, the two women couldn't contain their emotions, and their faces lit up with unbridled ecstasy. Their enthusiasm, in turn, brought a beaming smile to the Mayor's face, encouraging him to share even more passionately.

Time seemed to fly as the Mayor's secretary interrupted, entering with a delivery that brought even more excitement to the room. The Mayor revealed the blueprints, laying them out for all to see, and the women's excitement bubbled over, their voices rising with each idea shared.

The Mayor, with a pencil in hand, engaged actively with the

blueprints, scribbling notes, drawing lines, and adding numbers. The room became a hive of creativity, each individual's input combining to form a symphony of ideas.

Hours slipped away unnoticed, but their efforts bore fruit. Agreement was reached, and the meeting concluded with a feeling of accomplishment and camaraderie. Plans for a follow-up meeting were made, and the women left the Mayor's office with gratitude in their hearts.

As they departed, the Mayor couldn't help but reflect on the day's events. He made a call to ensure that the blueprints were swiftly collected, the sense of accomplishment mingling with the satisfaction of a productive day.

Alone in his office, Mayor Thomas sat back in his chair and gazed out of the window, a whirlwind of emotions swirling within him. A sense of deep joy welled up inside him, like springs of water bursting forth. A tear of fulfillment escaped his eye, and his face glowed with a radiant smile that outshone the sun itself. The Mayor knew that today's collaborative effort would pave the way for a better future, and that, for him, was the true essence of happiness.

The deafening roar of gunshots reverberated atop the parade float, sending shivers down John and George's spines as they desperately sought refuge beneath its towering structure. Amidst this symphony of terror, each passing moment was a silent prayer of gratitude that the bullets hadn't torn through the fragile shield of the float.

John's heart raced like a runaway locomotive as he clambered up to the forsaken driver's compartment, an abandoned throne overlooking the battlefield of festivities. George, his loyal comrade, followed suit, both of them wedged into the tiny space as if hiding within the secret heart of a mechanical beast.

From this concealed perch, the rhythmic hum of the engine was a lifeline. John's fingers curled around the steering wheel, a desperate grasp on fate itself. He exchanged a glance with George, their eyes speaking volumes amid the pandemonium. As the accelerator responded to John's touch, the float stirred to life, but its movement was hesitant, like a creature waking from a nightmare.

Slowly, inexorably, the float crept forward. With a sharp intake of breath, John's gaze plummeted downwards, landing on a lever. He seized it, wrenching it from its slumber, and the mechanical beast roared to life with newfound vigor.

An urgent cry from George pierced the air, his voice a poignant note in the cacophony of chaos. "We're going to plow into the crowd!" Fear and concern dripped from his words, casting a shadow over their desperate flight.

John's eyes darted to the fleeing crowd, the sea of humanity parting with agonizing sluggishness. In a heartbeat, a decision was made, a steering wheel turned, and the float veered into a narrow side street, a path less traveled and more perilous.

Their frantic escape continued, the relentless helicopter still their ghostly shadow, a reminder of unyielding pursuit. A jarring bump echoed through the float, a bone-rattling impact that detonated like a bomb.

"John, we're trapped!" George's voice was a piercing wail of despair, the hopelessness of their situation echoing through every syllable.

A heavy sigh escaped John's lips, resignation and determination intermingling in his eyes. "I know," he conceded, the weight of their predicament etched across his face. "I know."

Then John pushed the engine to its limits, a symphony of mechanical power merging with the symphony of gunfire. The float surged forward with newfound ferocity.

A wicked grin spread across Penkowski's face, triumph dancing in his eyes as he issued the triumphant decree to his men. The world around them transformed into a maelstrom of speed and danger, machine gun fire slicing through the air like a deadly hailstorm.

In a crescendo of chaos and carnage, the float collided with the walls of looming buildings, a brutal collision that tore through the float's defenses. The once-majestic float, the embodiment of a wild safari, was now a battered and wounded titan, screeching to a painful halt.

A frantic urgency hung in the air like a storm about to break as Penkowski's command sliced through the tension. "Over there, land, now!" His finger jabbed toward a sparsely used parking lot, the chosen arena for this impending clash.

The pilot's voice quivered with doubt, a trembling note of caution in the face of peril. "I'm not sure that our helicopter will make it in that small parking lot."

A tempest of frustration brewed in Penkowski's eyes, his impatience seething, his focus unrelenting as he fixated on the float below. The realization gripped him - they might have to venture into the open, a tantalizing prospect that could tip the scales in his favor.

With determined insistence, the helicopter touched down, a dance with danger that narrowly missed the swinging power lines and parked cars that crowded the makeshift landing strip. The gust from the rotor blades whipped the surroundings into a frenzy.

The float, now a shattered relic of its former self, bore the marks of their battle, its once-vibrant façade reduced to tatters. Penkowski's heart raced, a wild beast straining at its cage, as he and his men jumped out of the helicopter and surged toward the wounded behemoth. They resembled predators closing in, the scent of impending victory thick in the air.

"Find the driving compartment!" Penkowski's voice, edged with desperation, resonated through the chaos, a call to action that spurred his men into motion. Layers of camouflage peeled away, revealing empty seats.

Confusion and disbelief mingled in Penkowski's shout, a cry born of disbelief and frustration. Doubt gnawed at the edges of his mind, a lurking suspicion that he had been outsmarted, that two elusive figures had slipped through his grasp. Pointing beneath the torn remnants of the float, he galvanized his men, the collective effort to scour every hiding place for the quarry that had eluded them.

The search yielded nothing - an empty void where his vengeance should have been. A bitter taste of defeat settled on Penkowski's lips as he rose, the sun's warmth an ironic contrast against the cold realization of his failure. The world seemed to stand still as he surveyed the scene, silence echoing in his ears, mocking his impotent rage.

In the absence of victory, a primal scream erupted from deep within Penkowski's chest, an anguished cry that reverberated through the street, a lament for revenge denied. The buildings that flanked the avenue bore witness to his torment, the very walls seeming to shudder at the intensity of his fury.

Amid the fading echoes of his scream, the distant wail of sirens grew closer, a relentless march of justice encroaching on his domain. Urgency surged through the ranks of his men, a stark reminder of the consequences they faced if they lingered. Reluctantly, they retreated, casting lingering glances at the unvanquished float as the police sirens drew near.

Back in the helicopter, the throb of the rotor blades marked their hasty exit, a retreat from the brink of capture. As the urban landscape blurred beneath them, Penkowski's gaze remained fixed on the scene below, a tableau of shattered hopes and missed vengeance. The police arrived too late, their sirens' lament falling on empty streets, as the helicopter soared away, leaving a trail of unfulfilled retribution in its wake.

Virginia stepped into the Mayor's office during lunch, catching him in the middle of his workday. The receptionist looked briefly surprised but quickly returned to her usual professionalism. The Mayor, without a word, acknowledged his wife's unexpected visit and left his duties behind to join her.

They headed to a small restaurant in the town square, known for its cozy charm. Seated by a window, they enjoyed the view of the bustling square below. The crisp air outside was invigorating, and their smiles reflected a quiet gratitude for this time together after recent events.

"I'm so glad you're okay," Virginia said, her voice unsteady. Memories of him on the stretcher flashed in her mind, bringing tears she struggled to suppress.

"It's okay," he reassured her gently. His calm demeanor eased her worries, though he couldn't help but reflect on how the recent scare had brought them closer after years of gradual distance.

Virginia wiped her eyes and asked, "When they revived you, you were so eager to see the Pastor. Why? What happened?" Her tone was a mix of curiosity and concern.

Mayor Thomas knew it was time to share his hospital experience. He began recounting the dream he'd had and the moments leading up to his awakening. Though he chose to omit some of the more distressing details, he explained how Pastor Bruce's prayer had played a pivotal role, not only in healing Virginia but also in transforming his own perspective.

"I realized that Pastor Bruce's prayer healed you," he admitted, a hint of awe in his voice. That realization had given him the courage to trust God with his future.

Virginia, moved by his story, leaned closer. The distance between them—both physical and emotional—seemed to dissolve. She listened intently, touched by the change she saw in him.

Outside, life in the square carried on as usual, but for them, it felt like a new beginning. Virginia sensed that their journey together was far from over and that the road ahead held new opportunities for growth and purpose.

The darkness enveloped them, a cloak of obsidian that George clung to as he clutched the ladder beneath John. A silent hope whispered through the suffocating blackness, a plea that the ladder would remain a barrier against the unseen, scurrying rats that might crawl their way. The stench, a nauseating assault on the senses, was a relentless adversary, threatening to betray George's tenuous hold on his composure.

"Helicopter's gone," John's voice emerged from the shadows, a glimmer of hope threading through the murk. A stealthy hand lifted the cover of a manhole, revealing a small crack of the world above. With careful precision, the cover was lifted further, revealing a portal from their subterranean refuge. Side by side, they emerged from their noxious haven, blinking against the sudden intrusion of light.

Their emergence was met with a jarring sight - a sea of police cars and officers, their weapons at the ready. John and George raised their hands in a gesture of surrender, their eyes locking in shared bewilderment. The tableau hung heavy with tension until a commanding voice shattered the silence. "Put your guns down!" The police sergeant's order sliced through the air, and he advanced toward them, his authority an undeniable force.

As the sergeant approached, words began to flow, a river of explanation that washed away the uncertainty. Details poured forth, painting a picture of the events that had transpired, offering reassurance that their enemies were being pursued relentlessly. Penkowski's lair was encircled, and the sprawling expanse of the Advance Medical building was similarly cordoned off. The skies above bore silent witnesses in the form of police helicopters, vigilant sentinels searching for any sign of the fugitives.

Suddenly, figures materialized from the police cars, familiar faces imbued with a sense of hope. Pastor Bruce and John's sister,

Elizabeth, bounded toward them, their steps propelled by relief and urgency. Emotions swirled as they embraced, their voices a medley of relief and recounting the tumultuous events. As the narrative unfolded, their gazes shifted to the once-grand parade float, now a symbol of chaos and destruction. It stood as a monument to the trials they had faced and survived, a testament to the resilience that had carried them through the darkest hours.

In that fleeting moment, surrounded by the trappings of law enforcement and the loving embrace of family, John and George found themselves on the precipice of a new dawn. The shroud of danger and uncertainty was slowly lifting, revealing a future tinged with the promise of closure and healing.

Penkowski's meticulous planning had paved a path of escape, leading to the outskirts where the helicopter found its resting place amid the secluded embrace of the woods. The chopper's blades whispered their farewell, its metallic frame settling onto the earth as the train tracks stretched out like a lifeline.

As the train lumbered into view, it slowed its inexorable march, an unwitting accomplice in Penkowski's desperate escape. The box cars offered a sanctuary of anonymity, a haven for him and his loyal henchmen. In one synchronized movement, they leapt onto the box car's platform, vanishing within its cold, metallic embrace. It was a crude, yet effective stratagem, erasing their trail with every passing moment.

The train's relentless journey carried them through the tapestry of the landscape, rolling inexorably toward its predetermined destination. Eventually, its mechanical heart faltered as it nestled within a small town, just a stone's throw from Stapleton. With the precision of a well-practiced ballet, Penkowski and his men disembarked, their hurried footsteps echoing a rhythm of escape.

A weathered white old classic car awaited their arrival, a stark contrast to their former mode of transportation. Its battered frame carried the weight of their desperate bid for freedom as they sped away, the town's dust-covered streets bearing witness to their hasty retreat.

Within the cocoon of a humble motel room, neon lights flickered overhead, casting a crimson and cobalt dance upon the shadows. The room exuded an air of desolation, a fleeting haven for fugitives on the run. Penkowski's voice, a blend of authority and anticipation, reverberated within the room as he conversed over a cell phone. The promise of a rendezvous loomed, an exchange of power and loyalty that would shape their future.

"Stapleton is our final destination," Penkowski's words bore the weight of destiny as they hung in the air, a whispered oath to an uncertain future. The connection on the other end quivered with an overwhelming eagerness, the voice on the line echoing the reverence that Penkowski commanded. Promises exchanged like currency, he demanded assurance, a vow that all his followers would be there when he arrived.

"I will be there," the response was tinged with a blend of reverence and obedience, "but you must promise that you will have all the followers in Stapleton." A pause, a beat of anticipation before the voice continued, "I will come first." The gravity of this undertaking was etched in the voice's inflection, the weight of duty and loyalty vying for prominence.

"Yes," Penkowski's affirmation was tinged with satisfaction, his power reaffirmed in the echo of adoration, "I receive your adoration." The cell phone fell silent, the conversation ending as a shroud of uncertainty settled over the dimly lit motel room.

Mr. Robinson listened intently to the account of the escape, his expression firm as Elizabeth posed the question on everyone's mind. "So now what?" Her voice reflected a blend of uncertainty and cautious hope, resonating with the room's shared anticipation.

His response was clear and direct, leaving no room for ambiguity. "Simple. Once they find Penkowski, he's put in jail. No trial, no jury… he's already proven his guilt." The room seemed to collectively exhale, a subtle relief spreading as the weight of justice began to take hold.

Elizabeth, seeking more details, asked, "For how long?"

"Life," Mr. Robinson answered without hesitation, his tone underscoring the seriousness of the crimes Penkowski had committed.

The group exchanged small, relieved smiles, though George quickly brought them back to the immediate challenge. "But finding him won't be easy," he said, voicing the obstacle that lingered unspoken.

Mr. Robinson nodded. "This will probably be the hardest part."

John leaned forward, his voice steady and confident. "I don't think we need to look for him. We just dismantled his entire operation. Revenge will bring him to us." His words carried a weight of experience, his serious tone adding gravity to the conversation.

The room fell into a thoughtful silence as the discussion shifted, reflecting on the chaos they had endured and the steps ahead. Stan Robinson, drawing from years of legal expertise, noted the extraordinary nature of their situation. The conversation flowed naturally, blending moments of reflection with a shared determination to see justice served.

As they headed for the airport, a sense of finality settled upon them. The plane ride was a mix of relief and reflection, a temporary respite from the storm they had weathered. Seated together, John sensed George's unease, his nervous glances casting shadows of doubt. Concerned, John broached the topic, "You seem tense. You were looking all over the place when we were in the airport."

George's apprehension spilled forth, a confession of his haunting fears. The specter of Penkowski's vengeance loomed large, a past betrayal that seemed destined to culminate in an inevitable reckoning. John stepped into the role of comforter, his words carrying a blend of reassurance and empathy. "George, get a grip. Remember who is in charge." He shared his conviction. "God is. You heard Elizabeth... how everything just... came together." John shifted gears, revealing a more personal experience. "And I'm telling you, the last trip to California, it seemed I could do no wrong... everything was the right timing, the right person or lack of them..." John's voice softened, his concern for his friend genuine. George's struggle was evident, his mind racing through the echoes of his past.

John's voice became more insistent, his faith unwavering. "All I'm saying George is that... if God was in all of that, do you think He is going to back out now?" George's gaze turned toward John, contemplating his words, grappling with the meaning behind them. Looking out the window, George began to sift through his journey, the healing of his leg, the newfound friendships, and the providential meeting with John. The realization dawned on him.

"You're right, John. Thanks. Thanks for everything. You are a great friend." George's voice was imbued with gratitude, a recognition of the support that had bolstered him.

John's response was heartfelt, a testament to the bond they had forged through their shared trials. He placed a hand on George's shoulder, the gesture a silent reminder of their journey. "So are you. So are you." The words carried a weight of significance, a recognition of the transformation that their experiences had wrought in both of them.

Aware of the potential danger of seeking revenge in Stapleton, Penkowski shrewdly avoided that path, recognizing that the authorities would likely have their sights set on him there. Instead, he chose discretion, making the decision to lie low for a while. Departing the next morning in the nondescript white classic car, he led his loyal band of followers on a journey through the obscure byways of the countryside. As the miles rolled by, the stark contrast of his current situation weighed heavily on him, the luxury he once reveled in now replaced by discomfort and inconspicuousness.

Through the winding roads and hidden routes, they eventually found themselves in a town bordering the outskirts of Las Vegas. Penkowski navigated the intricate web of his contacts, ensuring his continued survival by securing both luxurious accommodations and a high-end vehicle. Set against the backdrop of a serene lake tucked away in the woods, their new hideaway provided an illusion of tranquility.

Penkowski's loyal henchmen remained by his side, assuming the roles of 24-hour bodyguards, shadows that clung to his every move. The veneer of luxury could not dispel the undercurrent of malevolence that radiated from their leader. Within their sanctuary, Penkowski resurrected a twisted altar, transforming a rustic living space into a macabre chamber. Candles flickered in the dimness, casting eerie shadows as he and his men began to chant.

The spirits they beckoned heeded their call, but their arrival was far from benign. A dark energy enveloped the room, tangible in the levitating objects that crashed against walls, windows, and light fixtures. Amid the chaos, Penkowski's voice remained eerily calm. "We need a sacrifice," he stated matter-of-factly, his unwavering demeanor a testament to the horrors that had become his reality.

His men promptly departed, returning with an offering—an animal sacrifice to appease the restless spirits. With the ritual completed, a sense of malevolent satisfaction seemed to permeate the air. The spirits, once displeased, were now quelled, their demands met. In their satisfaction, they whispered new orders, their chilling commands cementing Penkowski's descent into darkness.

A new day dawned upon Stapleton, a town that had been shackled by the looming specter of Penkowski's presence. Yet, in the wake of AFT's dissolution and the cessation of its immoral enterprises, a renewed vitality surged through the streets. The once-dreary atmosphere had transformed, replaced by a sense of cleanliness and vibrancy. Smiles graced faces, and an unmistakable buoyancy echoed in the steps of the townspeople.

The streets buzzed with energy, curiosity running high as construction crews diligently worked to transform the former AFT buildings. Gossip floated through the air, speculation taking root as rumors sprouted like wildflowers. The true owners of the buildings remained shrouded in mystery, and the city's silence only fueled the intrigue. John and George contemplated the possibilities, leaning away from the notion that Penkowski could be involved since his operations had been dismantled.

Amid the backdrop of the town's revitalization, Bruce found himself at home, seeking solace and clarity. The emotional rollercoaster of recent events had taken its toll, leaving him grappling with a sense of futility. The effort expended to incarcerate Penkowski now seemed futile as he evaded capture. Still, there was a silver lining—AFT's nefarious activities were no more, and the abortion clinics and manufacturing plants had shuttered. But a twinge of apprehension tugged at Bruce's heart as he considered the construction taking place at the former AFT facilities. Would a new force emerge to undermine the divine work that had blossomed in Stapleton? The question weighed on his mind.

Seeking guidance, Bruce lowered himself to his knees, his living room becoming a sanctuary of connection with the divine. Amid the flood of emotions, a sense of peace enveloped him, soothing the tumult within. A gentle whisper of assurance echoed in his mind, "Trust the Lord... and don't try to figure it out."

After his prayers, Bruce turned to his computer, ready to delve into the happenings of the world beyond his window. Just then, a knock sounded at the door. George's arrival was met with a warm smile, and Bruce welcomed him in.

"Pastor Bruce," George greeted with a genuine grin.

"George! Come on in," Bruce invited, pleased to see his friend.

George's voice carried a hint of regret as he spoke, recounting the time he had been tangled up in AFT's web. "I wanted to let you know that I am available once again for God's service. I have been tied up..."

Bruce cut him off, reassuringly. "I know, I know. But praise the Lord, you are not working for AFT any longer, and thanks to you, it is gone."

George's thoughts turned to the elusive Penkowski. "So is Penkowski unfortunately."

With conviction, Bruce replied, "God will take care of Penkowski, don't you worry about that." His tone shifted, becoming more hopeful and excited. "Funny thing, I was just about to get on our internet site to see what has been going on. Sue has been doing a great job managing it since you left."

Curiosity piqued, George inquired, "Has she added anything to it?"

"No," Bruce replied.

George's anticipation grew as he took his seat before the computer, his eyes beginning to sparkle with curiosity. Bruce observed his friend's excitement, marveling at George's extensive knowledge and ease with technology. As George navigated the digital realm, he shared his ideas for upgrading the internet site. His vision encompassed a way for Bruce to stay connected with the community, facilitating communication about needs, prayers, and miracles. With this platform, Bruce could share the works of God with the church, fostering a sense of marvel and praise among the congregation.

A smile spread across Bruce's face as he listened to George's plans. "You know George; it is good to have you back."

George exhaled deeply, leaning back in his chair with a sense of contentment. "Pastor, it's great to be back."

Bruce extended a cold beverage to George, the moment growing more intimate as they settled into conversation. With a quiet intensity, Bruce began, "George, I have a personal prayer request I would like to share with you."

Sensing the gravity in Bruce's voice, George halted his computer work and turned his full attention to his friend. The room seemed to hold its breath as Bruce continued.

"I have a friend, her name is Jennifer. We have been very close over the years. She was called to the mission field and I was not. I still am unsure why God chose two different paths for us, but He did."

Bruce paused, his struggle to express his feelings evident. George remained silent, offering his unwavering support.

"I have so longed to be with her, but I also want to follow God's will for me. Look at this, George. God has allowed me to be a part of the first revival America has seen in years…but my heart still aches for a soul mate...one that I already know exists."

With a deliberate pace, Bruce continued, "I dream about her, but my commitment to God's work helps me navigate through the tough times. But they still come."

George posed a question, gentle and probing. "Does she know how you feel?"

Bruce responded, "Yes."

"Does she feel the same?"

"Yes."

"Have you asked God to change His mind?"

Bruce hesitated, pondering George's words. "Well, that is where I am right now. I don't want to take Jennifer away from what God is doing overseas."

George's response was resolute and compassionate. "Ask Him to finish His work with her over there and then bring her back to the states."

Bruce expressed his apprehensions. "That sounds a bit self-centered, don't you think?"

George's confidence was unshakable. "Not at all, Bruce. Your faithfulness has brought God to this town. Making this request with a pure heart, wanting to share your life with someone... there is nothing selfish about that. If Jennifer feels the same way, she is probably having this very conversation with her close friend as we speak!"

Bruce looked at George, his smile growing as he recognized the truth in his friend's words. "I will be praying for you concerning this," George assured him.

"I'm flying back to California," Elizabeth informed her brother, John, over the phone. "Stan, Mr. Robinson that is, wants to get together with me to go over more trial information... over dinner."

John couldn't help but tease his sister, remembering her pre-date jitters from their childhood. "Well, well, well... Looks like you've got a date."

Elizabeth's response was swift, tinged with amusement. "John, I know what you're thinking! I'm not marrying the guy. It's just a date... a work date... dinner."

Chuckling, John reassured her, "Whoa, sis, it's okay. Let me know how it goes. Maybe he'll invite you to his church?"

Elizabeth's nerves settled as she realized her brother's approval. "Thanks, John. I'll keep you informed, both personally and business-wise... and if we hear anything about Penkowski's whereabouts, of course."

Meanwhile, John resumed his conversation with Maggie, recounting the events of their escape. "She's flying back to California. She has a date with the attorney general of California," he informed her.

Maggie playfully responded, "Wow, I'm impressed." Eager to hear more, she prompted him, "So, you were saying that the helicopter landed, and that's when you were trapped. What did you do?"

As the two friends delved into the narrative, time slipped away unnoticed, consumed by the tales and camaraderie they shared.

"Another prayer request I have, George, is that God would provide a larger church for our community," Bruce shared with George as they continued their work on Bruce's computer. He elaborated, "We have been blessed to use the school's auditorium, but it seems even the Tuesday night prayer meeting is outgrowing the space. Principal Benton offered the football field, but I'm hesitant to overextend our presence there. We've used the auditorium for a while, and now even their football field...they use it for football, track, and more."

George, ever the technologically inclined, urged Bruce to take a look at the screen, where emails poured in, echoing the very prayer request Bruce had spoken aloud. A grin formed on George's face as he indicated the flurry of emails. Clearly, the community had already been fervently praying for a larger church.

As they shifted their focus, Bruce asked George about his post-AFT plans. George's response was deeply heartfelt. He recounted the profound impact Bruce's preaching had on him, sparking a newfound sense of life and purpose. Working undercover at AFT had been soul-draining, witnessing firsthand the destruction caused by sin and feeling powerless to help. But this experience had crystallized his path upon escaping Penkowski's clutches.

George's eyes gleamed with passion as he spoke of his desires. "I want to free others... to be a part of what you're doing." He pointed to the computer screen and expressed his love for helping, renovating homes, and being involved in the revival. "I want to be a part of what God is doing in this community!"

Bruce's smile echoed George's sentiments. "There was a definite void when you were gone, not just in our friendship, but in the Lord's work. Your gifts have been invaluable. I'd love to have you work with me full-time!"

The idea resonated with George. He felt liberated and purposeful since his escape from AFT, and the prospect of being a full-time participant in God's revival energized him. In no time, George took charge, revamping the internet site to support a national revival. He devised a comprehensive plan, assigning leaders to different aspects of life, from business to evangelism, all with the goal of spreading God's healing and message far beyond Stapleton.

"Pastor Bruce, Stapleton is only the beginning! God wants to heal our land, not just our town!" George's words flowed with enthusiasm and conviction, resonating deeply with Bruce. As George continued to speak, Bruce leaned back, absorbing every word. He saw the passion in George's eyes, as if his voice was channeling divine energy. Bruce knew in his heart that it was God speaking through George, guiding their vision beyond the present.

"He has started a good thing that He will bring to completion. He wills that none should perish but that all should have life, forever!" George's words were almost ethereal, and Bruce could sense the spirit of God moving through their conversation. It was a reminder that their purpose was part of a grander plan, and the scale of their efforts was much greater than they had initially perceived.

Bruce, previously focused on the immediate needs of Stapleton, realized that their responsibility extended beyond their town's borders. He recognized the urgency of sharing God's glory and message on a broader scale. He pondered the idea that they were just one small part of God's plan for healing and restoration, not only in their community but across the nation.

George's revelation struck a chord with Bruce. He chuckled and said, "I guess we need to pray for a bigger church than I first thought we needed." The humor in his statement broke the intensity of the moment, and they both shared a hearty laugh. It was a reminder that their journey was a collaborative effort, filled with purpose, joy, and unexpected twists. As they contemplated the exciting possibilities ahead, Bruce and George felt a renewed sense of unity and anticipation. Working together was bound to be an exhilarating adventure, guided by the divine plan they were now more deeply aligned with than ever before.

TWENTY SEVEN

Under the cover of night, Penkowski had stealthily made his way to what was perhaps the most sinister congregation in all of America - the largest satanic gathering. A chilling aura pervaded the air as the clock struck three in the morning, marking the commencement of this ominous assembly. The attendees, shrouded in black hoods and robes, looked like a congregation of shadows in the dimly lit room.

The location, nestled on the outskirts of Las Vegas, provided an eerie backdrop for this unsettling event. The sprawling building had been transformed into a hub of dark devotion, drawing travelers from across the nation to participate in this ominous annual tradition. Among the congregation were the leaders of every satanic church nationwide, a sinister fellowship brought together by their shared beliefs.

Penkowski, a figure of prominence among the six highest-ranking leaders of the entire satanic network, had a storied history within the fold. His dedication had propelled the church's malevolent cause forward, making him a key player in their nefarious activities.

Tensions were high, and emotions were raw as Penkowski took the stage. He was incensed, his voice dripping with venom, as he began to recount the ongoing strife in Stapleton. The weight of his anger was palpable as he unleashed a torrent of words, his fervor evident in his spittle-laden speech. His grip on the microphone was fierce, amplifying the intensity of his message and the chaotic energy in the room.

The air was heavy with the scent of burning candles, casting eerie shadows across the dimly illuminated space. A bloodied sacrifice lay on the altar, a grim testament to the devotion these worshipers held for their sinister deity.

"I had the city! It was within my grasp," Penkowski seethed, his voice trembling with malevolence. The twisted satisfaction in his evil smile conveyed his pleasure in the deception that had ensnared the unsuspecting citizens of Stapleton. The darkness of his tactics was evident as he detailed the manipulation of the town's people and the subsequent unraveling of their lives.

A momentary calm washed over Penkowski, replaced by a sinister glee. "How I deceived them," he hissed, relishing in the memory of leading the town astray. The ambiance of the room seemed to intensify as he recounted the city's descent into moral decay, driven by his malevolent influence.

But then, like a storm unleashed, Penkowski's anger surged forth once more. His demand to regain control over the town for the glory of Lucifer reverberated through the room, drawing others into his fervor. The chant "For Lucifer!" swelled, filling the space with a cacophony that shook the very walls.

As the sacrifice was offered and the dark forces accepted it, Penkowski's fellow leaders joined him, adorned in elegant robes that contrasted their malevolent intentions. Each of them vowed vengeance for the wrongs inflicted upon their high priest, fueling their resolve to dismantle the progress of the Kingdom of God.

With fiery determination, they outlined their sinister plan. Their goal was to obliterate the town of Stapleton, to crush its inhabitants with a relentless tide of malevolence. Their devotion to their dark god was intense, an overwhelming force that fueled their mission.

The chilling chants of "For Lucifer!" once again filled the room, a collective mantra that surged like a sinister tide. Flames engulfed the altar, and the worshipers bowed in fervent prayer for the success of their sinister conquest. The stage was set for a battle between forces of light and darkness, the outcome uncertain, but the intensity of their malevolent purpose was undeniable.

In the dead of night, Bruce was jolted awake by an overwhelming sense of malevolence that seemed to pervade the air. The darkness was suffocating, wrapping around him like a shroud of blackness. A foreboding aura seemed to envelope him, sending shivers down his spine as he rose from his bed at the bewitching hour of 3 AM.

Unease gnawed at him as he ventured into the bathroom, where an eerie sensation of being watched sent shivers down his spine. Flicking on the light, he braced himself for the sight of an intruder, the tension in the room heavy. However, his fears were unfounded, and he found himself alone, yet still consumed by an unshakable feeling of dread.

The silence was shattered by a crashing noise from the living room, confirming his suspicions that he was not alone in his home. Bruce's heart raced, his every nerve on edge as he hastily extinguished the light. He offered up frantic prayers in his mind, desperate not to be heard by whatever unwanted presence lurked nearby.

Navigating the pitch-black hallway, he encountered a strange sensation against his hands, as if the walls themselves were tainted with a chilling dampness. Startled, he withdrew his hands, only to be startled again by another crash from the living room. His pulse quickened as he peered around the corner, his vision adjusting to the inky darkness, revealing nothing.

The living room, usually illuminated by a streetlight's glow, was now enshrouded in impenetrable darkness. Bruce's anxiety grew, and he recalled a scripture that brought him comfort. "God did not give me a spirit of fear..." he reminded himself, bolstering his resolve. Hastily retreating to his bedroom, he dropped to his knees and began to pray. A warmth spread through him as his fear slowly ebbed away, replaced by a newfound strength.

Amidst the praying, the room suddenly blazed with a brilliant light that seemed to radiate through his closed eyelids. Overwhelmed, Bruce couldn't bring himself to open his eyes, even as the light seemed to dissipate after a moment, leaving behind a lingering sense of awe and serenity.

As he finally dared to open his eyes, Bruce was greeted by a soft, dim light filtering into his home from the faithful streetlight outside. The oppressive darkness seemed to have been lifted, and the eerie presence that had gripped him had dissipated. With cautious steps, he ventured into the living room, flicking on the light to assess the aftermath.

Pictures had fallen from their perches on the wall, their frames shattered on the floor, but otherwise, the room appeared undisturbed. Just as he was taking in the scene, the phone rang, jolting him. With trepidation, he answered, his voice tinged with both relief and wariness.

"Hello?" he answered, the tension evident in his voice.

"Bruce, this is Wayne," the voice on the other end responded urgently. "I know it's 3:00 AM, but I just had an incredibly unsettling experience, and I need to talk to someone who won't think I'm losing my mind."

As Wayne began to recount his own eerily similar encounter, Bruce felt a chill run down his spine. The details of their stories aligned with uncanny precision, confirming that they had both shared an inexplicable and haunting experience that defied the boundaries of rational explanation.

The morning sun gently illuminated Bruce's study as he sat in contemplation, his Bible open before him. The events of the previous night lingered in his thoughts, casting a shadow over his tranquility. The intrusion of evil within the sanctuary of his home had rattled him deeply, an experience he couldn't easily shake off. As he surveyed the aftermath of the shattered glass, he couldn't help but wrestle with the question of why a benevolent God would allow such malevolent forces to encroach upon his safe haven.

In his heart, Bruce knew that he might never fully comprehend the intricate workings of God's plan. The silence he encountered in his prayers left him seeking solace in the assurance that God had a reason beyond his understanding. Gathering his thoughts, he turned to the task at hand, offering prayers for the leaders involved in the revival of Stapleton. A smile graced his lips as he mentioned George by name, appreciating the transformation in his life and his dedication to the cause.

Bruce's emotions swelled as he reviewed the countless answered prayers that had already unfolded. Tears welled up in his eyes, and he had to pause, humbled by the privilege of being a conduit for God's work in Stapleton. As the sun filtered into his office, he glanced at the rose bushes outside, their barren appearance a reminder that life often thrived beyond what the eye could perceive.

Taking a deep breath, Bruce resumed his prayers, now petitioning for a larger space to accommodate the growing congregation, for the safety of Jennifer who was abroad, and for the realization of the broader vision George had shared. Just as he delved into his earnest supplications, the phone rang, jolting him from his reverie.

"Hello?" Bruce answered, a note of curiosity in his voice.

"Pastor Bruce, it's Sue," came Sue's voice, tinged with excitement.

"Sue, how are you?" Bruce inquired, anticipation building as he sensed Sue's enthusiasm.

"Could you meet Maggie and me at Mayor Thomas's office around 8:00 AM this morning?"

Sue's excitement was electric, even through the phone.

Puzzled, Bruce sought clarification. "What's this about?"

"I promise I'll explain everything when you get here. It's really important," Sue replied, her determination evident.

Bruce's concern peeked. "Is everything alright?"

"Everything's more than alright. Can we count on you to be there?"

"I'll be there," Bruce affirmed, a mixture of curiosity and concern in his voice.

"Thank you, Bruce. See you soon," Sue concluded, her excitement still reverberating through the line.

As Bruce hung up the phone, a sense of anticipation settled over him. The upcoming meeting seemed to hold a promise of something significant, a development that could potentially shape the trajectory of their endeavors in Stapleton. With a renewed sense of purpose, Bruce gathered his thoughts and prepared to venture into the unknown, ready to face whatever revelation awaited him in Mayor Thomas's office.

It was a crisp 8:00 AM when Bruce arrived, a bit early, to Mayor

Thomas's office. His curiosity was piqued, and he couldn't help but wonder about the purpose of this unexpected meeting. Offering a bright "Good morning" to the receptionist, he was quickly ushered in as the Mayor's voice beckoned him forward.

With the door now open, Mayor Thomas stood before Bruce, welcoming him warmly. Sue and Maggie stood beside him, their excitement apparent in their beaming smiles. Bruce's own smile mirrored their enthusiasm as he greeted them all. His curiosity was reaching its peak, and he was eager to discover the reason behind this gathering.

"How are you feeling, Mayor?" Bruce inquired with genuine concern, hoping to initiate a conversation before delving into the heart of the matter.

The Mayor's response was nothing short of inspiring. "Pastor Bruce, I've never felt better in my life. For the first time, I feel alive, truly alive!"

As the conversation shifted, Mayor Thomas wasted no time in addressing the topic at hand. "Being a politician, I've made promises in the past, but this time, I intend to keep them. I want to make a positive impact, not just in our community, but in the lives of its people and the surrounding areas."

Bruce's pleasure was evident, a testament to the Mayor's genuine transformation. The anticipation in the room was undeniable as the Mayor shared his commitment to upholding the values of various faiths and promoting religious freedoms.

The Mayor led them out of his office, and Bruce couldn't contain his excitement, feeling like a child on the verge of unwrapping a long-awaited gift. Their journey led them to the old AFT building, and as Bruce puzzled over the purpose, Sue encouraged him to look up. Squinting against the sunlight, he followed her directive, his eyes widening as he saw what he had never expected.

"A... cross?" Bruce uttered, astonishment lacing his voice.

"That's exactly what it is," the Mayor affirmed, his smile growing.

"Why is there a cross on the AFT building?" Bruce questioned, still grappling with the sight before him.

The Mayor's response was nothing short of astonishing. "Because, Pastor Bruce, I thought you might appreciate a cross on your new church building."

Confusion mingled with disbelief, Bruce exchanged glances

with Sue and Maggie, trying to process the unfolding revelation. The Mayor's demeanor exuded confidence and playfulness as he disclosed that the building, fully renovated and furnished, was now theirs.

"But how... how did this happen?" Bruce stammered, his mind racing.

The Mayor's smile remained, his eyes gleaming with a mischievous twinkle. "It's all taken care of. Consider it your gift, free and clear."

Bruce was rendered nearly speechless, trying to absorb the magnitude of what he was hearing.

"Credit Sue and Maggie for the designs," the Mayor continued. "They collaborated with me on the blueprints."

Still grappling with the incredulity of the situation, Bruce found himself led to the entrance of the building. As the Mayor opened the doors, a rush of new carpet scent greeted them. The Mayor illuminated the room, and its beauty was breathtaking. Every detail had been meticulously arranged - the colors, the lighting, and even a charming fountain at its center.

Approaching the fountain, Bruce's eyes fell on a small plaque bearing a scripture verse. Kneeling down, he read the words etched there.

Bruce's tear-filled eyes gazed up at the scripture verse engraved on the plaque, 2 Chronicles 7:14. As the words etched into his heart, he closed his eyes in a moment of profound gratitude. "Thank you, Lord," he whispered, his voice trembling with emotion. He felt a deep connection with the divine, a confirmation that their journey, guided by prayer and faith, had led them to this pivotal moment.

In the presence of the Mayor, Sue, and Maggie, Bruce's heart swelled with appreciation. He wiped away a tear, looking at each of them in turn. "Mayor Thomas, thank you for your generosity. Sue, Maggie, thank you for your dedication and support," he expressed, his voice filled with genuine gratitude.

The Mayor's response held a sense of reciprocity and transformation. "You've shown me the Light, my friend, and for that, I'm grateful."

Maggie and Sue chimed in, echoing their own transformation and gratitude. "And you've shown me my salvation, Jesus," said Maggie.

"And for being the man of God you are," Sue added, her voice reflecting deep appreciation.

The Mayor's excitement was contagious, and as he led the way, Bruce, Sue, and Maggie followed. Bruce's curiosity heightened with each step, and he was both surprised and amazed as they entered a vast space filled with stadium-style seating. The sight was overwhelming, a testament to the Mayor's commitment to their cause.

Overwhelmed by the grandeur, Bruce took a seat, still processing the enormity of the gesture. Sue and Maggie joined him, their faces mirroring his sense of awe. As Mayor Thomas shared his vision, Bruce was brought to his feet, moved beyond words. "More?" he asked incredulously.

The Mayor's smile held a sense of purpose as he continued, "Much more." The procession continued, leading them to another area of the building. The view that greeted them was breathtaking - row upon row of seating that stretched as far as the eye could see. In the front, a simple yet elegant podium awaited, bearing a Bible inscribed with the very scripture that had guided their journey.

Overwhelmed with emotion, Bruce finally surrendered to the moment, sinking into a chair. Sue and Maggie held his hands, the touch a reminder of their unity and shared purpose. Mayor Thomas stayed behind, letting Bruce take in the sight before him. As he regained his composure, Sue and Maggie led him forward, the Mayor following suit.

Upon the stage, Bruce saw the Bible with its inscription, and his heart swelled. A sense of awe washed over him as he looked out at the sea of seats and the profound potential they held. With a trembling smile, he extended his hands, beckoning Mayor Thomas, Sue, and Maggie to join him. They formed a circle, united in purpose and gratitude.

Bruce's voice filled the air as he began to pray, the words a heartfelt offering to the Divine. His prayer carried the weight of their journey, their aspirations, and their faith. "Father, you've blessed me with these friends. They're my brothers and sisters in Christ," he began, his voice strong with conviction.

He continued, acknowledging the generosity of the Mayor, the dedication of Sue and Maggie, and the shared commitment to the revival. As he lifted their collective efforts to the divine, his prayer resonated with a sense of hope, faith, and reverence.

"Now, I pray that you take this revival beyond these walls, beyond Stapleton," he fervently prayed, his voice filled with passion. "Do great and mighty things that only You can do, in Jesus' name."

The echo of his prayer hung in the air, a tangible manifestation of their collective hope and determination. In that sacred moment, they stood on the cusp of a new chapter, united by purpose and propelled by faith.

Bruce's heart raced as he stared at the screen, his eyes fixed on the email that had finally arrived. The message he had dreamed about for years, the one that he had hoped to read someday, was right before him. He could hardly believe his eyes as he read each word, his excitement growing with every sentence.

Titled "Dear Bruce," the email emanated a sense of longing and anticipation. Jennifer's words carried a mixture of emotions that echoed his own. As he absorbed the contents, he couldn't help but feel the overwhelming impact of the moment.

"Though I have longed to be with you," the email began, and Bruce's heart skipped a beat. The realization that Jennifer was finally expressing what he had felt for so long filled him with a sense of joy he could hardly contain.

The message continued, revealing a surprising twist of events overseas. Their country had denied access to missionaries, resulting in every missionary being asked to leave. Despite the unexpected turn of events, Jennifer's faith remained steadfast. She saw it as a divine work of revival in the midst of adversity, a testament to God's sovereignty in even the most challenging circumstances.

Bruce's fingers trembled slightly as he read on, his eyes moistening with emotion. Jennifer's words about her feelings for him struck a chord deep within his heart. "My heart has ached thinking of you," she confessed, conveying the depth of her affection and her desire to be with him. Her faith in God's plan for their lives, alongside their shared devotion to their respective callings, resonated profoundly.

A Bible verse that Jennifer's friend had shared resonated in the email: "Delight thyself in the LORD and He will grant you the desires of your heart." The verse seemed to encapsulate their shared journey, the intertwining of their faith and love.

Jennifer's dedication to her work overseas was evident in her words. She had formed deep connections with the people she had been serving, training many in lay work and even identifying a potential pastor for the community. Her heart held both a sense of sadness at leaving and an overwhelming joy at the prospect of finally being with Bruce.

As he reached the end of the email, Bruce's emotions surged. Jennifer's words were filled with promise and urgency. The government's mandate had pushed them into a moment of decision, one that could alter the course of their lives. Jennifer's closing words brought a smile to his face, a mix of love and anticipation. "Oh how I look forward to seeing you. We must leave immediately or suffer the consequences of this government for not complying; therefore I will see you soon."

The weight of Jennifer's love and her decision to be with him was overwhelming. Bruce's heart swelled with gratitude and excitement. He closed his eyes for a moment, breathing in the reality of the email he had waited so long for. With a deep sense of resolve, he composed himself and began to type, his fingers dancing across the keyboard as he crafted a response that echoed his feelings, his faith, and his eagerness to finally be united with Jennifer.

Bruce sat back, a deep breath escaping his lips. A wide smile graced his face as tears of overwhelming joy welled up in his eyes. God had done it – He had granted Bruce's heart's deepest desire by bringing Jennifer home to him. The anticipation of their reunion filled him with an eagerness he could hardly contain. He dropped to his knees, his heart bursting with gratitude, and fervently thanked God for His incredible goodness. With a heart full of emotion, he composed a heartfelt email to Jennifer, eager to update her on the remarkable events that had unfolded. Despite the uncertainty of her travel, he felt compelled to share the blessings that God had poured out, including the provision of a new building for the believers in Stapleton.

Bruce's excitement was overwhelming, and he felt a surge of joy that compelled him to invite John and George to his home. Their presence magnified his elation, and as they gathered, he was practically bouncing with enthusiasm.

"Guys, sit down, please," he said, his voice bubbling with excitement, as he fetched some drinks for his guests.

The curiosity in John's eyes was evident as he asked, "What's going on, Bruce?"

"Yeah, Bruce, you've got us all curious. What's the big news?"

George chimed in.

Bruce could barely contain his secret any longer. He couldn't help but blurt out, starting with the church.

"I can't believe this!" John exclaimed.

"We were just praying about that!" George added, his surprise mirroring Bruce's when he first heard the news.

"Exactly! And guess what? It's all happening incredibly fast," Bruce shared, a sense of wonder still evident in his voice. "It's got me utterly amazed."

George, intrigued, asked, "What do you mean by incredibly fast?"

Bruce's excitement spilled over as he recounted how prayers were being answered with swift precision these days. He reflected on his lifelong journey with God, where answers to prayers often took time to materialize. However, in recent times, it felt as though God was responding almost instantaneously, leaving him both amazed and profoundly grateful.

Bruce continued his story, sharing the details of his meeting with Mayor Thomas, the appearance of Sue and Maggie, and the stunning gift of the new church building. He described the features of the building and how it was designed to accommodate everyone involved in the Tuesday night prayer meetings and beyond.

However, George's concern about Penkowski's ownership of the building and the potential repercussions weighed heavily. "What about Penkowski?" George asked, his voice tinged with fear. "When he finds out, we could be in serious trouble."

Bruce acknowledged the concern, having spent the day contemplating this very issue. But he remained resolute. "I've thought about this all day, and I've come to a conclusion: If God is on our side, who can be against us?"

George's face displayed a mix of understanding and worry. "I get that, but I can't forget that gun pointed at my head," he said, his voice betraying his emotions.

With unwavering simplicity, Bruce asked, "Did God rescue you?"

The question hung in the air, and George's response was steady. "Yes, He did."

Bruce's tone remained calm as he continued, "Did God rescue John from the imminent explosion in his car? Did He rescue you from that job that held you captive in fear? Did He rescue John and his sister from Penkowski's grip? Did He rescue this town from

Penkowski's corruption? Did He rescue John's sister from past regrets? Did He rescue both of you from a dangerous situation on that float? Did He rescue John from a life of emptiness? Did He rescue you from greed? Did He rescue me from a life of selfishness and separation from God?"

George met Bruce's gaze, his understanding deepening. He recognized the pattern of God's faithfulness in their lives. The risks were real, but so was God's power and protection.

John, injecting a sense of reason, addressed the potential danger of Penkowski's retaliation. "Bruce, I understand what you're saying, but let's be practical. If Penkowski learns about this, he won't hesitate to come after you and the entire church."

Bruce remained steadfast. "So be it. If he chooses to wage a war, he'll be warring against Almighty God." He drew strength from scripture, reciting verses that affirmed God's promise to fight for His people.

George's anxiousness found a measure of solace as Bruce prayed for their protection. His words conveyed the depth of their faith and unity, as well as their reliance on God's sovereignty.

With a glint of excitement in his eyes, Bruce mentioned, "I've got some great personal news to share too."

As Bruce began to talk about Jennifer, George's excitement was vivid, having recently prayed for their pastor and friend in this regard. For John, this was the first he'd heard of Bruce's girlfriend, but he couldn't help but share in Bruce's joy.

Their conversation flowed late into the night, a reflection of their shared faith and camaraderie. As they eventually parted ways, a common thread of excitement connected them – excitement about what God was orchestrating in their lives, in Stapleton, and even overseas in a land that had never crossed their minds before. In the face of uncertainties, their belief in God's power and sovereignty remained unshaken. Indeed, their God was truly great and capable of mighty things.

***"What an exhilarating day!" Sue exclaimed as she chatted with Maggie over the phone.

"Absolutely! I wish we could have captured Pastor Bruce's expression on camera," Maggie replied, her excitement evident in her voice.

"All the hard work and time we invested was so worth it. Even Jerry regrets missing that moment," Sue remarked.

"He was a huge help. You're lucky to have such a supportive husband."

Sue reflected on Jerry's transformation – from his past self to the dedicated partner he had become. His tireless efforts in collecting information from churches around the country and collaborating with his friends at work to ensure no detail was overlooked in building the new church were remarkable. The entire team had invested countless hours in crafting the perfect plans. Mayor Thomas had insisted on surprising Pastor Bruce, leaving no opportunity for input. It had all been entrusted to God, and the outcome seemed to have exceeded their expectations.

"Maggie, how's your recording going?" Sue inquired, shifting the conversation.

"I just wrapped up recording the vocals for the final song on the music project. I'll be sending it out today. The recording label assures me that the music should be added soon. They've provided samples of other rough tracks with added music, and it's been incredible!"

"Do you think you'll be pleased with the final result?"

"Definitely. The music they've shared so far has been amazing. I can't wait to hear the finished product."

Shifting gears again, Sue asked, "How's everything between you and John?"

There was a brief pause before Maggie responded, her voice a bit shy, "Good."

Sue seized the opportunity to dig for more details. "Come on, spill the beans!"

"We've been spending time together every day. He's changed so much since we first met."

"Any plans for his job?"

"He's considering a government job in the investigative field. The position he's eyeing would allow him to work from his home."

"In Stapleton?" Sue inquired hopefully.

"Yes, Stapleton," Maggie confirmed with a contented sigh. "It seems like everything is falling into place, doesn't it?"

Sue's mood shifted slightly as a concern crossed her mind. "I can't help but worry about Penkowski. He's still out there, and now we've purchased his former property and transformed it into a house of prayer."

Maggie offered reassurance, "Given that he's a wanted man, the chances of him showing up in public here are quite slim. Besides, John is actively working with the government to track down leads on his whereabouts. That's how he connected with the potential job I mentioned."

Sue found comfort in Maggie's words, and the two friends continued their conversation well into the evening. Before they wrapped up, Sue checked her email and found a message from Pastor Bruce, sharing not only the exciting news about the new church but also the arrival of his future fiancée – who would soon be making Stapleton her permanent home.

Time had passed since Bruce last received communication from Jennifer about her return home. However, a quick email arrived from her, notifying Bruce that she would be flying in on that day. Bruce had arranged to have his friends accompany him to the airport, and the group eagerly awaited her arrival.

As the plane approached the landing strip, Bruce's heart raced with anticipation. He hadn't seen Jennifer in a while, and this time, her return was permanent. The moment he had dreamed of, prayed for, and longed for was finally about to materialize. Imagining holding Jennifer in his arms, walking together, sharing dreams and life, it was all on the brink of becoming reality. Amid the excitement, Bruce continued to offer gratitude to his Lord for fulfilling his dream.

With the plane coming to a stop, its engines winding down, a face that resembled an angel appeared in the window – at least, that's how Bruce saw Jennifer. She smiled, wiping tears of joy from her eyes as she waved. Overwhelmed with happiness, Bruce struggled to hold back his own tears. Meanwhile, George, John, Sue, and Maggie observed their pastor's joy with delight.

Once the plane's doors opened, the passengers disembarked one by one in single file. Amid the crowd, Bruce's eyes locked onto Jennifer. He dashed over to the plane as his friends watched, and Jennifer navigated through the people to reach him. As they met, they embraced tightly, conveying their love through the warmth of their hold.

Walking back to his friends, Bruce beamed, still holding Jennifer's hand. He was eager to introduce her to each person.

"Bruce has filled us in about you." Sue said with a grin.

"We're thrilled that your work overseas is finished, as we could certainly use your help here," George added, with nods of agreement from the rest of the group.

"Thank you so much! Bruce has shared so much about all of you. I feel like I already know each of you personally," Jennifer replied, expressing her gratitude.

Bruce, Jennifer, and the group embarked on their journey. As they drove, Bruce eagerly recounted all the details about the church to Jennifer. Unable to email her while she was en route to Stapleton, he was now thrilled to share the news in person.

"I hear you, but it's just hard to believe. The entire amount paid off?" Jennifer exclaimed.

"Every single penny," Bruce confirmed.

As they arrived at the church, its beauty seemed even more pronounced than when Bruce had first seen it. The rest of the group pulled up as well. Stepping out of the car, Jennifer was utterly taken aback. She covered her mouth in astonishment, gazed at the church, then turned her eyes to Bruce, and let out an excited squeal.

"I can't believe this!" she exclaimed.

"Just wait until you see the inside," Bruce replied, his excitement electric. He marveled at how fitting it was to share this moment of awe with Jennifer, their first thrill together centered around God and His kingdom.

They ventured from room to room, and Bruce's excitement was infectious. He recounted the planning efforts of Sue, her husband Jerry, and Maggie. He spoke about Mayor Thomas's generous contribution, his enthusiasm unabated.

The atmosphere was joyful until a somber mood overtook Bruce. Recognizing that Bruce likely hadn't had the chance to inform Jennifer about Penkowski and the looming threat he posed, George and the others sensed the shift.

Bruce continued, "Penkowski was the one who originally erected this building. It replaced Reverend Stone's old church that was destroyed by a tornado."

Jennifer interjected, "He was pure evil. I heard bits and pieces from Bruce, but it's hard to believe something like this could happen here in the States."

"What do you mean?" George inquired.

"Well, Bruce can tell you about some of the unusual experiences I've had in the field, but these kinds of occurrences... you don't typically associate them with the United States."

As Bruce shared further details with Jennifer, a smile suddenly graced her face.

"Why are you smiling?" Bruce asked. "We just informed you about the serious danger we're all facing with Penkowski at large."

Jennifer's smile persisted as she responded, "I'm smiling because when I left my country and was flying back, I was sad to leave a place where God was working so powerfully. Now, I'm receiving the wonderful news that He's doing equally amazing things here in the USA. I'm grateful not only to be with the love of my life…" She reached for Bruce's hand, her gaze fixated on him before she looked back at the others. "...but also to be part of God's incredible work and revival."

Their conversation continued, and Jennifer was captivated by the news of abortion clinics closing in town, the bankruptcy of the large abortion industry, and the reintroduction of prayer and God's commandments in schools. As they sat together in the worship center, Jennifer took in the grandeur of what God had accomplished.

As they bowed their heads, each member of the group began to pray. They lifted up prayers for the ongoing revival, the dedication of the building to God, and the growth of new believers. They also brought their concerns about Penkowski before God, united in faith and confident in Christ's victory over the matter.

TWENTY EIGHT

The air was charged with anticipation on that Tuesday night as a gathering of people clustered around the new church, eagerly waiting for the ceremony to commence. Mayor Thomas and his wife stood at the front, flanked by Pastor Bruce and George. A bright yellow ribbon adorned the front doors of the church, its vibrant color symbolizing the hope and new beginnings that were about to be celebrated. Smiles graced the faces of the assembled crowd, filled with a mixture of excitement and gratitude.

Microphone in hand, Mayor Thomas stepped forward, his voice resonating through the square as it was amplified by the sound system, remnants of the same equipment Penkowski had installed for his own purposes. Emotions flickered across the Mayor's face as he began, "We are here tonight..." His words reached out to the multitude, his voice carrying a sense of profound gratitude and humility, intertwining personal stories with collective triumphs. He glanced at his wife, their shared journey evident in the glance they exchanged, as he continued, "…and for me personally."

Mayor Thomas's voice wavered, and his eyes glistened with emotion, revealing the depth of his sentiments. The crowd stood still, captivated by his words, witnessing his vulnerability and sincerity. "I am very grateful for His hand not only on my life, but on my wife's." He drew her closer, the love and appreciation between them evident to all. "I am grateful for God's servant, Pastor Bruce Hutchinson," he continued, acknowledging the bond between him and the pastor. "For his patience with me as I was not very accommodating to him, patience from each of you as I followed my own self-serving desires...yet here I stand in front of each of you…still your Mayor."

Mayor Thomas's voice grew stronger, carrying a mixture of humility and resolve. The crowd hung on his every word, feeling the weight of the moment. He looked back at his wife, his voice quivering with genuine emotion, "...and finally, patience from my wife who has seen the worst in me...yet stuck by me all these years."

The crowd's hearts were touched by the Mayor's sincerity, and a warm wave of applause resonated through the square as a show of support and appreciation.

"I want to say 'Thank You' to each of you and to Pastor Bruce," Mayor Thomas continued, his tone now a blend of gratitude and joy. The attendees leaned in, eager to catch every word. "By contributing this building as the new church for Pastor Bruce, to each of you, so that you now have a place to meet on Tuesday night, Sunday morning, and any other time." His words were met with nods of agreement and approving murmurs. "It is yours...may God bless and use it as He sees fit."

With a decisive snip, Pastor Bruce cut the yellow ribbon with oversized scissors, and the crowd erupted into cheers, their elation echoing in the night. Simultaneously, spotlights burst to life, casting a warm glow on the cross that graced the building's front. Bells began to chime melodiously, their sound interweaving with the joyful strains of music that filled the air. The atmosphere was electric, charged with a sense of divine presence.

As the cheers subsided and a reverent hush enveloped the crowd, Bruce took his place at the microphone, his heart overflowing with emotion. He gazed at Jennifer, then at the faces of his friends and fellow believers, their eyes alight with anticipation.

"I have longed for a day that I could be a part of a revival of God," Bruce's voice quivered with emotion, and he spoke with a heartfelt vulnerability. The crowd hung on his every word, drawn into his personal journey. "I have dreamed dreams, I have discussed with other pastors, friends, and I have pleaded with God for…as long as I can remember." His voice trembled with a mixture of gratitude and awe.

As Bruce continued, his voice became more animated, and his words ignited an exuberant response from the crowd. His words resonated deeply, connecting their hearts and souls. "Now, here...in this, my hometown of Stapleton...here I stand...we stand in the midst of the working hand of God." The cheers and exclamations of praise grew louder, echoing the collective joy and thanksgiving of the people gathered.

"Let us take this moment before we enter into this building and thank Him for all that He has done," Bruce's voice held a firm yet reverent tone. The crowd's energy softened into a solemn silence as they bowed their heads, united in prayer.

Mayor Thomas and his wife bowed their heads, their unity and devotion evident. Bruce's words, infused with deep spirituality, rose above the hushed expectancy. "Lord, we come to You humbly. We come to You in prayer. We stand before You, longing to glimpse Your face even tonight." His voice resonated with reverence and longing.

As Bruce continued to pray, the crowd's hearts and voices joined in unison, a collective "Amen" resonating through the night air, sealing their petitions with faith and unity.

At the airport, a small private jet touched down gracefully on the runway. Its engines hummed to a stop as six enigmatic figures, garbed in sinister black robes, disembarked from the aircraft. Waiting in the airport parking lot were five large buses, each ready to carry out a dark mission. These buses weren't just ordinary means of transportation; they were harbingers of ominous intent. Their interiors, capable of carrying up to 25 individuals, including the drivers, were cloaked in darkness.

With eerie synchronization, the buses pulled to a stop, and their doors swung open in unison. The leaders who had descended from the jet now stood in a foreboding formation before the buses, their presence radiating malevolence.

A figure among them, his voice dripping with a hellish resonance, began to speak, his words laced with malice, "I want the entire city cursed. Every house, every business, every street...even the garbage cans...everything."

As if guided by an unholy force, the buses dispersed, scattering in different directions, like sinister tendrils extending into the heart of the city. The night sky took on an ominous hue, darkness enveloping everything. The wind grew into a howling tempest, and lightning bolts cleaved the sky, illuminating it with sinister brilliance. Thunder echoed through the air, resembling the roar of artillery in a chaotic battlefield.

Each bus came to a halt at the entrance of a different neighborhood. The men in black robes emerged from the buses, their presence shrouded in an aura of dread. The wind intensified its fury, and the crackling of lightning seemed to challenge the very elements. However, the figures remained resolute, undeterred by the tempest they had unleashed.

From the bowels of the buses emerged a large wooden cross, a macabre emblem of their nefarious intentions. Chanting, guttural and haunting, resonated through the air as the cross was positioned in the lawns, symbolic sacrifices of the darkest kind placed at its base. The wood itself seemed drenched in kerosene, a sinister omen of the impending event.

As if in response to the malevolent incantations, the wind howled with a newfound intensity. Lightning, now striking closer to the figures, illuminated the scene in brief, eerie flashes. Thunder, reverberating like the detonations of a cosmic war, underscored the gravity of the moment. Yet, the figures remained steadfast.

With a convergence of sinister forces, the cross was ignited, flames leaping hungrily at the skies. The conflagration seemed almost alive, a manifestation of the darkness they sought to summon. The figures began to step away, the flames appearing to reach for them like ethereal fingers, a dance of pain and chaos.

Amidst the roaring wind and the cacophony of the storm, the chanting reached its zenith. The night had become a realm of darkness and menace, a place where the boundary between the natural and supernatural was blurred. The wind's ferocity intensified, as if in protest, but the flames held their ground, defying the tumultuous elements.

Across Stapleton, in every neighborhood, before businesses and schools, even in front of venerable old churches, this malevolent ritual unfolded in synchrony, a haunting symphony of darkness and ritualistic chaos.

Having completed their sinister work, the figures finally converged before the old AFT building in the town square, a place steeped in history and now shrouded in an aura of foreboding.

As the tour of the magnificent building came to an end, attendees gracefully found their seats, each awestruck by the beauty that surrounded them. It was a moment of sheer splendor, and the air was tinged with a mixture of reverence and excitement. Bruce stood humbled, his heart swelling with a mix of emotions. This dream, once just a flicker in his mind's eye, had materialized into a breathtaking reality. As he looked out over the sea of faces, his eyes met Jennifer's, and in that gaze, he felt an overwhelming surge of love and gratitude.

With the weight of the occasion upon him, Bruce knelt down in solemn prayer. His words, a heartfelt conversation with the divine, echoed through the grand space. His whispered petitions and expressions of gratitude resonated in the hallowed chamber, each word a testament to his faith and dedication.

Amid the awe-inspiring setting, a dark force gathered outside. The buses that had arrived earlier now stood ominously in front of the church building. As the men disembarked, an air of impending malevolence clung to them. Their movements were calculated and eerie, each step marking the progression of a sinister plan.

Amidst this grim assembly, Penkowski emerged from a black limousine, his aura oozing malevolent authority. His gaze fell upon the building he had erected, but his eyes widened as he saw the illuminated cross atop it. Rage coursed through his veins, his anger an inferno that threatened to consume him.

"Burn it down!" His command tore through the air, an order

that carried the weight of fury and desperation. The men sprang into action, torches blazing, intent on carrying out their dark master's wishes.

Around the building, fires were kindled, the wind howling with a malevolent force. The very robes of the men were whipped by the gusts, as if the elements themselves conspired against them. But the flames they ignited were repeatedly extinguished by the relentless wind, refusing to be bent to their malicious will.

Meanwhile, a makeshift cross was erected in front of the church, formed by pieces of wood from the buses. Kerosene drenched its form, as if anointing it for a sinister purpose. The wind raged, the robes of the men billowing, and the firebrands of the torches were poised to transform the night into a symphony of malevolence.

Touched by the flames of their torches, the cross erupted into fire, the night illuminated by its ominous glow. But the wind's ferocity defied their efforts, blowing the flames towards the very men who had lit them. A cacophony of chaos ensued, as fiery tendrils seemed to reach for them, a sinister dance of danger and retribution.

In the midst of this storm, lightning crashed down with a violence that matched the wickedness of the scene. Thunder roared like a vengeful god, as if the heavens themselves voiced their anger. The cross, now an inferno, bore the brunt of the storm's fury, a clash between the profane and the celestial. As the lightning struck, the cross exploded in a torrent of fiery debris, scattering embers in every direction. Men screamed as they were struck by the fiery shrapnel, the very air heavy with the scent of burning wood and scorched flesh.

In a twisted symphony of malevolence and destruction, lightning danced across the skies of Stapleton, obliterating every cross that had been erected. The echoes of its explosive strikes lingered in the air, leaving behind only fading tendrils of smoke and an eerie sense of the supernatural.

As the thunder rumbled and the lightning painted jagged streaks across the sky, the congregation within the church building remained blissfully unaware of the tempest brewing outside. Their minds and hearts were consumed by the beauty of the newly dedicated space, and the sounds of the outside world were muffled by the thick walls.

Meanwhile, Penkowski's rage knew no bounds as he clutched a torch, his fury a consuming force. "Follow me!" his voice rang out, a command that bore the weight of his malevolent authority. But the moment he stepped closer to the church's entrance, an uncanny sensation washed over him. It was as if an invisible barrier, an intangible force, was determined to keep him out. The creeping dread gnawed at his insides, his steps faltering as terror clawed at his emotions. His heart pounded like a drum of doom, and yet he pushed forward, a mix of determination and dark desperation compelling him to proceed.

Within the hallowed halls of the church, a congregation was lost in a moment of divine worship. Hearts overflowed with gratitude and voices soared in praise, each note and word an offering to the heavens. Their prayers intertwined, rising toward the rafters, and their connection with the divine was intense. Eyes closed, heads bowed, they were immersed in their devotion, the echoes of their praises a sweet symphony of faith.

Abruptly, the tranquility shattered as the doors at the back of the church were flung open with a deafening crash. The noise reverberated through the worship center like a shockwave, each person jolted from their reverie. Heads turned, eyes widened, and gasps punctuated the air as the unexpected disruption pierced the sacred space. The abruptness of the intrusion was jarring, a stark contrast to the serenity that had enveloped the room just moments before.

Bruce's gaze lifted, and in that heart-pounding moment, a surge of emotions threatened to overwhelm him. Just as fear was about to claim its grip, he found solace in a scripture, his voice carrying its weight like a sacred secret meant only for the ears of those following Christ. With a voice both resolute and fervent, he proclaimed, "...stand where you are and watch the Lord rescue you. The Lord himself will fight for you."

Jennifer's gaze turned toward Bruce, concern etching lines of worry onto her face. In the midst of the tension, Bruce met her with a look that held promises of safety and reassurance. His eyes, pools of calm amidst the storm, silently communicated a steadfast resolve. He then shifted his gaze to George and the others seated behind him, each exchange carrying the same message of unwavering confidence.

Amidst the unfolding chaos, Penkowski and his six formidable leaders led the ominous procession. The men, clad in obsidian robes with hoods veiling their identities, exuded an aura of dread. Their torches cast eerie shadows that danced like malevolent spirits, while the flames themselves seemed to hunger for more than just wood.

The onlookers, a sea of petrified faces, felt their limbs turn to stone as the cloaked figures methodically encircled them in every aisle. A suffocating fear settled over the crowd, choking back their voices and replacing them with heartbeats that thudded like drums of doom. Attempts to escape the advancing figures were met with threats as Penkowski's followers brandished the fire with sinister intent.

Penkowski neared the front, his voice erupting in an infernal outcry. "What is this? You take my building and pervert it with your putrid religion?" he spat, directing his accusatory finger at Pastor Bruce. His voice, like a searing brand, etched the weight of his indignation into the air.

His gaze shifted to George, the venom in his words echoing through the building. "And you! You traitor!" His voice reverberated, a relentless echo of betrayal. "I gave you years of job security, paying you more than you've ever earned in your pathetic life. And this is how you repay me? Dragging me off to court, causing me to lose everything I've worked for?" His words carried the bitterness of shattered trust.

Turning his focus to John, Penkowski's voice sliced through the air like a serrated blade. "And you, you troublemaker!" His finger aimed like an arrow of accusation as he closed the distance towards the stage. On that stage, John, George, Sue, and Maggie sat, shadows behind Pastor Bruce's standing form. "You started all this!" Penkowski's voice dripped with disdain. "I tried to squash you like a dreadful cockroach, but you kept scurrying into the darkness." He stepped closer, his voice a venomous hiss. "And then you break into my office building, steal my possessions... break into my house! Man, is there nothing sacred to you?" His scream pierced the air, carrying the weight of his violated sanctums.

"I'm sure that putting a wrench into your sabotage operation of your greatest competitor in the abortion industry, The Association for Fetal Research, your illegal sales of fetal tissue for research and other use, and your laundering operation used to cover illegal gambling was quite disconcerting," John said, brimming with his trademark sarcasm. George couldn't help but crack a smile, even though fear hung heavily in the air. No matter how dire the peril, John's ability to wield sarcasm remained unmatched.

"Lies! All lies! I see now why you hang around this group. They live, breathe, and move in lies. It is what makes this religion work. Weak people being duped into thinking that there is a God out there that loves them. Please! A god with great power has only one agenda, get more power. My god wants to share his power," Penkowski countered, his voice a mixture of frustration and derision.

Turning towards the crowd, Penkowski continued, "I offered this to all of you while I was here. I offered power for daily living... freedom from the strife and the legal laws traditional religion can only offer. I offered life. To live it to the fullest... not holding back or denying any of your deepest desires."

"You liar, what will God do to you? How will He punish you?" Bruce's voice suddenly boomed across the building, a forceful sound that reverberated within the chests of every person present. It caught everyone off guard, capturing their attention, including Penkowski's. On the stage, George, John, and the others stared at Bruce, eyes wide open. Jennifer, in disbelief, listened to the man she loved.

Bruce's voice continued to resonate with a deep intensity. "Through God's precepts I get understanding: therefore I hate every false way. What shall be given unto thee? Or what shall be done unto thee, thou false tongue? With a soldier's sharp arrows you will die. With red-hot coals and fire you will die!"

Penkowski's anger surged again, his voice erupting as he addressed Bruce and then the people. "Your own Bible says, 'Be not righteous over much; neither make thyself over wise: why shouldest thou destroy thyself?' That is what I have been telling you all along! This righteous living will destroy you! Are you all so blind and stupid not to see it right in front of you?"

"You follow the author of lies who has been twisting the truth since the beginning. 'You and your followers are all children of your father, the Devil, and you want to follow your father's desires. From the very beginning he was a murderer and has never been on the side of truth, because there is no truth in him. When he tells a lie, he is only doing what is natural to him, because he is a liar and the father of all lies," Bruce's words echoed with the same commanding tone.

"I have only quoted your Book!" Penkowski retorted.

"And so did the Devil when tempting Jesus! Why would you not use the same technique with God's people here today? You pulled out scripture from its context to suit your self-serving needs. It is balance God was looking for in a life, not becoming more evil!"

"You lie!" Penkowski's voice reverberated.

"Your so-called 'truth' you spread through this community via this building caused men, women, and children to suffer from lives that were destroyed and shattered… never to be remedied again! Now, God has taken over this building and He will rescue the lost, feed the poor, and clothe the naked. And He has said to His people even today…" Bruce's voice grew louder, his arms raised as he addressed the entire building, causing its foundation to tremble, "...stand where you are and watch the Lord rescue you. The Lord himself will fight for you."

Penkowski's demeanor spiraled into wild chaos. The air around him seemed to warp and shift, mirroring the unsettling transformation that had occurred during that fateful evening in the school auditorium during the Tuesday night prayer meeting. His human facade crumbled, replaced by a monstrous form, twice his original size. Rippling muscles strained against scaly skin, while his face contorted into a hideous mask of darkness and evil. Yellow sulfurous smoke billowed from his mouth, a venomous exhalation that tainted the air with an otherworldly stench.

As George, John, and the others shifted their attention to Pastor Bruce, a remarkable radiance began to emanate from him. In a split second, two angelic warriors, luminous as lightning, materialized on either side of Bruce. Their swords rested in sheaths at their sides, ready for the battle that lay ahead. George and his companions exchanged incredulous glances, torn between questioning their reality and embracing the astounding scene unfolding before them. As their eyes darted through the crowd of believers, they noticed other celestial figures emerging, sprinkled like stars in the night.

Penkowski's hellish voice commanded, "Burn them! Burn them all!" The men under his influence obeyed, unleashing flames from their torches that danced upon floors, walls, and every object in their path. Yet, despite the consuming fire, none of the items were consumed; they blazed but remained untouched. The flames danced through the aisles, yet Penkowski's followers managed to sidestep their perilous advance.

To everyone's astonishment, the fire met an invisible barrier, unable to harm the believers. It was as if an unseen shield had been erected, sparing them from the inferno's wrath. The fire's advance halted, halted by an impenetrable force. Even as it reached the stage, it retreated a foot away from Bruce and the two angelic warriors. George and the others behind them were shrouded in safety.

The creature that once was Penkowski bellowed and cursed, the name of the Lord contorted into a profane chant. He seized a fireball from the floor, hurling it towards Bruce. In an instant, the two angelic warriors drew their swords, unleashing crackling lightning as the swords soared through the air, obliterating the fireball in a blaze of red and white brilliance. This dance of celestial light continued as Penkowski hurled more fireballs, the angels countering each threat with their swords of divine protection.

The angels dispersed among the believers drew their swords as well, a symphony of flashing blades as lightning danced throughout the crowd. Each person stood firm in their faith, witnesses to a celestial intervention that held the line against the onslaught. The swords sliced through the air, extinguishing every fireball Penkowski launched, safeguarding the people's lives.

Even Penkowski's followers underwent a grim transformation, morphing into demons, twisted and malevolent. They too joined the fire-throwing assault, their demonic flames aimed at the crowd. The angels continued their battle, a divine choreography of protection, just as God had promised.

Penkowski's advance halted as he ascended the stairs, his determination clear. His sword emerged, and as its blade gleamed, it emitted a noxious sulfur smoke that seemed to embody his malevolent intentions. With each swing, arcs of maleficent green light burst forth, painting the air with a sinister glow as he approached Bruce.

Reacting swiftly, Bruce's angelic defenders shifted their stance, positioning themselves between him and the approaching demon. The clash was inevitable, and with swords drawn, the celestial warriors engaged their foe. The collision sent shockwaves rippling through the air, arcs of light transforming the scene into a mesmerizing laser light show. The sound that accompanied the clash resembled the crackling of thunder, an awe-inspiring symphony of power.

The demon's voice could be heard, a cacophony of curses and grunts, his outnumbered position placing him on the defensive. Bruce's angelic guardians fought valiantly, their skill evident as they pressed their advantage against the demonic threat. The demon's efforts to maneuver and counter were met with resistance, each attempt thwarted by the celestial prowess of the angels. In the midst of the fierce clash, Bruce remained steadfast, radiating an unwavering aura of confidence and faith.

As the battle raged, the watching ministers could only stare in disbelief, their eyes fixed upon the surreal spectacle unfolding before them. The sheer intensity of the clash, the dazzling arcs of light, and the tumultuous sound of the duel defied explanation. Yet, amidst the chaos, Bruce's presence stood as a beacon of hope and assurance.

No matter how the demon Penkowski attempted to break free, to maneuver and escape, he found himself trapped, his movements constricted by an invisible force. The angelic warriors' coordination was unyielding, their mastery of the situation evident as they held their adversary in check. The demon's desperate attempts to regain control proved futile against their united front, leaving him effectively immobilized in the face of their strength.

In an instant, two more demons materialized by Penkowski's

side, their presence meant to bolster his struggling efforts. Yet, their intervention proved futile against the seasoned and skilled warriors of God. Swift and precise, each celestial defender engaged a demon, their movements fluid and deadly. The clash was intense but brief, as the angels' swords struck true, and the demons crumbled to the ground amidst the flames.

One of the angelic warriors managed to strike Penkowski's side, sending him tumbling off the stage, his form now consumed by the all-encompassing blaze. As he staggered to his feet, his words were a venomous storm of curses. Amidst the chaos, Penkowski's followers ceased their fire-throwing, abandoning their malevolent attack and regrouping with the men in black robes.

Through the building, the angels withdrew their swords and returned them to their sheaths, the gleaming blades vanishing from sight. As Penkowski struggled to regain his footing, his anguished scream pierced the air, his desperate words an outcry to a forsaken power. "Satan! Why have you forsaken us? We have been loyal, given everything, even our souls! Curse this city of Stapleton! Curse this people of God! Curse this man of God and all he represents!"

The demon's form shifted, once terrifying and monstrous, now reduced to a mere man clad in a tattered black robe. His appearance was marked by a burnt hole and a grievous, bleeding wound, his gaze seething with unrestrained anger and hatred, directed squarely at Bruce.

Amidst the celestial display, the angels carved out a space for Pastor Bruce, gesturing for him to rejoin their protective ranks. Bruce stepped back between the angels, the light that emanated from him undiminished. In the same commanding tone that had echoed before, he intoned, "The wicked are doomed by their own violence; they refuse to do what is right. But what they have done to others will now be done to them. If you defy me, you are doomed to die. Thus saith the Lord."

As Bruce's commanding words ceased, a profound transformation swept through the room. The fire, which had danced menacingly yet spared every object, suddenly turned its hungry gaze upon the men in black robes. The air was rent with agonized screams, cries of anguish echoing throughout the building. The flames voraciously engulfed every man, their forms consumed by the relentless fire until not a trace remained.

Penkowski, too, became a figure of torment, his agonized shrieks mingling with his profanity-laden curses against the very

God he once scorned. The fire's fury raged unabated, reducing all to ashes in its unforgiving grasp. The consuming inferno painted the scene with a searing intensity, leaving nothing in its wake but the haunting echoes of suffering.

Amidst the conflagration, the angels emerged as beacons of ethereal light. Their wings unfurled from their backs, majestic and radiant. In a harmonious motion, the angels stirred their wings, generating a gentle, soothing breeze that swept through the building. The flames, once relentless, began to falter and wane, extinguished by the divine intervention.

As the breeze swirled through the space, an electric sense of divine presence permeated the atmosphere. The entire building seemed to vibrate with a sacred energy, a testament to the overwhelming power of the Almighty. The angels, radiant as the sun and as pure as the whitest snow, melded seamlessly with the celestial glow, their forms fading into the brilliance.

And then, as abruptly as it had begun, the fire vanished. Not a single trace of destruction marred the space. The building, once engulfed in flames, stood untouched, its contents pristine. There lingered no remnants of Penkowski or his followers, no scent of smoke to remind of the inferno that had engulfed the room.

Bruce's heart blazed with an intensity that transcended mortal experience. His spirit soared on celestial currents, and he contemplated the surreal thought that he might be amidst heaven's host even now. The grip of fear had been shattered, replaced by an overwhelming assurance of divine victory.

Bruce sank to his knees, a gesture of humble reverence in the face of the awe-inspiring display he had witnessed. His fellow ministers, breathless and awestruck, joined him. One by one, they knelt beside Bruce, their hands resting upon his back, a silent affirmation of unity. As they bowed their heads in prayer, the room resonated with the hushed symphony of their whispered gratitude and devotion.

The entire congregation joined in the sacred chorus, an outpouring of prayer, rejoicing, and gratitude that swelled through the room. They raised their voices in fervent appreciation for the divine promise fulfilled, for the Almighty's unwavering protection in the face of adversity. Bathed in the radiant glory of God, they basked in the divine presence that lingered long into the early hours of the morning, a resounding testament to the triumph of faith over darkness.

TWENTY NINE

Months later…

"Sit still! I'm going to stick you!" Sue's voice was both determined and gentle as she addressed Maggie.

"I'm sorry. I'm just so jittery," Maggie replied with a nervous laugh.

"Well, that's understandable... You are about to get married!" Sue's tone carried an undertone of excitement.

"Can you believe it?" Maggie's voice was filled with an infectious joy that was hard to contain.

"Sue, when you're done with Maggie, could you take a look at my dress? It's got a small tear at the bottom. It's my Mom's wedding dress, and I guess the years have caught up to it," Jennifer chimed in.

"It would be my pleasure," Sue responded eagerly, clearly invested in the preparations.

The women were absolutely stunning. Each was brimming with excitement about their impending wedding day, and the prospect of a double wedding had them positively thrilled. As both brides experienced fluttering butterflies, Sue took on the role of a calming presence, working diligently to ease their nerves. Her task was no small feat, as she navigated the delicate balance of emotions, ensuring that the excitement didn't overwhelm them. Indeed, she had her hands full with this endeavor.

Maggie's wedding dress was a vision of purity and elegance, a testament to her newfound spiritual journey. The gown, white as snow, boasted intricate lacework that adorned the bodice and gracefully trailed along the edges of a luxuriously long train. Around her neck, white freshwater pearls gleamed, adding a touch of grace, while her veil was delicately adorned with similar pearls, lending an air of refined charm.

"Oh, Maggie, you look absolutely stunning!" Sue's words dripped with genuine admiration and happiness.

"Thank you!" Maggie's voice quivered with excitement, a mix of joy and pre-wedding jitters.

After a warm embrace, Sue and Maggie moved over to Jennifer. They took in her appearance, their eyes reflecting the mutual pride and joy they felt. Jennifer's dress evoked a sense of timeless elegance, harking back to a bygone era. The cream silk material was adorned with delicate lace and white beads, carefully accentuating the gown's intricate design. Completing the ensemble were dress gloves and a petite pocket purse that complemented the dress impeccably.

Sue wrapped Jennifer in a heartfelt hug, a gesture of camaraderie and affection. Maggie, mindful of her delicate attire, joined in the embrace, her cautious hug conveying her excitement without disturbing the meticulously crafted dresses.

"You know, I have conducted quite a few weddings, and I have never been this nervous!" Pastor Bruce's pacing was a testament to his inner turmoil, his restless energy filling the room.

"Pastor, you're making me more nervous... sit still... please!" John's plea held a mixture of concern and humor, a lighthearted attempt to settle their leader's jitters.

"Guys, relax! You look great, and you will be just fine up there on stage." George's voice carried a soothing reassurance, his attempt to quell the escalating nerves. "Besides, everyone will be looking at your lovely 'Brides to be,'" he teased, aiming to bring a smile to their faces.

The duo of men stood resplendent in their black tuxedos, white shirts immaculate, belts and ties adding a touch of sophistication. Their appearance exuded a timeless elegance, as if they had stepped straight from the glossy pages of a men's fashion magazine. Every detail, from their impeccably coiffed hair to their polished shoes, had been meticulously attended to. All that remained was to wait.

Within the church, a transformation had taken place. The sanctuary was adorned with a profusion of decorations, candles casting a warm and inviting glow. As friends and family streamed in, their faces lit up by the flickering candlelight, an undeniable sense of anticipation hung in the air. The fragrance of fresh flowers mingled with the soft strains of music, creating an atmosphere both enchanting and intimate.

The guests signed the guest book and took in the sight of the stage, adorned with carefully arranged flowers and a pair of two unity candles, their flames dancing in harmony. The ambiance was one of serenity, an oasis of tranquility amidst the bustling excitement.

Among the attendees was John's sister, Elizabeth, who had

journeyed from California with her date, Attorney General Stan Robinson. Their presence added an extra layer of significance to the occasion, a testament to the healing power of time and renewed connections. Elizabeth's smile was a testament to her newfound contentment, her steps towards healing facilitated by her involvement with the church's pregnancy center, a path that ironically intersected with Stan's own ministry.

Amid the gathering, Pastor Wayne Miles arrived with a congregation that mirrored his own infectious enthusiasm. His radiant smile was a reflection of his contentment, a testament to the transformative power of his new church, made possible by the generosity of AFT's original manufacturing building and the support of Mayor Thomas. The connection between these elements was a poignant reminder of the community's intertwined journey towards redemption.

Embracing his role as a shepherd, Pastor Wayne reveled in the growth of his congregation. The seeds of faith he had sown were taking root, flourishing in the fertile ground of unity and shared purpose. A remarkable camaraderie had been forged among the churchgoers, their bond strengthened by their regular gatherings on Tuesday nights at Bruce's church. The convergence of souls under one roof spoke to the common thread of renewal that wove through their lives, a testament to the transformative power of faith and fellowship.

As the doors swung open, unveiling the radiant brides, the room was filled with an aura of ethereal beauty that only a bride could emanate. Maggie's entrance was met with Sue's exuberance, her grip on Jerry's arm a testament to the excitement that surged through her. Jerry, though feeling the tight grasp, couldn't help but share in her happiness, gently easing her fingers from his arm.

Following Maggie was Jennifer, a vision of timeless elegance in the wedding dress lovingly provided by her mother. The years seemed to dissolve, leaving behind a bride who embodied sheer magnificence. With each step, the brides graced the aisle, their journey up the stage a carefully orchestrated ballet of grace and anticipation. Veils cascaded, and hearts beat with an echoing promise of love.

"Dearly beloved..." George's voice resounded through the

sanctuary, his words carrying the weight of the moment. Bruce's heart continued to race, his silent prayers focused on George's steady delivery and his own ability to remain composed. He stole a glance at John, whose calm demeanor only amplified Bruce's own nervousness.

"...we are gathered today in the sight of God and His Son, Jesus Christ, and His precious Holy Spirit for the bonds of matrimony with Bruce Hutchinson and Jennifer Lewis, along with John Ivan and Maggie Fortunato."

The ceremony continued, George's words carrying the sanctity of the occasion. The brides and grooms stood hand in hand, their gazes locked in a timeless connection that spoke volumes of their commitment. The vows, laden with significance, were exchanged with unwavering conviction.

"Do you, Bruce Hutchinson, take Jennifer Lewis to be your lawfully wedded wife, your constant friend, your faithful partner, and your love from this day forward?" George intoned.

"I do," Bruce's voice resonated, his eyes unwavering.

George turned to Jennifer and said, his voice resonating with reverence, "Do you, Jennifer, take Bruce Hutchinson to be your lawfully wedded husband, your constant friend, your faithful partner, and your love from this day forward?"

"I do," Jennifer's voice was steady, carrying the weight of her commitment.

The atmosphere brimmed with emotion as George continued, his words infused with significance. "And do you, Jennifer Lewis, in the presence of God, your family, and friends, offer your solemn vow to be a faithful partner in sickness and in health, in good times and in bad, and in joy as well as in sorrow? Do you promise to love unconditionally, to support him in all his God-given goals, honor and respect him, to share in laughter and tears, to cherish him, and to set the example given to us by Jesus Christ? Will you follow His ordinances and leadership through His Spirit and the word of God for your family, for as long as you both shall live?"

"I do," Jennifer's voice rang out once more, her gaze locked onto Bruce's.

George's words then turned to John and Maggie, their solemn vows exchanged with the same unwavering conviction. As he pronounced each couple man and wife, the culmination of their journey echoed in the sacred space.

"You may now kiss your bride," George's words were like a

herald, granting permission for the long-awaited union of lips.

Bruce tenderly lifted Jennifer's veil, his eyes locking onto hers as their lips met in a kiss that sealed the promise of a lifetime. Years of anticipation and trials melted away, leaving only the present, where love, hope, and commitment blossomed.

Across the stage, John shared a similar moment with Maggie. Her veil lifted, their kiss held the power of forgiveness, redemption, and the promise of a fresh start. The past was cast aside, replaced by the bright horizon of their shared future.

The music swelled, and George's voice echoed through the space as he introduced the newlyweds, their union acknowledged by a symphony of applause. Hand in hand, they approached the unity candles, a symbol of their newfound unity and the beginning of their shared journey.

As the music continued to play, the newlyweds descended the stairs, a path lined with the heartfelt applause of their loved ones. The air was charged with a sense of wonder and joy, as the culmination of their love stories unfolded before their eyes.

Indeed, from the dawning of human existence, it was the hand of the Divine that ordained the sacred rite unfolding within those hallowed walls. The threads of destiny woven by the Creator led Bruce and Jennifer, John and Maggie, to this very moment, where vows were exchanged, and hearts united. It was His providence that had orchestrated their paths, guiding them through trials and triumphs to this profound union.

As the ceremony drew to a close, the truth became clear: God's presence was tangible, infusing every corner of the church with His grace. The beauty of the surroundings, the music that swelled through the air, and the love that radiated between the couples were all gifts from the Almighty, who had lovingly orchestrated every detail.

In the town of Stapleton, God's presence had manifested itself in the lives of its residents. His touch had healed wounds, shattered darkness, and ignited hope. Mayor Thomas and Virginia's rekindled love, Elizabeth's journey to healing, and the elimination of a once-dreaded man like Penkowski were all testament to the power of His intervention.

This small town had been visited by a force greater than itself, a force that had set in motion a series of events that led to this awe-inspiring celebration of love and commitment. As friends, family, and believers looked on, the resonance of their joyous union echoed in the heavens. Each life touched, each soul changed, was a testament to the glorious power of God.

And so, as the newlyweds began their shared journey, the spirit of gratitude and reverence filled the air. The town of Stapleton, once overshadowed by darkness, was now a place where God's light shone brightly. Every life, every story, every heart that had found healing and hope, whispered the same refrain: "To God be the Glory!"

THIRTY

Some time later, Bruce stood at the front of a church located far outside of Stapleton. The atmosphere was heavy with concern, for this city grappled with a deeply unsettling issue. The young local pastor who had recently assumed leadership of the church had heard of the transformative events that had unfolded in Stapleton. Filled with a mix of hope and desperation, he extended an invitation to Bruce, hoping that the divine intervention witnessed in Stapleton could extend to his own community.

Maggie's role as a musical leader had concluded, and she took her place beside her husband, John. His affectionate arm around her shoulders drew her close, a silent expression of pride and support. Their shared journey had weathered many storms, and this moment marked a testament to their enduring love.

Jennifer occupied a pew, her gaze fixed lovingly on her new husband, who was about to address the congregation. Silent prayers emanated from her heart, enveloping Bruce in a cocoon of support and divine guidance.

Bruce rose to his feet, a figure of strength and conviction as he addressed the congregation. His words carried the weight of his experiences and the transformation he had witnessed. His voice, steady and resonant, held the promise of hope and renewal.

"God yearns to extend His presence to each one of you. He longs to breathe life into your spirits, to bestow upon you a personal revival that stirs your very being. He eagerly awaits to hear your voices, to receive your prayers, and to hold your concerns close to His heart. He is the mender of wounds, the solace for your pains, and the architect of familial healing. Above all, His gaze is upon this town, waiting to bring forth restoration and renewal."

Bruce continued, his voice a conduit for the timeless wisdom of scripture. His words invoked the age-old promise of restoration found in humility and prayer.

"'If my people, who are called by my name, shall humble themselves, and pray, and seek my face, and turn from their wicked ways; then will I hear from heaven, and will forgive their sin, and will heal their land…'"

ABOUT THE AUTHOR

For nearly four decades, Tony Tona has passionately embraced his faith in Jesus Christ. His unwavering commitment to impacting lives through the redemptive message of the Gospel of Jesus Christ has left an indelible mark on successive generations, spanning both youth and adults alike.

Mr. Tona's fervent aspiration is to usher individuals into the divine realm of God's Kingdom, elevating them from their current spiritual journeys to a profound, more intimate, and spiritually mature communion with the Author of their souls.

Made in United States
Orlando, FL
22 December 2024